THE SENATOR

The Senator

by Drew Pearson

Doubleday & Company, Inc.
Garden City, New York

The author would like to express his gratitude to Scott Meredith, Kenneth McCormick, and Gerald Green for their assistance in the preparation of this book.

THE SENATOR

CHAPTER ONE

I have been in love with Washington since I was twelve years old. It is no source of embarrassment to me to admit that I have loved this city and will always love it, more than I could ever love any other human being, any other place, any idea. Awe, respect, affection—all these are part of my love. And nothing shall ever change it.

For example. In my thirty-five years I have enjoyed the company of several beautiful, charming women. It is possible that I may have been in love with one, and I am fairly certain I *was* in love with another. But no woman I have ever known, no matter how intimate our relationship, has ever affected me the way a fresh view of Washington has—from the comfortable interior of a taxi-cab as it cruises along the Mall at dusk, from the window of a low-flying jet as it lazily circles National Airport and the magnificent monuments below gleam in morning sunlight, from the steps of the Capitol at night, when all about the historic edifices glow with the promise of wise laws, reasonable dealings, the application of intelligence to affairs of men and states.

At moments like these (even so mundane a sight as a group of government workers, white, black, male, female, leaving the Interior Building for their buses, cars, taxis, in the haze of a late October afternoon) my heart quickens, my skin prickles, and I am again thrilled that I have been privileged to be a part of this "grand continuum" as one of my Government professors at Ohio Normal College used to say.

To return to my first view of Washington. The trip was a prize I had won for the best essay on "The American Way," sponsored by the American Legion. I was the runaway winner in my home town, Indian Mound, Ohio, population 1045. To this day I remember the way my winning composition began:

> *What is the American Way? It is as easy—and as hard —to define as Old Glory, or the clear sound of taps over Arlington National Cemetery.*

There were about a dozen of us on the trip, all regional winners from Ohio. The other winners were accompanied by at least one parent. I was the only one who went alone. My father, the late Charles Darwin Deever, was unwilling to leave his "business"— an unrewarding grocery store, slowly dying of supermarket competition. My mother was bedridden, weakened by the pernicious anemia that was to cause her death shortly thereafter.

To be honest I did not miss them. They were good people, but they were too much a reminder of my impoverished existence in that moribund small town. (Indian Mound's population today, twenty-three years later, is half what it was then.) My parents could never have shared the glory of Washington, D.C. with me. Their shabby presence would have diluted my vision of the awesome monuments, the elegant streets, the sparkling waters. It was all mine. I devoured it. I knew I would be a part of it some day.

These memories are so rich, so poignant, that even now, almost a quarter of a century later, they cause me to start, to send delicious shivers up my spine. How glorious it was! The Jefferson Memorial, that serene rotunda on the Tidal Basin; the quiet power of the Supreme Court Building (I marveled at the way these nine robed men dispense laws, wisdom, judgments, and we obey them, without the need for force); the busy corridors of the Senate Office Buildings, filled with authoritative young men and women, whom I envied; the gingerbread eccentricity of the Smithsonian; the grand view of the city from the lawn of the Custis-Lee mansion, a sight that made me blink my moist eyes and find my vocal cords knotted, so that I could not respond and averted my wet face when Sheldon Goldberg, the Cleveland essay winner, shouted at me, "Hey Eddie, c'mon down here, they're changing the guard for the Unknown Soldier!"

Later we were received by President Truman in his oval office. I remember the high windows, the elaborate scallop-style decorations in the lofty arches. It was just after the 1952 election. The President seemed a bit sad, a bit distracted. Soon he would be leaving the White House, the city he had known so well, and where he had served so long and so courageously. He was a bit smaller and a bit older in appearance than I had anticipated. But his eyes! They had an electric quality, an alertness, a fine sense of the power and authority residing in the great office he held. It was odd how the photographs and newsreel shots of him seemed to miss this all the time. When you saw Mr. Truman in person you realized you were in the presence of a brave, determined, sharply intelligent person. At the same time, he had that marvelous warm and friendly quality—like that of a kindly Midwestern pharmacist, a beloved country lawyer. So in spite of his august position, he appeared as "one of us"—a sturdy man in a squared-off gray suit, bifocals, maroon tie. I suspect every person in our Ohio group loved him at that moment, even Mr. Wade, the American Legion official in charge of us, who had earlier opined that while he liked "Old Harry" he was afraid the President was sometimes "soft on Commies."

We stayed but a moment with the President. I can recall, word-for-word, his final advice to us. His face was solemn, and his voice had that honest Midwestern quality as he said:

"Don't ever forget it, you young people. This is the greatest country and the greatest government in the history of the world."

Does it sound strange to you that I began to cry? Oh, I did not bawl, or wail, or make any noise. But as we left the President's office for a special tour of the White House, involuntary tears clouded my eyes. For the second time that day, I wept for the beauty and glory of my country. It was not until we had concluded our tour of the White House—the Green Room, the Fish Room, all those places so rich in our history—and we were once again out of doors in the bracing air, that I was able to stop the tears. (I do not cry easily; I pride myself on my self-control.)

What made me weep that day? Some simple truth, I suppose, uttered by a good man. And in spite of all I have seen these past few years, all I have been party to, the things I have observed and recorded, I still believe the President.

Believe it I do, in spite of what my lawyers, with a cynicism that I find offensive, keep saying: *It boils down to this, Ed. Steal a pile, a real big pile, and it isn't stealing at all. And even if it is, people don't get excited about it. Hell—what's a million, two million. Just paper. Somebody else's paper. And maybe it's just business. An ordinary financial transaction. But don't get caught with a fur coat, a rug, a color TV, a hi-fi. People identify with that. Or even a small bundle, like ten grand, twenty grand . . .*

I am in their hands, and I suppose that in some dreadful way, they are right. But if they are, the question will always puzzle me. What exactly is the line of demarcation between a (I shudder at the word) bribe and a business transaction? Is there any?

My former employer, the greatest man I have ever known, Senator Benjamin Bow Hannaford, would never have any difficulty making the distinction. Ben sees the world from an elevated throne. He is too rich to be bribed, too intelligent to be compromised, too honorable to be bought. By Ben's lights, *everything* he did was business, and business was a proper and fitting activity for a United States Senator, whether it involved the construction of a hundred million dollars' worth of pipeline and refinery in the Middle East, or pushing for an amendment to the Foreign Aid Bill.

These musings about that first visit to Washington and my current situation revive in my mind the event which my old Sunday school teacher would have called "that first fatal bite of apple." It was not really the first. I had been aware of many, many apples, many offerers of the fruit, and biters of same. But it *was* the first that involved me directly as a biter. Now you may find this hard to believe, but the bite was not a very big one and the fruit was not especially sweet or nourishing. And it proved to be a singularly indigestible apple.

Senator Hannaford had called me into his office. It was a warm June morning. The air was soft, the light outside hazed, as it so often is in Washington. He had turned off the air-conditioning and thrown the windows open. At heart, the senator was an outdoors man, a country boy. He liked nothing better than leading a party of guests—customers, fellow legislators—around one of his new construction sites, booted, helmeted, setting a rugged pace through mud, across fields that would soon be "processed" into airfields, cities, industrial sites.

I had brought in our latest file on the New Wilderness Bill, S.671, or the Hannaford Bill. When the bill had been introduced on the floor of the Senate some weeks ago, Lou Parenti, that vulgar journalist who has made it is his life career to attack, abuse, and vilify us, called it "Ben Hannaford's private hunting license in the national forest; you can hear the redwoods screaming already."

"I've a breakdown on mail on S.671," I said. "We may be in better shape than we thought, Senator."

He waved away my references to the New Wilderness Bill.

"Our persistent friend Mr. Blake was on the phone a few minutes ago," Senator Hannaford said.

"He doesn't take no for an answer," I said. Albon Blake was one of the leading "Industrial Consultants" in Washington. That meant he was a lobbyist, but one of Olympian stature. He dealt only with the very biggest clients, and handled only very special matters. A major industry like oil, or motors, or mining, would have its own massive lobbying or "educational" organization in Washington, but might also call on Albon Blake from time to time for certain discreet operations.

"There is no discouraging the likes of Albon Blake," the senator said. "Faith is the substance of things hoped for, Edward."

"Ah—New Testament?"

"The Epistle of Paul to the Hebrews," he said, pleased with himself. There was a rumor that Senator Hannaford's stepfather had been an itinerant Baptist preacher, as well as an oilfield rigger. He did not deny it and he was liberal with quotations from the Good Book, uttering them in round tones, as if addressing a Sunday school class. But he did it sincerely, with perhaps a slight air of joshing his listener.

"Is he still bothering us about the tax bill?" I asked.

Ben Hannaford's dark square face nodded solemnly. "The man, like many others in this city, will never learn that I don't need him. He can't change *my* mind. He can't buy anything for me. He can't even invite me to a cocktail party. But it is the essence of the lobbyist that he cannot be rejected, insulted, discouraged, or ignored."

"Then why did you call me in to talk about him?"

I was the only member of our considerable staff—perhaps with the exception of Cleo Watterson—who would dare talk to him in that manner. But he and I were close, very close.

Senator Hannaford spun about in his high-backed black leather chair and looked out across Constitution Avenue toward the dome of the Capitol. Freedom, feathered and robed, glistened in the morning sun. An ugly statue, I thought. I was glad she was sufficiently elevated as to be virtually invisible.

"I'm wondering if we can't accommodate Mr. Blake," the senator said.

"The tax bill?"

"Yes. Everyone knows I'm against the mortgage-and-loan tax increase. I don't need Albon Blake to convince me. I'm a builder, Edward. I know all about easy money."

"But for educational purposes?" I suggested. "To explain to some colleagues the validity of the mortgage-and-loan position?"

He turned to face me again. "That's a possibility, Edward," he said. "That is surely a possibility."

Across his wide burnished desk, he handed me a slip of paper with some scrawls in his own hurried slanting writing. His desk was free of papers. "You are to call this fellow at this number and arrange to meet him today. He is one of Albon Blake's people. Then come back here. Be distant, Edward. Be aloof. We can't let Blake or his clients think we really want to do this, or that we really need them."

The name on the slip of paper was George Paxton. The number was in the District of Columbia. I spoke briefly to Paxton, and when he seemed reluctant to name a place of rendezvous, I suggested the Washington Zoo in Rock Creek Park.

I don't know why I selected the zoo. Perhaps because of the glorious weather. Perhaps because of the need for some reminder of my first visit to Washington (we had gone to the zoo then) and my first innocent reactions to the city.

The exact point of rendezvous was to be opposite the gibbon's cage. If you have ever visited the Washington Zoo, you will know that this gibbon—a long-limbed dark brown fellow with an impudent black face—is one of the city's star performers. His act is an exciting one—wild breath-taking leaps around his cage, the acrobatics accompanied by deafening shrieks. As he shrieks, he puffs out a curious pouch on his throat, and each unearthly scream is punctuated with a resonant thumping. He reminds me, I regret to say, of some of the senator's critics in the press. The net effect of the gibbon's vocalizing is a sort of *Whoop-thump! Whoop-thump! Whoop-thump!*

A large crowd, mostly women and children, it being a weekday, had gathered around the cage. It was a lovely picture—the kids laughing at the ape's yells, the women pretty in cotton frocks, curlers in their hair, faces fresh and free of cosmetics. I found a bench a few yards from the gibbon's cage and bought a bag of popcorn. I munched, waited, and in a few minutes two men—not the *one* I had expected—appeared, walking from the direction of the reptile house. My instincts told me at once that the taller of the two was Paxton—something about his starched blue seersucker suit, his erect bearing, the assertive way in which he pumped my hand and looked deep into my eyes with two pale blue irises, told me he was Albon Blake's messenger.

"This is Mr. Krallis," Paxton said, "from New York."

Krallis—I think that was the name or at least something like that—was short, chubby, and well-tailored in a shiny blue-black suit of expensive cut. He had a soft moist face, blunted features and a hesitant manner. It was as if Paxton had been engaged as his mentor on how to act and behave in Washington. For there was in Paxton's crisp, Midwestern manner a certain ease—arrogance perhaps—that the likes of fat Mr. Krallis could never master in a lifetime.

"I can't tell you how happy we are that your boss has agreed to go along with us," Paxton said airily. His voice was too loud. "Mr. Krallis here is representing our clients. He's mighty happy, too."

But Mr. Krallis did not look happy. He adjusted a pair of thick eyeglasses on his damp face and then, suddenly, thrust at me a black attaché case he was carrying. "Take this goddamn thing," he whispered. "I wanna get the hell out of here as soon as I can, okay?"

Paxton patted his arm. "Easy there, Norton. It can't hurt to visit a little with Mr. Deever. You can go home and say you met Edward Deever, Senator Hannaford's right-hand man. And we are all aware of the senator's importance."

I wished he would lower his voice. These loud, self-assured

seersucker'd men bother me. One wonders that they are ever entrusted with anything.

Suddenly I found myself holding a heavy black attaché case. We sat on a bench—the three of us, like the Marx Brothers in A *Night at the Opera*—and as I placed the valise on my lap I felt obliged to say something appropriate to Paxton. Krallis I ignored. He preferred not to look at me, his eyes wandering to the gibbon, the neighboring chimpanzees.

"You are to understand one thing," I said firmly. "This in no way will influence the senator as he has told Mr. Blake many times. He's his own man. He's been opposed to the mortgage-and-loan tax all along. But it can serve certain educational purposes."

"Exactly," Paxton said. "We did not conceive of it any other way. To educate some of the disbelievers. Why, I'd be out of my mind, and so would Al Blake if we dreamed of trying to work on a great public figure like Ben Hannaford."

"Furthermore," I said, "you are not to count on anything. We'll apply this to educational uses, but we can't guarantee that the students will learn everything. But we'll try."

"Of course, of course," Paxton agreed—laughing. "May I?" He held his freckled red hand over my popcorn.

"Help yourself."

He grabbed a handful, and then nudged the fat figure of Krallis, who had turned his back on us. "Popcorn, Norton?"

"Nah, nah," the man from New York said. "Let's get outa here."

"Well I guess that does it Mr. Deever—may I call you Ed?" Paxton asked.

"I suppose so, if you wish."

Whoop-thump! Whoop-thump! Whoop-thump! The maniacal gibbon was shrieking again. Mr. Krallis cringed every time the air shivered. Paxton got up. So did his client. I remained seated, the black case on my lap. Both men shook my hand—Paxton with the firm grasp of the go-getter, Krallis wetly and weakly. Then they vanished in the sunlit crowd of women and children.

I rested a few minutes, then lifted the heavy case and started to meander among the exhibits. The zoo has some splendid rhinoceroses, and its small mammal collection is one of the finest in the world. I dawdled among the binturongs and kinkajous.

For some reason, I was reluctant to return to the office. At length I wandered south on the main path through the zoo, crossing the bridge over Rock Creek Park on foot, and exiting in the vicinity of Adams Mill Road and Harvard Street. It had gotten warmer and stickier. I was sweating profusely. My shirt was soaked. My legs ached. Had I been thinking clearly, I would have retraced my steps to Connecticut Avenue and found a cab. Now, stranded in a quiet residential neighborhood at mid-day, I knew I would have trouble getting back to the Hill. Only an occasional car went by. Not a taxicab was in sight, not a taxi stand. Panting, I climbed Adams Mill Road, toward a Bus Stop sign. The black case weighed down my right arm like a burden, a convict's iron ball. For about five minutes I paced in front of the Bus Stop, finding neither bus, nor taxi, nor a friendly face.

I set the case on the ground and straddled it. It was deep and wide—almost a valise—of a dull grainy material, and was closed with two shiny metal hasps. For some reason I imagined that it was attracting attention—even though the only people who walked by were a few schoolchildren and a woman pushing a baby carriage.

"Need a lift?"

A Negro was addressing me, a mahogany-colored goatee'd man, leaning from the window of a dirty pale green Buick. On his long head perched a yellow Panama hat with its short brim turned up all the way round.

"Ah yes, I need a cab—"

"You ain't gonna git no cab heah, man. An' that ole bus never comes. Git in, I run you over to Connecticut, you can git you a taxi theah."

Just for a moment did I hesitate, then walked toward the opened door.

"Don't fo'get yo' case, man."

"My goodness, isn't that stupid of me." I stumbled back to the sidewalk and got the attaché case.

"This is very kind of you," I said inside the car, as my dark Samaritan sped off. The rear seat was piled with crisp paper cartons—each bearing the label *Free-Hand Laundry*. "I was strolling through the zoo, taking a few hours off, and I made the mistake of thinking I could get a cab anywhere."

"Well you must be from outa town. Salesman?"

"Yes. Yes, I am."

As we cruised up Adams Mill, crossed Rock Creek again, and sped out to Porter Street, I felt ashamed of myself for having hesitated before accepting the ride. Warm weather was upon us and the papers, as usual, were filled with accounts of Negro crimes, Negro welfare chisellers, and assorted horror stories. My rescuer may have looked like a bad sort—the beard and the hat were rather suspect—but he was, after all, only a laundry delivery-man with a kind heart.

At Connecticut Avenue he stopped the rattling car. "Okay, man. Plenty cabs heah."

I dug my hand into my trousers pocket and fetched out a wad of money. I peeled off two singles and offered them to him.

He looked pained. "No, no, man. Jes' a favor. Heck, you don't have to lay on the bread."

I wasn't quite sure what he meant but I was humiliated. "Really, I'd like to show my gratitude. It was nice of you . . ."

"Okay, okay man. Jes' a favor. G'wan, you'll miss yo' next appointment."

I stammered my thanks, perhaps a bit too emphatically, and got out of the car. The pale green Buick screeched as he turned the corner.

What could he earn delivering shirts? Seventy dollars a week? Eighty? Could he support a family with that? For some reason I was unsettled by the incident. On the matter of civil rights I am neither a bleeding heart liberal nor an intransigent; I am a realist; I helped Ben Hannaford push through the Ghetto School Bill; and I will match our practical and consistent support of Negro aspirations with those of any group in Washington. So I had no cause to feel guilty. But it was disturbing to be patronized, rescued, put in my place, as it were, by a ridiculous fellow earning eighty dollars a week. My pity for him was mingled with a vague sense of unease with myself.

Settled in a cab, the black attaché case at my side, I wondered: "How long, oh Lord, how long, would my good-hearted delivery-man have to work to accumulate the amount I now carried in Mr. Norton Krallis' attaché case?"

An irrelevant question perhaps, but a plaguing one.

Senator Hannaford loved offices. He had three in Washington—his main headquarters in the New Senate Office Building to which I now hurried; a second suite from which he operated as Chairman of the Party's Senatorial Campaign Committee; and a third, in a brand new twenty-story building he had erected himself, in which his vast construction complex, the Hannaford-Western Corporation occupied two floors. But he liked the Senate office best. So did I. It put us at the center of things, "in the swim." And while by comparison with the Hannaford-Western offices downtown—or with the magnificent H-W Building back home in Ramada City—it was a modest suite of overcrowded rooms, short on desk space, but it was the office we loved, where we felt at home.

When I arrived the outer rooms were in their usual state of calm frenzy. "Calm" because most of our staff were relaxed Westerners; they seemed to operate better under stress than New Yorkers, or other big city people.

Cleo Watterson, the senator's secretary and office manager, was discussing the pile-up of mail with Marsha Treadway, our chief mail clerk. Both were good-looking women, even though Cleo was in her middle-fifties. She was rumored to have been "an old flame" of the senator's, but I did not believe it. It was sufficient that she was intelligent, hardworking, and resourceful. Cleo had iron-gray hair, fashionably bouffant, and was possessed of a remarkably fine figure. Marsha was something else again—young, soft, with a bosom like the Continental shelf, and a rump to match. She was half Cleo's age, and to my irregular tastes, not as attractive. There was a sense of something unfinished about Marsha—a strand of red hair undone, lipstick poorly applied, a stocking sagging.

"Hey Boy Wonder," Cleo called at me. "Senator Kemmons has been after you all afternoon. His Nibs doesn't want to talk to him, so it's your job."

Marsha looked at me moonily. We were involved at the time, an involvement I was uneasy with. Her large hazel eyes looked mournful, her soft mouth seemed to form a question.

"Senator Kemmons can wait," I said. "Is the boss free now?"

"All by his lonesome. Communing with the Great Spirits. He even refused a call from the White House."

That did not surprise me. Senator Hannaford treated the

White House and its incumbent with cavalier indifference—except when he needed them. More often than not it was the Executive Branch that needed *him*. They made the calls, they did the pleading.

In the inner office I was stopped by our Legislative Assistant, Matthew Fixx. Matt is a Ramada City boy, very young, very innocent, quite intelligent. But he is a little too infected with Washingtonese. He does this, I think, to compensate for not having gone to Harvard or Yale Law School, although there is nothing to be ashamed of in a degree from the Ramada University School of Law.

"Say Ed," he said eagerly. "I've been doing a little digging on the history of Wilderness Bills. I think I found us a viable fallback position."

Viable fallback position. That is Washingtonese. The words did not mesh with his stringy figure, his Southwestern drawl. But I indulged him. He was a hard-working young man, utterly devoted to the senator.

"What makes you think we'll need one?" I asked.

"Well, we're not exactly in a one-to-one relationship," he said archly, "with the rest of the committee."

That was a brand new one for me. A *one-to-one relationship*.

"I wouldn't worry about it, Matt," I said. "By the time the senator's finished explaining the bill to the others, they'll all be Christians."

"Hmmmmm. That could be. But the inter-face will be rough."

Inter-face? What in heaven's name was an *inter-face*?

"If you're so worried," I said, "you go ahead and get us a fallback position." I winked at him. "But no fallout from the fallback."

Matthew blushed. "Stop needling me, Ed."

I left him with his stacks of legal books, documents, committee reports, transcripts of hearings. He was a good detail man, but a very bad witness. Senators do not like to be lectured about "viable" positions. They are unhappy with "inter-face."

Senator Hannaford was in his shirt sleeves, his tie was undone. Someone from the corporation office had brought over a large, detailed plan of the new industrial park he was building around University City, and he was studying it with his shrewd black eyes, marking it with a red pencil, making illegible scrawls on a pad nearby. He sipped from a can of Dr. Pepper as he worked.

He could have been any millionaire builder, brawny, wind-burned, hard-handed, except for a certain quality of fine understanding that illuminated his face. I have known a good many wealthy men, through my association with the senator, and most of them are characterized by a bluntness, an inability to see beyond their work. They are very good at what they do, but at little else. Ben was different. I have no doubt he could have been a great teacher, or physicist, or doctor if he had chosen.

"Lock the door, Edward."

I complied. Then I placed the black attaché case on his desk. The senator stroked its grained surface. "Cheap. Purchased in a Peoples Drug Store or a discount house. Think of that, Edward. All the important things those people have on their mind, and look at how they transact business. A man should always go first class, even if he's on his way to prison."

"Maybe Mr. Paxton thought of it as a security measure. You know, an expensive thing with a Mark Cross label."

"We're dealing with cheapjohns. I detest cheapjohns."

"But you'll do business with them?"

"Only for my own—and the nation's—good. Not for theirs, Edward."

Briefly I described my meeting with Mr. Blake's agent, George Paxton, and with the sweating Norton Krallis. The senator did not seem interested in either of them. He was impatient with underlings—sometimes even his own, but never with me.

"I have little use for Albon Blake and his people," Ben said brusquely. "But he'll serve a purpose."

So saying he snapped open the two metal hasps and raised the lid. I blinked once or twice and felt a tightening in my throat.

"There should be twenty-five of them," the senator said. "Count them."

There were indeed twenty-five—twenty-five neat bundles of one hundred dollar bills.

"Count one of those stacks," he ordered.

I did. There were one hundred bills in the bundle—$10,000.

I said: "That would make $250,000. A quarter of a million dollars. That is a lot of money for an afternoon at the zoo."

The senator hunched his broad shoulders. "I hardly think so. Them as gave it can afford it. And them as are going to git it, needs it."

There was a trembling in my hands. My lower spine was going soft and boneless and my abdomen seemed to be parting at the umbilicus.

Senator Hannaford perceived my discomfort. "Easy there, Edward. It's only money."

"A lot of money."

"Not that much." He sipped his Dr. Pepper and his Indian eyes narrowed in good humor. Happy little wrinkles formed at the sides. So, I imagined, must his full-blooded Kiowa grandmother have looked when she watched a white man roasting on a slow fire.

"I would suggest we get rid of it," I said. My voice was a vibrato.

"No hurry. Let's just sit and admire it, as if it were a painting or a statue." He laughed softly. The transaction was a diversion, something to add spice to his day. "Yes, that mortgage-and-loan crowd didn't want that tax increase, did they?"

"So it would seem."

"But, I never wanted it either."

"They knew that."

"Oh, sure, sure they did." The senator chuckled. "This is for nonbelievers."

"It should help create some converts."

Senator Hannaford got up and paced the office a few times. He studied the plans for his new industrial park, opened another window, and waited a moment before commenting on what I had just said.

"Edward, no converts are needed."

"I beg your pardon?"

"That mortgage-and-loan tax increase never stood a chance of passage. Oh, it might have been close a few weeks ago. But it isn't going to be in the final version of the tax bill. The conferees have already just about buried it."

In four years in his employ, enjoying his confidence, I had become accustomed to his curious methods, his backdoor approaches, his talent for alternating direct action with the slyest of hidden maneuvers. But at this moment, with that black case and its quarter of a million dollars, resting between us, my bewilderment was total.

"You accepted this money from Albon Blake, on behalf of mortgage-and-loan interests, to see to it that the increase in the tax bill would be beaten—knowing full well that the increase was already dead?"

"Why not? The world is filled with people eager to dispense favors. They are unhappy if they don't. Why should I disappoint them?"

I thought of unhappy Mr. Krallis in his shiny blue-black suit. Was some of the money his? His father's? His father-in-law's? I consoled myself that the poor man was only a messenger. Bag man, I believe is the underworld term.

"But—but what in God's name are we to do with this?" I asked.

"You'll get us a safe deposit box at a friendly bank. We'll use the funds from time to time."

"But for what? For who?"

"Educational purposes."

"That's what Blake and Paxton keep saying, and I don't like hearing it from you."

"First let's divvy it up," Senator Hannaford said. "Then we'll think about it."

With those muscled brown hands—the hands of a high-steel man, a rigger, a crane operator—he began to shuffle the fat bundles. For a moment I understood the abstract power of the stuff. I was no longer thinking of what it could buy, what pleasures it could provide, but of the stiff crisp paper itself. It had a life of its own.

At length, after a few hesitant moves, he took seven bundles —$70,000 from the valise and set them in front of himself.

"Lemme see," Senator Hannaford mused. "How can we have some fun? Well, Edward, you got to start thinking about yourself one of these days. Can't stay a bachelor forever. Wife and kids will cost money. Here, that's for you." With that, he shoved two stacks across the desk to me—with no more perturbation than if he were raising the bet in a small poker game.

"For me? Why?"

"For loyal service. Go on, that's for you." He was giving me $20,000 of Mr. Paxton's clients' money. Then he did an odd thing. He took the five remaining bundles—$50,000—and dropped them in a side drawer of his desk. Noting the frown on my face, he laughed: "And that is for personal expenses in connection with this project."

"Of course. Now what about the rest?" I indicated the attaché case—he had now closed it—which held a residual $180,000.

"Find a safe deposit box. From time to time we will draw on it for educational purposes. Let's be candid. We have friends who will need campaign funds. I'd rather not mess up the books at the Campaign Committee with this. Let's regard it as a little kitty, we can go to as required." He shoved the case at me. I sat immobile.

"You ought to buy yourself some nice white shirts, instead of those ones with the little buttons on the collar," the senator said. "I never trust those Eastern boys with button-down collars, and I don't see why a small-town kid like you has to imitate them. *We* are in charge, Edward, not *them*."

His reference to shirts made me think of my bearded Negro friend, delivering his load of laundry. What would he make of all this?

"I'm puzzled by a lot of things," I said. "But one thing especially."

"What is that, Edward?"

"Albon Blake must have known what you've just told me—that the mortgage-and-loan tax was dead. He's got contacts in town. Why should he arrange this—for a measure that's beaten? What if his client finds out?"

He rose, his great chest bulging the expensive custom-made shirt. " 'Owe no man anything, but to love one another,' " the senator intoned. " 'For he that loveth another hath fulfilled the law.' "

"I'm not so sure I want to love Albon Blake *or* his clients, Senator. I still don't get it."

He arched his graying eyebrows. "Think of the New Wilderness Bill, Edward. Will it be a close run race?"

"I think so."

"Will we need help?"

"Indeed we will."

"Mr. Blake has just given us the bricks to build our house."

So—we were getting the suckers in the mortgage-and-loan crowd to help pay for passage of the New Wilderness Bill. Only Ben Hannaford could have dreamed that one up. "Is Blake aware of this?"

Ben held up a finger and frowned. " 'There are diversities of gifts, but the same Spirit,'" he said happily. "Sure he knows, Edward. He is representing the Conglomerate."

"Then—then—he's representing—*us?*"

"No one represents us, for we represent the people, the popular will. He's just there to help. Now I suggest you get on with your business before the banks close."

"I'm on my way, Senator."

"You might stop by the gymnasium, Edward, and tell Senator Stapp to expect a meeting of the Interior Committee any day. Keep our allies advised."

This would be Senator Sidney Stapp of California, handsome "Swinging Sid," a close friend of my boss.

"I'll do that." Senator Stapp was zealous of his lean, youthful figure; he worked out a lot in the Senate gym.

"But not a word to him, or anyone else about that black bag, Edward. St. John the Divine wrote that 'there was silence in heaven about the space of half an hour.' Our silence will have to last much longer. Perhaps eternally."

"I understand completely." I walked out with my attaché case. He'd made everything clear to me—almost everything.

At the door I hesitated. "Senator," I asked, "do you think Lincoln ever sent Harndon on such an errand?"

He laughed heartily and waved me off.

By now the reader will detect a certain—what shall I call it?— subservience, servility in my mode of speech, my attitude toward Senator Hannaford. I must advise the skeptics, those who would argue that in modern American society, bosses and underlings are all "pals," that a leveling process has endowed these relationships with an egalitarian veneer, that they know nothing of the United States Senate. Nothing at all.

A senator, within his small domain on the Hill, is a lord, a king, a potentate. Senatorial staffs are among the most respectful, admiring, unquestioning to be found anywhere in the world. Even those aides who know in their heart that their employers are less than they pretend to be, that they are perhaps fools and knaves, treat them with a variety of awesome worship that astounds the outsider. And Ben Hannaford was neither a fool nor a knave, and was a lot *more* than the outer man revealed. The truth of the matter is I enjoyed a close, warm and often informal relationship with him—at least in comparison with some of the administrative assistants on the Hill. You can hardly imagine the bowing, scraping, and forelock-tugging that goes on behind some of those doors. I sometimes think of each little senatorial enclave as a small monarchy, a petty principality, with its sovereign ruler from Iowa, New Jersey, or Georgia, and his attendant court of worshipful retainers. (And sometimes a few resident concubines.)

These reflections stirred me as I hurried to the private Senate gymnasium to talk to Senator Stapp. The attaché case weighed heavy on my arm. Outside the gym, a Capitol policeman greeted me. I knew them all quite well, and they knew that I was the number one aide to one of the Senate's most powerful members. A word about these police, for again, they reflect that insular and privileged nature of the Senate. The ordinary Washington, D.C. police have absolutely no jurisdiction on the Hill. They dare not invade the area to arrest a senator, a congressman, or indeed one of their workers. The truth is, the Hill is a place apart, a sanctuary, a world unto itself.

What better example than the hallowed gym, holier than any shrine, redolent of oil of wintergreen, sweat, and old sneakers? As the policeman greeted me and opened the door, I thought laughingly of the rigidly enforced rule—no photographer had ever been admitted to the gym in the entire history of the Senate. Senatorial paunches and haunches were not considered a fit subject for the probing lens.

"Is Senator Stapp here?" I asked a Negro attendant. I could see Walter Edgerton, the learned Chairman of Foreign Relations, clad in a gray sweat suit, working out with Indian clubs.

"Mr. Deever, he just left. I think he is at the barber shop."

Time was running short. I wanted to get to the bank before closing. But I hurried to the Senate barber shop. It was odd, how this rambling stroll through the most private, most privileged confines of the Senate Office Building, helped soothe me, helped arrange my confused thoughts. For the fact was, the black case at my side, and its potent contents, were troubling me. What would I do with that $20,000? Why had Ben suddenly decided to lavish it on me? What right had I to blithely accept this "cut" from the mortgage-and-loan people's "special fund?" In some curious way, my ramble through the holy corridors and stately rooms gave me assurance: it was all right because Ben said it was all right.

I found Senator Stapp getting a shave in the Senate barber shop. I suppose this barber shop would rank next to the gym in order of exclusiveness. Displayed on a huge shelf are shaving mugs for each senator, with his name painted on it.

"Hi there, Senator Stapp," I said. "Senator Hannaford has a message for you. He may be calling a meeting of the Interior Committee very shortly."

"Oh? Well, we'd best do a little homework. Thanks, Ed."

I liked "Swinging Sid." He had style, class. A bit too flashy for the Senate, but a shrewd, hard-working man.

Outside the old office building I got into a cab and told the driver to take me to the Riggs National Bank on Dupont Circle. As we sped off—it was early afternoon and there was very little traffic—I treated myself to a view of the great Capitol dome once more. I never tire of looking at it.

The massive, complex power it represented—particularly the lofty power of the United States Senate struck me full force. It was as if it had never been revealed to me, or outlined so starkly, as it had been by Senator Hannaford's actions that day. As the dome faded in the distance, I struggled to make some connection between the majestic building beyond, and the cheap attaché case on the seat next to me. *Power.* That was what my mind kept returning to. I thought of the Senate's staggering power. The power to sit in judgment on other branches of government. The power to impeach and remove judges—and even Presidents. The power to investigate any cabinet member, to make it so hot for them they had to resign. The power of subpoena. The power to haul American citizens before committees and whether they liked it or not, force them to testify under oath. The power of the libel-proof fortress of the Senate floor, where anyone in the world could be attacked, criticized, raked over the coals with total impunity.

And what of us, the worshipful party of senatorial servants? We, too, possessed distinct, unique powers, and we used them freely. We could sign our bosses' names to foreign travel orders, or to counterpart funds from U.S. embassies. We—I did myself many times—changed the language of our bosses' speeches in the holy Congressional Record, polished them to make them sound like oratory, deleted any slip that might cause embarrassment. We could even sneak on to the Senate floor and persuade a cooperative tally clerk that our boss had been on the floor, when in fact, he had not been there at all.

All of these exercises in power, we and our senatorial lords deemed necessary, indeed vital, to the so-called government of checks and balances. So what if our dedication to this principle often served to impede progress rather than to move us along? It was the use of our power, I now feel, that truly motivated some of us. One was not quite *drunk* with power, just a little giddy, a little lightheaded. I look back on that eventful summer and tragic autumn, and I realize now that some of us—senators, and their enchanted aides—sometimes became victims of this power and tended to play small god or petty king.

And it occurred to me, as the cab sped toward Dupont Circle, that Ben Hannaford's current acquisition of a quarter of a million dollars from "interested parties" was nothing less than a manifestation of this easy power. He had simply done what he wanted to do, because it would help his ambitions and goals, and because no one really had to know about it. So be it. I accepted Ben's judgments on just about everything else. Why not this time?

The black valise felt infinitely lighter, and not at all conspicuous when I got out of the cab at Dupont Circle and walked into the Riggs National Bank. A clerk gave me two sets of keys. I produced identification and filled out several forms. Then I asked for some letter-size manila envelopes, and in these inserted the $180,000 left after Senator Hannaford had taken his $50,000 for "expenses." The $20,000 he had given me remained in the black valise, but for the life of me I could not think of anything I wanted to do with it. So I put that also in an envelope, marked the outside "E.D." and shoved it into the box.

I am a meticulous, well-organized person. I had felt the need for some sort of record as to what went into the safe deposit box —the bank does not care and keeps none—so prior to entering, I had gone into a nearby drugstore and purchased a combination letter-envelope and a stamp. On this form I now wrote: *Riggs National Bank, June 25, $200,000 from N.K. and G.P. $20,000 E.D., $180,000 special fund.* The clerk obliged me by putting the bank's date stamp on the inside of the letter, which I then addressed to my apartment and mailed. The postmark too would verify date and place. Satisfied that I had served Senator Hannaford well, I returned to the office and cleaned up a backlog of telephone calls.

CHAPTER TWO

Across my morning coffee and orange juice, still in my silk bathrobe, I viewed Marsha Treadway with reluctant resolve. This was the morning I had chosen to sever our relationship. It would not be easy for me, and it would be a lot harder for Marsha.

"No toast? Shredded Wheat?" she asked. Marsha had a flat western New York State accent, as different as imaginable from a New York City accent. People from Rochester, Buffalo, the little places in that region, are really Midwesterners, basic bedrock Americans.

"No thanks, dear," I said. I scanned the front pages gloomily, but my misery did not stem from our newest "police action" in Djarak, or the Soviet Union's latest rejection of Pope Clement's appeal that they halt the bombing of Inner Mongolia. My mind was burdened with sex, and what to do about it. And across the formica table top from me sat the personification of sex, soft Marsha Treadway, her lush coppery hair tantalizingly mussed, her puffy face expressing satisfaction with the night's work, her flimsy pink peignoir barely concealing her ripe melons or the dark triangle. She was by no means completely unattractive at that moment, and had not my mind been set on a surgical end to our relationship, I might have suggested a reprise. But not quite.

Courage! I told myself. The deed had to be done. I tried not to reflect on my slobbering surrender to her last night—or all the nights we had spent together. For the past year or so, we had been loyal bedmates, enjoying our bodies on a regular schedule; but the joys had not diminished. In a sense, I was revolted by my own schoolboyish helplessness during our love-making—and perhaps that is one reason I chose to manifest my will power and discard her.

No sooner would we be in my bachelor apartment than I was at her clothes, on my knees, burying my head in her garments, clutching at a tricky garter, a clever zipper, my mouth searching, my hands grasping, my body consumed with roaring fire. I did not want to behave in this manner; I simply couldn't help it. I would all but rip the clothes from her, like a man peeling a banana, and then would pace the apartment in nervous anticipation as she took medical precautions in the john. The rhythmic rituals would follow, and at length I would explode into outer space, go into biological orbit, and fall into a sated sleep.

In these fevered joys, I sometimes thought nothing else in the world was worthwhile. But thank goodness for post-coital calm! After the heights of passion are scaled, what remains? Well, Marsha was a good-looking, voluptuous, good-natured young woman from a small town near Buffalo, not terribly bright, but knowledgeable in the ways of Washington, a woman in her late twenties, not given to expressing deep emotions, not exactly a "girl on the town" but a "fun date," a good gal to take to cocktail parties and on rides to the country. She dated a few newspapermen, including the columnist, Lou Parenti.

Of course I was not in love with her, and knowing Marsha, I doubt that she loved me. But I did like her very much. In fact, I owed her a good deal—and not only in terms of the erotic gratification she had given me so willingly. Before my employment by Senator Hannaford I had been a newspaperman, working for a small syndicate servicing a chain of Ohio newspapers. I was the chain's only Washington man, and that meant a twelve-hour day, work on weekends, and perpetual exhaustion—all for the grand sum of one hundred and fifty dollars a week. Marsha Treadway at that time was working in the office of the Secretary of the Senate. Both of us were underpaid, eager to succeed, and a little uneasy about our small-town origins. (People from western New York State are very much like Ohioans.)

Marsha and I started dating, and she became a friendly, helpful guide to the city and to the seats of power on the Hill. Her knowledge of the inner workings of the Senate and the House was considerable. Many senators knew and liked her; she was the pinchable, huggable kind of almost-beautiful, slightly overweight girl, one finds in government offices. I was astounded one day to hear the Vice-President himself address her by her first name!

I confess that at the time, early in my Washington career, I was something of a square, a country boy, who barely knew where to get a good restaurant meal. Marsha became my teacher. On our first date—at her suggestion—we rode in the swanboat in the Tidal Basin, then went to dinner at the Gangplank on the waterfront. I still can taste the tang of those cold martinis, the sweetness of the soft-shell Maryland crabs. Oddly, I did not try to kiss her on that first date, when I dropped her at the door of the Southwest Plaza. I was so astounded with my good fortune at finding her, that I did not want to be too aggressive and ruin what promised to be a fruitful relationship.

The next weekend she suggested that we rent a canoe and float down the Potomac to the Watergate concerts. It was delightful. We paddled down the river from Fletcher's Boathouse, and I remember the sun setting behind the spires of Georgetown, the modern high rise buildings opposite them, the lush foliage on Roosevelt Island, the handsome bridges, the distant alabaster beauty of the Lincoln Memorial. We had packed a picnic lunch— liverwurst sandwiches and cold beer—and we ate happily as the Army Band serenaded us with Debussy and Ravel. It was one of the grandest evenings I had ever spent.

Our dating continued. Marsha, in return for my friendship, began feeding me tips on Senate business, opening doors for me. Marsha was a minor figure in the Secretary of the Senate's office, but she seemed to know everyone, was always being invited to the right parties, and had a knack for getting senators and their aides to do favors for her. I'm willing to admit she probably did not even have to sleep around; she was simply a likable, busty, friendly girl, whom people were glad to help. And if she had a boyfriend, an ambitious young newsman who wanted an exclusive interview with Senator Henshaw of the Labor and Public Welfare Committee, the senator would be glad to oblige.

As I recall this early phase of our friendship, it was only after several dates that we went to bed. I don't know why. I'm not an overly aggressive fellow when it comes to sex, I suppose. I enjoy it very much, but I fear rejection; I am afraid I may be rebuffed. Marsha had another "regular" beau at the time, a Navy Commander, who claimed to be separated from an invalid wife in Charleston. (She had stopped seeing the aforementioned Parenti.) In any event, we did finally consummate our friendship. Then it lapsed, for reasons I cannot define—boredom, other interests—and then it revived, shortly after I returned her early favors by hiring her when I went to work for Senator Hannaford.

It was not an easy decision on my part to divest myself of her company. But the truth was, there was an unsatisfactory aspect to our coupling. It will sound idiotic, but it had something to do with these yawning, stretching, distracted morning-afters. There was something about the business of confronting Marsha across the coffee and orange juice that bothered me. Perhaps it was my puzzlement at my ardor of the night before. How? I would ask myself. How could I be reduced to a blob of quivering jelly by this woman? I suspect a man knows that he is really in love when he faces the object of his gasps of the prior night, over the box of Bran Flakes, and finds in his loins a passion equal to the one that ravaged him nine hours ago. That had never happened with Marsha. In some curious way I was beginning to resent the way she reduced me to a trembling schoolboy at night.

And, to be absolutely candid, I was suspicious that she was beginning to see Lou Parenti again. I am a stickler for loyalty—from all hands. Just as Ben Hannaford demanded it of his staff, so I demanded it from girlfriends. I had no real evidence that she had taken up with the columnist—I note parenthetically that this Parenti was a self-appointed crusader who specialized in blackguarding people—but I have a sixth sense in these matters. I would catch her in cryptic phone conversations, a word dropped here and there, a change of attitude. And once I saw her in what seemed to be tense, confidential conversation with Parenti outside the press dining room. There was something about the look on their faces that bothered me; the way Marsha hurriedly and nervously left him when she saw me.

"Marsha, darling," I said firmly, "I hate to tell you this, since I am so darn fond of you. But we are going to have to end this."

"End what?" She brushed a crumb of toast from her upper lip.

"You and me. I feel like a wretch saying this. A rat, an ingrate. But it's not right for either of us. We won't ever marry—I mean each other. It's holding you up, and it's wearing me down."

"You mean for good? End it?"

"I think so, dear." I reached across the yellow formica and patted her hand. Marsha had very small, very soft hands. "I've enjoyed our relationship enormously, darling. But, dammit, it doesn't seem to go anywhere. We know we aren't ready for a permanent, sanctioned arrangement . . ."

"You have another girl," she said, a whine creeping into her voice.

"Scout's honor, Marsha, I have not."

"You're sick of me."

That was a little closer to the truth, but not really the truth. I was, let us say, uneasy with the disparity between the morning-after Marsha and the way she made me melt, surrender, and slowly die at night. Or was that merely symbolic of something in our relationship that I resented?

"That is not so, Marsha, that is not true at all. I merely feel that these things, as wonderful as they are, run their course."

I had been mulling a termination of our friendship for a long time. Now, in some way I cannot truly define, the senator's odd act of generosity toward me—indeed the whole affair at the zoo, the heavy black attaché case—had hardened in me the need to be rid of her, to uncomplicate my life, to divest myself of confidantes, of involvements with co-workers in the senator's office. I would give up all those mad clutchings at skirts and slips, the moans and groans and sighs, in the interest of security.

"Well, you're frank, anyway," Marsha said. "It won't be easy for me." But she did not cry. There was iron in Marsha's soft pliable body. "You won't believe it, but this is the first time I've gotten the gate. I have a pretty good record. It's always been me who's told the fellow to get lost."

"I am certain of that, Marsha. And please don't feel it's 'the gate' as you put it. You still have your job. We'll see each other at the office and around town."

"You found another girl," she said flatly. "I know you did."

"I have not. I wish it were that simple. I'm overworked, Marsha. I have too many things on my mind."

"Hmmmm. Maybe you're telling the truth. You haven't exactly been one hundred percent lately."

"See? See? Even you've noticed it."

But she was hurt, deeply hurt, and I felt like a scoundrel. She got up to collect the breakfast dishes, loyal friend to the last, and I heard her begin to sniffle.

"Marsha dear, please don't cry . . ."

"Ah, go to hell," she whimpered softly. I tried to touch her, to console her, but she showed admirable dignity. She shoved me aside, and her brief tears stopped at once. "Go on, I'll clean up," she said.

That was loyalty! That was the essence of being a good sport! She would do her small housewifely chores to the end, and I sincerely hoped that soon she would find another mate for whom she could perform so well. Hearing her showering, I had a twinge of regret. In a few minutes her hair would be combed, her makeup applied, her soft body powdered, encased, strapped, shaped, by all that elastic, nylon, and lace. A final effort? A goodbye? No. Never again. Self-control has always been a strongpoint with me. Moreover, I really did not have to shed too many tears over Marsha. There was always Lou Parenti.

That same Parenti was after us in his morning column. His wide flat-nosed face scowled at me from the side of his column "View from the Hill," in the Washington *Truth.*

> Bible-quoting Ben Hannaford, the Big Builder from Ramada City, and the richest man in the United States Senate is up to something—and it may result in the most daring raid ever on the National Wildernesses, and perhaps even the National Parks. Nothing stops Big Ben when he's after something he really wants.

How Parenti learned things astounded me. People—senators, congressmen, top officials—had an uncontrollable urge to talk to him. There is something about Washington that makes people eager to tattle, snitch, inform, advise. Wait long enough and any secret becomes public knowledge. The fact of the matter was, the senator's decision to move on the New Wilderness Bill had just been made a few days ago. And already Parenti knew!

> Whatever happens, look for the taxpayer and the public to get burned. Hannaford has always claimed his bill is aimed at reinforcing the existing legislation protecting Wilderness lands from mining, timbering and oil interests. But a close reading of the Senator's bill reveals the

joker in the deck. Conservationists say it will be opening wedge to throw the National lands open to exploitation. When Builder Ben introduced the bill on the floor of the Senate—against his own party's wishes but with the blessing of President Kretz and his Interior Secretary "Giveaway Gordon" Hackensetter—public outrage was so great that the bill was put in cold storage. Evidently it's out again and Hannaford is ready to move.

I folded the paper. Enough of Parenti. He was the eternal crusader, the presumed guardian of the public interest—and a stiff pain in the neck. One senator, the aged Gabriel T. Tutt of Alabama, had once thrown a punch at him, and the Majority Leader, Senator Gage Hopewell of Wisconsin, had denounced Parenti on the floor of the Senate as "the fetid, foul breath of the scum and slime of American slums." (It was Lou Parenti who had bestowed on Senator Hopewell the nickname "Honey-Tonsils".)

Parenti would be at our throats on the New Wilderness Bill, and we would have to be prepared for him. But I had faith in my boss. Ben Hannaford had a talent for getting what he wanted—and what he wanted was good not only for himself, but for the country. He kept money moving. He built. He created jobs. It was no wonder that President Hayward Kretz, although in the opposition Party, leaned on him so heavily, trusted him so implicitly. "The point of this whole thing is," Ben Hannaford told me once, very late at night, "someone's got to be in charge. And that someone might as well be me. In fact, it *better* be me, because I'm what keeps this country going."

Listening to the dreary morning news on the radio, I knew the truth of Ben's creed—someone had to be in charge. The world had become terribly complex, terribly confusing. Who better than practical men like Ben Hannaford to run things?

". . . Pope Clement has again appealed to the Soviet Union for a halt in the bombing of Inner Mongolia, in a special letter to Chairman Gromyko. The Holy Father was joined in his plea by Secretary-General Ojukwa of the United Nations. Mr. Ojukwa said that he had reliable information from Imre Bator that if the bombings were suspended unconditionally, peace talks could begin at once . . . No statement has been issued by the Kremlin, but an editorial in this morning's *Pravda*, which reflects the govern-

ment line, states again that 'all the Soviet Union asks is that Inner
Mongolia let its neighbor, Outer Mongolia alone . . . ' "

I sighed. So went the world. We had been saved from folly in
Thailand by the blessed emergence of President Kretz. And now
the luckless Russians had been suckered into a meaningless adventure on the windy steppes of Central Asia. It was all very
well for Americans to sit back and snicker; but Ben did not like
the way things were going. It was bad for business, anyone's
business. He knew a lot of Russians, especially their engineers and
construction men, and he got along with them. They were being
led astray by bomb-happy generals, Ben felt.

"Meanwhile, in the crucial Arab sheikdom of Djarak, on the
Persian Gulf, an additional five hundred United States Marines
have landed. This brings to three thousand the number of Marines
now stationed in the tiny Arab state, where a revolution by so-
called Free Djaraki forces is attempting to overthrow the government of Prince Omar Aziz. A State Department communiqué last
night said the Marines were landed in accord with our bi-lateral
treaty with Djarak, and to protect American life and property . . .

"Thus far there no reports of injuries to any Americans, or to
the extensive refinery and pipeline operated by Longhorn-Mideast
Oil . . ."

Djarak. A dot of sand, sand covering billions of gallons of black
petroleum. Hannaford-Western had built the first pipeline there.
Longhorn-Mideast, run by Mrs. Hannaford's relatives, were there.
Well, we were defending freedom there also. Freedom came in
different shapes, sizes, and disguises, Ben used to say. And it included the right to pump oil, create jobs, build refineries. Were
the Djarakis better off, or worse off before Longhorn-Mideast
came in? Any fool knew the answer. They had starved over camel
dung fires and slit each other's throat in the old days. Now there
were doctors and teachers in the tiny country; Longhorn had
given them color television and a soft drink bottling plant.

Ben's power reassured me. Better in *his* hands than in the
hands of irresponsibles. Even the yesterday's transaction did not
dismay me. What was it that Ben used to quote to me? *"We do
evil that good may come."*

I went in to the bedroom where Marsha, in filmy pink slip was
combing her hair. Lust flickered for a moment, but I controlled
it. I kissed the back of her perfumed neck, ran my hands—for the

last time—down her girdled flanks until they reached the unencumbered stretches of soft thigh, and recalled all the splendid times we had had together. "Lock up, Marsha," I said. "And leave the key in the mailbox. See you at the office."

She made no response. I sensed that she was hiding her sorrow in deference to me. I never liked her as well as I did at that moment.

We made a point of taking different cabs to the office and arriving at different times. Not a soul, not even all-seeing Cleo knew of our affair.

In the calm interior of the taxicab, I concentrated my mind to the work ahead. Any day now, Ben would spring the New Wilderness Bill, S.671, on the Interior Committee. The screams would be loud. But he was going in confidently; the windfall of cash from the mortgage-and-loan lobby would be used to help the measure. It was a brilliant stroke, brilliant as only Senator Hannaford could conceive it: milking the zealous anti-tax people to defeat a measure that was already dead, and using the funds to push through something he wanted very much for himself, for his associates—and for the good of the country. The humor of the whole thing!

Well, the humor of it was never lost on my boss. No matter how big the stakes, Ben Hannaford was able to laugh. There is a cushioning quality about great wealth; it softens the falls; eases the bumps; greases the skids. You cannot really get hurt if you are rich enough.

Ben Hannaford had envisioned his Washington career as another challenge—another contract to be fulfilled, another job to be delivered, another means for—let me be frank—making a fortune. And the zest, the vigor he brought to his activities! What a joy to see him in action—handling suspicious reporters, especially those of liberal stripe, or in a committee meeting, answering arguments, rebutting his critics. But best of all, his performances on the floor of the Senate itself!

I thought back (as my taxi approached the Capitol, moving slowly through the morning traffic along the Mall) to that day when I first became intrigued with the senator, the day I saw him in action on the Senate floor, during the debate on the oil depletion allowance. Not to get bogged down in technical details, let me explain that traditionally the oil industry is permitted a tax rebate to the extent of 27½ percent on every barrel they pump. The theory is that they should be permitted to write off the diminishing worth of each well. After all, the supply of oil is not limitless, is it? Critics point out that the deduction—greater than that allowed any other mining operation—goes on *long after the oilman has recovered his original investment*. Liberals like Lou Parenti call it a "steal," a "giveaway," "a loophole" and are forever pointing out that giant oil corporations often pay less taxes than "charwomen" or *no taxes at all*, or actually get *tax refunds on millions of dollars of profit*. My answer to all of this is, that the finest, most respected men in Washington—including our last six Presidents—have supported the depletion allowance, as well as such august and beloved figures as Speaker Sam Rayburn. How can it be so evil?

In any event, liberals have been raging against this so-called loophole for years. During Senator Hannaford's first term, a congressional cabal of liberals decided the time was ripe to reduce the depletion allowance from 27½ percent to 15 percent. They rallied support on the Hill. They propagandized the press. They produced tearful testimony, including that eternal little charwoman who had paid more taxes in 1972 than Longhorn-Mideast Oil, and they were convinced that at long last the "villainous" oil barons would be brought to justice.

They did not reckon with Ben Hannaford and his connections with the oil industry. Ben was then a member of the Senate Finance Committee, which writes our tax laws. Into the Finance Committee hopper went the proposal to slash the oil industry allowance from 27½ percent to 15 percent. But before anyone could object, Ben worked a deal with the friendly committee chairman (who needed campaign funds badly) to substitute a measure that would *raise* the tax benefit for the oil industry to 33⅓ percent!

The liberals raged and screamed and the crusaders in the press came down on Ben with a vengeance. President Kretz reluctantly supported Ben's substitute bill, which was soon reported favorably out of committee.

A few days later, when the measure came up for debate on the floor of the Senate, I was to see Senator Hannaford in action, flexing every muscle, using every trick, bending and swaying the

Senate to his will by sheer force of personality, sheer nerve, sheer arrogance.

I was covering the Senate, new in my job as Washington reporter for a small press service for Ohio papers, and had just taken my seat in the gallery. As ever, the Senate Chamber filled me with awe: the severe black pilasters, the glass eagle in the ceiling, the dark brown desks with their traditional inkwells and sand containers, the brown leather armchairs in the corners—suggesting the waiting room of a country doctor—the rather hideous plum colored carpeting, the bronze-edged riser, the pages in shirt sleeves lounging at the edge of the long tables.

Senator Maury Eisenberg of Illinois was speaking. He was a wealthy real estate operator from Chicago, a down-the-line liberal, and an enemy of the oil industry. "This bill is an outrage against the American people!" Senator Eisenberg cried. "Already, the oil industry is refusing to bear its fair share of the national tax burden! And now this measure will give them an even *greater* inroad into the national treasury! Look at these figures, Mr. President, Harbinger-Dole Oil Corporation, on an income of 217 million dollars paid less than two and a half million dollars in taxes—a rate of 1.4 percent! Longhorn-Mideast Oil—"

He cried out his anger to a sleepy Senate. They had heard much of this before. I listened with half an ear—surprised at the mild rate at which the oil corporations paid taxes, but accepting it as part of the scheme of things. The Vice-President slumped in his great chair of office. No one needed to convince Vice-President Smead Beldock of the inherent right of any corporation to make as much money as it possibly could. As a right-wing congressman he had advocated abolition of the progressive income tax.

I saw Senator Hannaford—while Senator Eisenberg kept attacking tax benefits for oil, get up from his seat and begin to prowl, and prowl is the only word—the floor of the Senate, stopping here to gossip, grabbing this senator by the lapels, that one by the arm, haggling, laughing, waving his arms, in total disrespect for the man speaking.

Yet there was something so graceful and nonchalant about Senator Hannaford's performance, that I forgave him any discourtesy to Eisenberg.

". . . may I point out that the oil industry has *already* ducked its share of taxes by this unfair, undemocratic fiction . . ."

Ben Hannaford had grabbed both of Senator John Tyler Lord's lapels—Lord was a weedy patrician New Englander—and was lecturing him, evidently on the need for passing the tax bill as written. With a look of horror, Senator Lord tried to disengage. It was almost comic. After a moment Senator Hannaford released Senator Lord, and treading again in the aisles, set his sights on another of his opponents, scholarly Senator Royce Henshaw, a former professor of political science at Columbia. Henshaw was a powerful figure, a genuine intellectual who was rumored to have authored Senator Eisenberg's attack. Senator Hannaford was at Henshaw's desk. He pounded it twice, he gestured wildly under Henshaw's nose, he pointed to Eisenberg. It seemed to me he was saying, "I know you wrote all that guff for him, and I won't forget it."

". . . the oilmen admit it! Their own promotional literature brags about it! If they strike a dry hole, Uncle Sam pays. If they hit it rich, they keep the bulk of the profit! How did this outrageous state of affairs come to pass? Is there no longer a sense of fair play in American life?"

"You bet there is, Senator!" Senator Hannaford shouted—from alongside Senator Henshaw's seat.

Senator Eisenberg looked as if he had been stabbed. "I beg the senator's pardon?"

"You asked about fair play," Ben Hannaford called out. "There is no fairer square-shooter than an oilman! They are only asking their natural rights! Oil isn't going to last forever! It's a national treasure, a crucial resource. And those men who risk life, capital, energy, use their imagination and power to bring it to us, got to be rewarded! That's our system, whether the senior senator from Illinois likes it or not."

"May I remind the senator," Senator Eisenberg said, clearly shaken, "that under the rules of the Senate, senators are supposed to be at their seats when they speak. I appeal to you, Mr. President, to caution the senator from these outbursts from different areas of the Chamber. I rather feel like I'm being peppered with buckshot from ambushes."

Vice-President Beldock nodded at Senator Hannaford. "The senator will speak only from his own seat."

But Ben kept wandering. After working over Senator Lord and Senator Henshaw, he got over to the opposition side of the house, walking in that long easy stride, on the lookout for unbelievers to be won over to the cause of a 33⅓ depletion allowance.

Henshaw was now talking, reciting statistics on the tax bill, attacking the loopholes. From the distant corner of the chamber, Senator Hannaford suddenly snorted, "One man's loophole is another man's equity!"

"This legislation," Senator Henshaw went on, "is nothing more than one more loophole."

"Loophole! Loophole!" Ben Hannaford shouted from across the Chamber. "You fellows keep saying loophole! It is a legitimate benefit!"

For the first time Vice-President Beldock used the gavel. Hannaford shrugged. As the floor was given to John Tyler Lord of Vermont, Senator Hannaford stalked another victim, another subject for indoctrination. I believe it was Senator Ernest Wagenknecht of Iowa, a fence-sitter, who might be swayed. Senator Wagenknecht reacted differently. His round red face beamed. Wagenknecht was a small-town appliance dealer, and he was truly honored, to find himself a conversational partner for Ben Hannaford. As a flushed John Tyler Lord proceeded with his attack, Hannaford and Wagenknecht laughed and chatted.

"I beg the senator who has introduced this measure to at least listen to the arguments," John Tyler Lord pleaded. He was very blond, very thin, and he seemed to wobble a good deal. His blood had thinned over the years. He was too much the Harvard man, too much the Yale Law School graduate.

"I know all your arguments," Hannaford boomed, from his seat alongside Senator Wagenknecht. "You people have no understanding of what makes this country great!"

There was a hum in the press gallery. John Tyler Lord's father had been an Associate Justice of the Supreme Court. His grandfather a Governor of Vermont. Several antecedents had signed the Declaration of Independence. One had been burned as a witch. To question his lack of understanding about "what makes the country great" appeared to be the ultimate in effrontery.

We could see the veins pounding in Senator Lord's small head. The color rose purplish in his pale face. "The senator has forced me into a position I was reluctant to take," John Tyler Lord said, in a strained voice. He turned to Vice-President Beldock. "Mr. President, I call the attention of the Senate to Senate Rule 12—"

"Lord's making a mistake," someone in the gallery whispered. "Ben suckered him into it."

"Under Senate Rule 12," Lord said shrilly, "any senator who has a direct pecuniary interest in a piece of legislation must disqualify himself from voting on it. This is not a compulsory rule, Mr. President, but it has the sanction of precedent."

But Lord was gaveled down by the Vice-President. "The chair rules that the comments by the junior senator from Vermont are out of order and have no bearing on the debate."

Ben Hannaford was at his seat, finally. "If it please the chair, Mr. President, I'd like to respond to the distinguished senator from Vermont's attack on me," Ben said softly. The Vice-President nodded.

"The question from the junior senator from Vermont is, do I intend to vote on the proposed measure? And if I do, how do I justify it in terms of my interest in the oil industry?" Ben braced his feet and jammed his huge hands in his coat pocket. "The answer is, yes, emphatically, I do intend to vote for this measure, this means of ensuring our country's continued wealth and prosperity. The senator speaks of a direct pecuniary interest. Just how is that to be defined? The fact that my wife—whose name I would trust could be kept out of these debates—has interests in this industry, interests created by the hard work of her beloved father, the late A. J. Cudder—"

"A point of privilege, Mr. President," cried Senator Lord, sensing he was whipped. "Will the senator yield?"

"Not now," Senator Hannaford said firmly. "Mr. President, I make no apologies. We are all lobbyists, every single one of us. The junior senator from Vermont, the senior senator from Wyoming, we are all the agents, whether we like it or not, of these special interests of our states. Show me an interest that is *not* special! Let everyone in this Chamber step forth and disclose what special interests they have legislated for, lobbied for, done favors for! There is nothing to be ashamed of! This is an open society, may I remind my young friend from Vermont! Why should not our industrial companies which have done so much to build this country—as much, may I suggest, as Harvard and Yale —have a friend at court? I am dismayed by the junior senator from Vermont's attack on me . . ."

And so it went. By the time he was finished he had made mincemeat of John Tyler Lord, who squirmed and tried to get the attention of the Chair, but found no friend in Vice-President Beldock. Finally Lord left the Chamber in a rage. Senator Hannaford's triumph was complete when none other than the Majority Leader himself, Senator Gage Hopewell, rose, and to a hushed Chamber and gallery, intoned:

"Mr. Praaasident, whatever our feelings about the bill under consideration, I think the senators will agree with me, that the attack on Senator Hannaford was of a most unsporting nature, and that these personal matters are not a proper subject for senatorial debate!"

So sang the Majority Leader himself, in support of Ben Hannaford. There was more applause from the gallery. I was young and naive at that time, and I was puzzled by what I had just witnessed. Senator Hannaford had been rude, brusque, and had violated several rules of the Senate, but he had emerged the hero of the moment, or at least blameless. And poor Senator Lord, merely for suggesting a conflict of interest, had earned the disapproval of his peers. Later, when I had learned more of the folkways of the Senate, I understood what had happened. Cunningly, Hannaford had pushed Lord into an attack on another senator's motives, and thus forced Lord to violate the most precious of all Senate commandments: *Thou shalt not speak evil of a brother senator, anywhere, any time, but especially not in the Chamber.*

I can remember wandering through the press gallery later and hearing Lou Parenti tell another newsman: "Hannaford is something new, that big bastard, an original. He's got brains, brass, dough, ambition, and he enjoys himself. They better look out he don't buy 'em all."

Shortly thereafter I suggested to my wire service a profile on Senator Ben Hannaford, and they liked the idea. During the course of my interviews, the Senate defeated his bill for a rise in the oil depletion allowance. When I went to see him at his office I expected him to be downcast. But he was delighted.

"I don't understand, Senator," I said. "You've just gotten licked. Why are you so happy?"

He winked at me. "Licked? Son, that bill of mine never stood a chance. I knew it would get licked."

"Then why did you introduce it?"

"Well, we had to head off those crazy liberals. That bunch who wanted to chop us down to a 15 percent depletion allowance."

"But how—who—"

"Say, you are a young and innocent boy, Deever. Now don't you print any of this, but listen, because you'll learn something."

I listened. I felt that at that moment our lives would somehow be intwined.

"That gang in the House, and a few well-meaning but misguided crusaders like Lord and Henshaw thought they had us this time with that 15 percent deal. Well, there's only one way to fight back. Best defense is a good offense. So I introduced my bill to raise the allowance to 33⅓."

"And you didn't mind its getting defeated?"

"I knew it had to. But it kept the 15 percent crowd from getting theirs through. They had to fight my increase all the way, and to make sure it didn't get passed, they had to agree to forget their bill."

"Agree? With whom?"

"Me. Senator Hopewell. The administration. That crowd was so scared of my measure, they were willing to bury their own. You learn something, Deever?"

"I certainly have."

Shortly thereafter I went to work for Senator Hannaford, first as his press secretary, later as his administrative assistant. (My predecessor moved on to the Federal Power Commission; the senator knew how to take care of his own.) The job of press secretary was combined with my new over-all duties in the office. I was never happier.

These memories still flitted about me as I entered our office and was greeted by our legislative assistant, Matthew Fixx. "Ed," he said, "the capability factor on the New Wilderness Bill is very high. The name of the game is power."

"Are we still in a one-to-one relationship?" I asked.

He laughed. "A little better, I'd say. The arguments are well-structured. I think the senator will like what we came up with."

I patted Matthew on the back, pleased with his loyalty. Ben demanded more than loyalty. Only Cleo and I were allowed to argue with him, and then under special terms. The watchword of the office was obedience, unswerving obedience; he asked for it, he deserved it, he got it. It was said on the Hill that he ran the happiest of ships. (And, I may add, one of the best-looking. Senator Hannaford's girls were the prettiest in Washington. A fashion magazine did a piece on them once—and came to the conclusion that the loveliest, best-dressed women in the city were to be found not at a Georgetown cocktail party, not at any fashion show, but right in his suite in the New Senate Office Building.)

Let me expand on this a bit, lest there be misunderstandings. Senator Hannaford was not a skirt-chaser, like his colleague, Sidney "Swinging Sid" Stapp. Far from it. His fealty to Mrs. Hannaford was well known. It was simply that he appreciated thoroughbreds, that he believed in quality. The four thousand head of Black Angus cattle he had on the big ranch in Ramada City were thoroughbreds; so were the Gordon setters that Fern bred; and so were the attractive girls we hired.

At that time our staff numbered thirty-five, one of the biggest on the Hill. But we needed them all. No office was busier, more concerned with a multitude of functions—the senator's legislative functions, his work as Senate Campaign Chairman, his commitments to Hannaford-Western and its allied companies, and—why deny it?—the beckoning vista of the White House.

I checked phone calls. None was urgent. Senator Alford Kemmons had called, but then, he was always calling, always leaning on us, always after help.

When I returned to the outer rooms, Cleo Watterson was talking to a girl, one I had never seen before. I was certain of that, for had I seen her, I would never have forgotten her. She was beautiful. More than beautiful. She had that rare grace and freshness that women seem to lose so quickly after marriage, working too long in the same place, or an unhappy affair. She was in her early twenties, a tall, slender, superbly proportioned young woman. I admired the way she sat in the chair opposite Cleo's desk—long legs crossed, spine very straight and not quite touching the back of the chair. Good posture, good bearing in a woman is something that enthralls me.

"I'm sorry, Miss Valdez," Cleo was saying. "There are no openings on the senator's staff. But we might send you to see some friends of ours in town."

Miss Valdez. She was a Latin, a Mexican-American, as were many of the senator's constituents. She had about her that exotic look of the Latin. Her hair was not quite black; the morning sunlight endowed it with reddish lights. Her alert face was almost square—as wide as it was high—the nose short and charmingly dented, the eyes like polished onyx, the mouth broad and crimson. I stared at her a little too long, a little too intently. Aware of my scrutiny, she uncrossed her legs, and then re-crossed them, tugging at a short yellow skirt of some light fabric. She did this not in any flirtatious way, but as an act of self-assertion. *I know you are staring at me and I know I am lovely, and there is nothing we can do about it,* she seemed to say. Her dress was sleeveless; her arms were creamy tan.

"I'd hoped to see Senator Hannaford and give him this letter," Miss Valdez said. "My father worked for him for many years, and he was sure the senator would remember him."

"Well, honey," Cleo said, "many people have worked for the senator, but very few get to see him. He's terribly busy now. I hope you understand. Suppose I make a few phone calls for you."

I walked toward Cleo's desk. "You say your daddy worked with the senator?" I asked. "I assume that was back in Ramada City."

She smiled at me. Latin warmth radiated from that perfect face. The formula was so easy—sun, family love, simple food, a touch of Catholicism, guitar music. Why did it elude us?

"My father was one of his foremen. He worked for him first when they built Terrence Field, then on the Longhorn Refinery, and lots of other jobs. He only works on and off now—he isn't too well."

"The young lady brought this letter for the senator," Cleo said. She handed me a single sheet of white paper. It was neatly typewritten—Miss Valdez's excellent typing, I was certain.

Dear Senator Hannaford:

Please forgive me for bothering you. I am Joe Valdez who worked with you on Terrence Field back in the forties and lots of other jobs. The arthritis keeps me cooped up a lot, but your men down here have found work for me now and then, for which I am grateful. I have no kicks. You once said I was the best concrete man in the southwest, and I can still get out there and earn my money, when my back is okay.

I have a favor to ask. This letter will introduce my daughter, Maria Anna Valdez, who is 22, and just grad-

uated from Ramada U. She is a smart girl, graduated
cum laude, but also can take shorthand and type, since
I have always advised her to have a real skill to earn a
living, in addition to knowing history and literature.
Mrs. Valdez and I are very proud of her, and I think you
will get a kick out of seeing her, Senator, since you must
have seen her when she was a little kid.

Anything you can do to help an old iron hat will be
appreciated. We are all darn proud of you back here in
Ramada, especially us working stiffs, and most especially
us Mexican-Americans.

Sincerely,

Joe Valdez

The letter was neatly typed, not an erasure. But the signature
was that of a sparsely educated man.

"If this is your typing," I said, "you're pretty good."

"It is. But the composition is my father's. He wouldn't let me
change a word of it." She smiled—snowy white teeth, a dimpling
of her coffee ice-cream cheeks.

"Well, I do wish we could be of assistance," I said. "Do you
know anyone else in town?"

"No one. I just arrived last night."

The legs moved again—faultless knees. I felt chastised as she
tugged at the yellow skirt. She was exceptional, a rarity, a black
swan unexpectedly lighting in our pond of pale blond Anglos.
Our pretty girls ran to yellows and reds—lank hair, pale skin,
that slightly boiled-out aroma of the pure-bred Nordic. But Miss
Maria Anna Valdez was another breed of cat—a whiff of Myrurgia,
the scent of bougainvillea and oleanders at dusk. Distantly I heard
a mournful guitar.

"Cleo, why don't we tell the senator Miss Valdez is here?" I
used my most charming manner. Cleo and I observed a polite
neutrality—separate but equal powers. "After all, she's the daughter of an old friend. He might want to say hello."

"Senator Kemmons is in there. And the files for the Interior
Committee meeting aren't quite ready."

"Oh, just a minute of his time. Senator Kemmons won't mind."

Of course he wouldn't. Alford Kemmons had become so utterly
dependent on Ben that he would have permitted me to interrupt

their meeting to bring in the head of Americans for Democratic
Action, a group Kemmons regarded as very close to traitors. Poor
Kemmons! He wasn't a genuinely bad man; just a weak one. He
could not hold his liquor. Nor could he hold his tongue. There
was just something *missing* in Alf Kemmons, some essential
mechanism that prevented him from being much of anything.

I knocked, walked in, and greeted Senator Kemmons. "Senator,
hope you don't mind an interruption."

"Heck no, Eddie. The boss and I are just chewing the fat." His
round, balding gray head rotated atop his scraggly bird-like neck.
He suggested a cheerful undertaker. He smiled a lot—too much
for my tastes. Nor did I appreciate the way he played the syco-
phant to Ben, referring to him as "the boss."

"Senator Kemmons has made a big decision today," Ben said.

"Really?" I asked. "Giving up air travel?"

We all laughed. The senator was known as "Airborne Alf" to
some newspapermen. Lou Parenti had fixed the name on the
amiable senator from Nebraska. It referred to Senator Kemmons'
frequent use of military transport to take him to his home state.
It was alleged by Parenti that Senator Kemmons had set an all-
time record for using Air Force transportation, free of charge, to
fly him home just about every weekend, always on the pretext
of inspecting some new air base, some defense plant.

"That's a good one, Eddie!" Alf Kemmons gargled. "No, I
haven't done anything that rash. Matter of fact, I'm off to Hubbs
Field tonight to have a look-see. Part of the job." Hubbs Field was
an hour from his home town, where he ran a lucrative insurance
business—but judging from some of his operations, not lucrative enough.

"Senator Kemmons has decided to shelve his investigation of
the cement industry," Ben said. "He has come to this decision
after long and prayerful consideration."

"Yes, it was a dead end," Kemmons said airily. "No evidence
of price-fixing at all. I let those young wiseacres on the committee
staff sell me a bill of goods."

"I'm sure it was a wise move on your part," I said.

"Who really cares anyway?" Kemmons said loudly. "Oh, a few
minor violations, but that's not the business of a Senate Subcommittee."

There was a moment of silence. A knowing look passed between

Senator Hannaford and myself. Kemmons was up to his old tricks. He had been bought again. It was the cheapest, meanest of schemes—announce an investigation, get a lot of publicity, dig up some hot information, scare a few of the rich corporations, and then discover it was not worth the effort, that no real evidence had been found to establish this-or-that crime. And of course, somewhere in the process, one might be rewarded by the beneficiaries of the canceled probe.

"Yes, I get the feeling nobody really believes in those investigations any more," Ben said. "We've had too many of them. We all seem so righteous that the public is beginning to doubt we're all that good. Nobody investigates *us*."

"The Senate of the United States is above suspicion," said Alf Kemmons, laughing. "Any schoolboy knows that. It's like the church, or the press."

I marveled at Kemmons. No man wrapped himself more in that cloak of probity that the Senate prides itself on. Few men deserved the protective robing less.

"Hate to bother you, Senator," I said. "But a young lady's outside to see you—thought you might like to see this letter she brought along." I showed him the note from Joe Valdez.

He read it swiftly. "I'll be darned. Joe Valdez's kid. He was a great foreman, one of the old-timers. If the girl's anything like the old man, she must be a good one. Can we help her?"

"We're full up, sir. Cleo said she'd send her to some friends."

"Then I guess that's it." He leaned toward Kemmons, and I walked to the door and opened it. "If you have a minute sir, she's worth taking a look at."

Senator Hannaford, understanding the import of my remark, got up from his desk and strode to the door.

"That's her—the dark girl in the yellow dress."

Straighter than ever was her firm young back. The tilt of her head was astonishing. She was the kind of young woman in whom dignity and high quality were as normal as sweat and talkativeness in other women. And that quality would assert itself anywhere—in a Mexican slum, in the Senate Office Building, in the theatrical district of New York.

"So that's Joe Valdez's little girl," he said. "Good for old Joe. Sent her to college and everything." He was pleased that his old foreman had done so well by a daughter. "Hire her," he said.

"Wish I could make decisions like that, Senator," Kemmons gargled. He had a spongy voice—a terror to witnesses appearing before him. "But I gather that wasn't a hard one to make."

Senator Hannaford ignored him; as I left I heard him begin to query Kemmons about the Interior Committee's members.

Briskly I walked up to Cleo and Miss Valdez. "Well, Miss Valdez, it looks like you have been hired."

Cleo blinked—only twice. She knew me well. She knew Ben even better. He had looked upon Maria Valdez and found her beautiful.

"Oh goodness!" she cried. "I can't believe it!"

"You better believe it," Cleo said. "You're going to work hard here."

Maria got up. She was taller than I expected, and not quite as slender. Her waist and limbs were thin but her hips and breasts were pleasant ripe surprises. Far off in the desert night, beneath a purple sky I heard that guitar again, plunk-plunking around a fire of roaring mesquite.

"I can't thank both of you enough! Can't tell you how happy I am!"

"You thank Senator Hannaford, honey," Cleo said. "You'll never meet a man anywhere in this city, in this country who is more loyal to old friends. Your father had a lot to do with this. The senator must have thought highly of him."

No doubt he did. But Ben, in one swift glance, one hawk's view of the girl, had been impressed by daughter as much as father. I had seen that slight intake of breath, that spark in his eyes. He knew quality. And I imagined he must have felt, as I did, the need for a little Latin spice in our overly Anglo'd office. (I am of Scotch-Irish ancestry myself, pure-bred Nordic blood, thoroughly Protestant, so I hope I will be forgiven these half-jesting remarks.)

And so Maria Valdez came to work for us.

Her hiring, it now seems to me, was one more relevant event in the concatenation of dramatic incidents that took place that calamitous summer. Not that she was in any direct way connected with the fortunes of my boss. But she was part of the great tide that seemed to sweep over our affairs; the sea change in him, the surge of power, the cresting of the wave that he himself had created in the placid sea of the capital. Soon we would all be swept up in it, some succumbing, some striking out for the distant shore.

I had sensed it for the first time during the incident of the $250,000. Why had he thrust that outlandish bundle of money on me? (I refer to the $20,000 for my own use.) And why did he suddenly, capriciously, keep $50,000 for "personal expenses"? The balance of the money—now stowed in a safe deposit box in my name in the Riggs National Bank—was an understandable sum, a logical fund. But the odd way in which he had "cut the pot," bothered me a little as I went about my morning chores—after turning Maria Valdez over to Marsha Treadway for some indoctrination on office routine.

He had taken the $50,000—and had made me a gift of $20,000—for one reason, and one reason alone, I concluded. At the peak of his powers he was convinced that he could do anything he wanted to do.

But that was too simple. He was, in his own mind a reflection of the national will. The concept is a subtle one, and I shall attempt to develop it later. He conceived of himself, and many of his associates in the Senate, particularly those on whom he conferred his largesse, as buffers against something dark and bloody in the national character. He spoke often of the "tiger" that had been let out of the cage in the 1964 election. "That tiger got out," Ben said to me once at night, as we pondered the voting figures in our state, "and he is not going to be back in for a long spell." And he spoke of the people waving fists at reporters, the repeated references to "crime in the streets," the recurrent harping on "morality" by men neither more nor less moral than anyone else.

"When a man says to you he is against crime in the streets," Ben said to me, "it means he hates colored people and is willing to shoot them. Hell, I am against crime in the streets also. Who isn't? But that's code son, pure *code*. It means, to hell with niggers. I am no great friend of our black man, but he is an American, goddamn it. They got rights too."

It was against these new moralizing impulses that he imagined himself to be a buffer. "I can handle 'em," he winked at me, after a particularly exhausting session on the floor of the Senate with Senator Gabriel T. Tutt of Alabama, "the liberals will be eaten alive by them, but not me."

And in some arcane way, his pocketing of the $50,000 was a nod in the direction of traditional cupidity and arrogance; as if he were saying to himself, see, I do this, I am not ashamed, but I am not part of the tiger. The small act of thievery, moreover, kept him in shape, kept him alert, on the move, keyed to any windfall, any opening, any advantage that might be taken. He had taken the $50,000 in the same way a man takes a workout in the gymnasium before engaging in a weekend of tennis—to tone the muscles and get the juices flowing.

We cared very little about the tax bill at that moment, one way or another. Our energies were fixed on the New Wilderness Bill, by number, S.671. (The S. stands for Senate and indicates the bill's origin.) Ben had gotten "Swinging Sid" Stapp, the senior senator from California, to introduce the bill early in the session. All of this was routine. The bill was then forwarded to the Senate Interior and Insular Affairs Committee, of which Senator Hannaford was Chairman, and it was anticipated that Ben would bring it before the committee in short order.

At that point the Conservationists began to howl. There is no howl louder than that of some aroused do-gooder beating his breast on behalf of the California condor or the bald-headed eagle. We were bombarded; the White House was importuned; the press screamed. The New Wilderness Bill, they shouted, was the most vicious raid on the National Forests ever conceived, a violation of the spirit of conservation, a rape of our national wilderness. Ben retreated. He bided his time. He got to know the President a little better (goodness knows the President was delighted; he looked with wonder on Ben) and he cultivated the Secretary of the Interior, Gordon Hackensetter, a shipping tycoon from California, whom Lou Parenti had nicknamed "Giveaway Gordon."

We had just come from a hearing of the Interior and Insular Affairs Committee. Pork had been served. Large portions of pork —a harbor here, a river improvement there, a dam for this district, a monument for that. It is a mid-level Committee, not taken too seriously. Ben ran it with a firm but friendly hand. Most of the members were in his debt. Toward the end of the hearing —it was an executive session, closed to the public—he had mentioned the New Wilderness Bill. His allies were silent. His enemies fidgeted. John Tyler Lord, in particular, a great friend

of the northern hemlock and the western spruce, had stiffened
in his seat.

"I'd go easy," I said, back in our office. "Lord was ready to let
fly, Senator."

"He is too damned noble," Ben said irritably. "I can understand
any man operating out of sense of greed or self-preservation, or
cynicism. But these idealists will be the death of us. They stand
in the way of progress. Any man who is more concerned with the
nesting habits of the prairie chicken is not be trusted." He looked
out the window at the Capitol. It disturbed him that his power
over that historic building was being challenged by the likes of
John Tyler Lord, a sniffish aristocrat. "Hell, I like birds also.
Didn't I stock the ranch with doves, and pheasant and grouse?"

"You sure did. And shot what—one hundred and twenty-two
doves one day last month?"

"You joshing me, Edward?"

"You'll never win the Conservationists over. They know what
the New Wilderness Bill is. So do we. It's a blank check for mining
and timbering and God knows what else in fifteen million acres
of the National Wilderness."

"Now, now, Edward. The bill specifies only in times of *National Emergency*."

"And who decides that?"

"Secretary of the Interior," the senator said.

"And you are counting on friendly ones—forever?"

He stretched. His chest, the chest of a rigger, a tractor driver,
pulsated under the expensive shirt. "Well, we got us a friendly
one for the next few years." He leaned forward. "Edward, you are
right about the opposition to this New Wilderness Bill. There is
but one solution. Outspoken backing from President Kretz himself, and of course, the Secretary of the Interior, Mr. Hackensetter.
We will convince them."

The White House had agreed to a tabling of the bill. Now Ben
was ready to change their minds. "I think it would be nice," he
said, "if we entertained the President and his party at Ramada
Ranch this weekend."

"On such short notice?"

"Why not? We'll give him a good time. Barbecue. Some advice
on improving that herd of Black Angus he keeps in Nebraska."

"I doubt that he'll come."

"Doubt not, ye of little faith. Edward, President Kretz will not only be our guest at Ramada Ranch, he will dedicate my new road. He will bestow his blessing on Highway 602."

I concealed my polite skepticism. But Ben was not bluffing, not overoptimistic. That weekend, in the dry, enervating desert heat, President Hayward Kretz did indeed cut the blue ribbon on Ben's new road.

A word in passing about President Hayward Kretz. He had been, prior to his surprise nomination and election, the head of a medium-sized southern newspaper publishing chain. His family, the Kretzes of North Carolina, had owned and operated newspapers and trade journals in a half dozen southern states. As a young man in his thirties during World War II, he had served with distinction as a public relations officer in the United States Navy, and was still referred to, by his closest friends, as "Commander." Hayward Kretz had never quite gotten over the Navy; he loved it more than anything.

Thus, his credentials—Southerner, Navy, conservative publisher—were impeccable when, some months before the nominating conventions, he wrote a memorable article for *Commentary* magazine on our burgeoning military involvement in Thailand. The article was entitled "Let's Get the Hell out" and it attracted nationwide attention.

Wrote conservative publisher Kretz: "Before I say a word, I defy anyone to look me in the eye and call me a left-winger, a pinko, a liberal, a commie, a socialist, an internationalist, or any kind of muddled do-gooder. I'm an American patriot, first and last. Now that we've got that straight, let's talk about this mess in Thailand."

Here was what the American people had been waiting for! "Commander" Kretz—conservative, businessman, press lord, Navy booster. Who could question such a man's devotion to bedrock Americanism? When he said we should stop the imminent shooting in Thailand, people listened.

"That's how it goes son," I heard Ben Hannaford explain to a reporter. "It helps if you're a Southerner, or got an in with the military. Proves you're a real American. Look at Eisenhower. A great man, and a great President. He got us out of Korea, didn't he? But you know what would have happened to Adlai if he had made that kind of deal with the commies? Why, they'd have lynched poor Adlai in the streets, left him deader than a Hereford calf in a blizzard."

The reporter was no fool. "Well, where does that put you, Senator Hannaford? You're not a Southerner, you're from the southwest. And you've had no military service. And yet you are one of the leading bridge builders to Eastern Europe. Right now, your company is negotiating with the Hungarians to build super- markets and filling stations."

"Son, I'm something special."

And he was. And President Hayward Kretz knew it. The Presi- dent was not a stupid man, but the intricacies of government bored him, and the dirty work of politics repelled him. On the legislative level, the President leaned heavily on my boss, and on men like Senator Gage Hopewell, the movers and shakers in the Senate. That they were of the opposition party did not bother the President. He felt himself to be above party lines, much to the chagrin of his own right-wing, and the disappointment of the liberals. But the country prospered, and apart from a few troublesome foreign matters like the rebellion in Djarak—which our Marines appeared to have under control—a somnolent calm had settled over the nation.

Ben Hannaford had a lot to do with this happy state of affairs. Did President Kretz (or his advisers) want the Peanut Subsidy passed? Depend on Senator Hannaford to bull it through the Agricultural Committee, with a talk here, a shove there, a cam- paign contribution for this senator, an appointment for that one. Power gravitated toward Ben Hannaford naturally, just as Presi- dent Kretz—heir to a publishing fortune he never really bothered to run—preferred to shed power, the way an oak sheds its leaves in autumn.

In a sense, I suspect that President Kretz admired Ben because Ben was a self-made man of great wealth, while he, while by no means a pauper, had inherited all of his. The Kretz fortune was ready-made when it devolved upon him after his Navy service. And as I have pointed out, he rarely concerned himself with the intri- cacies of his family publishing empire. I think it bored him. "Senator," I heard him ask my boss one day, "how does a man start a multi-million dollar construction business? How do you begin?"

Yes, he admired and needed my employer, but I doubt very

much that the President wanted to make a command performance
in Ramada City to dedicate a county road. It seemed a trivial
matter for the most powerful figure in the world. Besides, the
Secretary of Commerce, Mr. T. E. Kape, who was even richer
than Ben (steel and alloys) had already invited the President to
his Maryland hideaway, Roaring Mountain, for a weekend of
cribbage and tennis, two pastimes the President enjoyed more
than anything. If I may digress for a moment, it is worth recalling how Mr. Kape, whose inherited wealth defies analysis, got
to be Secretary of Commerce. Learning that Hayward Kretz
enjoyed nothing better than an evening of cribbage or a morning
of doubles, he had his personnel department, on the basis of com-
puterized findings, hire two minor executives—jokingly referred to
as Vice-President in Charge of Cribbage, and Department Manager in Charge of Tennis—and these young men were always
present when Mr. Kape entertained the President.

In a sense, Ben "stole" the President from Mr. T. E. Kape that
weekend. The steel executive was unhappy; he disliked Ben, as
only a man of inherited wealth can hate a self-made upstart. Ben
returned his contempt.

So there we stood on that broiling Saturday morning, the new
road gleaming in the dusty desert, a straight black snake, with a
white stripe down its back, stretching from the U.S. highway that
led to Ramada City into the back country. The wicked summer
heat surrounded us like cotton batting, but it had a comfortable
drying quality, a relief after Washington's infernal stickiness. As
far as one could see, the hot baking land shimmered—mesquite,
creosote, sagebrush, all pale and dust-laden. I loved the heat. Dry
heated vacuums developed in my skull, cooked the moisture out
of my lungs, endowed me with energy. I chivvied the press, answered questions, greeted minor dignitaries, arranged positions
for the television and radio crews, as we awaited the arrival of the
President of the United States aboard Senator Hannaford's private
helicopter. The presidential jet had landed at Terrence Field,
some eleven miles distant and was due any minute.

The Ramada City Technical High School Band (well-integrated,
with sprinklings of Negroes and a lot of Mexican-Americans)
struck up "The Stars and Stripes Forever." A platoon of cuddly
teen-age girls tossed batons and shook their delectable little
bodies for the entertainment of the several thousand people. Their

pink-tan limbs made me think of our new girl in the office, Maria
Valdez. Was she once a baton-twirler? I doubted it. I saw her
rather as a member of the dramatic society, a soulful reader of
Shakespeare.

On the reviewing stand, amid a group of local matrons—poli-
ticians' wives, daughters—stood Mrs. Hannaford, Fern, somewhat
taller, a bit aloof, a serene and lovely woman of middle age. Mrs.
Hannaford's big-boned, well-formed figure advertised her essential
lady-like qualities. Her hair was wheat blond, newly set, a hard
varnished crown gleaming in the sun. She wore long white gloves
and a pale green dress of simple but flattering design. Fern
seemed to be forever encased in light armor beneath her outer
garments.

"Everything all right, Mrs. Hannaford?" I asked. She never spoke
much. Basically she was a shy woman, uncomfortable in Washington society, ill at ease even with the local ladies. After all, she
was a Cudder, a daughter of one of the wealthiest families in the
state, the heiress to part of an oil fortune, and hence an object of
wonder to them.

"Yes, Edward. Isn't it a lovely day?" Fern's voice was thin and
pat. I never heard her raise it. Or raise an eyebrow for that matter.
Her face had a splendid immobility, and yet it was a pretty face,
with its wide unlined forehead, straight nose, and perhaps just a
bit too much upper lip.

"We are so happy to have Mrs. Hannaford heah," a young ma-
tron in electric blue said to me. "We lak to feel she is one of us."

"And indeed I am, Mrs. Reardon," Fern said sweetly. But she
was not one of them. By no means. The money made her different and they all knew it. I felt sorry for her. The wealth had
meant little to her; a childless marriage; a back seat while Big Ben
wheeled and dealed and manipulated; the torture of endless re-
ceptions, parties, dinners at their Potomac mansion.

Distantly, I heard the hum of the helicopter. The band struck
up "Anchors Aweigh."

"Right on time," I said to Mrs. Hannaford. The crowd cheered.

"You can depend on the senator," she said serenely. "These are
his own people and they must never be kept waiting."

"Yup, that's our Ben," an oldster in a straw hat chuckled.

"Here it comes! Here it comes!"

"Wow—a brand new one!"

It was indeed a gleaming new silver chopper, with the huge letters HW on its side. Ben had told the local Air Force people to forget about their own helicopters—his was the latest model and had a more comfortable interior.

The noise became deafening. A small dust storm on the desert as the silvery aircraft settled gently to earth. Hearing nothing but the roar of the blades, I felt someone tugging at my sleeve. Turning, I saw the broad unpleasant face of the columnist Lou Parenti. He had not come down with the press party and his presence was bothersome to me.

"What is with this cockamamie road?" he shouted. "What kinda nerve is that, bringing the President of the whole United States down here to cut a ribbon, hah? Don't you know we almost got a war in Djarak? Or that the Russians are bombing Inner Mongolia?"

The noise of the helicopter drowned out his obnoxious remarks. But he was indefatigable. "Jesus, who ever heard of a President coming down to a lousy hick road. Twenty miles of *horseshit!*"

On the last word, the noise of the helicopter ceased, and the profanity hung loud and resonant in the desert heat. I saw a faint wincing on Mrs. Hannaford's face, and I hurried away from Parenti, shepherding the TV crews.

Cameras were grinding away around the helicopter as the President—white-haired, benign, waving—emerged.

The band struck up "Hail to the Chief."

"He looks great!" people cried.

"And there's Ole Ben—right in back of him!"

Parenti grabbed my sleeve. "What's he got—a gun in his back?" Parenti is a bulky, menacing-looking man, a year or two my senior, but far more mature in appearance. His black hair is almost white at the temples and he has a blunted, broken nose. Many women find him handsome. I find him to be an overbearing lout. He affects the manners and speech of an ignoramus, but I ran a check on him a few years ago through some contacts at the FBI and I learned that Parenti is a Phi Beta Kappa from Brooklyn College and has a Master's Degree from Fordham. He once taught Government in upstate New York.

"Lissen, Eddie," he persisted. "What's Giveaway Gordon doing here? What are you guys up to? Gonna toss the New Wilderness Bill into the hopper again?"

"If you are referring to Mr. Gordon Hackensetter, he is a good friend of the senator."

Secretary Hackensetter had just emerged from the helicopter and was trailing the President and Senator Hannaford across the desert toward the reviewing stand.

"Come on, Eddie, he hates Hannaford's guts. Almost called him a traitor last year, didn't he? For trading with the Rooskies and building department stores for the Romanians, didn't he?"

I tore myself away and joined the party following the President and Senator Hannaford. The President looked splendid. His flesh was ruddy, the short, firm features alert and intelligent, the stride manly.

Senator Hannaford was at the microphone awaiting a signal from the floor manager of the live TV crew from station KRAM-TV, Ramada City.

"We are honored beyond words," Ben began, in his clear, yet curiously gentle voice, "to have with us the greatest American of our generation, the man who brought peace to Thailand . . ."

The President grinned but seemed distracted. His green eyes sought the horizon. Release, perhaps was what he wanted. Some hunting at Kape's retreat in Maryland. An hour of cribbage.

"I have praised many times," the President said, "this great coast-to-coast network of highways, federally conceived but built by private enterprise . . ."

"Don't nobody tell him anything?" Parenti whispered to me. "This is no coast-to-coast highway. It's a lousy twenty-mile county road. And what is this private enterprise? The taxpayers got soaked for it."

Of course the President should have been better briefed. No matter. No one really heard what President Kretz said. His fatherly face was assurance enough. The shears gleamed in the morning sun, and he cut the broad ribbon to applause. Ben Hannaford nodded approvingly. The President was in his pocket for the country to see, and the President did not seem to mind at all.

Parenti was shaking his head in disbelief.

CHAPTER THREE

The purpose of bringing the President to the Ramada ranch was twofold: to show Ben's opponents—who included some violent right-wing lunatics who had once spit upon him in the parking lot of the Ramada Hotel—that he was as close to the Chief Executive as any man could be, and secondly, to secure Administration approval for bringing the New Wilderness Bill up for a vote.

That is why we had invited the Secretary of the Interior, Gordon Hackensetter. The approach would be made through him, thence to the President, and before the weekend was over, Ben would have the green light. As far as the Party leadership was concerned, we had already taken care of *them.* In a sense, Ben *was* the leadership, being as close to Senator Hopewell as any man could be, and carrying great influence with all the important party men.

The barbecue dinner at the Hannaford ranch house was small and informal. After dinner on the patio, we gathered in the living room. For a man of Ben's wealth, the Ramada ranch house was not at all "showy." It was Western in flavor—brick walls, railroad ties as beams, ceiling-high fireplaces, a liberal usage of copper, ironwork, native wood, and stone. It was a low, sprawling, multi-roomed house, bright with horse, dog, cattle and Indian prints, although the senator certainly was not a professional Westerner, one of those amateur cowboys. He preferred the wheel of a new Ford, and he hated those pointy-lapel "cattleman" suits.

Fern sat next to the President on a small sofa. President Kretz

enjoyed the company of dignified, well-mannered women. Fern's
blond serene head was pleasing to him, and she was the only
person in the room he looked at directly. They were discussing
Gordon setters, which Fern bred. She owned four national champions.

"The trouble is weak haunches," she was saying. "Many breeders
are irresponsible, greedy people. They have inbred the poor
creatures so much that defects are turning up, like weak haunches."

"Yours don't seem so."

"No, they are splendid."

Around the vast sunken living room sprawled three of Fern's
pedigreed dogs—sleek, muscled animals, as gentle as she was.

"Senator," the President said, "Mrs. Hannaford here is my idea
of a real woman. You will forgive an old man for being so blunt.
But her knowledge of animals, and her cooking, and her style
are my notion of what a woman should be."

Fern did not blush.

Ben smiled. "Mr. President, you will find no disagreement on
that score."

"And," said the President firmly, tapping Fern's stockinged knee,
with a little bit of sexy implication, "I want that chili and green
pepper wing-ding recipe that you served! Maybe Mrs. Kretz can
get those darn White House cooks to make it for me! My, that
was tasty."

"I'd hoped the cooking improved," Ben said. "They tell me it's
been poor ever since those Frenchies the Kennedys moved in.
Seems no one could get the kitchen functioning again."

The President's white eyebrows arched. "You just might get a
chance to straighten it out someday, Senator."

Everyone laughed. The President was the most decent of men.
In tweed jacket, gray flannel slacks, suede shoes, puffing at a
stubby pipe, he seemed a retired professor of mathematics.

An Indian girl wheeled a cart among us, dispensing coffee,
brandy, and cordials.

"Sarah, say hello to the President," Senator Hannaford said.

The girl curtsied, and smiled, not at all embarrassed. "How do
you do, sir."

"Why you are a lovely little thing," President Kretz said. "What
tribe are you?"

"I'm a Mescalero Apache," she said.

"Goodness, you are a long way from home," the President said.

"A lot of us are. The Cavalry saw to that."

The President guffawed. Ben laughed also. "Sarah is the direct descendant of Old Antelope, one of the last paramount chiefs," he said. "She's got a much finer lineage than I have. My Kiowa ancestors were marauders, not much better than Paiutes."

"Amazing, amazing," said the President. "I just wish we could do more for the Indians."

Gordon Hackensetter sat tight-lipped, a little out of everything. He did not particularly believe in doing anything for Indians or anyone else. ("What Is the Civil Rights Movement?" Giveaway Gordon had shouted at a meeting of Save America, before he was appointed to the cabinet. "The Civil Rights Movement is a conscious part of the Communist conspiracy!")

Page Tulliver, the President's press aide, came in from the library with a sheet of teletype paper in his hand. Direct lines to the White House had been installed.

"May I interrupt, Mr. President?" he asked.

"Why certainly, Page."

"Chairman Gromyko's speech on the Mongolian situation is coming through."

"Ah." The President's eyes glazed slightly. He was bored to death with the Russian war in Mongolia. What those birds needed was a Soviet version of honest publisher Hayward Kretz to end the bloody mess once and for all!

"Would the President like me to sum it up for him?"

"Yes, yes, Page. Is there anything new in it?"

"Not really, sir. But the full text isn't in yet."

Ben Hannaford shifted in his arm chair. I knew he was saying to himself: *You going to run a country, run it; you going to be President, be President.* The irony was not lost on him. He had practically forced the President of the United States to make a trip to Ramada City to participate in a ceremony, and now the Chief Executive was too tired to care about a vital international problem. Tulliver was still waiting for a signal to start reading.

"What did Gromyko have to say?" Ben asked in a loud voice.

The aide darted a look at the President, but the latter was lost in some reverie.

"Let's hear it, son," Senator Hannaford said.

"Hmm, let's see," Tulliver said. "Partial text of Chairman

Gromyko's address to the League for Cultural Freedom meeting in Moscow. He stressed that the Soviet Union desired no wider war with Inner Mongolia. All they asked was that Inner Mongolia let its neighbor, Outer Mongolia, alone . . ."

"Same tune," Ben said. "What else?"

"Well, he said that he would fly anywhere, any time to meet with the Inner Mongolian representatives, including Ulan Fong. He said, 'Let them show up in Geneva tomorrow, and I'll be there.'"

The President patted a yawn. Poor Gromyko, bogged down in a pointless land war in Central Asia, had nothing else to say. More and more Soviet troops were poured into the grassy wastes.

"Shall I go on?" Tulliver asked.

"Why surely, Page," the President said. "That is—if everyone else is interested . . ."

"Well, Chairman Gromyko said that there could be no question, at this time of negotiating with the Free Mongol Liberation Front, whom he described as murderers and torturers. He said that a suspension of the bombing of Inner Mongolia was out of the question, unless the Inner Mongolians indicated what they would do in return. 'This is not a one way street', Gromyko said. 'If we stop bombing Kalgan, what will they do?'"

"Do we have any reaction from the Secretary of State?" asked the President.

"No sir. The Russian Desk at State feels Gromyko is under heavy pressure from both the *sokols*, that is the Russian word for hawk, who want to escalate the bombing of Inner Mongolia, and the *golubs*, or doves, who want to stop the bombing, withdraw to Red Army enclaves, and submit the matter to the UN."

The young man left; everyone else in the room awaited some word from the Chief Executive. But his eyes were closing. A direct and simple man, a good-hearted man, he may not have known where the two Mongolias were, or what the fighting was all about, but he disliked bloodshed.

"That fellow Gromyko," President Kretz said thoughtfully. "I sort of feel sorry for him. Met him once. You remember, Gordon." He looked at the Secretary of the Interior. "When they moved the United Nations from New York to Geneva."

"I do indeed remember him," Secretary Hackensetter said.

I was certain he did. It was Gordon Hackensetter's right-wing

friends who had succeeded in driving the UN from the East Side
of New York to the old League of Nations buildings on the
shores of Lac Leman, in Geneva.

"Not a bad sort," yawned the President.

"Mr. President, you are too trusting," Hackensetter said, ad-
justing his pince-nez. "He is a Communist and no Communist
can be trusted."

The opportunity was too good to be resisted. "I am told, Mr.
Secretary," I said, "that in the Soviet Union they pass out cards
with Gromyko's photo on it, and the caption 'Would you buy a
used balalaika from this man?'"

The air froze slightly. The President darted a vague look over my
left shoulder, then his eyes sought the oak beams in the ceiling.
He had this odd habit, very odd, in a man in such high office. He
never quite looked you in the eye.

Gordon Hackensetter burned. He did not particularly want to
come to Ramada. He did not like Ben Hannaford. Hackensetter
was a torch, a flaming presence, and Ben was an accommodator.
"I will tell you about Gromyko and all those gangsters," he said.
"They are Communists."

"Why of course they are, Gordon," Ben said. "But they got
problems. I found that out when I was negotiating to build
the Ogotz pipeline for 'em. I told 'em they needed a good dose of
capitalism."

"Yes, and thank God an alert Congress prevented you from
dosing them," Hackensetter said.

"Yeah but I sneaked one past you birds in Romania," Ben said.
"And the Hungarians are next. I'll teach 'em capitalism yet."

Hackensetter sulked. I knew Ben would not goad him too much.
We still needed his approval to go ahead with the New Wilderness Bill.

The Apache maid walked in, padding on moccasins and whispered something to Mrs. Hannaford. Fern leaned toward me. "Edward, there is a phone call for you."

From the library, where I picked up the phone I could hear the
President marveling at Ben's dealings with the East Europeans.

"Eddie baby, Lou Parenti here."

He sounded surlier over the telephone. There was an understanding that the presidential party was to be left alone. The
press were quartered in a motel five miles away, and had been

assured that no news would be forthcoming from the President's brief visit.

"Can I help you?" I asked.

"Lissen, Eddie, I just found out about that important local road for which President Kretz was obliged to give up a weekend and shlep down to this horseshit community. I am at the newspaper office of Mr. Flood, publisher of the *Ramada Clarion*, and I have learned that the road for which our President cut the ribbon is twenty miles long—"

"That was well known—"

"—and ends, *ends*, right in Senator Benjamin Bow Hannaford's six car garage! For Chrissake, Deever, you guys forced the President to come down here to dedicate Hannaford's private driveway!"

He did not seem outraged. Parenti is a cynic. Nothing really arouses him.

"First," I responded coolly, "what is a liberal like you doing with Mr. Earl Flood?" Flood was a right-wing crank. It was he who organized the pickets who spat upon Senator Hannaford in the parking lot of the Ramada Hotel during the last election campaign.

"Well, I don't agree with Earl Flood," Parenti said, "on burning down Harvard, or hanging Judge Moscowitz, the distinguished director of the FBI, but I got to have my sources too. Jesus! Twenty miles of blacktop driveway—and the President gets to christen it!"

"I have to hang up," I said.

Parenti growled. "I'm gonna print what I found out. What a disgrace! We got Marines landing in Djarak, we got a war in Mongolia, the stock market just went down, and all the President has to do is come down here to bless Hannaford's road!"

"Are you finished?"

"No. I wanna talk to the senator."

The senator would probably enjoy the respite. The President and Hackensetter were not his idea of lively company. In the living room the conversation had turned to the breeding of Black Angus cattle and the President was asking about stud fees. I told the senator about the call and he excused himself.

Ben met the accusation head-on—no dodging, no evasions. The only concession he made was a thickening of his Western accent—he might have had a chaw of tobacco in his cheek, sharing tall tales with another cowpoke.

"You say you found out the road ends at my garage?" Ben shouted. "That it is my private driveway? Why shoot, son, why not? The first job I had in Ramada City was County Commissioner, and the first thing I did was build me a road to my little frame house. Louis, there is no point in bein' County Commissioner unless you can build yourself a road!"

Parenti was reduced to mumbles. ". . . President got other things to do . . . you're trying to show up the opposition . . ."

"Sure I am, son! The President loves comin' out here and stayin' with ordinary folks!"

"You're worth two hundred million bucks, at least! You're not ordinary!"

"Yes, I am, Louis. I got to go—"

"What about the Secretary of the Interior?"

"We are educating Mr. Hackensetter, but don't quote me."

"Can I quote you on that crack about getting a road built?"

"You bet you can, Louis." Ben hung up. "A good boy, Parenti. I wish we could work on him a little."

"How about something from Albon Blake's fund?" I asked—not meaning it. The money bothered me.

"No, not with people like Parenti. We have only one way to handle him."

"What way, sir?"

"Tell him the truth—up to a point."

The living room was silent when we returned. The color TV had been turned on for the evening news. All watched and listened attentively, although the President, exhausted by the trip and the long day in the hot sun, yawned a good deal. He even yawned through the brightly colored film of himself cutting the blue ribbon for Ben's road.

". . . and down in his Caribbean hideaway on the island of Almaza, former Congressman Angel López Garcia has vowed once again to appeal to the Supreme Court to reinstate him . . ."

On the TV screen, brilliant in tropic sunlight, his café-au-lait face beaming, was Congressman Angel López Garcia of Chicago, the first Representative of Puerto Rican ancestry, and a disgrace to his people. "The Big Spick," Ben called him affectionately. He liked Garcia. He had served on Senate-House conferences with him. And Ben had warned him repeatedly about flaunting his petty dishonesties in the face of his fellow legislators.

"They are going to catch you someday, Angel," Ben told him.

"They have to run preety fast, Senator."

Well, they had run very fast, a lot faster than Angel López Garcia had figured they could. And now he languished in the tropics, a king deposed. But in what mocking splendor! He puffed a foot long chocolate-colored Havana cigar (a gift from Cuban admirers) and with each arm he embraced a dusky island maiden. Bougainvillea splashed wild colors in the background, contrasting with Garcia's dark face, white teeth, his orange-and-yellow shirt.

Fern shivered. "Disgraceful," she said.

No one heard her because former Congressman Garcia was talking. He was like the devil himself, Mephisto, Old Scratch, evil personified, but an evil so charming to some, and so horrifying to others, that no matter what he did or said, he commanded attention.

"I dislike that fellow," the President said. "He is a discredit to his race."

What race? I wondered. Garcia had on more than one occasion informed reporters who questioned him on his background, "Leesten, Chico, I am Spanish, Indian, Negro, Dutch, and maybe a little bit Jewish on my mother's side." Then he added: "But you don't have to be Jewish to hate me."

As the film revealed Garcia swaggering about his bungalow— laughing, hugging his doxies, blowing clouds of smoke toward the camera, I could see the President stiffen. As for Hackensetter, he was ready to murder someone. "I would like to have that scoundrel back in my home town in California," the Secretary said ominously. "All I'd need is a tall cottonwood and a few yards of rope."

Ben cleared his throat. "And a bullwhip, Mr. Secretary? Mebbe a little branding iron?"

"I would not hesitate," Hackensetter said. "That mongrel is a threat to every decent value in this country."

"He is certainly a disreputable man," Fern said soothingly. "And the House of Representatives was surely within its rights in denying him his seat—all that cheating on airplane tickets and salaries."

On the lurid screen the camera followed Garcia to a small beach-side bar, where the ex-legislator collapsed at a table and sipped a tall tropical concoction.

"Good booze," Garcia told millions of television viewers. "Island rum. The best."

"Congressman—" The reporters still addressed him by his title; he insisted on it, insisted that his ouster was illegal. "—why do you think the House voted so overwhelmingly to exclude you?"

Garcia drank deep. "I tell you, Chico, it's because I am already an outsider, you dig?"

"How do you mean that, Congressman?"

"*Mira*, Chico, look at poor Garcia. Look at my skin. Pretty dark, *verdad?* Leesten to how I talk. Pretty Spick, *verdad?*" The grin widened; the big semi-Negro face looked as if it would break into song. "But there are Gringos up there in Washington, guys I could name for you, crooks and swingers and especially the beeg industrial guys in the House and Senate—construction, oil, timber —or lawyers who got plenty rich clients—and, Chico, they are all cutting the pot. They all got a leetle vigorish going, and with some it isn't so leetle."

"Would you name a few? One?"

"No, Chico, not yet. But you know how it is. They *white*. They reech. They in the club. They Establishment. Nobody going to deny them their seats, Chico."

"Why not, Congressman?"

"They are Insiders, Chico. Wake up. I been on joint committees, House-Senate conferences with some of them. There is one guy so reech, so powerful, he knows where every buck in Washington goes. He decides who gets what. He gets his relatives and his friends on every commission where they can do his money good. But they never will lay a hand on that beeg guy. Because he is Real American, Chico, and Angel is an outsider."

"Care to identify the person?" a reporter persisted.

"I identify *nada*, Chico. I still have a sense of honor. I don't go rat on colleagues. Time for my afternoon siesta, *amigos. Adiós.*"

Off he swaggered with his courtesans, making a mockery of our public officials, our government, or political system. He was like the old movie villain—was it Von Stroheim?—who was advertised as "the man you love to hate." Garcia filled some need; he was a lightning rod; he let us indulge our most righteous indignation in public.

"Arrogant, drunken lecher," Secretary Hackensetter fumed. "The House was too easy on him. He should have been strung up on a live oak."

"What puzzles me," President Kretz said, as the announcer gave the baseball scores, "is how those foolish people in Chicago keep sending him back to Washington."

Ben stroked his chin. He had listened carefully to Garcia's innuendo. The Big Spick, as Ben affectionately called him, had no evidence. And even if he had, if he ever intended to get back into the House, he would need Senator Hannaford's help.

"Mr. President," Ben said, "his constituents like him just as he is."

"Oh really, Ben," Fern protested—as she noted the President's eyebrows bristle. "You can't be serious. Mr. President, my husband claims he knows the Latin temperament. But I am certain a man like Garcia will not be respected for long."

"My dear," Ben said, "the more Garcia thumbs his nose at us White Caucasians, the more the voters love him. Now if he'd wear a sombrero and sing *La Cucaracha* in a funny accent on the floor of the House, his fellow legislators might let him back in. But they'd kill him at home. He's a proud man, Mr. President."

President Kretz sighed. "A shame, a shame. I guess he is well-liked. By people similar to himself, of course."

"He's worshipped," Senator Hannaford said. "To their way of thinking he is acting out a commentary on the white leaders of America. Right down to the whiskey, the cigars, the women—and the arrogance."

"But that is a damnable lie!" the President boomed. "This country's leadership respects virtue and honor and family life!"

"And those who don't agree, better learn it quickly," Secretary Hackensetter said. "If they won't, it's about time we started teaching it to them—with force."

President Kretz got up. "Early start tomorrow," he said. The senator had arranged a doubles match for him at the Ramada Country Club.

When the President left, Ben took Hackensetter's arm. "Mr. Secretary, give us a minute or two before you retire."

The three of us went to the den. It was 11:15. I estimated it would take Senator Hannaford until 11:45 to convince the Secretary that he needed the President's approval on presenting the New Wilderness Bill to the Interior and Insular Affairs Committee.

He had gotten it by 11:37.

Late the following afternoon, when we were making preparations for the departure of the presidential party, Senator Hannaford drove up to the back of the ranch house in his four-wheeled jeep. In the back was one of those aluminum freezing lockers that are often taken on fishing trips and the like.

"Ed," he said, "see that this gets aboard the presidential plane. Have the chopper run it out."

"Perishable?" I asked.

"It's packed in dry ice, but it'll last till Washington."

I assumed it was some kind of foodstuff, some barbecue treat, perhaps the beans and green peppers the President had admired so much—a going-away gift to the White House party. I took it to the helicopter and forgot about it.

CHAPTER FOUR

The following Monday I arrived at our office, as is my habit, at eight o'clock—I am invariably the first one at work—and saw our new girl, Maria Valdez pacing the corridor.

"No fair beating the Administrative Assistant to work," I said.

"I didn't sleep much."

"Nervous?"

"Excited." She was lovelier than I remembered. There were tiny golden lights in her black eyes. She favored pastels. A chartreuse shift, matching low-heeled pumps. The light hues did wonders for her tan flesh. Distantly, that teasing guitar went *plunk-plunk* again.

When I opened the door for her, and she walked by me, with a swish of her short skirt, a scent of perfumed soap, I swore to myself: *no more office romances.*

She went to the minuscule desk Cleo had assigned her and set to work reading a batch of mail left by Miss Andrus, one of the mail clerks.

At my own desk, I went through Matt Fixx's résumé of what to expect when we hit the committee with the revived New Wilderness Bill. He wrote the way he talked. *Viable. We can live with it.* All that interested me was his guess on the committee vote. *We are in the ball park of an even split, or with the breaks, nine to seven for our side.* He was being pessimistic. If party lines held, we'd get the bill out, nine to seven; and a few opposition people would surely go along with Ben.

More important than Fixx's report were my own little file of cards on senators. I studied the Interior Committee file for a moment. These cards were my own work and I enjoyed writing them in the manner of a football scout's report.

GOODCHAPEL, LESTER. Basically conservative, slow to react and understand, but hard to move when mind is made up. Too thick for the Club, but a prospect. Leans heavily on Establishment Types either party. Faithful to only wife; two sons, one a veterinary student, other dentistry. See no problem with him on our program. Tough on civil rights legislation which no concern to us. Lawyer but mainly involved real estate, mortgages.

The morning newscast told me nothing that last night's hadn't—the British Labour Party had asked Russia to stop bombing Mongolia, the Marines in Djarak had exchanged small-arms fire with rebel tribesmen, Congressman Garcia was threatening to sue Congress—and I asked Maria to order coffee for us. In the morning stillness, the office vacant except for the two of us, we sipped our coffee and enjoyed each other's company. She was good to look at in the morning. I envied any man who had ever enjoyed that privilege from the warm, private sanctuary of a double bed. A motel? I wondered. Some brute of a halfback at Ramada U? A campus radical, bearded and unbathed?

"I really didn't get a chance to thank you enough," she said. "And Senator Hannaford."

"He gave the word."

"I will work very, very hard. Honestly, I'm terrific typist and I have good shorthand."

"Your talents will get full use." I let the coffee fumes rise up my nose. No sooner am I back in Washington than my nasal passages clog. Down in the dry heat of Ramada City my head had been clear and well-vented. "Your father must have been close to the senator."

"Daddy was one of his foremen. But anyone who ever worked for the senator worships him."

"I'm the last one to be told that."

She blushed—a faint infusion of scarlet on the silken cheeks, her unlined neck. "That was silly of me. Trying to tell *you*. But

it's true. Ordinary people—truck drivers, bricklayers, secretaries.
I don't know how to say it. They identify with Mr. Hannaford.
They don't resent him because he's rich. He's rich—but he's one
of them."

Her scarlet lips went to the edge of the Lily cup. A poem—
Herrick, I think—flitted through my mind: the poet wishing he
could be the lady's garment. I would have settled for the rim of
that paper cup. Self-control, self-control, I cautioned myself. Having just sworn off Marsha Treadway I promised myself to never
again dally with office personnel. But I wondered if I would have
the necessary self-control.

"Fitzgerald said the rich are very different," I said, "but he
wasn't talking about people like Senator Hannaford."

"I know that story," she laughed. "I was an English lit major.
Hemingway said to him—'Yes they have more money.' Maybe
Hemingway was right—the senator does have more money, but
he doesn't act much different than ordinary people."

"Possibly," I said, "possibly."

She bent to her work—reluctant even to waste time with the
Administrative Assistant. "I'm so happy here Mr. Deever, honestly! I read these letters—and it's like being right at the heart
of the country!" Her eyes widened. "Some people say awful things
about the senator!"

"You will get used to it, Maria. Not everyone has ever worked
for him."

A difficult day, an exhausting week loomed ahead of us. In
addition to the New Wilderness Bill, there would be some work
on the Djarak Amendment, a post on the Federal Trade Commission for Fern's cousin, and a review of campaign expenditures.
I had to make sure that "Giveaway Gordon" would honor the
Interior and Insular Affairs Committee with his presence, as he
had promised. He was with us all the way, Ben had assured me,
on the airplane ride back from Ramada City. We had departed
an hour after the presidential plane, the *Anemone*, had taken off.
Senator Hannaford's corporate-owned HW jet was more luxurious
and there was no point in making invidious comparisons.

And finally—and this was a secret job that only he and I could
undertake—the members of the Conglomerate would have to be
notified that we were moving, and that all of them were to shut
up and let Ben handle the operation. Moreover, Albon Blake—

unless some unforeseen problem arose—was to remain in the background. We had discussed this on the plane.

"Edward," the senator had said, "if that fool Blake calls, warn him off."

"Yes sir."

He yawned, stretched. The muscular chest of the old rigger, the construction man appeared about to rip the shirt. "Damn fools think all you have to do is spread money around. I'm not against that. But there are ways of doing it. Don't raise the bet until you have to."

Cleo Watterson and Marsha Treadway arrived together. Marsha looked improved. Perhaps I had done her a favor by debedding her. Her hair was combed, puffed, and she must have gotten herself a new girdle. But she could not shake that aroma of perfume, sweat, and elastic.

Cleo settled at her command post, adjusted her bifocals (she wore them on a string, which I found engaging) and looked at me archly.

"Well boy-genius," she said, "you must have gotten Parenti's nose out of joint." She thrust the morning *Truth* at me.

"Good thing he's such a liar," Marsha said. "Imagine if people believed him."

"Maybe they do," I said. "And they just don't care."

Parenti had lived up to his threat. Sometimes I wondered whether Ben were wise to talk so freely with people like Parenti.

Chutzpah is a Yiddish word that the distinguished Chairman of the Interior Committee, Senator Benjamin Bow Hannaford, has probably never heard. It means nerve, gall, a colossal disregard for anyone else. It has been defined as the quality shown by a man who murders his parents and then throws himself on the mercy of the court because he is an orphan.

Big, Bible-quoting Ben Hannaford, the richest man in the United States Senate, and its most powerful member, because of his control of his party's purse strings (he heads up their Senate Campaign Committee) is the king of Southwest *chutzpah*.

This weekend he *forced* the President of the United States to make a command performance down in the Senator's home town, Ramada City, to dedicate a new road. But what a road! It is twenty miles long and it ends right at Senator Hannaford's six-car garage! It is Senator Hannaford's private driveway—and for this, the President was required to snip a ribbon!

Another sidelight: along on the presidential party was one of Ben Hannaford's pet hates in the cabinet, Interior Secretary Gordon Hackensetter. "Giveaway Gordon" infuriated Big Ben last year when he opened up valuable Wildlife Refuges to copper mining at the request of another cabinet member, the Secretary of Commerce, the multi-millionaire T. E. Kape. Not that Ben is such an avowed conservationist—he merely wanted some of those precious refuge lands for his *own* mining and oil buddies.

More on Ben Hannaford's operations in a later column; the man can't be believed.

Parenti was letting us down easy. If he knew anything about the New Wilderness Bill, he was holding his fire. He had excellent sources. Our opponents talked to him freely. And he needed material for four columns a week. Actually the piece wasn't too bad—Ben emerged as a kind of lovable rogue.

When Senator Hannaford arrived we discussed the Parenti column. He dismissed it. "The Wop can't hurt us," he said. "Nobody listens to newspapers any more. Not since old Harry Truman whupped Dewey."

"Not even the Washington *Post?*" I asked.

"Oh, a little," Ben went on. "But newspapers are for amusement, that's all. Look at Parenti—he's a clown most of the time."

Cleo sounded the buzzer on the senator's desk. "Senator," I heard her mashed voice say. "Mr. Albon Blake is on the phone."

"I can't talk to him," Ben said. "Tell him not to call today."

"He refuses to hang up, sir," she said. "He wants to talk to Mr. Deever if you can't."

Ben shook his head. "Cleo, advise him Edward is in a meeting with me. Impress upon him that he is to make himself scarce in the next few days. We will call him if he is needed."

The senator shook his head in disgust. "Mr. Blake passeth all understanding. Can't he learn to stay out of this until I settle it my own way?"

"Some of the Conglomerate people may be after him."

"They have been warned also. Greed will be their undoing."

It was odd how the senator could joke with a mortal enemy like Lou Parenti, and yet have contempt for people on our side, like Blake, or his business associates.

"It's about time I gave you the list of members," he said.

"Whatever you think is best from a tactical standpoint."

Ben reached in the breast pocket of his dark blue jacket and gave me a small file card.

On it were seven typewritten names: corporations. I read: *Petrol-Air, Longhorn-Mideast, Outerbridge-Mace, Jackwitt Copper, Halberstadt Inc., Dover Plains Chemical, Tramlett Hewes.*

"All old friends," I said.

"Or converts."

I pondered the list a moment. So these would be the members of the new "Conglomerate" that was being put together. It was interesting. All were in the second or third rank in their fields; companies not on the top level by any means. Longhorn-Mideast for example, old clients and friends of the senator, founded by Fern's family, was not one of the famed "Seven Sisters" of oil. Jackwitt was a small copper mining outfit, nowhere near the size of T. E. Kape's monstrous corporation. All were, in a sense, *outsiders.* But together, with someone like Ben running the show . . .

"I'll keep this confidential, of course. Not a word."

"That is understood, Edward."

"And all of them? Silence?"

"They'd damn well better," Ben said ominously. "That fool Blake'd better hold his fire also."

"I see his role now. I understand the transaction at the zoo. Robbing Peter to pay a lot of Pauls."

Senator Hannaford laughed. "In a sense."

He ordered me to get together the file on the New Wilderness Bill, and we went off to the committee hearing. Immediately we were in the marble corridors of the New Senate Building, I felt my blood race, my heart leap. The old excitement stirred me.

The executive session of the committee, which means it is closed to the public, was in room 3302 of the new building. My own favorite among the hearing rooms is the Senate Caucus room, 318 in the old building. This chamber with its lofty ceiling, marble pillars, and crystal chandeliers is truly impressive. Ben preferred the more compact rooms in the new building. He could control committee members better. "I like a small corral," he told me. "Keep the ponies from straying too far, and I don't have to spend so much time in the saddle."

At an executive session, the press is not in attendance. No lobbyists either, except when invited as witnesses. Only the senators and their staff participate. Needless to say such executive sessions are very important. Secrecy is demanded; but leaks to the press do occur. A good deal of the confidential business, including so basic a matter as preliminary votes, is not revealed, and is, indeed, deliberately left out of the record. Senatorial hair tends to get let down at these closed sessions.

I do not want to give the impression that these executive sessions are conspiratorial plots against the public weal. Hardly. We are still an open society. And the vast, nay the overwhelming, majority of our lawmakers are honest men. It is simply that the complex business of governing this complex country would never get underway unless a certain degree of privacy were permitted our legislators.

There were the usual friendly greetings, exchanges of jests, as the senators settled around the semicircular table. I kept the mimeographed copies of the letter to the President describing the bill inside my briefcase. Meanwhile, I tried to size up the members to see where we stood. Including Ben, there were sixteen on the committee—seven of the opposition party. But neither party would hold to the lines on a hot potato like the New Wilderness Bill. There would be trades, deals, crossing of party lines and the like.

As chairman, Senator Hannaford had an enormous advantage. I do not think the public is sufficiently aware of the power of the chairman of a Senate Committee. He is a king. He alone decides when meetings shall be called. He decides on the agenda. He approves staff appointments, often giving members of his *own* staff, or those on the staffs of friendly senators, committee jobs. (I was *ex-officio* staff director for Interior and Insular Affairs in addition to being Ben's number-one aide.)

A chairman also determines the membership of subcommittees, ignoring foes if he chooses, loading them with colleagues who see eye-to-eye with him. In the case of the Interior Committee, moreover, a lot of pork is available. In fact, it is probably, with the exception of the public works committee, the super-pork operation, or, at any rate, the most venerable and custom-bound. There is an easement for this nice fellow; a river project for that good soul; an improved park for that friendly chap who votes right.

Cynical? I think not. That is the way of the world and the way of the United States Senate, and a lot more good than evil comes out of the system. It has worked amazingly well all these years; let the amateurs and idealists show me a better system.

I checked off in my mind "sure things" on the committee—senators who would go with Ben, even if the New Wilderness Bill called for the filling in of Grand Canyon with cement.

Item, there was Sidney Stapp of California, dapper "Swinging Sid," scourge of the chorus line at the Gayety Theatre. He dazzled us with his white-on-white shirt and his white-on-white tie and his actor's smile. Senator Stapp was a theatrical lawyer, representing great chunks of the entertainment industries. We may have had the best-looking stable of girls on the Hill (decent, refined ladies, I add) but "Swinging Sid" had us beat when it came to conventions. He was in our party, a comer, a man with an eye open for the main chance.

Item, there would be support from Senator Alford Kemmons of Nebraska. Poor Alf. He was on the skids, and he didn't know it. He was in debt; he drank too much; he had wicked friends who were not discreet; he was in over his head, a man who had no right to be in the United States Senate. He listened to too many voices.

All over his native state, they were throwing testimonial dinners for Alf, and the question of where the dollars were going—into Alf's personal exchequer or into his political fund—was being raised. He had a weakness for people who did favors for him—no matter how trivial. I studied Senator Kemmons' lean figure, the wobbling bald head that seemed to rotate on a set of ball bearings, the roosterish neck, and I felt pity for him. He was in our pocket.

Item, "the meanest man in the Senate," Senator Gabriel T. Tutt of Alabama. He would support the New Wilderness Bill and he would swing another vote, probably Jack Mull of Georgia. I do not believe in stereotypes. Some of the most charming men I have

known have been racists. Certain scoundrels I have known are
do-gooding liberals. What a man professes and what he *is* are not
always congruous. But in the case of ancient Gabe Tutt, the man
himself was what he preached and believed. He was a bigot, a
drunkard, a bully, an intransigent who lent aid and comfort to
every violent strain in American life. He was the tiger incarnate,
and a drunken tiger at that. Once at a meeting of international
jurists, Gabe had started a screaming tirade against "Missus
Roosevelt, Adeline Stevenson and all them damn Jew liberals!"
and had to be escorted from the conference room.

But he was an old hand who by right of seniority and his protected status in the club (the club is a sort of Wildlife Refuge)
was untouchable. Senator Tutt crusaded against beards, pornography, divorce, and radicals. His Puritanism, though soaked in
bourbon, was sincere, and his colleagues feared and protected
him.

As I studied his blunt face, his white crewcut, his severe mouth,
the face of a hanging judge, a corrupt sheriff, I wondered who
was the greater menace to our institutions—Angel López Garcia
of Chicago, or Gabriel T. Tutt.

These were our three allies—Senators Stapp, Kemmons, and
Tutt. A cynic might remark that this trio consisted of a lecher, a
weakling, and a bigot. But that would be only partially true.
Senators are men, after all, and they have their failings. Each of
these colleagues of Ben's had something to commend them:
"Swinging Sid" was an excellent corporate lawyer and was a
crackerjack on entertainment industry problems; Kemmons did
well by his farm constituents; and Gabe Tutt could act swiftly
and intelligently in matters concerning national defense.

"Gentlemen, the committee will come to order," said Ben
cheerfully. "This is an executive meeting of the Senate Interior
and Insular Affairs Committee to . . ."

I held my breath, awaiting the reaction.

". . . to consider S.671, the New Wilderness Bill, introduced
June 4th on the floor of the Senate."

Even "Swinging Sid," whom I had forewarned, looked a bit
surprised. Everyone understood that the bill was dead, that the
President had acceded to the wishes of the conservationists, and
that Ben would not dare bring it up again.

There was a murmuration around the table. Then a few nervous laughs. Then they began to read Ben's letter to the President outlining the need for bringing the bill before the committee as soon as possible.

> A BILL to amend the powers of the Secretary of the Interior as outlined in the Wilderness Act of 1964 and to take account of the National Forests and National Parks as permanent heritages of the American people . . .

The flossy language was nonsense. What the bill boiled down to was a change in the procedure set up in the Wilderness Act of 1964 in which fifty-four wilderness areas in the National Forest were created. Under that act, every ten years, the Secretary of the Interior was to review every roadless area of 5000 acres or more—plus roadless islands in the wildlife refuges—and determine its suitability for preservation as a wilderness. Under our bill the Secretary could review the wilderness areas, *annually*, and could, if he deemed it *in the national interest*, and if the President and the Congress concurred, open certain areas to "multiple use." Multiple use meant a lot of things. To Ben it meant timbering, oil drilling, mining—all the things that the members of our projected Conglomerate were so good at.

"I don't understand this at all," Senator John Tyler Lord said uneasily. "I don't understand this one bit."

The Vermonter's eyes goggled. He had not addressed the Chair, as is customary, but had merely sent his voice curling up to the ceiling.

"I take it, Mr. Chairman, this is the same bill that was introduced in the Senate some weeks ago?" Alf Kemmons asked.

"It is, Senator," said Ben. "I open this meeting for consideration of the measure and to arrange to hear witnesses."

"Mr. Chairman," John Tyler Lord piped. "No one was advised that this was to be on the agenda."

Ben smiled, then waved a hand at me. "Senator, you can blame my assistant, Mr. Deever, who was supposed to notify committee members."

"I would have come better prepared had I known," Lord said.

Senator Hannaford beamed at him. "Senator Lord, I'm sure your assistant can run back to your office and bring you reams of handouts from the conservationist lobby. Why don't we proceed with discussion of the bill on its merits?"

Lord's back stiffened. He had never forgiven the way Ben had manhandled him on the debate on the oil depletion allowance. "Were I the chairman of this committee," Lord sniffed, "I would be the last man in the world to mention the word lobby—"

"Gentlemen, gentlemen," Senator Webb Urban of Wyoming said evenly. "This is pointless. The chairman has seen fit to introduce this bill again to the committee. True, he did not notify us. He acted alone in securing the President's approval to submit it. I am not happy with such a procedure. But the chairman was within his rights."

"What is the purpose of a yearly review by the Secretary?" John Tyler Lord persisted. "I asked that question three weeks ago, and I'm still not satisfied with the answer."

"The purpose?" Ben asked. "The purpose is to further protect the national wilderness from exploitation."

"Indeed?" Lord asked. "It would seem to me just the opposite. The key phrase here, the operative phrase is 'in the national interest.' Who is to decide what the national interest is? The 'national interest,' according to a Secretary of the Interior may involve the drilling of oil wells in Yellowstone Park. That may not be *my* national interest, but it may be the interest of the oil people—"

"May I inquire," asked Senator Webb Urban, "why the President changed his mind?"

Senator Hannaford nodded. "Certain aspects of the bill that he did not fully understand were made clear to him," he said. "The multiple use provision for example."

Webb Urban cleared his throat. "I take it the chairman was the one who made these points clear to him."

Ben looked at Urban. "Of course. That is one of my functions as chairman."

Inexplicably, Alf Kemmons began to laugh—that gargling, stupid laugh of his. "Yeah, you don't get invited down to Ramada City," Kemmons burbled, "without getting a little religion on the side!"

There was a shocked silence. Webb Urban's face froze. He was an elder of the Mormon Church.

"I am sure the Senator from Nebraska is joking," Urban said

coldly. "I am disturbed at the precipitous way in which the Chief Executive's mind was changed, and the precipitous way in which this measure is being presented."

"So am I," said John Tyler Lord.

Senator Lester Goodchapel, sitting next to Webb Urban shook his pumpkin-like head. His eyes were mangled behind extra-thick lenses. "Golly, I'm with Senator Urban on that one. I'm a little mixed up."

"Was it not decided, Mr. Chairman," John Tyler Lord went on, "that the case made by the Conservationist Society of America was sufficient to prove that this bill was a green light for exploitation of the National Wilderness, that it would mean opening up our forests and rivers to bulldozers and drilling machines and power saws? Was that not agreed upon?"

"Not by me, Senator," Ben said. "I have always rejected the Conservationist opposition to multiple use. I still do."

"And the President does now?" Webb Urban asked.

"He does," Ben said. "And Mr. Hackensetter will so testify in a few minutes on behalf of Administration."

"We will respect the President's wishes, of course," Urban said, "but the chairman will permit us to call witnesses of our own."

It was a bad omen, a very bad omen. Let me talk a little about Senator Webb Urban of Wyoming. He was of that breed of gray, quiet, discreet, rural men who are at the very heart of the Senate Establishment.

As I have mentioned, he was a Mormon. He was also a lawyer, a man of moderate means. Most of his clients were ranchers and farmers. He did not smoke, or drink alcohol, tea, or coffee. He retired at 9:30 every night and was up early to pray. Physically he blended into his environment, so that in the halls of the Capitol, he was almost invisible. Of medium height, medium build, clad in medium gray suits, and dark blue ties, bespectacled, gray, square-faced, thin-lipped, quiet-voiced, he reminded me somewhat of Harry Truman as Vice-President, the man I had seen in news-reels sitting silently beside Roosevelt.

I cannot ever recall hearing Senator Webb Urban say a single thing of consequence on the floor of the Senate. He never raised his voice. He steered clear of partisan arguments. Above all he was fanatically honest. Not that the vast majority of the men in the Senate are not. But honesty was part of Urban's religion. Two examples will suffice. He was sedulous about putting postage stamps, paid for out of his own pocket, on every single piece of personal mail. He refused to use the congressional franking privilege which is so often abused. Once he was known to have personally tracked down a letter to the Senate post office so that he might put a stamp on it—a new girl in his office had used a franked envelope. (It was his electric bill.)

On another occasion, a testimonial dinner for him was held in Cheyenne to raise campaign funds—although this phase of the dinner was not revealed to Urban. In his naïveté he thought all those nice people just wanted to get together for a nice evening of steak, beans, and soft drinks. When, a few days later, the dinner committee presented him with a check for $9000, he flew into one of his rare rages and gave the money to an orphanage.

And so, as the debate droned on I feared Webb Urban's polite antagonism. I sensed that Ben Hannaford was uncomfortable also—a rare situation for my boss. Let me explain. When it gets down to close votes, to issues that may swing one way or the other, one must normally have the support of the Establishment, the Club. There is very little to be feared from the zealous outsiders, the amateurs, the journalists, the patricians, the college professors —the John Tyler Lords or the Maury Eisenbergs. The men who really count are those quiet men from country constituencies, who through some heaven-made covenant, some hoary tradition, represent the mystical essence of the Senate. Webb Urban, in his Sears Roebuck suit and his two-dollar ties was the very heart of that mystical essence.

He would oppose the New Wilderness Bill and he would vote against reporting it out of committee. But we had not counted on his vote anyway. The question was—how many votes would he pull away from us?

"I was under the impression," Lord said shrilly, "and I said this weeks ago, that the act of 1964 is very clear on protecting the national forests. The order of declaring wilderness areas roadless in perpetuity is very simple—a review every ten years by the Secretary of the Interior, approval by the President, approval by Congress. The areas then become legislated wilderness areas. They can't be touched. It's worked so far. Why change it?"

"Times have changed, let me remind the junior senator from Vermont," Ben said. "We have world-wide obligations. The supplies of precious minerals, resources, timber are running short—"

"They are *not*," Lord snapped. "There is a five hundred page survey by the Conservationist Society that the chairman is quite familiar with to disprove that contention. The national forests are but a tiny fraction of our potential resource producing land. Why open them up?"

"Let me assure the members," Ben said, "that this need not be the final version of the bill. It can be modified as the committee sees fit." He paused. "To a degree."

I began to make notes on the committee line-up. We had to hold everyone in our own party. It would be rough. Lord was a lost cause. He was more adamantly against the bill than anyone in the opposition. That left Lester Goodchapel. We needed his vote. I was fairly certain that Ben could work on him and win him over. Lester was one of those eminently forgettable men, a member of the great army of "insulted and ignored." He was never asked to appear on TV panel shows, or the "Today" show. Once he had shown up at the NBC Washington studio and discovered he had been called by mistake.

"I shall oppose this bill in committee," Lord said finally. "And I shall oppose it if it gets to the floor of the Senate. And if it passes, I shall fight for its repeal."

"Afraid we're out to kill all your woodchucks and daisies, eh, Senator?" Kemmons asked brightly.

Lord ignored him.

"I'm against it also," Webb Urban said. "At least in its present form."

A few others joined in to state their opposition. Lester Goodchapel said nothing.

"I appreciate these expressions of opinion," Ben said. "I see that the Secretary of the Interior has arrived, so gentlemen, if it pleases the committee members, I'll call on Secretary Hackensetter."

There was "Giveaway Gordon," steel-rimmed glasses glinting, followed by two sour-faced young aides. Most Interior people *believe* in woodchucks and pin oaks. They were not happy with their boss Hackensetter.

The Secretary took his seat facing the Interior and Insular Affairs Committee, adjusted his spectacles and began to read.

"The President authorizes me to state that he is in accord with the principles of S.671," Hackensetter began. "And wishes me to convey . . ."

After Hackensetter spoke, Ben adjourned the meeting.

In the corridor I found Lester Goodchapel at my side.

"It was an interesting discussion wasn't it, Senator?" I asked.

"Oh yes, yes indeed. Gosh, I wish I understood the argument a little better. But if Senator Hannaford says the bill will protect the National Forests . . ."

"Of course. Except for an occasional ruling in favor of multiple use—when a National Emergency exists."

"National Emergency? Yes."

Was he with us?

Lou Parenti was lying in wait for the committee members. Normally the press ignores the Interior Committee. It is a pork operation, a joke of sorts. No reporter really cares about the expanding of the national forests or the regulation of grazing rights. But Parenti was on the track of something. And he knew that John Tyler Lord would be his best source of information —even though it is not considered fair to divulge executive session matters until the report is published.

"How'd it go, Senator Lord?" Parenti boomed.

"A disgrace," Lord said, "an affront to America."

"Ah, that's what I wanna hear," the columnist said. "What's the Master Builder up to?"

"He has resubmitted the New Wilderness Bill, the greatest raid on the national wilderness in history," Lord said. "And he has the backing of this administration."

"Hackensetter?"

"And the President." Lord wiped his high, domed head—an aristocrat's head, a head nourished on boiled dinners and brown bread. "I do not know what has impelled Senator Hannaford into this rash act, but I will fight it all the way."

I made it my business to listen carefully. Senator Goodchapel was at my elbow.

"Jesus, he can't build roads through *all* the parks," Parenti said. "Or put up refineries everywhere. Why risk getting so many people mad?"

"Senator Hannaford played fast and loose with the public when he tried to raise the oil depletion allowance," Lord piped. "Why should he not try to use the National Wilderness for mining and timbering?"

"I hope Senator Lord will forgive me," I said, "but there is every assurance that the terms National Emergency will mean just that—"

"It will mean whatever Senator Hannaford and his Big Business associates want it to mean!" cried Lord. A small group had gathered. The man was violating every Senate rule in the book. One simply did not impute bad motives to another senator. Anyone else in the world—Popes, Kings, Giant Intellects—could have bad motives. But never a United States Senator.

"I helped draw the bill up," I said. "And we feel—"

"Of course! Leave it to Senator Hannaford to put his court favorites on the committee staff! That bill was rammed down our throat! Mr. Parenti, you may quote me—I'll fight this outrage to the end!"

And off he loped, a wading crane, his seersucker coattails flying, his thin blood aroused, his New England conscience burning.

Parenti turned on me. "Deever, what is with this bill?"

"It is in the national interest."

"Jesus Christ on a raft. You must be smarter than that. You were once a newspaperman, Deever. You expect me to believe that?"

"You are determined to see devils everywhere."

"Know what I think?" he asked. "I think Hannaford is jealous that T. E. Kape got his hooks into the Wildlife Refuges. He'll show that fink! He'll get his hands in every National Park and Forest we own! Who's with him, Eddie? Uranium crowd? Longhorn? Hah?"

Did he know anything about the Conglomerate? He could not. It was the tightest of secrets.

"That is unkind, Lou," I said. "You know that Senator Hannaford operates open and above board. He made no secret of his connections with the oil industry during the debate on the depletion allowance."

Parenti's black mistrustful eyes darted this way and that. "Yeah. He's wide open where it don't matter. You guys are like the Commies. Never a word on what you really wanna hide."

As we conversed, Parenti's voice rising, a small crowd of Americans gathered around us. One was a huge fat man in rancher's tan

twill suit, tan wide-brimmed Stetson, three cameras, and a pur-
pling mottled face gathered around one of those twisty rum-
soaked cigars. He beamed at both of us.

"Howdy, friends," he said.

"Hiya, Jack," Parenti said.

"How do you do," I said politely.

"Name isn't Jack, it's Fred," the fat man said jovially. "I may
look lak a Texan but I'm from Ocala, Florida. I jes' dress lak a
Texan to confuse folks. How y'all?"

"Great, great, buddy," Parenti said, turning his back.

"Now you boys are doin' a mighty fahn job hyeah in the
Senate," Fred went on. "Ah'm a surgical dentist back in Ocala.
Got a boy at Georgia Tech and a gal at Florida State. And we all
proud of you boys in the Senate."

"Thank you, Doctor," I said. I shook his hand. It had three
rings on it, one a Mason's.

He waddled off. Our Americans. I liked him. Parenti did not.
And I knew that Parenti would be no match for Ben when it got
down to cases. Ben could reach our dentist friend. Lou never
could. And therein rested a crucial difference, a great advantage
for our side. Parenti strode off and I hurried to our office. Senator
Goodchapel, who had been on the edge of the argument all
along, waddled alongside me.

"Senator Lord was very upset," he said. His mouth barely
moved when he spoke.

"Yes, he takes these matters seriously."

Lester Goodchapel frowned. "But shouldn't he? I mean, we?"

"Of course, Senator. But he is always looking for windmills to
tilt at."

"Beg pardon?"

"Battles to fight, when there aren't any. He's like a Crusader
who has run out of Turks."

Senator Goodchapel smiled. "Say, that's good, Edward, very
good." He moved away. The corridors were filled with summer-
time visitors. Not a soul recognized him.

Young Matt Fixx, our legislative assistant, grinned at me. "I hear
the boss really zapped 'em."

"Yes, you might say that, Matt. But I wouldn't."

"Oh? Didn't it go well? I thought all systems were go."

"Matthew, if you will consent to speak the English language, I will oblige you with an answer."

His pinched face drooped. Deprive Matt Fixx of his lingo and he was lost. "Sorry about that. Damn, I did it again."

"No matter, Matthew. It was good hearing."

"Would you say our capability is high?"

"Not only that, it's viable."

He tagged after me as I hurried to my desk, brushing by Marsha's figure. It did naught to me. Christmas Past.

"Ed—does the senator still regard the bill as well-structured?"

"It has high potential," I responded.

"Built-in, I hope," Matt said apprehensively.

"Inherent."

The office buzzed with action. We were too many things at once—functions, duties, obligations were blurred. Senator Hannaford, Committee Chairman, Caucus member, Policy Committee power; Big Ben Hannaford the Master Builder, President of Hannaford-Western; B.B. Hannaford, the Chairman of the Senate Campaign Committee; not to mention all sorts of odds and ends—letters to cattle breeders' associations, helping Mrs. Hannaford with her charities, requests from Indians, Mexicans, Negroes, and union men back in Ramada City. I prided myself that we were able to handle all these functions in orderly fashion. We hired good people and demanded nothing less than total loyalty, high efficiency. These thoughts impelled me to look in on our new girl. Maria Valdez was seated behind a frosted-glass partition. A pair of wide oval eyeglasses framed her eyes. They made her even prettier, endowing her with a schoolmarmish quality which I found exciting.

"In the swing of things, Maria?"

"I hope so. Oh, this mail! It's unbelievable! What an insight I'm getting into our fellow citizens."

"Tell me so I'll know." I walked around the partition. "What is your impression?"

"Confusion. A lot of people like the senator. Most of them want favors. Some say he's Communist. And some that he's a fascist."

"Well, that's a good cross section. Appears we're doing very well."

Seated sideways, her chartreuse skirt hiked high, I found my-

self staring at her tan thighs. She adjusted her dress, gave me a
reproachful look. No, no, I warned myself. Never again. The
frenzied liaison with Marsha Treadway had been too much, too
wearing. The need for secrecy had proved exhausting. I needed
the comfort of a big-bosomed soft-spoken woman ten years my
senior.

"*El Jefe* calls," Cleo Watterson said. She poked her gray prettily
set head around the partition. "Make sure you remind him
about the reception at the Hungarian Embassy tonight. They've
called twice. Seems as if it's no real party unless they can get at
least one big bloated capitalist." She gave me the Indian sign.
"Plenty Red Brass wantum Shake Hand Big Bridge Builder."

Cleo did not approve of the senator's dealings with the Communist states of Eastern Europe. She had to spend a lot of time
fending off the zealots who accused him of "selling-out," when
Ben's sole notion was to get more American business. "If *we* don't
build 'em, son," I heard him tell an irate American Legion official
once, "the Eye-talians and the West Germans will, and all that
cash will go elsewhere. Besides, the more you give them, the
more they'll realize communism is for the birds."

He was on the phone with Albon Blake when I walked in.
"Not yet, Albon," he said. "If any of the members call you, merely
say it went well. A vote? I don't know. Couple of days. Yes, I am
optimistic."

"I'm not," I said, closing the door.

"How do you read them?"

Sitting down, I tilted my head. "Urban is bad medicine. People
listen to him. As much as they listen to you. I had counted on
Goodchapel to go with us, but I think we've lost him. Hopkins
is out. That means we lose nine to seven."

"I can't believe it," he grumbled. "Why the President is for it!"

"And more to worry about. John Tyler Lord was blabbing to
Parenti."

Ben scowled. He looked as if he had a mouthful of vinegar.
"The curse of inherited wealth, Edward. It endows a man with
guilt. I have no guilt. I've worked since I was thirteen and I love
every dollar I have. I don't owe anyone an apology."

I laughed. "Too bad you can't help Lord with his re-election
campaign fund."

"Yes, that would be nice. But he doesn't take. Impudent rich man's son."

"And utterly without manners. Doesn't he know a senator isn't supposed to talk about what goes on in closed sessions—unless the chairman and the others agree?"

Ben shrugged. "Lord can be ignored, Edward. Who among them can be swayed?"

I shook my head from side to side. "It's got to be Lester Goodchapel. If he's with us, we're home free."

The senator spun about in his high black chair. "I see no problem there. We'll reach him, one way or t'other."

In late afternoon, when the office was quiet—the senator had gone to his mansion in Potomac to change and to pick up Fern for the reception—I visited with Maria again. I was beginning to think of her as my charge. Who knows why? She didn't seem to need my help. Perhaps I am a frustrated father.

I saw her there in the fading light of a late June afternoon, her face dappled by sunlight lanced by a Venetian blind, the eyeglasses pushed back on her clear brow. She was sipping a soft drink. Every now and then she brushed aside a lock of ebony hair. To me she symbolized all the dear young girls who come to Washington to work with the mighty, to adorn this masculine city with grace and charm and sweet scent and lithe figures. I was grateful to her.

"Miss Valdez? Maria? How about getting initiated into what passes for night life in our town?" I asked.

"Am I being invited?"

"Part of your education. Your first Embassy reception. The idea is to convince you of the total dullness of these affairs, so you will spend your time better."

"I'm thrilled! What does one wear?"

"A dark dress and a look of wonder on your lovely face," I said. Then I was sorry I said it. There would be no pursuit of Miss Valdez by E. Deever. Or would there be?

CHAPTER FIVE

There is something depressing about the Eastern European diplomatic corps. I suspect they live in fear of their own people, or at minimum are painfully aware of the contempt in which they are held by them. They are full of excuses, cheeriness, nervous jokes, and envy. Oh, a lot of them are decent fellows. But they try too hard. They are like eager poor boys at a rich man's college.

These Communists seem to paint everything gray. Surely there are no more vivacious people than the Hungarians. Gifted, witty, talkative—they are most engaging. But make a diplomat out of a Hungarian, a *Communist* diplomat, and you get a gray pudding.

The new Hungarian Embassy was an imposing old stone mansion on Massachusetts Avenue, built by an American dowager before the days of income taxes, and now passed on to a Communist government, whose diplomatic immunity saved *it* from paying taxes. With some imaginative decorating, the building might have been stunning. But the cold hand of Karl Marx lay heavy in its cavernous chambers. Worst of all—and this is true of virtually all Communist offices—the lighting was dim and tended to flicker. "Socialism plus electricity," Lenin said, "equals communism." At the rate they were going, Senator Hannaford said, they would *never* have communism, since they apparently could not discover the secret of electricity.

I suspect the Hungarians wanted Ben to show them how. He was a great favorite of theirs, ever since building their model supermarkets, filling stations, and a pipeline far below their estimated cost. The pipeline was built with such ruthless efficiency that their Soviet masters were left breathless, embarrassed by the audacity of this American capitalist.

The right-wingers had been on Senator Hannaford's neck ever since, but Ben was too rich, too big and too typically American to get hurt. "Teach 'em free enterprise!" Ben had bellowed to an American Legion convention. "Make 'em throw out Karl Marx! And make 'em pay through the nose!" His rhetoric confused the rightists in our own land as much as it did the Soviet economists who listened to Ben and then went back to Lenin to try to find justification for his theories. "Take a good look, boys," Ben once told a convention of Czech economists, "you look long enough you can find anything you need in Lenin."

I was distressed to see that the conservative zealots had despatched two pickets to the Embassy. They were there for our benefit I was certain. Maria and I approached them in the warm June night. From the other side of Massachusetts Avenue I could see the senator, Fern beside him, parking their car. (He favored a souped-up Ford, eschewing Cadillacs and Lincolns.) We paused near the pickets. A D.C. policeman stood to one side.

"Who are you fellows picketing?" I asked.

"Commies," one said. He was a tall weedy man with the look of the intransigent in his eyes. His sign read: KILL A COMMIE FOR CHRIST.

"No American has any right to set foot in there, not while the Red butchers seek to dominate the world," the other added. He was short and bore a placard reading: NO HELP TO MURDERERS.

"Yes," I said. "I suppose you have a point."

As Ben crossed the street, the tall one nudged the short one. "There's a traitor. That's *him*."

The short one nodded. "Pretending he's a capitalist. I knew he'd be here."

Ben and Fern noticed the pickets. He motioned her to walk to the Embassy steps and wait for him. Then, in that hard stride of an old construction man, he walked toward the two. They saw him and stepped back a bit. Ever since Ben had been spat upon in the parking lot, he had an urge to confront these lunatics. He was without fear. He told me that he hoped someday to find the three or four wretches who had showered him with saliva and crack their skulls. The pickets saw the determination in his face. They retreated a step.

"Good evening, gentlemen," Ben said.

"Huuuuh . . ." the tall one muttered.

"You . . . you . . . have no right to g-g-g-o in . . ."

The policeman moved close. He recognized the senator and grinned. "Good evening, Senator. Nothing serious. They have a permit. They're the Save America Society."

"You boys are mighty busy Saving America. Who are you saving it from?" Ben's eyes flashed.

"P-p-people like you," the short picket stammered.

"You do business with Reds," the other said.

"Do I?" Ben asked. "Tell you what, boys. You go back and tell those two-bit tinhorn phony patriots who sent you here that Ben Hannaford never, never does business with Communists . . . unless he can make money out of them."

He turned away. The policeman chuckled. But the pickets were unmoved.

"Traitor," one of them whispered.

For a moment I thought Ben would turn and throw a punch. I saw him halt and rub his huge fist, and I started from the Embassy steps toward him. But Ben was only mulling the pleasant notion; he crossed the street and disregarded them, even as they hissed at his back: "Treason, treason . . ."

There was something awry in the country; it had gotten too easy, too simple to call people traitor, to cry treason.

In the dim lobby of the Hungarian Embassy, I realized Maria had not been introduced to Mrs. Hannaford, and performed the rites.

Fern studied Maria's face. "I welcome you to Washington, my dear. You will find it very different from Ramada City."

"I am already," Maria said. "Wasn't that awful . . . those people out there calling the senator names?"

"The senator cannot resist an argument," Fern said sadly. "He feels the need to confront some people."

"Those two deserved it, Mrs. H.," I said.

An Embassy flunky ushered us through the dim gray-yellow rooms to a vast chamber where the new Ambassador, the Honorable Imre Bator, was receiving guests.

As we pushed our way through the clotted rooms, I could see

Fern sizing Maria up. "Well, you certainly will uphold the office reputation for beauty, my dear," she said.

"You shouldn't compliment me like that, Mrs. Hannaford."

"No, my dear, you'll find yourself very much in demand. This is a man's town, but a pretty face is a great advantage. Women are mainly decorative here, aren't they, Edward?"

Fern's serene face looked at me curiously. Was she hinting in some vague way to my dalliance with Marsha? Fern was not as square as people imagined. She knew a lot more than the breeding of Gordon setters.

"I don't know, Mrs. Hannaford. Look at the last few First Ladies. More than decorative, I would say."

"Perhaps, perhaps." Her eyes roamed the room. Fern hated these large pointless affairs, and went only because her husband insisted. Senator Hannaford had detached himself from us and was shaking hands with the Director of the Federal Bureau of Investigation, Judge Samuel Moscowitz.

"Howdy, Judge," Ben said. "Doin' a little checkin' up?"

"Yes," the director laughed. "Three of my agents have already filed reports on me for being here."

Judge Moscowitz was noted for his sense of humor. He was also one of the most eminent civil libertarians in the nation, an expert on law enforcement, police administration and the inner workings of the Mafia.

"You got any idea who *their* cops are?" Ben asked.

"Of course I have. But I wouldn't tell you. You'd use it to your advantage somehow."

Senator Hannaford dug the judge in the ribs and winked at him.

Lou Parenti was on hand, guzzling vodka, clearing plates of Hungarian salami. Even in the din, his abrasive voice was distinct. "Marsha! Hey, Marsha baby, come say hello to the Tass guy!" Marsha Treadway was with him. She had lost no time in finding a new friend. The gossip had been true; she had been carrying on with Parenti.

Parenti spied me with Mrs. Hannaford and came lurching over, Marsha in his wake. A few Eastern European guests were studying Marsha's frontage.

"Eddie, baby!" he called. "Hiya, Mrs. Hannaford!"

Fern smiled bleakly.

"The word's out from the White House, Mrs. Hannaford,"

Parenti boomed. "The President just has to have that recipe for red beans and green peppers. Says he never spent a nicer weekend than the one you and the senator arranged for him!"

"That is very kind of you to report that to me," Fern said. "How do you find these things out, Mr. Parenti?"

"Connections."

"And what connections supply you with information about roads in Ramada County? Or the senator's committee hearings?" Fern asked gently.

"Touché, Mrs. Hannaford. Well, a boy has to make a living."

"Yes, I suppose so." Fern looked at Marsha. "What a lovely shade your dress is, Marsha. Is that puce?"

"Gee, I don't know, Mrs. Hannaford."

"I would call that puce."

Fern was like that. She was interested in the staff, especially the girls—Hannaford's Harem they were jokingly referred to, although not a breath of scandal ever touched our office. She worried about Marsha—whose dresses were too tight, whose breasts bulged, whose stockings were never quite straight.

The bulk of the crowd, those more aggressive, more attuned to VIP's, had gravitated toward the receiving line, where Ambassador Imre Bator was oozing Budapest charm on Ben.

"Here is our real American ambassador," Bator said loudly. He spoke flawless English and his clothes, unlike the dreary bags worn by his staff, had a foppish British cut. "Here is the real friend of the Hungarian people."

There was laughter, some of it nervous. The Tass man was standing close by. It was said he was a KGB operative. I noticed that the Director of the FBI was studying him with an amused look. Judge Moscowitz knew.

"Mr. Ambassador, that isn't necessary," Ben said. "I'll build whatever you want, if you'll pay for it. I'll cure you people yet. Marx has been wrong on everything, but you won't admit it."

"No, no, dear Senator," the ambassador piped. He was a tall man. Long service in London had made him almost English in appearance—horse face, ruddy complexion, big teeth. But what were Hungarians supposed to look like anyway? "Temporary setbacks. We are still building socialism. We will still create a true Marxist state."

"You better not tell your citizens," Ben said. "That surely isn't what they want."

"What do they want?" the ambassador said. The crowd pushed closer—the Tass man, a Romanian diplomat, a snotty Frenchman whom I had argued with over NATO, Parenti, a few other newsmen.

"They want *quality*," Ben said. "Shoes that don't fall apart. Toothpaste that tastes good. Suits that fit. You're trying, but not hard enough. Find the men who can run factories—and *give* 'em the factories. You tell 'em—make good shoes, or we try someone else!"

The Tass man was shaking his head. Like many Russians, he didn't look good indoors. He had a round oily face, lank blond hair, and he smelled like the lobby of the Bolshoi Theatre during a December intermission.

"Senator is wrong," the Tass reporter said. "Senator wrong because socialism is true to human nature. Socialism believes in good men, generous men, men who share with neighbors. We believe in need of men to cooperate."

"Do you really?" Ben asked. "And what about capitalism?"

"Ah!" the Tass man cried. His eyes widened. "Capitalism must fail because it believes in every man for himself—every man after all money he can get, no concern with welfare of neighbor. You care, Senator, for your competitor in road business? No. You happy if he fails, loses money. So capitalism is jungle society. It is doomed."

He folded his blue serge arms and grinned. There was a bit of applause.

"*Bien dit*," said the Frenchman. "*Nous sommes tous Marxistes*."

I detest these French intellectuals, so eager to display their ingenious logic. But I said nothing.

"Now son," Senator Hannaford said to the Tass man, "you have just stated your case, and I contend you are as wrong as poor Trotsky, waiting for some glorious workers' revolution to rescue him—when all he got was an ax in the head."

There was a shudder. Ben really did not know much about Trotsky, but he enjoyed shaking them up.

"You say capitalism is every man for himself?" he went on. "Why sure it is! It is based on *greed*. G, r, e, e, d. We believe in greed. We reward it. Man is a greedy animal. He wants things.

Earth, house, woman, food, comforts. And he wants them for *himself*. To heck with Charlie down the street. So we recognize this. We encourage it. You know what the prayer says. Give us this day *our* daily bread. Not give them *their* bread. Why, there isn't a greedier book than some parts of the Old Testament. All about how many sheeps and camels and goats those old desert people owned."

"We end all that!" the Tass man cried.

"You can't. You Marxist-Leninists expect people to act kind and generous and sweet and agree to cooperate. You are all too good for this world. But people are ornery critters. They want to *own*, to have, to plow their forty acres. So when people *don't* act generous and kind and cooperative, you have no choice but to kill 'em."

There were some gasps. The Tass man fingered his collar.

Ambassador Bator raised his eyebrows. "Surely the senator is jesting."

"I am not. You birds never learn. Farmers didn't want to give up their land—so Stalin shot 'em. Well, you finally got 'em on collectives, but they're still so mad two generations later they won't grow crops or raise chickens, except on a little private plot of land you let 'em have. They just wouldn't act as nobly as you want."

"Not true," the Tass reporter said, but he was grinning. Communists tend to grin a lot. Probably to cover up their embarrassment. "Collective farms are big success. People who refused to work on them were fascists, rich, exploiters of poor."

"Now you don't believe that, do you, son?" Ben asked. His swarthy head dominated the circle around him. They were as attentive as fellow committee members about to have some unpleasant truth stuffed down their throat. Ben had that power; he made you listen. "Mr. Ambassador you'll have to excuse my bluntness but I'm going to say a few words about what happened in your country in 1956."

"Ah yes," Imre Bator said. He was sounding more British by the moment. Confront a Communist about 1956 in Hungary and their eyes glaze, their throats constrict. "The regrettable events of October as we refer to them."

This was evidently an inside joke. There were a few uneasy laughs.

"Who do you think got shot down in the streets?" Ben asked.
"Fascists? Reactionaries? Conservatives? No sir. You and your
Russian friends shot down factory workers. Steel workers. Textile
workers. Your own proletariat, who'd had enough. Sure it was the
students started it and a few writers, and you shot some of them
also. But they weren't that army of people who went into the
streets with old guns. They were your own beloved working
class, who'd had enough, and just wanted a house, a suit of
clothes, a chance to laugh and have fun and go to church, and
not feel like some damn noble abstract ideal of a worker that a
bunch of theorists dreamed up at a Marxist school. In short,
gentlemen, they were greedy. And why not?"

"You have misrepresented the counterrevolution!" the ambassador cried. He was grinning idiotically.

"I've been to your factories. I know the boys at the Csepel
Steel Works and I talked to the men at that big plant on the
Danube. They want cars. Homes. TV sets. Good clothes. It's that
old understandable greed at work, but all you want is for them to
be noble architects of the great revolution. But you don't know
how to give 'em a decent bar of soap at a low price."

"What does Senator suggest?" a Czech asked.

"Turn them loose! A little regulated greed! Give the stores
back to owners! Take some fellow with brains and energy and say
to him—here's this department store—it's yours—make money!
Take a shoe factory and give it to the smartest worker. It's his!
Make money! Make good shoes! Then set another fellow up to
compete!"

They roared.

"I'd straighten your economy out in six months. Of course all
you Communist professionals would be out of work. Unless you
learned a trade."

Parenti nudged me in the ribs. "That guy could be King of
Romania if you let him. Or any of them places."

"No, it boils down to this," Ben said. "You must stop believing
in the innate nobility of man. It will kill all of us. You keep insisting on that, when he doesn't behave nobly, you have to gun
him down. Why not recognize his faults—and control 'em—just
enough to make virtues out of 'em? Does he want land—a wife
—fancy duds—a big car? Well, let him work for 'em!"

"C'est pas Marxiste, c'est pas Chrétien!" the Frenchman cried.

"Neither Marxist nor Christian, he says," Parenti offered.

"But it works," Ben said.

The little Romanian edged closer. "You, Senator Hannaford, you are motivated by greed?"

"Of course."

Parenti howled. "He's got you there, Senator. First time I ever heard you admit it."

Fern looked at the journalist with distaste. Maria too looked shocked.

"I'll admit it anywhere, any time, Lou."

"On the floor of the Senate?" Parenti asked. "Like when you tried to ram through the 33⅓ depletion allowance for your oil buddies? So the oil companies could cheat even more on taxes?"

There was a rising appreciative murmur from the assembled Eastern Europeans. There it was! The capitalist trapped!

"The President backed me on that, Parenti. I want money to move around. The Book tells us 'lay not up for yourselves treasures upon earth, where moth and rust doth corrupt, and where thieves break through and steal.'"

"Veech book?" asked a Bulgarian.

"Not *Das Kapital*," Parenti said.

"St. Matthew," Ben said. "I am greedy for building, for creating, for letting the earth produce. I am greedy for new cities, new factories, roads, bridges and great big stores where people can buy anything they want."

"And to what extent is your greed controlled, Senator?" asked Parenti. "Who controls it?"

"The great American public."

"Do they really have any control over you?" Parenti persisted.

"The ballot, son. You don't think I shot my way into the Senate? I was elected and re-elected by the biggest majorities in the history of our great state."

"Yeah, but once you get in, you kind of make it *your* government," Parenti said.

"No, there's lots who disagree with me, and who fight me, and who criticize me. One fellow's greed against the other fellow's greed, but a kind of understanding that everybody gets a share of it."

"Like the National Forests?" the journalist asked.

The Hungarian Ambassador appeared uneasy. Ben smiled at Parenti, but he was getting annoyed with him.

"Please, please, friends," Ambassador Bator said, "enough politics! Try some Hungarian salami—for export only! Like the senator says we are greedy too—for American dollars—so we export all the good salami, and our poor Hungarians must eat inferior brands!"

Parenti lost himself in gluttony. The Romanian, the Czech, the Tass man, gathered around Senator Hannaford. It was curious the way they were drawn to him. None of Parenti's thrusts had lessened their admiration for him.

"Dear, we should be getting home," Fern said.

Neither the senator nor Fern were night-owls. They usually avoided parties, dinners, and the like, and never went to the theatre or concerts. I saw Ben patting a yawn as we moved toward the gloomy foyer. A Japanese diplomat waved at him, so did Prince Malik, the Djaraki Ambassador.

Outside the air was soft, pleasantly moist. Moths whirred in halos around the faint embassy lights. I detained the senator a moment to review tomorrow's schedule—a campaign committee meeting, some planning for the Interior hearings, a session on the Djarak Amendment. Sensitive to his moods, I realized he was listening with one ear, looking intensely at Maria Valdez who was talking to Fern near the curb.

"Joe Valdez can be proud of that girl," he said.

He too was hearing that guitar. Who could blame him? There was a freshness about her, a Latin warmth, that was irresistible. I do not mean this in a purely physical sense. She had an aura, a quality, and any man who appreciated quality was doomed to respond to her. I studied the proud cast of her features—dimly lit by a street lamp—and I thought of certain stylized paintings of Indian children I had once seen in a Mexico City museum.

"She's bright also," I said.

"Old Joe Valdez," Ben said. "Got to find out if he needs help."

"Maria said he can only work part time. Arthritis."

"Check on it, Edward. Talk to HW tomorrow."

Ben and I approached the women. "What does Edward have you doing, Maria?" the senator asked.

"I'm second assistant mail clerk, I suppose."

"That will educate you. You will learn how thoroughly hated I am in some quarters."

"I can't believe that," she said.

"Looky yonder," Senator Hannaford said. The two pickets were still parading with their signs: NO HELP TO MURDERERS. KILL A COMMIE FOR CHRIST.

"But they don't really count," Maria said.

We escorted the Hannafords toward their car. "Maybe not," Ben said. "But there they are. And there is our friend Louis Parenti, not insane like those two, but out of touch."

"He is a disgusting oaf," Fern said. "I regret that Marsha, after all the senator has done for her, sees fit to go out with him."

"Doesn't mean a thing," Ben said. They got into the Ford.

"That's Washington," I said easily. "We don't *really* hate one another, except for a few misfits. Parenti admires the senator, Mrs. Hannaford. Someday we'll get him to say so in print."

Ben laughed. "It's getting so nobody has a good word for the old man," he said.

Maria looked upset. "They have down in Ramada, Senator," she said. "You know what the Mexicans say about you—"

"I can imagine," Ben said, smiling. "Mrs. Hannaford here understands Tex-Mex pretty good, Maria, so watch it."

"It's very complimentary. They say when you work for Hannaford-Western, *mucho trabajo, pero mucho dinero*."

"Yes, I recall that." He looked as if he wished he were back on the construction sites, laying out an endless pipeline, envisioning a huge refinery, away from the intrigues and pressures of Washington.

"One of the nicest things anyone ever said about me."

We said our goodnights. The Ford blasted off. He was in high spirits—his performance at the Embassy, the imminent battle for the New Wilderness Bill; the smell of conquest; the lovely young girl, newest addition to "Hannaford's Harem"; all these exhilarated him. There would be votes to change, opponents to frustrate, allies to accommodate.

Maria was not tired. She wanted to see Washington by night. Summoning a cab, I took her on a quick tour of the magic city. The white buildings glowed with unearthly splendor. Above us loomed the Lincoln Memorial.

"I'm going to cry!" Maria said. Her luminous eyes were wet at the edges. The city affects the young, the good in heart in this manner. Let the Gabe Tutts stagger drunkenly, let the Alford Kemmons engage in double billing, the Angel López Garcias pad their expenses—the grandeur remains. So much that is ugly and mean in our national life can be cleansed by a view of the great monuments. So I had felt those years back when first I saw the city with the other American Legion essay contest winners. It still moved and thrilled me, but not with the same intensity, I am sure, with which it moved young Maria Valdez.

The cab stopped in front of the alabaster shrine, the brooding statue of that kind troubled man.

As she gazed, transfixed, from the cab window, I said:

"In this temple, as in the hearts of the people for whom he saved the Union, the memory of Abraham Lincoln is enshrined forever."

"Such lovely, lovely words," she said.

I pointed toward the Capitol, gleaming like a pale jewel in the distance. "When Lincoln was a young Congressman Maria, he used to stand on the balcony of the Capitol and look down at a slave pen—a filthy, crowded corral, where Negroes driven up from the South were kept before being sent out to the Maryland tobacco plantations. They say it was this memory that impelled him to battle against slavery."

"Eddie, you should have been a teacher," Maria said. "You're wonderful!"

"No, it's just that I'm cursed with total recall of details. For example, the Lincoln Memorial wasn't dedicated until 1922, but why so late I don't know. Harding was President then. From Lincoln to Harding. There's a moral in that, but I'm not sure what it is." Old scandals, bribes, corruptions, cluttered my mind.

We drove through West Potomac Park, crossed the Tidal Basin and stopped at the Jefferson Memorial.

"I expect another quotation," Maria said. "You're better than any guide!"

"A smart schoolboy could oblige you."

The domed monument rose in the misty night. The Jefferson Memorial is impressive but it does not really capture the flavor of that noble dilettante—musician, scientist, intellectual, inventor.

"I'm waiting," she said.

" 'I have sworn upon the altar of God, eternal hostility against every form of tyranny over the mind of man.' "

I did not tell her that Jefferson had kept slaves and had worried a good deal about them. Was it true he had beautiful mulatto daughters who were sold at auction?

We halted the cab at the Washington Monument.

"The only thing I can think of by Washington," she said, "is something about avoiding entangling alliances."

"Yes, and the cherry tree bit. But it's likely Parson Weems invented that, and Mark Twain rewrote it." I thought of Congressman Garcia's women, of Gabe Tutt's drunken rages, of Alf Kemmons' testimonial dinners and I added: "Mark Twain also said, 'In America there is no natively criminal class except Congress.' "

"That nice man, who wrote *Huckleberry Finn?*"

"He was not a nice man at all. He was a cynical bad-tempered man, who said all sorts of terrible things. Such as, 'It is at our mother's knee that we learn our most noble principles, but there is seldom any money in them.' "

Maria applauded. The cab driver, too. I had not enjoyed myself so much in years. Back in the taxi, Maria moved closer to me —student to teacher.

We drove slowly through Georgetown and I showed her where President Kennedy had lived when he was in the Senate. She looked grave. She was a child when he was killed. He had had a special significance for the young—children had understood him, had sensed that he was a tolerant and fair man. He had no murder in his heart.

"Yes, I took him in my cab several times when he was in the Senate," the driver said. He was an elderly beige-colored Negro. One sees these mannerly well-spoken mulattos frequently working as waiters in old seafood restaurants in Philadelphia, Washington, and Baltimore. Vanishing Americans, their children either work for the government or are picketing someone.

"What was your impression of Mr. Kennedy?" I asked.

"I tell you what," the driver replied. "He did not get too friendly, talk too much. But he had quality. He didn't hate. You sometimes can divide up people in this city with those what hate and those what don't. I don't mean just on race, if you gather my meaning. And the sad thing is, those that do *not* really hate are

truly and deeply hated by those who *do*. Look at Mr. Stevenson.
Mr. Stevenson was truly a gentleman. He had no real hate for
anyone. Yet what I don't understand is, there was hardly a man
ever more hated than he was, hated by a lot of people who he
never did any harm to. Picked up a bunch of Georgetown students
one night. Oh, they were kids and maybe a little drunk. But the
names they called Mr. Stevenson! The way they hated him! And
what did he ever do to them?"

"I can't believe that!" Maria cried.

"It's true, ma'am."

I said nothing. The driver was right. He was talking about the
tiger, the one we let out of the cage in 1964.

We returned to Massachusetts Avenue. I decided to take Maria
to the Monroe-Plaza Hotel for a drink. Usually some interesting
types showed up at the bar late at night. We drove past the
stately façade of the Cosmos Club.

"Does the lady know that is the Cosmos Club?" the driver
asked.

"No. It's magnificent."

"Used to be the old Townsend Mansion. That was Pennsylvania Railroad money. Mr. Sumner Welles lived there. He was a
wonderful gentleman. Drove him around a lot. Seems there are
less real gentlemen here as the years go by. Lots of rich people,
but less gentlemen. Now it is the Cosmos Club. You got to write
a book to get in." He laughed. "Which means very few senators or
congressmen belong to it."

"There's a few can write," I said.

"Yes, but there is a difference. You know the story." He turned
his head and winked at me. "Guide was taking tourists around,
and he said, 'That there is the Cosmos Club, where they got lots
of brains but no money, and that there is the Metropolitan Club
where they got lots of money but no brains, and that there is the
Army and Navy Club, where they got neither.'"

At the hotel entrance, as I paid the driver, Maria asked him:
"And what do you think of Senator Hannaford?"

"Senator Hannaford? The big man?"

"Yes. You know him, don't you?"

"Yes, I know him. He been in the cab. From what I read he
has got money and brains. Not the brains to write a book, but
lots of other kind of brains. I don't think he hates, the way some

of them did. And I don't think he's afraid of anyone in the whole
world."

Maria seemed satisfied. I suspected I had a Hannaford-idolator
on my hands.

She drew stares in the lobby. The Monroe-Plaza is small but
elegant, a place for "insiders."

A few gray-suited men studied her mournfully. They sported
plastic-covered convention badges. The loneliness of those American nights away from home! I loved politics because one is
never without good friends, colleagues, stimulation.

We found a quiet corner in the mahogany-paneled bar. Not
that I had a thing to hide. I was simply in no mood for banter,
gossip, backslapping. But no sooner were we seated and had
ordered, than two men at the bar nodded at me and gestured for
me to join them.

One was Albon Blake. His white hair, lovingly waved (I suspect he had it set) crowned a lean, ruddy face. He was too handsome, too courteous, too friendly. He was a man who never
insulted anyone, and in turn, could not be insulted. Next to him
sat Senator Lester Goodchapel. The senator had a semi-invalid
wife, a shy woman who was almost never seen in public. They
lived quietly in a small apartment. Of an evening, the senator
could be seen shopping in a supermarket, porting huge paper
bags back to his flat. He was an unlikely drinking partner for
sleek Albon Blake.

I waved back at them, but did not leave our table. Blake could
not be discouraged. He walked over to us, a stylish man in the
narrowest dark blue suit imaginable.

"Edward," he said, "please join us in a libation. The young lady
is welcome also."

I introduced Maria to him and refused his offer.

"Well, come by for a moment," he insisted. "Senator Goodchapel is my guest."

Reluctantly I excused myself and walked toward the bar.

"Very Latin. Very exotic." Blake glanced back at Maria. "Local
talent?"

"She is the new girl in our office. A Ramada girl."

"The senator's high standards."

"She is an excellent typist, has good manners, and her father
was one of Senator Hannaford's foremen. Enough?"

"Goodness, Edward, I didn't mean a thing."

Senator Goodchapel's round lumpy face beamed at me. He was a lonely man. I don't think he had ever dreamed of getting to Washington. "Good evening, Edward. Mr. Blake was nice enough to ask me to have a drink with him. He wanted to give me some literature on the New Wilderness Bill." He plucked from his pocket a few slick handouts.

"Golly, things happen fast in this town. You know, Edward, I've made up my mind on the New Wilderness Bill. I called on Senator Urban this afternoon, and he convinced me I should vote against reporting it out of committee. I do believe, with all respect to your employer, Edward, that I respect Senator Urban more than any man in Washington."

"You won't even give us a chance to present some witnesses?" I asked.

"That's what I was telling the senator," Albon Blake intervened.

Glaring at Blake, I said, "Senator Hannaford will be disappointed when he finds out."

"Oh, he knows already," Goodchapel said. "I felt so bad after talking to Senator Urban that I called Senator Hannaford this evening. I told him I knew how important this was to him, and I wanted to let him know right away."

Ben had not mentioned this to me at the Embassy reception. Perhaps he counted the committee votes differently than I did.

"What did he say?" I asked.

"He thanked me for my frankness. He said he certainly would not hold it against me. He's a big man, your boss. I wish I could have helped him."

"You can still change you mind, Lester," the lobbyist said. "Why not look that material over—"

Goodchapel's misshapen head was nodding negatively. He had pitted cheeks, a pitted nose. "No, Senator Urban convinced me it is not a good bill."

Blake and I looked at each other. I wished he could be detached from our operation. I thought of his aide, freckled Mr. Paxton, and his client Norton Krallis, and the black case they had given me in front of the gibbon cage. *Whoop-thump! Whoop-thump!*

"I would say the prospects of the bill are not good," Blake said. "Unless we can advance with our educational program."

"I don't get this," Goodchapel said. "Is Mr. Blake working for the senator?"

"No, no," I hurried to say. "Mr. Blake has clients with parallel interests. Senator Hannaford has never used a lobbyist—"

"Industrial consultant," Blake grinned.

"—a third party, if you prefer, in his life. He is his own man."

"Amen," Blake said.

"When I was a boy back in the Great Smokies," Senator Goodchapel said dreamily, as if our conversation had been a trading of childhood reminiscences, "I remember clear streams full of bullhead and crappie, and piney mountains, and fresh air. It isn't that way any more. There's junk in the rivers and the pines have been knocked down for strip mining and the air is rotten."

"But the New Wilderness Bill will help preserve your boyhood woodlands," Blake said.

Senator Goodchapel shifted his bulk. "No sir, I don't think so. I don't really think so."

This defeat hardly seemed to dishearten the lobbyist. This was his job. Had Ben called him in—shock troops on short notice— to straighten Goodchapel out? Blake ordered another round of drinks. I returned to Maria.

I brooded a moment. She noticed and began to ask questions. It took some explaining to define exactly what Albon Blake did, and why he called himself an "industrial consultant" rather than a lobbyist.

Like a child at a Western movie, she wanted to know if he was "a good guy or a bad guy."

"Neither," I replied. "Just a functional guy."

As we talked in the quiet of our corner a third person, a woman, appeared at the bar. Blake introduced her to Senator Goodchapel, who rose as gallantly as was possible considering his heft.

The woman looked familiar to me. She had coal black hair, teased and lacquered into an inflated crown, several inches too high. She had a pale long face and rather slanted eyes. Her dress was discreet—a dark brown as I recall—and she had a bosomy wide-hipped figure.

Blake pulled a bar stool up. The woman sat between them and a drink was ordered for her. There was laughter, heads coming together. Lester Goodchapel said something that must have been funny, for she giggled and patted his hand.

Maria was yawning. "Excuse me. I've overestimated my staying powers. I am really exhausted."

"Overstimulated?"

"Yes. In love."

I winced.

"Not with anybody. With this city, with my job."

We made our way past the bar. I nodded goodnights to Blake
and Senator Goodchapel. The woman did not turn around.

"You must never lose your love for this city," I said to Maria
as we waited for a cab. "Strange and wonderful things happen
here. And sometimes strange and terrible things. But in the long
run it will merit your affection."

The words had a fatuous ring, but I believed them. And I am
certain she did also.

Senator Hannaford did not seem terribly upset over Lester Goodchapel's decision. "We'll get the committee votes somehow," he
said, and called the White House to pressure a presidential aide
on getting an appointment to the federal judiciary for a distant
relative of Fern's. I sometimes had the feeling that all Washington would be stocked with his friends, relatives, business associates.

After putting the poor White House aide into a sweat, he
revealed to me that the Secretary of Commerce, the monumen-
tally rich T. E. Kape, was rumored to be angry over the calling up
of the New Wilderness Bill, that the cabinet was thus split—
Hackensetter for us, Kape against us. Kape could mean trouble
—he was a fierce, independent, stubborn fighter—and President
Kretz respected him.

"That flinty son-of-a-bitch Kape has despoiled more forests
than any man alive," Ben said reflectively, "but he'll be damned
if anyone else will get a crack at them."

I said nothing. I did not like the way the opposition was
mounting—conservationists, Senate club members like Webb
Urban, millionaires like T. E. Kape.

Cleo's voice came over the inter-com. "It's Lou Parenti, Senator.
He insists on talking to you—nobody else."

Senator Hannaford nodded at me to take the extension.

"Good morning, Louis," Ben said. "What can I tell you that you can use against me today? Haven't you learned nobody believes you?"

"Maybe so, Senator," Parenti shouted. He is a true New Yorker —he shouts on the telephone. "I really got to thank you, the way you talk to me no matter how mean I am in the column!"

Ben leaned back in the black chair. "'He that is slow to anger is better than the mighty, and he that ruleth his spirit, than he that taketh a city.'"

"Very good, very good," Parenti laughed. "What's that about taking a city? Senator Hannaford taketh the city all right, and a lot of people in it."

"Don't get overfamiliar, Louis. What are you calling about?"

"A little agricultural information."

"Since when are you a farmer? You are a city boy."

"I have boundless curiosity, Senator, about all kinds of things. Like artificial insemination. Can you help me?"

"I know a bit about it."

"Frozen semen? Frozen bull's semen?"

"Yes. It has to be frozen for preservation."

"And shipped frozen, natch."

Senator Hannaford's eyebrows arched. "That is correct. Packed in dry ice."

"Like live lobsters, right? In a big aluminum cooler?"

"My, Louis, you have a lot of knowledge about artificial insemination. Have they assigned you to the Agriculture Department? If not, perhaps I can arrange that."

"Thanks a lot, Senator, but I'm happy on the Hill. Now is it a fact or not, Senator, that this weekend you had placed aboard the presidential plane a large aluminum cooler containing a glass vial chock full of frozen bull's semen from your national champion bull, Ramada Potomac Oaks Bandolier. True or false?"

"Sure I did."

"A gift to the President?"

"Indeed it was. He was my house guest."

"Fascinating. How do you get it out of the bull? I mean, I don't mean to be crude, but is it like a big jerk off? Or some kind of mechanical stimulation?"

"Louis, get to the point."

"Man, what a wad. Anyway, my informants say that this batch— load—quart—of bull's semen was sent out to Nebraska to impregnate some of the President's cows which were a gift, you'll remember, from Longhorn-Mideast Oil, and that if anyone else wanted a shot from Ramada Potomac Oaks Bandolier it would cost a grand —a thousand bucks. So a quart of semen might be worth about $50,000, right?"

"I put no price on a gift or favor to a man I esteem as much as President Kretz," Ben said.

"But you charged the Slanted-Bar-T Ranch ten grand when that prize bull knocked up some of their cows. What'd he cost you, forty-eight grand? That's a lot of bull, Senator."

"Don't push me, Louis."

"All I'm saying is, if I were putting my relatives and friends on every commission I could lay hands on, and if I was after the President to reverse himself on the New Wilderness Bill, a cause very close to my heart, I might think twice before showering him with frozen bull's semen."

Parenti kept repeating those three words like a litany, wallowing in his vulgarity.

"It was a gift. The President did not ask for it. Is that all you want to know?"

"Except for this," Parenti went on. "I checked with the Aberdeen Angus Breeder's Association. It is against their rules to impregnate a Black Angus cow artificially. The calf born of that illicit wedlock cannot be entered in the registry. It is not considered a registered Aberdeen Angus unless the calf is conceived in the old-fashioned way."

"Tell you what, Louis. We'll have the rules changed."

Parenti paused. "I figured. Not that I care whether Kretz's cows get knocked up or not, or how it's done. But you'll change the rules. Don't you always?"

"When I deem it in the national interest," Ben said.

"Which is always close to your own."

"You have put your finger on it."

"Look out, Senator. You may not make it on the New Wilderness Bill. If I see any aluminum coolers being hustled around the Senate Office Buildings, I may get suspicious. You gonna call an open hearing so's we can all hear how we're getting jobbed out of Grand Canyon?"

When the columnist had hung up, I warned the senator about Parenti. He could hurt us with ridicule. He would print all that nonsense about frozen bull's semen. It was the kind of trivia that the public loves. I thought of Truman's deep-freeze, Sherman Adams' vicuña coats, LBJ's hi-fi set. These were the petty symbols that people remembered—not the hundred million dollar contract, the two hundred million dollar mining rights, the multi-million dollar tax exemption.

"He's got an obsession with you," I warned.

I doubted that the Conglomerate secret could be kept from him much longer. Parenti had sources. He was known to bribe people. He was always getting secret, informing calls. Drunks, vengeful small-timers, disappointed favor-seekers. We would have to move quickly on getting the bill out of Committee. If the story on the Conglomerate broke, we would be dead.

The senator got up and began to pace the office. I am sure he was bothered by the same thing that was troubling me—the need for speed on getting the bill to the floor. He paused at the open door. He was staring into the outer office.

"I can't get over Joe Valdez' little girl," he said. "An exceptional young lady. Is she bright?"

"Outstanding. She attracts a bit too much attention, is all."

"So do I, but it doesn't bother me."

"I don't imagine it bothers her either. She's got natural poise. I suspect we'll lose her to marriage pretty soon. No one that good-looking will stay single long."

"You think so?" he asked. "How is her dictation?"

"Cleo says it's good—better than average."

"Send her in. We'll try it." This was a ritual with all new girls in the office. He enjoyed variety. All of our seventeen girls were expected to take letters from the boss from time to time.

I went outside for Maria. The eyeglasses were pushed high on her forehead. She was busily answering letters, working at a tiny portable.

"Halt all operations," I said. "Senator Hannaford is ready to try your dictation. Pad ready? Pencil sharp?"

She put a hand over her mouth. But she was not really frightened. Beauty is a marvelous source of confidence. I have known incompetent secretaries, girls who could barely spell their names, who sailed serenely through long secretarial careers, all errors nullified by clear skin and regular features.

"I don't think you're nervous," I said. "Stockings straight?"

"I'm not wearing any." Indeed she wasn't. Nor much else beneath another of those $7.50 cotton sheaths—this one pale beige. I thought of stately Fern Hannaford in her neck-to-knee iron maiden. Here was Maria Valdez, twenty-two, with that free smooth body beneath the thin dress.

Maria got up and walked toward his office. Her back was straighter than ever.

Ben took her hand as she entered. He was all gallantry. Women were idealized creatures in his world. He sometimes talked of his own mother, who had died when he was twelve—a shy, dark woman, part Kiowa, who had taught school at Kiowa Agency Reservation, a woman incapable of unkindness or meanness.

Maria sat down opposite his desk, her pad and pen at the ready. Ben began to dictate. As he paced the office I saw him pause once behind her chair. His left hand began stroking the bridge of his nose. His eyes were shut as he concentrated. Suddenly he placed his right hand on Maria's shoulder—almost as if trying to draw inspiration from her bare flesh. She did not move but turned and looked at him.

This brief communion ended, he turned and closed the door.

CHAPTER SIX

We held another hearing on New Wilderness. It went badly for us. Senator John Tyler Lord arranged for some professional conservationist types to testify and they made the bill look very bad, very wicked.

Our friends on the committee, Senators Stapp, Tutt, and Kemmons, gave us little help. They seemed willing to let Ben run his own ball game. But the boss did not seem upset. In spite of some pestering phone calls from two of the potential Conglomerate members, who were growing querulous, he exuded confidence.

A few days later I understood why.

Senator Lester Goodchapel of Indiana, who had missed the last hearing, and whom I had last seen at the Monroe-Plaza bar with Albon Blake, phoned to ask if he might call on us.

He lumbered into our office that morning, carrying a small portable tape recorder, which he set on Ben's desk. Senator Hannaford and I exchanged puzzled looks. Goodchapel settled his bulk into a black leather chair where he could reach the machine. Sighing, he spent an inordinate amount of time polishing his eyeglasses. The lenses were thick and tended to mangle his small dazed eyes.

"Is everything all right, Lester?" Ben asked. "Mrs. Goodchapel feeling all right?"

"Oh, yes. Felt well enough to go to the picture show last night."

"Fine. Give her my best."

We waited; he sat there stupidly, an elephantine, non-communicative man.

"Would the senator care for a drink?" I asked, moving toward the small mahogany bar. "A bit of bourbon?"

"Oh, no, thank you, Edward," Goodchapel muttered. He peered at the tape machine. "Little reel of tape I want to play for you both. But just you two. Can you make sure no one else will come in?"

Ben told me to lock the door. He buzzed Cleo and told her to hold all phone calls.

"Mr. Blake lent me this contraption," Goodchapel said. "It's his. Matter of fact so is the recording on it. Let's see. He showed me how to run it last night. Hmmmm . . . that's the doo-hickey that starts it."

Goodchapel's pudgy index finger pushed the START button. The plastic discs spun swiftly and silently. Senator Hannaford and I said nothing. Goodchapel sunk back in the seat and folded his hands on the rise of his paunch.

There were some mashed, muddled noises at first. Then a woman's voice emerged—faint, but the words clear and well-enunciated.

"Oh what a thrill, Senator Goodchapel!" the woman cried. "To be in Senator Goodchapel's very own office so late at night when nobody else is here! Gosh, I've never done this before!"

Ben scowled. "Senator Goodchapel, this isn't necessary . . ."

"Oh yes it is," Lester Goodchapel said. He smiled grimly at us. "It gets better."

"Yep, this is it, my office," a voice on the tape said. It was Goodchapel's voice, chuckling, a warm, self-satisfied voice. "Yep, that's my desk, and my picture there with the President . . . make yourself comfy, little lady, right there . . ."

My boss made a tent of his fingers and touched his lips. He leaned back in his chair, his eyes almost shut. I wondered what he was thinking.

"Goodness, what are you doing, Senator?" the woman's voice on the spinning tape said. "Golly, Senator Goodchapel, don't be so rough, so anxious! Goodness, right here in your office? In Senator Lester Goodchapel's very own office? Oh, I've never done anything like this before! Oooh, Senator you're so naughty!"

I could swear I now heard heavy breathing on the record—a man's heavy breathing. In my imagination, it almost seemed to be in time with Goodchapel's actual breathing at the moment. It was lunacy, sheer lunacy.

"No, no, let me, Senator, I'll do it . . . you'll rip my *dress* . . . there, that's easier . . . Ouch! . . . Oooh, stop it at once!"

"This is mighty nice of you, Clarice, mighty nice," Goodchapel-on-the-tape mumbled thickly. "I sure appreciate it, I do, and I want to thank you and that nice fellow Mr. Blake . . ."

Some giggles followed, some high-pitched laughing. "Oh darn it, my garter's caught!" the woman simpered. "Gee . . . right there . . . ooh . . . thanks . . . Gee, this leather is so cold! Oh, Senator!"

"Might as well go all the way and get it all off," Goodchapel's hoarse voice mumbled. "Ah, ah, say that's all right, that sure is something, Clarice . . . but not a word of this to anyone, you un-un-un-understand . . . Aaaaaah . . ."

"Warm me up, Senator! It's cold here!"

Goodchapel sat there motionless, a great clunk of flesh, a mound of mortification. There was a sort of harsh satisfaction on his lumpy face. Throwing it back at us. Beating himself in front of us, as if to show us how terribly we—Ben—or at least, Blake—had mistreated him.

"Oh, to think of it . . . the two of us without a stitch of clothing on, right here in Senator Goodchapel's very own office! In room 611!"

(I actually sensed that the woman was directing her voice toward Albon Blake's hidden microphone. She was well-instructed. Probably she had performed these services for the lobbyist before.)

"Say that's fine, oh, that's real good, Clarice, you sure are nice to a fat old man, like me . . ."

"Oh, golly, Senator Goodchapel, you aren't fat and old, you're very distinguished. But, gee, think of it, here we are making love right in a senator's office in the middle of the night! Oh, it really is so exciting for me . . . honest, I've never done this . . ."

Senator Goodchapel leaned over and turned the tape recorder off.

"Well sir, that's the heart of it," he said to us.

"Why have you played it for me?" asked Ben.

"Senator Hannaford, I think you had something to do with this," the fat man from Indiana said glumly.

"What makes you say that?"

"Last night Mr. Deever saw me at the Monroe-Plaza bar with Mr. Blake and a young lady. The young lady whose voice you just heard. Is that right, Mr. Deever?"

"That's so, Senator Goodchapel."

"Mr. Blake seems to have some relationship to you, Senator Hannaford. At least he is working in behalf of the New Wilderness Bill. He tried to get me to change my vote, then when I was adamant, he advised a little recreation. You have just heard the results of that recreation on this machine."

"Are you saying that Mr. Blake made this recording of your nocturnal rendezvous?" I asked. "That's scurrilous."

"Oh, he admits it," Goodchapel said. "In fact he played it for me this morning. He lent me the tape recorder when I challenged him on it and said I wanted to play it for Senator Hannaford."

"But what did Blake say he'd do with it?" I asked.

Goodchapel hunched forward, squinting at the discs. "He said that unless I was prepared to change my vote in the Interior Committee on the New Wilderness Bill, that is, to vote favorably on it, he would play this tape for Mrs. Goodchapel."

Ben inhaled deeply. His great chest inflated and he stretched. "Why have you played it for me?" Ben asked again.

"Senator Hannaford, I know you are the only one who can stop this man Blake from going ahead with this. For all I know, and I feel awful saying this, you put him up to it."

Ben shook his head slowly. "Not so, Senator. Blake is working for other parties who want the bill passed. I'm interested in getting it out of the committee. And he's aware of my interest. But I never told him to involve you in this sort of mess. I don't work that way."

"I was certain of that," Goodchapel said—and he beamed at my boss. "May I depend on you, sir, to advise Mr. Blake that it is your desire that this tape, and the original of it, which he has kept, be destroyed, and never, never revealed to Mrs. Goodchapel?"

Senator Hannaford waved an assuring hand at him. "Absolutely. As soon as you've recorded your vote in favor of the New Wilderness Bill."

Goodchapel's lower lip drooped. He lifted those mangling eyeglasses and his confused, vague eyes darted at Ben, at me, at the damnable recorder with its evidence. "You mean, sir," he whispered, "that you expect me to bow to this—this—blackmail?"

"Don't look at it that way," Ben said lightly. "Look upon it as an experience, an adventure. Is the issue really that grave?"

"There is a principle involved," Goodchapel muttered.

"Of course there is. But I'm afraid, Senator, you were suckered in. Hell, it only hurts a minute."

"Sir, I am disappointed in you."

"Many people are. I needed your vote, Senator, but I sure as hell did not want Albon Blake to set you up like that. I'll speak to him about it. And once we get your vote, I'll kill those tapes."

With great effort, Goodchapel hauled himself to his feet and then closed the portable recorder.

" 'Though your sins be as scarlet,' " Ben said to him, " 'they shall be as white as snow.' Let that be our text for today's sermon."

Goodchapel gathered up the case and plodded toward the door, shaking his stunned head. Ben called to him: "Tell the truth, Lester. She was almost worth it, wasn't she?"

And with that, a lewd smile lit Goodchapel's homely face. "Now that you ask, Senator . . . yes, yes, indeed." He chuckled to himself, opened the door and left.

I turned to Senator Hannaford. "Well?"

"Not my idea, Edward. Blake's notion of how to change a vote."

"It worked," I said.

"Yes, it did." He spun about in his high-backed chair. "And it looks like we all win on this one. Blake. Us. The Conglomerate."

"And Lester Goodchapel?"

Ben laughed. "He loved every minute of it, Edward, including the confession. If Blake doesn't look out, our friend will be back, asking to be corrupted again."

That afternoon, satisfied that a major hurdle was overcome—a favorable committee vote—Senator Hannaford revealed some details of his daring plan for the "Conglomerate."

From a locked side drawer in his desk he took out a dark green folder and handed it to me. I had never seen it before.

"This is top-secret, Edward," he said. "Just you and me in this office know about it. Not even Cleo. Blake knows the basics, and of course so do the future members. It stays locked in here at all times."

He had already shown me the card with the names of the seven corporations that were to form the Conglomerate. I noted again that each was an organization of the second or third rank. Petrol-Air was a relatively new natural gas company; Longhorn-Mideast was not in a class with the "Seven Sisters." And so on. But all were comers.

A basic memorandum at the top of the file disclosed that the scheme was hatched at a secret meeting in Colorado Springs in March. Ben had been the chairman. The key provisions were as follows:

1. Longhorn-Mideast would buy out Ben's corporation, Hannaford-Western, and would then become the parent corporation. (It was all in the family; Fern's people, the Cudders were the founders and majority stockholders of Longhorn.)

2. A new corporation, for working purposes to be known as the "Conglomerate" would then be formed. Ben would become board chairman of the new umbrella corporation.

3. The Conglomerate would proceed, over a period of not less than eighteen months, to buy out the remaining corporations—Petrol-Air, Tramlett Hewes, Dover Plains Chemical, the others.

4. Ben would then be Chairman of the Board of the entire group. The Conglomerate would be in a position to compete with the giants in their fields. "One hand can wash the other", a memo from the president of Dover Plains Chemical said.

5. The new industrial giant would focus its energies on "development of natural resources everywhere in the world."

That was the gist of it. There was a lot of attendant stuff, letters, memoranda, résumés, surveys, statistics that bored me, but essentially the plan was to combine a group of second-rank and third-rank corporations—and thus compete with the truly monstrous ones, such as T. E. Kape's.

"So that's the Conglomerate," I said. "I take it it's your child?"

"The little bastard is all mine."

"The New Wilderness Bill is part of this," I said. "The Conglomerate will get first crack at any timbering, or mining or oil drilling, or road building when the national forests are opened up, correct?"

"I am inclined to think they will."

"This presupposes a friendly Secretary of the Interior, who will decide that a National Emergency exists, let us say, requiring more oil, or copper, or whatever."

"Once we establish a precedent with the incumbent Mr. Hackensetter, I think we will be in good shape."

"That will be quite an advantage for the Conglomerate."

Ben yawned. " 'The zeal of the Lord of hosts will perform this,' " he said.

It was ingenious. From his seat of power he would see to it that the Conglomerate got the lion's share of new contracts, mining rights, trading rights. He had never hesitated to use his power and he would now be in position to utilize it for a complex, all-pervasive industrial empire, not just Hannaford-Western.

"And this ties in with all those new bridges you are building to Eastern Europe?" I asked.

"Of course. I tell you, son, old-fashioned capitalism will do more to end the cold war than any two-bit diplomacy. By the time our Conglomerate is through, we'll have Sofia, Bulgaria, looking like Detroit, and lights burning bright all over Moscow. I'll give 'em their electricity—without Lenin!"

No wonder he had refused to let Lester Goodchapel off the hook. Ben was a kind man and he did not like the way Blake had blackmailed his colleague. But when it got down to cases, what was really more important—not just for Ben and the Conglomerate, but for the country as a whole—whether Goodchapel changed a vote he really did not understand, or that the progress be served?

"You'll excuse a cliché," I said, "but someone like Parenti might say that the stakes are enormous."

"They are, Edward. Now you see why I have been so anxious about the bill. It is my gift to the new corporation, a sort of bridal shower."

"When will the Conglomerate be made public?"

"First we have to get S.671 locked up. Once we have it out of committee I know we can get it through the Senate. The House will be no problem. Their mood is favorable. The way they jumped on Garcia was the tip-off. They are in a splendid mood. We'll wave the Free Enterprise flag at them, and they'll come around. Are you a Christian? Then you are in favor of using God's bounty for man's use! Are you an American? Then you are in favor of chopping down redwoods and mining copper!"

"So the bill is passed. What then?"

"At that point Longhorn-Mideast buys me out. I will retire for a brief period, to emerge, newborn as board chairman."

"Are you sure you want to do this much? Hold down your Senate seat—take on all these extra chores—and have to fight for them all the time?"

"Edward, that's what life is all about. The Ethiopian can't change his skin, nor the leopard his spots. If I'm not in the thick of it, I'm not happy."

"Of course you'll run for the Senate again," I said. "The Conglomerate, at least as it gets started, will want you right here to keep an eye on things."

"Maybe. Maybe not." He gazed out at the Capitol. Night had fallen on the city. The dome glowed in unearthly light.

His term was up the same year as the next presidential election. We had assumed all along that he would run again.

"Edward, how would you like to be administrative assistant to the President of the United States?"

"You won't run again. A nice offer, Senator, but I don't think I'd enjoy working for President Kretz."

Ben smiled at me. "I didn't mean that at all. I meant working for President Hannaford."

Why not? How odd that the thought rarely occurred to me. He was aiming high. Thus far his shots had been true and straight, a kill each time. The presidential goose soared above him, and he had it in his sights.

"I'd enjoy *that* very much."

"We'll crank it up pretty soon."

I could hardly wait; the newly won battle over S.671 seemed a small matter at the moment. Greater struggles loomed on the horizon. My heart pumped a bit faster when I left the office that night.

I had observed for some time the manner in which Senator Hannaford's eyes followed Maria about the office. Nothing remarkable in that. She was quite simply stunning. I recalled too the first
time she had gone into his office to take dictation, and the warm
possessive manner in which his hand had rested on her bare
shoulder. What of it? The senator was that kind of man. Not a
libertine, but genuinely affectionate where his employees were
concerned.

To the best of my knowledge—and I confess I am not infallible
in these matters although I knew him as well as any man—he
had always been faithful to Fern. He was a man of vigor, in excellent physical condition, but I believe he put sex very low on
his priority list. As a young buck in the oilfields thirty years ago,
perhaps he was something of the Lothario, a conquerer of
lithe young Indian girls, white-skinned Anglos, dusky Mexicans.
I don't know. He never talked much about his youth, except to
remind liberal critics that he had been poorer than any of them
as a boy. But I had the feeling that once married to Fern, the richest girl in town, heiress to the Cudder oil money, he practiced
fidelity to her in deference to her high position. Their relationship was an odd one—formal, excessively polite, with no outward
signs of affection, none of the "lovey-dovey" business I have observed in some middle-aged couples, and which can be both
nauseating and a hint that all is not well in their marriage.

"There is no finer woman in the world than Mrs. Hannaford," he
used to say. "She is the key to whatever success I have had,
whether in business or politics." Well, not quite. I think he was
being gallant. Ben would have achieved eminence no matter
whom he had married. That compulsion to succeed was bred in
his bones. What *is* true, is that Fern's modest fortune helped him
make the ascent faster. I suspect these tributes to her were
partial compensation for his busy expanding way of life, his constant motion, and her own placid existence.

But that there was authentic devotion between them I cannot
deny. Nor can I recall, have I ever had the slightest hint, that he
strayed from the straight and narrow.

After that first day that Maria took dictation, he asked for her
every day. When Ben wanted something, he simply did it—
with no excuses, explanations, or embarrassment. "Send Miss Val-

dez in," he would say to me or to Cleo. "She's darn good. Not a
mistake in those last letters."

It was a natural reaction in a virile man in his middle fifties.
The young fresh girl, in her light summer shift—bare-legged,
bare shouldered, her black hair with its tantalizing red highlights,
tied in a sassy ponytail. Perhaps memories of her as a little girl, or
at least the memories of his old comradeship in the boondocks
with her father, piqued his interest. The door would remain open.
I could see him circling the office, pausing to form sentences, gaz-
ing out the window, occasionally stopping to place a hand on her
shoulder. He showed a good deal more interest in her than in the
other girls in the office. (And we had some "knockouts"—prettier
than Marsha, perky young things, including one blond pedigreed
Washington society type, who was not in the least backward at
thrusting her perky breasts forward at the men.)

"The boss has taken a fancy to you," I said to Maria late one day.
I had been in conference with Matthew Fixx, our tireless legislative assistant, and my head was swimming with "inter-faces" and
"nitty-gritties."

"Really?" she asked. She was assembling her gear for departure.
I am a sort of fetishist and I watched, envious, feeling lonely and
bereft of that woman's world of sweet-smelling trivia, as she
stuffed lipstick, a packet of Kleenex, a small automatic pencil, a
book of matches, one of those tiny folding plastic rain hats, into
her cavernous Op-Art handbag. I envisioned her riding home
alone on the bus to the small apartment she shared with another
Ramada City girl she had met at the YWCA. I saw her lonely, in
shortie pajamas, her lush hair down, settling down for an evening of television and letter-writing. Even very pretty girls are
not out on the town every night. "The senator says my shorthand
is the best in the office—next to Miss Watterson's."

"He's a good judge," I said. "Excuse my nosiness, Maria, but
I did hire you—"

"The senator did."

"On my recommendation. Be that as it may, how is your social
life? Any interesting young men? Any bachelor congressmen?"

She shook her head. A mock frown wrinkled her clear brow.

"It's not that easy. I'm really not much of a swinger. Back at
Ramada U., I was considered something of a drag. I start to yawn
at ten o'clock—"

"Maybe you had yawn-inducing friends."

"No, no, I have low metabolism, low blood pressure. Isn't it awful?"

"I can't think of a greater waste of natural resources. The thought of you being forced to play the wallflower, Maria, is almost as appalling as one of Lou Parenti's columns."

"That's how it goes," she laughed.

"I'll try to change it. But . . ."

She cocked her lovely head at me. "But what?"

"Well . . . your friendly guide to Washington here recently took the pledge. No dating of office personnel. Which doesn't mean I'm not ready to backslide."

"You're sweet, *amigo*. But I won't suffer. There's this Marine captain I've been seeing. A good Joe, if something of a square."

Suddenly I was annoyed with the captain, whoever he was. Oh, I knew what he was like—crewcut, ramrod-back, blue eyes, bemedalled. Did she let him paw her, cover her mouth with wet kisses? It was getting harder and harder to play the role of disinterested big brother.

We found ourselves working at night in the office more frequently. Sometimes I would be there, sometimes Ben, sometimes both of us. When he stayed, he often asked for one of the girls, usually Cleo, but sometimes Maria or Pat Kelsey, to remain for dictation. We were reasonably sure that we would have clear sailing with the New Wilderness Bill, now that Lester Goodchapel was with us. But the senator was always prepared with a second line of defense, in this case, the sandy Arab principality of Djarak.

I became the Djarak expert, burying myself in old Foreign Aid bills, Congressional Records, reports of the Foreign Policy Association, Facts-on-File, several Encyclopedias, and Bockelmann's *A History of the Islamic Peoples*. Ben was especially intrigued with a Foreign Aid Bill of the Sixties in which the pro-Franco lobby had tacked on a special amendment insuring continued U.S. dollars for Spain, a gilt-edged guarantee that the dictator would not be cut out.

"If the good old R.C. Church, bless 'em, could do it for Franco," Senator Hannaford said, "a couple of good Baptists like us can do it for Prince Aziz."

"The prince is hardly my idea of a Fundamentalist," I said.

"We'll make him one," Ben laughed.

One night several of us worked late. Maria took some letters, Cleo spelled her for a while, and when we were finished, I escorted her through the building. Maria wanted to see the inside of the Capitol. I had had such a good time playing guide a short time ago—the memorable evening when we saw Lester Goodchapel about to be entrapped—that I agreed.

We used our passes to enter the rotunda, and we strolled about, while I showed her the three-armed girl in the painting of Washington resigning his command at Annapolis; the six-toed Indian in the portrait of Pocahontas saving Captain John Smith; the three-legged horse in the frieze above these. I told her about the Italian artist Brimidi, who fled his country after plotting against the King, and who, in the twenty-fifth year of lying on his back decorating the Capitol, slipped from the scaffold and was killed.

We wandered among the statues of the states' Hall of Fame, and I showed her where Will Rogers' toe was worn down by the caressing hands of tourists, as well as the similarly eroded trouser-leg of Senator Bob La Follette of Wisconsin.

She was silent, absorbing it all.

"Yes, my dear, this is one of the great shrines in the world—magnificent and mighty, yet still possessed of the common touch," I told her. "Do you know that the west wall of the Capitol moves four to eight inches on a hot summer day? Or that this whole building was once lit by pine torches, or that it's supported entirely on arches? No matter."

"It does matter, Eddie. Everything about it is important."

"Yes, I suppose so," I said, as we walked in the half-lit corridors toward an exit. "And do you know that the basement of the great building is a maze of labyrinths, and a favorite hideaway for lovers? Why one of the biggest jobs of the Capitol police is ferreting them out. They don't actually quite have an anti-vice squad, but close to it."

Maria laughed. She didn't blush or look shocked—she laughed. As we emerged into the warm night, and I hailed a cab, I experienced a deep and soulful change in my attitude. She would have to be mine. All mine. Not right away. I would nurture the relationship. As we stepped into the taxi—and I almost swooned at her bending lithe figure—I decided I would pursue the delicate goal with finesse, with style. I've often been like that. I save my pleasures for such a time as I feel I've earned them. As a boy, I would do all my hardest homework first—math, science—and save the easy, pleasurable reading chores for late at night. So I would arrange my imminent joyful relationship with Miss Valdez. What could be more natural for both of us?

We approached the final hearings on the New Wilderness Bill. Ben was now convinced that our opposition—the conservationists, the Secretary of Commerce, press scolds like Parenti, could not prevail against his argument that these precious forests would not be touched except in times of National Emergency. Like the bloated, fat, graft-ridden Defense Budget, which no man dare question or oppose, the term National Emergency was one of those shibboleths that serves anyone in just about any way he wants it to, and is very hard to oppose.

But my own certainty was shaken one morning when Matthew Fixx stopped me in the outer office. Matt, I might add, knew that Senator Goodchapel had switched his vote for us, but he had no idea why the Indianian had done so.

"Ed, are you sure of the body count on S.671?" Matt asked.

I ticked off the favorable votes. "Yes. I think we'll just make it."

"No no-shows?"

"No. It looks solid."

"Hmmm." Matt's lean face twisted to one side. He tended to be shy and inarticulate with everyone except the senator and myself. "Ed, I would start checking all systems. We may not be in orbit yet."

"What do you hear?"

"The body count may be wrong. Couple of IC's in with the VC's."

"Now what the devil does that mean in English, Matthew?"

"Oh, sorry, Ed. Innocent Civilians in with the Victor Charlies."

"Such as?"

"Kemmons may be getting ready to bug-out."

"Airborne Alf?" I was stunned. We had always assumed we owned Senator Alford Kemmons of Nebraska. That finagler, that chiseler, whom Ben had bailed out of trouble a half dozen times!

"You or the senator better check it out," young Fixx said

tensely. "I know he's been huddling with Secretary Kape's janni-
zaries, and that could mean trouble. Some guy named Mulrooney,
a front man for the Kape interests."

"When did you hear this?" I asked. I was perturbed. The loss of
Kemmons' vote could kill us.

"Yesterday. Look, Ed, it doesn't surprise me. It's no secret
about Kemmons."

It was no secret on the Hill, that was certain. Alf was in deep
trouble. The gentleman's conspiracy among the senators had protected Alf, for a long time. No man had more testimonial dinners
in his honor—and no man accounted in more slovenly fashion for
the funds. Letters for favored clients poured from his office—a
good word for anyone who could help him financially, a hint to
this federal agency, a threat to that State Department desk, a
request from this cabinet member—all for an odd bag of favor-
seekers. All senators, I might add, do this sort of thing, and
most of it is legitimate, understandable, in the nature of actions
on behalf of constituents. But in Alf Kemmons' case, the "con-
stituent" might be a lobbyist for the Haitian government with
an office in New York, rather far removed from the senator's native Nebraska, or a tax favor for a TV manufacturer in Ohio,
hardly a hometown friend.

Then there were those maddening on-again-off-again investigations of Alf's. The most recent was to expose price-fixing in the
cement industry. Alf had kicked it off with a big press conference
and a ringing call to "once and for all determine who is behind
these continual rises in the price of cement." The big companies
denied any guilt. The story ran for several weeks. Then, inexplicably, there was not another word about Senator Kemmons'
crusade. When Ben Hannaford heard about it, he winked at me,
and said, "Alford had better go easy on that old dodge. One of
these days he's going to start an investigation of some people
who don't care if they are investigated. He might even have to
go through with one."

I told Senator Hannaford about Matt Fixx's suspicions. At once
he telephoned Kemmons.

"Alf, I've heard a disturbing rumor," Ben said. "I'm told you
may change your committee vote on the New Wilderness Bill."

"Did you? Who the devil told you that?"

I listened in on the extension. Kemmons had a spongy voice.

He drank too much and he had developed a tremor in his right hand. The man was falling apart.

"Never mind, Alf," Ben said easily. "Now, you should know I will move for a vote on S.671 at the next committee meeting—day after tomorrow. I do not intend to move unless I am certain that I can get a favorable vote."

"Haaargh, haaargh," Kemmons said. "Ben, you know I respect you more than anybody on the Hill."

"Then I can forget those rumors? You're with me?"

"No, I'm afraid—ah—I'm afraid not, Ben."

"I'm not sure I heard you correctly, Senator."

"Ben, I know you'll understand what I have to say . . ." A fit of coughing convulsed him. He finally got the obstruction from his throat, blew out his breath a few times and stammered out: "I—I—I changed my mind, Ben. I'm voting No in the committee. A—a—a question of conscience, Ben. I'm sure you understand."

"I don't understand at all."

"Well, a variety of considerations. First, I was pretty certain you had the votes . . ."

"I don't."

"Golly, I didn't know that. Ben, be that as it may, I can't go with you on this. Those arguments against the bill are pretty valid—an unscrupulous Secretary of the Interior, an unfriendly administration, they could wipe out the National Forests in a generation—"

"Senator, you don't give a good goddamn about the national forests," my boss said. "You never have. You forced through those pork barrel dams in your own state that destroyed Sioux Valley. Didn't you?"

"L-l-l-local issues, Ben . . ."

"I hope you will reconsider, Alf. I want your vote."

"I'm sorry, I'm really sorry, Ben. It just wasn't in the cards . . ."

He began to blubber, his watery voice, interrupted by coughs and hacks, explaining, excusing himself.

"Anything else, Ben, *anything* else, I'm with you!" Kemmons cried. But Ben was not listening. After he had hung up, I saw him studying, for a moment, the Conglomerate folder. That morning there had been a call from one of the Petrol-Air contacts in Washington. They were applying pressure.

"That whining son-of-a-bitch," Senator Hannaford said. "He's been bought off."

"How is that possible? After all he owes you?"

He slammed his fist to the desk—almost wishing it were Alford Kemmons' booze-soaked face. "If there's anything I hate, it's a dishonest man who can't be trusted! When I buy somebody I expect him to stay bought!"

"We've been outbid."

"I know who did the bidding. That friend of the White House, T. E. Kape. He looked at the committee list and picked himself a winner."

"The way we picked Goodchapel?"

"Yes, Edward, you might put it that way." He pointed a finger at me—almost a defensive gesture, a move very unlike the boss. "But we had *firsts* on Kemmons! It isn't fair buying someone already purchased!" Then he roared with laughter. The humor of the situation was not lost on him.

"Well," I sighed, "it's too bad Kemmons isn't interested in a batch of frozen bull's semen."

We both laughed, Ben till his eyes were filled with tears.

"That won't help," Senator Hannaford said. "But the fish hasn't gotten away yet." He hunched his shoulders forward. "Edward, where is the Special Fund?"

I told him about the safe deposit box in the Riggs National Bank.

"We have $180,000 there, do we not?" he asked.

"Actually $200,000. I've put my own there also."

"Why?"

"Oh, until I decide what to do with it."

"Invest it, Edward. Make a soldier out of every dollar. Why not let me give it to Longhorn? Risk five thousand and bring in a well. If you lose, Uncle Sam pays. If you win, he pays anyway."

"Thank you, but I'll wait."

He was trying to estimate exactly what would be needed to change Alford Kemmons' mind. The boss was a wizard at these things. He could read someone's credit rating like a cashier at a Las Vegas casino. "Senator Kemmons is in deep trouble," he said.

"I can't understand it," I said. "Apart from that dusty old mansion he rents in Cleveland Park, his expenses can't be that high."

"He is a damn drunkard."

"I keep hearing that drunks go into debt," I said, "but they can't really drink *that* much. How much does it cost to get inebriated?"

"Initial cost very low. It's the incidentals—like bad investments. The senator is a fool. He has been led astray by evil companions."

"And I assume we'll show him the road back."

"Edward, go to your hollow tree at the Riggs National Bank," Senator Hannaford said, "and extract from it one of those fresh, crisp bundles."

"Ten thousand dollars?"

"That is correct. I will telephone Senator Kemmons' office and advise him you are en route with some new data on the New Wilderness Bill. I will tell him to await your arrival."

He buzzed Cleo Watterson and had her call Alf Kemmons' office. To our annoyance Kemmons' secretary said that the senator was not feeling well and was in the process of losing his lunch.

As I reached the door, he stopped me. "Edward, listen carefully. This may be one of the crucial errands of your life. You are not only to deliver that bundle to Senator Kemmons, you are to make certain that whatever it was the Kape people gave him—and I would guess it is about half of what we are offering—is returned to them *immediately*." He pounded the desk again. "We'll teach *them* a lesson."

I paused a moment. "Is there any reason we can't wait a while? I mean, do it out of campaign funds, or some other way?"

"No, no, Edward—that's what the fund is for—our reserve. It's for emergencies. Hell, when you got an oilfield going up in flames, you don't wait for the downtown fire department, you run in your own fire-fighting rig."

A half hour later I was at the Riggs National Bank branch on Dupont Circle. Just before entering, I repeated the procedure I had employed when I had deposited the $200,000 a few weeks back. At the adjacent Peoples Drugstore (sometimes I marvel at the number of drugstores in Washington; it seems the major business of our city) I purchased one of those self-sealing combination envelope-letters.

In the vaults, I produced my identification and my key, and was given access to D.789. In the air-conditioned silence, with only an elderly guard standing nearby, I withdrew one stack of bills—ten thousand dollars. I put it in my inside jacket pocket. Then, on the self-sealing letter I wrote the date, and the words: *Ten thou-sand ($10,000) taken from safe deposit box D.789, this day, for personal transference to Senator Alford Kemmons,* and signed my name to it.

I asked the guard if it would be possible to stamp the inside of the envelope with some identifying mark. He obliged, using a rubber stamp showing the bank's name and the date.

Then I affixed a stamp and mailed the letter to my apartment from the mailbox standing just opposite the bank. The postmark would of course show the date and the station from which it would be handled.

Hailing a cab, I returned to the New Senate Office Building, to meet with Senator Kemmons, and ensure the happy future of the New Wilderness Bill.

Alford Kemmons had a small staff. Nebraska is not a populous state, and Alf was not an ambitious man. He had a modest suite of rooms tucked away in a corner of the building.

Some hometown booster had tacked a colored poster to the outer door, a brilliant photograph of a sheaf of corn, with the legend: *NEBRASKA, CORNY AND PROUD OF IT.*

I entered. The office was as silent as the stacks in the Library of Congress. Compared to the noise and bustle in ours, it was disconcerting. There was a lone girl at a desk, a plain young woman in spectacles (I learned later she was Kemmons' niece) who did not recognize me. I asked for the senator, identifying myself.

"He isn't feeling very well. I think he's taking a nap."

"I'm afraid I'll have to awaken him." I had no intention of carrying ten thousand in cash around with me until Alf Kemmons sobered up.

"I'll ask Miss Craigie." Ellen Craigie, a middle-aged nervous woman was the senator's private secretary. I knew her slightly.

Miss Craigie came out, looking distraught. Her gray hair was coming undone. She had the look of a fatigued Midwestern schoolteacher vexed by a rowdy class. "Oh, Mr. Deever. Senator Hannaford called a little while ago and said you'd be coming over. I'm sorry, but Senator Kemmons is feeling ill. He can't see anyone."

I looked about. The niece was listening to us. A young man

entered. He was Kemmons' legislative assistant. We nodded at each other.

"This is rather important, Miss Craigie. May we go inside? Just you and I."

I steered her to the inner office, to the horrified stares of the niece and the young man. There are few secrets from an office staff. Living cheek by jowl, they know all and see all. They knew that their boss was dead drunk.

The shades were drawn in the inner office. No lamps burned.

On the long black leather couch against the side wall, below several autographed photographs from colleagues, governors, Presidents, Senator Alford Kemmons lay prone, in the blissful sleep of the sot. His tie was undone, and his buzzard's neck rose and fell as he snored stertorously. To tell the truth, I rather liked him at that moment. He had the courage of his drunken convictions.

"Really, Mr. Deever, I shouldn't have let you in here," Miss Craigie whimpered.

"Don't worry, Miss Craigie. You know I'm a friend, and I would never breathe a word to anyone. And does the senator have a better ally than my boss?"

"Yes, that's true."

"We are in this together, Miss Craigie. We both work for great men, and we both bear grave responsibilities. May I make so bold as to ask you to observe secrecy—the utmost secrecy—concerning what I have to do?"

She nodded her head. She was all right, Miss Craigie, a decent old-timer.

"First, I am going to have to wake Senator Kemmons up," I said.

She groaned. "That's impossible. When he's off on one of these, all he can do is sleep it off. He won't wake up for hours. He threw up before, and then he took his pills, and that means he'll sleep all afternoon."

I studied Alford Kemmons' splotched face: mouth open, nose twitching, the bald dome a sickly gray in the half-light.

"Draconian measures are indicated," I said. "Miss Craigie, we cannot shrink from our duty as servants of the elected representatives of the people." With that I began to shake Senator Kemmons. His meagre arms and skinny chest bounced like a

Halloween skeleton. And still he snored, and still his eyes remained locked. I slapped his face while Miss Craigie whimpered. I rubbed his wrists. I slapped his face harder.

"I warned you," she said. "He is the hardest sleeper I have ever seen."

Desperate, I looked around the room for something. I did not want to waste time on black coffee and floor walking. On the senator's desk stood a large carafe. Hesitating not a moment, I seized it, uncapped it, and walked toward his insensate form.

"Oh, please, Mr. Deever . . ."

"Lock the door, Miss Craigie."

As soon as I heard the *click*, I let him have it—a good hard *whoosh!* The damned carafe was deceptive. It contained a veritable Niagara—and the rush of water not only soaked his face, but drenched his jacket and his shirt. He gasped, threw his arms out, and sat up.

"Whah? Whah? Jesus . . . whah this?"

He was awake! I shook him roughly and propped him against the black sofa.

"Senator, you must wake up," I said. "This is Deever, Edward Deever. Senator Hannaford sent me here with some important business that has to be handled at once. *Wake up!*"

His eyes focused. The damned fool actually smiled at me. How could anyone dislike Alf Kemmons? "Edward, Edward, how are you? Had upset stomach. Took in a bad clam at lunch. Everything okay with the boss?"

I looked at Miss Craigie. Should she witness this or not? I decided she should. As I have pointed out there are few secrets from private secretaries.

With no more ado I reached inside my pocket and took out the packet of bills. "Senator Kemmons, this is a campaign contribution from Senator Hannaford," I said loudly and clearly. "The party wants you to have it per your request."

Kemmons smiled idiotically. "My lucky day," he said, still half-boozed. "Looky here." And with that he reached inside his *own* breast pocket and extracted a wad of bills held together with a large paper clip. "Never rains but it pours," he said. "Or, you might say, it's a feast or a famine."

Miss Craigie clapped a hand over her mouth.

"*Soaked*," Kemmons cried. "Absolutely soaked! Look at 'em."

His money was drenched, so wet, so sodden, that the bills were sticking together.

"Fair exchange?" I asked him. "Mine for yours? I think you'll do well on the transfer."

He seemed to be ready to conk out again. I swiveled my head toward Miss Craigie. "How much is it?"

"Oh, dear. Oh, dear, this is terrible. Five thousand."

"There's ten here."

I relieved him of his drenched stack. The fool! To carry that around with him! I felt his trousers. They were dry. Pushing his slender body sideways, I inserted the paper-bound stack of new money—our money—in a trousers pocket. "There you go, Senator," I said. "For your campaign expenses. So that there will be no mistaking the nature of this transaction, I am going to return this amount to its donor. Senator Hannaford feels we will all be better men for doing it this way."

"Yes, yes, Edward," Kemmons mumbled.

With that, he fell back on the couch and was asleep again in a matter of seconds. The five thousand dollars in my hand—a stack of fifty hundreds—was soaked. I was under orders to "return to sender" immediately. By now I had entered the spirit of the chase and was enjoying myself. I pondered the soaked bills in my hand. I had trouble prying them apart. Currency has a tendency to absorb water with great tenacity, to turn limp, sticky and disagreeable when drenched.

"We've got to dry this," I said. "Dry them out before I return them."

"How?" wailed Miss Craigie.

"On the air-conditioner, for one thing. Here, help me." So mad, so wild had been the rush of events, that—as I look back upon that day—I can only recall it with a sense of hilarious joy. Miss Craigie and I began draping bills on the air-conditioner. When we were out of space, we draped them on the edge of Senator Kemmons' desk, and then we stretched a string across the room, tying one end to a lamp, the other to a plaque from the Cornhuskers' Association, given to Senator Kemmons as the "annual Ambassador of Corn." On this improvised clothesline, we hung the balance of the bills. For a while I tried blowing at them. The ones on the air-conditioner appeared to dry quickly. But those on the desk and on the clothesline were still wet.

"A fan!" I cried. "Do you have a fan?"

The stunned woman produced one from a closet. I plugged it into a socket in the distant corner of the room. It was a small table fan with rubber blades. "Here goes nothing," I said, and turned the switch. The fan whirred: its power surprised me.

In the air-conditioned confines of the office, the fan created its own blizzard—a storm of swirling, dancing, green hundred-dollar bills. Before I turned it off, I enjoyed the mad sensation—the tormented old maid and I standing amid the snowstorm of legal tender while Kemmons snored through it all.

Then, aware of my mandate, I turned it off, and we began bringing in the sheaves. They were more or less dry by now.

Before leaving Senator Kemmons' office, I elicited from Miss Craigie the information that the five thousand dollars had come from one J. J. Mulrooney, an "Industrial Relations Counselor" with an office on K Street. I knew him slightly—an errand-runner and lunch-eater, not in the same class with Albon Blake.

From a public phone booth I telephoned Senator Hannaford, to tell him that the deed was done. He grunted his pleasure. Then I located Mr. Mulrooney ("Hi there Eddie, this is Jack Mulrooney, doncha remember me, pal?") and arranged to meet him in the lobby of the Hay-Adams.

He was a chubby man, sharply tailored in one of those curious jackets with vents at both sides, flaring at the hips.

"Howsa bouta drink, Eddie?" Mulrooney asked.

"No thank you." The meeting would be surgical, direct, and without social niceties. "Mr. Mulrooney, this sum of money was given to Senator Kemmons this morning by you."

I took from my pocket the somewhat damp stack of hundreds, clipped together. "The senator is returning it. He has thought better of the whole affair and is not interested."

We stood there—two foolish young men in expensive suits, scented with after-shave lotion, two young men very much "in" on things—with our manicured hands joined on a wad of wet money. I withdrew mine first.

"It's all yours. Or Mr. Kape's. Or whoever gave it to the senator."

"I take it this will affect the voting on the New Wilderness Bill?" Mulrooney asked.

"You will have to read the Congressional Record to find out.

Or attend a committee hearing. They will be open next week."

He had poise. He did not panic. After all, he was only a messenger—like myself.

I telephoned my boss. Senator Hannaford was pleased with the dispatch with which I had handled the assignment. I left out the lunatic details about drying the money, the windstorm of greenbacks.

The day was clear and fine, so I walked to the Capitol. A few pickets of mixed hue, one Negro, some Latins, white bearded types, were demonstrating for Congressman Garcia. WHY PICK ON ANGEL? one read. And another: OUR FALLEN ANGEL WILL RISE AGAIN.

My sympathies were with them, but Garcia had only himself to blame. One did not flaunt one's defiance of Congress. One did not make a *joke* of minor corruptions. One denied them, made excuses, and acted humble. Every time Garcia appeared on television in loud shorts, embracing bosomy island maidens, he only dug his grave deeper. It was too bad. He had been an intelligent, constructive member of the House. Ben had always liked "the Big Spick."

A tall old man was sitting in our outer office when I returned. He looked familiar, but I could not place him. Marsha, tugging at her girdle, came from behind her desk and took me aside.

"He says he's an old friend of Senator Hannaford," she whispered. "I think he's nuts. He says he's Senator Atherton."

There was no Senator Atherton. I looked at the old man. He wore a black, shabby suit and needed a shave. But his face was dignified, the jaw firm and the eyes, under snowy eyebrows, were alert and intelligent.

"May I help you, sir?"

"I wish to see Senator Hannaford," he said in an old man's sparse voice. His lips had a habit of parting, closing, opening again before he spoke. "I am Senator Atherton of Oklahoma. Former senator. Long before your time, sonny."

The name registered. I knew a little bit about him. A giant of the New Deal era—confidant of Roosevelt—author of a half dozen pieces of major legislation. I recognized the craggy, rough-hewn face, the long brushed-back hair. But what in heaven's name was he doing here? He was a vestige, a dinosaur, a man long passed from history.

"I'm sure Senator Hannaford will see you," I said and guided him through the rooms to Ben's office.

"For goodness sake," Ben said, when he saw the old man. "Senator Atherton. I did not know you were back in Washington."

The ancient smiled. "I have never left."

Ben looked puzzled. "But . . . all these years . . . when was it? Nineteen forty-four?"

The history of this unique man began to come back to me. Atherton had been a monument in the Senate—a frontier democrat, a founder of the New Deal, an old-fashioned Populist, scourge of the monopolies, a true friend to the dust-bowl farmers and the depression poor. He had chaired several key committees and one national convention.

Then, in the election of 1944, he had parted company with FDR on the conduct of the war. A strong foe of "Imperialist" Britain, a partisan of MacArthur and a greater effort in the Pacific, he neglected to campaign in the mistaken notion that he was assured of re-election—and was beaten. He had been in the Senate for twenty-four years—a landmark, an institution. He had no life beyond the Senate. I recalled reading about him—a dignified ghost, sitting in Lafayette Park, lost in dreams of his vanished eminence. The truth of the matter was, I had assumed he was dead. It almost seemed I had read his obituary.

"Yes, 1944, Senator Hannaford. You were a mere boy."

Ben got up and gently ushered Atherton to a comfortable chair. "I am honored to see you, sir. What business brings you here?"

Atherton's tongue darted to his lips, the lips opened and closed with an old man's uncertainty. "May I speak in front of sonny?" He nodded at me.

"Mr. Deever is my Administrative Assistant."

"Yes. I had some good ones, too." He stroked his unshaven chin. "I lost my job today, Senator. They fired me. I don't know why. I've always been on time."

"Your job?" Ben asked incredulously. "Where were you working?"

"In the Patent Office. For the past six years. I'm on time every day. I do my job, modest as it is. Why did they have to fire me?"

Ben's eyebrows arched. It was inconceivable.

"I suspect the Secretary of Commerce's office may have done it. Not intentional. Just to make room for someone else." His eyes studied the photographs on Senator Hannaford's wall. "I like the Old Senate Office Building better. Higher ceiling. The wood is darker, too."

"Senator Atherton," Ben said. "You will get your job back. If not that job, a better one. I promise you that."

"You will? Why, thank you, Senator. They speak of you as a man who gets things done. I'm sorry we never had a chance to work together. You know, I wrote every one of my own speeches. Never had a single one written for me."

"I am sure," Ben said. "I've read some of them. We don't get that kind of oratory on the floor any more."

"No. A lot of things have changed. For the better I guess. Most of you fellows are pretty well off. You are a millionaire, I'm told. Fine, fine. In our day, when I started, not many of us were rich. If we were not re-elected, it meant back to some small town law practice. Well, I even neglected that. So I stayed around Washington. I just couldn't leave. I couldn't believe they'd gotten rid of me. Do you know what I did, Senator, the day I was supposed to move out of my office across the street? I barricaded the door. Now that is hard to believe, isn't it? I pushed my bookcase against the door—Senator Fray of New Hampshire was taking my office—and I sat down and I wept. I could not leave the building. I could not leave this city."

"And you've been here since?" Ben asked.

"Oh, yes. For a while the party took care of me—National Committee—odds and ends. But I became a pest to them. You see, I was once very famous, very powerful. And it was unpleasant seeing me wandering around the halls of the Capitol, too stubborn or too stupid to pack up and go home. I could have had a dozen jobs lobbying—the big cattlemen, the big wheat growers —but I had nothing but contempt for them when I served in this great body, and I would not join them."

He fingered his collar. It was soiled. His tie was unraveling. The curled lapels of his old black suit were threadbare.

"Senator Atherton, you'll forgive my ignorance, but I had no idea you were still in Washington," Ben said. "Had I known, and had you made known to me your desire for a position suited to your talents, I would have taken care of the matter."

"Of course. I know you would have. You were a freshman congressman when we met, isn't that right?" Old Atherton's eyes gleamed a bit. "Yes, I certainly recall you. We were on a Senate-House conference on the agriculture bill. You were a pretty snappy kid. I guess it's all that money, and success made you that way. Not being critical, Senator Hannaford."

"You may be if you wish," Ben said. "I have had the deepest respect for you for years. Wasn't it you who said to the President, 'My heart is always with the people even if my vote may not be?' "

"Yes. I think it helped lick me in 1944."

"No, people admired the frankness. I think we tend to be a bit holier, to take ourselves too seriously here these days."

I studied old Atherton: a ghost from the recent past. He had been a legend, an archetype of the senator, in his severe black suits and long graying hair. But Ben was right: he was much better than a lot of them—he had never taken himself seriously in that tiresome, hypocritical manner that so many of Ben's colleagues assumed. I recalled that on various bills creating the Office of Price Administration, he had voted twice *for* them, and twice *against* them. "At least," he winked to a reporter, "I was right 50 percent of the time." I wondered: could this cavalier quality, this blunt candor, this capacity to laugh at himself, could this have reduced him to penury, to begging for work? I thought of him sitting in Lafayette Park watching the leaves fall.

Old Atherton's eyes roamed the wall behind Ben's desk, lost in nostalgia: old comrades, old victories. One photograph showed Senator Hannaford with Harry Truman. It was taken in Independence, some years after Mr. Truman had left the presidency.

"Old Harry," Senator Atherton said softly, his thin voice edged with tenderness. "No finer man ever walked these halls. Loyal. Decent. His word was gold. I had the knack to make Harry laugh. When the right-wing zealots were after his hide on the Hiss business, and the left was still angry with him for the Marshall Plan, he told me of the vile insulting mail he received. He asked me, 'Senator, do you get such mail?' 'Indeed I do, Mr. President,' I replied. 'I get angry letters on three things—Communists in government, the war, and Henry Wallace. I read them all, Mr.

President, and then put them in three separate boxes.' 'But how
do you answer them?' Mr. Truman asked. 'I don't,' I said, 'I just
leave 'em in the boxes.'"

Ben and I laughed. Senator Atherton had told the story with
gusto, licking at his dry lips, laughing in a shrill, cracked voice,
after we had stopped.

"Do you know, gentlemen," Atherton went on, "Harry Truman
loved the United States Senate more than anything in the world.
Even after he was President, he used to come back here and visit
with us. He loved the Old Senate Office Building and the Capitol
and he loved all the men there—except maybe one or two who
got to calling him a traitor. Imagine that. Harry, a traitor. Yes,
we'd meet Harry in someone or other's office, sip a little bourbon
and branch water, and we would all be in agreement."

"On what, sir?" I asked.

"That there was no place in the world like the United States
Senate."

"I would subscribe to that sentiment," Senator Hannaford said.

"It is all anticlimax after you have left," Atherton said. "Nothing
means very much if you cannot walk these historic halls as one of
that great number."

"I am certain that is so," said Ben.

"I'm not so sure you younger fellows understand. Oh, you'll
regret it when you're gone. But many of you are rich, powerful,
you have careers beyond your government work. Many of us were
senators, and that is all. Trained for it, worked for it, dreamed of
it, all our lives. Today . . . Like yourself, Senator Hannaford. I
know all about you." A sly grin crinkled his mouth. "You have a
finger in a lot of pies."

Ben chuckled. "I don't deny it."

"Why should you? And that bright Jewish fellow, Eisenberg.
Say, I like him. Real estate millionaire. Or young Henshaw, who
was the professor at Columbia. And I like that, too. About
time we got some educated men here. Or Johnny Lord. Knew his
daddy. A snobbish fellow, but bright as a copper. But the point I
am making . . ." His voice melted down to a mumble. "Damned
if I know what point I *am* making."

"You make yourself very clear, sir," Ben said.

"All anticlimax once you've gone. The steak has been served
and eaten and there is no dessert. The bourbon bottle is empty.

After you have served in this great body, Senator Hannaford, and you are again out in the world, no matter how rich or great you are, it is as if you have loved your only love, the only woman whose grace and beauty and form could truly delight you—and now she is gone, gone, gone forever, and you know you will never know her again, the touch of her hand, the color of her hair, the curve of her thigh. Gone. She is still around. But she is no longer yours."

The three of us sat there a moment, letting the soft gold of the late afternoon sun settle on Atherton's heartfelt words.

"Senator Atherton, do you want that job in the Patent Office back?" Ben asked. "I need only call. Or would you prefer something with the Campaign Committee? I can arrange either, and Mr. Deever here will advise you. In any event, there will be a job for you."

Atherton waved a withered hand. "It doesn't matter, Senator. Whichever is less trouble for you." Creaking, he got up. "All anti-climax, after you've been here. The woman you love—still there, still there for you to admire, and long for, and dream about, to feel the pinch in your heart, and the pump of your blood—but not yours any more."

I escorted him to the door and got his address—a hotel I had never heard of in the Northeast section. Then he shook my hand, walked through the door and vanished down the corridor. No one recognized him.

"A ghost," Ben said to me. "A great figure in his day, Edward, but he made the mistake of hanging on here. This town can't afford ghosts. You have to go home, get out when your time is up. When my time is up here, I will clear out. Atherton didn't understand that." He reached for the buzzer. "But we'll land him a job."

"I'd go easy on Commerce, Senator," I said.

"Yes. No need to push Secretary Kape any further than we have to. That lion will be shot another day. Mr. Kape probably did not even know that old Atherton was supervising a supply cabinet, or a water cooler over at the Patent Office. No, we won't badger Mr. Kape—not yet, and not on so trivial a matter."

He told me to call the personnel director of the party's Campaign Committee. Not only would we get Senator Atherton a job, but we would publicize it and get a little mileage out of it.

CHAPTER SEVEN

It was decided by Ben that a junket would be in order, a committee-paid trip, to one of the national forests, in order to *prove* his point—that wilderness areas could be opened to "multiple use" such as timbering and mining, and still not have their grandeur diminished.

To this end, I huddled with one of Gordon Hackensetter's assistants, a young former Park Ranger named Wilson Blades, trying to decide which particular forest would suit our purposes. Blades' heart was not in the job. He knew the bill for what it was—a blank check for industry to ruin the forests. And he knew "Giveaway Gordon" for what *he* was—the man who endangered the whooping crane and opened the refuges to oil drillers. He cooperated reluctantly, and for several afternoons, I joined him in a dark office in Interior, poring over maps and photographs. I envied Blades. His love was for sequoias and red foxes, dune primroses and cactus wrens. Some boyhood memories of my scouting days—merit badges for bird watching and butterfly collections—saddened me. We narrowed the choice down to California, a wilderness area already containing a mining enclave and near enough to San Francisco so that the committee members would be comfortable.

As I left the Interior offices late one night, I was suddenly delighted by the prospect of a few days in San Francisco. It is a romantic, evocative city, a city made for secret trysts and the fulfillment of dreams. Maria was to accompany the subcommittee as a member of the staff; she would take notes, serve as the girl-of-all-work for our group, and especially for Ben. There it was! There was the opportunity to make my move! Maria—myself—San Francisco. I would be her friend, guide, companion—and lover. No matter that it meant breaking my vow of abstinence where office girls were concerned. The time was ripe; the painful math and science homework was finished; and now I could settle down to the joys of *The Scarlet Letter* or *A Tale of Two Cities*.

Who could tell where this would lead? Was it not possible that I was ready for more than another romance? In this exhilarated manner, I walked briskly into the New Senate Office Building, nodding at the guard, and took the elevator to our floor. So good did I feel, that I wanted to place a memo on the California junket on Ben's desk immediately.

I was not surprised to find the outer door unlocked. Ben was probably working late, or perhaps Matthew Fixx was spending a few hours brushing up on clichés. Someone had left a small lamp burning on one of the girls' outer desks. I did not turn it off, but walked toward the door leading to Ben's private office.

As I approached the door I heard a rush of water—the toilet flushing, or possibly the sink—from Ben's small private bathroom. Well, I would not have to type the memo after all. The boss was in, and I could tell him of the arrangements for the trip out West. We would share a drink and look forward to a successful vote on the New Wilderness Bill.

I opened the door with my master key and walked in.

"Good evening, Edward," the senator said softly.

His office was dimly lit—only the small fluorescent desk lamp glowed. But Ben was not seated at his desk. He sat in a black captain's chair in front of his desk. He was in his shirt sleeves, tieless, the top two button sof his shirt undone. Did I imagine it—or was he sweating, his swarthy face finely oiled?

"Good evening, sir," I said. "I've worked up final plans for the California trip . . ."

"Good. Miss Valdez and I were about to finish some related memos . . . some material you and Matt Fixx can work on. History of mining claims before the Wilderness Bill."

"Miss . . . she . . . ?" I am normally not tongue-tied; it was only that my weary eyes had suddenly located her in the gloom. She had been seated in the corner of the long black leather sofa, her legs tucked beneath her, her smooth knees gleaming white in the darkness. Now she slowly shifted from this informal, coiled position, lowered her long legs to the floor, brushing at a strand of black hair.

"Oh hi, Maria," I said stupidly.

"Hi."

"Maria and I have another fifteen minutes of dictation," Ben said. "What time is it anyway?"

I was staring at her. Normally I am the most self-contained, the most prudent of men. Where was her dictation pad? Not on the couch. Not on the mahogany end table.

"Oh. The time. Yes, it's eleven-thirty, sir."

Ben stretched. I found myself studying his massive chest. In his mid-fifties, he was still a potent virile man. For a lunatic moment, I saw myself locked in mortal combat with him—a battle to the death over Maria. (He would surely break me in two.) As cool as I am, my mind has a tendency to race ahead to final solutions, to ultimate confrontations.

"I'm about finished," Ben said. "Maybe you want to leave your notes with Maria. She can add them to mine in the morning." He got up and walked to his swivel chair. I had the sensation that he wanted to be back in his seat of authority—the better to dominate our uneasy trio.

"No, I'll do it first thing in the morning," I said. "I actually came by to pick up some of the Interior Department materials I'd left here. I realized what I'd worked up for you was incomplete." I was searching for an excuse to leave, to get away as soon as possible.

In the gloom I watched Maria: she was immobile, aloof, above all of this. In some maddening way she was asserting that superiority of the flesh which youth and beauty afforded her. My eyes flashed across the long, cushioned sofa, looking for . . . what? She crossed her elegant legs and I stared. But Ben was indifferent, scanning papers on his desk, checking his calendar.

"Well, I'll be on my way," I said—with too much easiness to be convincing. "Can I take Miss Valdez home?"

She looked at the senator; I caught the motion of her head.

"Oh, I can do that," Ben said. "We've got a few more items to take care of. Ready, Maria?"

She got up. Was her dress wrinkled? My throat was constricting, my eyes blurred. At last, that damned dictation pad! Yes, it was on the edge of Ben's desk. She turned the captain's chair to face him, took up the pad and a ball-point pen and waited.

"Anything else, Edward?"

"Ah, no sir, I think we're in good shape. We're getting a fine response from the subcommittee on the junket."

He gave me that short, characteristic wave of the hand to indicate he approved, and that he was finished with me for the time being. I said my goodnights and left, closing the office door, walking softly (why? because I felt like a voyeur, a footpad?) through the outer rooms and into the bright corridor.

And in the bright, almost hurtful glare of those marble walls, I began to conjure up painful visions. "The old goat," I said aloud. "The old stud." Jealousy—admiration—frustration—wonder —awe—caution—all these made a muddle of my usually well-ordered mind. *Steady, Deever,* I told myself, *steady there.*

I considered the evidence. And I did not need a Matt Fixx to tell me that no court would ever convict either of them of adultery on the basis of what I had seen. So, he was in his shirt sleeves, appeared to be sweating, his thick black hair mussed. So, she was coiled, kitten-like in a cozy corner of the office couch. Were her shoes on? I tried to remember. On? Off? Yes, they must have been off—two frail chartreuse pumps, resting on the carpeting. When she had swung her legs about to a more decorous position, she had probably inserted her feet in them. *Inserted.* The word made me gag, as I walked through the revolving doors into the warm moist Washington night.

Had they? Hadn't they? Could they have not been merely observing a five minute break from a long evening of work? Many a legislator found himself working nights; many a secretary stayed late to aid her overworked boss. And where on the Hill was there a man with more duties, obligations and interests than my boss? Logical. Believable. Nothing out of the ordinary.

It was no use. By the time I approached the mall, my mind was swarming with terrifying detailed images. I need not describe them. I was convinced that it had happened. If it had not, it was going to happen. And what a joke on young Edward Deever, the Boy Wonder of the Senate! What a grim, ironic note at this point in my career! I thought of my ambitious plans in San Francisco . . . the way I would court and win Maria . . . the culmination of my romantic scheming in some lush, carpeted, silent suite of rooms. And now, the man I most revered, the man to whom I owed my career and my livelihood, and in whom resided the power to fulfill all my hopes, had beaten me to it.

Now as insane as this will sound (I have already pointed out the potency of the senatorial image, the grip these princelings have on their serfs) my sense of loss, my self-pitying frustration, was immediately mingled with concern for Ben. Suppose the rumors got out? Suppose there was gossip? Even if he had never touched her (I now refused to believe that) people would talk. A scoundrel like Lou Parenti could find out . . . And official Washington would whisper about the exotic Mexican pearl who spent evenings on Senator Hannaford's couch. No. It would not work that way. Ben could not be hurt, I assured myself. Presidents, some in recent memory, had had their little flings, and it had not hurt them a bit. Indeed, it gave them a certain panache, a certain dash. Besides, your average American citizen would never believe it about old Bible-quoting, rich-as-Croesus, Ben Hannaford. He was too American.

So thinking, I now began to reject my convictions of five minutes earlier. But not for very long. Ben was vigorous, handsome, domineering. He took what he wanted. Ah, Deever, I argued, but not where women are concerned. There is Fern. There is always Fern—tall, calm, serene, corseted, silent. And Ben had never been a garter-snapper, a skirt-lifter, a buttock-pincher. Never. He had too much dignity, too much natural class. But now?

I crossed the mall, noting the arm-in-arm lovers, a few tourists, a band of kids playing cops-and-robbers. Our Americans. Our people. And Ben, not least among them. The secret, if ever revealed, could not hurt him. It might be whispered, repeated, heads would nod, tongues wag, eyes wink. But it could not hurt him with his colleagues, and the chances were that his amiable constituents back in Ramada City would never know. Ben was too much of this world—this country, this time—to be hurt by a scandal. And I would do my utmost to deny it, to see that it was laid to rest. Above all, I vowed, I would attempt to terminate the hot connection.

Abruptly I realized the ludicrousness of my attitude, the powers with which I was now endowing myself. I would not dare go to Ben and say, Sir, you must stop this liaison with Miss Valdez.

But I could, very easily, go to Maria. She was my protégé, my ward. She would have to be discouraged in this folly. Moreover, I would win her young limbs and breasts for myself!

Yes, I was jealous. Hopelessly, agonizingly, wrenchingly jealous. I cursed the Marsha Treadways of this earth, the free-and-easy women I had slept with, the office loves I had pursued, the romances—if that is what they were—that had made me foreswear the muddling of profession and ecstasy. Having taken the pledge just at the time of Maria's arrival, I had left her open to the field— and the field proved to have included one purebred champion in it, one charging thoroughbred, who had raced to the wire ahead of everyone. I had chosen not to enter the sweepstakes, and now I cursed myself for failing to win the silver plate.

Nor did the late movie on television help me. For hours I could not sleep, troubled with visions of Maria Valdez's slender, shining body, the crown of black hair. Normally an untroubled sleeper, I slept not at all, arose with a throbbing head, and irately turned off the *Today* show when I saw Senator John Tyler Lord attacking the New Wilderness Bill as "legal rape." He soured my orange juice.

No more than a curt exchange of greetings passed between Maria and myself the next morning. She was a strong one. Let me digress for a moment to make an observation about beautiful women. Beauty endows them with uncommon strength. Beauty is a shield and a sword against all other failings in a woman— stupidity, meanness, cowardice, selfishness. It has its own inherent (as Matt Fixx would say) mechanism that operates to bless its possessor with "the strength of ten." Never mind the poetic nonsense about the powers of the pure heart. No amount of noble character ever served a woman better than a lovely profile, kissable lips, smooth skin, lush hair, wide dark eyes. These are the elements which afford a woman substantial power, a capacity to overcome obstacles, defeats and entrapments. Not for one moment, may I say, did I ever harbor an ill thought about Maria Valdez's character. In the time of our brief friendship, she appeared to me (she still does) a young lady of exceptional kindness and generosity—a warm-hearted, candid and uncomplicated person.

I merely make the point that had Maria *not* been a beauty, had she not enjoyed that perfection of flesh that is the grandest weapon of all, had she been a Plain Jane, the exchange of greetings on that morning-after might not have been so innocently casual. She might have betrayed her shame with a blush, a shying away from my probing eyes, a batting of those long eyelashes, an averted glance. But of these there were none. Not a sign. Nothing. She was all frankness, down to her pre-occupation with her letters. Do I make myself clear? She could carry this off because she was *beautiful*, and beauty has its own potency.

Her calm, cool attitude toward me only deepened my sense of loss, of defeat. Like any normal vigorous male, I am in need of sexual gratification. I will not patronize professionals. I like sex to be accompanied by a friendly "associative" feeling. But what I cannot stand are the interminable preliminaries—the date-making, wining, dining, phoning, entertainment-providing that must precede and accompany an affair. In giving up Marsha, for whom I had gone through all the accessory boredom (I dislike most restaurants and tend to doze through movies, plays, and concerts), it meant I would have to start all over.

And now having decided to pursue Maria Valdez—and what a prize she was!—I had made the discovery that the boss had pre-empted her. I begrudged him Maria. I begrudged him not a red cent of his millions, his corporations, the thousands who labored for him, his power to lobby and pass laws, his cattle, his oil, his pedigreed dogs, his earth-movers, giant cranes, and pipelines. I was delighted that he owned all these things. But deep down I resented the swift, total manner in which he had seized my protégé. No one else had even been allowed a second look. And he, old stallion, old stud, old Ramada Potomac Oaks Bandolier, had enjoyed a good deal more than a stare or an ogle. By now I was convinced of that.

But I resolved not to let the matter affect our strong, functional relationship.

Cleo handed me the Washington *Truth*, opened to Parenti's column.

"Your pal is after us again," she said.

"He'll never lay a glove on us." But as I scanned Parenti's report on my way to Ben's office, I began to wonder. His sources were good—Senator Lord, and perhaps even a tap on one of Senator Kemmons' employees. And he had become obsessed with Ben.

Pity poor Senator Alford Kemmons. Alf is a likable, easygoing sort, who likes to please everyone. But Alf can never really make up his mind as to who are his best friends. At the moment Kemmons is torn apart deciding how to vote on Senator Benjamin Hannaford's notorious New Wilderness Bill, an outrageous raid on the national forests. Originally, Alf backed the bill, because he has always been close to Big Ben Hannaford. But recently, the distinguished Secretary of Commerce, T. E. Kape, got in on the act. Kape is even richer than Ben Hannaford. His fortune in mining dwarfs Ben's construction millions. And normally Secretary Kape regards any hunk of American land as valuable only in terms of how much ore can be gouged out of it. But lo! The Secretary is opposed to Hannaford's pet bill! Why? Well, Mr. Kape had got his, but he isn't so sure he wants Ben Hannaford and his mining, oil-producing and timbering friends to get *theirs*. So Mr. Kape's representatives went into action, put pressure on Alford Kemmons and got him to promise to vote *against* the New Wilderness Bill in committee—and possibly kill it there. Big Ben Hannaford, the Master Builder, is said to have gone into orbit over the Senate Dining Room. His own counterattack is expected momentarily, with Senator Kemmons caught right in the middle. It will be interesting to see just how the Senator from Nebraska votes.

It was not as bad as it might have been. Parenti was a little behind in his schedule. He had no idea that I had already undone Kape's work, and that Alf Kemmons was back in line. I shuddered. What if Parenti learned about that mad comedy we played out in Alf's office—the money drying like laundry, the cyclone of hundred-dollar bills?

"Sit down, Edward," Ben said. "We have big decisions today."

He went on to explain that he was still not absolutely certain of getting the bill out of committee. Moreover, a close vote and a protracted committee debate might affect the bill's chance of passage.

"This trip will prove to the nation that a national wilderness can be beautiful, serene, a source of joy and wonder to the beholder," Ben orated, with comic emphasis, "and also create money and jobs and lumber and useful metals at the same time."

He had gone through my recommendations for the ideal site for the inspection by the Subcommittee on National Forests (Chairman Sidney Stapp of California) and had settled on the Cavite National Forest in California's eastern range.

"A wise choice, I observed Mr. Kape hoist with his own petard."

He darted an annoyed glance at me. Ben, whose education stopped in the eighth grade, resented displays of learning. I was usually careful to avoid such locutions; but for some reason—Maria?—I felt impelled to parade my degree from Ohio Normal College.

"What in hell does that mean?" he asked.

"Blown up by his own bomb."

"We hope it will work that way. Kape Corporation has been digging holes in Cavite for fifteen years," he said. "Hasn't seemed to bother anyone. When the Secretary and his men make their next move against us, we can say, 'Judge not, lest ye be judged.'"

Ben had that sixth sense. He knew that Kape, richer, tougher, greedier than any conservationist, was shaping up as the real opposition to the New Wilderness Bill. "A case," Ben said, "of our modest, controlled greed against Kape's unlimited greed."

A word of explanation as to why the Kape Corporation was allowed to mine at all in a National Wilderness like Cavite. At the turn of the century several private mining firms had staked out claims in that wilderness area. Mining laws were free-and-easy then, conservation a dream. Over the years the Kape juggernaut had bought out these claims, and even *after* the Cavite area had been declared a National Forest by Act of Congress, the Kape people possessed these holdings.

Under the Wilderness Act of 1964 (the one we now sought to replace) areas such as Cavite are protected from road building, mining, lumbering and so forth. But—and a big but it was—*previously existing mining claims* could be exploited and prospecting permitted until 1984. Ignoring the screams of the conservationists, the Kape people had plunged ahead and started its open mine in the heart of the Cavite Wilderness Area. Tons of iron ore were gouged out of the awesome mountains. They had set a precedent. And Ben hoped to profit by it. Using Kape's mine as an example, he would blunt their attacks on him.

He outlined the trip to me: we would fly to San Francisco, spend a night there, meet a Department of the Interior man, and then go on, by charter flight, to Cavite.

"Get us some good press coverage," he said to me. "By the time we leave California, old Kape'll be groggy. The subcommittee won't have any more doubts."

He took a phone call from the White House—the President, through an aide, begging for Ben's help on the Housing Bill— and called to me, as he placed a hand over the mouthpiece: "Tell Miss Valdez to bring along a warm coat and boots. It gets cold up in those mountains."

I nodded, thinking to myself: she will have more to keep her warm than a coat and boots. Suddenly the trip to California depressed me. It was to have been a grand climax for me, the start of a new romantic adventure.

At the airport, the following morning, I handled the luggage, tickets, and so forth, keeping an eye on old Gabe Tutt, reeking of bourbon at nine in the morning, jesting with younger men like Royce Henshaw and John Tyler Lord, who flirted like ardent schoolboys with Maria. How she adorned our dull group!

At the check-in counter, Senator Hannaford said to me: "Edward, you sit with Miss Valdez. Make that standard procedure. Everywhere."

Airborne over the city, the great white Capitol appeared to rotate on a giant's lazy Susan, as the huge plane wheeled in the morning sky. I realized there was a name, a not very nice name for the new job I had been assigned.

"*Beard*," I muttered as I checked my seat belt, and glanced at Maria's wondering face. She was staring at the city below.

"Did you say something, Ed?" she asked.

"Just mumbling. Takeoffs make me nervous, so I mumble."

I was to be Senator Hannaford's beard—the safe, single fellow, who is hauled along, forced to appear in public, who gathers the lightning and absorbs the gossip, to protect the reputation of the highly placed philanderer. I shut my eyes and felt nauseated as the hostess approached. I did not want tea, or coffee, or milk, only some self-respect.

"I've never been to San Francisco," Maria said. "I hear it's marvelous!"

"It is if you can avoid San Franciscans."

"What's wrong with them?" She turned her glowing face toward me. Her upright bosom, beneath another of those damnable $7.50 sheaths—this one was cobalt blue—made me tremble.

"They spend an inordinate amount of time congratulating themselves on being San Franciscans. But don't let that interfere with your enjoyment of the city. It is no mean city."

"You're bitter today," she said. She acted as if we had never had that embarrassing encounter-by-night. But as I have been at pains to point out, beauty makes its own rules.

"No, it's just something I ate," I said archly. "A few nights ago."

There was a faint raising of her adorable chin, and then she bent to her *New Yorker*. Very little conversation passed between us on the flight. Ben did not come to speak to us at all. He sat with "Swinging Sid" and they played gin rummy.

My sullen state of mind was not relieved by the fact that across the aisle from us—me in my new-won beard-dom, Maria insulated in beauty—sat Senators John Tyler Lord and Royce Henshaw. It took them no time at all to take notice of her and to start a two-headed, four-handed flirtation. Need I add that she responded?

"Change seats with Edward, Maria," Lord piped. "We see enough of him."

"That's right," Senator Henshaw added, "too much. And usually he's beating us on the head for his boss."

"Do you mind, Ed?" she asked me. "After all, two important committee members. Don't we need their votes?"

"Maria," I said, "you will find that all your smiles and womanly wiles will not sway those two. A Harvard lawyer and a Columbia economist. They suffer from a high idealism count. They are not of our persuasion."

Royce Henshaw, the professor on holiday, Montana's contribution to Economics and the United States Senate, winked. He was a good-looking young man, rough-hewn, ruddy-faced, with a wavy mop of rich brown hair. "I may just be able to switch my vote, if Maria explains the reasons for the New Wilderness Bill to me."

"Count me in!" shrilled Lord. (Who could begrudge him his schoolboyish trifling? I had seen his wife—tall, lank, homely, one of those angular, asymmetrical New England ladies, full of flat vowels, short answers, and inherited wealth.)

We changed seats, I to stare from the window at the cloudless sky and the changing landscape below, she to be flattered by two respected members of the Senate. Senator Lord, it developed, spoke excellent Spanish, and proceeded to converse with her in the tongue of her ancestors.

"*Señorita*," I heard Lord lisp, "*le gusta la cocina mejicana? Conozco un buen restaurant en San Francisco . . .*"

"*Gracias, no*," she said, laughing. "*Pero, comía muchissimos frijoles y tacos cuando era niña. Ahora, prefiero el steak.*"

They both laughed. Now I could hear Senator Henshaw say to Senator Lord, "Boy, she is a charmer." Then in a lower voice: "Hannaford travels first class, I'll say that for him."

I felt like shouting to them: *No beards need apply, gentlemen! That job has been filled!*

California was "Swinging Sid" Stapp's home grounds and the committee received enough press attention to appease the senatorial egos. But Sid wisely called off the reporters when the members desired privacy. When one was Sid's guest, privacy could be a sweet and special thing.

As I have mentioned, Senator Stapp, prior to his election—and still—was an affluent "show biz" lawyer. It was curious how he decided to run for the Senate. At least five of his clients—four actors and an actress—had successfully run for public office. One had been elected to the Senate—the late Senator Slim Coker, the beloved cowboy balladeer. Two others had made it to the House of Representatives. All had leaned heavily on Sid's professional advice, and so he had decided to run for high office himself. A handsome, almost beautiful man, Senator Stapp was something of a rogue, and I liked his insouciance. "Actors," he once told me, "are barely members of the human race. But when you get right down to it, Edward, that may be of great help to them when they run for the Senate."

We were lodged at the magnificent Sutter Hills Hotel. Its owners were Sid's clients, and we were treated with lavish hospitality. Our group dined that night in the Gay Nineties Bar, amid imitation gaslights, red-flocked wallpaper, cushioned leather seats. Voluptuous waitresses in waist-pinching red corsets and black net stockings minced about us. It was Sid's kind of place. But in truth, the Gay Nineties Bar impressed me as the kind of place that is so doggedly wicked, that it is innocent, a sexless imitation. No one would dream of pinching those black-netted flanks or tweaking a bursting pink satin bosom. Whoever had created the dining salon (no doubt some mincing homosexual) had so overstated his case that all desire was dissolved in the hyperbole of costume and those big-busted, full-rumped girls serving martinis and bourbon sours.

What was really needed to enliven our group, was Senator Stapp's flamboyant wife, Judy, a former "starlet," partygoer, party-giver, more than a match for "Swinging Sid." She was a loud, brash, sharp-tongued celebrity-seeker, and great fun. But she preferred running off to New York and her "thinky crowd" every chance she got, and she was probably there now, at some corduroy-and-tweed literary brawl, where Beautiful People rubbed knees and elbows with Establishment Critics.

About ten minutes after our party had assembled—John Tyler Lord, Royce Henshaw, silent Harold Erlenmeyer, Ben, myself, and Maria—Senator Stapp appeared in the arched doorway of the Gay Nineties salon, with two companions.

"Gentlemen," the Swinger said, "I would like to introduce Lila and Louise, two students of political science at Lobo Junior College."

There was a lot of sophomoric gallantry—Lord and Henshaw and Stapp vying to buy drinks for the two blond bookends. I noticed that Senator Hannaford sat a bit apart from it all—a fatherly tolerant figure. (A bit cynically, I told myself. He *had* his.) A piano tinkled some of those meandering tunes that appear to have been written only for dim cocktail lounges in San Francisco hotels.

I studied the girls—both of them young, blonde, one tallowy gold, the other a wheaten yellow, with lank hair and long legs, skins tanned, eyes wide, voices loud and clear, their blood activated by tennis, surfing, horseback riding, and conservative politics. Ah, Lobo Junior College! Some day I would retire and teach political science at Lobo J. C., and admire the flash of their nude tan flanks and the elongated curve of their thighs and legs. But at the moment, I was less concerned with them, edible as they were, than I was with dark Maria, who sat next to me, by Ben's mandate my date, consort. The beard was growing longer. Soon I would part and pomade it.

"The gals heard me lecture at Lobo last month," Sid said. "And

I promised to give 'em an Insider's look at the world's greatest deliberative body at work."

"I would observe, Senator Stapp," Royce Henshaw said loftily, "that their own deliberative bodies merit attention!"

Not bad for a former professor of economics at Columbia. I really like Henshaw. He was one of the brightest men in the Senate, dedicated to his work, a crackerjack at social legislation, honest and outspoken.

Drinks arrived. The two young girls had that All-American healthy look, but they did not draw the line at booze. Both were bourbon drinkers. We raised our glasses to "Swinging Sid," to California, to the Cavite National Forest, to the New Wilderness Bill. Even John Tyler Lord and Royce Henshaw, our opposition, drank to it.

People kept coming by to shake Sidney Stapp's manicured, beringed hand. He was well known in San Francisco—and Reno and Las Vegas. Nobody recognized Lord, or Henshaw or Erlenmeyer, but a few people recognized Senator Hannaford and pumped his hand.

"What a lucky gal you are!" one of the blondes—Lila or Louise, I could not keep them apart—said to Maria. "How do you get a job like that?"

"Good shorthand and typing," Maria said.

"Boy, to travel around with these famous men," the other said. "Honestly, I can't think of a more exciting life."

"Well—this is the first trip I've made."

"A reward for good work?" Lila-Louise asked.

"Yes, you might say that."

The other blonde child darted a look from me to Maria back to me—and the implication was clear. Ben looked bored. He ordered another round. Lord and Henshaw resumed a harmless flirtation with the "girls." Apparently they were available as dinner companions for whoever wanted to have dinner with them—a variety of Anglo-Saxon geisha.

"Goddamn Roosevelt!"

In the tinkling whispery gloom of the Gay Nineties Bar, Senator Gabriel T. Tutt's raucous bellow shattered the air, as rude as a belch.

"Damn mongrelizing New Dealers!" Tutt roared.

"Edward," Ben said. "Get him." He nodded toward the arched entrance to the cocktail lounge.

"Goddamn Eleanor also!" shouted Tutt.

I sprinted to the entrance. Senator Tutt was tottering in front of a padded crimson booth in which sat an astounded, offended couple. The man was a handsome caramel-colored Negro. His date—his wife, for all I know—was a white woman with pert features. She looked terrified.

"Hi, Senator," I said in a low voice. "You're late for the party. Come along."

I hooked an arm in his and started to pull him away.

"You see that? You see that example of what this country is becoming?" he cried. "It goes back to that crippled son-of-a-bitch Roosevelt and that Eleanor! I knew it when I was a Congressman! That kike-lovin' Socialist tried to get my job! But I showed him!"

"You certainly did, Senator."

The Negro had risen from his seat. He was tall, and I could see in his purposeful manner an earnest desire to smash Gabe Tutt's sodden purple face. But fortunately the woman got up, pleaded with him, and drew him back to the sanctuary of the booth.

"Nothin' to stop 'em now," Senator Tutt moaned. "They will mongrelize and bastardize the white race beyond hope!"

How to control this lunatic? How to deal with this vial of venom, this garbage can of old hatreds, fears, rancor? I steered him toward the table. Fortunately Sid Stapp was a diplomat. Moreover, my own boss was one of the few men in the Senate who could handle Tutt, who could shut him up, or even, on occasion, reason with him.

"Senator Tutt, the girls have been dying to meet you," Sid said. "This is Louise and this is Lila—two political science students from Lobo Junior College. Ladies, the eminent Senator Gabriel T. Tutt of Alabama!"

"Ladies," Gabe said—and bowed.

They exchanged smirks. They were no dopes, those two girls. They were sharp little California cookies, and they knew a drunken old bum when they saw one—senator or no.

"And no finer public servant ever lived," Senator Hannaford said softly. "Girls, this is the man who really runs the Finance Committee. A much loved and much respected figure."

Gabe had already been at the bourbon, but he ordered a double. He stared at Maria, stared at the two girls, and his train of thought evidently returned to the sexual prowess of Negro males, and he cried: "You see that big buck back theah? With that white gal?"

Louise and Lila giggled. Maria looked horrified.

Tutt started to wobble to his feet, about to shout at the couple, when suddenly Ben's big, hard hand reached out and pushed him, with terrible firmness back into the red plush seat.

"Now, Gabe," Senator Hannaford said, "we are here for an evening of relaxation before the trip tomorrow. Let us not excite ourselves. Now go on and drink up, 'cause if you keep fussin', I'll tell Miss Emmy on you."

Miss Emmy was Gabe Tutt's aged wife. She adored Ben Hannaford. Senator Tutt's reptilian eye studied my boss—not trusting him entirely, but somehow respectful. He sat down, grumbling, and like a good baby, drank his bourbon. Ben prevailed.

We had no more embarrassments from Gabe until much later in the evening, and in much more harrowing circumstances.

Senator Hannaford arranged for the group to break up the way he wanted it to. I was commissioned to take Maria to dinner and have her back at the hotel early. Our plane was taking off at nine in the morning for Cavite. Ben decided to have a quiet dinner in his room, with the San Francisco manager of Hannaford-Western, a civil engineer. I knew the kind of dinner it would be—bourbon, steak, coffee, and a lot of hard, practical talk. The local man would come away from the session with dozens of problems solved, dozens of good suggestions.

"Swinging Sid," host though he was, had his own secret plans. The rest of the party would squire Louise and Lila. Henshaw and Lord and silent Harold Erlenmeyer seemed unhappy at playing chaperon to Tutt. The man had to be watched at all times, lest he cast discredit on their total image. But the young ladies would provide diversion.

I took Maria to a small place on Fisherman's Wharf, very strong on atmosphere, very low on quality. There is something missing in Pacific Ocean seafood. The fish do not have the tang, the bite, the spice of their Atlantic brothers. But we managed with a respectable white California wine, some Dungeness crabs, broiled sandabs.

Maria ate very little, but finished more than half of the wine. Her dark face glowed. We had avoided the tender subject. As I have noted, she possessed the iron of beauty. To my surprise, it was she, who, after a third glass of Riesling, referred to the nocturnal encounter in Ben's office.

"I keep waiting for you to make some comment," she said.

"About what?"

"Oh, you know. The other night. When you walked into the office."

"Why should I comment?"

"Because you've been acting strangely. Your whole attitude on the plane . . . the way you've been making supposedly funny remarks. All that mumbling about your beard."

"You've got it wrong. I *am* the beard."

She arched her kissable eyebrows. "Don't evade the issue, Eddie. Why don't you say exactly what you think?"

I gave the waiter my credit card, and waited until he left. Then I looked at her with what I fancied to be lofty virtuous skepticism. "All right, I'll be blunt. There was something in the atmosphere that night. The way you were nesting in the couch. The senator's casual attire, let's say. But beyond that . . . a scent in the air, a presence."

"I know what you think," she pouted. "You think he made love to me."

The waiter returned. We suspended our conversation as I signed the chit, tipping him too liberally for indifferent service. Maria and I got up and walked out to the wharf.

"Yes," I said, "I'm pretty good at gauging what people have been up to. It's part of my job. I would say that you and the boss had consummated a joint conference."

"You can be cruel," Maria said. "But I don't care."

Was this the breathless young innocent I had escorted around the illuminated capital? The maiden who *ooh'd* and *ah'd* at my learned quotations?

On the wharf it was misty and cool. Cormorants and gulls shrieked, wheeled and dipped into the gray baywaters for offal.

"I don't mean to be cruel," I said, taking Maria's arm, "but you must not get involved in anything you'll regret."

"You're impossible," she said. "We're not involved. Nothing

happened. Nothing at all. My goodness, for a cool type like your-self, you certainly have a wild imagination."

"Very well, we'll interrogate you. Did he make love to you?"

"Absolutely not."

"Did he suggest it?"

"No."

"Did he, as the saying goes, make a pass at you?"

"No, no. Eddie, you are a nut, a plain nut."

"Stroke your hair? Touch a knee? Try to steal a kiss? Pat a shoulder? Out with it, woman." I tried to make a joke of the matter, but I ached with envy.

"Nothing. You don't know him at all! You claim to be so close to him. Eddie, he's a gentleman, a gentle, kind, polite man."

"Why were you on the couch?"

"We were resting. From our work, damn you! He suggested we take a break."

"And what were you discussing?"

"If you must know, Ramada City. He was asking me about the feelings of the Mexicans down there."

"Ah, purely political discussion."

"Yes, and some personal."

I widened my eyes. "Now we're getting somewhere. Confess, woman, confess!"

"He just wanted to know if I were happy in Washington, if I liked my job, if I had enough money. Eddie, don't be so thick. My father was an old friend of his. He's taking Daddy's role, don't you see?"

"I don't accept that, not for a minute. Tell me more. What did he say specifically?"

"You *are* a pest!" But she seemed to be enjoying the interroga-tion. If I were right, and they had, in fact, become lovers, she would want—sooner or later—to talk about, to be consoled, to seek advice. "He said I was the best thing that had happened to the office in years. That I made the place brighter and happier."

"Ah," I said. "Now we're getting somewhere. Then what?"

"Then *nothing*. You came blundering in, we worked a bit more, and he drove me to the Y."

The soft fog caressed us. We strolled back, past the restaurants, the curio shops, the wandering tourists. I did not believe her. I did not believe her for a minute. Maybe they had not gone "all the way" but I had too much confidence in my powers of observation, my knack for analysis and divination to think that he had talked to her about Mexican attitudes and her father.

"You're engaged in a bad show, Maria," I said. "I don't deny I'm jealous. I saw you first. But he's seen you also. And whether you're telling me the truth or not, whether the two of you are, at this moment, as pure as driven snow, the whole picture can change any moment. I see the way the big man looks at you. He can't hide it. I've got his interests at heart, Maria, and I'm almost tempted to find another job for you."

"I am afraid you're stuck with me, Edward." She pulled my arm closer and smiled at me.

"Yes, I suppose I am. And so is Benjamin Bow Hannaford." We stopped near the cable car station, and I drew her close to me. "Don't get hurt, Maria."

"I'm tough," she said. Tough? She was leather and steel. There was much to be said for the Latin style, I decided, and for childhood diet of frijoles.

We rode in silence up the steep incline, through the shifting mists, and entered the busy lobby. It was early evening. San Franciscans spend a lot of time in hotel lobbies. They are invariably well-groomed, over-groomed one might say. The men tend to be tall and graceful, the women rather horsey and awkward. Mink jackets and sable capes are standard garb. (I have always wondered why, when Jews in Miami Beach wear mink people sneer, but when pure-bred Christians wear expensive furs in San Francisco, it is deemed appropriate.)

We started across the ornate lobby toward the elevators, when I saw Senator Hannaford emerge from the bar, shake hands with the local HW manager, and bid him goodnight. The senator had been waiting for us. He strode toward us, and asked Maria if she enjoyed her tour of the city. She did. She was effusive, bubbling. Then all three of us rode up in the elevator. A middle-aged woman recognized Ben and squeezed his hand. He smiled.

Our rooms were all on the same floor—Ben's a corner suite, Maria and myself in smaller rooms on the main corridor. We started to go our separate ways, Ben toward his rooms, we toward ours, when the senator stopped us.

"It's only eleven," he said. "Maria, would you mind taking some dictation?"

"Not at all. I'm wide awake."

"I made notes for the past few hours. HW business." He reached in a coat pocket and took out a wad of scratch paper, envelopes with scrawls on them. "Unless I get these in shape while they're fresh in my mind, I won't be able to make sense out of them tomorrow. Bring your pad and portable." He turned and strode off.

We trod the inch-thick green carpeting, each bound for our room. Something about hotels elicits the erotic in me.

"So," I said. "He isn't even bothering to hide it anymore." But that was like Ben. What he wanted, he wanted. Subterfuges, camouflage, secrecy—all these would be impediments to the direct pursuit of the goal.

"Can't you accept that he really has dictation for me?"

"I'm certain he has. You'll be expected to do it without error, as well as the typing. The boss demands nothing less than top performance."

Our rooms adjoined. She paused at her door, I at mine. We glanced at one another. "Eddie, I'm disappointed in you," she said—and for once the steel of her beauty buckled a little. She sounded defensive.

Then she went in. I heard her fussing, gathering together her materials, and then leaving. As her door clicked shut, and I envisioned her walking the corridor toward Ben's suite, I cursed my foolish hesitancy, my lost opportunities.

A scream—more a controlled shriek. Then another. Then swearing, a shouted curse. I leaped from my bed with its silken sheets, switched on the bedlamp, and raced to the bolted door.

"Get away! Get away from me!" It was a young woman's voice, more angry than frightened. Then I heard the growl of a drunken male, the coarse bleat of a rutting goat, the grunt of a boar in heat. One of my jobs on these junkets is keeping everyone out of trouble. I am good at that sort of thing. And I sensed trouble as I unbolted the door, and in my blue paisley pajamas went into the bright corridor.

The hallway was empty. My bare feet sunk into the lush carpeting. I waited for the next sound. It was not long in coming.

There was another high-pitched woman's shriek. "Get your dirty
hands off me!" I heard. Then: "Yowwwwww!"

Around the corner, running as fast as her athletic young limbs
could propel her, came either Louise or Lila, one of those nubile,
blonde, All-American geishas.

"What's wrong? What's wrong?" I cried.

"Get that old bastard away from me!" she yelled. As I turned
my puzzled head, she hobbled by me. She had one short-heeled
pump on, and carried the other. After a few steps she halted and
rested against the corridor wall to affix the other shoe to her
dainty foot. She was only a few yards from me and I could see
that her short-skirted maroon dress had been unzipped down the
back. Beneath its flapping halves I saw a touch of pink brassiere
and the elastic band of her pants. "Goddamn that old shit!" she
hissed at me as I came forward. "Some senator!"

As she fiddled with the shoe, anger rendering her more lovely
by the minute, I asked if I might help her zip her dress.

"Yes. But hands off. I've had enough."

As I offered my services, there was an animal noise, and around
the corner, stumbling, half-falling, fouling the air with the bad
breath of soured bourbon, and mashed maledictions came the
Honorable Gabriel T. Tutt, defender of American Morality, foe
of pornography, hater of beards, beatniks, pinko-lefto-liberals,
intellectuals, college professors, and any Roosevelt that ever lived.

"Lemme at her!" Gabe Tutt roared. "Lemme at that bitch!"

"Jesus I'll kill that old bastard if he touches me again!" Lila-
Louise cried. She was reaching to take off her shoe. Evidently it
had been her weapon against Gabe.

"Goddamn Roosevelt!" Senator Tutt bellowed. He staggered
sputtering toward us, and the young lady ran for the nearest
elevator. I prayed there would be no delay in the lift's arrival. At
this moment, as I braced for Gabe's charge, I became aware of his
garb. He was in his BVD's, and they were of a curious, old-
fashioned cut, a style probably available only in certain Southern
general stores. They were one-piece combinations of heavy
knitted stuff, the upper part featuring a V-neck and elbow-length
sleeves, the lower half terminating just above the knees. I believe
they also had a drop seat, luckily buttoned up. (In that mad
moment, all that raced through my fevered brain was the recollection of a mock headline in our college humor magazine:

LEWIS DROPS UNION SUIT.) The senator's costume included red garters, black silk socks, and black shoes. I had the notion that it was probably his archaic underwear that had frightened the girl off. After all, she *had* gone to his room. And her dress *had* gotten unzipped in back.

"Damn bitch!" roared Senator Tutt. "Dirty whore! Trifle with an old man lak that!" The aging defender of white Southern womanhood reeled into my arms. We stepped off in a lunatic waltz down the corridor, I pajama'd, he BVD'd, the two of us uncertain as to where our midnight minuet would lead. "Strangle the bitch! Tar an' feather her!"

"Steady there, sir," I reasoned. "That girl may very well be a pinko-liberal. A spy from the ADA. You don't want any part of her!"

As we rested against a red-flocked wall, his rheumy eyes recognized me. "Deever," he belched at me. "Deever, you young coon hound, whut you do with my gal?" My hair parted as his fermented breath formed a noxious cloud around my head. I gagged, swayed, but still held him.

"You young sunvabitch," he said. "You stole mah poon-tang. Whut you do with mah poon-tang?"

"I'd never do a thing like that, Senator."

"Yeah. You putty smart, Deever. You and Ole Hannaford. Couple of smart uns. Wheah mah poon-tang?"

"I think the young lady has left."

"Possum shit." With that colorful phrase, he lurched from my arms, and with that crazy vigor that infects drunkards he blundered around the corner. I ran for him, hearing Lila-Louise shriek again.

After him I sprinted, a barefoot Galahad. Arms raised like a swamp monster, the Honorable Gabriel T. Tutt went for "Swinging Sid's" houri. She flew away once more. He pursued. There was a stairway at the distant end of the corridor. The girl was fast and young, but bubbling hormones propelled Gabe. Sports have never been my forte, and I hate football. But I gauged the problem and the distance, and halfway down the hallway—a few doors opened and guests were peeking out—I shot forward, aiming for the old man's knees. We hit the carpeting with bruising impact.

Lila-Louise reached the doorway, studied us prostrate on the

floor and before she vanished down the stairwell, her field trip
into political science concluded, she sneered at us: "Screw both
of you." She had a point.

I lifted Gabe from the carpeting—he was in a semi-stupor—
and like Aeneas bearing Achates, ported his old bones to his
room. As I marched down the hallway, a few heads were poked
out to witness the tragedy.

"My daddy," I explained to a sleepy-eyed woman in curlers and
a scarlet wrapper. "The poor old fellow is a sleepwalker." She
nodded her sympathy.

No heads were thrust from Senator Hannaford's suite. *That*
door remained locked, shut, chained.

Tenderly, I put Senator Tutt to bed, removing his garters,
shoes, and socks. He was asleep at once, violating the atmosphere
with flatulent snores.

"Sleep well, Senator," I said. "You have earned your rest."

For a moment, I studied his corrupted face, and I wondered
how this mean old man would have fared had he been the color
of Angel López Garcia. The answer was obvious. But Gabe was one
of the untouchables. Firm on the rock of militancy, Puritanism,
and bigotry, he had built his reputation, and it could not be
shaken, least of all by drunken forays in hotel hallways.

The next morning our party boarded a chartered Lodestar to
fly us out to the government landing strip at Cavite National
Forest. We assembled at San Francisco Airport, an eye-rubbing,
aching group. "Swinging Sid" had begged off—he had business
in town. But the rest of us were on hand—my boss, Senators
Lord, Henshaw, Erlenmeyer, and Tutt. Yes, Tutt. I had to hand
it to the old goat. He was an indestructible. I concluded that
booze made him strong. Where it would rot one man's gut, it
strengthened and hardened his. His turtle's eyes were almost
closed, but he snorted and brayed his way through a pancake
breakfast, cussed at the cab driver, and allowed as how he hated
San Francisco because it was filled with "beatniks and pinkos."

My role as beard, at Ben's insistence, was enlarged. I found
myself sitting opposite Maria at breakfast in the hotel coffee shop,
riding in the same taxi with her, beside her on the plane. Not a
word passed between us apart from formalities. I buried my nose
in the *Chronicle*, affecting disdain for this world and its pleas-

ures. Not a word would I utter about where she had spent the night. That was her business. (But it was mine too, and I ached with a jealous hunger.)

The flight from San Francisco International Airport to the northeastern mountain ranges where Cavite nestled, was less than two hundred miles. Most of our party dozed. Ben sat with the young Interior Department official, Wilson Blades. It was Blades who had helped me set up the trip, and who had arranged the transportation. He was a former Park Ranger, a muscular man in his early forties, wind-burned, seamed, an odd combination of rugged outdoorsman and scholar. He had a Ph.D. in botany and had taught at a California State College. In some vague way I had a guilty admiration for the man and what he stood for. I suspect Ben did also.

"You're not happy with this, are you, Mr. Blades?" I heard Ben asking him.

"I won't try to deceive you, Senator," Blades said. "I'm opposed to the Hannaford bill. I've told the Secretary that."

"We got to be in favor of progress," Senator Hannaford said.

"Progress for whom?"

"The nation. Jobs. Products. Development."

"Is that really progress, Senator? Maybe it's gone too far already. Maybe what you call progress should have stopped years ago. Maybe it isn't even progress."

"You're a philosopher, Wilson."

"No, Senator. Just a botanist. One who's opposed to multiple use."

I glanced across the aisle to where Senator Hannaford sat, going over maps, trails, the route we would take with Blades, and I realized how much Ben too admired that dedicated friend to redwoods and ferns. Something Ben had lost, something irretrievable, was mirrored in Wilson Blades.

"Beauty is in the eye of the beholder, son."

"I suppose so. A mine shaft or a timber mill is beauty to you, Senator. An unspoiled forest is to me."

"A mine shaft is beautiful to the people who have jobs here, who get jobs from the use of the metals, to the stockholders . . ."

"And especially the owners—like you." Blades was solemn.

"Wilson, I would be the last one to deny that."

So we hummed across the Western skies. Below us the great

carpet of giant trees unfolded—ancient redwoods, Ponderosa pine, Douglas fir. I could hear Wilson Blades waxing ecstatic over it, and my boss listening. Next to me Maria slept soundly.

We bounced on to a dirt strip some distance from the heart of the Cavite National Forest. The day was bright, clear, and cool. It was July but the air was tangy with a mountain chill. Maria wore a lined gabardine parka and short boots. She had a knack for making everything she wore look tantalizing, lending it a "just right" quality.

Several Park Rangers were on hand to supply us with rough boots and heavy coats. We were loaded into four-wheeled drive jeeps, and proceeded up the mountainside toward where the Kape enterprise had its mine. Around us rose the glory of our Western wilderness—brooding old trees, scraping the clouds, rich with birdsong, insect buzz, the essence of life.

Somehow the vista silenced us. Even Gabe Tutt shut up. Lord and Henshaw seemed transported. They reminded me of two Eagle scouts nudging each other, crying at each new vista of mountain range, waterfall, thick green forest, here a patch of apple-green lindens, there a stand of dark green pine. They would come home and harvest a pile of merit badges, those two. But I checked my sarcasm. Once, I too, had been a scout and had respected the code. Did I still? For a moment I thought of my day at the zoo, my moments with N. Krallis and G. Paxton, and I decided that perhaps the scout code had died that day.

We arrived at a switchback in the winding red dirt road, where the jeeps were parked. We disembarked, and Wilson Blades led us to a fenced-in promontory, a lookout point hewn from the mountain rock. From it we could look out on T. E. Kape's iron mine—a vast spreading open pit, a huge bleeding wound in the mountainside. If Ben wanted to prove that multiple use did not harm the forests, this seemed a terrible place to do so. But I knew his strategy: he anticipated Kape's opposition, and was making an advance move to neutralize the Secretary of Commerce.

"Now is that so bad?" Ben asked our group. We all stood at the edge of the promontory. Below us, in and around the dirt-red pit, midget trucks, payloaders, bulldozers and tiny men scurried about, drawing iron wealth from the earth.

"It is appalling," said John Tyler Lord.

"A nightmare, Senator," Royce Henshaw added. "A scar."

Senators Tutt and Erlenmeyer said nothing. Ben paced back and forth, his fists dug into the pockets of the khaki parka. "Damn, that isn't bad at all. Wilson, how many tourists come up here to look at this particular hunk of forest?"

"Very few. There's only this dirt road and we don't allow vehicles up except for maintenance and official forestry duties. They have to hike in or come by horse."

"How many this year?"

"Several hundred, I suppose."

"But the other side of the range—the southern and western parts of Cavite, they are more accessible?" Senator Hannaford asked.

"Yes. There's a dirt road at the southern end. The view isn't as awesome, but the road is open seven months of the year and there's a small parking area."

"Hell, that's all I'm talking about," Ben said patiently. "These places are big enough for you nature lovers and also for those of us who have to keep the country clothed and fed and with houses over their heads. That's what I mean. This Kape operation does use a small hunk of forest and mountain. But there's lots left."

"That is not the point, Senator," John Tyler Lord said. "It is a desecration."

"Says who? Nobody except a handful of people who can get up here anyway, if they really want to."

"And I say," John Tyler Lord said fervently, "that the needs of that handful must be respected!"

Ben waved his arm out over the mine below. "A lot more than a handful benefit from what Kape is doing down there—and, as you know, he's no friend of mine."

The rest of the afternoon went quickly. We paused for lunch at the Rangers' compound halfway down the mountain-range. Again, I played dinner companion to Maria. The trip was tiring her and she was not very communicative. But I could not help noticing on several occasions the arch glances that passed between her and the senator. No man, no matter how discreet, how circumspect, can hide these signs of infatuation. Once, when Maria walked ahead of us, her willowy figure more desirable than ever in the sassy parka, the exciting boots, I saw Ben's eyes follow her, like a hawk watching a baby quail hopping across a meadow. His eyes were locked on her—possessive, magnetized. I knew she told me the truth about the depth of his affection. I trusted I was the only one who noticed the way in which his glance followed her, the lost moments when he studied her profile, or turned his head to observe her climbing a rock. Senators Henshaw and Lord, still acting like scouts on a hike, alternated in flirting with Maria or trying to impress her.

"A monarch," Senator Lord said, as a beautiful orange-and-black butterfly dipped by us. "I used to collect them."

"And what do you collect today?" Maria asked.

"Losing causes," the New Englander said. "To people like your esteemed employer. There goes a Red Admiral."

When we had concluded our starchy lunch, Wilson Blades suggested that we take a short stroll to the edge of Cavite Canyon, to the site of an Interior Department monument—a plaque to the memory of Kibi, the last wild Indian known to have lived in the state of California.

We followed the Interior Department man down a winding, aromatic trail. Shafts of afternoon light pierced the cathedrals formed by the soaring trees. It was soberingly still, a place of wonder and joy, and we all—even Senator Tutt—were affected by the indescribable beauty.

The monument to Kibi, the last of the savage Indians, was a bronze plaque, set in a granite outcropping twenty yards from the edge of Cavite Canyon, at one of its most dramatic points—a deep gorge, laced with foamy waterfalls, half-hidden in pale evanescent mists.

Wilson Blades led us to the marker.

"We had this put up two years ago, gentlemen," he said to us. It was turning cool. We stomped our booted feet and were silent. Ben's swarthy face was brooding. Was that trace of aboriginal blood, that one-quarter of Indian essence reacting to the memorial to the dawn man?

Blades squatted beside the marker and read: "At this boulder, on April 8, 1912, a Kakita Indian named Kibi, last of his savage race, and believed to be the last Wild Indian in the State of California, appeared half-starved and naked and presented himself to two trappers, I. E. Metcalf and John Tubbs. Kibi later was taken to the Anthropology Department at Stanford University, where he lived until his death, in 1916, of pneumonia. He was believed to have been a chief, survivor of a band of wild Kakita Indians who lived in Cavite Gorge."

Blades had taken off his hat as he read—tribute to the vanished Red Man. "The experts at Stanford were amazed," Wilson Blades said. "They'd assumed the Kakita were extinct."

"Well," Ben said, with finality. "There's no doubt they are today."

"I don't know," Senator Lord said, "I like to imagine that maybe they are still roaming these wild hills." His blond head rotated, searching the sky for a wild bird. "'I would rather never taste chickens' meat nor hens' eggs than never to see a hawk sailing through the upper air again . . .'"

"Thoreau," Blades said approvingly.

A sad glance passed over my boss's face. His eyes darted from Senator Lord to Wilson Blades. They had some secret communion, some shared knowledge. It was not only that they *knew* Thoreau; they would touch one another with whatever wisdom Thoreau dispensed. He could not. Even if he memorized Walden it would not reach him.

As we turned from the monument I saw Senator Tutt, huffing and blowing, bundled up in his army parka. He was in remarkably good shape for an old drunkard. Bourbon was his vitamins. One of the Forest Rangers was a lanky Negro, a man named Simms, who had driven one of the jeeps. I suddenly saw Senator Tutt lurch toward this Simms and I shuddered—but Gabe was not being unfriendly. Negroes as servitors pleased him.

"Hey boy," Senator Tutt gargled. "Gimme a hand heah."

Ranger Simms obliged. He took the senator's arm, and they began to descend the narrow footpath to the canyon's edge. I felt a little better about things. Even Gabe Tutt was reacting to the glory of the setting. His manner toward the Ranger was not abusive.

"Yes," John Tyler Lord was saying, as we started a slow ascent toward the Rangers' cabins where the jeeps were parked. "Yes, Thoreau," Senator Lord said. "And I hope my friend Senator Hannaford will forgive me if I try to influence the subcommittee with some of his words . . ."

"Not at all, Senator," Ben said. "I am always glad to be taught. I envy you your education." There was no hint of sarcasm in Ben's voice.

"Thoreau wrote," John Tyler Lord went on, " 'When I consider that the nobler animals have been exterminated here—the cougar, the panther, lynx, wolverine, wolf, bear, moose, deer, the beaver, the turkey—I cannot but feel as if I lived in a tamed, and, as it were, emasculated country. Is it not a maimed and imperfect nature that I am conversant with? As if I were to study a tribe of Indians that had lost all of its warriors.' "

No one spoke. Lord's thin aristocratic voice with its flat New England accent had a charm and a sweetness that hypnotized us. We halted on the pathway. The senator from Vermont was suddenly embarrassed by the attention paid him. A self-effacing man, he reddened, and then grinned sheepishly. "Well, now. I didn't mean to make it a recital."

"Oh, please!" Maria cried. "That's so beautiful! More! He must have said more!"

"He said many things, Miss Valdez," Lord said. "Let me see if I remember the rest of this . . . something about . . . 'I take infinite pains to know all the phenomena of spring, thinking that I have here the entire poem, and then, to my chagrin, I hear that it is but an imperfect copy that I possess and have read, that my ancestors have torn out many of the first leaves and grandest passages, and mutilated it in many places!' " Lord stopped and walked ahead of us. "I forget the rest."

We began the slow ascent up the pathway, except for Senator Tutt who had wandered off with the Negro Ranger, Mr. Simms. I had a sudden mad vision of Huck and Jim on the raft. Would old Gabe end up on the roaring river below with his colored guide?

Senator Lord sighed. He was still lost in Thoreau. "The passage ends 'I wish to know an entire heaven and an entire earth.' "

"You say those lines so beautifully, Senator Lord," Maria said. "You'd have been a wonderful English teacher."

Lord lowered his head. Ben was listening carefully, saying nothing.

Wilson Blades shied a stone into the woods. "I'm a John Muir man myself," he said. "You know what he wrote after his first trip through the Sierras." We all paused to catch our breath at the head of the dirt trail. Blades looked out at the grand vista. " 'I have crossed the Range of Light, surely the brightest and best of all the Lord has built, and rejoicing in its glory, I gladly, gratefully, hopefully pray I may see it again.'"

Royce Henshaw nodded. "An eloquent thought," he said. "And I would hope all of us would agree with John Muir."

Ben was silent. He knew better than to take on Thoreau, John Muir, and the pure, shining love of the wilderness that possessed men like Blades and Henshaw and Lord. But as we approached the jeeps, Senator Hannaford, having mulled over their arguments, said, "That business about knowing an entire heaven and earth, gentlemen. I'm in favor of that. But I want the earth to produce. I want people fed, clothed, housed. I want life made easier so people like Thoreau can sit alongside of a lake all day and write poetry."

"It was a pond," said Senator Lord, "and it was a book."

"No matter," Ben said, "who do you think permits people like him—or the artists—or scientists—professors—to spend time doing what they do? I'm not against them. I just say, I'm the one who supports them. I make the wheels go."

"I wonder if the price is too high," said Blades. "Maybe some of us don't like open pit mines in the middle of virgin forest."

Ben grunted. "That's what virgins are for." He proceeded then to dictate seating arrangements for the trip back. Naturally I was to sit with Maria. Then he noticed that Senator Tutt was not with us. He ordered me to fetch him.

Hurrying down the footpath, I felt at peace with the world. Senator Lord's homage to Thoreau, the silent wilderness about me, all these reassured me. I found nothing contradictory in what men like Blades wanted and what my boss wanted. Compromise was the answer: progress *and* conservation at the same time. And who better than Ben to effect such a happy union?

The trail ended at the canyon edge, twisting and turning in a series of switchbacks, running between stunted pines and juniper. I hurried past the plaque to Kibi and found myself on a small projecting plateau perched over the gorge. There I sighted Senator Tutt standing at the brink, in the arms of the Negro, Ranger Simms.

"Senator!" I called. "We're ready to go!"

"He'll be right up," the Ranger responded. He had Senator Tutt in a tight embrace, a lover's grip.

"He'll be finished in a second," Ranger Simms said. This time he turned his head and winked at me under the broad-brimmed hat.

I trod the twisting path to the edge of the chasm. Modesty cautions me to delete this, but honesty insists on its telling. Senator Tutt's fly was open and he was urinating into the canyon. That was all there was to his enlistment of the Ranger. Ranger Simms was holding the old man tight, keeping him from tumbling into the gorge from which rose wisps of mist, and the hushed roar of the cascading stream.

"Goddamn them last few drops," Senator Tutt mumbled. "Lak to wet mah britches."

And so, amid the glorious trees, the boundless sky, he shook himself dry, and zippered up.

At that altitude, oxygen was in diminished supply. He huffed and puffed as the Ranger assisted him upward. I went down and joined them, taking the senator's other arm. Gabe Tutt grinned at Simms.

"You a good boy," he croaked. "You a good ole boy. Where you from boy?"

"Indianapolis, sir."

"Yeah. Educated, too."

"That's right, sir. I have two degrees from the University of Indiana. I was a geologist before I entered the Park Service."

Gabe nodded, absorbing this. His lizard-like eyes fixed themselves on me. "You see? You see?"

But that was all he said. Granted his enigmatic remarks could be taken either way. But I chose to believe he was registering his pleasure at Ranger Simms' achievements. There are times when I rest confident about our future.

The junket to the Cavite National Forest had been window dressing—a demonstration of Ben's insistence that the commercial use of public lands in times of "national emergency" was not inconsistent with the preservation of their scenic wonders. He had convinced only those who had been convinced before the trip; the doubters remained in doubt. But the photos and stories looked good in the papers. By now we were convinced we had the committee votes.

But no sooner had we assumed that there would be safe-sledding for the New Wilderness Bill than danger signals in a related area cropped up.

It started, as did so many of our headaches, with an item in Lou Parenti's column.

A king-size scandal is in the making involving a leading Senator and the lobby for a group of financial institutions. All the facts are not in, but it is known that the lobby forked over an enormous sum of money to influence a section of the tax bill. The "campaign fund" was not only set aside for the personal needs of the recipient, but it was a totally unnecessary gift. Seems the particular amendment to the tax bill never stood a chance of passage, with or without the largesse. Needless to say, the donors are raging—at the lobbyist who led them on and at the important fellow who got the loot.

I thought of my safe deposit box in the Riggs National Bank. Ben studied Parenti's assault and, for the first time in many months, I noticed that he seemed upset.

"Now how the devil did the Wop learn that?" he asked. "Edward, lock the door."

He had the Conglomerate file in front of him—it seemed to get fatter, to grow with a life of its own, inside the green plastic binding.

"Blake wouldn't dare spill it," I said.

"No, not Albon. But his clients."

"There was a fellow named Krallis that day. He carried the attaché case. Little fellow from New York in one of those shiny dark blue suits."

"Don't keep any records on the special fund," Senator Hannaford said. "Our friend Kemmons wouldn't say anything, would he?"

"Not a word. I think Alf is airborne again this week, at the Navy's expense. Off to look at an Ordnance factory near his home town."

"Alf won't be any trouble," Ben said. He shut the Conglomerate file. It was very much on his mind. "Ask around and see how much Parenti knows. Take him out to lunch. I have a feeling he's bluffing. Besides, he won't be able to prove a damn thing, no matter what those mortgage-and-loan cheapjohns tell him. It's our word against theirs, if it gets down to cases, and who'd trust *them?*"

I tried to arrange a meeting with Lou Parenti, but his secretary advised me he was out of town on another of his secret crusades, trying to track down some terrible injustice to appease his liberal guilt feelings about America. Fortunately, nothing else appeared in his column concerning the alleged "pay-off" to a "leading senator." But we were soon under attack from the other end of the political spectrum.

One of my friends in the Senate Press Gallery, a network correspondent named Fred Goldstein, sent me a small four-page newsletter with a note, reading *"See page four, the NUTS are after your boss."*

The "newsletter," if one may give it so dignified a name, was the weekly mailing of a group called Save America Now. Need I describe who they were and what they were? The leading article on the first page read: TRAITORS AND COMMUNISTS IN HIGH OFFICE. And it went on to state, as a fact that from the White House Staff down, the government was infested with "the scum and slime of America."

I read the article—no names were mentioned—and I could only sigh in resignation. For these lunatics to go on insisting that the government was crawling with treason, defied anyone's imagination. President Hayward Kretz was one of the most honorable, courageous, patriotic gentlemen of our time; he was politically a conservative; much-beloved by the people. And yet his administration, his cabinet, his appointees, as well as the leaders of the Congress were deemed to be prone to "treason."

Indeed, two of the leading members of the President's official family were themselves close in spirit to the authors of the Save America Now newsletter. The Secretary of the Interior, "Giveaway Gordon" Hackensetter, for one, had often told reporters that "civil rights is a front for communism." And the untouchable, unreachable T. E. Kape, Secretary of Commerce, although more discreet, less given to extreme pronouncements, was of a marked far-right coloration, who had cut off his Alma Mater, Princeton, without a penny of the Kape fortune, because he deemed the professors at Old Nassau "a bunch of International Socialists." (He had later set up his own fount of higher education, Kape

College. I often wished he would spell it Kape Kollege. It seemed more in keeping.)

These people, of course, were part of the tiger Ben always spoke about. It was easy to dismiss them as "nuts," "cranks," and "lunatics." But they did not go away; and over the years, perhaps in the last twenty-five in American public life, and notably since the elections of 1964, they seemed to feed on their own venom. "Maybe they can't swing elections," Ben said, "or really knock off the Supreme Court. But they have accomplished a good deal."

"Like what, sir?" I asked.

"Like making it easy to call any man a traitor. When I was a boy you were careful who you called a traitor. It could get you shot dead. No more. The word traitor comes easy to them, and they have made it part of the political language."

I turned to the last page of the Save America Now newsletter. There was a small item at the bottom. (It followed a list of pro-Red sympathizers in the broadcasting industry, and I could see Fred Goldstein among those cited.)

> Trading with our sworn enemy is usually defined as TREASON. But that does not deter Senator Benjamin B. Hannaford, the big construction man. He claims to be a conservative businessman, an enemy of socialism. But he is always rewarding the bloody murderers of Eastern Europe by building their factories and pipelines. Who is protecting him? What traitors in high places are giving this man the right to strengthen our enemy? A letter to Senator Hannaford telling him what it means to be an American would be in order! SAVE AMERICA NOW!

Something about this attack on Ben bothered me, and I offered to take Fred Goldstein to lunch at Harvey's to see if he knew any more about it. Being a sensitive Jewish intellectual from New York, Fred is well briefed on the tiger's prowling. Although a liberal, he had a great respect for Ben, and I flatter myself in thinking that Fred liked me also.

"What about this?" I asked him, as we luxuriated in the magnificent Shrimp Louis and sipped the Musty Old Ale. I waved the newsletter.

"Don't tell me Hannaford is upset by that," Fred said. He pushed his amber glasses—taped with a Band-aid across the bridge

—up his nose. "Me, a neuroteic Semite, I worry about them. But they can't lay a hand on your boss."

"Of course not. But I'm curious as to why this turned up at this time."

"Yes, they have sort of laid off that bridge-building business. Some of them even admit we aren't at war with Romania."

"Fred, you're the expert. Theorize."

We settled into our Nesselrode pie and coffee. Goldstein ruminated a moment. "You know, Eddie," he said, "these right-wing nuts tend to be inter-connected, like the lefties. They all learn from Lenin. You know what Lenin said, don't you?"

"He said a lot of things, and I hardly think Harvey's is the place to be quoting him."

"Hell, you have to know your enemy. Lenin said 'Confidence is good, but control is better.' These assholes figure they need some kind of central control, but being psychopaths and schizoids to a great degree, it's usually hard for them to give up control. But they do have connections, and sometimes they are instructive."

One could laugh at some of the outward forms of Ben's tiger, but he had been eating people for a long time, and he probably would always be lurking in the underbrush.

"Now this sheet of crap, Save America Now, is actually printed in Bayou Blanc, Louisiana, by a certain Reverend Al Hucks. He heads up Save America Now and is believed to be the man who coined the phrase Kill a Commie for Christ. Well, that's an aside. My files tell me that Hucks gets a good hunk of change every year from something called Inform America, a so-called educational group that sends out canned hate broadcasts. Inform America puts up a respectable front—prizes for patriotism, sponsors contests, and so forth. They in turn are part of a corporation called Under God, which is a tax-free outfit, operating out of Hubbardsville, Texas, and furnishes speeches, pamphlets, and money to interested parties. All for learning."

"I'm getting dizzy."

"I'm just about finished. Under God is supported by voluntary contributions, a lot of it dollar bills sent in by frightened old ladies, but the bulk of it in big chunks from corporations."

"Now wait a minute, Fred. Are you going to tell me that my boss' outfit Hannaford-Western has been a contributor to this outfit, which then ends up financing the nasty attacks on him as a traitor?"

"Nope. But T. E. Kape is."

I almost choked on my Nesselrode pie. Blinking, I sipped ice water.

"Kape helps them out?"

"Not directly, but through a front—the Kape College Foundation. He's too smart to ask where it all goes, and he'd rather not read some of the results. After all, it's a bit much. Him with the administration. And this rag calling your boss a traitor—when the White House needs Hannaford so badly."

"It is confusing," I said to Goldstein. "We've never really had any quarrel with Kape."

I paid the check, said goodbye to Goldstein and walked a few blocks, mulling the matter over. No, there was nothing coincidental about the attack in Save America Now, the nasty mail— and the crisis of the New Wilderness Bill. T. E. Kape was moving to stop us in our tracks—in spite of "Giveaway Gordon," the President, or our own considerable power.

There was another bad omen when I got back to the office. The senator was at lunch in the Senate dining room, entertaining some friends from the House side. Ben had a few ideas on appointments to the Senate-House Joint Atomic Energy Commission.

The bad omen was in the nature of a large aluminum cask sitting ominously in the foyer of our office, a few feet from Marsha Treadway's desk. It was the cooler which I had had placed aboard the presidential plane the week before.

My first assumption was that the White House was returning it, having made use of its contents. In my mind's eye I envisioned some lucky Black Angus cow of President Kretz's getting the aristocratic injection, seed that would have cost anyone else $10,000 a shot.

"What the devil is that?" Marsha asked, crinkling her nose. "Page Tulliver at the White House made a big fuss about it— had it sent over with a Secret Service man. He said to make sure it was called to the senator's attention."

The truth would have brought a blush to Marsha's cheek. For a moment I was tempted to reveal what the cask held—or had held—and describe the awesome powers of Ramada Potomac Oaks

Bandolier. "Some documents," I said, "probably stuff we sent Tulliver on the New Wilderness Bill."

"Documents? Eddie, that's a cooler—for beer and soda pop. We going on a picnic?"

Morosely I took from her the note on White House stationery that had accompanied the metal box. It was addressed to me, not the senator, and it was from young Tulliver.

> Dear Mr. Deever,
>
> The White House has decided to return the accompanying item to Senator Hannaford, although he appreciates the senator's interest in his farm stock.
>
> Use of the material is impossible at the moment. Moreover, breeding experts advise us the use of such materials is against standards set by the Black Angus Breeders Association.
>
> We have kept the contents packed in dry ice and trust there has been no diminishing in its value. The President thanks the senator for his interest.
>
> > Sincerely,
> >
> > Page Tulliver
> > Assistant Press Secretary

Reader, have you ever had the problem of getting rid of a dry ice-packed aluminum cooler containing a jug of frozen bull's semen, on a July afternoon in Washington, D.C.? But I handled the crisis—I called a friend at the Department of Agriculture Laboratories, invented a story about a misshipped batch of the stuff, and had them pick it up.

Like Onan, we had spilled our seed on the ground. And it did not augur well for the President's support of S.671.

Later, I talked to Matt Fixx. Our legislative assistant was just about finished with his plan for presentation of the "Djarak Amendment" to the Foreign Aid Bill.

"We're down to the nitty-gritty, Ed," he said proudly. His nose was flecked with carbon.

"Master Plan finished?"

"All systems are go."

"Brief me."

"Ed, as I see it, the element of surprise will be crucial," he said earnestly, "the operative factor."

"And how do you propose we move?"

"Stay out of the committee hearings. Play dumb. Let the senator spring it on the floor of the Senate smack in the middle of debate."

"Is that wise?" I asked.

"It's proper. Amendments can be offered right off the floor. No need to try to fake out the committee members. Who knows? They might kill us. Let's not hit the line, let's run the end."

"And when would you suggest we submit it for printing?"

"When the debate is getting hot. When they're snarling. Remember, any unchanged portion of a bill is open or subject to amendment at any time during its consideration. *Any* time. We'll pick our time, when we're ready for the *crunch*."

I pondered the wisdom of this. "We may get hung up. You know the Senate has to consider all committee amendments and dispose of them, before a floor amendment can be offered. We may get sidetracked."

Matt Fixx smiled—a sly smile. "Ed, isn't that your department? I hear we are in great shape. I mean, I have a feeling we'd be able to arrange to keep committee amendments off the floor."

His hint at secret knowledge did not please me. No one was supposed to know about our special fund, including office people. Yet I had the feeling there was a leak, that word was getting out.

"Well, don't be so sure. Edgerton runs Foreign Relations with an iron hand. He might not appreciate being pressured."

"See what you mean. Don't want to get into a one-to-one relationship there. But we'd have other capabilities."

"Such as?"

"Well, we could arrange with another committee to submit a general amendment, say Armed Services—Tutt should be willing to oblige us—something about a defense appropriation for Djarak—and then we could have Senator Hannaford, from the floor, submit his amendment to *that* committee amendment. That would be perfectly in order, and we wouldn't have to wait until all committee amendments were disposed of. Say! That sounds very viable, very viable indeed!"

I left him, convinced that Djarak, that spit of sand, would get its special attention in the Foreign Aid Bill—just as Franco's

Spain had gotten his some years back. When I thought of the lobbying pressures—church, business, military—that had been brought to bear on behalf of Spain, I was proud of Ben Hannaford. He and he alone would take care of plucky little Djarak and Prince Aziz.

Later, I checked mail with Maria. We were catching hell from the right. If Fred Goldstein was right, Kape's money—even if austere Mr. Kape himself had no part of it—was after Ben's hide. Between them and Lou Parenti, the scratchy voice of liberalism, there would be no place to hide. Not that it bothered Ben. He gloried in the challenge.

"Now here's a beauty," Maria said. She handed me a letter from Dallas (for some reason right-wing campaigns often stem from there—the same script, the same illiterate handwriting, the same venom) on cheap ruled yellow paper.

> Sentor Benjamin "Bolshevik" Hannaford:
> You dont fool us one minut posing as a patriot we reel patriots know you for what you are a lying trator trading with godless enemy.
> we have you in the sights of the rifle right in the crosshairs so be careful.

Like all of these mad threats, it was not signed. How wise Sam Johnson was! Patriotism—how saddening that it was so often the last refuge of scoundrels! Any such letters that contained specific threats I turned over to the Federal Bureau of Investigation, sending them directly to the director, Judge Samuel Moscowitz.

"Things like that give me the creeps," Maria said.

"Rest easy, child," I said, thumbing through the cards and letters. "They don't bother the boss. I'll quote Harry Truman to you if you're upset—'If you can't stand the heat, get out of the kitchen.'"

"But—whoever wrote *that*—they're saying they'll kill the senator!" Her black eyes blazed. *She* could have killed someone.

"Yes. There are lots of nuts on the loose."

"The tiger?"

"Members of the tiger fraternity. The way-out ones. Thank 1964 for that. Once let out of the cage he's hard to get back in."

The senator came out of the office in his shirt sleeves. I caught that exchange of knowing glances between them.

"Mrs. Hannaford's in today," Ben said. "She's got some correspondence she'd like to dictate." Fern—serene, silent—came by once a week to avail herself of office facilities. Everyone liked her. "You free, Maria?" he asked.

Yes, he would like that. His possessions all in one place—wife and mistress, a yard apart, old love and new love, the anchor and the sail, while he would sit in his shirt sleeves and make deals, change votes, manipulate men.

"I'd love to, Senator," Maria said. "But Miss Watterson is letting me go home early this afternoon. I'm moving to a new apartment."

"You're lucky," he said. "Nearby?"

"Not too far. Just below the Cathedral. It's tiny but real cute."

"Don't work too hard moving. Marsha, you available?"

Marsha slouched into the inner office as the senator held the door open for her. Ah yes, a new apartment. Without the roommate—the other Ramada girl. Ben, sly fox, acted surprised.

CHAPTER EIGHT

Secretary of Commerce T. E. Kape eventually appeared before the Interior subcommittee. It came about in curious fashion. Kape had called a press conference to announce some new statistics on our Merchant Marine. It was a routine matter, interesting only in that Kape avoided confrontations with the press, no matter how bland. He refused to go on *Meet the Press* or to allow any magazine or newspaper to "profile" him. In a way, I admired Mr. T. E. Kape's old-fashioned insistence on privacy.

I was not, of course, at the press conference, but Fred Goldstein was, and he reported it to me in full later, and I then asked for a transcript from Commerce. (They were reluctant, but came around. Sometimes they seemed to act as if there were no such person as Thomas Eells Kape.)

Secretary Kape read his report on the healthy state of the Merchant Marine, answered a few routine questions, and was then startled to his pince-nez, to hear Lou Parenti bellowing at him:

"Mr. Secretary, is it true the administration is split on the Hannaford bill? That you and Secretary Hackensetter are on opposite sides of the fence?"

"I don't think I have to answer that," Kape grunted. At this point, as Fred Goldstein related it, the Secretary began looking around for an escape, but Lou Parenti was under his nose. "Listen, Mr. Secretary, I happen to know that the right-wing press, including some outfits that your foundation finances, is

attacking Senator Hannaford, accusing him of being soft on Commies, and that this is a way of making him drop the New Wilderness Bill. Right or wrong?"

As I read the transcript, I had to chuckle. Kape—that unreachable multimillionaire, richer by far than Ben, subjected to one of
Parenti's assaults!

Finally after more badgering, Kape adjusted his pince-nez and
sniffed: "My own view is that S.671 is a bad bill. But the administration sees fit to back it. That is the way things go in a
democracy."

"Then why are you attacking Senator Hannaford?" Parenti
persisted. "Didn't your own corporation get drilling rights in
fifteen of the Wildlife Refuges?"

"There is precedent for that," Kape sniffed. "And that is all I
will say on the matter."

"What's good enough for your boys isn't good enough for
Hannaford-Western, hey?"

At this point, Fred told me, Kape sprung from his seat, a tiny,
trim, pink-bald man in a black suit and shook his fist at the
uncouth columnist. "Who do you think you are? Has the senator
put you up to this? Are you on his payroll, like a lot of others?"

There was a gasp, then a shocked silence in the conference
room. Kape's aides hustled him out, but the damage was done.
The man was simply not used to the practices of a democratic
press conference.

"Now we've got the son-of-a-bitch," Ben said happily, as I
showed him the report on the press conference. The papers, of
course, hit the story—but not quite as hard as one would imagine.
There was something about Kape, and the power he represented,
that kept the press away. The attack on Ben, the reference to
people "on his payroll" were not stressed. Only Parenti, who had
initiated the contretemps kept hammering at it.

First, let me deny that I am on Senator Hannaford's,
or anyone else's payroll other than that of the Washington *Truth*. But I am flattered that no less a person
than the Secretary of Commerce himself would pay me
such a compliment. But that's neither here nor there.
The intriguing question is—who is going to emerge top
dog between these two fat cats, if we may mix animal
life?

Secretary Kape eventually appeared before the National Forests Subcommittee of the Committee on Interior and Insular Affairs. At first, he refused. Point-blank refused our invitation. If you are T. E. Kape you can do such things. You can tell the world to go to hell. (He had already sent one investigating committee, a group looking into stockpiling into confused retreat. Was one of his subsidiaries paid millions for stockpiled uranium the government no longer needed? They were, Kape testified. Did he think it proper that while he held high office in the government, his corporation should so profit? Why not? Kape had snapped back. And then to the confusion of the miserable committee counsel, he added: "I'll do anything I please, if that's what you want to know. And I'd like to see you or anyone else stop me." And he did. And they didn't.)

Yes, Kape was an original. He walked smartly into the hearing room—3302 in the New Senate Building—with a platoon of bright young men to the rear. But he really did not need them. When you are as wealthy as T. E. Kape, you don't need anyone. I think Senator Hannaford respected him for his colossal arrogance, his refusal to play the part of a public-spirited man of wealth. Kape was different from those whining executives I have read about, who came hat in hand to Roosevelt during the depression, or those more recent figures in the automotive industry who mumbled their apologies during the auto safety scandal. Kape would come hat in hand to no man—the President included. He was no mere manager of wealth. He *was* wealth.

And there he sat—dark blue suit, bald pink skull, pince-nez, manicured hands folded in front of him. No smile creased his hairless head. No gesture, motion, fidget betrayed nervousness. The air in the high-ceilinged floodlit room crackled with tension. The press was out in force. Parenti had seen to that. He occupied a seat at the long press table, his face bright with anticipation. While we waited for the subcommittee to assemble I distributed handouts to the press—another statement from "Giveaway Gordon" claiming that the administration still put the New Wilderness Bill high on its list of priorities.

"Hey, Eddie baby," Parenti growled, "I hope your boss is properly grateful to me."

"Why should he be?"

"Look what I promoted! Dempsey and Firpo! The Green Bay

Packers and the Baltimore Colts—sudden death overtime. I would call this the Battle of the Century if I dealt in clichés."

Parenti counted heads on the subcommittee. "Stapp, Hannaford, Henshaw, Lord, Erlenmeyer, Kemmons." He grinned. "Yeah, they're all here. What a lively crew. How come Hannaford give the gavel to Swinging Sid?"

"Senator Stapp has always been chairman of the subcommittee."

"Yeah, it'll look better this way." Lights flashed. Cameras whirred. Secretary Kape was getting impatient. He put a hand to his mouth and conferred with his counsel.

Senator Stapp gaveled the hearing to order. Ben was seated at his right. The usual informality prevailed—some smoked, a girl assistant came in with coffee for Royce Henshaw, one of Senator Erlenmeyer's aides arrived with a note for him. But nobody noticed. All eyes were on Kape.

"Mr. Secretary, the subcommittee apologizes for taking you from your important duties," Sid said fawningly, "but we are anxious to get full testimony on the Hannaford Bill to amend the Wilderness Act of 1964, and we are honored by your presence."

"I'll second that," blurbed Alf Kemmons. "We are honored, yes indeed, Mr. Secretary."

Couldn't that man keep his mouth shut? The last time I had seen Senator Kemmons had been through a blinding windstorm of flying hundred dollar bills—Mr. J. J. Mulrooney's gift from the Kape interests. I liked him better that way—dead drunk on his office couch.

"It is my understanding, Secretary Kape, that you have a statement to read," Sid went on. "Whenever you are ready, sir."

No smile, no acknowledgment of Stapp's boot-licking softened the scowl on Kape's face. Oh to be that rich and that arrogant! In a way, it was zoologically exciting, as if one had suddenly come upon a live Triceratops!

"Very well," Secretary Kape said. He had a tiny voice, but it had snap and authority. Having inherited his wealth, he had spent a lifetime building up the image of a man who had made it on his own. At least in this respect he bowed to our egalitarian mythology. "This will be short, and I will have only a few minutes for discussion."

Diplomacy, deference to the power of the Senate, humility—all these were alien to Secretary Kape. No labor union official, no egghead professor would have dared address the subcommittee with such consummate arrogance. Senator Hannaford's eyebrows arched meaningfully, and he shot a glance at Senator Stapp. Swinging Sid, in turn, bent his head slightly as if to say—*we have a beauty on our hands*. One could almost sense a fluttering, a mild electric shock passing among the six men around the burnished horseshoe table. United States Senators were simply not treated in this insolent manner.

Kape read his statement. It wasn't much. He read it swiftly and without emphasis. He was eager to get it over with, to convey to public, press and Senate that these affairs were beneath him. How odd he must have felt, assuming the role of a protector of the public lands!

"Now I am ready for a few questions," Kape said. He looked at his watch.

"That is most generous of the Secretary," Chairman Stapp said. "Swinging Sid" looked at Ben.

My boss edged forward in his seat. The broad blue worsted shoulders never looked more potent to me. The one-fourth Kiowa eyes fixed themselves on Kape's small figure. There they sat— eye-to-eye, Ben's one hundred and fifty million dollars, earned from the time he was an uneducated fourteen, all by his own guile, strength and vision, confronting Kape's five hundred million, inherited in huge casks from three generations of high-handed robbers, wheelers, dealers, employers of Pinkertons, the paradigms of what FDR used to call "malefactors of great wealth."

"Mr. Secretary," Ben began, "I assume you are familiar with the operations of your company in Cavite National Forest?"

"Of course I am."

"I take it you have no objections to that enterprise?" Ben asked.

"I do not."

"Do you regard it in any way as a rape of the national wilderness, a blot on the landscape?"

"I do not."

"Does the Kape open pit mine in the Cavite range present a threat to the untouched forests surrounding the mine?"

"Absolutely not."

"Then why, Mr. Secretary, are you so opposed to other industrial enterprises, of a limited nature, screened and carefully selected with a view toward preserving natural beauty, from being occasionally introduced in our forests?"

Kape's back straightened. His aide leaned to whisper something to him, but the old man shoved him aside with his pink hand.

"Because, Senator," he said, "I don't trust a lot of people who claim to be industrialists."

"Would you care to identify them?" my boss asked.

"I don't have to. There are a whole lot of these new operators trying to get a foothold, and they don't care how they do it."

There was a momentary pause. No one needed to be prompted, no lines had to be pointed to Ben, to make clear just whom T. E. Kape was talking about.

"Now, Mr. Secretary," Ben said, "I have before me a report from the Secretary of the Interior's Office, dated June 15, 1970, which you will recall was the period during which mounting public pressures were being put on the Kape Corporation not to, I repeat *not to* start the mine in Cavite National Forest. I should like to read . . ."

Kape's face tightened into a grimace. "Anybody knows the history of that," he said. That secret voice was getting louder, angrier. "We had those mining rights since 1903. They were ours. We owned those enclaves of land outright. We had every right in the world to mine them."

Ben nodded his head. "You had a legal right, but did you have a moral right? Every conservation group in the country opposed it. The administration opposed it. Congress opposed it. The people opposed it. But you went ahead and mined."

Kape leaned back and set his fists on the witnesses' table, bookending the microphone. "We certainly did. And we would do it again and again."

"Let me if I may return to this report by the Interior Department," Ben said. "I quote: 'The Kape Corporation has stooped to the worst kind of tactics in forging ahead with its campaign to use its acreage in Cavite National Forest. Department investigators have evidence of at least a dozen bribes offered to conservation experts and to vilification when these fail. At least one congressman opposed to the mine was branded a Communist sympathizer, another found himself the target of an organized hate-mail campaign. Deliberate falsification of statistics, concerning the extent of the proposed mine and its productive capacity was resorted to. In one instance, a Park Ranger in Cavite was . . ."

"That'll be enough!" Kape shouted.

The room gasped. No one—*no one*—spoke to a United States Senator in that manner. Ben smiled at T. E. Kape. "Did I hear the Secretary correctly?" he asked.

"Yes. That report is a pack of lies. It was discredited years ago. Can I leave?"

Senator Stapp leaned forward in his best courtroom manner. His white-on-white tie gleamed in the newsreel lights. "Mr. Secretary, we know you are a busy man and we will not detain you." But not a word of warning—no reprimand—no explanation that one did not give orders to the U. S. Senate.

"Senator," Harold Erlenmeyer said politely, "it has been the subcommittee's understanding that the administration wants our bill passed, and passed in its present form. Are we correct in so assuming?"

Kape tapped the table top with his right knuckles. "I am recommending that the administration ask for an amended version of the bill."

Senator Hannaford put his hand to his mouth. Kape meant business.

Parenti dug me in the ribs. "Hey, Deever. Got any frozen bull's semen handy? You could send a gallon to Kape and see if it helps."

Ben showed his concern. "All I have tried to point out, Mr. Secretary," he said, "is that we have no objection to the Kape mine in Cavite Forest. Why do you think I took the subcommittee out there for an inspection tour?"

"I don't care what you did!" Kape cried.

"May I finish what I have to say?" Ben asked. "I know you're a lot richer than I am, but that doesn't give you call to be abusive."

At once the atmosphere changed. Kape's tiny eyes opened wide. His shriveled lips parted.

"These personal remarks have no bearing on anything at all," said Kape. The man could not be insulted, frightened, moved. Wealth had inured him to all. "And I don't mind telling this committee, that I don't like the way this hearing is proceeding at all."

Sid Stapp's face turned as white as his fifteen-dollar shirt. He

had the feeling that anyone connected with the subcommittee
would be on Kape's bad list from now on. And Sid needed his
White House connections for his clients.

"You may not like it, Mr. Secretary, but this is the United States
Senate," Senator Lord said patiently, "and we have asked you to
participate because we need guidance on legislation."

"What do I care?" snapped Kape.

Ben Hannaford raised his eyes toward the high cream-colored
ceiling. By now the packed hearing room was a-stir. Parenti
grinned like a madman.

"No, you wouldn't care at all," my boss said. "Now I'm a rich
man also, Mr. Secretary, not in your class but, mighty rich.
But there is a difference. I went to work when I was fourteen,
I was a poorboy." (He pronounced it thus, as if it were a single
word.) "So I am concerned with the American people. But
you were born to wealth, Mr. Secretary, always had it, always will,
which is fine, and in the American tradition."

"I don't have to listen to this," T. E. Kape muttered.

"I do not believe," Parenti whispered to me, "that a group of
United States Senators have ever listened to such horseshit in
their lives. If that man was a pinko-liberal-lefto, they'd have him in
jail already."

Sid Stapp looked helplessly at Ben, who, as usual, had taken
over. "I suppose inherited wealth has its advantages," my boss
said easily. "I suppose it taught you to be impolite for one thing."

Kape leaped to his feet. "That is enough. I won't listen to another word."

There was a collective gasp, a rising muttering. Sid banged the
gavel. He was a lamb caught between two lions.

"I shall clear the committee room if there is further disturb-
ance," Senator Stapp said weakly.

Kape shook a finger at Ben. "I'm not just another witness
for you to browbeat, Senator," he said. His aide was at his side,
whispering advices in his ear. Kape listened, thrust his jaw out
and sat down again.

"Mr. Secretary, you did own *that* land," Ben Hannaford continued. And now his voice rose, the voice of the chief rigger
in the Ramada oilfields. "But did you own the land in the Tulipa
Wildlife Refuge, which the administration, in defiance of all
precedent, saw fit to open up to your mining engineers? Did you

have any claim at all to the Habaji Bird Sanctuary, which is now
the site of a Kape sulfur mine? Or did you wangle it out of the
Interior Department with threats and pressures? Who gave you
the right to drill for natural gas in the Great Black Snake Refuge?
What makes you think you have the right to rape every square
foot of the American continent?"

By now the room was in what I can only describe as quiet up-
roar. Sid Stapp banged the gavel. But it was to no avail.

"You'll all regret this!" Kape cried. And with that—something I doubt anyone had ever said to a U. S. Senate subcommittee
—the Secretary of Commerce stamped out of the room, followed
by his troops.

"Beautiful, beautiful," Parenti said to me. "One of the great
moments in Washington history."

"We sincerely regret the Secretary's sentiments," Senator Stapp
was saying, "and we thank him for his frank statements to the
subcommittee . . ."

"You know what we just witnessed?" Parenti muttered to me.
"We just saw the whole United States laid out like a dead zebra
on the plains, the whole vast country. And there are two lions
tearing at its guts, fighting over who gets to eat more, Lion Hannaford and Lion Kape, two of a kind, liver for one, heart for another. Deever, this is one of the finest moments of my life."
He was scribbling wildly.

The silence was appalling. Not only had they been insulted,
abused, snubbed, told off by the millionaire cabinet member. But
what in heaven's name could they do to him? He was no Negro
militant, no addled left-wing agitator, no hoodlum union official
who could be cited for contempt. And what gleaming scorn for
all of them he had exhibited!

"Got to hand it to Big Ben," Parenti said, as the room began
to clear, "I don't think anyone ever talked to Kape that way in his
life. The old fart is going to go home and cry, I bet."

I found no consolation in Parenti's view of the confrontation.
The power of people like Kape is not to be minimized. As I gathered my documents together, I felt that our bill was a dead bird.

Ben was not ready to surrender. He called me aside in the corridor. "Set up a press conference," he said, "I'm going to lay into
Kape a little."

At the office I made some calls to reporters. There was a lot

of interest. The Hill loves a good fight, and the battle royal between two titans, two of the richest men in Washington was
something to enjoy.

Yet what could Ben say? Kape had shrewdly painted him into
a corner. The great T. E. Kape, with all his millions had now
assumed the pose of a protector of the national forests! The press
conference was not a success. Ben left it frustrated, brooding.

That afternoon I heard him tell Cleo to call Mrs. Hannaford
and tell her he would be working late in the Hannaford-Western
offices downtown. He would not be home, he said, before midnight.

Alone in my apartment, bored, uneasy, I turned off the television and called the HW number in the big office on K Street.
There was no answer.

I then called Maria Valdez's number—the new apartment she
had been so excited about a few days ago. There was a busy
signal. I tried again in ten minutes. Still busy. And again. Then
I called the operator and had her try. "That number is tempo-
rarily out of order," she said. "Or the phone is off the hook."

Of course. Off the hook. But I was not. Nor was Senator Hannaford. The man was hooked as he had never been. I tried to close
my mind to visions of her bed, their bodies, what they said, what
they did, but I failed. Gifted as I am with a creative mind, I saw
it all, clearly, in detail, smelled the sweat, heard the sighs, listened
to the endearments and the promises. Maria's denials, I told myself, were lies. And I was more miserable than I had been since
my senior year at Ohio Normal College, when I was beaten out
for valedictorian by a crippled girl by the name of Lala Jenkins.

Senator Royce Henshaw of Montana, the former Columbia professor, telephoned one day to invite Senator Hannaford to lunch
at the Cosmos Club. As I have pointed out, they were quite different breeds of men, but they respected each other. Senator
Henshaw was a genuine intellectual, a bookish man who lived
modestly and augmented his income with magazine articles and
lectures. He and Ben were on opposite sides of most questions,
but like most of the men in the Senate, they kept a dialogue
going.

You will recall the badgering manner in which my boss treated
Senator Henshaw during the debate on the depletion allowance

bill. When the debate was over, Senator Henshaw had stopped
Senator Hannaford in the cloak room, and said to him: "Senator,
I resent the manner in which you spoke to me on the floor. It was
not that you were rude, it was simply that by your hectoring, you
may have given the impression I was a man easily swayed. I assure
you I am not easily swayed—by wealth, or power, or pressures."

Ben had looked at him with new respect. "I am sorry, Senator," he had said, "I am truly sorry." And they had gotten
on reasonably well since.

Henshaw was a well-built man with a great mop of rich brown
hair. He often displayed a melancholy, distracted air, his long,
rough-hewn face appearing to reflect disappointment with Washington, with the Senate, a sad awareness of what he had expected
of the great republic, and what it had boiled down to. I suspect
the realization that his textbook theories, his idealism, did not
always flower in Washington's muggy air, had much to do with
his lugubrious mien.

As chairman of the Senate Labor and Public Welfare Committee, Royce Henshaw had been much concerned with racial
matters, the poor, the new poverty program. These were aspects
of legislation that did not interest Ben very much. So we did
not quite understand what Royce Henshaw wanted when he
invited us to lunch at the Cosmos Club. I believe I mentioned
that one must have written a book to belong to Cosmos. Henshaw was one of the few senators who qualified. He had written
six, including the best-seller *Punishing the Poor*. This was a remarkable work, which set forth the theory that the American
government, notably the legislative branch, with the backing of a
majority of the people, had come to fear and despise the poor,
most of whom were colored people. The white majority, grown
sleek and fat through the social legislation of liberal Presidents,
now were determined to deny the good life to Negro citizens. It was, Henshaw argued forcefully, the final evil matu-
ration of the Protestant Ethic, the Calvinist conviction that the
poor are sinful. *Punishing the Poor* had created a stir, and was
largely responsible for rousing a sullen Congress to pass the New
Works Progress Administration Bill.

I have always liked the Cosmos Club. The high ceilings, the
dark mahogany panelling, the polished floors and heavy rugs
remind me of an age that is gone, of the lush era when one could

afford to build and maintain such palaces because taxes were low and servants plentiful. The Cosmos Club had been built by a certain Mrs. Townsend, who owned most of the Pennsylvania Railroad stock. It had, in the old days, featured a grand ballroom half the size of a football field, and on its hardwood surface had waltzed General Douglas MacArthur. His dancing partner had been Louise Cromwell of the J. P. Morgan fortune, and he had stolen her from General Pershing and wed her—much to MacArthur's subsequent regret. The marriage did not last long.

Now professors, scholars, the wise men of Washington dined in the lofty, fresco'd ballroom. Truth to tell, these learned writers and experts looked a bit out of place in the awesome room. It was not really their sort of place; nor was it Ben's.

We were told that Senator Henshaw and a guest awaited us in the dining room.

"I feel educated already," Ben said. "A man could get a degree just wandering around here." But he did not sneer; he respected men of learning, and especially Royce Henshaw.

Senator Henshaw was seated in a distant corner with a very black Negro. This did not surprise us. I recalled a story about a crisis at the Cosmos Club over Negro members, and how a boycott by influential white members ended the color bar.

"Senator Hannaford, Mr. Deever," Henshaw said, rising, "I would like you to meet Mr. Dalton Warfield."

We all shook hands. I knew who Warfield was, and so did the senator, but we had never met him. He was blacker than in his photos and television appearances. Warfield was the leader of the newest of the Negro civil rights groups, the Triple-O, which stood for On Our Own. It had its headquarters in Los Angeles.

Triple-O, On Our Own, was an outgrowth of "Second Watts." It is unpleasant to review these instances of terror and torment in our national life. But I suppose that the Negro insurrection that followed the "Get Tough" administration of Governor Verne Sparrier was inevitable, and the stuttering machine guns of the National Guard which put the rebellion down was equally inevitable, and that the final death toll in Second Watts of 237 was inevitable also. It is not my purpose here to review tragic history. There had been conservative governors before Verne Sparrier, but none had made the campaign promises he had —"*Orders will be shoot to kill*"—and the people had elected him, and when rioting ravaged Watts, the governor delivered on his promises.

Out of that bloody tragedy arose a new kind of Negro leader —stubborn, aloof, dedicated, tough, determined—and one such was Warfield, a former high school teacher and the recipient of a Silver Star from Vietnam. His idea was for the Negro to progress on his own—a notion previously advanced by such early leaders as the Black Power people and Malcolm X. The difference was that Dalton Warfield played it "cool." He had no time to hate "Whitey." He did not engage in polemics against "blue-eyed devils." He went into the streets and talked to his people. Block captains were appointed. Parents were forced to be responsible for sending kids to schools. "I don't want to see a single damn scholarship go begging, or an empty seat in a classroom, or a job that's available unfilled," was his doctrine. He was not one hundred percent popular with many rank-and-file Negroes, who wanted more blood. But Warfield had a calming effect on them. I could see why.

He was a large, broad-shouldered man in a cheap, ill-fitting brown suit. His tie was spotted. His eyes were sad. But he breathed leadership.

"Read some about you," Ben said. "And I see you on the television quite a bit."

"Yeah, we are both public figures," Warfield said. His sombre eyes—the round mahogany irises appeared to have run, staining the whites—studied Senator Hannaford. "Wish sometimes I wasn't."

He affected a certain uneducated manner. Warfield was actually a graduate of a state college in California.

Warfield's brother, a social worker, had been killed by machine-gun fire in Second Watts. Later, his store-front office of Triple-O was fire-bombed. His oldest daughter had been beaten up. His home had been dynamited three times.

"Dalton is an old friend," Senator Henshaw explained. "I helped draw up the manpower survey after Second Watts. He says he likes to come to Washington because he's got someone to talk to. Back home, Verne Sparrier and the rest of the State House people won't give him the time of day."

It was odd, exceedingly odd, that the governor of a great state should so act toward a minority leader. But had not the handwriting been on the wall in the middle sixties—the riots, the polarization of voting blocs? A Negro could win a local election now and then, but the Negro bloc votes could not, could *never* swing a state where racial antagonisms had been exacerbated. All the rosy predictions of "a new era," of "moderate views prevailing" had been shattered by the bloody riots. It had been proven that a white racist candidate could win anywhere. The only question was how far would he go after he won. Governor Sparrier had shown the world how far, although I was reliably informed by "Swinging Sid" Stapp, a fellow Californian, that there had been deep disgust and revulsion among much of the white community. The state population, after all, was not entirely composed of retired generals who dreamed of a military coup, or those who cried "Kill a Commie for Christ," or those who still screamed of "traitors and communists" in President Kretz' cabinet of millionaires, or those who shrieked "Nuke the Chink!"

"You are a brave man," Senator Hannaford said.

"He's the bravest I know," Royce Henshaw added.

Dalton Warfield shrugged. "It isn't bravery, it's despair. Oh we are getting some good done. But it drags, it drags."

"The job picture is better, isn't it?" I asked. "The voluntary industrial plan is working pretty good, I'm told." I was referring to a group of large corporations who had undertaken the training and hiring of Negroes in a wide variety of jobs.

"Yeah, I have no kick about them. Most of them are pretty good." And again Warfield's big ebony head lowered itself as if the burden he bore was sometimes too much for him. I thought of his dead brother, his dynamited home, and I wondered where he summoned up the courage to keep going.

"Hannaford-Western, Senator Hannaford's company is part of the industrial volunteer plan," Royce Henshaw offered—hoping to raise Warfield's spirits, and to establish our own *bona fides*.

"I'm aware of it," Warfield said. "HW is okay."

"They'd better be," Ben said. "You let me know if there's any problem."

"It's not HW. It's not the companies. Heck, it isn't the government." Warfield sipped at his martini.

"What is it, then?" I asked.

"It's the people of the United States," the Negro leader said gloomily.

"Not all of them," Senator Henshaw said.

"Enough of them to elect Verne Sparrier. Enough of them to keep us out. I don't understand it. All those laws, all those programs, even with the way we were set back during the Punish-the-Poor Congress. Still, they don't want us. Yeah, to win the Olympic high jump. But not next door. Not at the next desk." He sighed.

"It takes time," Ben said.

"Too long," Warfield commented. "Too damn long. And you know what? Things like Triple-O may be doomed, Senator. On our own we painted the houses, kept the garbage cans shut down, dressed our children neatly, tried to keep the fathers sober, and I don't think it's helping much. Senator, we are still niggers."

"You're always a pessimist, Dalton," Royce Henshaw said.

"Royce, you know nothing's really happened all these years. Yeah, we got a lot of laws on the books. Even got the Federal open housing statute through, thanks to you. But the damn thing can't be enforced and when it is everyone catches hell."

"It beats not having a law at all," Ben said.

"I suppose it does," Dalton Warfield said. He sighed deeply. I marveled at the man. What right had he to be so calm? "Nope. There's no consensus for us. There never has been. Somehow the laws get passed, but ever since 1964, something's been different. So we rioted in the streets and hollered Honkey and Whitey, and we gave 'em all the excuse they needed."

"Not everyone feels that way," Senator Henshaw said. "The Congress has acted generously."

"That's the funny thing," Warfield said. "It could be worse. If you left all this race legislation up to public referendum, I suppose the American people in their infinite wisdom would have us back in chains, or in zoos, or shipped off to Africa. I'm thankful for any help. Congress, the universities, corporations, like Senator Hannaford here, even the unions finally. They all helped. But I think it really isn't helping. Of those 237 who got killed in Second Watts, 218 were Negroes."

"Mr. Warfield," Ben said firmly, "you started the riot. Your people anyway. I didn't want those machine guns to open up. But when they did, it was you folks who were in the streets burning and looting."

Dalton Warfield studied my boss. There was no enmity in his

gaze, but a kind of grudging respect. "I've heard about your reputation for blunt speaking, Senator Hannaford."

"It's the damn truth," Ben said. "We got a wild and violent country here. Always has been."

The Negro afforded himself a bitter laugh. "One of our early rabble rousers said that and got himself cursed and damned all over the place."

"I have the advantage of being rich, white, and a senator," Ben said. "I can say anything."

We ordered our lunch. While I always enjoy going to the Cosmos Club, I find its menu uninspired. It seems to me to go with a lot of other things about Washington—all those drugstores, for example, and the endless advertisements for used cars in the newspapers.

"It's the people that hate us," Warfield said suddenly, as he stared at his liver and onions. "They are sick of us. Fed up. We have tidied up our lawns and put white shirts on our kids and learned trades, and it has done no good. Deep down we are not wanted. We remind too many of them of their guilt. And we incite fear."

"That isn't entirely so," I protested. "Mr. Warfield, you can eat in any restaurant in America and check into any hotel. Why, you can even eat here."

"Not what I'm talking about," he said. "Laws made hotels and restaurants accept us. Money talked. And here—well this is an elite place. The elite doesn't fear us, or even hate us. It's the people—all of them."

"But, Dalton," Senator Henshaw said, "education, understanding, time, all those things are working for you."

"I doubt it," the Negro said. "Who is to say that the vast bulk of Americans will not remain racist for another hundred years? Two hundred? All those marches and demonstrations made people hate us more. And you know what those marches were about, back in the sixties? They weren't for open housing or buses or lunch counters or schools. It was just us saying, stop hating. We were crying, we know what's in your mind, Jesus, *stop it.*"

"As I recall, Mr. Warfield," Ben said firmly, "some of your people did some pretty good hating also."

"*Some?*" Warfield asked, opening his sad eyes. "*Some? All* of us, Senator. But when you are outnumbered ten to one, it doesn't help. Yes sir, we are skating on very thin ice."

"You got yourself the New Works Progress Administration. Training. Better schools. More jobs." My boss tapped the table as he enumerated these.

"True." Warfield ran a hand over his nappy black poll. "But we know what the whites are thinking."

"You can't do a thing about it," Ben said. "Royce, you're a college professor, and I never got past eighth grade. You tell Mr. Warfield here if that isn't the truth. Not a damn thing. You may just have to wait two hundred years. Meanwhile, take the job, send the kid to school, buy a house, and do your best. I suspect maybe some of your black extremists are right. Go on, live among your own. Marry your own. There are worse things."

"We still know we are not wanted. So long as we *know* that, we are only partial citizens, we are semi-human. The self-hate that every black man grows up with has intensified."

"But that is the way of the world, Mr. Warfield," Senator Hannaford said firmly. "You can't expect to be loved. Nobody has that right."

"Not loved. Respected. Looked upon as a fellow human. Given a smidgin of dignity—not in stores, or schools, or factories—but dammit to hell, *in the mind of the white man!*"

"No law can do that," Ben said.

"Senator Hannaford is right," Royce Henshaw said.

"Then," Warfield said, "we got to figure out ways of changing it. Royce, that's why you said we'd meet the senator. We got to force ourselves on the white man, rough as that sounds. *Make* him respect us. Change his mind."

"How?" Ben asked. His tone was skeptical but he looked at Warfield with sympathy.

Royce Henshaw pushed back his mop of brown hair. "Ben, Mr. Warfield and his colleagues are pushing for a revision of the Federal Low Cost Housing bill. He came to me, because I co-sponsored it with Senator Eisenberg. But we want your support also."

"What sort of revision?" Ben asked.

"We, Triple-O and others, want a firm provision in the housing bill," Warfield said, "that would make it mandatory for all new construction to be on a *scattered sites basis*, that is, in predominantly white neighborhoods. We don't want a nickel of federal money given to putting up low cost housing in existing ghetto areas."

Senator Hannaford was shaking his head negatively. "Not a chance, Mr. Warfield."

"Now, just hear me out," Warfield said. "The only way we are going to change white people's minds is to live among them. We've made strides, thanks to the laws and some corporations and the universities. We have made progress everywhere except with Mr. Average American with his car and his job and his color TV set. But if you keep sticking us in apartments, far away from him, he'll still hate us. Let us live next door. Mix up the people in the new housing. Scattered sites or nothing."

"Senator Hannaford," Royce Henshaw said. "I intend to support Mr. Warfield's request. I'm calling a meeting of the Labor and Welfare Committee this week to discuss it."

"You'll succeed in killing the bill altogether," Ben said grimly.

"You sound pretty sure of that, Senator," Warfield said.

"The history of scattered sites is a rough one, gentlemen," Ben said. "It's killed off more good men than I care to think of. It is poison. It is death. It is a certain way to get *any* low cost housing bill killed. Those little house owners, those Eye-talians and Greeks and Ukrainians and Poles and in the big cities, they do not want it. They will fight it. They will kill it. And if they can't, they will destroy any politician who supports it." He looked at Henshaw. "Royce, it won't hurt you, you're from the boondocks, out in Montana, where there are damn few of those people and less Negroes. But it will destroy any big city senator who votes for it."

Warfield's eyes opened wide. "Not if you back it, Senator Hannaford. They will listen to you. I suspect the country will listen to you if you support scattered sites. You are a builder."

"This isn't my field."

"That's why I decided to ask you to help," Royce Henshaw said. "Mr. Warfield is right. With your power, you could rouse the whole Senate in favor of this."

Senator Hannaford looked pensive. He sipped his coffee. He was delaying, unwilling to commit himself. But I knew what was going on in his mind. Ben was a born trader, a man out for himself. He didn't mind doing noble and good things—if they paid off.

And he could see no payoff, no return benefit, no margin of profit in supporting a bill that would be enormously unpopular and divisive.

Dalton Warfield understood this. He was no fool, that black, troubled, burned-out man. "Senator Hannaford, you flew in the face of public opinion when you pioneered trade with the satellite countries. They damned you as a Red and a traitor, but you did it."

"Yes, I did," Ben said. "Because I made a lot of money on the deal. You know what I said. I would never trade with a Communist unless I could make money from him."

"It didn't keep you from being re-elected. Or lessen your reputation with the folks in Ramada." Royce Henshaw sounded plaintive—as if aware that grasping, unlettered types like Ben Hannaford could act in an "un-American" way and get away with it, while he, poor professor of economics that he was, had only to appear at a Foreign Policy Association seminar and the maniacs of the right were after him with torch and spear.

"I will tell you why," Ben said. "Hungary and Romania are four thousand miles away. But the colored man who is going to move into a low cost housing development is next door."

Warfield got up. He said he had an appointment with some congressmen. He suddenly looked out of place in the Cosmos Club, with his rumpled cheap brown suit, his huge black head and gnarled hands. He grasped Ben's hand firmly. "Maybe you'll change your mind," he said. And he left.

"He is one hell of a man," Ben said. He turned to me. "Edward, you have just witnessed pure unadulterated courage. I wonder whether I'd have the guts to keep at it."

Royce Henshaw nodded. "You should spend some time with him out there in L.A. I would say he averages twenty obscene and threatening calls a day. Yet he keeps going."

"Yes, he is to be admired."

"And he deserves our help, Ben."

Across the busy dining room, I could see the Director of the FBI, Judge Samuel Moscowitz, waving at us. (He surely qualified for the Cosmos Club. He was the author of many learned law texts, but was best known to the reading public for his dissertation on civil rights, *Enforcement for What?*)

"Senator Hannaford," Henshaw was saying, "I'll make a final

appeal to you. If you would get up on the floor of the Senate, or just call a press conference and say you'll back me and Maury Eisenberg on a scattered sites provision in the Federal Housing Bill, I know it would pass."

My boss waited no more than a second to respond. "Suppose I do, Royce?" he asked. "Will you vote for the New Wilderness Bill?"

There are some men who never lose their innocence. Senator Royce Henshaw was among them. I say this not to demean him, but with a kind of respect. Poor Henshaw! He was still in some misty land of textbooks, faculty teas, lectures, booklined studies, foundation grants, everything covered with tweed and redolent of pipe tobacco. The man had been in the Senate for some time. He knew that trades and deals were part of the game. And yet here he was, acting stunned when my boss proposed to him the most logical *quid-pro-quo* imaginable.

"But—but—you know, Senator, I am opposed to the New Wilderness Bill. It's a bad bill, and I have always been surprised at the zeal with which you pursue it."

"Senator," Ben said, "you want this scattered sites housing deal pretty bad, don't you?"

"Yes. I think Warfield has put his finger on what we need."

"If you want it that bad, you have to give Benjamin B. Hannaford something he wants just as bad."

"But I can't. S.671 is against my principles. It is what John Tyler Lord called it—a raid on the public lands."

"That's debatable, Senator. You give me a break in the committee, and I'll push for a revised housing bill."

Henshaw shook his shaggy mane, as if to clear his head. "Impossible. I'm sorry, Senator Hannaford, but that's impossible."

"Principles?" Ben was smiling.

"Exactly." This seemed to give Henshaw an opening he sought. "But that's just it! Principles! You don't have any where scattered sites housing is concerned. I don't think you care one way or another. Why not give us the vote?"

"I care a speck," Ben said. "Got my troubles with the tiger. I don't want to make them more savage than they are. But aside from that, Royce, I am a trading man, a profit-and-loss man. Let's trade."

Henshaw called for his check and was signing it. "No, I can't," he said. "I simply can't. Maybe it is a failing on my part, but . . ."

Ben held his palms up in a "that's that" sort of gesture and we got up.

"That fellow Warfield," my boss said. "He will be a mighty disappointed man." He seemed to be speaking to himself as we walked out of the dining room. "Too bad we won't be able to reward that kind of courage. Not much left of that any more."

"Yes," Henshaw said—with faint bitterness—as we headed for the ornate curving stairway. "Yes, too bad."

CHAPTER NINE

One morning, arriving early as was my habit (Maria was no longer beating me to the office door—it probably had something to do with her new apartment, and her regular guest), Cleo Watterson took me aside into her cubicle and closed the door.

"I want to get rid of Treadway," she said.

"Marsha? What's wrong?"

"She's useless. Worse than useless. She can't even spell her own name any more. She's messing up the mail and driving me crazy. Wrong letters going out all the time. She sent a batch of form letters thanking people for supporting the senator on Foreign Aid—sent them to people who had written in to complain about the Agricultural Committee lowering price supports for alfalfa. The girl is hopeless."

I hesitated before responding. For some reason I was reluctant to let her go. Was it some old bedroom loyalty? Good and faithful servant she had been. Cleo, wise old hen, knew what I was thinking. No secrets were kept from Miss Watterson. She knew, I was certain, what was developing between Maria Valdez and the boss. Both of us were born observers, people blessed with keen intuition. Ben no longer made any effort to keep from following Maria's willowy figure with his demanding eyes. In the midst of a conversation with me, if she were to walk by, his attention would wander, his face momentarily lost in contemplation of her sweet body.

"Can we get Marsha a job somewhere else?" I asked.

"Marsha will have no problems," Cleo said sourly. "She may be a bust on correspondence, but she has other talents."

I raised my eyebrows. "That's not like you, Cleo."

"Ed, you're at your most distressing when you play the prude. As a matter of fact, one of HW's clients needs a girl. We'll send her there. Shall I tell her, or shall you, Exalted Administrative Assistant?"

"I would prefer it if you would," I said. "And if you wish, I'll add a few grace notes."

The deed was done. To show my interest in her, I took Marsha to a farewell lunch at Frances' in Georgetown. At first she refused to go, advising me she wanted no favors from me. But I convinced her, stressing that I could still be helpful. We sat on the outdoor porch, finding little to say to each other. The goodwill gesture had been an error on my part.

"I hope there will be no hard feelings," I ventured. "There was nothing personal, Marsha. But Cleo insisted your work was falling off. Maybe you need a rest, a change."

"Since when are you so concerned with my welfare?"

"But I am, Marsha. Please count on me as a friend. If that job with Petrol-Air doesn't work out, we can find you another one."

A forced smile crinkled her full mouth. I realized Marsha was quite pretty; one was always distracted by her great projecting bosom, her high rump, or set off by the loose strand of hair, the botched lipstick. For a fleeting moment I remember those savage bouts we had enjoyed in my bachelor diggings. A Sinatra LP on the Hi-Fi . . . a faint light from the half-closed bathroom . . . the two of us tumbling and laughing, gasping, reaching. Consolation came to me with the assurance that poor Marsha, cruelly called the "New York State Open" by some, would not want for male companions.

"Are you still seeing Lou Parenti?" I asked.

"On and off."

"He's bad medicine, Marsha. You know he's been married twice already."

"So? You've never been married. And were you such a bargain? You know, I'm just beginning to realize what a lousy thing you did to me."

"That is unfair, my dear. I thought our relationship was a good one. It was what I promised you it would be." Again, I toyed with visions of our first coupling. She had been good to me—warm, soft, pliant, responsive.

"Well, in any event, Marsha," I said, "your past services to the office and to me are deeply appreciated."

"Thanks for nothing, Eddie."

Her bitterness disturbed me. I was obliged to warn her: "You may feel resentful toward me, but please be careful of what you say to Lou Parenti. I'm afraid he will try to use you."

"Oh, boy, the way your mind works! Could it ever occur to you that we find one another attractive?"

"I'm certain that's the case. But Parenti will keep his eye on the main chance. He lives in hopes of discrediting the senator. Just be careful. Try not to work off your anger at me by telling him things he shouldn't know."

Marsha made a slight grimace of vexation. "I don't need you to tell me what to say or do."

"Maybe not. But think carefully before you tell Parenti anything—anything at all—about the office, the senator or myself. No matter what you say to him, he'll find a way of twisting it against us."

"I couldn't care less about any of you," Marsha said, with hauteur. "Not that everyone around doesn't know—about the boss and that hot tamale. Who cares?"

"Let's keep it that way. Who should care?"

I breathed a little easier. So long as she imagined I was concerned about the senator's amorous dalliance, we were safe. Even if she told Parenti, it could not hurt us. Such juicy bits of personal gossip about senators or congressmen are never, never printed. One just does not indulge in these wicked asides. What had concerned me was anything she may have overheard about the Conglomerate, or the safe deposit box in the Riggs National Bank, or my meeting with Messrs. Paxton and Krallis. Evidently she knew nothing about these, or if she did, had no idea they would interest Parenti. Marsha was not terribly quick. A decent enough girl, but a dullard, thank goodness.

A week passed. We moved cautiously on the New Wilderness Bill. Ben decided to hold no more hearings until he could get a commitment from the White House. He was worried. For the first time in all the years I had known him I had sensed hesitance in his moves. T. E. Kape had proven a match for him and he was disturbed by it.

It angered him that the White House kept calling for favors on its legislative program. "Senator, the President would like a good word from you on the Air Pollution bill; Senator Hannaford, the President sure would appreciate some help from you—maybe five votes—on the Emergency School Appropriation." Ben set his jaw, performed favors for President Kretz and would growl at me: "Seems like the President looks at this as if it's a one-way street."

"Maybe he figures you owe him a few for dedicating that road in Ramada City."

Ben laughed. "The trouble with our President is, he loveth the uppermost rooms at feasts and the chief seats in the synagogues. But he doesn't care about others getting their seats."

"Senator, a lot of people are saying the same thing about you."

We were seated in his office late in the afternoon. The radio newscast droned on. We listened with half-an-ear as the announcer described the newest crisis in the Soviet Union. Rioting mobs of young people—long-haired, flower-bearing, barefoot—had tied up downtown Leningrad with demonstrations against the Mongolian War. "Mongolniks," the Soviet press had named them. Young men had burned draft cards on the steps of the Defense Ministry in Moscow. One rumor said that the ringleaders had been arrested, convicted of treason and executed. The Mongolian adventure was tearing Russia apart. All the leaders in the Kremlin could do was keep mumbling about "Inner Mongolia letting its neighbor alone." Gromyko had promised to go anywhere in the world, if he could find a single, solitary Inner Mongolian who would talk to him.

"Congressman Angel López Garcia says he will sue the House of Representatives for refusing to seat him," the announcer went on. "All is quiet in the Arab sheikdom of Djarak on the Persian Gulf. The U. S. Peace Keeping Force in the desert state reports no incidents in the past twenty-four hours . . ."

Ben switched off the radio. "World has sort of settled down," he said. "They got their problems, we got ours. But we are the ones who will straighten the whole thing out."

"How?"

"The proper use of greed. That is the basis of man's existence, and we are the ones who know how to use it."

"Is that why you are so intent on the Conglomerate?" I asked.

He looked at me quizzically. The boss' face was more lined than usual. Even a powerhouse like Ben Hannaford runs down after a while.

"That's one reason."

"Will the Conglomerate operate under a policy of controlled greed?"

" 'Freely ye have received, freely give,' " Ben replied.

"I don't understand. Why is the Conglomerate so important to you? You are rich enough. You have six corporations under your thumb already. Hannaford-Western seems to get bigger every day. Why do you really want all those others—Tramlett-Hewes and Petrol-Air and whatnot?"

He leaned back in the black leather chair. "Edward, that's a good question. There are times when I'm not really sure. The beauty of it, though! All those big ones! Create jobs! Build new cities! Big roads. Oilfields. Use that damn timber and copper and oil and iron for useful things. I like to see things in *motion*."

"A commendable list of desires, Senator," I said carefully. "But is it worth carving up National Forests?"

"We'll hardly touch 'em. Besides, I promised the Conglomerate I'd deliver it."

"Sort of a wedding present?"

"In a package with a ribbon on it. Now dammit, Edward, if a bastard like T. E. Kape can move into the Wildlife Refuges, why can't I get some good hunks of land also?"

"No reason at all. Except some people might not like the idea of *either* of you doing it."

"They are without vision. I tell you, we must permit greed to function, or we are through. And we must teach the Communists greed, and the Orientals and the Latin Americans."

"What if we lose on S.671, Senator?"

"I won't be happy. I may not be able to hold all those hosses in line. I tell you, Edward, I want them very much."

"No wedding present, no wedding?"

"It would appear that way." He winked at me. "Although, we just might get them another present."

"Such as Djarak?"

"Yup. A whole dang Arab country. Just for us."

Maria Valdez—prettier, perkier than ever—stopped me at the water cooler. I had the feeling that the smart, brown-and-gold dress she wore was out of the $7.50 class.

"Are you free to take me to lunch?" she asked.

"Frankly, no. I would love to, Maria, but the senator is driving me up a wall."

"Please. I must talk to you."

How could any man resist those limpid brown eyes, that red parted mouth? We compromised on a fast picnic in the mall. Maria ordered hero sandwiches and soft drinks and we sat on a bench in the summer heat, with the white monuments all around us. Tourists jammed the paths, clogged the benches, shouted, pointed, lost children, found inspiration. The city would never lose its magic. Once I saw a ghostlike, black-clad figure glide by fussing with his old-fashioned tie. It was former Senator Atherton, now safely established in a sinecure with the Senate Campaign Committee, thanks to Ben.

"This will have to be a brief meeting," I said.

"I need your advice," she said. A crumb of Italian roll clung to her lower lip. I brushed it away, envying Senator Hannaford's freedom to touch, caress, stroke, and know her.

"I'm not sure I can be of any help, Maria. You know, when you came to work here, I saw you as an innocent, a waif, a quivering bird. *Pajarito?* Is that the word?"

"Yes."

"But you're not. Not by a long shot. You are a tough little cookie, Maria. Don't look offended. I don't mean you are hard or cruel. But you know your mind. You know what you want."

"I didn't want a lecture, Edward. Only advice."

"They come together. With the salami-and-provolone heroes."

She crumpled up the wax paper wrappings and stuffed them into the brown bag.

Seymour! I heard a stout woman with frizzy blond hair shout. *Seymour! Get away from them taxis!*

"I think I am in trouble," she said.

Gagging, I spewed forth a mouthful of Diet-Pepsi. No, not this. Not Ben. He was too smart, too careful.

"Steady there, Maria. We'll run up to New York over the weekend, I know this dentist who knows a . . ."

"Oh, Eddie! You and your dirty mind! Not that. Damn you,

you still won't believe that we've never, never . . . not once . . . not even close . . ."

"You asked me for advice, Maria. Leave. Get out of town."

"Your attention span is terribly short. Now listen to me. Mrs. Hannaford knows. Do you hear me, she *knows*."

"Knows what, for God's sake?" I cried.

"How he feels about me," she said—with almost a touch of pride.

"And how is that?"

"Eddie, he's in love with me."

Deep, deep I slumped on the hard slatted bench. So that was it. The lion in love, the bull of the woods led by the garlanded heifer. Old Ramada Potomac Oaks Bandolier himself. Well, at least I had been faked out of position by a true champion.

"Tread carefully, Maria," I said. "Men say things in the grip of passion that they don't really mean. The words come easily during those hot embraces, during those wet kisses and gymnastics."

"Shut up!" she cried. "How many times do I have to tell you that hasn't happened? That he hasn't even suggested such a thing? It's . . . it's . . . different. And he told me he loves me."

"Just like that? With no demands made?"

"Yes. You couldn't think of anyone loving anyone else unless there was a deal, an exchange, a trade of some kind."

"Don't accuse me of that. Big Ben wrote the book on that kind of operation. Mr. Wheeler-dealer himself."

"Well he's thrown the book out." Her lovely face twisted in a grimace. "Eddie, he told me so that night in San Francisco. It was so sad. He didn't touch me—just put his hand on my shoulder —he didn't kiss me—he never has—and he said he loved me. Loved me, more than anyone . . . and that he would have to find some way to have me. But that with Fern . . . so loyal, so good to him . . ."

"And so rich, and so proper. Christ in Heaven, Maria, I don't believe you. Yes, I believe he told you that, but he told you that while the two of you . . . the two of you . . ." I choked on a remnant of salami and turned away. "Ah, why pursue it. I'll hate myself no matter what I say."

"Can we forget about your problems for a moment?" Maria asked—with monumental self-concern. "Honestly, Eddie, I need help. I can't be bothered with your romantic moanings. Really, Eddie, you're supposed to be the Big Brother." She patted my dark blue knee. "Please help me."

The nerve of that little Latin bird! The appealing gall! "Okay, I'm here. Old Reliable Deever. Now you said what—that Fern knows Ben professed his love for you?"

"Well, at least she *suspects*."

"I'm sure she does. She's no dope, old Fern Cudder Hannaford. Don't be deceived by that bland blond head. I think that at night, when she undoes that steel corset she wears, she is capable of cool, analytical thought. Now why do you think she suspects the senator is hooked?"

Maria arched her smooth neck. "You won't believe this. She wants me to move into their house in Potomac . . . to live with them!"

I digested this. Yes, she knew how Ben felt about the girl. She was not a woman to be underestimated. Gordon setters, my eye.

"Last weekend I went out there to take some letters, and she pulled it out of the blue, announcing that she thought it would be just swell if I moved in with them!"

"What did the senator say?"

"He didn't like the idea. But he's always so polite, so considerate, almost in awe of her, that he didn't argue too much."

That was dear Fern. She had seen the way her husband's eyes had followed the lithe young creature, his scrutiny of the beautiful head, the erect breasts, the long legs. He could not hide it at the office. He did not hide it in his home. And so she would end it all, by inviting Maria to live with them. An adopted daughter. One of the family. Close enough to home so that Fern could keep an eye on her, and perhaps close enough so that Ben, in time, would grow tired of her.

"But why? Why the devil should she want you around?" I tried to feign ignorance.

"She kept saying it was terrible the way I had to live by myself, all alone, someone so young and helpless. She didn't like the neighborhood, with all the muggings going on, and since Ben had such a personal interest in me . . ."

"She said that?" I asked incredulous.

"She really was wound up. Which is hardly like Mrs. Hannaford. Gosh, most of the time, she just sits there with her hands folded, looking elegant and not talking."

"She knows, Maria, she knows." I leaned back on the park bench, letting the sun caress my weary face. "And I must say I find her strategy ingenious."

"I don't," said Maria peevishly.

"Naturally, you refused to go along with this scheme."

She turned that marvelously formed head to me in profile. Her dark, waved hair was gathered in a short pony tail that fell just to the top of the new frock. Beneath the hank of soft hair rested the head of the cunning zipper, the gateway to ecstasy.

"I haven't said yes or no."

"And what was the senator's reaction?" I asked.

She pouted. "That was the funny thing. He almost seemed to be agreeing with his wife. He didn't say he was *against* my moving in with them, and he did keep saying that my neighborhood was perfectly good, and I was a big girl, but he sort of hesitated."

"You'll find, Maria, that the senator has a healthy respect for Mrs. Hannaford's wishes."

"Pooh. Sometimes I hate her."

"It won't help. If she wants you occupying one of those adorable chintzy sunlit third floor bedrooms, you'll occupy it. Maybe you'd better start packing."

"But it's awful! She *knows* the way he feels about me, and there she is inviting me in!"

"She wants you under her clear cold eye, señorita. It will present problems to both of you, but none, I daresay that the boss will not be able to resolve."

I chuckled to myself. This was Fern's way of telling Ben that he had no secrets, nor did she fear the new competition. She would challenge it, invite the challenger to her home grounds, and beat her all hollow, age-for-weight, in an allowance race.

"Eddie, what am I going to do?"

"I'm no good at this sort of thing," I said. We got up, strolling like two tourists, down the mall, toward the magisterial dome of the Capitol. Freedom—awkward lady—waved to us. "Does he really contend he's in love with you?"

"Every time I am with him."

"He's, let me see, thirty-one years older than you are."

"Thirty-two."

"What has he said about marriage?" By now I was enjoying my role. I suspect it is my colossal indifference to most people that makes me such a good listener, that endows me with fraudulent compassion.

"He doesn't talk about that. Just that he needs me so terribly, that he doesn't know how he can go on without me."

Ah, I thought, just like the Conglomerate. He needed both— her naked young limbs, her soft creamy flanks, her honey breasts; just as he needed Tramlett-Hewes, Petrol-Air, Dover Plains Chemical, Longhorn-Mideast, and the others. The man talked a lot about Controlled Greed, but I wondered who exercised any controls over *him*. Fern, perhaps.

"He'll find himself in trouble one day, and so will you, Maria," I said with clerical authority. "The two of you may be having a ball now, but it can't last."

She sighed. "Damn, I'm not sure I want it to. It's . . . it's an incomplete relationship."

"Then clear out, Maria. Beat it, before it's too late for both of you. Go on to New York. You will dig the big town. I'll ask some of the news magazine people here to get you a job up there. Or a network."

"I will not. I like it here."

"Then sweat it out, child. Ben will never divorce Fern for you or anyone else. If he did, it would kill his political career. He's got White House notions. He's had them a long time, but he's smart enough not to discuss them with anyone except me. And there'll be no room in the mansion for an exotic Latin mistress. Never forget, 1600 Pennsylvania Avenue is no Byzantine Court. It's not Versailles. It's respectable middle-class America."

"Oh, that's such a long way off," Maria said.

"Very well. *Carpe diem.* Live for each moment. And good luck to both of you."

"I wish you didn't sound so cynical. Eddie, I have to discuss these things with *someone*."

"And who better than old reliable?"

We crossed in front of the Capitol and walked toward the New Senate Office Building. I nodded a greeting at Senator Lester Goodchapel, fat and friendless, as we passed by. How marvelous were the ways of our world! He bore us no ill will, none at all. For all I knew he had returned to the sinful well. Perhaps he now regarded Albon Blake as the nicest man he had ever met in Washington.

"I'm supposed to let Mrs. Hannaford know before the week is out. About moving in."

"Naturally. She wants the room tidy. Also give her time to get some extra keys made." Then, maliciously, thinking about Lester Goodchapel I added: "And probably to have the tape recorder installed."

She pulled her arm away. "That isn't nice and hardly what I expect." She hurried ahead of me a few steps—unquestionably the most desirable twenty-two-year-old woman of Mexican ancestry in the whole city.

A few nights later, having retired earlier than usual after an exhausting evening with the senator and Matt Fixx—we wrestled with the Djarak Amendment—my telephone rang. I was only half-asleep, my mind swarming with floor amendments, committee amendments, substitute amendments, germaneness of amendments, orders of offering, and orders of voting.

"Ed? This is Fred Goldstein."

Fred often did a late night news spot for his network, and he occasionally called me.

"Yes, Fred. Can I help you?"

"Eddie, have you seen Lou Parenti's column? The *Truth* just hit the streets. Has your boss seen it? Or said anything?"

"This is the first I know about it."

"Brace yourself, kid. He's dropping the heavy bombs. The nerve of that guy." I sensed a tinge of envy in Fred's voice; as an old newsman I knew the feeling—he was appalled at whatever it was Parenti had done, and achingly jealous.

"I called to see if I could get a statement from the senator, or at least from you, but seeing as you haven't seen it . . ."

"Read it to me."

"Sure, sure, Ed. FYI, the wire services are holding up doing anything on it until your boss says something, and my guys in New York feel the same way. I also got word from Parenti's syndicate that a half-dozen papers, including the Ramada City *Times*, won't touch it."

"For God's sake, Fred, read it to me!"

"Okay, here it goes." I heard Goldstein's flat New York voice drone on, filling my ears with what proved to be Parenti's first salvo in that long bitter struggle.

Goldstein read: "'The mystery as to why Senator Benjamin Bow Hannaford has been pushing so vigorously for his pet project, the New Wilderness Bill, has at last been revealed. If this measure is passed it would mean a multimillion dollar windfall, for years to come, for a new corporate giant the senator is working to create.

"'This latest raid on the government by the senator, richest man in the Senate and one of the most powerful, is evidence of Hannaford's contempt for the American people, for the public good and for the body in which he serves—the United States Senate.

"'The New Wilderness Bill would in time, open the National Forests to brutal exploitation by mining, timbering, and other commercial interests. It would in the opinion of conservationists, ultimately destroy our national forests. Even so liberal a dispenser of public lands as President Kretz has blown hot and cold on the Hannaford bill. His own cabinet is known to be divided on the wisdom of its passage. And Senator Hannaford, as ruthless as he is, has had trouble pushing the measure through the Senate Interior Committee, of which he is chairman.

"'But the big question has always been, why has Ben Hannaford, a construction magnate (his net worth is said to be in excess of 150 million dollars) with family connections in oil—Mrs. Hannaford's family founded Longhorn-Mideast—why has he been so determined to get the measure passed?

"'*View from the Hill*' can now supply the answer. We have in our possession a file of secret correspondence between Senator Hannaford and a half-dozen large corporations. Texts of these incriminating documents will be released in the next few days. What they boil down to is a scandalous use by Senator Hannaford of his office, a disgraceful perversion of the legislative process and a greed rarely seen in American life. Senator Hannaford's plan is to unite these giants—including his own Hannaford-Western Corporation into a huge "Conglomerate." He himself would eventually be named Chairman of the new group. The dowry for this wedding of great wealth would be nothing less than the notorious Hannaford bill, a free ticket to exploiting the national lands, a guarantee of limitless drilling, mining, timbering and construction rights in the National Forest System!

"'Needless to say, Senator Hannaford is in violation of every Senate rule on conflict of interest, of lobbying, and other types of misconduct, which we will bring to light in due time. For the moment the following letter from the senator to Mr. Winston M. Doak, Board Chairman of Petrol-Air (a natural gas operator, one chosen for Big Ben's Conglomerate) should reveal the brazenness, the crass greed of the man!'"

Fred Goldstein stopped to catch his breath. I was surprised to discover my hands bathed in sweat.

"Jesus, Eddie," Fred said slowly. "He's out for blood. Parenti really latched on to something."

Irrelevantly, with all the problems, crises, aggravations I saw multiplying in my mind, I was annoyed with Fred. "You sound as if you believe everything he says," I commented.

"Eddie, you know Parenti wouldn't run this, unless . . ."

"Unless it were true?"

"He's got this text of a letter, and he says he's got a whole batch of them to back up his charges."

"He does?" I asked stupidly.

"Yeah." Goldstein read on. "'This letter is the first of dozens that have come into our possession and which will be released in the next few weeks.' That means he's got a batch."

Marsha. That whore! That quasi-nymphomaniac! How she had deceived me! With her wet-lipped assurances that she "couldn't care less," with that sly response to my warnings—claiming she thought I had been talking about Ben's romance with Maria, and not the crucial matter of the Conglomerate! The woman scorned, the woman discarded, she had had her revenge. Who would think that dim-brained, big-bosomed, slow-talking girl was capable of such vengeance?

"Here goes," Goldstein was saying. "'The letter is on Senator Hannaford's stationery, dated June 18. Dear Winston, the passage of S.671 is virtually assured. The Interior and Insular Affairs Committee regards it with favor, a wise amendment to the Act of 1964, and a forward-looking step in conservation. You may so advise your board members, and I would appreciate some sign of their reaction. Once the bill is reported out of committee—with the President's backing—I see clear sailing in Congress. With this in view, the finalization of the Conglomerate structure is mandatory. We want to be in business, the store open as they say, once the

New Wilderness Bill is law. The next step will be a prudent approach to the Interior Secretary. But all this is contingent on our group being in agreement, and functioning as a unit. Sincerely, Benjamin B. Hannaford.'"

Goldstein sucked his breath in. "Man, unless that's a forgery, he's got a lot of people by the short and curlies.'"

"Anything else?" I asked.

"One sentence. 'This reporter feels we are about to see revealed a scandal that will rock Washington for years to come. The evidence is in our hands.'"

What could I say? I mumbled my thanks to Goldstein, trying to formulate statements, modes of action, in my troubled head.

"Listen, Ed, I need a statement from the senator, quick. Your phone is probably humming right now. You know these editors who wouldn't use the column—they'll wait only so long. What can you tell me?"

"Not a thing, Fred. I'll have to talk to the senator."

"Like right away? Right now? And I'll call back?"

"Yes. Give me ten minutes."

"Sure, Eddie. And listen, kid. Whatever happens, I sure hope you don't get hurt. That Parenti." He said it with hushed admiration—a reporter's awed respect for the great scoop, the grand score.

Immediately I dialed the senator's unlisted phone in Potomac. A drowsy Fern got on the line. "Why this is the fourth call, Edward," she said wearily. "The Associated Press . . . the Washington *Post* . . . that nice man from NBC. Is anything wrong?"

"Nothing that we can't handle, Mrs. Hannaford. Parenti is attacking us again. Has the senator spoken to any of the reporters?"

"Goodness, no, Edward. He isn't home yet."

"I see. Do you know where I can locate him?"

"He said he was attending a private dinner with some Hannaford-Western clients."

"Did he say where, Mrs. Hannaford?"

"No, I'm afraid not. Travis took the message. I wasn't in when he called. But he should be home soon."

The man could rig votes, appoint relatives, push legislation, lobby for his own money—but he was an amateur at carrying on an affair. He had lied badly and incompletely to Fern, and I was certain she knew where he was and what he was doing. I thanked her and told her that if the senator wished he could call me on the matter of the Parenti column as soon as he got home.

"I certainly will, Edward," Fern said.

"I'm awful sorry to have disturbed you, Mrs. H."

After hanging up I took the phone off the hook. It would ring again and again—the papers, the press associations, the networks, the newsmagazines. As for trying to reach him that night, I gave up. I knew where he was, and whom he was with, and what they were doing. It almost seemed he had a right to enjoy himself fully and freely. Moments of untroubled bliss would be few and far between for a long time.

The green-covered folder lay on Ben's desk in front of us. He opened it and began to leaf through the file. I watched from the opposite side of the desk.

"All there," he said.

"And all copied."

"Yes," he said. "I suppose I forgot to lock them in the drawer one night. Someone borrowed them. Someone Xerox'd them. Someone got them to Parenti. Someone returned the originals."

"And I guess we know the someone," I said.

"The Treadway girl?"

"Who else?" I shook my head. "An irresponsible woman. I should have fired her long ago. But those weak unstable ones rarely do anything so rash. Parenti must have twisted her arm to get her to do this. She's liable to prosecution for something like that."

Ben stretched. "I suppose so. But we haven't proved it was Marsha. What the hell, Edward. How will it look if Ben Hannaford persecutes some little gal on his staff?" He looked at me with that questioning glance, and I knew what was in his mind. Was I the truly guilty one? Sleeping with Marsha, enjoying her favors, abandoning her, firing her, so that in feline vengeance, she ransacked the office and gave Parenti his ammunition?

"You're right. Besides, we can't even prove she was the thief. Not that it matters. But we might hang it on Parenti. He's, at minimum, a fence, a purveyor of stolen goods."

Ben asked me to call in Matt Fixx. Matt entered, paler than ever, his long, meagre face dripping sorrow, shock, outrage. He could barely summon up the "viables" and "capabilities" he needed so badly.

"Matthew," Senator Hannaford said, "call our boy at the Justice Department and see if Parenti can be stuck on stealing documents, or using them. Might as well give him a few uneasy moments. I'll buzz Judge Moscowitz for an opinion."

Matt Fixx nodded and went out. As he did Cleo Watterson stuck her gray head in. Of all our staff members—aside from myself—she was taking the blow the best. A tough old bird Cleo. She had been through a lot with Ben.

"The phones won't stop. Every reporter on the Hill, and all the big columnists. They want a press conference. They want a statement. They're all going to run Parenti's next column."

Ben waved a hand at her. "Hell, let 'em. Tell them we stand on what we said first thing this morning. We deny any wrongdoing of any kind. Documents were stolen illegally and the thieves will be prosecuted. There is nothing illegal about a conglomerate, and the New Wilderness Bill is the best thing that ever happened to American Conservation."

"It won't keep them happy, but I'll try," she said.

When Cleo had left Ben kept thumbing through the Conglomerate file. He was remarkably in control of himself. Lesser men would have wavered, been filled with doubts and fears. But he was firm in purpose, convinced of his rightness. "What the hell do these letters prove anyway?" he asked me. "They prove we were starting a big new outfit, a damn good one. Suppose we open a few national forests—because of a national emergency? That's no crime, is it?"

"None at all, from our standpoint."

"Get me Hackensetter. I want to make sure this doesn't scare off the administration."

But I had the feeling—and I think he knew it also—that President Kretz would no longer back us. The administration did not like messy quarrels. They were sensitive to criticism. T. E. Kape would rub his pink hands in joy.

Well, the administration was one thing. The Senate was another. Senator Gage Hopewell, the Majority Leader, and with Ben a real power in the Senate, dropped by to make clear his outrage.

"That creature is a serpent, a parasite on the body politic," old

Gage intoned, his red-rimmed eyes popping. "Veritably a throw-back, a foul memory of an earlier day of irresponsible yellow journalism. Yaaaaas."

Old Riverboat Gambler, old dealer-from-under-deck, old medicine man Gage Hopewell, knew—he had to close ranks with Ben Hannaford. Outside our office, where a friendly death watch had been set up—three TV crews, some radio reporters, the wire service leg men—Gage Hopewell blended his trebles and basses and turned on the full stereo to voice his faith in Senator Hannaford.

"This is nothing less, nothing less I say," old Gage groaned, "than an attack on the integrity of the United States Senate itself. Is there a harder working, more respected, more beloved man than Senator Hannaford? There is not. Has any man done more for our country in the way of imaginative industrial development? No one has. He is a prince, yea, a king, a leader. The reporter who has started all this is malevolent, misguided, and misinformed. Yaaaaas."

Alf Kemmons, who himself had known Parenti's cruel lash, issued a cautious statement supporting Ben. So did Senator Gabriel T. Tutt, who resented Parenti's frequent charges that the South's leading bigot, enemy of pornography, leftists, and Asians, was a drunkard.

"It's the Commonists," Gabe bawled to a UP man. "The Commonists are after that man's scalp because he's a real American. I don't hold with Senator Hannaford on a lot of things, like those deals he makes with the enemy, but he's a real man, and he hasn't done anything wrong. Parenti is a liar. He's been called liar by every decent person in this city, and I suspect he is worse than a liar!"

A few others voiced their faith in Ben. But there was silence from Senator Webb Urban, the Chairman of the Senate Ethics Committee. "I shall have to study the matter," was all Urban would say.

We bided our time. Ben was remarkably calm. The office staff reflected his courage, his confidence. But I confess I was troubled, more troubled than I had ever been. Perhaps it was Webb Urban's equivocal comment.

The following day the storm worsened. It was not only that Parenti ran his second column, releasing more of the purloined letters. It was that the press in general, which had treated the story cautiously the first day, fearful of getting mired down in one of Parenti's crusades, now accepted the "scandal" as front page copy. All the Washington newspapers featured the attack on us; the radio and TV newscasts led with it; our telephones never stopped. Parenti wrote:

> Serious questions of conflict of interest, of senatorial ethics, of plunder of the national lands, are involved in the sensational correspondence that this reporter has received, letters revealing the nature of Senator Benjamin B. Hannaford's wheeling-and-dealing to push through the New Wilderness Bill. This is the notorious measure whereby the nation's precious wildernesses would be thrown open to rape by commercial interests—but mainly a corporate octopus headed by none other than Senator Hannaford himself.
>
> On June 21 of this year, the senator wrote to the president of Dover Plains Chemical, Mr. Kenneth Yancey, a prospective member of the proposed "Conglomerate" which was to be formed with the purpose of getting favored treatment in mining, timbering and other despoiling operations.
>
> "Dear Ken," Senator Hannaford wrote, "we are certain now of administration backing and therefore your agreement to the formation of the Conglomerate is essential. Please keep in mind the favored position we will have for fruitful development of carefully selected enclaves. Contrary to what the conservationist cranks say, none of these operations will detract from the beauty of the forests. The areas are isolated, out-of-the-way, and useless to anyone. You must, however, make known your decision immediately. I would suggest you deal with our Ramada City office if you want more details. It is better not to call Washington, or to depend too much on Blake."
>
> The Blake mentioned by Senator Hannaford is genial Albon Blake, free-lance lobbyist and partygiver. Which leads to all sorts of interesting speculations. It is known that several senators switched their votes in the Interior Committee. One such changeling was Senator Lester Goodchapel of Indiana, the silent man of the Senate. Senator Goodchapel has been seen a good deal in Mr. Blake's company. And it was shortly after this

friendship blossomed, that Senator Goodchapel decided
that he liked the New Wilderness Bill very much indeed, and would change his committee vote from yea to
nay. More tomorrow on the Hannaford case. We hope
the Senate Ethics Committee is paying close attention.

"He hasn't said a damn thing he didn't say yesterday," Ben
said. "I think he'll hang himself."

"How?" I marveled at Ben's composure.

"Because we haven't done a thing that's illegal, that's why. Edward, the Senate doesn't care for this sort of publicity. Men have
done disgraceful things here—and gotten away with it. And I
find nothing disgraceful, illegal, or unethical in a single thing
we have done."

"Then we'd better hold a press conference and say so. These
offhand statements in corridors and outside the chamber are no
help. The press is screaming for a full-dress statement."

"They'll get it when I'm ready."

Ben would work slowly, carefully. His counterattack would be
as shrewdly planned as a military campaign. He would let
Parenti seethe and spume, let him release his letter-a-day (I
calculated he had several dozen papers, and could go on for
another month) and then fight back with all the strength and
cunning he possessed.

When Parenti's third column broke, he summoned me to his
office.

"The Wop is walking into it," he said. "He will not quit. He
will not learn."

I nodded. Parenti, in today's poisonous piece, announced he
was sending photostats of the Conglomerate documents to the
Senate Ethics Committee and the Justice Department for study.
Furthermore, he expected responses from them.

The columnist wrote:

> It will be interesting to observe how the august, and
> untouchable gentlemen on the Ethics Committee
> react to this. Indeed, we await congressional reaction in
> general. Only last month, the congress, the White
> House, and the Washington Establishment in general
> rose in mighty wrath to denounce and expel Represent-
> ative Angel López Garcia of Chicago, for some penny-

ante stuff. But then again, Congressman Garcia is dark, foreign, left-wing, and contemptuous of his peers. Big Ben Hannaford is as American as apple pie. Will the Senate dare to even ask him a few questions?

That morning there was an agitated telephone call from Mr. Doak of Petrol-Air. Another from Mr. Yancey of Dover Plains. Then a flurry of them from the other potential partners in the Conglomerate.

"There is nothing as frightened as a million dollars," Ben said with disgust. He regarded all these rich men, his future partners as yellow-bellies, small-timers. He wanted their companies, and their resources, and he wanted the fun of manipulating them, of creating wealth upon wealth. But he had a lively disrespect for them.

Albon Blake was on the phone—interminably it seemed.

"Anything I can do to help, Senator," he bubbled. "Say the word, and I'll go into action. What if I take Parenti to lunch and straighten him out?"

"You take him to lunch and he'll eat you alive, you damned fool."

"Yes, yes, I suppose he would!" Blake agreed energetically.

"You tell our future partners to sit tight," Ben advised him. "That's the best service you can perform."

"I will! I will, Senator!" The lobbyist paused. "Say, I hate to bring this up at a time like this, Senator, but that fellow Krallis has been pestering me."

"Krallis? Who is Krallis?"

I remembered Krallis too well.

"Norton Krallis sir," Blake went on. "A nice chap, Senator, a swell guy. He was the one arranged for the special fund. You remember. Eddie met him through George Paxton."

That entire mad incident, that casual gift of a quarter of a million dollars was long banished from Ben's mind. He had much bigger, fatter fish to simmer—crisp, golden, succulent.

"What about him?" asked Ben impatiently.

"Senator, God knows how he found out, but he claims that the money shouldn't have been paid, that the provision they wanted beaten was dead already, and they paid the money for nothing."

"And?" Ben asked.

"Well . . . Mr. Krallis feels he should get it back." Silence from Ben. Bleak silence.

"Half of it?" Blake asked. More silence. "A token return?" the lobbyist queried.

"Good Christ, Albon, do you have to bother me with this crap when I'm up to my neck in serious matters?" Ben shouted. It was rare for him to raise his voice. "Now tell this Kravvis or whatever his name is, to take his medicine like a good boy. He paid. He got what he paid for."

Blake, not a whit dismayed, promised he would so advise Mr. Krallis.

This conversation concluded, Ben picked up the phone and called the Director of the Federal Bureau of Investigation, Judge Samuel Moscowitz, formerly of the New Jersey State Supreme Court.

At this point, I must point out that the eminent jurist—like so many Washington figures—was in Senator Hannaford's debt. A little recent history is in order. Judge Moscowitz was a lifelong battler for civil rights and for the enforcement of civil rights legislation. By no means a "total" liberal, he was on the liberal side of many causes, although he had always kept his lines to the conservative establishment open. But when his name was put forth by President Hayward Kretz (the judge had been a supporter of the wealthy publisher) to succeed the incumbent director, who after long distinguished service had decided to retire, an ugly and unseemly debate erupted in Congress. No less than three investigations were conducted into Judge Moscowitz's fitness to serve the Republic. A wild stampede ensued to see which committee, which chairman, which party spokesman could lead the assault on Samuel Moscowitz' fitness to serve. (As I recall both the House and Senate Judiciary committees, and the Senate Government Operations Committee got into the act.) Never in Washington history did a more disorderly, sleazy, ill-favored, and foul-mouthed parade of witnesses appear to denounce the judge as everything from an agent of Mao Tse-tung to a believer in compulsory abortion. The spectacle was not reassuring. President Kretz, nudged by Secretary Kape, was almost prepared to withdraw the appointment. (I remember Senator Gabriel T. Tutt, safe in his senatorial immunity, gargling to an empty

Senate chamber: "That fellah Moscovitch is no better'n a Commonist! He he'ps Commonists, an' he talks lak one!")

Judge Moscowitz, as the saying goes, "kept his cool" and was a dignified witness. Yet the storm did not abate. No evidence introduced to show that the judge was not an automatic liberal, that he had been tough on Negro rioters, that he had supported local police forces, seemed to do him any good.

The President, through the Attorney-General, then made an appeal to Senator Hannaford. My boss barely knew the judge. But he asked Matt Fixx to prepare a report on him in detail—biographical data, attitudes, connections, his career. Ben spent an evening studying it. When he had finished, he said to me: "He is a goddamn good American, every bit as good as Gabe Tutt. He'll get that job. I'll see to it he does."

Do you understand now why I felt that Ben was so important to the body politic? That he could get things done that lesser men, more liberal men, better educated men, could not, in a million years? A Royce Henshaw (an intelligent dedicated man) a John Tyler Lord (a high-minded idealist) could never have secured congressional approval for Samuel Moscowitz. But Ben Hannaford—so close to the American heart—did it in one tough, explicit, outspoken speech on the floor of the Senate.

"Once and for all!" Ben thundered, "once and for all let us stop these cowardly attacks on a great public servant! I beseech my distinguished friend, the senior senator from Alabama, to cease and desist! I know his motives are of the highest, and I respect his desire to keep the FBI free of subversives, but Judge Moscowitz will do just that! Let us take a vow not to make sneak attacks on those who serve, let us be guided by a man's record, his character, his service—not by wild rumor, rank emotion, and blind prejudice!"

The gallery exploded in applause. Senator Gage Hopewell lumbered across the dark maroon carpeting to pump Ben's hand. After that it was a matter of dropping all the cruel investigations to appease the madmen. Yes, Ben was a tiger-tamer. He did not even get a rise out of Gabe Tutt. That particular tiger growled, bared his fangs, allowed as how he still had no use for "Moscovitch," but if Senator Hannaford wanted him in the job, that was all right with him.

Although Judge Moscowitz was not a man to play favorites,

he had an understandable affection for my boss. We always got through to him on the phone. As I waited alongside the desk, studying out-of-town papers—we were front page news everywhere—the senator spoke with the FBI chief. It was agreed that I was to go to the director's office that day and present a detailed report on the theft of the Conglomerate papers.

"I'm not so sure this is a wise move," I said.

"Got to fight back," Ben said. "Maybe we'll drop this strategy later, but it won't hurt to shake Parenti up a little."

I frowned. "I don't think he can be shaken, Senator. Not this way."

That afternoon found me in the office of the FBI director. Judge Moscowitz was a short barrel-chested man in his late fifties. He had played guard for Columbia under the great Lou Little and was still in excellent shape, a squash and tennis expert. His hair was iron gray and thick, and he had a pugnacious look about him, except for his eyes which were a warm hazel.

"I must confess to you," Judge Moscowitz said, "I don't quite know how to proceed. I want to help the senator. But I'm not sure whether I have any jurisdiction in this matter. Perhaps I can function as a friend—if nothing else."

"We'll be grateful for any help."

"Did the senator tell you that the White House is much interested in this matter?" the judge asked me.

Ben had not mentioned that to me. But I said he had.

"From the President's office," Judge Moscowitz went on. "Nothing specific—just a request for an advisory from the Justice Department to see if any laws have been violated."

Raising my head I asked: "By who?"

The judge smiled. "You would make a good lawyer, Edward. The President didn't specify. But I gather just in general—any laws violated by anyone involved."

I was uncomfortable about this. That was the trouble with a decent uncommitted man like President Kretz. One was never sure just where he stood, apart from the certain generalized sense of his being in favor of "what was right." Nuances, subtleties, eluded him. I consoled myself with the knowledge that he would have to, in the long run, back Ben. His legislative program would be a shambles without Ben Hannaford to grease it through the Senate.

"As I told the senator," the FBI director said, "it would be helpful if I had a statement from you concerning the documents. That's really all that concerns me. I won't take any notes, I won't record you. You must take my word for that."

I laughed. The judge had been a bitter opponent of bugging, wire-tapping, any form of invasion of privacy.

"But you will permit me to invite one other person to be present when you make your case," he said.

"Of course." I assumed it would be one of his bright young aides; perhaps a Justice Department lawyer.

With that, he pushed a button on his desk. The door was opened by a secretary, and in walked Lou Parenti.

"Hi, Eddie baby! Good afternoon, Judge. Always a pleasure to be up here. Makes a man feel safer just to walk around. You gonna let me go down and see the boys shoot machine-gun bullets at the dummies later?"

Judge Moscowitz laughed. "If that's your pleasure."

"You could use a lesson or two," I said coolly. "Your own marksmanship leaves a lot to be desired."

"Wait, Eddie. I'm gonna start knockin' down ducks every day. I'm just beginning. And there's a great big fat drake I'm after especially."

The judge's broad face turned grave. He did not care for Parenti.

"Why are we here?" Judge Moscowitz asked rhetorically. "Well, the question has been raised, Mr. Parenti, just how you got access to Senator Hannaford's private correspondence. You are now using these papers in a campaign against the senator. I am not about to argue any of the issues raised in these letters, or the senator's recent activities vis-à-vis S.671, or his business affairs, or any connection between the two. I'm concerned only with the theft of those papers."

Right to the point! I said a small prayer to myself in loving thankfulness for Judge Moscowitz. He was on our side.

"I don't say a word without my mouthpiece," Parenti said . . . a crude attempt at humor. "Come on, Judge, you can't scare a newspaperman, anyway not a rat like me."

"It is not my intent to scare you, Mr. Parenti," the FBI director said. "But merely to advise you that you are under investigation for the possible theft of documents from the files of Senator Benjamin Bow Hannaford."

"Says who? Who ordered it?"

"At the senator's request."

"He doesn't run the FBI. Or the Justice Department."

"He has made the request and we will honor it."

Better and better! Ben was way ahead of me, way ahead of Parenti.

"Okay, okay," Parenti said carefully. "Lemme ask this. Is it a crime for a newsman to get his hands on evidence which documents charges of corruption in high places?"

"It is a crime to steal from a senator's private files."

"A federal crime? Come on, Judge."

Parenti was shrewd. I had the feeling—I cannot say why—that the FBI chief was approaching the assignment with less than total enthusiasm.

"I can be of help on this matter," I said. "It's our opinion, Judge Moscowitz, that the documents in question were stolen from the senator's desk by a young lady named Marsha Treadway. This woman was discharged from our staff for incompetence some days ago. She has been seen in Mr. Parenti's company."

"You can prove them last two statements," said the newsman—how I detested his deliberate use of bad grammar—"but you can't prove she stole a rubber band from Ben's boardingschool. Go on, prove it, Deever. Yeah, I date Marsha. And I'll defend that little lady's honor or my name isn't Luigi Massimo Parenti!"

"That is most gallant of you," the judge said. "But the little lady, as you call her, will be interrogated."

"Sure. Why not? Nothing stops you guys. While I'm at it, Judge, how often has the good old FBI raided desks, stolen letters, jimmied open file cabinets, heisted corporation books, documents and what not? And what about the way tax informers get paid off? Who's stealing from who?"

"A newspaper is not a law-enforcement agency," said the FBI chief firmly, "nor is a journalist a law officer."

"I would like to know what Mr. Parenti *paid* for those letters," I said. "And whether he himself, perhaps, was playing cat burglar in our office at night, with the help of Miss Treadway's duplicate keys."

Parenti grinned at me. "Didn't have to, Eddie. Besides, I'm told it's dangerous to go prowling around that office at night. Might embarrass some people."

Did he know about Ben and Maria? I could not believe it.

"As a matter of fact," the judge said, "we doubt that Mr. Parenti was the actual thief. We found no evidence of his fingerprints anywhere in the senator's office."

"Miss Treadway's?" I asked.

"Yes. But she did work there for a long time."

Parenti tried a new tack. "Judge, I got to admire your thoroughness, and like all red-blooded American boys I have always venerated the FBI. But let me ask you a coupla questions. You know, when you were up for appointment, it was proven that some nut assistants to Senator Gabriel T. Tutt, those Save America Napoleons, went through *your* files, tapped *your* phones, stole *your* letters, and did everything but pass obscene notes to your grandchildren. The idea was to get the goods on you and block your appointment. Right or wrong, Judge?"

The FBI director did not respond. Parenti had cut close to the bone.

"Yes, you know it's the truth, Judge," the journalist went on. "Senator Tutt's storm troopers, all those super-patriot gumshoes he's got on his staff, they were after your hide, and they didn't stop at anything. But you never said a word. No one in the United States Senate objected because it was good old Gabe Tutt's men who were doing the stealing."

"You are in error, Louis," Moscowitz said. "I denounced those actions at the time they took place."

"Didja investigate them afterwards, when you were in office?"

"No. It was water under the bridge."

"Who appointed Senator Tutt sheriff?" Parenti boomed. "What makes him a better judge of right and wrong than you or me?"

"That's not the issue, I'm afraid," Judge Moscowitz said, and he laughed—a bit hollowly I thought. "The only issue is did you conspire to steal private documents from Senator Hannaford's office?"

Parenti frowned and slouched deep in the green leather chair. He was not frightened or even annoyed. I suspected he loved the encounter, and there was no doubt in my mind that he would write about it. "It's the old story. If you're a United States Senator, you can get away with it. If you're a poor struggling member of the press, look out."

"Our office has no apologies to make," I said. "Senator Hannaford does not stoop to rifling desks."

"He doesn't have to!" Parenti boomed. "The guy can buy the whole country if he wants!"

Judge Moscowitz stroked his lips. His hazel eyes wandered to the ceiling. "Louis, do you want to admit to me now that you stole those papers, or arranged with Miss Treadway to have them stolen?"

"Nope. I did not put anyone up to it. Not Marsha nor anyone else. I paid not one cent for those papers. I stole nothing. Where are they now, Eddie baby? They are on the senator's desk or locked in his drawer."

"Your knowledge of those papers betrays your guilt," I said. "I suppose you even know the color of the folder."

Parenti's eyes narrowed. "Mauve? Puce? Oyster?"

"You have an obnoxious habit of playing the fool when you're guilty," I said.

Parenti assembled his great hulk and got up. "I never been so insulted in my life. But if you think this will scare me off, forget it. I'm too thick-headed to be afraid of a little FBI muscle. Or the Justice Department. Or the White House. Or Big Ben and his hundred and fifty million bucks. It's not that I'm brave. I'm a Calabrese—that's the hard-headed kind of Italian."

"You have a journalist's right to pursue these matters," the FBI chief said. "But I must warn you not to violate any laws."

"Not me, Judge. See ya, Eddie." I nodded at him, glad that I had seen the last of him—for a while. "Come to think of it, what did you guys do to Lester Goodchapel to get him to switch his vote?" He left.

Judge Moscowitz shook his head. "An impetuous and impertinent young man."

"What can be done about him?" I asked.

The FBI chief leaned back in his chair. "Nothing for the moment, I'm afraid. And perhaps never, unless we can prove theft."

"And that would appear difficult."

"Probably impossible. Edward, our agents have interrogated Miss Treadway. She is a stupid, emotional young woman, and while she was evasive it was our guess that she did this on her

own with no prompting from Parenti. As it were, an act of vengeance."

"Against the senator?"

"No. Against you."

What a price we pay for the pneumatic feel of woman's flesh!
What disasters lurk in scented nylon and lace! Never in my life did
I feel more foolish, more exposed, more betrayed. In a sense it
was I who had brought this disaster on Ben's head. Although, as
I left the FBI chief's office, I had the notion that we would weather
the hurricane. After all, who was Parenti, and what was his power,
when arrayed against the might of the United States Senate, the
Justice Department, the White House itself?

The barrage from Parenti intensified. He hoarded his ill-
gotten documents—the copies of them—and released them one at
a time, sometimes just a section of one. He made of the so-called
"Hannaford Affair" a cliff-hanger, a tease here, a hint there, an
innuendo at the proper time, an outright charge, a touch of guilt-
by-association. No one was spared his poisoned pen. To my
astonishment a good part of the American press saw fit to publicize his charges, to demand interviews with Ben, to hang us before the trial.

I scanned Parenti's newest blast at us sipping my orange juice
in my apartment—alone, ever alone at breakfast, now that I was
free of Marsha.

Not a word has come from the Senate Ethics Committee concerning the Hannaford matter. Ever since this
reporter exposed the brazen conflict-of-interest involving
Senator Benjamin Hannaford's arm-twisting pushing of
the New Wilderness Bill, so that his corporate buddies
could get rich despoiling national forests, the Ethics
Committee has been curiously quiet. Is it because Senator Hannaford is a key member of The Club, that
worshipful party of Senate elders who can do no wrong?

To prod the Ethics Committee along, we submit the
following new bit of evidence concerning Builder Ben's
exercises in self-interest. You'll recall that the so-called
Conglomerate included a variety of big corporate interests, who were to be headed by—you guessed it—Senator Hannaford. Here is a memo from one potential
group member, A. T. Loving. Mr. Loving is Board

Chairman of Jackwitt Copper. It is amazing the way these people avoid subtleties and get to the heart of the matter. Mr. Loving's note to Senator Hannaford is in answer to the senator's letter, printed yesterday, inviting comments from the potential Conglomerate members.

"Dear Senator," Mr. Loving wrote on July 21, "we remain favorably disposed to the merger, but it will have to be contingent on Jackwitt's securing exclusive mining rights in Starved Horse Forest. Only such a provision could put us in a competitive position vis-à-vis our rivals. We will continue to assume that passage of the New Wilderness Bill will be realized at this session of Congress."

We await some comment from the Senate Ethics Committee and its chairman, Senator Webb Urban, the rugged Mormon preacher from Wyoming. Considering the blinding speed with which the House of Representatives ran Angel López Garcia out of their chamber on a rail, we are puzzled by the Senate's lethargy. More on the Hannaford scandal tomorrow.

For a moment I wondered if Parenti were overplaying his hand, that his one-note harping on the Conglomerate and Ben's alleged misdeeds might only serve to bore the public, bore the Senate, and defeat his purpose. But the news columns kept covering the case; the radio and TV people were eager to follow his lead. It was disheartening.

At the end of a brutal week Ben decided to move. Thus far we had issued denials, ignored Parenti's personal affronts, and conducted ourselves with reserve. Ben would go on *For the People*, the nationwide Sunday afternoon television program. He was at his best in these informal give-and-takes. While not a polished speaker, Ben was straightforward and a shrewd arguer. Reporters respected him. The program was taped at the United Broadcasting Company studios just before noon. Fern decided it would be nice if we all watched it out at the Potomac mansion that evening and she arranged an intimate Sunday night dinner.

The party included Senator and Mrs. Gage Hopewell, Senator and Mrs. Sidney Stapp, and the Secretary of the Interior, Gordon Hackensetter. I was also invited, and so was the adopted child of the Hannaford household, my protégé, Maria Valdez.

I was thumbing unhappily through my Sunday *New York Times*—they had given too many columns to the "Hannaford case" and had run one of those "nothing less than a full and fearless investigation is needed" editorials—when my phone rang. It was Maria, asking for a lift out to the Potomac mansion.

"And Eddie," she said, "do you mind doing a little manual labor?"

"Such as?"

"Helping me with my valises and junk. I'm moving in with the Hannafords."

"So. Fern has had her way."

"Not really. I decided it would be fun for a while."

She did not sound convincing, not by a long shot.

"I see," I said. "Do you sign up for a certain period, sort of a short-term lease?"

"No. Mrs. Hannaford and I agreed we'd try it out for a while. She was very much concerned about me walking around those dangerous streets at night. There were two muggings on my block this week."

"Yes, that's considerate of her. Nobody gets mugged out at Potomac. But you might get bit by a Gordon setter if you're not careful."

I drove to Maria's apartment and helped her load her meagre belongings into my pale blue Pontiac convertible. She was packed and ready for me, standing in the apartment lobby when I drew up. I had the feeling she did not want me to see the cozy flat where she and the boss had enjoyed one another's company. I could not blame her. And I wondered: What now? How would this work when all were under the sloping slate roof of Potomac Oaks?

I put down the top of the convertible and we sped out of the city—two handsome young people, smack in the middle of important events, two people close to the seats of power.

"Is he in trouble?" she asked, as we whizzed down Massachusetts Avenue, past the American University toward the district line.

"I doubt it, Maria," I said. "We will be smeared but I can't see any lasting harm coming our way. Ben is a charter member of the club."

She frowned. The lines on her clear forehead made her even lovelier.

"But is that fair? I mean—should we get away with whatever it is we're supposed to have done, just because of that? It's like saying a rich man shouldn't be convicted of a crime just because he's rich."

"That's just part of it, Maria. What I really meant to say is we've done nothing wrong, violated no laws, broken no traditions. That is where our real strength lies. The fact that the senator is widely respected will only facilitate our case."

"I hope so." She looked at me solemnly. "He's very upset about it, Edward. He confides in me."

"I would imagine he does."

We sped into Maryland, the humid summer air enveloping the car, making us languid and restive. I drove through Wood Acres, past the Amusement Park, and on to the George Washington Memorial Parkway, with the river on our left.

"Is he still in love with you?" I asked.

"He tells me so all the time," Maria said. "He said he can't imagine being without me."

"Maria, dear child," I said, "men say extreme and improbable things when they are devoured by passion."

"But that's just it . . . There hasn't been any passion. He won't touch me. And I'm sick of denying it to you. You're a bore, Eddie."

"Senator Hannaford is a complex man. Don't be deceived by his blunt manner or his lack of education. There are deep untapped wells in his nature. Maybe he is in love with you. But I think he knows it is a hopeless business, and I would advise you to look upon it the same way."

"I won't."

"Then at least, I beg of you, be prudent in your conduct at Potomac Oaks. You know what I mean."

"I don't need any lessons in prudence." She looked at me with a defiant stare. "He's as much mine as he is *hers*. And he's in love with me, not with her. She's had him long enough."

I took one hand from the wheel and shook a finger at her. "And she shall have him all his life. You are pursuing a will-o'-the-wisp, Maria."

"Maybe I am," she said, "but I'll settle for that. It's better than waiting for phone calls from junior chamber of commerce members and Marine lieutenants."

"Or senators' administrative assistants."

She laughed—no gloom in that girl. She was enjoying, *enjoying,* her wicked game. "They're the worst, Eddie!" She stuck her tongue out at me and I shivered. "You didn't even try, so there. But you're not a bad sort at all. A little wound up in your own affairs, but a good egg."

"That's what the girls say."

Maria giggled. "All except Marsha Treadway. Wow, is the office buzzing over *that* one. I heard Cleo telling Matt Fixx off yesterday —she acted as if Matt was at fault for not handling Marsha any better."

I sighed. "No one is at fault. Marsha deceived us all. And let that be a lesson to you. Work out your destiny with the great man as you wish, Maria, but for God's sake stay out of the confidential files."

Potomac Oaks was spurious Colonial in style, but enormously impressive. In fact, it was far more luxuriously appointed than the Hannaford ranch home in Ramada City. There were soaring columns, an endless gravel driveway, rows upon rows of high windows, all in spotless Colonial white. The house had been built in the twenties by a millionaire bootlegger, a showplace for his wife, a former *Follies* girl. The bootlegger was subsequently convicted of tax evasion, the showgirl wife went dotty and was confined to a nursing home, and the huge white house, with its attendant lawns, stables, forests, and splendid view of the river, fell into disrepair. During the war it served as a training school for Army nurses. It had twenty-seven rooms and fifteen baths all with gold fixtures, and when Ben purchased it from the bank that had held on to it from the early sixties it was a wreck. But he was a builder, a construction man, and his expert carpenters, plumbers, electricians, and masons worked it over until it emerged as the showplace of the Potomac. Everything was electrified, strengthened, buttressed, scraped, painted, and rendered impervious to termites, wind, rain, and criticism.

I always had the suspicion Fern did not like the house. It was too big. It was excessive. She was a rich woman, but she was a Ramada girl at heart—horses, dogs, long rides across the prairie, quiet evenings watching television. It almost seemed that in her quietly resentful way, she had spent double what was necessary, furnished everything in the extreme, as her revenge on the house. For example, there was a piano in the living room that made it almost impossible to conduct any sort of business there because of its intrusive presence. It was a concert grand, an antique, and finished in cream, with a gold stripe, the creation of some Georgetown homosexual who knew a sucker when he saw one. Fern had not played the piano since she was sixteen, and Ben was totally unmusical (even cowboy and hillbilly ballads bored him) and the piano sat there on the royal blue carpeting, a sullen white whale. It was extravagant, and Ben and Fern were really not that way. Back in Ramada City they lived in comparative simplicity for people of their wealth. It was almost as if the Hannafords, on arriving in Washington to set up residence, decided to lead from strength in the hostile environment—and their strength was their money.

I crunched the Pontiac into the porte-cochère. Two of Fern's Gordon setters, muscular, snuffling beasts, came running to us, slobbering and waving their behinds indecently, as I unloaded Maria's valises. Travis, the Hannafords' butler, immaculate in his starched white coat, came out of the enormous doorway to help me. I often wondered where Travis had come from. That kind of Negro seemed to me outdated, a model no longer made, one for which no spare parts were available, vanished from the catalogues. Not that he was an Uncle Tom. Quite the contrary. He was a mahogany-colored man of indeterminate age, of exceeding politeness and efficiency. Yet he was unlocatable, unreal in some way. I suppose all the race agitation of the past twenty years has made it hard for us to understand Negroes like Travis.

"Let me take those, Mr. Edward," he said. "Good day, Miss Maria. Welcome to Potomac Oaks."

"Travis," I said, "I must ask you not to address me as Mr. Edward. Mr. Deever if you will, or Edward will be fine. After all, we are both employees of the same man."

But Travis said nothing. A flat knowing smile turned his thin lips upward. No riots or revolutions for him, thank you.

While the exterior of the Hannaford mansion was a pure Colonial white, the inside was a melange of deep blues and rich golds. So had decreed Fern's fagot designer. It was all very American, very Colonial and very costly. But neither of the Hannafords enjoyed the grandeur. They were Westerners. They liked sky and sand and hot sun, native woods, and redstones.

"Ah, the young folks are with us," Senator Gage Hopewell said as we entered. Ben came forward and greeted us. Fern bussed Maria lightly on the cheek and I had the sense of them both recoiling slightly.

"I am so happy you will be staying with us," Fern said. "That city is just not safe any more for anyone."

Mrs. Hopewell—Rachel—came waddling forward. She was stern Midwestern stuff—broad-beamed, bandy-legged, frizzy-haired, and smart as the devil. Everyone liked her. "Hi honey," she said pumping Maria's hand. "I'm Mrs. Hopewell. Boy, I can see why Ben and Fern want you under lock and key out here in Potomac! Those Washington wolves wouldn't give a beauty like you a minute's rest!"

No one reacted to Rachel Hopewell's blundering sense of humor. She waddled off in that stride that told of a thousand church suppers, PTA bridge games, United Fund coffees.

I shook hands with Senator Stapp and greeted his wife, Judy. Mrs. Stapp was a former actress who had never made it, tall, black hair teased and lustrous, her face a bit too firmly defined and apprehensive. She was a publicity hound; she hungered for celebrities and "In" people.

"How do you do, Mrs. Stapp," I said. "We are sorry you didn't join us on our trip to Cavite. It was fun."

"Good Christ," Judy Stapp sniffed. "Tramp around those goddamn redwood forests and freeze? Now if you'd been surveying Palm Springs or Las Vegas you might have twisted my arm."

Swinging Sid wandered off and I was left with his spouse. When he was out of earshot (did it matter?) I said: "Twisting your arm would come under rare erotic practices, ma'am."

Her green eyes went wide. "Ha-ha. Funny boy. Does Senator Hannaford keep you around for laughs, or do you really know something?"

"I try hard, Mrs. Stapp."

"Judy."

"Of course, Judy. I enjoyed that piece in the Washington *Post* about the think-in at your home in Georgetown. Took a lot of courage to invite all those crazy bearded poets and musicians. What did the neighbors say?"

"*Neighbors?*" I liked that brazen quality in her voice. She was rumored to be the daughter of an Italian restaurant owner in Sausalito.

"Some neighbors! Those old society Washington creeps need a goose every now and then! Why, they were sick with jealousy! I had every inside poet and artist I could lay my grubby hands on." She nodded her lacquered head toward "Swinging Sid," elegant in a gold turtle-neck sweater and white linen hacking coat (it was Sunday afternoon) who was swapping gossip with Majority Leader Hopewell and my boss. "Of course, lover-boy out there thought it was a disgrace, especially when Farbelman, the black art poet—he's the one with the yellow whiskers—stood on a table and recited, 'Screw my Senator, screw me.'"

"I can understand Senator Stapp's concern," I said.

"Oh can you? Listen, those Georgetown crumbs were hanging over our back fence with their tongues dangling. They were jealous. Boy were they jealous."

"Perhaps only curious."

"Envy, Deever, envy. Listen, I hate this town and all those official people in it. They think they run things. Well, maybe they do, but not the really important things. I'm a San Francisco girl, and believe me, there's nothing in this country between San Francisco and New York."

"I rather fancy Fort Wayne, Indiana."

She turned her large-boned head sideways, one green eye fixing me with wary contempt. It had dawned on her, much to her regret, that someone in the room might be wise to her posturing. And it was unsettling that I—a callow Administrative Aide—might be that someone.

"Aren't you cute?" she asked. "Well, like I was saying they've sort of distilled all the small town crap in the middle west, and boiled Washington out of it."

"Your intolerance doesn't become someone as lovely as you, Mrs. Stapp," I lied.

"Who's intolerant? I'm bored! Bored, bored until I could shriek! You think I care how the hell the Labor and Public Welfare Committee is going to vote on rent subsidies? Or who got invited to the President's luncheon for the Peruvian Ambassador? Or why some old drunken Southerner full of grits and hog-jaw got the fattest federal court appointment? Why do you think I run off to New York every chance I can get? To keep my blood circulating, that's why. I'd congeal down here!"

"I am certain your blood is rich, red, and free-flowing," I said. Travis passed by. I took a martini from him, and asked for another scotch for Judy Stapp. "But let me suggest that you don't like Washington, because it hasn't accepted you. Don't get offended. You're right. This *is* a rural town run by rural people, or at least people who like to pretend they are country folk. Correct?"

Judy Stapp rolled her eyes around the vast living room of Potomac Oaks, then jerked her head toward Fern's hard blond figure. Fern's lady-like hands were clasped about her middle as she sat in a wingbacked chair conversing delicately with Mrs. Hopewell. "Dig them. Do I sound like I'm jealous of that crew?"

"It isn't jealousy. But I submit there is a good deal of pique on your part that people like the Hopewells and Hannafords, don't care for you."

She accepted a fresh scotch on the rocks from Travis. A warm smile illuminated her face. "Yes, I guess you've put your finger on it. It's bad enough getting the old snub from someone you admire, someone you want to be like—but it's murder getting it from those you can't stand. You are a bright boy."

"That's from Hemingway," Maria said. She had joined us— prettier, younger than Judy Stapp. A Judy Stapp before cynicism hardened the beauty, before ambition left its scars.

"What's from Hemingway?" Mrs. Stapp asked.

"You keep calling Edward 'bright boy.' That's in *The Killers*. The two men who come to murder Ole Andersen keep calling the man in the restaurant 'bright boy.'"

"Oh. You're a new one. Beautiful and intelligent. Your talent, Edward?"

The woman was impossible. When she was younger, I suppose, this air of sassy insult became her. Or at least she could get away with it. But a woman of forty-two, who has "kicked around" and been married three times, only demeans her charm with an overly bellicose manner.

"Maria is a home-town girl," I said. "She is from Ramada City. One might say she is a ward of the Hannafords."

"Crazy," Judy Stapp said.

"I don't think so at all," Maria said. "Mrs. Hannaford has invited me to come live with them—for a while anyway."

"Yeah, no Potomac mansion should be without one," Judy Stapp said. Her sly eyes studied Maria's exquisite face, the slender body in the simple blue frock. I don't know what her thoughts were: perhaps memories of a lost, wasted, intolerably sweet youth.

When she was silent and pensive—as she was now, scrutinizing Maria's face—there was a good deal of beauty, mystery, a touch of the occult in her. But in its insistent, abrasive way, Washington had dulled her sharp edges. Truth to tell, Judy Stapp was becoming a bit matronly, a bit respectable, suspicious of any woman younger and prettier than she was.

We drifted toward the television set, to watch Ben's taped appearance on *For the People* on United Broadcasting. The three senators came in from the patio. I could see Judy Stapp looking at Ben with a kind of fascinated appreciation. She, wife of "Swinging Sid," friend to fag poets and bearded artists, had always regarded my boss as the ultimate square, the total Washingtonian-cum-Southwest, a lucky millionaire with a lot of nerve and old-fashioned manners. Her husband respected and feared Hannaford, she knew, and the Swinger did not frighten easily. But she really had no use for the likes of Ben. Now she viewed him with what I could only think of as new understanding. In her hot female mind, she had divined some relationship between Ben and his heavenly young ward. Judy Stapp approved. Judy Stapp understood. She wished them both well.

As we assembled chairs in a semicircle to watch the program, she winked at me, and whispered: "Got to congratulate your senator. Maybe he's got troubles with the press, but he sure has taste."

"In everything," I said.

"Let's watch the man from Ramada handle four reporters at once," said Gage Hopewell. "Oh, I have faith unbounded in our friend. Yas."

I observed that Senator Hopewell's medicine man routine was largely for public consumption. Here, in a circle of close friends, his orotund style, his flamboyant elegance, his ruffles and flourishes were almost non-existent. His speech was normal, his choice of words not excessively florid. I noted the simple "Yas" as opposed to the full-throated, retarded, "Yaaaaaas" which he pumped out for the public and the TV cameras. Good old Gage!

"It was easy," Ben said. He sat next to Fern and patted her hand. "Comfortable, dear?"

"Yes, yes, Benjamin. Are you?"

"Fine, fine."

Did the small talk betray a trace of nervousness? Could the Parenti affair and the possible break-up of the Conglomerate fill these Lords of the Earth with doubts, tremors?

Ben's performance on *For the People* was nothing short of brilliant. He did not deny the correspondence with the Conglomerate corporations; he did not deny the letters were his; he did not deny that the passage of the Hannaford bill might afford him and his associates economic advantages. But he stuck to his guns—the Conglomerate was perfectly legal, the New Wilderness Bill was a good bill. The fact that the two circumstances might benefit him was irrelevant.

"Son," he told Wyatt Schoen of the Associated Press, "son, every law ever passed got to benefit *some*body." (He was layering his speech with a bit more cornpone and chili than usual.) "Let us assume it benefits me and my associates mightily. But it will also benefit millions of Americans in creating new jobs, goods, services, articles, and in every way increasing the gross national product and the national growth rate. That's the real key to all this."

"But Senator Hannaford," Schoen said, "isn't it against Senate tradition, indeed, is it not considered unethical to lobby for, to promote, to push laws which will give you personal gain?"

"I have never seen such a law in writing. Tradition? Precedent? Why there is not a man in the Senate who at one time or another has not voted for a law that would benefit him personally."

"B-b-b-but," said the UBC congressional correspondent, "it's a question of degree. You stand to make millions of dollars out of the National Forests."

"Son, somebody's got a right to make money out of all that useless land."

"The conservationists claim all you want to do is plunder it," the AP man commented sorrowfully.

My boss cocked his head at the reporter. "*Plunder*. What a terrible word. I hate that word. Would any of you gentlemen regard the father of our country, George Washington, as a plunderer?"

"Oh dear, oh dear," Gage Hopewell moaned. He turned to Ben, who was smiling enigmatically. "Dear Ben, you stop at nothing, yaaaaas . . ."

The reporters looked puzzled; no one responded to Senator Hannaford's challenge. He sat back, very much in command of them. "Well, then, gentlemen, let me give you all a little history lesson. Not the kind you will find in the schoolbooks, but important nevertheless. Now then, why did General George Washington move out to western Pennsylvania and Ohio and pick a fight with the Indians and the French? Now, don't look so upset, Mr. Schoen, I'm part Indian and I *know*. They weren't bothering Washington. No sir. But you will remember that Mr. Washington was a surveyor, which was a fancy way of saying he was a real estate operator, a land buyer. The great man was not motivated by patriotism, he was motivated by profit. He wanted more land for himself."

The panel of reporters laughed nervously. "Swinging Sid" shook his head and chuckled. "Only you could get away with that one, Ben. And on the air, too."

We listened—as transfixed as the reporters on the TV screen.

"Oh I'm not through with 'em yet," Senator Hannaford said, digging an elbow into Gage's side. "Professor Hannaford's history course is just beginning."

On the multi-chromed TV set, Ben's head looked wider, ruddier, than normal; the hair was coal black, edged with silver. "Now gentlemen, why do you think our beloved first President ordered a canal built from the Potomac to the Ohio River? I'll tell you why. Because for six of his eight years as President of the United States, he was also President of the James River and Kanawha Canal. Conflict of interest? Maybe. Depends how you look at it. But that, friends, is the way this great country got built—by men of vision and industry, in government and out."

"But that was a long time ago, Senator Hannaford," protested the UBC man.

"Correct! My mode of operation is condoned by precedent! By precedents established by the father of our country. Mr. Schoen and you other fellows—do you know why the west side of the Capitol is crumbling and may fall and bury us some day? I'll tell you why. Because George Washington sold the government the stone for that wall from his own quarry on Aquia Island in the Potomac. So happened it was soft sandstone. I'm a builder and I know about these things. Yes, President Washington shipped that inferior stone up here by barge and sold it to the very government he founded! You can look it up in the records. Conflict of interest? Not by my standards. Business initiative, enterprise!"

"Controlled Greed, Senator?" asked Wyatt Schoen.

"If you prefer," Ben said.

In the living room we all laughed, reveling in Ben's brash, shrewd performance. What a move! Summoning up Washington's old business transactions to defend his own wide-ranging deals!

Soon he was attacking Lou Parenti as a "small time thief and a poison pen artist." The panel of newsmen seemed to enjoy this; they were all fearfully jealous of Parenti. "I have nothing against that boy personally," Ben said generously, "but he has a long, distinguished career as a liar behind him. Why should anyone believe him now?"

From the corner of my eye, I saw Senators Hopewell and Stapp relishing each of Ben's sallies. They were wallowing in his defense. And with good reason. "Swinging Sid," as I have pointed out, still maintained his lucrative law practice in Los Angeles, representing much of the entertainment industry. He often pushed tax legislation favorable to them ("tax reform" it was known as) and was not above using his influence to squelch investigations harmful to them. And old Gage, back home in Wisconsin, was senior partner in a law firm that represented all the important dairies in the state, as well as railroads and tool manufacturers. Need I explain that legislation favorable to these interests was always looked upon with a grandfatherly eye by wily Gage? He himself would convulse the Senate with his funny sayings and windy bravado in support of price supports for butter fat, stockpiling of heavy cream, tax credits for railroads. It was a show worth seeing when Gage Hopewell lit into the enemies of his pet bills. Yaaaaaas!

But was it a conflict of interest? My own sentiments favor the Hopewells, Stapps, and Hannafords. What is a conflict? And what is an "interest?" Whose interest? Suppose the law firm of Dickens, Clerk, Manfried and Hopewell get a big fee from the dairy farmers for "service A," while Senator Hopewell himself pilots through the skim milk bill? What's wrong? As Ben pointed out, *someone* has to push the legislation through. It is my own feeling that *without* these "special interests," nothing at all would ever get done in the Congress.

While I am on this matter, let me say I do not for a minute regard this sort of senator-client relationship at all dishonest. Why should it be? A senator represents a constituency. Perhaps his constituency, like Maury Eisenberg's of Illinois, is poor Negroes; naturally he will push for laws to help them. If that is all right, why cannot Gage Hopewell go to bat for his dairy farmers? Or Sid Stapp for the TV and movie corporations? Or my boss for mining, oil, and timber people? Why is it a "conflict of interest" when Ben Hannaford tries to open useless wild land to productive purposes—and "public service" when John Tyler Lord tries to get a New Works Progress Administration appropriation for jobless Puerto Ricans?

"Well done, Ben, well done," Gage said proudly when the program was over.

"You were splendid, dear," Fern said. "The senator is often at his best when he is under unfair attack."

"We should almost thank Parenti," Sid Stapp said.

Judy Stapp crossed her legs. The whole business bored her. Her eyes took in all of us—with varying degrees of revulsion. At that moment she would have preferred to be in the midst of a hyperthyroid New York party, rubbing elbows, knees and behinds with Inside Artists and Pederast Writers. She knew all about values. No three senators, not even if they included the richest senator, the Majority Leader and her own dazzling hubby, were worth one fairy novelist.

"I'd be hesitant about thanking Parenti so soon," I warned. "He's going to keep at it."

"Let him," Ben said impatiently. "Nobody believes him."

"Of course," Gage said carefully, "we may have to tread warily on the New Wilderness Bill. Not to say that you won't have my full support on it, Benjamin. Right down the line."

Ben's wide face darkened. I saw the pulsating in his lower jaw. Gage had given the game away. We all knew S.671 was as good as dead. But Ben had hoped Gage would back him a bit stronger.

"You think so, Gage?" my boss asked.

"Weeeell . . . the President . . . you know how he hates fights.

He simply doesn't want to be bothered with any bloodletting, anything that someone might interpret as scandal. He is despondent over the split in the cabinet."

"What if Sid and I hold the votes in the committee?" Ben asked.

"If you can . . ." And Gage's airy voice trailed off, as Fern got up and invited us all into the dining room for an informal supper.

Dinners at the Hannafords could not be described as scintillating affairs. I'm not sure why. Perhaps it was because Fern and Ben were never at home in that palatial house. They were country folk and they lacked the capacity to adopt attitudes and adornments of the very rich with ease. Oh, they were not exactly uncomfortable with Travis' punctilious service, with the vintage wine, the choice cuts of meat and the sparkling silver. By no means. It was simply that they did not show any great interest in their affluence. They accepted the house, the servants, the grounds as a form of unnatural but not unpleasant environment, in the manner of a man shipwrecked on an abundant fruitful island.

I suspect the vastness of the house, the perfection of furnishings, food, and domestics, tended to dampen relaxed table talk. Moreover these dinners tended to become heavily male in emphasis. Although guests were dutifully alternated, male and female, and husbands and wives were separated, the men tended to keep up a political crossfire, shooting their comments and arguments past the bored and sometimes offended faces of the ladies. More than one Washington wife has complained to me about this. In effect the women were like those empty spaces on bookshelves where one stows a ceramic piece, a glass zebra or whatnot. The men were the volumes themselves—hard-covered, full of meaning and ideas.

"Gage," Ben was saying, "I know you're down on the New Wilderness Bill, but I have a hunch a little rewriting might change your mind."

"Yaas, yas, so it might," blew the Majority Leader. Consistency was not one of Gage Hopewell's hallmarks. Fickle, unpredictable, he could dance with a variety of partners, to all sorts of tunes. About the only issue on which Gage was immovable was the defense budget. That hallowed, bloated, fat, graft-bedewed, sack of contracts was untouchable, sacrosanct, holy. Old Gage stood in

its defense like a lion. Not a cent was ever cut from the one
hundred some-odd billions appropriated for missiles and warships.
When it was pointed out to him by Senator Maury Eisenberg,
that one particular defense contract for a metal shaft used in an
obsolete helicopter was priced at fifteen times its cost in any
spare parts catalogue, and that the government could save $100,-
000 by striking the item, Senator Hopewell had responded (to the
delight of the whirring TV cameras): "Yaas, perhaps it is a bit
excessive. But I would remind the junior senator from Illinois
that I would rather be shafted than dead." And that ended the
argument; Eisenberg never again opened his mouth about the
outrages committed in the name of national security.

"We may be past a rewriting," Gage said craftily. "Dear Ben, I
have a feeling that our esteemed President has developed a case
of frigid pedal extremities, that is to say, cold feet."

"That's the way I read it," "Swinging Sid" added.

"You're probably right," Ben said. "Mr. Hackensetter found it
convenient not to show up tonight."

"That damn Parenti," Senator Stapp said.

"Oh, Parenti, pooh," Gage Hopewell blew. "We fear him not,
do we, Ben?"

"Maybe not," Ben said, "but I'm sorry that it takes so little to
scare the White House off."

"Let us give the chief a bit more credit," Hopewell said. "What
he really needs is your firm hand at the tiller, Ben. I know for a
fact that President Kretz was upset that you were devoting so
much time and energy to the New Wilderness Bill—when he
needed your help on the Foreign Aid Bill, the Housing Bill, and
goodness knows what else."

I thought to myself: they will get Ben's help on the Foreign Aid
Bill, all right. In the form of a little surprise amendment.

"That federal housing thing will be rough," Sid said. "The
Negroes won't accept it unless it's got a provision for scattered
sites housing. Even with most of the Black Power nuts out of the
picture, we're going to get static. I've been catching hell from
Los Angeles."

"What do those people want?" complained Mrs. Hopewell,
bobbing her parakeet's face. "What do they want? Why Gage here,
my little sweetie, fought for every darn civil rights bill that's come
up, and they still hound him!"

Ben shook his head. "Got to do what we can, within the limits of what the people will allow. I mean the people, the plain folks. They all got a little of the tiger in them. And that tiger is not prepared to melt down to butter for—" He looked across the room to see if Travis was around and continued "—Little Black Sambo."

"If you ask me," Senator Stapp said, "the Congress, the Executive, and certainly the Judiciary have been way ahead of what the country wants to do for colored people. Way ahead. So have the corporations. And the churches. And the universities. But . . ."

"Say it, Sidney, say it," Gage Hopewell puffed. "It is the people themselves. The great swarming multitudes who elecet us to office. They have been the foot-draggers, yaas. We could build us a shining city for black and white people—and the white people would move away."

"Fellow named Warfield talked to me about scattered sites," Ben said. "Royce Henshaw took me to meet him. Head of an outfit called . . . what was it called, Edward?"

I peered up from my roast beef. "Triple-O," I said. "It stands for 'On Our Own.'"

"I know them," Sid said. "They were started after Second Watts. A good group, but they're beating the same dead ponies. I suppose he bugged you about scattered sites?"

"That's right," Ben said. "I told him no go. I won't back it. I won't back anything that the welder at River Rouge won't back."

I received—and rather appreciated—a sexy nudge of the knee from Judy Stapp. She had been downing the estate bottled Bordeaux with great gusto and her cheeks were flushed.

When she spoke, she twisted her red mouth, Hollywood gangster style, and let the words out *sotto voce*. "I don't know about you, bright boy, but I've never listened to so much crap in my life."

"Really?" I asked. "The affairs of state don't interest you?"

Her hard orbs circled the guests. "There's only one kind of affair here that interests me, buster." She stared at Maria—silent, eating very little, noticing no one, as the heavy male talk hummed about her. "And I bet it interests you too." In her mocking, actress' voice, she whispered in my ear, in a baby singsong: "They've just about adopted me."

"That Warfield," Ben was saying. "I would have liked to have helped him."

"We cannot move mountains, Senator," Gage Hopewell said piously.

"Look what happened to my sweetie," his wife added.

But you can give the admirals and generals anything they want, I thought. The notion of that $110,000,000,000 defense budget deadened my appetite—I'm not sure why. I kept thinking of those overpriced shafts for obsolete helicopters.

Travis approached me and said: "A Mr. Goldstein is on the telephone. He wished to speak with the senator, but I told him you would take the call."

I followed Travis into Ben's study. "Eddie?" Fred asked. "You guys are off the hook. Congratulations."

"I didn't know we were ever on one."

"Come on, kid, the Ethics Committee's been reading Parenti's column like it's the Bible. Haven't you heard the latest?"

"No."

"Couple of us called Webb Urban after your boss made his appearance on *For the People*. Senator Urban has come out four-square for the big man."

"Simpler language, please."

"Senator Urban, Chairman of the Senate Ethics Committee, says that there is absolutely no evidence of wrongdoing of any kind in regard to Senator Hannaford's activities, and that the charges raised in the Parenti columns do not warrant an investigation. How do you like them apples?"

"I like them very much, Fred. He say anything else?"

"Nope. You know the old Mormon missionary. Just a few short snappy comments. He said Senator Hannaford's explanation of his activities were candid and that there was nothing for the Ethics Committee to discuss."

"Fred, you are a dear friend. We all thank you."

"Any statement from the senator?" the journalist asked.

"No. He isn't even aware of this. But you might quote an aide —me—as saying that we never took Parenti's charges seriously, and that we intend to prosecute him for the theft of those letters."

"Good-O. Keep me advised, Ed."

I went back to the dining room feeling elated, triumphant. How good to be the bearer of happy news!

There was a burst of applause when I announced that Senator

Webb Urban, old honest Webb, that stickler for rectitude and decency had come out in support of Ben.

"Never thought he'd do otherwise," Ben said.

"Yaas, one of the giants before the flood, Senator Urban," Gage intoned. "A great believer in tradition and propriety."

"We can all breathe a bit easier, can't we?" Fern said. She tinkled the bell for Travis.

I got a silken nudge from Judy Stapp's knee again. Once more her mouth twisted toward me. "They sure cover up, don't they?" she asked rhetorically. "Guess no one is ever gonna catch the Builder with his overalls down, hey, bright boy? Except Señorita over there."

Shocked, I pulled my knee away. All I could think of to say was: "I'd go easy on the wine, Mrs. Stapp."

She jerked her lavish head. "Up yours, too, Jack."

CHAPTER TEN

Parenti reacted to Senator Urban's decision with rabid screams.
In his next column he wrote:

> Well, the world's greatest deliberative body is up to its
> old tricks. Is it any wonder that the prestige of the
> United States Senate has never been lower? When a
> man with Senator Webb Urban's reputation can lend
> himself to a whitewash of one of the worst scandals in
> Senate history, something is rotten on Capitol Hill. This
> column has revealed in the past week the outrageous
> manipulations of Senator Benjamin Bow Hannaford,
> Chairman of the Interior and Insular Affairs Committee,
> in his attempt to ram through a bill that would reap
> hundreds of millions in profits to a corporate monstros-
> ity he has been putting together. Every pressure imagi-
> nable has been put on committee members to vote for
> the Hannaford Bill, which would open our National
> Forests to unlimited exploitation.
>
> But these revelations apparently did not move the
> Chairman of the Senate Ethics Committee, Senator Ur-
> ban, who is supposed to be the watchdog of the es-
> teemed one hundred. Senator Urban says he has found
> nothing to investigate, no conflict of interest. We sug-
> gest he stick around. Why, we ask, why did Senator
> Lester Goodchapel of Indiana change his vote so sud-
> denly? Why did Senator Alford Kemmons of Nebraska,
> dear Airborne Alf, change his vote? We will have more
> to say about these curious developments, and then per-

haps Senator Urban and his Ethics Committee colleagues will see fit to abandon their old creed, "Thou
shalt not speak ill of another United States Senator."

Ben and I agreed that Parenti was bluffing—that he did not
know the inside of the Goodchapel affair or the switch in Kemmons' vote.

"Besides," I pointed out, "Senator Goodchapel's change of
vote had nothing to do with *us*. Albon Blake arranged it."

As for Kemmons, I could say nothing. He had been bought
twice. Once by the Kape people; once by us; he was probably available for purchase by anyone willing to cough up the price. But
truthfully, neither of us were overconfident. If the Ethics Committee had cleared us, we were evidently dead on the New Wilderness Bill.

Thus troubled—and troubled particularly by Ben's unease—I
was surprised by an anonymous caller late one afternoon. "Some
nut," Cleo said to me. "You can tell they're nuts when they
mumble into the phone. He wants you."

"Mr. Deever?" a nasal voice asked.

"Yes. Who is this?"

"Yew don't know me. Got some information yew might want.
No charge. Tellin' yew this because I like your boss. I hate that
damn Wop who's been after him in the papers." The accent was
southern; possibly Tidewater.

"May I ask your name?"

"Don't matter. Now listen. I know how them letters got stole
from your office. Girl named Marshy Treadway stole them. Little
ole girl with big tits who used to work with yew."

"We are aware of that." I felt like an idiot. Was I agreeing on
the size of Marsha's bosom—or the fact that we knew she had
stolen the Conglomerate papers?

"Yeah, but how she done it. She snuck 'em out at night, and
then she took 'em to the Pennsylvania Insurance Building to my
gal's office. My gal is a friend of Marshy. The two of them and me
got drunk on beer and then we Xerox'd all them papers."

"Why did you lend yourself to this?"

"Shoot, man. I had no idea what was in them letters. Marshy
said it was just some office stuff. She dropped one, and I read it,
and I figured she was out to get something on your boss."

"Is that all you have to tell me?"

"Well, you ain't checked that file too careful. I kept that copy she dropped. Letter to Petrol-Air. Yew want it back?"

"Yes. If you could mail it to me."

"Sure, sure. Ole Marshy really put the blocks to you boys. One other thing. After I called her on these here letters, and asked why was she behavin' so bad to the senator, she said, 'I know lots more, only it ain't on paper.'"

"Well, thank you, thank you very much."

He hung up—one of those faceless drifters on the edge of life in the great city. In my mind's eye I saw him—lean, slack-jawed, perhaps a motorcycle driver, a chauffeur, one of those fringe people. I knew he would tell me little else, and I knew he could not be depended upon as a witness. But he had given me a warning: *I know lots more only it ain't on paper*. It could only be the safe deposit box; the strange incident of the $250,000 from N. Krallis. But what was I to do? Warn her off? Threaten her? Pay her fare out of town?

Clearly we had not heard the last of Parenti. He would dig and pry and bribe and threaten until he was able to abuse us again. The Senate Ethics Committee's failure to act had inflamed him. Nor was my state of mind soothed when the senator, as we lunched in the Senate Dining Room, surrounded by his peers, the eminent men who respected him, who needed him, leaned toward me and said, in a hushed voice:

"You get yourself some good investments with that twenty thousand?"

I was so shocked that I almost choked on my Crab Maryland.

"No sir, it's sitting with the rest of the special fund."

"How does it stand?" he asked. Across the room Senators Maury Eisenberg and Royce Henshaw waved at us.

"Well sir," I said, in a small voice, "there are one hundred and ninety thousand dollars in the box. We gave ten thousand to our airborne friend."

"Yes, but twenty thousand of that is yours. Young man like you should be thinking about the future. Why not let me invest it? Stick it in oil wells. If it comes up dry, Uncle Sam pays. If it comes in, he still lets you keep most of it. You can't lose."

It was at that, for the first time perhaps in our long affectionate relationship, that I think I truly resented him—just a little. I don't know why. It just seemed to me that there were limits to how much a man could reasonably want to take out of his country's wealth. And perhaps that is why I had kept the "gift" in cold unproductive cash.

"Stick it in certificates of deposit, son, do something with it. It'll just get mossy there in the Riggs National Bank."

"I will, Senator. Soon as I get around to it. What about the rest . . . the special fund?"

"That must remain liquid. Shortly we'll be putting it to use. Like manure it will be spread around."

Seersucker jacket properly rumpled, his patrician face flushed, John Tyler Lord rushed into the dining room. He shot a pained puzzled stare at us, started toward our table—both Ben and I greeted him—and then executed a sloppy right-face, and hurried toward Henshaw and Eisenberg. I had the feeling he wanted to tell us something but lacked the resolve.

Back in our office, Fred Goldstein called me from the Senate Press Gallery. "You better get down here, Ed. Maybe your boss better get into the chamber too. John Tyler Lord is unloading—on him, on the Ethics Committee and on the whole United States Senate."

The senator was sitting in on a Foreign Relations subcommittee meeting at that moment. I hesitated. Should I tell him of the Lord attack—and have him wade onto the Senate floor in full fury? Then I thought better of it. If Lord were out for blood, it would be better for Ben not to sit there and take abuse: let him answer Lord on his own terms, on his own time.

I hurried down to the basement, hopped on the subway and got to the Senate in a few minutes. At the door from the cloakroom to the chamber I saw a group of pages, whispering and nodding at me. The little monsters! They always knew when something was up, when someone was in trouble. As I walked by them, through the double doors into the great chamber, I thought I heard one say: "Fearless Fosdick to the rescue." And this was followed by a rude titter.

Senator Lord was at his desk, in mid-speech, as I entered and walked quietly to one of the long dark brown couches in the corner of the chamber. Depressing items, these couches, rather like the furniture one would find in the waiting room of a disreputable doctor.

"Mr. President," Lord was saying, "Mr. President it is with great reluctance that I make these statements, but someone must make them. This is an unpleasant matter. This is an embarrassing matter. And I am well aware that I am violating one of the oldest rules of the club . . ."

From my seat in the corner I scanned the hall. There could not have been more than a dozen senators present. Most of them were busy with committee assignments. No bill was under debate. I imagined that the presence of even *that* many—twelve or thirteen —was due to Lord's advertising his intention to a few sympathetic ears. Senator Jack Mull, the good-natured farmer from Georgia was presiding. I'm not sure that Senator Mull had strong feelings about anything except price supports for agricultural products grown in his home state. But he was one of that group of amiable, middle-roading men who were awed by Ben.

"Mr. President," Lord went on, "I am sick to my stomach about all this nonsense about 'the club,' about 'the establishment,' about some vague, semi-secret, self-perpetuating mysterious group that is alleged to run this great body and set the rules. I have had enough of this club, and I suspect the American public has also!"

I looked up at the Press Gallery. Parenti was there, in a front row pew. He rarely attended sessions of the Senate unless some important debate was in progress. I could only conclude that Lord had tipped him off in advance. Indeed as the senator from Vermont continued, I had the notion that collusion was evident —that Parenti had put the pale aristocrat up to his destructive speech, or perhaps had written it for him.

Next to Parenti was my friend Fred Goldstein. I caught Fred's eye, as if to thank him for calling me, and he, in turn, clapped a palm to his cheek, as if to say: *Oh boy!*

"We witnessed last night, Mr. President," Senator Lord went on, "the club at its best, working as always to protect, to insulate, to preserve the sanctity of its own—with no regard for the American public, or indeed, for truth and integrity. I refer, Mr. President, to the remarks of the distinguished senior senator from Wyoming, the widely respected chairman of the Senate Ethics Committee. In a statement issued last night, the chairman of the Ethics Committee said he saw no reason to pursue an investigation of Senator Hannaford."

There was a buzzing from the floor. One did not address another senator by *name* on the floor. It was always the distinguished, or the respected, or the esteemed senator from this or that state. But Lord was intent on smashing idols, and thus far, he was succeeding, although I had the feeling that he himself might be the ultimate smashee.

"Yes, Mr. President, I realize I have just violated another club rule. I have dared to address a colleague by name. Well, I am fed up with this hypocritical formalism. I am particularly fed up with it when it is a façade for unethical, corrupt, and devious behavior!"

At this, Senator Gabriel T. Tutt who had wandered in, staggered toward his desk, waved his arm at Senator Mull, the latter burrowed deeply into his chair of authority, unhappy in his role of presiding officer.

"Mr. President!" bellowed Senator Tutt. "The senator from Vermont is out of order. He—"

But Lord was on fire. There is something to be said for the reckless nerve, the drive of these thin-blooded New Englanders. He spun toward Tutt, shaking his finger. "I did not yield! I will not yield! Mr. President, I will not be interrupted, and I ask the chair to permit me to finish my remarks!"

"Ch-ch-chair so rules," Mull said. And he banged the gavel once. But Gabe Tutt was aroused: he saw what was coming. As a high-ranking club member, a true Establishmentarian, he was not going to see his beloved group of insiders under attack. He stumbled from his desk and plodded toward Senator Henry DiFalco of Connecticut—a hard-working little fellow who had absolutely nothing in common with Gabe Tutt, but happened to be the nearest to him. He leaned over DiFalco's desk and began to harangue him. Lord tried to ignore him and continued.

"Mr. President, this means that the Senate Ethics Committee will not even deign to look into the charges brought out in the newspapers, charges documented with photostated letters between Senator Hannaford and members of a group of corporations, who would benefit to the tune of millions, through the passage of Senator Hannaford's New Wilderness Bill!

"I suggest that there is a conflict of interest here of such overwhelming proportions, of such naked obviousness, that it demands our attention, it screams for investigation. And what has happened? Senator Hannaford has blithely denied that he has done anything wrong. He simply states, over and over, that he has a right to push for the bill but also boasts that he will do anything he wants in the way of corporate business! He said so himself yesterday, on the television, and I quote 'My business is my own business, and it has helped this country grow rich and strong!' Yes, perhaps it *is* his business—but not when it forces itself upon this great body, influences legislation, affects our national heritage, and results in Senator Hannaford playing the triple role of lobbyist, legislator, and legatee! Do we have revealed here a new Trinity, Mr. President? A new triple godhead?

"The American public is fed up with a lot of our doings! If we have an Ethics Committee, for God's sake, let it concern itself with Ethics! I suggest that Senator Hannaford—"

With a roar, Gabe Tutt spun around from Senator DiFalco's desk and bawled at the chair: "Mr. President, if you won't shut that man up, Ah will! He is in violation of every tradition of this great body! He dare not foul this great chamber with pussonal attacks on another senator, one of our greatest Americans! I demand, Mr. President, you tell the senator his remarks are outa order, that they were outa order from the start, and that they will be stricken from the Congressional Record!"

Mull went into a whispered huddle with the Secretary of the Senate. Lord, sensing that the ax was about to fall, resumed his speech:

"Mr. President, we have a right to ask the Ethics Committee to look into the questions raised by Mr. Parenti! I don't care whose reputation is at stake! If it is mud Mr. Parenti has thrown, let's establish it as mud and throw it back at him! But if he has revealed the truth, let the truth be known! Let us not shirk! We must look deeply inside ourselves! Who are we? What are we? By what right do we drape ourselves in the mantle of virginity, of spotless, blameless probity? Who says we are all that pure?"

He went on for about thirty seconds or so: there was a lot of agitation on the floor now. Senator Tutt staggered away from Di Falco's desk and began to berate Maury Eisenberg and then lurched toward the presiding officer's table. Poor Lord! He had violated a most sacred Senate rule and was about to be punished for it. Of course, in his erratic way, he had accomplished what he set out to—to keep the fires going under the so-called Hannaford case. But I knew he could not prevail against the massed will

of the mighty body. Senator Mull was now gaveling Lord down.
I saw Parenti guffawing and talking loudly to Fred Goldstein.

"The Chair rules," Senator Mull said huskily, looking at the
Secretary of the Senate, "that the remarks by the junior senator
from Vermont are out of order. The Chair asks that he be seated,
and the Chair further rules that all his remarks be stricken from
the Record."

"I c'ngratlate the Chair," mumbled Gabe Tutt.

Lord was still on his feet. His pale head was splotched with
rage. "Of course, Mr. President, I will abide by the Chair's
ruling."

"You damn better," Tutt belched—loud enough for the gallery
to hear. Naturally, he was not reprimanded.

"As I was saying, Mr. President," John Tyler Lord went on,
flashing an aggrieved look at Tutt, "I will abide by the ruling, but
I do not withdraw a word of what I have said. I also advise the
Senate that I am about to distribute to the press the full text of
my remarks, including the parts I have been forbidden to deliver
here on the floor. I shall have more to say on this matter both on
the floor of the Senate and in the Interior Committee."

Sweeping up his papers, Lord hurried out, his head down. There
was a momentary hush. Then Jack Mull recognized Gabe Tutt.

"Mr. President," Tutt roared, "we have witnessed a disgraceful
spectacle. A member of the Senate pussonally insulting another
member right here on the floah. In my twenty-two yeahs heah
I have nevah witnessed such downright villainous behavior. And I
say to you, Mr. President, it is the result of Commonism, pornography, liberalism, and Harvard University that we find such disrespect for tradition!"

On he mumbled, meaningless, meaningless mumblings, until
through the main doors came the rotund figure of Gage Hopewell, the Majority Leader. There were *Oohs* and *Ahs* from the
public gallery. Everyone liked Gage. And I must confess, it was
good to see Old Honey-Tonsils sailing across the maroon carpeting—oily, suave, helpful, reasonable, all things to all men—
and toward Gabe Tutt, to whom he whispered something. *And lo!*
Gabe Tutt shut up and sat down.

Consoling myself with the knowledge that Hopewell and all
the other lords of the club would be very much on our side, and
that Gabe Tutt's blasts on our behalf could not do us much dam-

age, I hurried up to the Press Gallery to pick up a copy of Lord's handout. There he was, full of Vermont integrity, sitting in the tiny television booth with its electric blue curtains, reading his statement for the TV cameras.

I pushed my way through a mob of reporters, studied Lord's self-righteous face for a moment, and got an extra copy of his attack on my boss. He had pretty much said what he wanted to say before being gaveled down.

But my eye caught one paragraph that seemed to me below-the-belt stuff, not worthy of a man of Lord's education and breeding.

"In the past few weeks," he wrote, "there have been reports in the press and rumors in congressional circles about some very odd vote changes, peculiar about-faces by members of the Interior Committee vis-à-vis the New Wilderness Bill. They are worthy of study, if only to put the rumors at rest. It is too much to hope that the two senators whose attitudes toward the bill have taken such unpredictable turns would come forth with a frank explanation as to why they changed their minds. Perhaps they did so out of an honest appraisal of the bill's merits. What else is one to think of a United States Senator? But if that is the case, let them explain so, publicly, and put the rumors to rest."

He was getting at Goodchapel and Kemmons; how much he knew I was not certain. But I suspected he knew a good deal, and that he was working hand-in-glove with Parenti. And Kemmons worried me. Airborne Alf drank. When he drank he talked.

"Your boss gonna answer this?" Fred Goldstein asked me, as I elbowed my way past reporters and cameramen into the anteroom of the radio-TV side of the Press Gallery.

"It's rough stuff, Ed," a man from NBC said. "Lord must know more than he's letting on to."

"I can't speak for the senator, fellows," I said. "Senator Urban has obviously read all the Parenti columns, and he disagrees with Senator Lord. And I doubt that any man in Washington is more respected for his honesty than Webb Urban."

"I know, Eddie," Fred Goldstein persisted. "But is Hannaford gonna say anything?"

"I thought he said whatever had to be said on *For the People*," I replied.

Senator Hannaford read Lord's address and I noted an unusual gravity on his face. "Damned fool Yankee blue-blood," Ben said. "He'll get himself in trouble. He and Parenti are working together on this. Let's go after the easy one—the Big Wop. You have any notions, Edward?"

"Let me see if I can get a confession from Marsha that she stole the letters. Maybe she'll say he put her up to it. Or bribed her. It's bound to make him look bad."

Ben nodded his agreement. "I don't want the girl hurt," he said. "But see what you can do." Then a bit of the old Hannaford shone through. Undaunted, he winked at me, and said: " 'Go to the lost sheep of the house of Israel.' Edward, 'Be ye therefore as wise as serpents and as harmless as doves.' "

"Not quite that harmless. I have a feeling Marsha may be Parenti's—forgive me—soft underbelly."

From one of Albon Blake's cronies I borrowed a small tape recorder which fitted inside my interior coat pocket. The tiny microphone rested underneath the second button on my Dacron shirt. Thus armed I met Marsha for lunch at Duke Zeibert's.

I must confess she looked good, and for a moment I had a twinge of old lust. The memories were sweet: it was good to have all that dependable, available, uncomplaining flesh—generous, warm, accessible—and suffer so little emotional involvement with it. I have a notion this is what ruins a lot of marriages. The sex is splendid for a while, but when these ineffable physical joys, those exquisite titillations of nerve endings become dulled with emotion, with fear, hate, jealousy—yes, with *love* if you will—the fun goes out of it. A cynical view, I know. But at least I am candid. Perhaps it explains why I have never married.

"Marsha, you look marvelous!" I said, rising, and kissing her. She did, too—a new dark green dress, her hair, for a change, smartly set in little curly puffs.

"Thanks, Eddie. Can't say the same for you. No kidding, you look pale. I think you work too hard."

"I am a bit harried. Thanks to your new beau." I like the old-fashioned word. It seemed to me to describe perfectly Marsha's male friends. They were indeed "beaux." I suspect some of them referred to her as their "sweetheart."

We ordered, and chatted about minor matters. She was not working yet, but had no worries about finding a job. I had the feeling that Marsha's family was pretty well-fixed. Her father ran a hay, grain, seed, and feed business in western New York State and she was an only child. I think she got remittances from home as needed. This knowledge helped ease any guilt I might have had. Yes, she was still seeing Lou Parenti. He was "a lot of laughs, a real fun guy."

"We hardly think so," I said. "I'm afraid he does not come across to us as an Art Buchwald."

"Well, you wouldn't. Not now that he's got the goods on you." She smiled over her Bloody Mary. Our friendly lunch was becoming embittered.

"Has he really?" I asked.

"Don't you know it."

"If he has what you refer to as 'the goods' on us," I said, "maybe you were the one who supplied the goods."

"Maybe." She cocked her head—defiant, enjoying her revenge.

"You will regret your rashness, Marsha. You have broken the law by stealing those letters."

"I never said I stole anything. That's not a nice accusation to make to an ex-girlfriend. You're as bad as those FBI squares." She took a hefty swig of her Bloody Mary and her eyes flashed. "And by the way, you can tell your friends at the Justice Department to call off the bloodhounds. They interfere with my social life. They're a couple of drags, anyway."

"The FBI has been questioning you?"

"And I'm sick of them. They're so polite I could vomit."

Ben was really putting the pressure on the Justice Department, on Judge Moscowitz. Though I confess, I did not feel too much pain for Marsha. One FBI man, two, or a platoon of them—she could handle them.

"Marsha, if you will level with me, I'll see to it that the FBI leaves you alone."

"Making deals all the time, aren't you, Edward? Boy, you never change."

"Unless you've already told them you *did* steal the letters and *did* give them to Parenti."

She smiled, her full lips spreading across her chubby pretty face. Inhaling, her projecting bosom inflated, and I thought with fleeting sorrow of the hours I had spent cuddling in that warm pillow.

"Nuts to you. I won't say a thing."

She ate voraciously, devouring her crab cakes and potatoes au gratin, ordering another drink while I toyed unhappily with my Health Salad.

"Marsha, I happen to know a lot more than the FBI about your misguided favors for Parenti," I said. "You stole those letters from the green folder on the senator's desk last week. You took them to the Pennsylvania Insurance Building at night. You have a girl-friend there who works late now and then. She drinks a lot of beer and she has a boyfriend, a fellow with a southern accent, who is also a beer drinker. The three of you got tanked, and then you and this girl Xerox'd the Conglomerate file, and turned the copies over to Parenti the next day."

Her cheeks reddened and she stopped eating, her eyes fixed on me—mocking, sullen, the eyes of a wicked child found out.

"Now as it happened," I went on, "neither of your beer-swilling chums had any idea, nor did they care, what was in the letters. But you happened to drop one of the originals. It was a note to the Petrol-Air Corporation. The male member of your trio picked it up, saw Senator Hannaford's name on it, and was nice enough to telephone me about it. He identified you as the redheaded gal with the big tits. The way he pronounced your name it came out Marshy, a common error among culturally deprived southern whites."

Marsha pouted. "The dirty bastard." Yet she was not really angry.

"Yes he is, Marsha."

"Drunken bum."

"And that."

"Why'd he snitch to you?" she asked. "What was it to him?"

"Marsha, people in this town have an uncontrollable need to shoot their mouths off. I don't care what the subject is, who is involved, how secret the proceedings. Someone will blab. This town is a spy's dream because no one can keep their mouth shut. I don't know. Maybe it's that swampy air we live in. At least three times a day I get calls from helpful tipsters, some of them worth-less, some lies, some lunatic mutterings, but every now and then someone has a jewel for me. We are a city of blabbermouths—your-self included. We are a community of gossips, rumor-mongers, tattle-tales, snitchers and sneaks. You snitched on *us*. Your friend snitched on *you*.

"So right now, I want you to admit to me the following: a)

you stole the Conglomerate file from Senator Hannaford's office, and b) you Xerox'd them and returned the originals, and c) you gave the Xerox'd copies to Lou Parenti of the Washington *Truth*. Speak, child."

She hesitated. I had activated the tiny tape recorder. Now I could feel the silent spinning of the clear plastic spools against my heart. The mechanism was like a second heart, one that would have given me a lot less ache than the one of muscle and blood that had driven me to Marsha's embraces.

"Why should I tell you?" she asked. "You're the all-time rat in my book."

"We'll make a deal to help you. The senator and I are very fond of you, Marsha, and we don't want you to get into trouble."

"You don't even lie well any more."

"It is the truth. If you admit to me the items I have mentioned, I can promise you very little will happen."

Marsha turned her head sideways, an impudent gesture. "You two really think you run the whole world, don't you?"

"Not quite. But we're on our way."

"Okay, what do I care? Sure, I took the letters. I knew all about that file and the deals you had with those other companies. One peek into the folder was all I needed and I knew about the New Wilderness Bill. What a robbery!"

"Did Parenti get you to steal them?"

There was a moment's hesitation—and I could not tell whether she was lying or not. "Nope. I took them on my own."

"And out of a deep concern for the profession of journalism, you then took it upon yourself to have the documents photostated, and then you handed them over to a surprised Mr. Parenti?"

"Yes. If you say so."

"I want you to say so."

"Yes, I did. Eddie I got fed up with you and Hannaford getting everything your way." She grimaced. "Oh, that's baloney. I did it to get back at *you*—for throwing me out the way you did. You were lousy to me, Eddie, the lousiest any man has ever been."

"Dear child," I said, letting my paw rest on hers. "I had no idea I had hurt you."

"No, you wouldn't. You have no emotions. You're Senator Hannaford's machine, that's all."

"'That is unkind. I am very fond of you."

"Ah, cut it out, Eddie." I detected a sniffle. That I had hurt Marsha, I was sorry. But dammit, she had landed on her—feet?—with Parenti. What I was sorry about was her nerve in stealing the letters, her ingratitude.

"Well, you admit it then—you took the letters, photocopied them, and gave them to Parenti as an act of revenge against me?"

"Yes, yes, I did. So what?"

I called for a check, shaking my head sadly. "You have done great harm to a great American, a noble public servant. I don't care about myself. I'll survive. And so will the senator. But you made a lot of trouble for him. He should be working hard at affairs of state, on the needs of government—and now he has to be defending himself against the wild charges of a scoundrel like Parenti."

She stared at me as if I were blaspheming. "Cut the crap, will you, Eddie?" Marsha asked rhetorically. "Jesus, don't you listen to anything except your own voice, your boss', and his pals up there on the Hill? Everyone—I mean *everyone*—knows him for what he is. A crook. A lousy crook."

"That's a terrible thing to say."

"You better get used to it. Everyone is saying it. Y'know, Ed, you're too close to your work. You should get out and talk to people. It's gotten so people'll believe the worst about anyone in Congress, and they're believing it about Big Ben. Ask anyone. What is he? And they'll tell you. A crook."

So ended a disheartening lunch. I shut off the minirecorder, satisfied that I had her confession. I would have to decide whether to edit the tape or not. Did I want it disclosed that this girl was driven to her act of revenge because I had discarded her? But the goods were there; and we would need them. Yes, she was a vengeful thief. She was in cahoots with an irresponsible journalist, a scavenger, a man who had long demonstrated his hatred of Senator Hannaford.

After leaving Marsha I hailed a cab. An elderly man with a Maryland accent was at the wheel. He had that dead-center middle-class quality that I liked. Perhaps he was a retired cop or fireman, many of whom drove cabs. He was polite and not unintelligent.

As we drove through the steaming streets we chatted about

various people on the Hill—Senator Hopewell, President Kretz, others.

Suddenly I said to him, as if to take up Marsha's challenge: "And what do you think of Senator Hannaford?"

"Who?"

A good sign: if we were not well known, we would be less in danger.

"Ben Hannaford."

"The one Parenti's been writing about?"

"Yes, that's the man. How do you think he stacks up?"

The driver laughed. "You ask me," he said, "he's a crook."

Depressed, I presented the tape of Marsha's confession to Ben, but he seemed uninterested. He had come to the conclusion that he had to face up to his opponents in the Interior Committee. He would force a vote on the New Wilderness Bill. Let Lord bluster and Henshaw wring his hands, let Urban sit there sniffishly, he would ask for a vote—and he told me, he would *win*.

The vote that doomed the New Wilderness Bill was close but it was foreordained. The Parenti columns had done their dirty work. While the Senate leaders had rallied behind Ben, while Webb Urban and his five colleagues on the Ethics Committee had argued that he was blameless, it would have been impossible to report the bill favorably at this point.

We went into executive session, all sixteen committee members. Ben made some preliminary remarks. He cited our trip to Cavite National Forest as evidence of his fair handling of the argument. He stressed the fact that one could mine and drill and cut trees without injuring the beauty of these places. Not once did he allude to Parenti's attacks on him.

The vote to report the bill favorably out of committee was defeated nine to seven.

Senators Urban, Lord, Erlenmeyer, Henshaw, Putnam, Ussery, and Hopkins all voted against us. We had never expected to carry them. What stunned us was that Lester Goodchapel and Alford Kemmons joined them. Nine votes and S.671 was dead.

When the clerk of the committee called the roll, Lester Goodchapel, shifting his lard in his shapeless suit, drew his breath in and peering at Ben through the rimless glasses that scrambled his eyes, said loudly: "No."

That loud "No" meant one thing. He was not afraid of Albon

Blake, or Ben, or the tape that recorded his night of passion. He was saying, in effect: *You are a crook and I am not afraid of you.*

And he was calling our bluff. He knew Ben Hannaford was not a mean or evil man; he knew that the way things stood, the tape would not be shown to Mrs. Goodchapel. And in that curious manner in which intelligence is communicated on the Hill, the manner in which the ups and downs of prominent people are all but wafted on the air, like the odors of fear and rage which animals are able to detect, even Lester Goodchapel understood that Ben was in trouble, that the big man was on the defensive.

As for Alford Kemmons' negative vote, what can I say? Cheapjohn manipulator, seller of his vote—what could we expect? I wondered where the money was—that ten thousand from Mr. N. Krallis' coffers which I had stuffed in his breast pocket that lunatic afternoon.

"Your sentiments are noted, gentlemen," Ben said with regret. "I will make no further attempt to press for S.671 at this session. I still feel it is a constructive measure. A curious combination of opponents—from the ends of the spectrum, men of great power and wealth, malcontents, professional bird lovers, and relentless enemies of mine in the press, have seen fit to defeat this measure."

"Mr. Chairman," Senator Urban said tautly. "Many of us have opposed this bill from the start, myself included. I do not feel that any of the categories you have listed would cover my vote. Nor that of other committee members."

"I did not include the senior senator from Wyoming in my comments," Ben said. "Nor do I question the motives of any member of this committee who voted against the bill. I merely deplore the atmosphere generated by opponents of the measure."

John Tyler Lord fidgeted in his seat. "I remind the Chair, that I opposed this bill from its inception. I've always argued for a bill to strengthen the Act of 1964—but with due respect to the Chair, S.671 was not designed with that in mind."

I expected Ben to counterattack. But he only shuffled papers in front of him, and looked around the table. At that moment I sensed he was tired. The Ben Hannaford I had known some months ago, would have waded into John Tyler Lord—with humor, Biblical quotations, a threat, an insult. But Ben was running down—just a little.

Kemmons kept covering his wrinkled face. What a betrayal! After all the trouble we had gone to to straighten him out! He had difficulty looking at Ben, as the committee business droned on—Erlenmeyer wanted a dam built back home, Ussery had some questions about water rights in his state. All of them were much concerned with home folks. What was wrong with that? As Ben pointed out everyone had a constituency he had to satisfy. Well, his was a little bigger, a little more complicated. Why was he subject to attack because of it?

After a half hour, he turned the Chair over to Senator Stapp and nodded at me. We walked the corridors in silence.

In the office, Cleo came toward me. "Been some shooting in Djarak. Three Marines killed." I went to my cubicle and turned on the station that carried round-the-clock news.

"*. . . loss of American lives is reported from the Persian principality of Djarak. A mortar attack by the rebel left-wing Communist guerrilla group, resulted early this morning in the death of three Marines, members of the 451st Mobile Assault Team, who were landed in Djarak last month to support the regime of Sheik Aziz, the tiny oil state's pro-Western ruler . . .*"

I reported the news to Ben.

"Going the way I said it would," he said. "Get hold of Albon Blake and arrange for us to meet with him. Tell him to figure out some neutral ground. We've got to push the Djarak Amendment. Edward, we are not dead yet. By no means."

"I never thought we were."

"Get after Blake. Find out why that son-of-a-bitch Kemmons double-crossed us for the second time."

"I will. And I think we're in good shape, Senator. In spite of what just happened in the committee."

His rugged face was suffused with humor, with the expectation of a new battle, a new foray. You could not get the man down. He took off his dark blue jacket. In his tailored white shirt, he had the torso of a line-backer, a college wrestler. "Our text is from St. Matthew, Edward. 'He that endureth to the end shall be saved.'"

An hour later a manila envelope was delivered to me by a Capitol policeman. It bore Senator Kemmons' return address. I knew what was in it. There they were, snug, stacked, rubber-banded. All ten thousand. With the money was a note.

Dear Edward,

The enclosed was delivered to my office evidently by
mistake. Miss Craigie advises me that you were the one
who brought it here, and I therefore am returning it.
As you know, it has always been my intent to vote
against S.671, not that I do not have the deepest respect for Senator Hannaford and feel he has presented a
good case for the bill. But my conscience dictates that I
oppose the bill.

Sincerely,

Alford Kemmons

It was a bad year for gift-giving. First, the White House had
sent back that damned cooler with its precious cargo of bull's
semen; and now, our special fund would be richer by $10,000
thanks to Alford Kemmons. Whether the Kape interests had
bought him off once more; whether he had begun to worry about
the new "campaign gift"; or whether he was due for another windfall as the result of calling off another of his abortive "investigations" I do not know. At this late stage I hardly cared. Ben had
dropped the New Wilderness Bill. But he had not dropped his
determination to create the Conglomerate. And to that end we
found ourselves that night in a three-room suite in the Monroe-
Plaza, guests of the elegant lobbyist, Mr. Albon Blake.

Blake was always at his most optimistic, his most obsequious
in the presence of Senator Hannaford. I think he understood
Ben's deep-rooted contempt for him, but Blake was a man who
refused to accept scorn. The more you insulted him, the broader
his toothy smile, the cheerier his greeting, the gayer his manner.

"I am sorry we lost the battle, Senator," Blake said, after we
had removed our coats and settled down in the luxurious Regency
furniture. The suites at the Monroe-Plaza are superbly adorned.
Blake used them often to concoct his schemes, to make payment,
perform favors, educate the uneducated. "But after all, it's only
a battle, not the whole war." Again, that shellac smile froze his
wide mouth, his big white teeth.

It bothered me that Ben had decided to go to Blake, to function
through him. All through the struggle to pass the New Wilderness
Bill, he had warned Blake to remain hidden, to move only when

told to, to keep hands off the committee. Only once had he been called upon—in the Goodchapel matter—and even then, he had angered Ben with his *modus operandi*. I took it as a measure of Senator Hannaford's impatience that he would now approach Blake and work hand in glove with him.

"I assume you've contacted all the participants," Senator Hannaford said.

"I took care of that today," Blake said.

"And their reaction?"

"Splendid, splendid!" the lobbyist said. He clasped his smooth hands on his narrow chest, the manicured fingers laced on his twenty-dollar French tie. The monstrous gold cufflinks blazed. "They are wary, Senator, but I would say we're in good shape."

"In plain goddamn English," Ben said, "what do they think?"

Blake was still grinning. Nothing daunted him; nothing discouraged him. "Dover Plains wants out. Tramlett-Hewes wants out. Jackwitt is unhappy and would like out. Petrol-Air is dubious. And Longhorn will go down the line with us."

Ben got up and prowled the thick gold carpeting. He kicked his shoes off.

"That is one hell of an optimistic report," he said. "We lose on the New Wilderness Bill and they run like scared quail. Every millionaire I ever knew had a little crap in his blood." He looked at me. "Don't ever forget that, Edward. Blake here knows it, but he wouldn't admit it."

"Senator, they are a little apprehensive," he said. "You know . . ."

"Know what?" snapped Ben.

"We did promise them the New Wilderness Bill. In fact, Senator, some of them understand the Conglomerate as being dependent upon development rights in the National Forests. Their feeling is that was the *only* inducement."

"We never spelled it out in so many words," I offered. "They have to understand there are limits to what the senator can do."

"We had that bastard Kape beaten. We made a fool of him at the hearings. It was that Wop who killed us." Ben shook his head. He was seething, and this was unlike him. No man had better control of his emotions—and now they were getting the better of him. "If that Treadway girl hadn't gotten ideas . . ."

"We've got the goods on her," I said, feeling a twinge of guilt even as I said it. Was not my rejection of Marsha the cause of our present crisis?

"Too late for that, Edward," Ben said. "We can save that tape to use on Parenti."

"It will need editing," I said.

Blake grinned. That was his department—phonily edited tape, stolen films, faked photographs, bugged bedrooms. "We'll handle that, Edward. I've got a fellow who can snip and patch so it sounds absolutely foolproof. He runs it through an echo chamber and lays in some background presence."

Ben was pacing, his arms folded, his corded hands kneading his great biceps. I had the sense that he wished he were back on a construction site, amid the cranes and hoists and earth-movers, shouting orders to the payload driver, the man on the grading machine.

"Dammit, I want those companies," he said. "I want it more than I've ever wanted anything."

"We're not dead yet," chirped the lobbyist.

Senator Hannaford ignored him. "I wanted those damned fool companies to teach 'em a lesson. To show 'em how business is done. To show 'em how to build, to make real money, make more jobs. Why is it that every motive is misunderstood in this country? Edward, you are a former journalist, enlighten me."

"We are by nature a suspicious people. We are suspicious of most power, and people who want power."

"I don't accept that," Ben said.

"It's true. I'm convinced as I study the history of the thirties that Roosevelt got the New Deal passed because he kept attacking the rich and powerful."

Ben scowled. "Hell, if that were true, we'd have gone Communist long ago."

"No sir," I said, "what happened was that people like you saw to it that most Americans became rich—and acquired some power. As the Gilbert and Sullivan song says we live in a time 'When everyone is somebodee.'"

I did not finish the rhyme: *"Then no one's anybody."*

He smashed a fist into his open palm. "By God, I'll put that damned group together."

I knew the details of the Djarak Plan. Blake did not, or if he had any knowledge of it, it was just some vague notion that Ben was interested in a construction contract there.

"Albon," he said, "when I outline what I have in mind, you can get in touch with our partners. You tell 'em they may have lost out on the National Forests, but Ben Hannaford is about to offer them a whole foreign country."

The sheer audacity of it, the wild, ambitious plot, thrilled me. As for the lobbyist, he assumed Ben was joking, and his perfumed face wrinkled in a noiseless laugh. "Say, that's a good one, Senator. I'm sure they'll get a charge out of that."

"I don't want them to be amused," Senator Hannaford said, "I want them to know what they're getting. They are getting the Arab principality of Djarak. Their toy. Their showcase. Ours to develop, build, make money on—and turn into a moneymaker. And that will just be the start. Once we show those Ay-rabs what we can do for 'em, the whole Middle East will open up to us. We'll settle the peace with the Israelis, and we'll be the people who run things out there. The British ruined it. The Russians can't do it. The Chinese are hated. The Arabs want to destroy the Jews. The oil companies tried, but all they care about is oil. Well, it's time for Controlled Greed to take over. Nobody knows more about Controlled Greed than I do, and I intend to get my big foot into Djarak, just like it was the door to the richest bank in the world. We won't just take out oil and whatnot. We'll put in. And by the time we're through, we'll make Djarak into Houston, Texas."

"Senator," I said, "there are only 22,000 people in Djarak. There's a million and a half in Houston."

"Yeah, but there's seventy million in the Middle East. And they can grow anything they want—look at what the Jews did. The Arabs can get washed, learn to read, learn to work, make money and get the eternal message of Controlled Greed."

Blake was shaking his silvery head. "I must say, Senator, you are a man of unlimited vision." He laughed without sound, twirled his scotch and appeared to gargle with it. "I'll have a lot to tell the members tonight."

"A whole damn country," Ben said. "Just for them. And a whole part of the world, if they'll come along."

"And the legislation?" Blake asked. "May they assume there will be no obstructions?"

"There will be none," Ben said soberly. "The Djarak Amendment will be part of the Foreign Aid Bill."

The lobbyist whistled. "The senator will pardon my playing devil's advocate. But Foreign Relations is a tough bunch. Walter Edgerton is not very sympathetic to you."

"He'll come around," said Ben.

"And there are enough votes?" Blake persisted. "You realize, the Conglomerate people will be wary this time . . ."

"The votes will be there."

Ben went on to explain the most ingenious aspect of the Djarak plan. It would not be enough to pass a five-hundred-million-dollar appropriation for development, construction and defense of the oil-rich principality. The amendment would specify that *all* construction and development there would be on a cost-plus basis, to be undertaken by a single corporation, *without competitive bidding*. There were precedents for this, he explained, as witness the special amendments to the Foreign Aid Bill to help Franco Spain. No problem there. But Blake saw a joker in the deck.

"Yes, all that is fine, Senator," the lobbyist said as Ben paced impatiently. "But how will you guarantee that the government will give the Conglomerate—or Hannaford-Western acting for the Conglomerate—exclusivity or even part of the contract?"

"Careful preparation, Albon. Even Edward here isn't aware of the relationship I have with our Air Force."

"Air Force?" asked the puzzled Blake. "I thought Djarak was mostly a Navy show."

"Exactly. The Air Force is sick and tired of being shut out. Not out of the military operations. Out of the construction business. One more example of the beauty of Controlled Greed. Navy Greed and Army Greed have distressed the Air Force for a long time. I did some reading on Vietnam. Air Force took a terrible beating from the Navy Facilities Engineering Command and the Army Corps of Engineers. Those two negotiated all the construction, development, and housekeeping contracts and never gave the poor Fly-Boys a crumb until near the end of the war. The Air Force is still mad about it. Hell, if Admirals and Engineer Generals can make deals for a billion dollars' worth of ports and airfields and depots and barracks, why not the Air Force? Well, the answer is they're the youngest, so they get less. But they are as greedy as the others. I've been negotiating, with some high level blue hat boys, and I am assured that once that Djarak Amendment is passed, the first contract to be awarded will be for jet bomber facilities. The Air Force will insist that Hannaford-Western build it."

"Amazing, amazing," Blake said.

"Brilliant," I added. Ben had kept all of this to himself. No one, not a soul in our office had any idea that he had been pursuing this ingenious line.

"You may also inform Petrol-Air and Longhorn and Dover Plains and all those other chicken-hearted people," Ben went on, "that we will be awarded a cost plus contract at a full ten percent profit guaranteed."

"*Ten percent!*" cried Blake. "The most any of the Vietnam contractors ever got was *six!*"

"Yeah, that was another war. That damn two-bit rebellion in Djarak is just an excuse to let us move in and make that country into something worthwhile. To wake up that whole part of the world. Gentlemen, I'm not just going to put up airfields and ports. I am going to build the Ay-rabs schools and hospitals and office buildings. Drag 'em into the twentieth century."

In my mind's eye I had a mad vision of sandy, burning, treeless Djarak—bright with Peoples Drugstores and MacDonald Hamburger Stands.

"A clever move," Blake said. "Playing off the Air Force against the other two."

Ben shrugged. "They're like kids. Air Force is sore because the big Navy and Army kids got their personal contractors to build 'em docks and barracks and depots. So the Air Force kiddies got to have theirs. We will oblige them. Albon, you got work ahead."

The industrial relations consultant had been jotting notes in a small black leather booklet as Ben spoke. He smiled at me. "I must say, nothing stops your boss."

"Nothing," I added.

Ben picked up the phone and asked for another room in the Monroe-Plaza. As he waited, Blake said to me: "I hate to bother him with this, but I might as well tell you. Mr. Krallis is on my neck again. About that money."

Krallis! That shifty man in his shiny blue suit! Would we never be rid of his nagging? "What did the senator tell you last time?" I asked the lobbyist.

"To forget about it," he said.

"Well, that's good advice. Mr. Krallis got what he wanted. So did the senator. So did you. I would imagine, Albon, it's your job to handle people like Krallis. Or maybe George Paxton's."

I heard Ben say to someone in the other hotel room, "Come over right now, dear. I got us a mess of dictation. Lots and lots of notes, letters." He paused and turned his back on us—a weak deception. "Oh, only an hour or so. Two hours the most."

Blake and I rose and put on our jackets. Ben would of course want privacy. I studied Blake's boyish face; he was one of those beautifully groomed men, who rather indecently refuse to grow old. What he lacked, I decided, was a beard. But evidently Ben was giving him one. In fact, Blake could have worn mine. We both served the great man.

The lobbyist and I said our goodnights to Ben. In the plushy corridor we passed Maria, hurrying along in quick steps, bearing her dictation pad, a folder, a purse, very businesslike, almost prim in her secretarial dedication. Of course! A little midnight dictation. Absolutely necessary to get all those ideas down while they were fresh in the boss' mind.

"Howdy," I said sourly.

"Evening, Miss Valdez," Blake beamed.

She smiled at us. "Hi. Meeting went well, I hope?"

As I have always said, beauty is its own strength and shield. She evinced not the faintest embarrassment, unease, or shame. They would be alone for a few hours, and then they would drive back to Potomac Oaks, where Fern "could keep an eye on her."

The cry of the heart, I concluded, had come late in life to my boss. But it was a loud clear cry, and it was one he could not resist. And I knew Ben was sincere, as deeply in love with Maria as he was that day a month ago when he had told her so. All the years of faithfulness to dependable Fern, that prim river Baptist wedding, those eternal vows, had been forgotten.

I suppose he had never encountered another woman who interested him. His physical needs were probably lower than that of most men. Sublimation was perpetual in his case—all that muscular and nervous power manifested itself in politics, in business, in building. To the best of my recollection I never heard the man make a lascivious remark about a woman, ogle a twitching behind, stare at a proud bosom. It is true we had the prettiest collection of girls in any senatorial office. But this was not an indication of concupiscence on Ben's part. It was nothing more than a reflection of his insistence on quality. Homely girl? He would no more hire homely girls than he would breed inferior strains of cattle. A model of propriety he had ever been with our ladies— courtly, considerate, but only rarely a pat on the arm or a squeeze of the hand. Madge Callahan, the leading Washington hostess— "ox-eyed Hera" a columnist had nicknamed her—once confided to me: "There is no more attractive man in this town than Senator Hannaford, Eddie. Those dark eyes, that tough face, the broad shoulders! But what does a woman have to do to get a rise out of him? I always get the feeling he's bored talking to me, that it's a waste of time, an intermission between one big deal and the next!" How right Madge was.

With one exception. His conversations with Maria were more than intermissions. They were main acts; featured performances; and for all I knew a grand finale. I was of two minds regarding the achievements of my beautiful protégé. Naturally I was jealous. Having waited too long to drink deep of her beauty, choosing to wear my winter garments of repentance and refrain from warming myself with the fires of spring, I had but myself to blame. I could have overlooked any romance she might have found with the square Marine captain or some young chap at NASA. But the senator was my idol, my symbolic father and I could not suppress the envy that gnawed at me whenever I imagined their couplings— which she still denied. I was loyal enough to understand that he needed her; that operating under perpetual pressure, always in crisis, always extending his energies toward new contests involving millions of dollars, diverse personalities, wrenching public debate, he needed comfort, periods of relaxation. I had to, in spite of myself, wish him well. I only hoped that this emotional strain would in no way dilute his powers of concentration, his talent for grand stratagems.

Some time later, during the period in which we began our sounding out, or "educating" of the Foreign Relations Committee vis-à-vis the Djarak Amendment, I ran into Fern in Brentano's. It was something of a surprise. As far as I can recall, I never saw Fern reading a book. (Ben for that matter had no use for books of any kind; one would think he would have immersed himself in volumes on politics, government, and history, the way many senators do. Not Ben. "I play it by ear," he told me. "Politics is in your blood, bred in your bone.") Apart from *Good Houskeeping* and certain journals published for dog breeders, I doubt that Fern even read magazines. My bafflement was set to rest—Mrs. Hannaford was in the doodad department purchasing cocktail napkins.

"Good morning, Edward," she said pleasantly, as I approached. She looked splendid. At forty-six there was nothing frowzy or middle-aged about Fern. Her wheat-blond hair, as always, was shellacked, shaped, and impeccable. A tall woman, firm in her foundation, her figure was pleasing and comforting. Many a young punk—myself included—might have entertained notions of an adventure with her. Her legs were splendidly long, the ankles thin, and the calves full and prominent as a result of much time in the saddle.

I offered to carry her packages and we walked toward the door, my eye surveying some of the non-fiction titles. Washington bookstores seem to stock an abundance of obscure volumes which have apparently been written and published with the ultimate purpose of resting unread and unbought only in Washington bookstores. I saw snappy items like *The TVA Plot, Wit and Wisdom of the Cabinet, Harding Re-examined,* and *A History of the Bureau of Weights and Measures.*

It was one of those sickening summer days in Washington—a choking haze hovering over the streets, the temperature in the high nineties, people moving irritably through the miasma, spending as little time out of doors as possible, seeking the cold blessing of air conditioning.

"May I drop you anywhere, Mrs. Hannaford?" I asked.

Fern, bless her, did not sweat, did not suffer the devastating heat. "No thank you, Edward, I'm just here for a few errands. Travis is waiting at the garage." Then she paused, shading her pale eyes. "But you might buy me a soft drink."

"My pleasure, Mrs. H." The request was unlike Fern. I suspected she wanted to talk to me.

We went into a drugstore (not at all hard to find in Washington, truly our leading city in terms of mammoth cut-rate all-encompassing drugstores; we are the Florence of drugstores) and settled into a chilled green plastic booth. For a few moments we made small talk—Judy Stapp's unfortunate language, Marsha's treachery— over our Diet-Cola drinks. Then I saw Fern's face advertise a distinct anxiety.

"Edward," she said, "you are as close to the senator as any-one . . ." Her voice trailed off. She was not an articulate woman, and her native shyness confounded her attempts to talk freely.

"I'm complimented if either of you feel that way."

"You are the son we never had. The senator regards you as the one person in whom he can truly confide about political matters. All those people back in Ramada City at HW—all his colleagues on the Hill—they don't count the way you do."

"Mrs. H., I can only say I am flattered."

"The senator always says you get right to the heart of the matter."

"High praise, ma'am. You know that's what Churchill used to call Harry Hopkins—Lord Heart of the Matter." A sense of being set adrift passed over Fern's smooth face. It was entirely possible (why not? it was years and years ago) that she had never heard of Harry Hopkins. "Hopkins was a special assistant to President Roosevelt and he handled a lot of crucial jobs for him during the war. That's where Winston Churchill got to know him and named him 'Lord Heart of the Matter'."

"Oh. How fascinating."

"That must have been an exciting period." I did not pursue the topic. She had been in her early teens then, a rich little girl back in Ramada City, daughter of the best family, the oil-laden Cudders. They probably had sat around the dining-room table cursing FDR. Some of her relatives regarded Ben Hannaford as not much better than "an international socialist."

"Edward I am worried about the senator. He is working too hard."

"He always works hard."

"Yes, but he manages to regulate his work, to arrange his duties so that they do not exhaust him or make him short-tempered."

"Do you find him so these days?" I asked cautiously.

"I'm afraid I do. He is terribly tired. . . ." Her voice trailed away, as if wanting to say something else, but reluctant.

"I am sorry to hear that. You know, Mrs. Hannaford, the senator is not one to spare himself. He would never indicate to any of us that he is overworked or in bad temper. I am sorry that you have to be witness to this. I wish it could be me."

A flat smile stretched her thin lips. "Oh, don't misunderstand me, Edward. You know the senator. He is not a man to ever be rude or short with me. But he does seem . . . well . . . tired and preoccupied all the time."

"He gives himself totally to everything he does."

"To a fault, Edward."

"I don't see how he can live any other way. This battle over the New Wilderness Bill, for example. He hated to lose it. He put every ounce of energy he had into it. And it is a big disappointment to him. But now we're getting into the Djarak matter, and it's the same thing all over again. I don't think either of us could convince him to spare himself, to work a slower pace."

"Yes, he seems to be spending more and more evenings away."

I sipped busily at my dietetic drink. "You need not tell me. I spend a good deal of those evenings with him."

"I know you do."

Ah, the curse of non-communication. Her pale eyes, faintly rimmed with wrinkles—a horsewoman's outdoor wounds—nailed me, trying to elicit something from me, unwilling to press the unspoken.

"If it isn't Senator Edgerton or someone else from Foreign Relations—you know we need them on our side for the amendment, it's Senator Hopewell, or the campaign committee, or Albon Blake. I assure you, he'd rather be spending a relaxing evening at Potomac Oaks with you, than arguing and explaining his way through these conferences."

With a suddenness that surprised me, she asked: "Does Maria go to some of these meetings?"

In the open. Out at last. But what could I say? "Sometimes. She's an excellent secretary, a most efficient girl . . ."

"And so lovely."

"Yes if you care for those dark types."

"So she does attend some of these conferences?"

"Sometimes."

"Recently?"

"Ah . . . I think . . . the, ah, meeting with Mr. Blake as I recall, last week, with Prince Malik."

"Where?"

"Where? At the Monroe-Plaza. Mr. Blake keeps a business suite there."

"And any other times?"

"Oh, two or three . . . I think she kept the minutes of the last Campaign Committee meeting. Once when we had a late session with Senator Hopewell. Of course, you'd know . . . whenever she came home with the senator . . ." What was I to say? She didn't need confirmation.

"Well, Maria does not always come home. She often spends the night in Washington with a girlfriend."

"I would imagine she would from time to time," I commented.

"And very often those happen to be nights when the senator is working in town."

"Well, that has a certain logic," I said. "Perhaps she doesn't fancy the long ride back to Potomac. Or she might have a date."

"Probably. A girl that pretty. I bet she has lots of beaux."

"Oh, many, many," I said quickly. Thank God! An excuse, an opening! I would have happily put on my beard at that moment, worn it proudly, accepted all praise, or blame, or whatnot, to relieve Ben of suspicion. "As a matter of fact I know some of them."

"I am glad," Fern said. "I was a little worried when I asked her to live with us that she would be lonely out there. But I'll take your word that she does have boyfriends. I suppose she'll marry one of them one of these days and we'll lose a fine secretary."

"That would be a natural sequence of events," I said, feeling like a fool. I was terribly sorry for Fern, this shy, isolated woman, breeder of Gordon setters, horsewoman and heiress, forever lonely and unhappy in official Washington. I guessed that the truest joy of her life had been the vigor that Ben had brought to their nuptial bed. Whatever residue there was of that joy—and it was really none of my business—was now threatened with obliteration by Maria. She knew. Ah, how well she knew. She knew when she had insisted that Maria come live with them. *Poor child, she is all alone in the city, with all those muggings and beatings taking place every day* . . . Fern had taken the viper to her bosom, with the hope of mothering it, and as vipers will, it had bit her.

"The senator has a genuine and admirable interest in Maria," she said.

"That's perfectly natural. Joe Valdez' little girl."

"He's so loyal to his old friends."

"Like President Truman." She looked blank. "*Harry* Truman. He was the essence of loyalty. He never forgot a friend." I tried to make her laugh with a story about President Truman, how he had been spurned by his party leaders, by the California Democratic bigwigs, and had gone to Los Angeles in 1948—the year he was so unpopular and was being advised not to run again—and was met at the airport by only one person, the comedian George Jessel. From that day on, Jessel remained one of Truman's favorites, a man dear to his heart, a treasured and honored friend. But I did not tell it very well and I suspect the point was lost on her.

"It's funny," she said. "I don't even remember this fellow Joe Valdez."

"I guess he was just one of many who worked for the senator."

"He must have been a remarkable fellow," sighed Fern. "Goodness, the way the senator favors that girl. He never takes his eyes off her."

The entire conversation was painful, humiliating. A proud woman, she had to tell her sorrows to someone. How distressed I was that it had to be me! What could I do to help her? Nothing. Nothing at all. All I could think of was that she was lucky he had delayed his philandering this long. And was it mere lust, the lechery of a middle-aged man? Maria insisted he was in love with her; hopelessly in love. (And still denied that they slept together.) That his fixation was that strong, I doubted Fern suspected. A fling was one thing, infatuation another. I would say nothing. I would offer inconsequential comments. But I could envision the strained scene of an evening in the vast white parlor at Potomac Oaks: Ben and Fern seated silently at the fireplace, flanked by black Gordon setters couchant, the senator going through some HW papers—he did a lot of his corporate work in his spare time —and Maria moving lightly from dining room, to his study, to her upstairs bedroom, her willowy figure a reproach to Fern and a magnet for his dark eyes, his gaze helpless to control its direction, darting toward her form caressing her young breasts and thighs, while Fern, frozen, unbudgeable, nourishing terrifying thoughts, sipped her coffee.

"That is a perfectly natural reaction, Mrs. H.," I offered. "Maria is beautiful. I stare at her a good deal myself. She's got that perfect sort of face, the cheekbones and the wide eyes."

"I do suppose a man is a better judge of that."

And we sat there in the reviving cold air, she seeking solace, a listener, someone to share her misery—and me, unequipped, wrong for the job. There is something unsettling about the unhappiness of the very rich. It is as if they have no right to be unhappy about anything. We like to assume that their wealth renders them impervious to grief. We like to believe this because it gives us a goal toward which we can work. If we wax wealthy we will be similarly armed against suffering. Thus we are upset when we find them joyless. We resent it. I resented Fern's misery a little. No one with that much money, no one who had enjoyed all those benefits since her childhood, had any right to be disconsolate.

"It's part of the general lack of concentration he seems to show," Fern said. "Edward, he is very upset by the possible loss of the Conglomerate."

"I'm aware of it. I'm doing everything I can to help him."

"I think at one point in his career, maybe in the last few months, the senator realized he would never be President. When he realized this, he addressed all his strength toward a new industrial combination that would beat anything the country's seen yet."

"He'll get it, too," I said.

"I hope so, Edward." She sounded like a mother hoping that her son would make the honor roll. "He deserves it. And perhaps it would—perhaps it would make him less tense and preoccupied."

And keep his eyes from following that girl around the room. Fern thanked me for the drink, and for being a tolerant audience, and we left, she to be driven back to the lonely house on the Potomac, and me to my labors on behalf of the Djarak Amendment.

CHAPTER ELEVEN

The senator himself undertook the early "educational" campaign to tag an amendment to the Foreign Aid Bill, an amendment which would eventually make the sheikdom of Djarak his own fief, to exploit, develop, mold, improve, and uplift with the aid of his Conglomerate partners.

The Air Force had already been taken locked up. A certain general in Air Force Procurement, a former halfback at Ramada U., was with us all the way. Ben had gotten his brother a job in the Bureau of Fisheries and Wildlife, and had put his wife on Senator Ziegler's payroll. The general was delighted with what was to be a grand coup for his branch of service—independent contracting for major construction, a function long denied his people, a lush area normally reserved for Army Engineers and the Navy's Facilities Engineering Command. So much for the Air Force. (Gabe Tutt, as a ranking member of the Senate Armed Services Committee agreed to back Ben all the way; whatever Ben wanted, he'd get. I liked to think that his concurrence had something to do with the night in the Sutter Hills Hotel when I rescued him from public shame in that mad sprint down the corridors.)

Next, there was Senator Gage Hopewell, the Majority Leader. Old Honey-Tonsils arched his bushy brows, widened his red-rimmed eyes, and found much to his liking in the Djarak Amendment. "Is it essentially a defense measure, this special appropriation for our little Arab friends?" he intoned. "Or is it for economic betterment? For as we all know, if it is for defense against Communism, yea, it shall pass and readily. But if it is for some new-fangled cultural do-good scheme to make entrepreneurs and voters out of ragged savages, I fear for its success."

Ben had put a brawny arm around Gage's shoulders and said: "Old friend, it is for both. And where draw the line? Isn't every dollar spent in bettering their lives a defense against Communism? The appropriation will be wide open. For everything. For airfields and agriculture, for deep-water ports and dams, small-arms factories, and sewage systems! *The works!* Anything American ingenuity can build. We will build a new Jerusalem in that sand-blown strip of desert!" Gage nodded drowsily. He really did not care one way or another whether the Djarakis were saved from Communism or not. What really interested him was the selection of his home town—Milwaukee—as the site for the party's next presidential nominating convention. And Ben, as a big cheese on the Campaign Committee would have a lot to say about that. Old Honey-Tonsils would not mind at all if Senator Hannaford were to offer an amendment, his own personal amendment, to the Foreign Relations Subcommittee. He'd even say a good word for it on the floor of the Senate when the time was ripe. Medicine Man and Master Builder, they understood each other.

I know it will sound odd, but the attitude of the administration, specifically the State Department, the President, and the Defense Department, were not of much concern to my boss. As I have explained, President Hayward Kretz, the old conservative newspaper publisher, was a "hands-off" President. "That government is best which governs least," he opined. "The country is sick of Presidents who make everything their business."

A meeting was arranged with the Secretary of State via our man in the Department, a former official of Longhorn-Mideast Oil, whom, as I have mentioned, Ben had placed at the State Department's Mid-East desk. He was a bright young fellow who spoke Arabic and knew the ruler of Djarak, Prince Omar Aziz, personally. The day before the meeting we benefited by a widening of the conflict in the desert state. The "Free Djaraki" rebel movement, financed by the Chinese, attacked our Marines in force, dropping five mortar shells on an ammunition dump, killing three more Marines and wounding fifteen. These raiders then vanished into the sandstone hills beyond the capital city of Tel

Djarak. Pursuit proved fruitless, but for the first time considerable American airpower was brought to bear. Medium bombers dropped their loads on the desert hideouts of the leftist rebels and a body count revealed later that no less than forty-two of the "Free Djaraki" tribesmen had been killed. (A cynical network correspondent claimed that the body count included ten camels, five donkeys, and three Arab shoeshine boys.) In any event, it was bruited about Washington that "the die was cast," that we were in Djarak to stay, and that the attack on our Marines at Jebel-el-Souk was to be the "Tonkin Gulf Incident" of the Middle East.

The State Department was saying little. President Kretz was saying even less. I had it on good authority that the Department was preparing a stiff protest to the United Nations in Geneva. The gist of it was that we would merely ask that Djarak's neighbors "let her alone," although *what* neighbors they were not quite sure.

In any event, the Secretary of State, his minions and a Defense Department liaison man indicated their accord when Ben presented his case for a rider to the Foreign Aid Bill to insure the independence of Djarak, and to assist in its economic, social and cultural development. He suggested an appropriation of $250,000,000 to get it started. The secretary replied that $100,000,000 would be a better figure to start with. Ben nodded his head, but was unhappy. After the meeting, Matthew Fixx asked the senator: "Can we live with that, sir?"

"I doubt it, son," Ben said. "But we'll raise the ante."

"In the ball-park of a quarter of a billion?"

"Hopefully, Matthew."

"It'll be an interesting inter-face," our legislative assistant said.

So we had touched bases with the Majority Leader—no objection; the Air Force, who would be our main client—no objection; and the Executive—confusion more than objection, but willingness to go along. There remained the toughest hurdle of all—the Chairman of the Senate Foreign Relations Committee, scholarly Walter Edgerton of Ohio. Senator Edgerton was another professor-turned-politician, like Royce Henshaw. He had taught American History at Oberlin. An erect, slender, handsome, and articulate man, he admired Ben. Edgerton liked the way Ben had stood up to the right-wing when he had contracted for the pipeline in Eastern Europe. And my boss had, I think, a sneaking envy for Edgerton's intellect, his background in international relations. He liked the way Edgerton, in his writings, saw certain historical developments as growing out of personal eccentricities or pet manias of national leaders.

"Great national and international decisions," Professor Edgerton had written, "are often not the result of logic, or historical forces, or economic necessity, but are nothing more than the rash, arbitrary and imperfectly understood reactions of leaders. They may be termed Exercises in Ego and until we study them, and try to learn what caused them, we will continue to be deluded by the myth of historical imperatives. Not all historical events are imperative, or mandatory or predictable, because men are fickle, conceited, and driven by secret, often self-destructive impulses."

"I like that," Ben said, "and I understand it. That Edgerton is all right."

But our meetings with Senator Walter Edgerton of Ohio were not successful. All of Senator Hannaford's powers of persuasion could not move the chairman to regard the Djarak Amendment as anything more than one more ill-advised involvement for American arms. I gathered too that Edgerton saw at once that my boss was after Djarak as a piece of private real estate, a gift to the Conglomerate. But he never raised the question. One was permitted to *think* all sorts of things about fellow senators, but never to say anything. (That is why John Tyler Lord's intemperate attack on Ben on the floor of the Senate had been stricken. The man had violated the oldest rule.)

"Ben, I am afraid this amendment is misguided and wrong," Senator Edgerton said. "The people are sick and tired of these commitments to illiterate subsistence-level tribesmen. We got burned, and badly burned in Vietnam. Oh, I know, we were stopping Communism and so forth. But what are we stopping in Djarak? Yes, I'm advised that the Free Djaraki movement is financed by the Chinese, but so far it consists of maybe two hundred guerrillas. I think our Marines can handle them and keep Sheik Aziz in power."

"No, Senator Edgerton," my boss said patiently, "Marines are not enough. You know that. Those countries have to be overhauled, made strong economically. You pull the Marines out, and some other murdering slob, with Lin Piao's writings in one hand

and a machine gun in the other will start shooting up the place."

"Perhaps. But I'm not sure it's worth a quarter of a billion dollars to stop him. Or the life of a single Marine."

Ben hit Edgerton's desk with his fist. "That's what I mean! Let's try it my way!" The chairman leaned back and clasped his hands behind his head. A Phi Beta Kappa key twinkled on his creased vest. The only thing lacking was a spray of chalk marks on his jacket. His office was barren of any kind of political adornment—none of the usual hand-shaking, back-slapping, autographed photos of men in power. But his library was formidable. One threaded one's way through stacks of *Foreign Affairs*, *Atlas*, and the *Annals of the American Academy of Political and Social Science*.

"Now look here, Walter," Ben said. "You remember the Model Cities program? Where we selected some cities with race problems, slums, economic distress, and pumped money and brains into 'em, to prove it could be done, that we'd make 'em work?"

"I do indeed. It was a limited success."

"That's the trouble with you intellectuals. You want it all to work at once, first crack out. Here's the solution, why doesn't it solve everything? Walter, life is no math problem, it's no college examination. No one gets grades. You got to settle for little gains, for a little bit at a time. And you can't get discouraged."

"Yes, I suppose I've been something of a Cassandra and a pessimist ever since Second Watts," Edgerton conceded.

"Well, we had a Model Cities program," Ben went on, "and it did a lot of good. What I'm after is a Model Countries program. I aim to start with our friends in Djarak. I intend to make that little place the showplace of the Middle East—we'll build us a Pasadena right in the middle of the desert, with American money and know-how. We'll knock off those Free Djaraki terrorists in no time. With what? Marines? Well, yes for starters we'll need security. But we'll make the place function with factories, schools, hospitals, housing developments, roads, airports, docks, and everything that's needed to drag 'em into the twentieth century."

Edgerton hesitated. "I assume the Hannaford Conglomerate will be a main participant—with the United States government—in effecting this Cinderella change?"

"Why not?" Ben responded. "We can do it better than anyone."

Walter Edgerton frowned. "Ben, you don't stand a chance. The public reaction to the New Wilderness Bill was not good."

"You give me a chance to explain this amendment before an open session of your committee, and you'll see what the public thinks." Ben was getting tense, a bit angry.

"It's possible you could convince some people that this amendment is a wise move," Senator Edgerton said patiently. "But I must be frank, Ben. I dislike it for a variety of reasons. First, there is conflict of interest here. Please let me finish. You and I have always enjoyed mutual respect and I hope this doesn't end it. It will appear to be another melancholy coincidence—you pushing for a special rider that will benefit your business associates, and trifling with the foreign policy of the United States while you go about it. If you think the press will let you pursue this untouched, you are mistaken."

"They have never scared me and they don't now."

"But many of your colleagues feel otherwise," Edgerton said. "I doubt you could muster the committee votes to get this tacked on as a committee amendment. And you won't get mine, Ben. Or my cooperation in presenting it. I can let you come before an open session and offer the amendment. You've done me favors and I'm ready to do one for you. But I object to this amendment and the philosophy behind it for an entirely different reason— one that has nothing to do with how many billions you and Longhorn-Mideast and Dover Plains can milk out of the United States government in the name of defense, saving the world from Communism or uplifting the Arab tribesmen of Djarak."

Senator Hannaford clasped his powerful hands on the slight rise of his paunch. He had not anticipated such complete opposition from the professor. I could see the lines hardening in Ben's face, the jaw protruding slightly.

"Senator," Edgerton said, "we are playing a mugg's game trying to make capitalists out of these people. What worked in Western Europe was one thing. We had a base to build on. I have a hunch you will also succeed in Eastern Europe, if the Soviets ever give you enough elbow room. You and I know that Budapest is a lot closer to Paris than it is to Moscow. Again, there is a base to build on. But in many of these places in the world we are deceiving ourselves. These half-naked people are no more fit to be freedom-loving, consumer-oriented citizens of a capitalist democracy than are we, to give up this rich technical society we have created, to live in igloos or Kaffir kraals. Ben, we deceive ourselves, and this grand plan of yours, as well-motivated as it is, is another deception. Look at South Vietnam. It is a shambles. All we succeeded in doing with our airfields and docks and soft drink bottling plants was to destroy a century-old way of life."

"Yes, open drains, disease, malnutrition, and seasonal floods," Ben said. "Walter, you liberals have become the pessimists, the defeatists. Used to be that you were all fired up to change the world. Now it appears you want the world to sort of rock along. I say we got to prove that American capitalism is the greatest force for progress ever conceived! I mean the new kind! My kind!" He leaned forward—his face intense, then he smiled. "And of course, I intend to make some money for myself while I'm going about it."

Edgerton laughed. "Ben, at least you're open about it. Even when I disagree with you I enjoy our sessions. Will you say this to the committee? On the floor of the Senate? In a press conference? That one of the reasons you want the Djarak Amendment is to make money?"

It was almost a challenge, and challenges were irresistible to Ben. I saw him mulling the notion over in his mind, the corners of his eyes crinkling, his lips turning upward at the notion. "Walter," he said, "I do believe you have given me one hell of a good idea!"

"You can't mean it sir," I protested. "I mean—you just can't go out and say, I want this amendment because I will make millions of dollars out of it."

Senator Edgerton ran a hand through his crewcut. "He's joking, Edward," he said to me.

"I am not," said Ben. "I believe I have found the key to rallying the people behind me! I will say, yes, I will get rich off the bill. My partners will get rich! But at the same time, we'll make ourselves a Model Country in the Middle East! We'll knock off these Communist attacks once and for all! Teach 'em capitalism! A supermarket in every village! Why, we can change that whole part of the world! And you know why? Because there'll be *money* involved. That's how things get done. Not for virtue or honor or goodwill or ideals—but because of *Greed*. Controlled Greed, Walter that's the answer. I'll admit I want money—but I want money in a good cause! Electric ranges instead of camel dung!"

Senator Edgerton was not convinced. "Your enthusiasm is admirable Ben, but I will oppose you down the line. You don't stand a chance on the committee. This Conglomerate business is just behind us, the fuss over the Hannaford bill. And while the administration may have given you a green light, they won't back you if there's a battle."

"There's gonna be a battle," Ben said.

"I was afraid of that," Senator Edgerton sighed. "I must warn you, Ben. You have to lose this one."

"Maybe," said my boss, "and maybe not."

Edgerton's reaction did not deter Ben's insistence that we set in operation a swift campaign to rally support for the Djarak Amendment. To this end it was decided to cultivate and bring before the public, His Excellency, the Djaraki Ambassador, Prince Malik.

The contacts with Malik had already been made by Ben's lieutenant, Senator Stapp. "Swinging Sid" gravitated naturally toward people like the Arab diplomat. Malik was a pleasant enough chap, if a bit dim-witted. Just why a dot of burning sand like Djarak needed a full-blown ambassador eluded me. The story was that at the time the United Nations, by vote of Congress and a national referendum initiated by Save America, was told to clear out of the United States, and all those beautiful buildings on the East Side of Manhattan were taken over by New York University, Prince Malik was stranded. The UN moved to Geneva, to take up quarters in the old League of Nations Building, while people like Gordon Hackensetter cheered.

The ruler of Djarak, Prince Aziz, a distant cousin of Malik's, decided he did not need representation at a diluted United Nations in Geneva, and turned his country's UN representation over to a Swiss bank. This left Malik afloat in New York City in a twelve-room apartment on Park Avenue with a fleet of black Cadillacs and a Jaguar for weekends only. He was said to know more girls than a well-known quarterback for a New York professional football team. In any event, Malik was told to liquidate his assets and get back to Djarak. But the young prince had drunk deep of the cup of the decadent West. He would have no more of those hot days and dull nights. It then occurred to him to suggest to his sovereign that Djarak get itself an Embassy in Washington. At the time they were represented by a trade mission. The notion appealed to Prince Aziz, and shortly thereafter, there was young Malik, and a staff of leggy American girls—he favored tall blondes with lank hair and pale skin—throwing parties, escorting celebrities, and serving his tiny homeland energetically along Embassy Row.

I had met Prince Malik several times at dinners, parties, and other functions and had found him to be a merry little fellow in his thirties, always smartly tailored in navy blue. He favored a kind of iridescent pale tie—lavender, silver, blue—a style usually associated with Mafia captains. Round-headed, curly-haired, moist-handed, he always appeared to have been sprayed with scented oil. He was jovial, sociable, and usually agreed with anything that was said to him. I gathered that at some time he had been exposed to the United States Army, for his speech was peppered with GI slang.

Judy and Sid Stapp had known Prince Malik for a long time. I think that when the United Nations was still in New York, Judy had met him at one of those glittering parties she was always bragging about. Senator Stapp, or at least his law firm, had performed some contract work for the Djaraki government and a California-based oil company. When the Prince was transferred to Washington, Judy and Sid included him in their retinue of regulars, although I must confess, she behaved toward him in an atrocious manner, as I will soon illustrate. Fortunately, Malik was un-insultable. He would appear at these Washington brawls, bearing on each tailored arm a blond giraffe-like girl with vacant eyes and bad manners. These were camouflage. He lusted for Judy Stapp and she regarded him as a worm. One must remember that he was an Arab nationalist, and she, although an Italo-American, was very "show-biz" and numbered many Jewish persons among her close friends. She was also infected with that unformed fuzzy liberalism that taints so many theatrical people. In her hard green eyes, Malik, no matter how rich and important, was "a goddamn Ay-rab"—and worse.

The idea of the cocktail party in the Prince's honor was a good one. Ben knew him slightly, and it was deemed proper that any man whose country was about to be bought by an American corporation, should know the purchaser better. Actually both Ben and Fern detested cocktail parties. But Judy Stapp insisted on one. She loved a mob. She loved a smorgasbord of disparate, even antagonistic people. And pretty soon, the guest list, like just about everything Judy was involved in, got out of hand.

"Hell, I can meet him in my office," Senator Hannaford complained to me. "Besides, I get all my information about Djarak from Wiggins out there. He gets me news faster than the State Department gets it."

T. C. Wiggins was the resident manager of Longhorn-Mideast Oil in Tel-Djarak. The ruler of Djarak, Prince Aziz, did not make a move without consulting him.

(It was this Wiggins who arranged the famous "goldlift" of two and one half million dollars in gold bullion aboard a United States Air Force bomber during the 1970 crisis, when Prince Aziz, under threat from the United Arab Republic, was warning he might go under President Fawzi's wing unless an emergency gold payment was made. Wiggins personally flew out with the gold, and free enterprise in the Middle East was saved.)

But Judy's party was deemed expedient—I was inclined to agree with the Stapps—and we all went our dutiful way to the imposing Georgetown mansion, rather two mansions, that breathless Sunday afternoon.

I say *two*, because that is exactly what the Stapp home on Dumbarton was—two ancient red brick edifices, artfully but confusingly joined at the seams. The surgery was erratic. One was never quite sure where one was in the Stapp house. Doors led to nowhere; what one imagined to be a john turned out to be a closet; a presumed corridor leading to a living room deposited one in the garden; a wrong left turn found one face to face with Judy's alarming Filipino cook; steps led nowhere; rooms revealed themselves grudgingly like the inside of a Chinese puzzle; and guests, awakening at night in search of a bathroom, were known to wander in aimless circles like a tenderfoot scout lost in a pine barren.

But handsome it was, chock full of antiques and modern art, in splendid disarray, all reflecting Judy's flamboyance. I arrived early, as is my habit, and was greeted in the lobby by Senator Stapp. We both had to duck to escape decapitation by a low hanging chandelier, something Judy had salvaged from a Jamestown mansion.

"Ed," Senator Stapp said, "Judy's giving me fits on this. She invited Parenti."

I gagged for a minute. That was Judy, all right. "Maybe he'll be on his good behavior," I said.

"I couldn't handle her hollering any more," the Swinger said. "Not only Parenti—but some of her nut New York friends—what she calls her 'thinky crowd.'"

"It should make for an interesting evening," I said sourly.

Sid—resplendent in white silk turtleneck shirt and a rust brown silk jacket—led me into the garden amid the fragrance of magnolias and honeysuckle. Washington is, after all, Southland.

Ben, Fern, and Maria were standing, ill-at-ease, in a corner of the flowery garden, nursing drinks. Prince Malik, the guest of honor, was talking to Maria—effusive, friendly, gracious. Ben looked annoyed; Fern bored; Maria excited. Judy Stapp bustled amid the throng, wearing some sort of harem rig—billowing emerald green bloomers, dangling iridescent beads, a pearl tiara.

Wisely, Senator Stapp had invited a half-dozen friendly journalists—columnists, network chaps, fellows from the news magazines, who almost always gave Ben a good press. He handled them well, and they liked him. *Big, bluff Ben Hannaford, the millionaire construction man* . . . Thanks to them, Parenti's attempt to "get us" with the revelation of the Conglomerate letters had failed. So what? had been the general reaction. Yes, Senator Hannaford is rich. Yes, he would like to be richer. Yes, he is putting together a corporate giant. Yes, he might benefit by the New Wilderness Bill. But the conclusion in most of the press seemed to be—*what of it?* Besides, the bill was a dead pigeon. Why beat it to a second death? Senator Hannaford was still one of the most active, productive, intelligent men on the Hill. Why, reasoned the editors and publishers, weaken his usefulness to the White House, the nation, the Congress, by badgering him over what was at worst a misguided bit of special pleading for friends?

"Eddie baby," I heard an uncouth voice mumble, "howsa boy?" Parenti was in back of me, on the brick steps leading from the rear of the Stapp mansion to the lush steamy garden.

"Hello there, Louis." I tried to sound aloof.

"Some bash, hey kid?" Parenti said admiringly. His charcoal eyes surveyed the scene. He was the worst-dressed person there—in a tan suit purchased off someone's plain pipe racks. He saw Judy Stapp flitting among the guests, and ran a hairy hand across his mouth. "Eddie, dig them green bloomers. Man, I'd like to peel them down. Jesus, she'll drive me up the wall before the evening is over."

"You are a subtle fellow," I said. On the garden path, we studied each other. "Your revelations about your erotic needs don't interest me. Any more than your lying columns do." I looked around. He had had the good sense not to drag Marsha along.

"Ah, Eddie. I don't tell lies. I make trouble, but I don't tell lies. Listen kid—what was the final vote on the bill? I hear Kemmons double-crossed you guys, not once but twice. You can't trust a drunkard, Eddie. The big guy should know that. Kemmons is up to his asshole in trouble—bad trouble. His vote is for sale, you know that. One of these days I'll nail that chiseler, I swear I will."

"I refuse to discuss anything with you. Anything at all."

He thrust a huge arm around me. "Come on, kid, I always liked you. Listen, wasn't we news buddies once?" He was mocking me. "When the time comes, kid, I'll go easy on you."

I suddenly was afraid of him. I was fearful of something that was bound to involve me, some deal, some fix, some arrangement that Ben would drag me into—something that was bound to fail, but that Ben, in his one-track determination about the Conglomerate, would force through to a dreadful conclusion.

"Hiya, Judy baby," Parenti said. She offered a powdered cheek. Parenti kissed it, then turned her chin and kissed her full on the lips. "Man, you turn me on," he said. "Listen Judy. Whaddya wear under that rig? I mean how do you get inta them pants?"

"With money," she sneered. Parenti howled; I blushed. These were not my kind of people—and certainly not Senator Hannaford's. I noted that there were very few congressional or White House "insiders" attending. Senator Eisenberg, who had endowed a museum in Chicago, was there, with his lovely wife, the heiress to a printing fortune and an artist in her own right. Young Alvin Martinson, Sid Stapp's junior senator from California, a mild-mannered former president of a state college, was present, and a few California congressmen. Courtly Judge Moscowitz, the FBI director, was on hand, and so were some local Washington officials, including the city's Negro mayor, Homer Murphy, the former All-League middle linebacker with the Washington Redskins. Murphy was an enormous smiling man with a strangely high-pitched voice.

Parenti trailed me—pumping Mayor Homer Murphy's hand—and faking a punch to Murphy's iron chest. "Got to watch that Luigi," Murphy winked at me. "He is a terror."

"I'll kick the shit outa ya, ya big creep," Parenti laughed. "Think ya so tough? How about when Leroy Kelley faked you outa the ball park, hah? You landed right on yer keester in front of forty million people!"

"An error of judgment on my part, Luigi," Mayor Murphy said easily. He introduced us to Mrs. Murphy, a handsome woman, lighter than he was. She had once been a militant in the civil rights movement. "Say Parenti," the huge Murphy said, "you must come speak to my friend Dalton Warfield—the Triple-O man from Watts."

"Yeah, sure, when I get through with a few second story men." He darted a look at me.

"I have met Mr. Warfield," I said. "He is an impressive man."

"He is the future," Homer Murphy said.

Parenti prowled his way toward Ben, Fern, Maria, and Prince Malik. I followed him. For some reason, I kept finding Parenti not only repulsive, but an object to be feared. There was something so uncompromising about his pursuit, that I saw him now not as simply another "crusading" journalist, but as a force of nature, a howling wind, a drowning flood.

Fern turned her back on him. She wandered off, nursing a drink, toward Mrs. Eisenberg and Mrs. Martinson, who sat primly at one of the little white garden tables that had been set up under the pleached bowers of leaves and blossoms.

"Hiya, Senator," Parenti said. "Guess you showed me up."

"It wasn't hard, Louis," Ben said warmly. There was no fear in Ben. An army of Parentis could not frighten that man.

"Anyway, I got that lousy New Wilderness Bill killed," he said.

"Maybe you did. Maybe you didn't."

"Senator," I said, "I don't see why you have to be subjected to this. If Mr. Parenti were a gentleman, any true representative of his profession, he would not resort to these rude tactics."

"That's all right, Edward," Ben said, smiling. "The man is practicing his trade. If his methods are irregular, so are mine sometimes."

Parenti roared. "Wow! That is what I love about the Big Guy!"

Sid Stapp wandered over, so did Judge Moscowitz, so did two of

the friendly syndicated columnists—second-rank Washington
writers who could be depended upon to be nice to anything concerning business.

"Man, he is the greatest! *Irregular!*" Parenti howled.

"What's so funny?" I asked.

"Irregular! Like taking over a whole country! Senator, you are
the most refreshing person I have ever met in my wicked career!"

"Who is taking over what country?" Judge Moscowitz asked.

"Senator Hannaford here," Parenti boomed. "He's got a bid in
for Djarak. Whaddya say, Prince!" he shouted to Malik. "Lissen
—you could do worse! Let the senator run the whole place—he'll
do a great job."

Someone had probably leaked the details to him. Senator Edgerton? It was no matter, we would be publicizing it soon—Ben's bid
to include Djarak by name, in the Foreign Aid Bill, and establish
a special Djarak fund for the tiny country.

"Yes, you are quite right, Louis," my boss said. "I will make
Djarak into a *model country.*"

"It will be our pleasure," Prince Malik said. "And you better
believe it."

"I believe it," Parenti said. "Longhorn-Mideast is out there already, and you know who they are—the senator's friends and
associates."

"Sorry about that," Malik said stupidly. Where had he picked
up that pseudo GI lingo? Probably by watching television.

"We'll hide nothing," Ben said. "Yes, we'll be in Djarak—assuming the Defense Department selects us to do the work."

Parenti grinned. "Now let's see—during Vietnam, the big contractors got cost plus three percent, except this one outfit wan-
gled a deal with the Air Force under the table and got six percent.
What do you expect to bring it in for, Senator? I mean, if you
would be willing to speak as the Chairman of Hannaford-Western,
or the Conglomerate, instead of Senator Hannaford . . ."

Ben shook his head. "Louis, you'll push me too far. But keep
this in mind. I never short-change anyone. If Defense selects my
people for the work, no matter what the financial arrangement is,
the good citizens of Djarak will benefit by our labors. Whatever
the cost, there'll be value returned for every dollar spent."

"And a big fat profit, a big fat contract for your people," Parenti
said.

"It may work out that way," the senator said.

Maria's eyes were blazing; she was furious with Parenti. The air was getting tense, a certain unpleasantness was manifesting itself. The heat was no help—that damnable Washington miasma, the fetid breath of the Dismal Swamp enveloping us, forcing us to reach for more and more vodka-tonics, scotch-sours, bourbon highballs.

"Listen joker," Prince Malik said to Parenti, "Senator Hannaford is aces with us. He's a good Joe, a good buddy. And you better believe it."

"Who said he wasn't?" Parenti cried. "I think he's the greatest guy in the world! He'll have all you Arabs driving Mustangs and going to PTA meetings before he's through!"

Prince Malik looked stupefied. The oil seemed to ooze from his round olive face. "Honey, let's you and me heist a few brews," he said to Maria, offering her his arm. They walked off, Malik complaining to her about "that big joker."

There was a considerable press of bodies in the Stapps' garden now. Ben was getting uncomfortable—less because of Parenti's boorish needling than because he hated these mixed grills of humanity, these assemblages of unrelated tiresome people. He remained rooted to his post, his back against the high white-washed brick wall of the Stapps' garden, under a magnificent magnolia. Parenti lingered at his side. So did the FBI director and a few others. And now I had a troubling feeling as Parenti continued his sniping. I had the feeling that Ben was cornered. How does one corner so rich and powerful and influential a man? I don't know. Perhaps he had done it to himself. But I had the terrible notion that he *could not escape* from that right angle of brick wall and hard earth, that he, who strode with royal confidence across the barren fields on which he built cities, was now restricted to a mean corner of ground. Suddenly a line from Shakespeare flashed through my fevered head—Prince Hal commenting over the dead Hotspur—"And now two paces of the vilest earth is room enough." My morbid mood would not vanish. I am an indifferent drinker and get no lift out of alcohol, but the guests around me, women in flimsy summer wear, men in brazen colors, all of them seemed to be rising on a high liquored cloud.

"If I had the nerve, Senator," Parenti was saying, "I'd betcha you won't get that amendment through. No sir."

"This man can't be discouraged," Judge Moscowitz said to Senator Stapp. "I'm glad he's not after me."

"Louis doesn't mean any harm," Sid said suavely. But he also seemed uneasy. Only Ben, rooted to his corner of the garden, a tethered bear bullyragged by a terrier, seemed oblivious to Parenti's barbs.

"I don't think you can get this one past Walter Edgerton," Parenti was saying. "Not after what John Tyler Lord said in the Senate."

"He was not permitted to say it," I said. "He was gaveled down and those remarks were stricken from the record."

Parenti eyed me with contempt. "Natch. He broke a rule. But I break 'em all the time. I ran the full text of his speech. And so did the AP. You see, boys, this club crap has got to go. You got to stop acting like you are the True Blessed Recipients of the Word. People have a right to blow the whistle on the United States Congress also. And it shouldn't only happen to gooks like Angel López Garcia."

"I'll say amen to that," said Mayor Homer Murphy, his giant black figure looming at the edge of the crowd.

"This Djarak deal will go down the drain," Parenti said, almost unhappily. "It's too much—even for the Senate."

The small group around Ben seemed to gasp collectively. I could only conclude that Parenti was drunk—if not on alcohol, on the power he wielded with his poison pen.

"Louis, you need not be so rude," Judge Moscowitz said lightly.

"Excuse me, Judge, but all I can think of is, look who's talking," the columnist boomed. "You were the one sigged your FBI guys on me for telling the truth. And listen. I didn't care for the last two who questioned me. They were uncouth. You are getting a low element into the bureau and I might have to write my congressman. Also, that bug on my telephone is a pain in the ass. It clicks too much and it interferes with the obscene phone calls I get from Save America."

"Nothing personal, Louis," said the director of the FBI.

Ben was studying Parenti with a kind of grudging respect— the hard look a prize-fighter gives a rugged opponent before blasting him with the right cross. I almost had the notion that Ben was going to punch him. Back in his construction days, he had hit scores of men, and they usually went down. Malcontents, union agitators, shakedown artists, drunks—an army of these had reeled under Ben Hannaford's fists. But as Parenti blabbered on, all Ben did was yawn and turn his head to the hazed hot sky. I think he wished he were back in Ramada City under that clear blue desert ceiling, splattered with crsytalline stars. Did he really enjoy the frenzy of Washington—the eternal back-slapping, elbow-grabbing, conniving, convincing? Or was it nothing more than a tropism, an involuntary extension of the aggressive, hard-driving life he had led since he was fourteen and went to work as a rigger in the dusty fields? Did he sometimes weary of this endless quest for power and wealth?

"I had enough of your gumshoes, Judge," Parenti shouted. "And I know who sigged 'em on me—Senator Hannaford right here. There is nothing in the world he can't fix, if he tried hard enough. Right, Judge?"

"I'd stop right there, Louis," the judge said.

Parenti's hooded eyes fixed themselves on Ben—as if they two alone were joined in some mortal combat, some battle that had to be fought until one or the other were destroyed. "Me, and Senator Hannaford, let's say we're engaged in a collaboration—writing footnotes to American History. Sort of a record of the Golden Age in which the entire United States government, after much planning and precedent, became an agent of the Free Enterprise System."

"No, not footnotes," Ben said wearily. "Volumes. You may not realize it, in your blind liberal brain, Louis, but it is my intention to change the face of the globe. As the book tells us, 'Behold, I shew you a mystery! We shall not all sleep but we shall all be changed!'"

"Well, to hell with that for the moment," Parenti cried. "That Holy Roller stuff don't cut any ice with a Brooklyn boy like me, Senator. Save that for the State Fair Strawberry Social. What I want to know is, won't the American taxpayer get stuck for the bill on this deal, and second, won't all the profits wind up in Hannaford-Western's pocket and the pockets of all your capitalist friends, like Longhorn and Petrol-Air and the others? Isn't that a fact? What are we talking about, Senator? Cost plus eight percent? Nine? Jesus—I wish I could figure out how you're gonna mousetrap the Defense Department into this. Those hard hats over there got their own favorites."

At least he did not know about our secret arrangements with the Air Force. But he would in time.

"My, you really got your nasty clothes on tonight, Louis," Mayor Homer Murphy said jokingly. The former football star towered over Parenti. "Why can't we just have a nice fun party for a change, instead of all this hostility?"

"Homer baby, you're right." Again, Parenti made that half-jesting aggressive move toward the giant Negro, as if trying to block him, or keep him away from a passing quarterback. "Tell us about the day you dumped Tarkenton five times, Homer."

"He was a gent about it," Murphy said in that squeaky little voice. "Which is what I wish you would be. And lay off Senator Hannaford. He's one of the best friends we got in town."

"Yeah?" Parenti asked. "Since when?"

Ben smiled at Mayor Murphy. "That's all right, Mr. Mayor, you don't have to defend me."

The towering black man shook his head. "No sir, I'll tell anyone. Senator Hannaford can get things done for us, because he is the real America. Others can't. The public won't listen. But people listen to the senator. He is one of *them*. And I tell you what else he does, although you can't find it on paper anywhere . . ."

"Tell me, tell me, Homer baby," Parenti crooned.

"He protects us," Murphy said.

"You?" cried Parenti. "Colored people? Who the hell are you talking about?"

"I am talking about anyone who can be victimized by the tall strangers with the shotguns, Louis. There is always something worse around the corner. I get the feeling the senator keeps us from succumbing to our own worst impulses." Murphy looked at Ben with what I could only call a kind of tribal gratitude. "Yeah, I've seen him subdue the tiger and I thank him." He jabbed Parenti in the ribs. "And you'll thank him one day, also."

I seem to recall several women applauding a few times as Murphy walked away, his enigmatic tribute to the boss concluded. Parenti looked puzzled. He called for a drink and lurched off. Ben walked quietly toward Fern—poor Fern, sitting stiffly at the garden table and sipping bourbon with Mrs. Eisenberg and Mrs. Martinson.

A three-piece rock and roll combo was violating the steamy

Georgetown night with loud noises. Guests formed in sweaty groups. "Swinging Sid" moved from journalist to congressman to business associate, dispensing goodwill, jokes, gossip. Prince Malik was exhibited, made a member of our happy community. He glistened amid the lantern glow, and everyone was impressed.

A finger tugged at my sleeve and I was pulled toward a leafy bower, a trellis covered with ivy, in a corner of the garden. It was Maria.

"I'm going crazy in Potomac," she said. "If I don't get out, I'll end up in a sanitarium."

"Who told you to move in?"

"Oh damn, I couldn't help it. They insisted—they wanted me as one of the family—the same way Travis and his wife are, or Cleo, or all the others they adopt. But I'm not adoptable."

In the glow of a paper lantern, her face was a vision, like a sad Madonna of Guadalupe in a church in a crumbling Mexican village. The Mexicans made the prettiest, saddest Madonnas—they had marvelous models to work from.

"Move out," I said.

"I may have to. It's awful . . . just awful . . . the way he feels about me . . . and the way she knows, but never says anything. Not a *word*."

"It sounds grim," I said. "What do you do for conversation in a house like that?"

"I've become good friends with Travis. God, I think he must know the way the senator feels also."

"Well," I said cruelly, "I suppose you and Ben can make up for all that silence with some lively dialogues in Mr. Blake's hotel rooms."

"Eddie, I've despaired of denying this to you. You have to punish yourself all the time. Why do you insist on it? He's never, never touched me. He can't."

"Maria, I don't accept that, not for a minute."

"You know, I keep thinking of asking you to forgive me, and it's all so crazy," she said. "I stop and say, what for? What am I to be forgiven? That a wonderful, kind, good man fell in love with me?"

"You've got it all wrong. I'm the one I can't forgive. For passing you up. For letting him make his move. Dammit, I saw you first. I had prior rights. Remember that night I showed you the city?"

"It was beautiful, Eddie."

Couples danced around us, the idiotic shaking imitations of chorea that passed for dancing. I saw the Chairman of the House Appropriations Committee, a silent old crank, swivelling hips with the wife of an Interstate Commerce Commissioner. I suppose there is still a good deal of the Ohio Baptist in me, a bit of the American Legion essay contest winner. The city to me should always be serene and dignified, even a little sombre. Outdoor performances in a Georgetown backyard, especially Judy Stapp's backyard, depressed me. A bit of the bluenose, I am, and maybe that's why I believed the worst about Ben and Maria.

"I'll have my memories," I said. "Cab rides and all that."

"I'll share them," Maria said.

"Why did I give up so easy?" I asked. Swarms of night insects wove wreaths around the lanterns.

"Because you respect him so much," she said.

"Yes, he's got that power to command it," I conceded. Then I added: "Curse him." I looked at her intensely. "Do you love him, Maria?"

She pressed her hands to her temples. "I don't know. I don't know. Oh, but Eddie, he needs me so terribly. And not the way you keep thinking, the way you keep torturing yourself. He just has to have me around. He says I give him hope, I give him joy, that all the work, the pressure, the decisions, the duties he has . . . he just couldn't cope with them, without knowing he'd see me in a few hours. That he couldn't get through another day . . ."

"I don't believe it." I grabbed her wrist. "You sleep with him."

"No, no, no, no. He told me he never could. That he simply couldn't do this to Fern . . . If they could be divorced . . ."

"Which would never happen . . ."

"Yes, he said so . . . or if things were different . . . but it's a kind of crazy loyalty to her, and he won't change."

"Well, then what he's doing is even worse. Keeping all of you miserable. The man is beyond my comprehension." I studied her distraught face in the soft lantern-light. Was she telling the truth? What a grim irony if she were! Big Ben, who got whatever he wanted, who grabbed, took, influenced, dominated, manipulated!

But halted at the edge of ecstasy by some blind, unwavering obedience to his dull wife!

But I did believe one thing. I believed that he was in love with her. And as firmly I believed this, I knew that the relationship was doomed, hopeless, the deadest of dead ends. Even without the beckoning White House, I sensed, there would be no divorce. There was something about rich rural folk like the Hannafords; they did not think in terms of divorce. They were as entwined as a live oak and a creeping vine.

"A mess any way you study it," I said gloomily. "And I'll tell you something, *pajarita*, it's not doing you any good. I don't think you are in love with him."

"But I could be," she gasped. "If Fern weren't there . . . if he were single, or widowed. But she's got this hold on him. The Rock of Ages. Yes, that's it. And he wants us both."

My eyes narrowed. "I'm sure of that. And I give him another few weeks. That pained loyalty to Fern will end. If it hasn't already. And I may not want to be around when it happens."

"It won't," Maria said. "I'm quitting. Getting out."

"Of Washington?"

"Perhaps. I've told him. I can't see him suffer like this . . . I admire him, I like him enormously, I don't regret a minute we've spent together, and maybe I'd do it again. But I can't go on like this. It's not fair."

"And what did he say?"

"He cried," she said.

I was dazed. My boss? Big Ben Hannaford in tears? "Maria, I find that hard to believe."

"It's true. He said he needed me more than anything in the world. That I was what he had always wanted in a woman, that he had dreamed of someone like me. And he cried and said I could not leave him."

When she raised her head I could see that her luminous eyes were moist. But she did not cry much. I was certain that his tears were fuller and more prolonged than hers, and I was terribly sorry for him.

"But you will leave him anyway?"

"I'll have to . . . but I don't know when. Damn, Eddie, why did I get involved, why did I let it happen!"

All I could do was pat her hand and murmur inconsequential

comments—"It will all work out"—"It will be for the best"—"He will understand." Meaningless, meaningless. Big Ben had wept. And I felt my heart go out to that power-hungry man, that mover and shaker of governments and legislators and executives. No payoff, no appointment, no arm-twisting could relieve that empty straining in his iron chest, that fear of impending loss.

We sat in silence a few moments—and then both of us started at the sound of commotion of some sort at the distant end of the Stapp garden. People came running by in the lantern-glow—women in miniskirts, men in summer suits—and Maria and I joined them. I have heard it theorized that our world, even the sedate and stratified world of Washington, is a surrealist one, and I suppose it is not an especially original theory. But I am always astounded to see it borne out. In this flowering garden, this plot of fragrant earth and greenery in hallowed Georgetown, just a few minutes before great affairs of state had been tautly debated, and now all was reduced to a kind of despairing absurdity.

There was a small swimming pool at the other end of the Stapps' combined gardens (you will recall they had married two mansions) and at the poolside patio, in the glow of yellow lanterns, Prince Malik was being reviled by a very drunk Judy Stapp, and a fellow new to me, a bearded, long-haired bespectacled scarecrow of a young man, with pitted cheeks and a pronounced New York accent.

"Ya stink, ya stink," the bearded man was saying, "the Israelis'll kick the shit outa ya next time, too!"

"Settle down in there, soljer," Prince Malik was saying uneasily. "All I said was the Zionists stuck my people in concentration camps."

"Ah, balls!" Judy Stapp screeched. "Yer an Ay-rab, a lousy Ay-rab!"

I edged next to Mayor Homer Murphy. His soaring figure dominated the horrified audience—like some Nubian guard at a Byzantine court.

"Who is that loudmouth?" I asked him. "The man, I mean."

"Guy named Farbelman," Homer Murphy said. "Establishment poet. The King of the Acid Heads. Got himself a big rep when he shot his girl friend. Bastard's been patronizing me all night."

"My God," I gasped, as Maria and I drew near to witness the mad confrontation. "*That* made him famous?"

"Why sure, Edward," the Negro official said, winking. "If you are a black man in Watts and you shoot up your girl, you git hell from Mr. Charley. But if you an Establishment poet, you beat the rap, and you have extended the limits of human experience. Dig?"

"I'm afraid I do."

"Yaaah, and keep your grubby hands off me!" Judy Stapp shrieked. Her eyes were wild, her hair undone. "You try to yank these bloomers down once more, I'll kick yer ass!"

Prince Malik held his hands out, palms up, in supplication. "No sweat, kids," he said. "No sweat, I was just trying to find out if they were government-issue, that's all."

"Lousy Ay-rab!" Judy shrilled.

"Yeah, and you haven't made a single contribution to history, either!" the bearded poet Farbelman cried. As he spoke, I saw hordes of NYU students, guitar-strumming, folk-singing acolytes, hailing him.

"That is not quite true," Homer Murphy said pleasantly. "And you, Mr. Farbelman, should know better. Arab scholars were the envy of the Western world—Averroes, Avicenna, Ibn-Khaldun. Please show a bit more respect for our guest of honor, even though you may have certain differences."

"Oh, I gotta argue with you too, hey, Fat Stuff?" the poet crowed. Whatever he was high on—LSD, marijuana, heroin—was lifting him into lofty orbits where he would surely lose control, and fall. No retrorockets would help him. On the edge of the now considerable crowd—I could even see some neighborhood children peeking over the high wall—I noticed Ben and Fern, disdainful southwest Americans, alien to all this rococo nonsense, this Versailles decadence.

"No argument is necessary," Homer Murphy said. "I merely ask for a trace of good manners."

"We'll kick the shit outa ya!" Farbelman cried.

"Please, I don't want to talk politics," Prince Malik said. "As a matter of fact, what does a guy do to get out of this chicken outfit?"

"That's a good one, Prince, that's a good one," Homer Murphy chuckled.

Senator Stapp diplomatically tried to come to the rescue. He put his silky arm around the Djaraki Ambassador's shoulder. "No hard feelings, Malik," he said. "Judy is just kidding . . ."

"Like hell I am. He makes one more grab for my butt and he gets a knee in the groin!" Judy's beads clanged. They seemed to me to have a ring of doom about them.

"Yeah, you're right, Sid," Prince Malik said good-naturedly, "but I won't accept that crack about us Arabs not contributing anything. Listen, soljer," he went on, addressing the bearded poet, "we Arabs invented every damn way of making love known to the human races, that's right, you read our books and you'll find out there isn't a position or an arrangement or a combination we didn't think of first, so nuts to you, and if I had a chance, I'd show you, but I'm not sure you're man enough—"

"I'll kill the fink!" cried the bearded man. And he went for Prince Malik's short oiled neck, which part of the ambassador's body was extremely hard to find. The two wrestled for a moment —the literary man high on his trip, the confused desert prince tormented beyond reason—rolling this way and that, amid the horrified audience.

"Dammit, this is quite enough," Homer Murphy said. And with that, the enormous colored man, the savage linebacker who had stopped the entire Green Bay Packers singlehanded on three memorable occasions, picked up both contestants, and like a man dropping fish to an aquarium shark, tossed them into the Stapps' swimming pool. The splash was loud, final, convincing.

"Bravo!" cried an Italian embassy counselor.

"That was great!" boomed Senator Eisenberg. "Homer Murphy for President!"

"Hurray for Homer!"

Suddenly a fevered madness seized the party of celebrities. I saw Albon Blake flying off into space, fully clothed, and into the water. *Splash!* Then a Yale economist, a chubby, pipe-smoking, shy man. *Splash!* Next a member of the Pakistani military aid mission. *Splash!* After him Congressman Verlon Peacock, a bespectacled man, whom I had not heard utter a word in my Washington career. *Splash!* And several others. *Splash! Splash! Splash!* The splashes sounded loud and jarring in the night silence. The band struck up "Down by the Riverside."

Astounded by the mass hysteria, I saw Senator Hannaford guiding Fern toward the house. I took Maria's arm and led her away also.

"Everybody in the pool!" Judy Stapp screamed. "That's what I call a good party!"

Then borne aloft on the inflated wind of those emerald green bloomers she sailed up over the edge of the waters, holding her nose.

The scandalous party made the newspapers. Parenti, who had remained dry and land-based, better to record it, had written at length about the affair, making sure to point out that the party for Prince Malik, the distinguished Djaraki Ambassador, was a wicked farce.

Parenti went on: "And wicked farce is the best way to describe Senator Hannaford's attempt to make the American government and taxpayer foot the bill for his scheme to develop the sandy Arab shiekdom of Djarak. Everyone stands to lose by this, except Hannaford's big business pals, and the betting is that the Senate Foreign Relations Committee won't even hold a hearing on the proposed amendment. It doesn't look like a good year for the richest man in the Senate. He is learning that money isn't everything."

There were other reports on the wild party at the Stapps, but they were decent enough not to use the occasion to lambaste the boss. They were reported in a tolerant way, as if to say, well, these people are under pressure, why not let them relax? In fact, Mayor Murphy was quoted as saying, with a grin: "Man, it was a hot night, that's all."

In the weeks that followed we worked very hard trying to establish a favorable atmosphere for the Djarak Amendment. We were helped by two things—an increase in guerrilla raids by the Free Djaraki terrorists, and by a growing attitude in the press that the time had come to "get tough" with those leftist-inspired tribesmen who were troubling the peace of the world.

In this respect, the Russians, up to their elbows in a wasting war in Outer Mongolia, where the National Liberation Movement was giving them fits (it was rumored that the Soviets had committed no less than 400,000 men in trying to subdue the Chinese-backed rebels) were eager to shove us into a new adventure to draw attention away from their own headache.

"The United States, with its Marines committing atrocities on the innocent people of Djarak," Radio Moscow lied, "is in no position to criticize the peace-loving Soviet Union in its attempt to secure peace and freedom in Mongolia. As is well known, the Soviet Union supports the democratic aspirations of the Free Djaraki Liberation Front and denounces the American Imperialist aggressors."

Aggressors! We had less than five thousand miserable Marines sweating in fly-blown tents around the Sheik's palace in Tel-Djarak. Every now and then a rebel would lob mortar shells into their camp, and some poor lad from Texas or Georgia would be killed or maimed. We would send out a punitive force and find some Arab miscreant or kill a few of them. It was hardly a Vietnam; it was a tragic parody of a war.

But many newspapers began to demand a firmer line, and so did much of the public. "If we do not fight in Djarak," cried one bold editorialist, "we will have to fight in Cleveland!" Some of the extreme crowd dropped hints that the time had come once and for all to "lob a few big ones" into Lin Piao's latrine. One thing reassured me that the desert *opéra bouffe* would not get out of hand—as yet. The State Department had decided not to demand that the Free Djaraki movement "let its neighbor alone." It would have been difficult in any case; it was not a neighborly sort of war but an old-fashioned bandit foray.

In any event there was more shooting in Djarak. Encouraging advices came also from the Longhorn-Mideast man on the scene, "Tex" Wiggins, who reported in coded cables to Ben that the Royalist army of Prince Aziz could more than hold its own against the Free Djaraki guerrillas, particularly if a bit more American military aid were forthcoming. Ben felt ready to battle for his outrageous amendment and so did his Air Force friends.

"Anyone opposes this," he said to me, with a sly smile, "is selling out a plucky little ally to Communism."

But how start? We mulled over the notion of again approaching Senator Walter Edgerton of Ohio, the tweedy, pipe-puffing, obstinate Chairman of the Senate Foreign Relations Committee. But Ben sometimes knew his limitations. Edgerton was not for him, would not have his shoulder pummeled, his elbow bent, his chest nudged. Edgerton was a loner—much admired by his colleagues, but a loner. Not only was he not in the club, he did not care. Edgerton would be a tough nut to crack, and conceivably the Djarak Amendment might never even see the light of day in committee. We might have to settle for a floor amendment, always a chancy business. But we needed allies, another voice.

"We'll get to Henshaw," Ben stated. "He is a good boy and he will help."

I could see his strategy. Royce Henshaw, like Walter Edgerton, was an intellectual, a liberal, a respected voice, a leader of much of the nation's academic community. Although Henshaw was not on the Foreign Relations Committee, if he could be prevailed upon to deliver a "hawkish" speech on the floor—or perhaps at the National Press Club—calling for a hard line, a massive aid program in Djarak, Ben's cause would be much buttressed. It would indeed, be an "end-run" around Walter Edgerton.

I was with Ben when he stopped Henshaw in the corridors, greeted him effusively, and asked, "Royce, how is that fellow Warfield doing?"

"Dalton? Well, much the same. He was shot at a few days ago."

Ben grabbed Henshaw's right arm. "Royce, I'm ready to do that fellow Warfield and you a big favor."

The senator from Montana withdrew. He knew all about Ben's favors. "On Scattered Sites Housing, Senator?"

"That's right. You set a date and I'll read the Pentateuch to the Labor and Public Welfare Committee. You'll get just what you want from them, Royce, you and Warfield. One blast from Mr. Private Enterprise here, and they'll write the housing bill the way you fellows want it written. Even old Eisenberg will smile!"

Henshaw's craggy face beamed. "Senator, this is the best news I've had in years! I'll call a meeting for—"

"Hold it, hold it, Royce," Ben said. "Now I have a small favor to ask of you."

"Well . . . if it's another version of the New Wilderness Bill . . ."

"Oh hell Royce, that's Christmas Past. This won't be any problem at all. You know about that little amendment I want to tack on the Foreign Aid Bill, a special rider to give us a foothold in Djarak, protect American lives and property, and—"

Henshaw laughed and stroked his long nose. "I'm sorry, Ben, but there isn't a chance."

"I thought you wanted that Scattered Sites deal more than anything. It's dead Royce, dead unless I fight for it."

"Then it will be dead," Senator Henshaw said morosely. "No, I can't lend myself to this Djarak affair. It simply goes against my grain. Walter Edgerton has mentioned to me already that he knows what you have in mind, and he's very upset. Walter tells me he won't permit you to offer a committee amendment, and he'll battle you all the way on the floor of the Senate on it. And you know Walter when he's aroused."

I thought I saw a shimmer of respect light Ben's eyes as he studied Henshaw's rough-hewn face. "All right, Royce," he said. "But you may change your mind. The offer stands."

It would be a hard battle. Frankly I had no idea what his tactics would be now. And meanwhile, the nervous Conglomerate members clamored for results. They waxed impatient. Two of the weak sisters—Tramlett-Hewes and Jackwitt—hinted to Albon Blake that they would want out if he failed to deliver in the near future.

Late one autumn evening, the senator and I sat in his office and studied the list of members of the Foreign Relations Committee. I felt I had lived through this once before. I remembered us studying the membership of the Interior and Insular Affairs Committee.

The committee had nineteen members, including Chairman Walter Edgerton. Party lines would be meaningless. Ever since the Vietnam war, the usual political divisions had been shattered. It had been said of the committee, whose members were in a very real sense a senatorial elite, that they constituted 19 members and 21½ points of view. No longer did the Senate Foreign Relations Committee automatically respond to White House edicts. It snubbed the Secretary of State, flouted the State Department, and engaged in protracted debates of a controversial, disputative character. And scholarly Walter Edgerton was the least controllable of its members.

"My colleagues and I learned something during the Vietnam affair," the chairman said, "and we will never forget it. We must be originators of foreign policy, not mere rubber stamps for the adventures of an activist President."

Edgerton was a liberal on most issues, and it was curious how he and so many liberals like him had become opponents of the strong executive. The committee had become fragmented, kaleidoscopic, shifting shapes and colors with each shake of foreign policy. Senator Edgerton for example, was a "neo-isolationist" on matters such as the presidential edict that sent Marines into Djarak. That he saw as an infringement on congressional powers. On the other hand, he backed President Kretz' attempts—with the aid of powerful men like Ben Hannaford—to trade with Eastern Europe, even to hint at military help for the Romanians and Czechs if they became sufficiently disenchanted with their Soviet masters.

The committee, like a badly trained horse, reared and kicked and showed its teeth. It drew a good deal of criticism from the press—from leftist-liberals and from conservative journalists—and Chairman Edgerton found himself the subject of more attention than he cared for. He was essentially a shy and retiring man, much respected in the Senate, a puzzle to the White House, and particularly to cabinet members like Gordon Hackensetter, a gloomy millionaire who distrusted anyone with an education. He looked upon Edgerton's Phi Beta Kappa key as an affront, a symbol of his membership in some conspiratorial order aimed at the overthrow of the republic.

But able men often have a way of getting the top jobs in the Senate. And Edgerton was one such honest and able man. It was as if his colleagues, even the corrupt Alf Kemmonses and the millionaire Ben Hannafords had to concede that a college professor could be an intelligent, creative, patriotic person—and so they rewarded him with a prestigious post. I have always sensed a kind of admiring envy for the Edgertons and Henshaws of the Senate, by the Hopewells and the Hannafords and even the Gabe Tutts. They seem to see in the Walter Edgertons some of their lost ideals, something of the men they might have been. I'm not sure. I may have misread them completely. But that is the feeling I get. A man like Royce Henshaw represents to them *another* America—the America of Emerson and Jefferson and Wilson—and although they would never admit that *that* America is superior to the one built by the Hopewells and the Hannafords, I suspect they know it is there, and they are obliged to honor it.

Our work was cut out for us. And I entered this new effort with a despairing heart. Not so my boss. Ben studied the nineteen names and biographies I had had Maria type up for us on several sheets of white paper. Nineteen good men and true.

"I study this list," said Ben, "and I'm not overjoyed. I'm glad Gage is on the committee. He'll be for us. Right down the line. Maybe he can even swing it. 'Know ye not that a little leaven leaveneth the whole lump?'"

"I admit Senator Hopewell is full of yeast. But he won't make this loaf rise. Senator Edgerton's got his people also. Foreign Aid is simply too complex an issue. The opposition—and I mean the opposition in our own party more than the other fellows— will grab something like this amendment and use it to discredit the whole package."

"Stranger amendments have crept in," Ben said. "I've read the history of that Franco Spain Amendment. That was the damnedest thing I ever heard of. Priests grabbing senators in the corridors. A big mail drive. Cardinals getting on the phone to congressmen —just to make sure old Franco wouldn't be done out of a single dollar. And by God, it worked. I have to hand it to the Roman Church, they are the greatest organization in the world."

"The Conglomerate and Albon Blake and you aren't quite the Roman Catholic Church," I said. "Not yet, anyway."

Ben laughed. "Yeah, they are a great bunch. I've always said the Jews have the best theology, the Catholics have the best presentation, and we poor native American suckers, poor Protestants everybody jumps on, we've got nothing."

Again he scanned the lists, frowning. "I wish we had five Gage Hopewells on this committee. What a fine old gentleman. Hasn't been a single measure to make free enterprise more free he hasn't gone along with, and there hasn't been a single piece of creeping socialism he hasn't knocked for a loop. Name it—Truth in Packaging, Food and Drug Act, Oil Depletion Cutback, Anti-Monopoly—old Gage has murdered them all. And that little law firm of his in Milwaukee hasn't suffered a bit from Gage's kind heart. Not at all."

"But there's only one Senator Hopewell on this committee," I said despairingly. "Maybe we should drop this foray against the committee and offer the amendment on the floor when the bill is called up."

"That won't be until November the way things are going. We can't wait. The Conglomerate will be dead by then. The heat may be off in Djarak—we'd never get another crack at it. Wiggins says this revolt is a joke—fifty Arabs with rifles."

"But suppose you don't put together the Conglomerate? Is that so terrible? Does it really matter that much to you?"

"Son, it's *all* that matters."

He was goaded, pushed forward by some force I would never understand, some consuming need to own, control, acquire, dominate, influence. Motion, that was the key to it. He wanted everything in motion—money, men, matériel, ideas, plans. I think it was this more than anything that intrigued him, that drove him into rash and willful acts. Tranquillity infuriated him.

"Give me your reading on the committee," he said.

"Fourteen to five against us. I count only Hopewell, Erlenmeyer, O'Gara, Mayes, and maybe Guillaumin."

"A small team," he sighed. "I figure six—got my money on Dierking also. We have to move four."

"Impossible. We just can't do it."

"Edward, nothing is impossible."

"No sir, not this time. Edgerton will hold the line against you. You can't get this through, not after the bad publicity on the New Wilderness Bill."

"To hell with publicity. I'm going to get this into the Foreign Aid Bill. If the Catholics could do it for Franco, I could do it for Prince what's-his-name."

He could not be dissuaded. I had visions of Albon Blake, his tape recorder, his hotel suites, his hired ladies.

"We'll start modestly," Ben said. "Chip away at the soft earth before we start hacking at the hard rock. Looks to me like we got two easy ones."

"No one will be easy."

"Easier than the others," he said.

"They elude me."

"Goodchapel and DiFalco."

I groaned. Not Lester Goodchapel again, not poor Lester. Goodchapel's seat on Foreign Relations was a fluke, part of an interparty deal, which resulted in several members of his own party being forced to take lesser committee assignments. The odd thing was Goodchapel had proved a good committee member. In his plodding way he read everything, and had one of the best attendance records, never missing a committee vote or important debate. The reason was that members like Gage Hopewell, as Majority Leader, or Forrest Mayes, as Finance Chairman had other important duties that pulled them away. But Senator Goodchapel never missed a session.

As for Henry DiFalco, he was a hard-working, intelligent little fellow from Connecticut, a former district judge, a popular and aggressive politician. I believe he had eleven children and seventeen grandchildren. Once he had been mentioned as a possible vice-presidential possibility to run with President Kretz, but the right-wing of the party had dumped him in favor of Smead Beldock. Some of his fellow party members—the "you're a traitor" mob—had never forgiven DiFalco for having attended Harvard on a scholarship. The very word "Harvard" made them slobber with hate.

"Now, Edward," Senator Hannaford said, "tell me something these two men have in common."

"They are both up for re-election in November."

"Correct. What else?"

"They are both in trouble. DiFalco barely won his primary against that lunatic who accused him of treason. Goodchapel has gotten the Farm Lobby sore at him and was barely renominated. If you were to ask me I'd say they were both losers."

"And how do you rate them as members of the World's Greatest Deliberative Body?"

I hesitated. "Just as senators? Not as targets?"

"As senators, Edward."

"DiFalco is outstanding. He's honest, a hard worker, and he's been a genuine fiduciary—he works in the public interest. Any man who stood up to the right-wing the way he did, has to have guts. What's more I like him personally. It will be the Senate's loss if the little fellow is beaten."

"Goodchapel?"

"A lost soul. But oddly enough I think he may develop into something. He's no fool. He's awed by the majesty of his surroundings. I think the way he voted against the New Wilderness Bill may have been his coming of age. He was telling us something. If you ask me he's got potential."

"And they will both be beaten this November," Ben said. "Unless they get help."

"And you believe that help from us will move them to support our amendment?"

Senator Hannaford closed his eyes. "The help will be preceded by an extensive educational campaign."

"If we swing them, Senator, it will still only give us eight votes."

"We'll find two more—somewhere."

He was determined, single-minded about his amendment. And it would be fun. He would help two decent men win their seats, with the help of a big contribution! And best of all—it would be from our secret special fund, the gift from shifty N. Krallis.

"Edward, what do you regard as a decent figure?" he asked.

"Well, we gave Alf Kemmons ten thousand—and we got it back. That was to ensure New Wilderness. We should at least do the same."

"Let us say twenty."

"And how shall I describe this to them?"

"As contributions from the Campaign Committee."

"But they aren't . . . the committee may ask . . ."

He made a lateral gesture with one hand. "Hell, let's keep 'em *all* confused. You tell our friends that while this is from the committee, an additional sum for campaign purposes, they are to be quiet about it since it involved certain complicated bookkeeping arrangements that only I am privy to. They'll get their regular committee allotments just the same."

"They aren't that dumb. They'll suspect something."

"Of course they will. They won't suspect. They'll *know*."

"Where the money really came from?" I asked, raising my eyebrows.

"No. Why they are getting it, and what they are expected to do."

"They may not like the idea at all."

"No one turns down that kind of money. Leastwise, not most people. Do you realize how that can help poor DiFalco, with those assassins on his back? Or Goodchapel, with the farmers out to string him up?"

I was hesitant.

"There's something wrong with this," I said. "Maybe it's the men involved. Alford Kemmons was one thing. But you and I know he was an exception. You yourself have said, there aren't more than two or three Kemmons' in the United States Senate.

I mean, men who are buyable. You can't compare him to a fine man like DiFalco or a simple one like Goodchapel."

"I'm not. I merely want to help them. I will convince them by honest argument that they should support me. As St. Paul tells us, 'Let every man be persuaded in his own mind.'"

And so he went to work on Senators DiFalco and Goodchapel. They were lunched, dined, escorted, invited in for an evening's libation—"striking a blow for liberty"—and most of all talked to, as only Ben could talk to his peers.

Both men enjoyed this look-in on the seat of the mighty. Goodchapel appeared quick to forgive the incident of Albon Blake's recording. I think he felt that by finally voting against us he had established his independence, and in a way he had.

But Henry DiFalco, representing an eastern industrial state, a rather thorough-going liberal, was even more intrigued by being taken into Ben's confidence. DiFalco was often a lonely outsider on race and labor matters. He and Maury Eisenberg and John Tyler Lord battled valiantly for funds to help Negroes, but ever since the "Punish-the-Poor" era of the middle sixties, these had been harder to come by. Now, as Ben pointed out, the tiger was after Henry DiFalco.

I recall a lunch we had with DiFalco, in which the tough little Italian American—his grandfather had helped build the New Haven Railroad, and his father had owned a fruit store in Norwalk—talked about himself. At one point Senator DiFalco looked curiously at Senator Hannaford, and said wistfully, "Senator, I hope you will not take this amiss, but I often have the feeling that men like you—and goodness knows you and I have differed on many issues—that men like you are protecting us from something dark and evil in American life. Whenever my super-liberal friends start complaining about men of wealth I tell them, 'If you don't like Ben Hannaford, you should see who is waiting around the corner for you—with a noose in his hand.'"

Ben nodded his agreement. "Yes, there are some rough ones around. They still calling you traitor?"

"It amounts to a small industry in Connecticut. I am 'Red Henry.' I am the traitor to the great middle class that elected me. I am denounced because I am a director of the Harvard Alumni Association. My children, now my grandchildren, are handed obscene notes at school referring to me as 'the little commissar.' I long ago had to arrange with the phone company to do something about obscene phone calls."

It seemed to me that Senator DiFalco almost absorbed courage sitting next to Ben, that Ben's friendship was a testimony to his own patriotism, that a man close to this rich, potent figure, this essential capitalist, could not be accused of treason. You laugh? You say that these mad acts do not happen? I assure you that Senator DiFalco heard that word more often than he cared to think about. Soon he and Ben were good friends. At which point my boss got into the matter of the Djarak Amendment. DiFalco did not like it and said so. But he listened patiently—through more friendly meetings, a formal dinner at Potomac Oaks, whenever Ben could get him alone.

He worked his same rough magic—we hoped—on Lester Goodchapel. Bygones were bygones. Ben disavowed any part of the plot in the Monroe-Plaza. The tapes had been destroyed. Albon Blake was a scoundrel. Ben had long ago told him off. Senator Goodchapel was flattered. As far as the Farm Lobby was concerned, why Ben knew the head of it. He could be talked to. He might be convinced. He was not the only voice for Indiana's farmers. And so on. Then, when Lester was feeling better about things—my boss would bring up the Djarak matter. "Sure it's unusual, Lester," he would say, "but that is an unusual situation there."

"Well, Senator Edgerton keeps telling me we have no right to get involved. That it was a mistake for the President even to send in those Marines. That maybe we're asking for another Vietnam."

"I respect *Professor* Edgerton as much as any man in the Senate," Ben said, "but he can be wrong too. What I want to do, is build up that little place until no Communist dare go in, until the people are as rich and happy as Americans."

"That isn't what Senator Edgerton says. He thinks, I hate to say it, but that your amendment is nothing but—it's his word Senator not mine—a *ruse* to let you and your associates take the country over. I overheard him saying to Senator Lord and I know this is telling tales that maybe you wanted the Senate to name you the next King of Djarak."

"It's not original," I said. "Parenti said it first."

"I certainly don't approve of such insinuations, and I'm sure it isn't the case," Senator Goodchapel said. He melted forward, a shapeless man, his eyes mangled by the lenses. "But, darn it, I have to listen to people like Walter Edgerton and Webb Urban. Golly, Senator Hannaford—and you too. It's just a question of which of you is more persuasive."

"Let me suggest that none of us persuade you, Lester," Ben said warmly. "You are man enough to reach your own decisions. That is all I can ask of you."

We let the indoctrination of DiFalco and Goodchapel lapse for a while, although Ben was still attentive to them—some advice on a vote here, a hint on how to handle the Veterans lobby there, a tip on a job opening for a loyal party worker. The lines were kept open and we could only hope. Moreover, if we were able to swing their votes, it would just be a start. We would need two more changelings, as Ben read the committee. I felt we would need three.

At last D-Day arrived. My orders were the usual. I was to go to the Riggs National Bank and draw from the safe deposit box a total of forty thousand dollars in cash. I was to make up two envelopes, each containing twenty thousand dollars. And I was to present the money, in person, to both senators, explaining that it was a "special" donation from the Campaign Committee, but one about which total silence was advisable, in that it involved important committee contributors who had to remain anonymous. Naturally I was to stress that Senator Hannaford was responsible for directing the money to two loyal friends, two valued members of the Senate.

"But are they committed to us?" I asked.

"Not yet," he said.

"Then . . . shouldn't we wait . . ."

"They've asked for help," he said. "They need help. I've promised it to them."

"But they won't promise their vote in return?"

He spun around in his black leather chair and looked across Constitution Avenue. "They will. People like DiFalco and Goodchapel are fair men. They won't take a sincere campaign gift without giving something in return."

I blinked once or twice at this. Only the boss could state it so beautifully. Yes, they were *sincere and honest men*. But were they not sincere and honest in their original conviction that our shabby amendment (and I had reluctantly come to that conclusion) was a trick to give the boss and his friends economic domination of the Middle East? That the starveling sheikdom was no more worthy of this American largesse than were the oil companies for whom Ben had labored to kill the cut in their depletion allowance?

"Well . . . then you want me to get the money and go right to them?"

"Might as well have it in readiness," Ben said. "Then wait till I give the signal. In a day or two."

I wanted to talk further with him about the matter. For reasons which elude me I was disturbed. But an urgent phone call from the Dover Plains people interrupted us. The participants were increasingly restless.

I followed the procedure I had already established when we had arranged to send $10,000 to Alford Kemmons. At the Riggs National Bank, I produced my key and my identification card, and from the safe deposit box, counted out two stacks of $20,000 each, in one hundred dollar bills. Each stack I inserted, neatly bound with rubber bands, in unidentified manila envelopes. Then on two self-sealing combination letter-form envelopes, I wrote down the date, the amount, and the name of the recipient. Before sealing them, I added, hardly knowing why I did, the initials "D.A."—to signify "Djarak Amendment." I then asked the uniformed guard to date stamp each letter with an official bank stamp. He obliged me. I took up my two fat manila envelopes, nesting them in my interior coat pocket (they made a mighty bulge in my gray silk suit—it was of Italian design and not constructed to accommodate thick items) and outside the bank mailed the letter-envelopes to my apartment.

So tense had I been that morning that I did not notice Maria was not at work. I asked Cleo about her.

"Called in sick," Cleo said. Her eyes were full of suspicion, of unhappy visions. As I think I have said, Cleo was rumored to have been "an old flame" of the senator's. She still maintained an old-maidish proprietary attitude toward him.

"Nothing serious, I trust."

"Maybe she's getting ready to quit," Cleo said, busying herself with some newly arrived publications on the Middle East. We were all taking crash courses in Arabic history.

"You sound as if you want her to leave. Isn't she doing a good job?"

She did not look up from her desk. "Too good. And don't push me on this subject."

In late afternoon Maria called me. For some reason, I was glad the boss was out of the office—at a Senate Campaign Committee meeting.

"Feeling better?" I asked.

"I'm not sick. I've moved out."

"Ah. Back to the old apartment?"

"No. The YWCA. Back to where I started."

"That will make things difficult. They are singularly illiberal when it comes to the matter of guests in the rooms."

"Don't be cruel. Eddie, I've got to talk to someone. I've been going crazy. I couldn't stand another day in that big, empty, echoing house—with both of them staring at me like I was some kind of prize possession. I couldn't hurt him any more, and I couldn't stand her. They're—they're—not like other people. They're bigger than life . . . they react differently. It must be the money."

"Unless you are hypersensitive."

"Could you meet me here, at the Y? I'll be in the lobby."

All roles seemed to suit me where she was concerned. I had been employer, guide, father-confessor, beard, and now lay analyst. It was the sort of liaison with a woman that I have always sought to avoid. It is too much like being married. My notion of a female associate is a bedmate, pure and simple. Marsha Treadway had been perfect—a good sport, an undemanding and uncomplicated type. (I even forgave her her treasonous behavior with Parenti. That had been a lapse. In my current frame of mind, I would have welcomed Marsha back to my bachelor diggings.)

Maria hardly looked ill or pained. She was waiting for me in the austere lobby. Immense fashionable sunglasses hid her eyes. Something had changed about her, and the sunglasses were symptomatic. She seemed—I don't know—flashier, sexier in an extravagant way, an almost defiant way. The manner, for example, in which her legs were insolently crossed, disturbed me, and, although I scarcely know why this should have bothered me, she was smoking a cigarette. Now Maria did of occasion smoke in the office, but I had never noticed it, or if I had, it had meant nothing to me.

"The career of Maria Valdez comes full cycle."

Two tall spinsters cast reproachful glances at her—she was too much the tropic bird for the Protestant confines of the YWCA.

"Just about, Eddie. I couldn't take another day there!"

"Does the senator know you have flown the coop?"

"No. I just picked up and vamoosed. I got Travis to call me a cab. Fern was out shopping—I often wonder what she buys—I never see any of it. I didn't even leave a note. I didn't know what to say."

"Yes, it was an odd arrangement. You were ordered into the coop, so that hen number one could keep a cold eye on the new chick. But she forgot there were roosts all over town, and the rooster had no trouble."

"Eddie, shut up. Didn't you agree not to talk about your dirty suspicions?"

"Sorry." I sighed. I stared at her neck, a creamy tan column, with the kissable indented V just below the throat. How satisfying it must be to caress that small concave area with one's lips! I was jealous of Ben, furious with him. All his abstinence over the years, all his puritanical fidelity to Fern's bulletproof body, had been nothing more than watchful waiting, a holding back—until the perfect pearl was found. And he had found it. And he had loved it.

"I think I'm going to quit. I mean give it all up."

"The job? Washington?"

"Oh . . . just the job. For the time being. I'm not comfortable in that office any more. I think everyone knows. Do they, Eddie?"

There was almost a note of cocky pride in her. She hoped they knew. She was *glad* they knew!

"I think most people know, or at least have made educated guesses," I said. "But Fern's move threw them off. Maybe that's all Fern ever had in mind. But don't let it worry you. You aren't the first secretary whose boss has fallen in love with her. Not even the first senator's secretary."

"He really loves me, Eddie. He's desperate. I can't stand having all that power over him. It isn't right. He's—he's helpless when he's with me."

But my little oleander blossom did not seem distraught. A clear skin, fine features, luminous eyes, soft hair—all these endow their possessor with a resiliency that is the essence of life. She was not overwrought by their relationship. It was he—more than twice her age—who suffered. Were there moments in their fevered lovemaking, I wondered, when he contemplated his paunch, studied the corded veins on his arms, dwelt on the fact that in fifteen years he would be seventy years old?

"He will not give you up?" I asked.

"He says he can't. He can't do another day's work without me."

"Then I would suggest," I said cruelly, "that it is your patriotic duty to stay on the payroll. The republic demands nothing more than your acquiescence. Not to mention our noble Conglomerate. Why the entire future of the Middle East rests in your hands."

"You're being mean, Eddie. For the first time since I've known you. I don't like you this way."

"I'm playing the monster. But I can't help myself either. Maria, give him up if you have to. He'll manage. He always has."

"No, this is different. He told me so. He says that people like he and Fern aren't given to grand passions. That their world is a world of *things*—land, oil, cattle, cars. He understands himself pretty well. But now . . ."

"Ah! You are another *thing!*"

"No! Not at all! He loves me, Eddie, loves me!"

That driven, domineering man. So bent was he on having his own way, on accumulating, on bending others to his will, that he was ever at pains to hold his deepest passions in check. Lust was not permitted to diminish strength, to compromise, weaken, or betray. When these men strayed, they strayed within careful limits —the expensive whore in the hotel suite, the carefully planned assignation at the mountain camp, the faceless bedmate. But not for Ben! Now he was clutched by shuddering adolescent passions. Fulfilled or unfulfilled? I was no longer certain.

"I can't take much more of Fern," Maria said. "Those pale eyes! She's like a bereaved cow. Those eyes look at me—hurt, appealing. It's awful."

This, too, did not surprise me. Fern, poor woman, had never in her protected life had an original thought. Her marriage threatened, she had invited the serpent in but the serpent went on biting her mate.

"I walked in on the middle of a conversation one night," Maria said. "Something I wasn't supposed to hear. It was late. I'd had a headache, went upstairs to that damned chintzy bedroom—"

"I warned you what it would be like—"

"Ugh. Bird prints on the wall. I couldn't find any aspirin, and I started down the hall, and padded by a sort of little dressing room off the senator's bedroom, and I heard his voice first, not quite sure what he was saying, but then Fern, very clearly, in a kind of mean tone that I didn't associate with her—"

"I can imagine she has a rough side."

"And she was saying, 'I know what you want, and what you have in mind, but you have to remember one thing.' And he said, 'What is that, dear?' And this is what rocked me Eddie. She said to him, '*If you want to go to the White House you have to take me with you.*'"

"Say, that isn't a bad line. Did the senator respond?"

"He said, 'Maybe the White House no longer interests me.'"

What was I to tell her? It must have been gratifying for a Mexican-American foreman's daughter to have so much power.

"I just don't believe he intends to surrender his presidential dream. Although the way things are going it may be done for him."

"More troubles?" she asked.

"When sorrows come, Maria, they come not as single spies, but in battalions."

"Then I'd best uncomplicate his life and get out of it. He'll survive."

Her cold-bloodedness astonished me. I had thought of Ben as the dominant figure in their relationship—the aggressive male, the cock-o'-the-walk. How I had underestimated her!

"Shall I tell Cleo you've resigned?" I asked, getting up.

"No. Say I'm not feeling well . . . a virus. Give me a day or two to think about this thing. But I can't go on in that office, and I've had that twenty-seven-room house."

"Look here, Maria. Suppose Ben were to tell you he was going to divorce Fern and marry you. It's unlikely, but nothing shocks me any more. Would you agree?"

She cocked her head, and it was an effort for me to keep from caressing it, from touching the lustrous crown of dark hair, strok-ing her soft cheek. "I don't know, Eddie. I just don't know. He's sweet, and kind, and considerate, and he's one of the best men I've ever known. Maybe it would work. There's something . . . something . . . easy and comforting about a man his age. I never believed I'd feel that way, but I do."

"When you would be thirty-eight, he would be seventy," I said idiotically.

"Oh, spare me that arithmetic. You said yourself it would never happen, that he'd never leave Fern."

"But if he would?"

"I don't know what I'd say. But I'd be tempted."

Nothing I could say or do would be of any help to her, or Ben, or myself. I had the feeling that she, and she alone would resolve the matter. Kissing her lightly on the forehead—to the reproach-ful stares of a YWCA functionary—I left Maria in search of our two beneficiaries.

CHAPTER TWELVE

Senator Henry DiFalco, that courageous little man from Connecticut, was at first baffled, then reconciled, and finally, grateful.

We sat in the senator's inner office. The dark paneling on the walls were devoid of an empty spot. Signed photographs and citations covered every square inch. We sipped black coffee and I studied the photos. DiFalco apparently knew anyone of importance everywhere in the world.

"His Holiness signed that one for me when I attended the race-in-religion conference in Rome two years ago," Senator DiFalco said proudly. He offered me an enormous cigar—black, aromatic, thick. "President Otero sends me these every month from Havana. God, was I grateful the day we knocked Castro over. I hadn't had a decent cigar in months."

Around me gleamed framed photos of fellow senators, governors, four Presidents, two heavyweight champions, a half dozen professional football players (including Mayor Homer Murphy) and television, movie, and theatre personalities. Senator DiFalco was a public man; he knew all about communications. And he was a first-rate public servant, an honest and hard-working chap.

I placed the manila envelope on the table. "This may seem a little irregular," I said. "But Senator Hannaford tells me he has had several conversations with you concerning campaign needs. This may be of assistance."

Senator DiFalco blew a cloud of rich smoke toward the ceiling.

"Well, he is a man who tends to do things in an irregular way. Edward, I'm of two minds about this."

"These are funds from the Campaign Committee," I lied.

"Why in cash?"

"The senator has instructed me to say that he has set up a special fund for people like yourself—who need help urgently. He prefers that the specifics of the transaction remain confidential."

"I see." Again he hesitated. Then his small hairy hand patted the envelope. "That should help." He took a letter-size printed brochure and tossed it at me. "Take a look at this poison."

On the cover, in red and blue lettering was the legend:

HENRY DIFALCO—INTERNATIONAL SOCIALIST
HOW LITTLE HENRY CODDLES COMMUNISTS
AND TIPTOES AROUND TRAITORS!

"I don't have to read it. This kind of poison is always in the body politic. I'm sorry it has to be you."

"You know, Edward, they can swing an election now. One more riot in Hartford, one more crime wave in Bridgeport, and I'm through. They'll never forgive me for having gone to Harvard, no matter how often I tell them it was on an athletic scholarship." He chuckled a little. "What the hell, if I can't face up to them, I don't deserve to win. My grandfather swung a pick to build the New Haven Railroad, and my old man and my uncles built the retail stores, and I don't owe any super-patriot loudmouth an apology."

"Senator Hannaford would be proud to hear you say that."

"Yeah, the big guy is okay. You know I held a card in the bricklayers' union once? Worked summers when I was in college. I told your boss a few things about masonry—he got a kick out of it."

I was proud of Henry DiFalco and my boss.

"Well, I've got to move on," I said, rising. Next stop: Lester Goodchapel.

"Look Edward, I told Senator Hannaford that there are no strings with this campaign help. When that amendment comes up, I'll have to vote my conscience."

"I'm sure he understands, Senator."

When I left him, he was staring at the fat envelope—somewhat troubled by its presence. I did not blame him.

Senator Goodchapel was at a subcommittee meeting—Agriculture, I think. He was probably trying to shore up his relations with the Farm lobby. I gave the envelope to his secretary, then requested a slip of paper, on which I wrote:

My dear Senator Goodchapel:

The enclosed is from Senator Hannaford. It is a Campaign Committee contribution though not through normal channels.

The senator has been very much gratified with his recent talks with you.

Edward Deever

It is curious how men of great power know, through some sixth sense, some inner telegraphic system, some extrasensory sensitivity, when disaster is about to strike.

To this day I am confounded by the fortunate coincidence that led Senator Hannaford to be out of Washington, attending to HW affairs in Ramada City, in the protective fortress of the ranch, when the "iron ball hit," as Fred Goldstein put it when he telephoned me that warm September night.

"I won't even read it to you," Fred said gloomily as I ate a lonely bachelor's supper—one charred lamb chop and canned lima beans—and felt the urge for a soft thigh or a round hip to caress. "It's rough, Eddie, rough. Parenti must have the right dope, or else he's sucking for the biggest fattest libel suit in the history of journalism."

"What does he say, for God's sake?"

"He says you took a bribe—a big one—two hundred and fifty grand—from the mortgage and loan people for your boss. And he says the money wasn't even needed—the provision of the tax bill was dead already and Hannaford knew. Parenti says he got it from a guy named Norton Krallis."

N. Krallis! That shiny-suited, shifty, sweating man with the thin mouth and the darting eyes. I thought of the three of us—Krallis, George Paxton, and myself, sitting idiotically in front of the gibbon's cage as the black attaché case changed hands. *Whoop-thump! Whoop-thump!*

"Don't tell me anything else," I said. "I'll go out and get a *Truth.*"

"Any statement? Anything Eddie?"

"Not until I've read it and studied it."

"Can I call the senator?"

"I can't stop you. He's in Ramada City. But I don't think he'll have anything to say. Give me a chance, Fred."

I felt lightheaded, ballet-footed. In some lunatic manner, I felt free, unburdened. I was like a man who has long suspected his body of harboring a malignant disease, and is at long last gratified to learn the truth that he *is*.

I put on a sweater and hurried down to the warm misty street. At the corner there was an all-night drugstore (is there anything else in our great city?) with a newsstand. There I purchased the early edition of the newspaper and sat at the deserted counter, ordering a cup of tea.

With trembling anticipatory hands—almost like a man disrobing a woman—I turned to the inner pages to Parenti's column. Well, I had small favors to be thankful for. They had not transferred it to the front page.

I read. And I felt released, delivered. But this sense of deliverance, this masochistic euphoria, was short-lived. As I sipped my bitter brew, tasting bag, leaf, and purified water, scalding my lips, the precariousness of my position revealed itself. Indeed as the words leaped at me, the cold accusatory print, I thought of all the people who would read them—our friends and associates in Washington, the people all over the country who knew the senator, his constituents, his business associates, the hard-nosed members of the Conglomerate—already burned once on the New Wilderness Bill—and even Sheik Aziz of Djarak and his sheeted minions.

The words were daggers and each one pierced my side. I hated Parenti's guts. I could have murdered him.

A scandal that will rock the highest circles in Washington has come to light. It involves Senator Benjamin Bow Hannaford, the construction millionaire from Ramada City, his administrative assistant, Edward Deever, and others, whose names will be revealed in due time.

View from the Hill can report exclusively that a gift, fund, bribe—call it what you will—amounting to $250,000 in cash, was given, in person, to Edward Deever, Senator Hannaford's aide, last June 25, in the Washington Park Zoo, by two men representing certain Mortgage and Loan groups.

The two men were George Paxton, a lobbyist in the employ of King Lobbyist Albon Blake, an old friend of Senator Hannaford's, and Norton Krallis, representing the Mortgage and Loan crowd.

The deal was arranged by Blake. Krallis, who has made a full revelation to this reporter, is the head of the Morningstar Mortgage Corporation of Hillview, Long Island. He is a millionaire, but not in the same class as Big Ben Hannaford, whose net worth exceeds $150,000,000.

The payoff of $250,000 was aimed at killing the mortgage and loan provision of the new tax bill, a provision that would have upped tax rates. The money was to be used to influence congressional votes.

But here is the cream of the jest: At the very moment that Krallis was forking over a black leather attaché case with the money to Edward Deever, Senator Hannaford had confidential information that the mortgage and loan tax had *not the slightest chance of survivng the joint Senate-House conference on the final bill!* In short, Mr. Krallis and his associates paid $250,000 for nothing!

Some weeks ago Mr. Krallis learned how he had been cheated. He and his associates went into orbit. Krallis recently contacted this reporter with the story. He had irrefutable evidence, including a tape recording of his conversation with Deever and Paxton.

There are still gaps in the story, which only Edward Deever or Senator Hannaford can supply. Specifically: What happened to the $250,000? Where did it end up? One rumor is that it has been used as a "lubricant" on such Hannaford-backed measures as the notorious New Wilderness Bill. More on this sordid matter tomorrow.

NOTE: In short order, *View from the Hill,* is going to honor the Senate Ethics Committee with the transcript of conversation at the Deever-Paxton-Krallis meeting, and with a record of everything Norton Krallis has told us.

It will be interesting to see how fast the Ethics Committee moves on this one. Last time around, when *View from the Hill* made known Senator Hannaford's hanky-panky regarding the Wilderness Bill, nary a word of protest issued from the Ethics overseers. Indeed, Senator

Webb Urban of Wyoming, its Chairman, actually defended Big Ben. How long can this whitewashing be tolerated?

Ah, Norton Krallis. It was a fitting name. That stocky, impatient man in his metallic blue suit, a Miami Beach nightclub suit, in dramatic counterpoint to George Paxton's spurious Ivy League seersucker. Well, N. Krallis had had his day. I wondered about Ben. How smart had he been to leave himself open for this kind of attack? I suppose it was the confidence of *real* money —his pipelines and airfields and urban complexes—against fake money, the inflated dollars of Krallis and his people. Ben had naught but contempt for them. And they were going to prove to him that they were not objects of derision. And a tape recorder! Hidden no doubt in that electric blue suit. In his tie clasp perhaps?

I ordered a second cup of tea from the colored girl behind the empty counter. It is curious that whenever I am in situations like this, I find myself almost envying people who lead uncomplicated lives. Perhaps you will not believe this, but I envied that colored girl. She earned her weekly stipend, went home, watched a late movie on television, slept, took a bus to work, day after day of simple routine. My life had become unbearably complex; I longed for simplicity, green fields, a cloudless sky. Long long ago, perhaps when I was just learning to walk, I could remember toddling off into a wild green meadow—sunflowers and goldenrod and pepper grass—in back of my father's grocery store. With great vividness, with a kind of color photo clarity, I remembered myself wandering amid high foliage, a midget in a jungle, and even then, at the age of what—two?—feeling mysterious inspiration. I needed that open field right now; I would wander for days, living off the land.

But as the reader has surely learned by now, I am not a quitter, or a defeatist, nor do I lack courage and resiliency. There was nothing at all I could do that night, except go back to my apartment, disconnect the telephone and go to sleep.

A morbid silence hung over our office the next day. I had the feeling that I had contracted some terrible disease, one symptomized by an ugly sore, a suppurating lesion on my face.

"That rat is after us again," Cleo said thinly. "He'll get *his* some day."

"Professional liars are hard to trap," I replied. I asked if the boss had called in. No, it was only seven in the morning in Ramada City.

Matt Fixx came into my office, his pale narrow face whiter than skim milk, his jug ears wilting. "A bad show, Ed," he said. "I'm fractured."

"It'll blow over, Matt."

He tilted his slender face. "I mean—is Parenti leveling? Don't misunderstand, Ed. With the senator away for a few days, we have to be prepared for the questions. Did it happen?"

I made a tent of my fingertips and put them to my pursed lips. "Yes, and no. Don't look shocked. Yes, it happened, but not the way he's phrased it, and it was not at all underhand in any way."

Of course the phones began to sing. United Press, AP, Fred Goldstein from his network, the other networks, all the Hill reporters, the newsmagazines. They were enraged with Parenti for "scooping" them; furious with the way Norton Krallis had selected him as the recipient of goodies.

I took a few of the more important calls myself—the *New York Times*, the *Washington Post*, AP, telling them that we denied the story out of hand, and that Senator Hannaford and I would have a statement soon. What else was there to say?

Then I began to think of that money resting in fat bundles in the Riggs National Bank. Wild thoughts raced around my brain: should I take it all out? Destroy it? Deposit it in different accounts under false names, the way, I have been told, the comedian W. C. Fields used to do? But as I reflected on my dilemma I grew weary. I simply had run out of ideas. On something as complex as this I needed Ben. Only Ben could help me.

I telephoned the ranch house in Ramada City. He knew about Parenti's column. How calm and unworried he sounded!

"Have the reporters been after you?" I asked.

"Yes, but I'm not saying anything."

"Nothing at all?"

"Just to deny the whole story. I've said it simply isn't true, and we'll back up our case when I get back to Washington."

"When will that be, Senator?"

"Oh, two or three days."

Two or three days! The storm broke over us, the waves smashed against us, and he would remain warm and dry in his fortress in Ramada City. And who would be left to face the storm?

"But . . . but . . . what am I to do in the interim, Senator? Those reporters won't give me a minute's peace."

"Tell 'em it's a pack of lies," he said.

"Well, if it is," I ventured, "we'd best get our version of the truth set, so there are no discrepancies."

"Parenti is a liar," he persisted, "everyone knows that. That's as good a defense as any."

"He may have been telling lies all his professional career, and this may be the first time in his life he is being truthful. We have to do better than that."

"Maybe you're right." Did he sound tired, as tired as I was of this mess? I could not be sure. But he paused, and he was thinking things out. "For the time being, you say that the report is inaccurate and misrepresents the facts. Say there's a conspiracy out to get me, that I've made a lot of important enemies—people who stoop to stealing documents from my office, spreading lies—and we'll present our side in due time."

"That's not good enough, Senator. Parenti claims he has a tape of my conversation with Paxton and Krallis."

"He's lying."

"I doubt it. Parenti, whatever you may think of him, is a professional. People will ask why we aren't going to sue him."

"We are, we are, Edward."

I gulped. On what basis? It seemed to me that Parenti and Krallis had the evidence. We were naked, unarmed. And then I realized what the senator's reaction had been. He was a king. He had done just about anything he had wanted to do with his money. He was a man who forced the President to sweat his way down to the desert in July and dedicate a road to his garage. It did not matter to Ben who was telling the truth, how much evidence Parenti had, what underhanded dealings we were involved in. He would simply inflate his iron chest, set his hard jaw, and say, *I am right because I am rich and powerful and a senator, and you are wrong because you are a lying newspaper ghoul!*

"May I tell the press that you—we—intend to sue him?"

A pause. Then he said: "Yes. I'm going to sue him until his

head spins. And just keep telling 'em we'll have a full statement in two or three days."

"They'll claim you're hiding out in Ramada City," I said. "That isn't like you, Senator. They'll say you're evading the issue."

"I don't give a damn what they say. When have I ever?"

"But that will leave me alone to answer questions."

"Edward, you are a grown man. You answer them the way I said. Deny it all. Parenti is a liar. He steals documents. Play that tape of Marsha admitting she stole them. Get something on Krallis. He's no good. And he's yellow. Get after Albon Blake to make a statement. He can deny it also."

"I'll have to admit there was a meeting."

"You can say you met with them, but that it was a routine meeting."

"They will ask if money changed hands."

Again, he paused. He was, I realized, somewhat uncertain. This was not the Big Ben Hannaford I knew. And with this awareness, I felt my guts tremble a bit, my knees turn watery. I did not like what was happening. I no longer was so positive that we could brazen our way out of whatever it was we had done.

"Don't answer that. Say we'll get around to it when we prepare our response. Do you remember exactly what you said to those birds? Was anything said about money, how much there was involved?"

I racked my brain. I had trouble concentrating. "No, I don't think anything was said about money. I'm certain of it! Of course I had no idea how much was in the attaché case until we opened it on your desk!" I was jubilant.

"There. You see how easy this is going to be?"

"Right, right! As a matter of fact very little was said. This Krallis character didn't say much at all—he just wanted to get out, back to New York. I made sure to keep telling Paxton that this was purely for educational purposes. That it wouldn't affect our feelings one way or the other."

"Son, we are as free as birds," the senator said. "What in hell's name can they make of that? Sure, we took a contribution—something for the campaign committee—special fund for special purposes. Anything wrong with that?"

"Not a thing. Yes, I remember—I said specifically that I promised them nothing—nothing at all. And Paxton said he and his client understood."

"Good, good. Now you jot some of this down. We can always accuse them of doctoring that tape. Doesn't prove a thing."

I felt much better after that. But the press kept hounding us. They came to the office, they phoned, they stopped Matt Fixx and me in corridors. "We'll have a statement soon," I said, "Senator Hannaford thinks so little of this latest set of lies by Parenti, that he isn't even coming back to Washington. He's busy with personal matters in Ramada City."

It did not sit too well. I could tell by the mocking leers, the sideways glances, the knowing nods, that the journalists were not convinced.

If the press acted in a hostile manner, I was invigorated no end by the support we got from Senate leaders.

"A damnable, vicious slander!" Majority Leader Gage Hopewell chanted. "Yaaaas, the man who attacked my dear friend and colleague Senator Hannaford, is a revolving, vibrating, motorized, four-wheeled liar! I dare him to attack me! I know that wretch, and he has been on the back of honest legislators who disagree with him ever since he set his cloven foot in our city! Yaaaas!"

The reporters applauded, roared. They had made a pet of old Honey-Tonsils, our dear Gage. He was so funny, so show biz, so colorful! So what if he had gone down the line for every corporate favor, every easement for big business, every tax boon for the rich, every loophole for the powerful, every evasion for the banker? He was lovable old Gage, bless him.

"I'll defend Senator Hannaford against these jackals and vultures till my last breath!" sang Honey-Tonsils. "That scoundrel, that rascal, that scurrilous hound who stole papers from his office, who eavesdropped, bought tape recordings, bribed witnesses, how can anyone believe his word against that of our beloved Benjamin Bow Hannaford?"

On the edge of the mob of reporters, Lou Parenti, his dark, gray-templed head bobbing with mirth, called out: "Me, Senator, me! I believe him!"

"Yaaaas, you would! You are a disgrace to the honored profession of the Fourth Estate! And you may all quote me!" Off he floated.

Senator Gabe Tutt also defended Ben, although I began to

wonder—and wondered even more as our ordeal dragged on—
whether we needed him. To be candid, there was serious doubt
as to whether old Gabe, that avenging angel of the Old South,
that foe of pornography, miscegenation, Mrs. Roosevelt and the
Luce publications, was all there. It was suspected by even his
friends, that Gabe was losing his marbles, that booze, hatred, and
lechery, not to mention the unlimited power he exercised over
the Armed Services Committee, were taking their toll of his febrile
brain. Gabe was close to eighty. He had been hating people so
long—Al Smith, Roosevelt, Truman, Kennedy, LBJ, that I wondered that there was room left in his skull for anything else.

"A damn conspiracy!" Gabe bawled to the roving packs of reporters, hot after anything new on "the Hannaford case." "A
damn conspiracy by traitors and Commonists! Senator Hannaford
is a great Amurrican! I'll defend him to the end, against Commonists and traitors!"

Others were less outraged. Some senators said nothing at all.
Some were cautious. Royce Henshaw said merely, "I can't make
any comment, gentlemen. Not from a single column by a single
journalist. I've always respected Senator Hannaford and I find the
charges hard to believe. Let's have the facts before us before we
render any snap judgments."

"Is this a matter for the Senate Ethics Committee?" asked Fred
Goldstein.

"At the moment, no. Nothing at all has been adduced as evidence to support the charges. I am opposed to trying people in
the press."

"But maybe that's where the trial will have to take place," Goldstein persisted, "if the Senate Ethics Committee keeps ducking
its responsibility. They didn't say a word when the story of
Senator Hannaford's Conglomerate came out—the way it was tied
in to the New Wilderness Bill."

Royce Henshaw shook his brown mane. "I don't think Senator
Urban and the other members of the Ethics Committee saw any
need to pursue the matter. Senator Hannaford had certain business connections. He also had a right to sponsor the New Wilderness Bill."

"Isn't that a conflict of interest?" Goldstein asked.

"It depends on how you look at it," Senator Henshaw said
enigmatically.

So far, so good. Even John Tyler Lord held his fire. I had the feeling that his puritanical New England blood was so stunned by Parenti's accusations that he could not find words to express his fury with Ben.

The only outright attack on us came from former Congressman Angel López Garcia. Safe on his island retreat, a tropic maiden on each arm, "the Big Spick," as Ben called him, summoned eager reporters and advised them: "Chico, we see how those beautiful senators go to work on the Big One. I tole you once, I knew plenty dirt up there on the Hill. *Amigos*, we in for some fun. I make you a bet right now, Hannaford beats the rap. You see, Chico, he's one of *them*—right down to his accent and his cowboy boots. They let him off easy—but not before we learn a lot of cute stuff."

But no one listened to Garcia any more. He was a dark ghost, crying foul from his beach house, wondering when he would be let back into Congress. His insinuations only aroused sympathy for Ben—at least on the Hill.

I said nothing. I followed Ben's orders. We denied the truth of the columnist's remarks. We would make our own statement in due time. But Parenti was after our jugulars. After a few more columns hinting at further revelations, he ran what he claimed was a transcript of Norton Krallis' secret recording.

The unbelievable story of how Senator Ben Hannaford and his aide Edward Deever bilked a group of Mortgage and Loan people of a quarter of a million dollars grows more fascinating all the time. The money was given to Deever, for the senator, as an "educational" fund to help defeat the Mortgage and Loan tax increase in the tax bill. But the joke was that the measure was already dead. Norton Krallis, a New York businessman, who represented the Mortgage and Loan group made a tape recording of his meeting with Deever in the Washington Park Zoo when the money changed hands.

View from the Hill can report exclusively that the tape reveals a most intriguing conversation. In addition to Krallis and Deever, George Paxton, a Washington lobbyist who acted as go-between, was present, and did most of the talking for Krallis.

PAXTON: *This is Mr. Krallis from New York.*

DEEVER: *How do.*

KRALLIS: *Hiya.*

PAXTON: *I can't tell you how happy we are that your boss has agreed to go along with us. Mr. Krallis here is one of our clients. He is mighty happy, too.*

KRALLIS: *Take this goddamn thing. I wanna get the hell out of here as soon as I can, okay?*

PAXTON: *Easy there, Norton. It can't hurt to visit a little with Mr. Deever. You can go home and say you met Edward Deever, Senator Hannaford's right-hand man. And we are all aware of the senator's importance.*

DEEVER: *You are to understand one thing. This in no way will influence the senator, as he has told Mr. Blake many times. He's his own man. He's been opposed to the Mortgage and Loan tax all along. But it can serve educational purposes.*

PAXTON: *Exactly. We did not conceive of it any other way. To educate some of the disbelievers. Why I'd be out of my mind, and so would Al Blake if we dreamed of trying to work on a great public figure like Ben Hannaford.*

DEEVER: *Furthermore, you are not to count on anything. We'll apply this to educational uses but we can't guarantee that the students will learn everything. But we'll try.*

PAXTON: *Of course, of course. May I?*

DEEVER: *Help yourself.*

(Note by Louis Parenti: Mr. Krallis advises me that at this point Mr. Paxton helped himself to some popcorn Mr. Deever was eating from a paper bag.)

PAXTON: *Popcorn, Nort?*

KRALLIS: *No, no. Let's get the hell out of here.*

PAXTON: *Well I guess that does it, Mr. Deever. May I call you Ed?*

DEEVER: *I suppose so, if you wish.*

Parenti went on, repeating some of the things he had already said. I read the transcript again. How damaging was it? Did it prove anything at all? To begin with no sum of money was mentioned. No money at all. They might have been giving me a case full of leaflets explaining the need for lowered taxes on mortgage-and-loan associations. Moreover, we talked about the senator, but what proof was there that he had anything to do with the transaction? Could not it have been my idea? Thinking this, I began to worry. *What an out for him!* Was it possible that his prolonged stay in Ramada City was related to this? The same notion, I was sure, would occur to him when he read the column!

Our bustling office assumed a funereal air. The nattering of young girls, the bang and slam of desk drawers and typewriter carriages, filing cabinets were muted. Ben's authoritative voice was gone, and there seemed a diminution in the number of visitors. Cleo grew somber and distant with me. Her hair seemed grayer, her manner cool. Marsha had long gone. Maria was still "out sick." The other girls appeared afraid to speak to me.

Only the phones were raucous and insistent. The press gave us not a moment's peace. When would the senator be back in Washington? When would we answer Parenti's charges? Would we sue? For how much? Has the senator discussed the accusations with the White House? Had the President said anything—knowing how highly he esteemed Senator Hannaford, and how much he needed his help for his legislative program? To all of these, I hedged, offered evasions, summoned up charm, told jokes.

Only Matt Fixx offered me solace—and it was cold comfort. "We've got a bad inter-face here," he said to me, as we sat, like two marooned seamen, in Ben's huge office. "Our capability will be tested, Eddie."

"The senator will settle this in his own good time," I assured him.

"If attrition doesn't kill us first. I mean, we need a viable defense. I'd like to activate Parenti's destruct mechanism."

As if Matt's locutions were not sufficiently depressing, I had to contend with phone calls from Prince Malik, our Djaraki friend, and Imre Bator, the Hungarian Ambassador.

"Hang in there, soljer," Prince Malik said to me. "Don't didi out, Eddie. I talked to Djarak today. Wiggins says all systems are go. We're A-OK down there, you tell the senator."

No sooner had I thanked him (for what?) than Bator, with his quasi-British accent was on, to sympathize with me. "Who is this Parenti?" he asked. "What is his aim? Why should he attack a man like Senator Hannaford?"

"You might call him a revisionist, Mr. Ambassador," I said wearily.

"Revisionist! Hah! Very, very good!" But there was a hollow ring to his laughter. He was thinking of all those housing developments and department stores Ben wanted to build for the

Eastern Europeans. No doubt it worried him that if Ben were to
fall, to be bereft of power and influence, they all might have to
go back to wearing shoddy Communist-tailored suits and living
in crumbling Communist-built flats.

It was late afternoon when the senator called from Ramada
City. He sounded sanguine, not at all downcast. I was ashamed of
myself. In his absence, I had permitted a pall of gloom, a sickening defeatism to descend on the office.

"How are you, sir?" I cried eagerly. "And Mrs. Hannaford?"

"Fine, fine, Edward. We are all fine."

"I assume you have read Parenti's latest."

"Yes, yes. It's nothing to worry about."

"I wish I could be so certain, Senator."

"Edward, no one is going to believe two cheapjohns like this
Krappis or whatever his name is, and a liar like Parenti. People
will simply not accept that nonsense."

"They have that tape," I said, and my voice grew ragged.

"It could have been faked."

"Those things are hard to fake. I know."

"Suppose the tape is an actual one made when you met with
those people. What does it prove? It was a contribution. We say
it was for the Campaign Committee."

"But people will ask why it didn't go through regular channels
to the committee. Why was it never recorded at committee headquarters? And why did only the two of us know about it?"

"Details, details. This whole thing will blow over, like a lot of
others have. Hell, if we'd done something *really* dishonest"—and
I could hear his voice change as he smiled at his own roguishness
—"like double billing the Senate for plane rides, or putting a relative on the payroll, or using testimonial dinner money to pay
our liquor bill, they might have something to holler about. That's
rotten. That's *dishonest*. That casts discredit upon the United
States Senate. But we did nothing like that."

"Sooner or later you will have to come back here, and say as
much."

"I intend to be in Washington day after next. You schedule a
conference for me in the caucus room."

"Wonderful! We'll show them, sir!" But even as he said it, I
had tremors of doubt.

"And to set your mind at ease, Edward, I had a long talk with

Senator Urban this morning and with several of his colleagues. The feeling is that the Ethics Committee won't touch this until we tell our side of the matter. And believe me, our side will give them pause. I'll have that chiseler Kravvis and our friend Parenti howling Uncle before I'm through!"

That was the fighting Ben Hannaford! I was wroth with myself for having accused him of hiding out in Ramada City when the storm broke. Not my Ben! And how good it was to know that the good old Senate was closing ranks, that the mighty Ethics Committee, with its six upright members, would not countenance any slanderous attack on one of their most esteemed colleagues!

We chatted a bit more, the senator undismayed, still anxious to press for the Djarak Amendment as soon as the storm over my meeting with Paxton and Krallis blew over. "We got lots to do, Edward," Ben said expansively, "and we'll get it done."

And so we might have. Except for President Kretz' press conference the following day. As I have stressed, President Kretz was an amiable, peaceable man. As head of a publishing empire, he had always permitted underlings to make harsh decisions. His only competitive interests were cribbage and tennis; he could not bear argument, conflict, raw tempers, ill-feeling.

For all that he had an unpredictable strain in him. I can't explain it. Every now and then he felt impelled to "take a stand," to be firm, to make an issue. These sudden outbursts were as unpredictable as summer storms; and more often than not, they resulted in action—from Congress, the cabinet, local governments, the United Nations, the public. The reasons were twofold: President Kretz was a respected figure, and moreover, he spoke out strongly so rarely, that when he did, all assumed the matter was of great urgency. Publishers tend to act in this capricious manner.

"I'm sick and tired of these reports about a decline in our lobster fishing industry!" he shouted one day at a press conference, to a reporter from a New England newspaper chain. "I want something done to increase the lobster catch and lower prices!" And something was done. A concerted program initiated by the Bureau of Fisheries soon doubled the catch of lobsters and sent prices down.

We were the lobsters this time. It had begun as a routine press conference—the President reporting he had offered once more to act as a mediator for the Soviet Union in the Mongolian War and that Chairman Gromyko had rejected the offer, being now according to the President overly influenced by the USSR Joint Chiefs of Staff or *sokol* faction, the Russian word for *hawk*. He then meandered about the tax bill, the Foreign Aid Bill, the proposal that he go to Geneva to address the opening session of the United Nations, when suddenly a network reporter popped a question about Ben.

I watched the conference in my apartment at mid-morning. The office had grown intolerable, the stares and whispers of the girls a source of grief to me.

"Mr. President, a Washington columnist, Louis Parenti, has run several columns charging that Senator Hannaford and one of his aides took a large sum of money from a special interest group to influence legislation. Do you have any comment?"

The white eyebrows bristled, the pale eyes flashed. "I have not read the columns, Mr. Holland, but I have been informed of the matter."

"Do you think, Mr. President, that Senator Hannaford's actions should be investigated?"

The President looked puzzled. "By whom?"

"By the Senate Ethics Committee."

A dull glaze came over the President's eyes. I doubted that he knew that there was a Senate Ethics Committee. "Let me say this," he responded. "I don't know anything about these charges. I have great respect for Senator Hannaford. I have a great respect for everyone in the Senate. I have great respect for all the Congress. And I find it very hard to believe that any senator, any congressman would accept money to influence legislation. I don't believe it. I think Senator Hannaford will answer these charges in due time."

I breathed easier. The President's attitude—despite his non-committal manner—stood for much on the Hill. I was sure Senator Webb Urban and the other Ethics Committee members were watching. The storm was over, I felt. Then another reporter was on his feet. His name was MacGowan, and he had served in Navy Public Relations with the then Commander Kretz, during the Second World War.

"Not to belabor this, Mr. President," MacGowan said, "but suppose the evidence produced by Mr. Parenti is true—that this is an actual tape of an actual meeting between Edward Deever

and someone giving Senator Hannaford money to kill part of
the tax bill. Wouldn't it be something for the Senate to look into?
I'm thinking, sir, of the U. S. Navy's experience with the black
market operation at Kum Sak."

I could see the ruddy color rise in the President's face, the fists
clench, the sharp jaw thrust forward. He pounded the lectern
once. The eagle on the great shield shivered.

"I'll tell you this, Jack," he said to MacGowan, "I personally
backed that investigation at Kum Sak, and I didn't give a darn how
many high ranking Navy men were involved! The honor of the
Navy was at stake, and when I had the evidence I ordered the
book thrown at them!" His voice was a roar; he was truly furious.
"And I'll tell all of you this! If what this reporter says is true, I
don't care who is involved, or how high up he is! I'll back up
any investigation anyone wants to make! And that goes for the
Senate Ethics Committee! I'll give them all the help they need!"

A block of ice formed in my chest, replacing my heart. Cold
water pumped through my veins, and my hands and feet were
frigid. For all the jokes that were made about President Kretz,
his failure to lead, his deferral to Congress, his indifference to
issues, the fact remained that when he exploded, people's ears
hurt. They moved. They *ran*. And just as one outburst had produced lobsters, so another would produce an investigation, I
was positive.

I took the phone off the hook and waited, and wondered. Surely
Ben had watched the presidential press conference. The afternoon
papers would lead with his remarks. I could see the headlines:
PRESIDENT BACKS HANNAFORD PROBE.

But for the time being I was powerless, aimless. What was there
to do except wait for the ax to fall? And yet as I showered, shaved,
dressed, had the doorman bring me the newspapers, and otherwise wasted time, I had the feeling that Ben and I would survive.
No one could bring down Benjamin Bow Hannaford. He was of
the Senate, and he was in the American grain, builder, bargainer,
benevolent bully.

I answered a few calls from the press. Most of them had given
up on me. I was a poor source. Once I called the office—Cleo
told me that the senator had not phoned in.

"I'm not feeling so hot, Cleo," I said. "I may just stay at home
and think a lot."

"I understand. Do you want anything sent over—anything you want to work on? Matt has some new information from Djarak. Report from Wiggins."

"No thank you, Cleo. I'll just rest. If there's word from the senator, let me know."

Every hour I tuned in the radio news. John Tyler Lord and Royce Henshaw had both called on the Ethics Committee to investigate, but Gage Hopewell had opined as how there was hardly any basis for an investigation, and that Parenti could not be believed anyway.

In late afternoon, my phone rang, and a woman asked for me.

"This is Edward Deever speaking."

"This is Kevin Shanahan's office calling, Mr. Deever." My heart, almost thawed by now, turned icy again.

"Mr. Deever?" The voice was a Boston Irish voice.

"Yes."

"Hi there, Edward. We met a while back. This is Kevin Shanahan, counsel to the Ethics Committee."

He did not have to identify himself. I knew him: red-headed, freckle-faced, a clever New England attorney, a young man on the make, the man who had run the headline-making probe of the Defense Department contract scandals.

"How are you, Mr. Shanahan? I believe we had some dealings when you needed data on Jackwitt."

"Right. May I say you and Senator Hannaford were most co-operative. I wish everyone I had to deal with was like that."

"Our pleasure." Where was my voice? Where was my strength?

"Edward, Senator Urban has called an urgent meeting of the Ethics Committee for tomorrow morning and we would like you to appear."

"A-a-a-bout those Parenti pieces? You aren't really . . . ?"

"Well, you see, we have been studying them and making inquiries of our own, apart from anything Parenti has printed. Senator Urban feels strongly about these matters. I might add the committee was unanimous in calling for these, you might say, preliminary hearings. Nothing to be concerned about. I'm sure you've got your side to tell."

"I have indeed. Does Senator Hannaford know about this? Has Senator Urban informed him?"

"We tried reaching him in Ramada City, but they said he's en route back to Washington." Ben was coming back sooner than he had intended.

"Yes of course. I forgot."

"We'll try to contact the plane and tell him that the hearings are scheduled. There is no need for him to appear. We just want to get a few things straight with you. Ten A.M. tomorrow? In room 3302, Ed?"

"I'll be there, Mr. Shanahan."

The truth of the matter is, that at certain points in our lives, we simply don't know what to do. I rested on my sofa, keeping the radio humming with its recital of bad advices. As yet there was nothing about the Senate Ethics Committee hearing. But it would be out in due time. What else could we expect after the President, that blameless, much-loved man, had come out in favor of an investigation?

It was remarkable how the matter of the Conglomerate had not moved the committee a millimeter. Webb Urban had studied the charges, had perhaps winced, and had ignored them. The Conglomerate—all those giant corporations, those self-ruling, self-perpetuating, rule-making entities—had been too close to the heart of American life to be challenged. But I was not. I was Edward Deever, ambitious young man. And the whole notion of three men passing a quarter of a million dollars in front of the gibbon cage at the Washington Zoo, was overdramatic, too highly colored, to escape attention.

But what was I to say? Would I deny it? Claim the tape was a fraud? Say that the money was a campaign contribution, a gift to the party committee to help men get elected? That could be disproven. Webb Urban was close enough to the campaign committee to find out. Then where had the money gone? Who had it? Who was using it? I thought of leaving town; of hiding; of pleading insanity; of everything in the world except my rendezvous with the six stern men and the redheaded counsel.

I tried calling Maria at the YWCA. She was not in her room. I had no idea why I called her. Perhaps I would have considered inviting her to my apartment. I even would have settled for Marsha, that betrayer. The truth of the matter was I was agonizingly lonely.

Normally I am a sound sleeper, but agitated as I was, I took a sleeping pill after the eleven o'clock news—the Senate Ethics Committee had announced it would hold a closed session the next day but had not mentioned my name—and was soon in drugged sleep.

Almost at the moment of my falling asleep, my door buzzer sounded. It must have rung several times, for the blast that awakened me was protracted and insistent. I stumbled weakly from bed—these sleeping pills have a dreadful numbing effect on me and I never succumb fully to their false comforts—found a bathrobe and blundered, half-blind to the door. I undid the chain and opened it slightly.

"Good evening, Edward," Senator Hannaford said. "I thought I'd drop by to discuss our problem."

Never in my life was I so happy to see anyone. "Thank goodness, Senator," I said. "I was hoping we'd get a chance to talk before tomorrow."

"I took Mrs. Hannaford back to Potomac Oaks," he said. "She's upset about this business. Then I came out here. Didn't want to bother her with us meeting out there. I preferred not to go to the office."

It was the first time he had been to my apartment. I felt honored. Like a fussy housewife, I switched on lamps, offered him a drink, straightened my bathrobe, ushered him to an easy chair. It was half-past one in the morning.

How Ben generated confidence and hope! Here he was beset with racking troubles—the press hounding him, the Ethics Committee sniffing about, his dreams of industrial empire possibly doomed, his status and potency threatened, and he was calm, unmoved, his strong face betraying not the slightest care.

"It seems we stand at Armageddon, Edward," my boss said, smiling.

"And battle for the Lord, Senator."

"And we shall win that battle."

"I'm sure of it, Senator. I had my doubts these last few days, but seeing you now, I feel cocksure."

He asked for a drink of water, and while I hacked at the ice cube tray in my kitchen and let the tap run, I heard him call: "By the way, what's happened to Miss Valdez?"

Ah, he was fine, fine. The old bull in him was not dead yet; he still breathed and kicked and his hot blood pumped. "She was

staying at the YWCA. I'm sorry it didn't work out—her living
with you and Mrs. Hannaford. I know how fond you both are of
that girl."

"The YWCA?" A bit more eagerness than was usual in his voice
was revealed.

"Yes. And she's been feeling poorly the past few days—a bad
cold or a virus. She hasn't been to work, although I spoke to her
yesterday. She may be in tomorrow."

"Good, good. Mrs. Hannaford has been worrying about Maria.
Running out of the house like that, hardly saying goodbye."

"I'm sure Maria will be all right. She's young and tough."

"I suppose she is."

Sly fox! Mrs. Hannaford was worried! Precipitously, he banished her from his mind. He sipped at the water. "Edward, I think
we trust each other."

"Assuredly."

"And understand each other."

"I would hope so, Senator. After all these years."

"I've been trying to see my way through this mess that the
Wop has gotten us into. I think I'm on the right track. If the
President hadn't suddenly had memories of the way he threw the
book at some black marketing naval officers, we'd have had no
trouble. I have a feeling Webb Urban, with some help from Gage,
would have ignored this idiotic business. But the President . . ."
He shook his head, cogitating on the way that bland man could
swing national sentiments so easily. "Well, you're going to have
to testify tomorrow and you'll be under oath. I'll probably have
to say a few words later. So we might as well discuss our approach."

"Whatever you say, Senator." How stupid of me to be concerned!
The way out of the wilderness was visible now. Ben would lead
me.

"As I see it, Edward, we have three approaches to this mess.
First, we can claim that Krallis and Paxton are liars, that they
invented the whole thing, that their tape is a fake, and that Parenti was in cahoots with them to get after me. We might make it
stick. Look at the way he slandered me on the Conglomerate—
but the Ethics Committee wouldn't touch it."

"That tape. If it's any good at all, Senator, experts can testify
that it's my voice. They do this with those voice-prints."

"I said that was just a possibility. I've rejected it. Secondly, we can admit the whole thing. I sent you there. The money was for our special fund. It's our business what we do with it. The Mortgage and Loan people have a right to be represented and to contribute to a senator's campaign fund."

"Campaign fund?"

"Why yes, that's what the money was."

"But . . . we called it a special fund . . ."

"No matter, I've rejected that also. There's a third possibility and it's the best, Edward."

"It eludes me."

He got up, took off his dark blue jacket and walked slowly about my living room. "Edward, I am to ask a favor of you, and I expect you to agree. It won't hurt long."

"You know how dedicated I am to you."

"That's what I like to hear. Edward, you are to go before the Ethics Committee tomorrow and advise those six fine men, my six colleagues, that this matter of taking a quarter of a million dollars from Mr. Krallis through George Paxton was your idea and yours alone."

"But that isn't true."

"I know it isn't. But they don't." Did I see his eyes twinkle? Was there a merry wickedness in them? "Edward, you will tell them that Mr. Paxton approached you, and you alone, that you and he agreed this would be a fine way of getting a little extra cash, and that unbeknownst to me, the two of you arranged to milk Mr. Krallis and his friends."

I digested this for a moment. "But what about Paxton? He knows this was something Mr. Blake arranged with you. The committee will surely rake Paxton over the coals."

"Don't worry about Paxton. Albon Blake is seeing to it that he supports your story in every way. You see, he will be to Blake, as you are to me."

"Ah . . . I see. Two underlings who cooked up a little money-making scheme without their bosses being aware of it."

"Yes! Blake won't *deny* that Krallis' crowd were after him, and after me. That'll merely back up our case. The point will be that Paxton told you about this and both of you decided it was a good time to go into business for yourself."

I covered my eyes and tried to think clearly. "Senator, I believe that among criminals, this is called taking a bum rap."

Senator Hannaford held wide his hands. "I prefer to think of it as a religious exercise, Edward. 'Where sin abounded,' the Book tells us, 'did grace much more abound.' Not that any of us have sinned. But Edward, we need your grace."

"I may go to jail," I said.

"Never! What are you guilty of?"

"Well . . . I will be guilty of perjury if I tell this story."

He snorted. "Do you think those six friends of mine on the esteemed Select Committee on Standards and Conduct of the United States Senate, could believe I put you up to this? Never. I've already arranged with Senator Urban to postpone your appearance for a few days . . ."

Nothing stopped him. "You did?"

"I called him tonight. They'll call other witnesses first. They're going to give us every break there is. By the way, you're entitled to counsel. Matt Fixx will go in with you. Matt will be briefed first thing tomorrow. You aren't to appear for a couple of days. We have to get together with Paxton and Blake and set this up."

"Jail . . ." I mused. "I may end up in jail."

He walked to the back of my chair and put his muscled hand on my shoulders. "Edward, I would never let that happen. You were just a little eager. You looked for a chance. No crime there. Moreover, you are sorry and you are going to return that money to Mr. Krallis. By the way, where is it?"

"Well sir, you've got fifty thousand of it. The batch you slipped into your desk drawer."

"Did I? Yes, I guess I did. Hell, that was just for a laugh." He chuckled.

I laughed with him. "To see if you could get away with it, right, Senator?"

We giggled like school kids—my falsetto, Ben's hearty boom.

"Yes, that's just what it was. I'll get that back to you—when you need it—when the formal ceremony takes place. Where's the rest?"

"It's complicated. Forty thousand went out to Senators Di-Falco and Goodchapel—campaign contributions. The ten that we gave Senator Kemmons came back, and I deposited it in a savings bank using a fictitious name . . ."

"Good, good. You were trying to hide something. The rest?"

"In a safe deposit box. Ten is—was—mine. You remember you gave me twenty thousand for myself."

"Well," he mused, "that forty thousand out to DiFalco and Goodchapel is a problem. But I'll think of something."

"I'm sure you will."

"Yes, we'll see to it that Mr. Krallis gets it back, with an apology from me." He was satisfied—one more arrangement, one more deal.

My head was swimming. The blood thundered in my ears. It was as if some distant ocean, some crashing surf was transmitting its rolling booming roar into my tormented skull. "Senator, I will be dead after this, dead," I protested. "I may go to jail. In any case, I'm through in Washington. I can never work here again."

He turned his head sideways. "Says who? Edward, I would never let you down. You won't go to the hoosegow, and you'll work if I say you'll work. Some of the biggest crooks in this town are happy, employed and respected, and richly rewarded."

As I studied his undaunted, swarthy face, I wondered if he were making a bitter joke about himself. But was he really a crook? Or was he *everything*, a kind of amalgam of our national life—wheeling, dealing, fixing, legislating, benefiting, building, joining, and oiling the joints of progress?

We spent two days in meetings in one of Albon Blake's secret suites—not in the Monroe-Plaza but in one of those ornate decaying apartment hotels a few blocks from the Sheraton-Park. Blake, Paxton, the senator, Matt Fixx, and myself were the only ones present. We rehearsed our roles, studied our lines, made sure we would not be tripped up by anything.

I remember very little of these meetings. My mind was elsewhere—perhaps back in the oval office of President Truman when I was twelve, perhaps in that undulating green meadow, bright with yellow butterflies, in back of my father's grocery store in Ohio.

I do recall one curious incident. At one point, Matt Fixx, that whey-faced young man, whom I had always regarded with a sort of contemptuous tolerance, and who now emerged as a shrewd shifty fellow, turned to Senator Hannaford and said: "Senator, if the deal is that George and Ed cooked this up, there's a piece missing."

"What is that?" Ben asked.

"Well . . . a payoff to George. He didn't get into this for laughs."

Paxton's freckled face looked shocked. Thus far he was an innocent victim. But Blake's silvery head was nodding in assent. We were all in shirt sleeves, except Blake who kept on his tailored Italian silk jacket.

"Right you are, Matthew," Blake said.

"Yeah," Ben said. "We got to make this as logical as possible." He thought a moment, rubbing his chin. Then he walked to the chair on which his jacket was draped, reached in the inner pocket and came back with a thick manila envelope. At the coffee table around which we sat he dropped the packet. "Paxton, there is fifty thousand in there," Ben said. "Go deposit it in a bank somewhere in your own name and bring the bankbook to the hearings. As needed, you will produce it. When no longer needed, that money comes back to *me*."

Poor Paxton! He gulped, yanked his tie open, pleaded with terrified eyes at Blake, at the senator, and fingered the packet. "But . . . this is even worse. I agreed to go this far, but this . . ."

Blake patted his arm. "George, do you think the senator would let a friend of mine down? They can't even get a conviction against a Negro mugger in this town, so someone like you will be sure to beat this."

Unhappily, Paxton took the money—surely the most extraordinary loan on record—and fell silent. We resumed our deliberations as if the passing of $50,000 was the most normal thing in the world.

CHAPTER THIRTEEN

And so I appeared before the Senate Ethics Committee or to give it its formal title, the Select Committee on Standards and Conduct, United States Senate.

The hearing, thank goodness, was closed. Open sessions would come later, with all the usual nonsense about the public's right to know, and the photographers getting two minutes, and then being ordered out. In deference to Senator Hannaford it was advertised quite early in the game, by Chairman Webb Urban, that there would be *no* live television, *no* films, *no* radio reporting of even the open hearings. As for the closed sessions—at which Senator Hannaford would also appear—no members of the press at all would be permitted.

The so-called Ethics Committee was established by Senate resolution, and consists of six members, three from each party, who then elect a chairman and a vice-chairman. Among certain capital wags such as Lou Parenti, they are known as "Whitewash, Inc." This is unfair. The committee is charged with a grave responsibility, and they must act with deliberation, rectitude, and be free of outside influences at all times.

Senate Resolution 338 of the 88th Congress which set up the committee, states that the Select Committee shall "receive complaints and investigate allegations of improper conduct which may reflect upon the Senate, violations of rules and regulations of the Senate, relating to the conduct of individuals in the performance of their duties as members of the Senate, or as officers or employees of the Senate, and to make appropriate findings of fact and conclusion with respect thereto." Further, the committee is authorized to hold hearings, and it may then recommend to the Senate disciplinary action, or additional laws and regulations.

My morning started badly when I read an AP story—evidently a leak from prior hearings—to the effect that the committee was broadening its field of inquiry to include the matter of the Conglomerate, the purloined letters, and the New Wilderness Bill. This stunned me. I recalled the way Chairman Urban had summarily dismissed Lou Parenti's accusations. Now they would be after Ben on several counts. But the burden of their probe would still be the $250,000 mulcted from the Mortgage and Loan people. It was a bad omen. They were evidently intent to make up for lost opportunities—a tendency often observed in the Senate.

A mob of reporters, TV cameras, some confused members of the public, blocked the entrance to the room. Soon I was surrounded, crushed, microphones thrust at me, cameras whirring at my strained face, lights flashing and blinking around me.

I found Fred Goldstein sticking a mike almost up my nose. "Eddie, anything to say?"

"Nothing, nothing. Really fellows, I can't say a thing until after I testify."

They shouted, importuned me, grabbed at my coattails. I could see Parenti at the edge of the mob. He was studying me, almost with pity. He was responsible for the ugly mess, but I had been informed that he would not be called as a witness by Kevin Shanahan, the committee counsel. This seemed a good break for us. Chairman Urban was, after all, a fellow senator of Ben's. And Parenti was a widely hated scandalmonger.

As the lights kept flashing, and the crowd churned around me, the guards opened the doors wide, and I was half shoved, half dragged into the chamber, room 3302 of the New Senate Office Building. The cameras followed me—the usual two minutes would be allowed for picture taking. As I moved toward the seats reserved for witnesses with Matt Fixx at my side, muttering something about "a viable position," Fred Goldstein elbowed alongside me, and whispered in my ear. He was trying to tell me something—something no one else could hear.

"*Ed, Ed . . . listen . . . that tape. I didn't hear it, but I got*

the word . . . you can hardly hear it . . . nobody would know it's
your voice, or anyone's . . . it's lousy . . . indistinct . . ."

I absorbed this at once. The tape was a poor recording. Mr. N.
Krallis' cheap equipment. Krallis himself was in the room, seated
across the chamber and flanked by two young men in black suits
—his lawyers. I had been informed that he had already testified
at great length.

Matt and I sat down. The room was cleared, the doors locked.
Senator Webb Urban of Wyoming, the Chairman, entered the
room. His creased, frosty face was non-committal—it was not cruel,
it was not mean, but it had a demanding quality about it, and I
feared him. No man who refused to use the congressional franking privilege or insisted on paying every single bill with his own
money could be trusted.

"The committee will come to order," Webb Urban said. "The
photographers and press are all gone? Thank you. We can proceed. First, let me remind all present that these are preliminary
hearings in executive sessions. Because of the complex charges
raised by certain newspaper articles, this committee has decided
to expand the scope of its inquiries to two matters. First, the
relationship between activity on behalf of S.671, and secondly
charges of acceptance of funds from a mortgage-and-loan association, to influence a provision of the tax bill.

"I remind all present that witnesses will be sworn, that these
hearings are quasi-judicial in character. This is a fact-finding session, gentlemen. Facts control judgments, and we are after
facts . . ."

As he droned on, a flat-voiced gray man, I studied the other
five committee members to see how we would stand with them. I
was not discouraged, but not too enthused either.

Webb Urban was in our party, and so was Royce Henshaw, the
eminent economist, and so was Maury Eisenberg, the hearty
real estate millionaire from Illinois. The three opposition members were tough nuts—club members, gray, quiet, self-effacing,
honest men, men whom the public rarely saw, or heard from, but
men whose views and behavior was at the very heart of the Senate
establishment. They were, Clyde Furman of Kentucky, a stolid
lawyer, Carl Mullendore of Tennessee, a conservative old gentleman, who had come up the ranks through the statehouse and the
House of Representatives, and George Owens of Delaware, a ruth-

less rooter after tax evaders and government contract chiselers.

Webb Urban was winding up his remarks. ". . . will weigh all the evidence taken and determine the course it should follow under the terms of Resolution 338 and in all the matters related to the case." He then turned to Kevin Shanahan, the red-headed committee counsel, and said, "Proceed with the examination of witnesses."

Shanahan nodded and said: "I request, Mr. Chairman, that we start today with the testimony of Mr. Edward Deever, and I request, Mr. Chairman, that he be sworn."

Matt Fixx and I rose, he with his voluminous brief cases, and we took our seats at the oblong table facing the magisterial horseshoe at which sat the six stern men and the counsel.

Webb Urban looked at me—an impartial unprejudiced look, and in his nasal voice, asked, "Do you solemnly swear that your testimony in these hearings will be the truth, the whole truth and nothing but the truth, so help you God?"

"Yes, I do."

"Be seated. Counsel proceed."

Shanahan smiled at me. "You are represented by counsel?"

"Yes sir. This is Mr. Matthew Fixx at my right."

Shanahan grinned—lawyer to lawyer—at Matt Fixx who managed a crooked grimace in return. Shanahan had me state my name and address, then asked if I testified voluntarily to which I replied that I most certainly did. He fiddled around a bit more—my education, my age, how long I had worked for Senator Hannaford, what other jobs I had held, how much I earned as the senator's administrative assistant.

"Mr. Deever, are you acquainted with a man named George Paxton?" he asked.

"I am."

"And who is Mr. Paxton?"

"He is, I suppose you would call him, a lobbyist in the employ of Mr. Albon Blake, the industrial relations consultant."

Those six fatherly faces looked at me with kindly indulgence. I suddenly had the hopeful notion that they would never dream of hurting me, surely not of hurting their comrade, Ben Hannaford, surely not besmirching the name of the Senate. I thought of the contesting forces—on one side, the sneaky likes of Norton Krallis (damn him in his shiny gun-metal suit!) and slippery George Paxton and Lou Parenti. On the other side were Ben and myself—real Americans, corn-fed, hard-working, dedicated men, part and parcel of our national life. And now I was not afraid. I knew that anything I said would be accepted; that simply because of what I *was*, and what they *were*—I would prevail. At that moment, with Kevin Shanahan's Hibernian face smiling at me, I was convinced I would escape.

"When did you first meet Mr. Paxton?"

"Let me see. He telephoned me a few times last June, about meeting some clients of his."

"Yes, go on."

"And that is all I can think of."

"You are saying," Shanahan said, and the smile was gone, "that you have never met Mr. Paxton?"

"Oh, I may have seen him around Washington—a restaurant or a bar, yes."

"Mr. Deever, did you or did you not on June 25 of this year meet with George Paxton and Mr. Norton Krallis in the Washington Park Zoo?"

I inhaled deeply. I was not nervous at all. I recalled Fred Goldstein whispering to me that my voice was barely recognizable on the tape. That was it! I would barrel my way through. I would save both Ben and myself, by denying it all! After all, who was more credible, slimy Norton Krallis, or me—Eddie Deever, All-American Young Man on the Go? Matt Fixx suspected that I was about to change the script. He covered the microphone and was whispering in my ear frantically. "Ed, the fallback position. Remember the senator said . . . you and Paxton."

I took the microphone from Matt's shaking hand.

"Mr. Shanahan, could you repeat that question?" I asked.

"I ask you, Mr. Deever, did you or did you not, on June 25th of this year, meet in the Washington Zoo in Rock Creek Park, in early afternoon, with Mr. George Paxton, whom you have already said you know, and Mr. Norton Krallis?"

"No sir, I did not."

Krallis, seated on my left with his lawyers, gasped and started to rise, his shiny figure bursting with outrage. His lawyers had to drag him down. There was an agitated buzzing in the room. Matt Fixx was working valiantly to control his emotions. I had to hand it to the kid. I had thrown out the script, without a word of warning. I would fight this out on my terms, for a change, make people do it my way. Including Ben Hannaford.

Webb Urban glowered at me. "I remind the witness he is under oath, that he is open to a charge of perjury unless he answers the questions with the whole truth, and nothing but the truth."

"I am aware of that, Mr. Chairman."

Urban nodded at Shanahan. An aide brought in a small portable tape recorder and placed it on the table in front of me. The discs were set spinning, the volume raised, and in the grave-like silence, a mashed noise became audible, the general sound of a crowd. It was indeed a very poor recording.

Then the first voice emerged—Paxton's. *This is Mr. Krallis from New York . . . How do . . . Hiya . . . how happy we are that your boss has agreed . . . as soon as I can, okay . . . you can go home and say you met Edward Deever, Senator Hannaford's right hand man . . . in no way will influence the senator . . .*

I was now convinced I had won my wild gamble. For as I listened, as all in the room bent forward to hear the recital of the alleged meeting of conspirators, it became clear that the tape was indeed dreadful, the voices hoarse, off-speed, barely decipherable as human voices. Even though the aide pushed the volume knob to the limit, and fiddled with others, the sounds, though fairly clear in terms of what was being said, were extremely difficult to identify as the voices of anyone in particular.

. . . can't guarantee that the students will learn everything but we'll try . . .

That, of course, was me speaking. But it sounded more like Donald Duck, Donald Duck with a bad cold.

The tape whirred to an end, with me saying, *I suppose so if you wish . . .*

"You deny," Kevin Shanahan said, "that that is your voice?"

"I deny it completely."

"How do you explain this recording and the conversation that takes place?"

"I have not the faintest idea. I suggest someone was out to make trouble for Senator Hannaford and myself."

Senator Eisenberg leaned forward. He had a sad drooping face, and spoke very slowly. "Mr. Deever, this is a very serious matter. Two witnesses, Mr. Paxton and Mr. Krallis, have testified under oath that that is *your* voice, and that you were present at that meeting."

"Senator Eisenberg, that meeting never took place."

Silence. A fearful silence. Shanahan bent his long ruddy head toward Senator Urban and they conferred. From behind his seat, the committee counsel then produced a cheap black attaché case. It was the one Paxton had given me—or a duplicate of it. I had stowed it next to a filing cabinet in our office and had forgotten about it. Shanahan's gumshoes—I knew he had a staff of sneaks—had found it.

"Mr. Deever," Shanahan asked, "is this your attaché case?"

I paused. Careful there. "Yes. It is."

"And where did you get it?"

"Get it? I believe I bought it in a luggage store in New York. One of those discount places. On Lexington Avenue. I'd forgotten my case during a business trip up there."

"Are you certain?"

"Yes. I don't recall the store, but I can check on it."

"You don't use this every day, do you?" the counsel asked.

"No, it's a cheap case."

"Is it not your recollection, Mr. Deever, that this black attaché case or one exactly like it—lined with red plastic—was given to you by George Paxton in the Washington Park Zoo last June 25th, and contained a quarter of a million dollars?"

I sat up and looked noble, unafraid. "Absolutely not. That meeting never took place, and I was not given that case, or any other, or any money."

Once in the cold water, the shock was not so bad. I found it invigorating. To the side I could see Krallis, sweating freely, muttering to his bookend lawyers: "He's a liar, he's a goddamn liar, the bastard is lying." One of them was restraining him from getting up again.

Again Shanahan huddled with Senator Webb Urban. The Chairman looked at me with that bleak face. "The witness will return to his seat for a few minutes. Counsel will call another witness."

One of Krallis' lawyers was on his feet. "Mr. Chairman, may I request that my client, Mr. Krallis be allowed to testify again?"

Webb Urban squinted across the chamber. "He will have such

an opportunity momentarily. The Chair would like to hear a new witness with no further delay."

"Thank you, Mr. Chairman." The lawyer sat; he looked satisfied.

Matt Fixx and I retired to the long table at the side of the room.

The rear door was opened by the guard. In walked a tall, thin, very black Negro, a youngish man, sporting a mustache and goatee. He had dressed for the occasion—a well-cut Ivy League suit in a clayish color, a high-necked white shirt, a black knitted tie.

Senator Urban looked at the colored man and asked: "You swear to tell the truth, the whole truth and nothing but the truth, so help you God?"

"Yes suh, Senator."

He sat down, a trim and self-assured figure. Shanahan asked him, "Could you state your name, age and address, please?"

"William Truscott, twenty-eight, 1415 Kentucky, Southeast."

"Your occupation?"

"Well, by profession I'm a clarinet player. But things bein' slow now, I drive a delivery car for the Free-Hand Laundry. Deliver shirts and stuff."

"Mr. Truscott," Shanahan went on, "on the 25th of June this year, while you were driving your car near the Washington Zoo . . ."

And now I knew fear. Cold destroying fear. They had found him. It was not too easy to guess how. Krallis, or one of Krallis' spies, or Paxton, or one of *his* aides, had trailed me, to make sure I went right to Ben with the money. They had seen me waiting for a bus or a taxi, they had seen me get into Truscott's delivery car, and being thorough fellows, had jotted down the license number. For all I knew, they had followed me all the way to the Hill.

I looked at Matt Fixx, and his eyes were dull, his lower lip drooping. He could never be a trial lawyer. Krallis was staring at me—a pugnacious, contemptuous stare.

" . . . I repeat, did you give a lift to a gentleman carrying an attaché case, and then drop him off at Connecticut Avenue, where he waited for a taxi?"

"Yes suh, I did."

"About what time of day was it?"

"Can't be sure. Late afternoon, two, two-fifteen."

"Mr. Truscott, will you please rise, and if the gentleman you gave that lift to, the gentleman you picked up outside the Zoo on Adams Mill Road, is present here, could you please walk to him and point to him."

William Truscott, that dark angel who had befriended me on that warm afternoon, got up and walked toward me, pointing a black finger at my white head. "That's him."

Shanahan asked: "You are certain?"

"Yes suh. I saw him waitin' at the bus stop, pacing back and forth, and he look lost, like a stranger in town. So I pick him up. I remember he offer me two bucks tip, but I tole him it was just a favor, like I do a favor for anyone."

"Thank you, Mr. Truscott," Shanahan said. "Could you take your seat again, please?" He did.

Shanahan nodded at a young fellow in shirt sleeves—a committee aide, and muttered something I could not hear.

The young fellow then went to a table at the rear of the room, and from beneath it, wrestled out five different attaché cases— brown, tan, black, zippered, locked, and so on—including the cheap black one that Shanahan had shown to me.

The aide carried them to the witness table and lined them up in front of William Truscott.

"Mr. Truscott," Shanahan said, "there are five attaché cases in front of you. Which one was the one that gentleman was carrying that day?"

"Well, Ah ain' gonna say hit that one for sure, but if you ask me which hit most like, it this black one heah." And his hand went right for my case.

"I have no further questions," Shanahan said.

Senator Clyde Furman of Kentucky, who had a habit of moving, steady-on-course, for the irrelevant, asked the witness: "Why did you pick him up?"

Truscott looked startled. "Why not? He an American citizen, isn't he? Me too. I always he'p out."

A titter of laughter relieved the tension. Neither the Chairman nor any of the other senators had anything to ask the witness. Nor did Krallis' lawyers, nor did Matt Fixx.

But Matt was on his feet, and was addressing Urban. "Mr.

Chairman, we obviously have a variance in testimony here. Mr. Krallis' against that of Mr. Deever—"

Urban scowled. "Mr. Fixx, the variance in testimony is between your client on one hand, and Mr. Krallis, Mr. Paxton, and Mr. Truscott on the other."

"Yes sir, I understand sir," Matt Fixx said wanly. "This is a most serious matter . . ."

"You understate it, Mr. Fixx," Senator Urban said bleakly. "There is a clear case of perjury here, and I do not intend to let it be fudged or shoved aside."

"I am certain of that, Mr. Chairman. But in view of the seriousness of the situation, I request a recess for an hour so that I may confer with my client."

Shanahan leaned forward. "Mr. Fixx, did not prior conferences take place between the two of you? Was this a surprise?"

I felt I was somewhere else. I did not belong in there. I was not part of these proceedings. I floated outside myself on a soft, billowing cloud of amnesia. I recall Matt Fixx mumbling apologies and Webb Urban banging the gavel as he ordered the recess.

In silence, I trailed Matt back to our office. Ben was waiting for us.

After Matt had told him what had happened, Senator Hannaford studied me—not in anger, but with a kind of stunned incomprehension.

"What the hell happened to you, Edward?" he asked. "We went through this whole thing. I even talked to Shanahan to go easy on you. All you had to do was follow orders. Paxton had set it up already—you and he cooked up this deal. He's sitting there with a bankbook showing you gave him $50,000 as his part of the deal. You can't throw the game now."

"I lost my head, Senator."

"You are going to lose that and a lot else if you don't go back in there and tell the truth."

"The truth?" I asked, feeling as if I were narcotized, deep in a morphine-induced dream.

"Yeah, the truth the way I see it. Son, you have no choice. You will go back with Matthew and admit you lied, you panicked, you lost your head." He smashed at the desk with his fist. "Damn it,

Edward, it's the little things kill us. You have to keep an eye on the goal ahead."

Matt Fixx gulped a few times, then said, "Senator, why doesn't Ed go back and say he lied to protect you?"

"Hunh?" Ben asked.

"He could say," Matt went on, "that while you had no involvement in that transfer of funds, you were completely innocent, he was upset by the possibility that you might be wrongly charged with the matter and therefore lied to protect you—to dissociate our entire office from the alleged bribe."

"Think you can manage that, Edward?" Ben asked.

"I'll try, sir."

"You got to do more than try. Remember how we went through this all with Paxton. You and he rigged it. You took the money. You gave him fifty thousand. I never knew a damn thing you were up to. You have that?"

"Yes sir, I do." Fixx and I got up again. It was odd, as we walked the halls once more, to stares and whispers, and with a retinue of harassing newsmen, all I could think of was Mr. William Truscott. Strangely, I was not mad at him at all.

Again I was called to the witness chair at the oblong polished table in front of the horseshoe.

Was it my febrile imagination? Or did I sniff frost in the air, an iciness around the table? You could not tell with Urban. That Mormon elder's face was always forbidding and barren. But I sensed a freezing, a coldness of eye among the others—Senator Eisenberg, whom I admired, a warm and genial man; Royce Henshaw, that soft-spoken intellectual; the moderate dead-center Americans, Mullendore, Furman, and Owens . . .

Shanahan was again at me. He was not smiling this time. I resented his youth, his good health and that exquisite red hair—a rooster's comb.

"Mr. Deever, you have had your recess and before I put any questions to you, I shall give you the opportunity of making any statement amending the statements you made earlier, specifically your denial that a meeting in Washington Park Zoo took place between yourself and Messrs. Paxton and Krallis."

"Thank you, Mr. Shanahan." I cleared my throat. I placed my hands flat on the table. Matt smiled at me. It would be all right.

I would say I lied. I lied to protect Senator Hannaford. He was innocent, he had done nothing. But I wanted to protect him.

"Perhaps the witness would like the questions repeated, just as the record shows them, Mr. Shanahan," Urban said.

"No, thank you, Mr. Chairman," I said. "I think I can get this cranked up on my own."

Matt winked at me. "We're viable, kid. It's down to the nitty-gritty."

"Mr. Shanahan, I have done something for which I am truly ashamed. I lied to you and to the committee during the last session."

There was a mass exhalation of air, a shifting of behinds, a flexing of fingers. Everyone in the well-lit chamber seemed to move, except Webb Urban, who remained as stolid and lifeless as the bronze sconces on the wall.

"Gentlemen," I went on, "that meeting did take place in Washington Park Zoo, exactly as Mr. Krallis has described it. He did, through Mr. George Paxton, give me a black attaché case containing a quarter of a million dollars. And that other gentleman, Mr. Truscott, did indeed, out of kindness, give me a lift."

Senator Urban frowned. "Yes, yes, get to the point."

Shanahan pointed a finger at me: "You did, then, accept that money from the two men in question?"

"I did."

"Now can you tell us what led to that meeting? How did you learn that this money was being offered to you? Was this done through George Paxton?"

"Beg pardon?" My skull reverberated with thunder.

"Mr. Paxton has testified that he contacted you and said he had interested clients, people who wanted a provision of the tax bill killed, and that you then suggested this meeting. Is that correct?"

"I'm trying to recall the exact sequence . . ."

"Perhaps this will refresh your memory, Mr. Deever," Shanahan said. "Mr. Paxton says he called you on the 21st of June, that you called back a day later, that you then suggested a sum of money, and that you said you would see that Senator Hannaford arranged to have the mortgage-and-loan provision of the tax bill killed in committee, but that Senator Hannaford had no knowledge of the deal and would never allow it if he did . . ."

On he droned, vomiting back to me the lies Ben had concocted to save himself. I half-listened, nodding my head like a marionette.

"Do I take it, Mr. Deever, that those nods of the head indicate you are supporting this testimony from Mr. Paxton? That you are in agreement with it?"

Matt Fixx's knee nudged mine beneath the table.

"No," I choked out. "No. It wasn't that way at all. He put me up to it. He made me do it. That is, he *told* me to do it. He arranged the whole thing." I spoke through someone else's voice—a high-pitched womanish voice.

"Who? Who did all these things Mr. Deever?" Chairman Urban thundered.

"Senator Hannaford."

There are momentous occasions, when, at the very climax of events, a wild, comical sideshow takes place. It is rather like a woman giggling as her mate comes to orgasm. And as I uttered Senator Hannaford's name, a wild uncontrollable *whooooooop!* issued from Matt Fixx's mouth. Everyone ignored him. He turned crimson, blinked his eyes and seemed to recoil from me. The others in the room were stone silent. I could see a self-satisfied oily grin turning up the corners of Norton Krallis' mouth.

"When did the senator first broach this matter to you?" Shanahan asked.

"That day. June 25th."

"What exactly did Senator Hannaford tell you?"

"He said that Mr. Albon Blake, the industrial relations consultant, wanted help for some clients on the mortgage-and-loan provision of the tax bill."

"Did he mention that you were to receive money from Mr. Blake or anyone else?"

"He did not."

"But you assumed that."

"Mr. Shanahan, we had had prior discussions. Albon Blake had been persistent with the senator. I was not privy to all their conversations but I was aware that Mr. Blake was offering money from these clients to make sure that the legislation was killed."

"How did Senator Hannaford phrase this transaction?"

"Well . . . he didn't. He said he thought we could accommodate Mr. Blake, and then I said I suppose we'd use his help, whatever it was, for purely educational purposes, and the senator said that was a possibility."

My head was clear. How good it was to tell the world! My eyes swept the table, and I saw Senator Eisenberg's sagging face moving slowly from side to side in sorrowful contemplation of my tale.

"What else did Senator Hannaford do?" asked Shanahan.

"He gave me a slip of paper on which were written Mr. Paxton's name and telephone number. He told me to call him and arrange to meet him."

"And you did?"

"I did. I suggested the zoo. In front of the gibbon cage, that long-armed ape that keeps going *whoop-whoop!*"

The stenotypist, pecking away at his machine, darted a look at me. So at ease was I, so free and airy, that I smiled at him: "I guess that should be spelled w, h, o, o, p."

He nodded his thanks.

"Now then, Mr. Deever, will you now state that the tape recording played for you two hours ago in this room, purporting to be the voices of Messrs. Paxton and Krallis and yourself, made on the 25th of June, by Mr. Krallis, is indeed a recording of that meeting?"

"It is. That is my voice."

"It is not a forgery, or a fake?"

"No sir. And I was eating popcorn, and Mr. Paxton helped himself to some."

"Describe what you did on leaving them."

"Mr. Truscott has described part of it. I tried getting a taxi or a bus, and then Mr. Truscott picked me up and took me to Connecticut Avenue, where I got a taxi to our office in this building."

"Then what happened?"

"I went immediately to Senator Hannaford's office and he had me lock the door."

"Was anyone else present in his office other than you and he?"

"No sir."

"Describe what happened."

"The senator opened the attaché case, the one you showed me before. I remember the senator commented about the cheap valise, saying that it was typical of the people we were dealing with.

What he said exactly was, 'a man should go first class, even if he's on his way to prison.' "

"What was in the case?" asked Shanahan.

"There were twenty-five bundles of currency. Each bundle contained ten thousand dollars in hundred dollar bills. The senator checked one of them to make sure. There was a total of $250,-000 in the valise."

"What did the senator say?"

"He said he himself was always opposed to the tax increase, but the money would help convert non-believers."

Matt Fixx, who had turned sideways in his seat, his back to me, his legs crossed, his fingers dancing on his thigh, got to his feet. "Mr. Chairman . . . I beg of you . . . I do not think that Mr. Deever should be permitted to continue . . . he . . . he . . . he . . . clearly is not himself . . . he . . ."

Senator Urban nailed him with a glare. "Why don't we let your client decide if he wants to continue?" he said. "Do you, Mr. Deever?"

"By all means."

Matt sat—sank, rather is the word, or melted, or dripped—into his seat. He darted one lost grieving look at me, and then turned his back on me.

"Go on, Mr. Deever. Did Senator Hannaford say anything else?"

"He said no converts were needed, that the tax measure was dead already, that the people who had given him the money were eager to dispense favors, and that we should not disappoint them."

"What else did he say?"

"He told me to place the money is a safe deposit box and that we would use the money from time to time."

Shanahan leaned forward. "Did he state for what purpose?"

"Yes sir. For educational purposes."

"And you took all that money, a quarter of a million dollars, and put it in a safe deposit box?"

"No sir. Senator Hannaford detached two bundles of money, $20,000 all told, and shoved them toward me. He said that was for me, since I had to start thinking about myself. Then he removed five bundles more, that is, $50,000, and said, these were for personal expenses."

"What was done with that sum?"

"He dropped it into a side drawer of his desk."

"So you then had $180,000 to put in a bank?"

"Actually $200,000. I decided to put the $20,000 he had given me in with the rest of the money."

"Did he say anything further about the use this money would be put to?"

"Yes. He said we would use it to help get the New Wilderness Bill passed."

Now the gasps from several people in the room were audible.

Senator Carl Mullendore pushed his rimless eyeglasses up on his head and his eyes bugged. He leaned toward Clyde Furman and they whispered. Senator Eisenberg's lugubrious face looked as if he had just learned of a friend's death. Webb Urban put a hand on Kevin Shanahan's arm, restraining him.

"I warn the witness," Chairman Urban said, "to exercise prudence in anything he says from now on. He must be most careful in using the names of other senators, other public figures."

Ah, the good old club, the dear old establishment. Yes, we would have to be very careful.

"The New Wilderness Bill," Shanahan said, "that is the Hannaford bill?"

"Yes sir, S.671. It was voted down in the Interior Committee a few weeks ago."

"Was any other senator aware of this educational fund, this money received from Messrs. Paxton and Krallis?"

"No sir. Neither as to who gave it to us, or of any of the transactions that followed its deposit in a box in the Riggs National Bank."

Almost in unison, all six of my judges seemed to settle back and breathe easier. I so wanted them to feel good! "In fact, Mr. Shanahan, until today, no one in the world knew of that money except Senator Hannaford and myself—and as of three days ago Mr. Paxton and Mr. Fixx."

Shanahan frowned. "Mr. Paxton?"

"Yes. Senator Hannaford decided that I was to inform this committee that the deal with Krallis was cooked up by George Paxton and myself, the two of us operating without the knowledge of the senator or Mr. Blake. Well, we had to tell Mr. Paxton what had happened to the money, and we had to make it seem he had been rewarded."

"Yes?" Shanahan asked. "So you—"

"The senator gave Mr. Paxton the $50,000 he had taken for himself. Loaned it, I guess. He told Mr. Paxton to deposit it in a bank and get a record of it. I would imagine Mr. Paxton has already testified why he got that money. That I gave it to him as his cut."

Webb Urban barked at me: "The witness will make no attempt to divine or guess or imagine the testimony of other witnesses."

"I am sorry, Mr. Chairman. I will be more careful."

Shanahan went into conference with Senator Urban. I had so filled the room with poisonous vapors, with a miasma of evil, that they had to clear the air before continuing.

This time the discussion was prolonged. Senators Eisenberg and Henshaw got up from their seats and it became a four-way huddle, with Senator Mullendore, who was Vice-Chairman of the Ethics Committee, bending his head into the group. I could see Webb Urban's head moving, like a metronome from side to side, a gesture expressing negation, misery and shock in equal degree.

In the interim Matt Fixx stared at me. "*Why?*" he whispered. "*Why?* Why are you betraying him like this? Damn you, damn you!"

"I'm sorry, Matt. I can't help it."

"Yes, you could have. Oh God, what have you done?"

Tears should have misted my eyes. But I have a good deal of bounce in me, call it a fatalistic resiliency, a trait that is less courage than indifference.

The conference at the burnished table ended. Senator Urban leveled a finger at me. "Mr. Deever, I have instructed Mr. Shanahan to resume his questioning, as that is the wish of the committee, but I will rule that you are not, I repeat *not*, to mention the names of anyone—anyone at all—whom you allege to be the recipient of funds from this money which you say you deposited in a box in the Riggs National Bank. Is that clear?"

"Yes, sir. There actually were only three recipients."

"Not a word as to their names! You have made a series of grave statements about Senator Hannaford. For the time being you will refer to no other senators."

"As a matter of fact, sir," I said, almost gaily, "the three people I mention were senators also."

Clack! Clack! went his gavel. "I warn you! Make no further references to anyone alleged to have received money from that fund!"

"If that is the ruling, Mr. Chairman, there is very little else for me to relate. The bulk of that money is still sitting in the safe deposit box."

"The Chair will decide whether your testimony is to continue."

A giggle tickled my innards. Old Urban was up a tree! There is nothing more amusing than the sight of the righteous undone. Not that Senator Urban was not a totally honest, forthright man. But he was of the club, of the establishment, and any attack on the establishment was an attack on him. It was all right to throw accusations at the single man under investigation—Ben Hannaford—but if the tar were too liberally splattered, who knew, who really knew where dirty black stains would alight?

Again they huddled. Then Senator Urban clasped his hands on the table and announced: "The Chair wishes more time to examine this witness' testimony and study it in conjunction with the prior testimony of Mr. Krallis and Mr. Paxton, before further questioning of this witness and other witnesses."

Senator Eisenberg requested that the committee wait at least two days before summoning Senator Hannaford. This was agreed upon and Webb Urban adjourned the closed session.

Matthew Fixx leaped from his chair, his spindly figure propelled by wrath and turned on me. His eyes brimmed with tears. "You rat," he whispered, "you dirty rotten rat, you lousy traitor, you're a traitor, that's what you are." And he flew from the chamber.

I got up, alone, isolated, but feeling liberated. For some nutty reason, I kept feeling good about William Truscott, my deliverer. He at least, would emerge clean and innocent—he had done a good deed, now another. I was glad I had not contested his sworn testimony.

On the way out, Norton Krallis in his iridescent suit, looked at me with a greasy grin. So did his sentinel lawyers. They were thinking about that money and how to get it back. But I said nothing and marched through the great carved doors into the swarm of shouting, churning reporters. On the edge of the mob was Parenti. He would learn soon enough what he had wrought. Some friend on the committee would leak it to him. But Lou was not grinning. He looked morose, perturbed, even a bit guilty. After all, he and I had been fellow members of the Press Gallery not too long ago.

By now we were on the front pages: headline stuff. We practically pushed the Djarak action and the Mongolian War out of the newspapers. Who cared about our Marines shooting back at Arab snipers, or Gromyko's pitiful appearance before the United Nations General Assembly in Geneva? AIDE CHARGES HANNAFORD ACCEPTED $250,000 AND KEPT $50,000! the headlines screamed. There were photos of me, of Senator Hannaford, of Webb Urban, of Parenti. Lou had not only broken the story, he was part of the news.

I lolled in bathrobe and slippers in my apartment—a man with no friends, no hope, nowhere to go—and watched the evening newscast on television. I watched myself running past the cameras, the grasping, shoving reporters, watched Webb Urban announcing the delay in the hearings, and the fact that Senator Hannaford would appear to give his side of the testimony in a few days, and that the committee was unanimous in its determination to pursue the hearings "come what may." (He did not feel all that "come what may" that afternoon, I thought bitterly, stopping me dead in my tracks when I was about to mention who were the lucky recipients of our dividends.)

The only laugh I got was watching a miserable, stammering Gromyko in front of all those black, cynical, distrusting faces in the General Assembly in Geneva. "Mr. President," the Chairman of the USSR cried, "there are pickets outside this building, dirty, bearded, barefoot youths, the scum of Europe, although they claim to be pacifists and peacelovers, and I say to them, where is the representative of Inner Mongolia? I have come here to Geneva to talk with him—with anyone—with any person representing the aggressors in Inner Mongolia—why don't they come here to talk? We say again we will stop the bombing if there is even a hint, a hint that they will do something in return . . ."

The cameras switched to the bearded demonstrators outside. (*Hey, hey, Gromyko, your dirty bombs will have to go!*) A blond youth claiming to be a former bomber pilot for the Red Air Force mounted a lamppost and burned his draft card.

Apart from insistent reporters, no one called me. I was truly in Coventry. I did not even go to the office to collect my papers and personal possessions. (Luckily, the receipted postmarked letters describing my transactions at the Riggs National Bank were with me in the apartment.) I did not hear from the senator, from Maria, from a soul. I tried calling her at the YWCA. She had checked out—no forwarding address. "My what a popular girl," the switchboard operator said. "Just about every half hour someone calls asking about her." It was Ben of course, pining, bereaved, like the "devious cruising Rachel" in *Moby Dick*, looking for a lost child.

Two days later I was back in room 3302, this time without benefit of counsel. I was seated at the rear of the paneled chamber. Chairs were left empty all around me: the leper incarnate.

By now the press had stopped badgering me—both outside the hearing room, and during the strict two-minute interval which Senator Urban permitted for photo taking. Oh, they took a few photographs of me, a few TV newsreel shots—for which I smiled wanly—but the big news was Ben himself, Senator Benjamin Bow Hannaford, calm, joking, his huge chest squared off in a dark blue suit, his temples appearing a bit grayer, his handsome wide face a bit more lined.

Krallis was gone. Paxton was not present. But Albon Blake, accompanied by a lawyer, took a seat at the rear of the room. I gathered he would be called. And Marsha Treadway materialized, also with an attorney, a stooping man named Bookwalter whom I knew to be a buddy of Lou Parenti's.

As for the senator, he was accompanied by two lawyers, Matthew Fixx, and a tall bald man with a white fringe, an older patrician type, P. K. Aubusson, of Aubusson, Tuck, Fernald and Jacobi, Washington's most prestigious law firm. Aubusson wore a black suit, vested, key-chained, and sported a lapel decoration, possibly a medallion awarded by some king. Aubusson was by far the most distinguished-looking person in the room. Even the six senators of the Select Committee were rendered rather ordinary by his aristocratic presence.

Ben's lawyer also frightened me a little. I patted the envelope in my inner breast pocket. It contained the postmarked, bank-stamped records of transactions involving our mighty $200,000. I had a feeling I would need them this hot October day. The night before I had told Shanahan about them; he was very much interested.

"The committee will come to order," Senator Urban said, and banged his gavel. A few cameramen lingered and he barked at them: "You people get out when you are told. This is a closed hearing. The public's right to know will be honored when this committee is good and ready."

They scurried for the door. It slammed shut. The guards took up their positions. The stenotypist alerted himself at his machine.

"Now gentlemen," Webb Urban said, "before asking Mr. Shanahan to call his first witness, I would like to set up a few rules for this hearing. The committee has already adopted rules of procedure, but I am impelled to repeat some of them. Let us understand that Senator Hannaford will have all his rights protected at this hearing."

Ben raised his manly head and stared at Urban. I had the feeling that he even resented having the chairman describe his rights and privileges. Ben was above all that.

"The senator may attend all hearings, if he wishes. That is up to him." Senator Urban looked at my ex-boss. Ben looked at the ceiling.

Ben was picking his spots. Thus far he had disdained the proceedings—Krallis' testimony, Paxton's perjured words, and my own on-again, off-again performance. But now he was here, ready to counterattack, and, I assumed, ready to testify.

"Senator Hannaford may be accompanied by counsel of his own choosing," Chairman Urban said, "and he or his counsel will be permitted to cross-examine witnesses and offer evidence in his behalf."

Clyde Furman, surely not one of the brightest members of the Senate, but a decent uncomplicated man, was trying to say something. "Excuse me, Mr. Chairman," he interrupted, clearing his throat, "but does not rule 13 of our rules of procedure limit the rights of a person who is the subject of investigation, to submit to the Chairman and the Committee questions for cross-examination?"

"That's my impression of the rule also," added Senator Mullendore.

Webb Urban nodded his accord. "It does, Senator Furman, but I feel that rule to be rather narrow. I'm amending it for this hearing. I've often said that it is unthinkable for us to give people appearing before us less than the basic principles of American justice."

Senator Furman cleared his throat again. "But will this privilege apply to *everyone* appearing as a witness? Will all witnesses or their counsel be permitted cross-examination?"

"No," Senator Urban said.

"Why?" asked Furman innocently.

"Because Senator Hannaford is a United States Senator."

I blinked. We would all be subjected to interrogation. But only Ben would have the right to hit back. A little voice inside me cried, *unfair, unfair*. Yet in some perverse way, I found another voice agreeing with Urban's ruling. Of course Ben had to have extra privileges.

"Moreover," Webb Urban said, "the committee counsel, Mr. Kevin Shanahan, will have the right to cross-examine witnesses offered by Senator Hannaford. We're not prosecuting anyone here. This is not a trial. We will weigh all evidence and then decide what course to follow under the terms of Senate Resolution 338."

As Urban droned on, setting up ground rules, favoring Ben at every opportunity he had, amending rules so that Ben would never be at a disadvantage, (Did I hear him say that any witness whom Senator Hannaford did not want in the room would be sent out?) I wondered what tack Ben would take.

There were now three versions of the $250,000—George Paxton's involved lie, namely that he and I had conspired to cheat Krallis; my first, hopeless lie that the meeting never took place; and finally, my corrected version, which agreed with Krallis' account, with the scratchy tape recording. This last, of course, was the truth, albeit incomplete. I had been stopped from disclosing the name of Ben's three beneficiaries.

And of course there was the involved matter of the Conglomerate papers and the New Wilderness Bill, although I now had the feeling that the committee did not care much about *that* old chestnut. After all, only a month ago Webb Urban had dismissed the Parenti columns as unworthy of investigation. The whole Conglomerate matter lay on their polished horseshoe table, like a dead cat. Yet they did not smell it, did not see it.

That is why I was surprised when Ben's attorney, the genteel

P. K. Aubusson asked to have Marsha Treadway sworn as a witness. I now saw part of their strategy. Ben and his attorneys would claim a plot, a diabolical plot involving Marsha, Parenti, me, and all sorts of people. Nothing would shake up a fellow senator more, they reasoned, than the terrifying spectre of traitorous employees who pilfer papers. All of them would suffer if that wretched girl went unpunished!

Marsha, old bedmate, officemate, that gentle thief who had started this whole appalling business, walked toward the oblong table with her lawyer, the stoop-shouldered Bookwalter. She was sworn and took her seat. I could see Ben whispering to Matt Fixx, and I knew his mind: he did not like the idea of having her called as a witness. It had probably been the decision of the high-priced, high-powered Aubusson.

Since Senator Hannaford had called her, Aubusson proceeded with the interrogation. Her *curriculum vitae* were quickly established. I was surprised to learn she was thirty-three, not twenty-nine as she had told me. Aubusson, essaying a fatherly manner, then began his examination of the witness. Despite the black vested suit and the heavy key chain, for some lunatic reason I saw Lawyer Aubusson, in long winter underwear, wool socks and high button shoes, stomping around a brownstone house of a winter morning, stoking a woodfire in a stove.

"Miss Treadway, do you recognize this green folder?" Aubusson asked.

"Yes."

"What is it?"

"It's the Conglomerate File from Senator Hannaford's office."

"On August 3rd of this year, did you steal it?"

"I borrowed it."

"Did anyone give you permission to borrow it?"

"No."

"Did you know it to be Senator Hannaford's personal, private property, almost always kept locked in his desk?"

"Yes, I think so."

"Then why did you borrow it?"

Marsha paused, rolled her eyes upward, pushed her heavy lips forward, and said: "I felt it was my patriotic duty."

Aubusson reacted as if a wet towel had been slapped against his doughy face. "Your *what?*"

"My patriotic duty. I was troubled by the conflict of interest between Senator Hannaford's deeds in the Senate and his private interests."

Webb Urban looked dyspeptic. "The witness will limit herself to answering the questions."

"Mr. Chairman," said Marsha, "I thought that was an answer. I had already said patriotic duty, and when the lawyer said 'your what,' I felt I had to explain what I meant."

Ben folded his arms. He was a better judge of witnesses than Aubusson. He was displeased that they had started with Marsha Treadway.

"Is it not true that Mr. Louis Parenti asked or told you to steal those papers?" Aubusson asked.

"Not really."

"He hinted at the idea?"

"Well, I didn't steal, I only borrowed. And Mr. Parenti didn't force me to do anything."

"He suggested?"

"I guess you could call it that. He explained to me the way the senator and his associates were planning to exploit the national wildernesses with a new corporation and I—"

Webb Urban—good old Webb!—slammed the gavel. "I must direct the witness not to elaborate. Just answer the questions."

"Yes sir." Marsha almost winked at the old Mormon deacon. For a moment I thought I saw that frosty face smile. Well they had asked for it. There she sat, appropriately garbed for the occasion, a modest beige dress, a white collar, her red hair set in a neat bob, minimal make-up, low heeled shoes. She was one of thousands of pretty, sexy, rather simple-minded girls from humble homes who worked in Washington offices, good company at a party, fun at lunch, maybe even a lover. I had the feeling that old Aubusson would never succeed in painting her a knave, traitor, or thief to people like Clyde Furman and Carl Mullendore.

"And are you romantically involved with Mr. Parenti?" asked Aubusson.

"He's a friend."

"How close a friend?"

"I see him a couple of times a week."

"Are you engaged?"

"No." Marsha turned to her lawyer, Bookwalter. "Do I have to answer all this? That isn't any of his business."

Bookwalter nodded his assent. He was no dope. The more Aubusson martyred her, the more the committee would like her. Besides, they were operating in what I suspected was a "soft" area (I intend no pun or unkind reference to Marsha's attributes). The Conglomerate papers were small potatoes to the committee. But Aubusson was an old courtroom pirate. He evidently was convinced that if he could prove Marsha a *small* thief, nobody would care about the *big* thief he was representing.

He fiddled and faddled with her another few minutes, and suddenly his manner was minatory, angry. "Are you aware, Miss Treadway, that you committed a crime? That you violated a confidence? That you betrayed your kind and generous employer?"

"You make it sound so terrible," Marsha said. "I only borrowed the papers. And—what was so great about them?"

"Your friend Mr. Parenti thought they were important."

"Yes, but the Ethics Committee didn't," Marsha said innocently. "They didn't even care about investigating Senator Hannaford, so how important could they be?"

Kevin Shanahan was chuckling. I thought Eisenberg would start to laugh out loud. Chairman Urban stroked his forehead. "I must remind the witness not to argue with counsel or to offer opinions, or to make judgments."

"I'm sorry, Mr. Chairman."

Aubusson was lost, trapped in his own drop-seated longjohns.

"Young lady, this is a harsh thing to say, to so pretty a young lady, but I am forced to. You are an ingrate and a thief, you stabbed this good man in the back. You stole his private files to sell to a scoundrel, a parasite, sold them to betray a great public figure!"

"I never sold a thing! Lou didn't give me one red cent for those papers! And he never asked me to take them! It was my idea!"

"But why? Why, Miss Treadway?"

"Because I'm a patriotic American."

"Very well," Aubusson sniffed. "But we shall see to it, and I call the committee's attention to Miss Treadway's confession, that you will be prosecuted to the limit of the law! Such crimes, Mr. Chairman, cannot go unpunished! Such shameless assaults on law and order, on the very pillars of society, on our great public servants cannot be permitted!"

His indignation seemed excessive. Ben looked impatient. He was huddling with Matt and from my lonely seat opposite him, I could see the pique on his face.

At this point Marsha's lawyer, Bookwalter, got to his feet. I soon realized why Parenti had chosen him. "Mr. Chairman, sir?" he asked in the purest of New York accents. "May I raise a point concerning the threat to my client by Mr. Aubusson?"

"Yes, but be brief Mr. Bookwalter."

"I should like to ask Mr. Aubusson, Mr. Chairman, under what Federal or District statute, Mr. Aubusson would seek prosecution of my client. In short, what law will he recommend be operative when he presents his request to the Federal Bureau of Investigation, or the Director of Safety of the District of Columbia?"

A second wet towel seemed to strike old Aubusson in the face, and he appeared to stagger. "Law? Ah, law? Well, there is surely a law to cover thefts . . ."

"Borrowed, borrowed," Bookwalter sneered.

Chairman Urban frowned. "This is neither here nor there. But now that it's been raised, what do you think, Mr. Shanahan?"

"I can't think of any law," the committee counsel conceded.

"Well, I can," Bookwalter said. "The only crime for which my client is liable, if she is at all, Mr. Chairman, is mentioned in a memorandum dated June 24, 1966, from the American Law Division of the Legislative Reference Service of the Library of Congress on the subject of criminal liability for removal of documents. The criminal statute most likely applicable is a provision of the District of Columbia code which states that the taking and carrying away of the property of another without right is a *misdemeanor*."

Misdemeanor. With that trivial word, Bookwalter had squelched the effort to paint Marsha as the villain of the piece. Poor, dumb, big-busted girl, she had triumphed. I was glad.

"I suggest, Mr. Chairman," Bookwalter went on, "that your distinguished committee has other matters on its mind than the prosecution of misdemeanors, equivalent to the snatching of a milk bottle off a front doorstep. Besides, where would our legislative process be without the public's right to know? Documents are borrowed in this manner regularly by official and quasi-official investigators, and the issue of the District of Columbia code is never raised. Thank you, Mr. Chairman."

And that was the end of Marsha's testimony. Aubusson tried a few more questions, but the old codger had failed. I prided myself on the secrecy of my six-month affair with Marsha. Not once did Ben's lawyer hint that he suspected that Marsha had stolen the Conglomerate file to get back at *me*.

Shanahan waived cross-examination and Albon Blake was called to the stand. The silver fox would, of course, point the way the wind was blowing. He was too deeply involved with Ben to strike out on an independent course.

Blake was sworn. He also had two lawyers with him. I formulated Deever's Law of Committee Hearings—anyone earning six figures a year or more is entitled to *two* lawyers.

There was the usual fencing, and since Blake had been called by the committee, Kevin Shanahan started the questioning.

"Mr. Blake, who is George Paxton?"

"He is—was—in my employ. He is a public relations consultant, he handles certain industrial accounts."

"Why is he no longer in your employ?"

"Because I have reason to doubt some of his testimony before this committee."

"What testimony specifically?"

"For one thing, the matter of that $50,000 in his bank account."

"The money which he claims Mr. Deever gave him as part of his share of the quarter of a million handed over by Mr. Norton Krallis?"

"That is correct."

"Why do you doubt his version?"

"Because Mr. Deever and Mr. Paxton did not, as we say, cook the deal up between themselves. They aren't that intelligent. Mr. Deever denied it ever happened, then changed his story. As for Mr. Paxton, I can only conclude he is suffering serious mental lapses and possibly something worse."

"Where did that $50,000 come from?" asked Shanahan. "The bank records show it was only deposited a few days ago."

"I haven't the faintest idea. That's one reason I fired him."

Shanahan surveyed his man. I doubted he had much use for the lobbyist. "Mr. Blake, did such an actual payment, or transfer,

of that $250,000 take place in the Washington Zoo on the 25th
of June?"

"To the best of my knowledge it did."

"Why do you think so?"

"I arranged it."

"Give us the details, if you will, Mr. Blake."

"The Mortgage and Loan Associations are clients of mine. The
money was given for educational purposes, better to acquaint
members of Congress with the inequities in the new tax bill concerning their business enterprises. Mr. Krallis had been in contact
with me for many months on the matter, and was designated
spokesman for the group. It was he who helped raise the money."

"And who was the money to go to?"

"Why, to a variety of senators and congressmen, as campaign
contributions."

"But, I mean, to what *specific* agency, or *specific* person?"

"To Senator Hannaford."

Truth would be their weapon. There were simply too many
people to fix, to straighten out, to cover up. They would tell the
truth up to a point—then depend upon the closed ranks of the
world's most exclusive club to protect Ben.

"Describe how this was decided," Shanahan said.

"I decided it. I called the senator and raised the question. He
sided with the mortgage and loan people. He felt they had a
legitimate case, and that they deserved a fair shake from the Finance Committee. He agreed he would be the agency to distribute
the educational funds."

"And you then arranged for Mr. Paxton to meet with Mr.
Deever."

"Yes. I left the details to Paxton."

"And he reported to you that it was accomplished—that the
money had passed from Krallis to Deever?"

"He did."

"And did you hear further from Senator Hannaford on the
matter?"

"Just an acknowledgment that he had received the funds and
would put them to use for these—these educational purposes."

"He did not give you a breakdown—a dollar by dollar accounting of who was to get what?"

"Mr. Shanahan, I would not injure my long and warm relationship with Senator Hannaford by asking for that. If there is one man in Washington I trust with all my heart, it is Senator Hannaford."

"So you don't know how this money was distributed?"

"Nor do I care."

Senator Urban leaned forward. "Are you aware, Mr. Blake," he asked in that gray voice, "that at the time this money was given to Mr. Deever, presumably for the purposes you mention, that the mortgage and loan provision of the tax bill had already been defeated by a vote of the Senate Finance Committee?"

"No sir, I am not aware of that."

Senator Eisenberg interjected: "It appeared in the paper a few days ago."

"Excuse me, Senator Eisenberg," Blake said smiling, "but it appeared in Mr. Parenti's column, which is the only place it did appear, and we are all aware of that person's reputation."

The holy mantle, the glowing mantle! Angelic Albon! He was one of the most corrupt men in Washington, and here he sat denouncing Parenti.

"You say you had no idea that this provision of the tax bill was already dead, or that your clients were donating a quarter of a million dollars for nothing?" asked Shanahan.

"None whatsoever."

"Did they complain to you at any time?"

"Well, Mr. Krallis did raise the issue some weeks ago. I assured him he was wrong, that his contribution had helped defeat that part of the tax bill."

"Mr. Blake, isn't that what is called lobbying?" asked the counsel.

"Of course, Mr. Shanahan. I'm an industrial relations consultant."

"Did Senator Hannaford at any time tell you that he believed the mortgage and loan provision dead? That is, before the payment?"

"Sir, we did not discuss it again, after the transfer of the funds. As you know, Mr. Shanahan, I was also representing various partners in the so-called Conglomerate, which Senator Hannaford was interested in, and we were concerned more with that."

"I see," Shanahan said. "Was there—is there—any connection

between the money handed over by Mr. Krallis and the legislation referred to as the New Wilderness Bill?"

"None that I'm aware of."

Aubusson was on his feet. "Mr. Chairman, I ask that you instruct the committee counsel not to ask witnesses about these presumed connections. These wild reachings for the moon can only create suspicion and fear. In fact, I move that his question and the answer be stricken from the record."

The Chairman pondered a moment, then said, "Mr. Aubusson, I think you have a point. Mr. Shanahan, I think for the time being it won't be necessary to ask Mr. Blake what happened to that money after it was given to Mr. Deever. He may have no direct knowledge of the manner in which it was dispensed—"

"None at all, sir," Blake said.

Urban glowered at him. "But we will let the record stand. Proceed, Mr. Shanahan."

"Mr. Blake, do you also represent the government of Djarak here in Washington?" the counsel asked.

"Not directly, sir. I do represent Longhorn-Mideast Oil, which has been developing oil rights in the Sheikdom of Djarak. Only when my client is involved am I involved with Djaraki matters. They have an able ambassador here in Prince Malik."

"Have you worked at all with Senator Hannaford in matters concerning the so-called Djarak Amendment?"

"Oh, only in that—"

Aubusson was up again. "Mr. Chairman, Mr. Shanahan is doing just what you told him not to."

This time, the red-headed counsel had gotten a little close to the bone. How gracefully the club danced around its members!

"It would seem," Webb Urban said, "that we are on thin ice. Mr. Blake's professional chores are so multi-faceted, that I'm reluctant to see him questioned at length or in detail about every single senator and every single piece of legislation he's ever been associated with."

Yes, I thought, *because some of you would be spotted with bits of tar.*

Albon Blake's lawyers did not care to cross-examine their silvery client. The lobbyist would neither hurt nor help Ben. He would say he knew so much; he would back up everything Ben said. But the main defense would be the one Ben almost always took: *truth*. He should have had this raw courage a few days ago, I thought, before he had cooked up the scheme to have Paxton and me lie about the quarter of a million. But for once in his life he had wavered. Paxton's lies still stood—and that seersuckered sucker would probably be hit for perjury, unless he became a Christian. For that matter, I too was motley with perjury, even though I had retracted my reckless denial of the meeting.

I saw what was coming. Ben would admit he ordered me to take the money, admit that it was in a vault, and then cook up some story of the manner in which it was to be dispensed. They would arch their senatorial brows, *tsk-tsk* a little, decide he was imprudent and perhaps overeager in his desire to pass the New Wilderness Bill and the Djarak Amendment, but find no ground for censure. As for the three recipients of the largesse, they could be depended upon to remain silent. Kemmons, DiFalco, and Goodchapel would abide by the rules. And since Webb Urban had already ordered *me* to obey the unwritten law—"Thou shalt speak no ill of a senator in this committee room"—Ben would make his escape. But perhaps things would not be quite the same for him again; I suspected he would not be bending elbows, grabbing shoulders, bullyragging federal agencies, demanding judgeships, forcing his favorites on to committees, but he'd be around a long long time.

Blake was excused. There was some hemming and hawing about the next meeting—presumably the one at which Ben would testify—and then we were recessed until the next day. Alone, the pariah dog, I got up and walked out wearily. The exodus found me a step in back of Ben's broad back, but we were men from different planets, strangers, enemies, aliens, men who had nothing to say to one another. All commerce was suspended.

Outside the hearing room, the reporters made their ritual attempt to get me to talk, but I was silent. I smiled for them, waved and said "No comment," as easily as if I were President Kretz leaving a meeting of the National Security Council. But I owed Fred Goldstein a bit more. He had been a good friend, and I agreed to have dinner with him at a small Italian place around the corner from my apartment.

He came with an early edition of the *Truth*, opened to Lou

Parenti's column. Over the Clams Casino and the bitter Chianti, I read the columnist's sarcastic account of what I suspected was developing:

> A distinctive odor emanates from room 3302 of the New Senate Office Building, where the Ethics Committee is probing the tangled activities of Senator Benjamin Bow Hannaford, the Master Builder from Ramada.
>
> It is the odor of whitewash.
>
> Everything indicates that the six honorable men on the committee, Chairman Webb Urban included, will hear the senator's testimony and decide that while he may have acted imprudently, he did no wrong in acting as combined lobbyist, legislator, and beneficiary for the New Wilderness Bill (which died in committee because of administration opposition) and the pending Djarak Amendment, which would make that small country Senator Hannaford's private domain to exploit.
>
> Chairman Urban has already warned the key witness, Hannaford's former aide, Edward Deever, against mentioning any other senators, particularly any who may have received so-called "campaign contributions" from Senator Hannaford.
>
> *View from the Hill* knows for a fact that three senators did receive such contributions, as rewards for voting the way Senator Hannaford wanted them to vote. Now how do the august members of the Ethics Committee feel about that? When is a campaign contribution a campaign contribution and when is it—whisper the word— a *bribe*? How about it gentlemen?

I asked Fred what he thought would happen.

"He'll beat the rap," Fred said cautiously. "At least that's the betting in the press gallery."

"And me?"

"They might hang the perjury charge on you. Eddie, what is the real story? I swear I won't use it."

"What I told the committee, Fred. He asked me to get the dough, to keep it available and ready for use."

"And it was used?"

"Only a few times." I sipped the sour red wine. There is something about Chianti that doesn't go with Washington, D.C. Or any kind of exotic foreign food or drink. This is basically a southern town. Attempts to endow it with style collapse.

"And of course you won't say?"

"Only to Webb Urban and his five friends."

"They won't let you, Ed. They shut you up good when you started to mention the beneficiaries. Why not spill the beans to the press?"

"As crazy as it may sound to you, Fred, I love the Senate and everyone in it. Just about everyone. I'm not sore at Ben. He's too big, too grand to get sore at. It—it's like getting mad at God. You do that, you're damned for life."

Goldstein looked at me strangely, his dark eyes studying me through a curtain of steam arising from his spaghetti in white clam sauce. "Dammit, I believe you, Ed. It's sort of like your religion, isn't it? Even when it gets you down, you won't curse it."

I nodded.

"And that business about not mentioning the senators' names —I swear that's out of the Old Testament. You know, it's like the Orthodox Hebrew religion, in which I was bar mitzvah'd. You know, in the Hebrew texts, you never say God's name— *Yahweh*, the four letters. They call it the Tetragrammaton. You use substitutes—Lord, King of the Universe, Master. But never Yahweh. It's the unutterable. I think that's the way that old Mormon preacher Webb looks at it—no names of the gods, please."

"It is an interesting parallel," I agreed.

"Not to ruin your lasagna any more than I have to, but I think the little gods are going to run with the big gods. Hannaford will have some story about the dough being part of the campaign fund, and that will be that. You can't stop people from being generous. Besides what did Krallis think he was buying— insurance? It was a bet. He won his bet. So what if the race was fixed?"

"True enough. I'll tell you something crazy, Fred. I almost hope Hannaford does, as you said, beat the rap."

"Almost?"

"Yes, almost hope. He is still one hell of a man. It's just that— that—"

"You hate his guts?" asked the TV reporter.

"No. It's just that that damnable urge to control, run, operate, dominate and own, has finally gotten on my nerves. Just for once I'd like to see him set on his rear end."

Fred turned out his lower lip and looked glum. "Not a chance, Eddie. Not the way that committee has been sounding." He grinned. "They might want everything to look so great, they might let you off also. But then, there's the Justice Department and the Internal Revenue Service to worry about. Ah hell, Eddie, I shouldn't ruin your dinner. Have some more Chianti."

"No thanks, Fred. I think it's soured, or maybe I have."

Late that night, Matt Fixx called me. I gathered he was being groomed to be the new Edward Deever. "All your things have been put into cardboard boxes," he said, his voice shaking. "I've left them with the superintendent in the basement."

"All my things? Every letter, Matt? Maybe a few papers you and the senator can use?"

"That is not our bag, Deever. No sir, we aren't hung up on stealing papers, like certain people I know."

"I stole no papers, Matthew. Besides, you heard what Marsha's lawyer said. It's a misdemeanor under the District of Columbia code. Why that's almost as bad as bribing a senator."

"You keep that up, Deever, you'll regret it."

"Recording me, Matt?"

"I assure you, it will be a superior tape, much better than Mr. Krallis', so you won't be troubled with lying about the event having taken place."

"I asked for that. All right, I'll pick up my stuff. Did you include the framed photo of me and the senator at Ramada Day Cere-monies last year?"

"I destroyed that."

"And you hope to destroy me too, Matthew?"

"People like you destroy themselves. You have your own built-in destruct mechanisms. Deever, I don't enjoy these debriefings with you. I find them distasteful, but the senator can't get him-self to even look at you, much less talk to you. He wants informa-tion."

That was Ben! That was my nerveless, gutsy, unabashed, brutal Ben! He wanted information! From me! From *me*—Judas, Bene-dict Arnold, and both Rosenbergs, all in one!

"I'll be glad to help."

"He wants to know where Miss Valdez is."

Old Goat! In the midst of turmoil, he could still lust for that satiny skin, those cool limbs! Well I owed him something.

"She's staying at the YWCA," I said.

"She's not. She checked out."

"Then I can't help you. That's the last place I saw her."

"Are you sure she isn't with you?" Fixx asked.

"No, Matthew, she's not here. Or as you would say, negative."

"Any help you can give us in finding her will be appreciated. The senator has instructed me to tell you, he'll go easy on you, perhaps see to it that there are no criminal prosecutions, if you can help locate the young lady."

My brain danced. There was Ben—still wheeling and dealing in the shadow of censure, still trading, making bargains, bending elbows, twisting arms, pummeling shoulders.

"If she's flown the coop at the Y, Matt, I honestly don't know where she is. The *pajarita* has gone. *Adiós, muchacho.*"

"You aren't funny at all. You've been obsoleted, Deever. We've programmed you out of existence." And he hung up.

The next morning Senator John Tyler Lord was on the floor of the Senate, blasting the Ethics Committee, Ben and the traditions of the great deliberative body. He spoke to three members of the Senate—Senator Charles O'Gara of New Jersey was presiding, a young fellow, a Trenton lawyer, and he let Lord say a lot of things for which other men would have gaveled him down.

"Mr. President," Lord cried, "we hear disturbing reports from our Select Committee on Standards and Conduct concerning their current hearings. The word whitewash appears. Are we to go down that well-trodden primrose path once more? Are we once again engaged in that act of sweeping our own dirt under our own rug? When in the name of heaven is the Senate going to face up to the fact that United States Senators have the same obligations—indeed greater obligations—than ordinary citizens? Just who do we think we are—acting shocked, and outraged and screaming about ethics and morality all the time, when some of our own members get away with murder?

"Mr. President, it's now or never for the Ethics Committee! Even in those rare instances when it acts, the worst offenses of our members are glossed over, buried, dismissed. We have gotten into the habit of acting holier than any church, more secretive than a spy ring, more resistant to reform than a Byzantine court.

"It will be argued that the senator now appearing before the Ethics Committee engaged in nothing different from what many of our members engage in—only on a more ambitious scale. Does that make it right? Are we forever to be told that all 'special interests' are in the national interest? That the personal profit of one of our members justifies special legislation? Or that these acts are permissible because everyone does it?

"Mr. President, everyone does *not* do it. The vast majority of senators do *not* do it. And those who do, must be troubled with second thoughts. Whether these second thoughts occur to the senator now under investigation I cannot say. But apparently the Ethics Committee is handling this hearing as if the senator were the judge, and that the other witnesses, those who have firsthand knowledge of his operations, are the guilty parties . . ."

At this point Senator Gabriel T. Tutt stumbled on the floor of the Senate, and through his alcoholic morning haze, slowly got the drift of John Tyler Lord's speech. God knows what impelled him to rush to Ben's defense. He and Ben had never been particularly close, although Ben had used him frequently to keep the Southerners in line, and Tutt had gotten many favors from Ben via the pork barrel.

"Mr. President!" roared Tutt. "That man is outa order! You got to stop him!"

"I have not yielded, Mr. President," said Lord.

"Will you yield now?" cried Gabe Tutt.

"Not now," Lord sniffed.

"Mr. President," Tutt shouted, "that man is attackin' the fabric, the structure of our beloved body! He is poisonin' the very air we breathe, he is eatin' at the roots of our Republic, with his vile insinuations! If there's one thing senators got to do it is to stick together! I demand you declare him outa order, and order his words stricken from the record."

Lord was no sissy. Blue his blood may have been, spindly his body, but he had a patrician courage that is not lightly dismissed. "I suggest to the senator from Alabama that he go out and sober up and rest his voice," Lord shouted. Surprisingly, he outshouted Tutt. "I do not debate with irrational, inebriated men! Mr. President, I was speaking, and I have not yielded, and I shall continue my speech!"

Gabe Tutt lurched toward Lord—as the Press Gallery gasped, as the few early morning spectators goggled at the fracas. But luckily Senator Stapp had just entered, presumably on Ben's orders, and with the express job of responding to Lord in a civilized manner. (He did later on.) "Swinging Sid" was able to halt the drunken Tutt in midpassage. I had to hand it to the Swinger —white-on-white shirt, twenty dollar tie, crocodile shoes—but a good man when you needed him. After all his years as lawyer, agent and counselor for a host of actors and actresses, he was adept at handling drunks.

"That's all right, Senator Tutt," Sid whispered, "you and I can answer the senator from Vermont when he's finished. Come along, now."

And he led him back to his seat. Lord was not through. He went on lashing out at the Ethics Committee, at Ben, at the Senate, at the public. Like most ideologues, he ruined his case by overstatement. But he made some telling points. I had a hunch the Ethics Committee would be affected by them.

CHAPTER FOURTEEN

At long last Ben was sworn and called to testify. He sat at the oblong table, flanked by Matt Fixx and P. K. Aubusson, and immediately, the impression one got was that *he* was trying the six senators above him. He was several feet lower, but somehow it seemed he was higher, that he was the judge, and they were looking up to him. Don't ask me how he did it; he just did. In the same manner in which he had—somehow—hinted to several committee members that he did *not* want open hearings, and so closed they had remained.

"Senator Hannaford," said Webb Urban, "has requested that he be called at this time, and we have honored his request. We realize he has many duties and obligations, and we are anxious to conclude this matter as soon as possible, for all concerned."

Ben nodded. "Am I to be sworn?" he asked.

Ah, the magnificent gall of the man! Suggesting that perhaps he was of such high station, that his word had to be taken!

"Yes, Senator," Chairman Urban said, "do you solemnly swear that your testimony in this hearing will be the truth, the whole truth and nothing but the truth, so help you God?"

"I do," Ben said.

Aubusson leaned forward. "Mr. Chairman, may I suggest that in the interests of saving time, we dispense with direct examination by counsel. Senator Hannaford will submit himself to any questions the committee might have."

What consummate arrogance! By skipping direct examination,

the probing queries of Kevin Shanahan, Ben would have an enormous advantage. The committee members could be depended upon to handle the witness with care.

Webb Urban blinked his eyes. His gray face turned grayer. He looked at Shanahan. "What is the opinion of counsel?"

"I am opposed to that Mr. Chairman," Shanahan said. "When a person does not testify directly, and is then subjected to cross-examination with direct examination having been skipped, much time is wasted and much confusion results."

Webb Urban took three seconds to decide. "We will proceed then with direct examination. Counsel may proceed."

If Ben were hurt by this, he concealed it. He folded his thick arms on the table and waited for Shanahan's queries. I patted the envelope in my pocket—those letters to myself with names, dates and sums of money. Shanahan had that morning studied them, and photostated them, but refused to say a word about what he would—or could—do with them. No doubt the committee had seen them. I wondered if any of them had told Ben.

Aubusson was more perturbed than Ben over Urban's ruling on direct examination. He and Fixx exchanged a few words, and then the old lawyer addressed himself to the Chairman. "Mr. Chairman, there is ample precedent for skipping direct examination of a United States Senator. In previous investigations conducted by this committee, direct examination was dispensed with. That is to say, committee counsel did not, I repeat did not, interrogate the senator appearing here, and said senator was merely questioned in a frank and friendly manner by his colleagues."

There was the appeal direct to the club. But had John Tyler Lord's shrill calls for a full investigation been heard?

"I do not consider all precedents binding," Senator Urban said cheerlessly. "The chair has already ruled in favor of direct examination, and we will thus proceed. Mr. Shanahan."

"Senator Hannaford, concerning this green file, known as the Conglomerate File—why did you consider it a secret matter?" asked the counsel.

Ben at once betrayed some annoyance. "Most corporate matters involving mergers have to be kept secret, Mr. Shanahan. You've been a corporation lawyer, you are aware of that."

"The charge has been made that the plan for this merger, this new corporation, was contingent upon passage of the Hannaford bill."

"Not true," Senator Hannaford snapped. "The bill was beaten. The merger will take place anyway."

"Did you promise the members of the proposed Conglomerate that they would have special favors regarding multiple use of the National Wilderness, after passage of S.671?"

"Absolutely not."

"Did you order Mr. Albon Blake to make such promises?"

"Absolutely not. But if you must know, Blake is an impulsive fellow, and he may have said some things to them along that line."

"Do you consider such promises a conflict of interest—in that your association with Mr. Blake was very close?"

"I do not. I've never been that close to Blake. I've never hired him for anything. I don't need him."

Aubusson squirmed—were his long woolen drop-seated pants itching him? "Mr. Chairman, I object most vigorously to this line of questioning. Everyone knows that Senator Hannaford is an industrialist, one of our most eminent. Everyone knows he was working to put together a more efficient, more productive organization by combining related corporations. Why does counsel keep dwelling on facts that are already known?"

"They were not known, Mr. Aubusson," said Senator Urban, "until the folder was stolen from the senator's office and the information made public in a newspaper column."

"Mr. Chairman, you will excuse my asking this, but are you condoning that theft?" Aubusson asked.

Poor strategy, poor strategy, I knew as I sat by myself, leper, outcast, untouchable. One did not make such statements to committee chairmen, especially to Senator Webb Urban. The trouble with people like Aubusson, I reflected, is that they begin to believe in the power and glory of their own public images. Senators, of course, do that all the time. But within the confines of the establishment it usually works. Aubusson may have been hot stuff in his aristocratic law firm, or in a lower court, but here he was just another special pleader.

"I said nothing of the sort, Mr. Aubusson," Urban responded, "and I will be obliged to you if you will refrain from drawing unwarranted conclusions about the motives of the members of this committee. Go ahead, Mr. Shanahan."

The references to the Conglomerate apparently at a dead-end, Shanahan proceeded to ask Ben about our legendary $250,000.

"Did you, Senator Hannaford, instruct Edward Deever on June 25th of this year, to meet with a George Paxton and receive, through him, the sum of $250,000 from a Mr. Norton Krallis?"

Ben raised his head. "I did. The only inaccuracy in that statement is that I did not know who would be bringing the money. I have never met Mr. Krallis."

"But you were aware that it came from a group of Mortgage-and-Loan people who wanted a provision of the tax bill defeated?"

"Yes."

"Who made these contacts?"

"Mr. Albon Blake."

"And what were you going to use this sum of money for?"

"As a special campaign fund for members of my party in need of campaign funds."

"Why *special?*" asked Shanahan. "What does that connote?"

"I wanted the funds in liquid, accessible form, readily available."

"I don't understand. Why did you not turn them over to your party's Campaign Committee? You were the Chairman of the Senate Campaign Committee."

"That's exactly why. I'm Chairman so I run the committee the way I want. They gave me the job, they have to trust me."

I could see a dour look cross Webb Urban's face. At the same time, the two other members of Ben's party, Royce Henshaw and Maury Eisenberg, looked a bit heartsick.

"Mr. Deever has testified that you took $50,000 of that money and set it aside, and that you gave him $20,000 for his private use. Is that correct?"

"Yes. The $50,000 I wanted handy for emergency dispensations. The $20,000 was a gift to Mr. Deever for long and faithful service."

Webb Urban looked appalled. He raised his arms and rested his fists on the table. "Senator Hannaford," he said mournfully, "was that not an irregular procedure? Should not campaign funds be strictly accounted for, carefully dispensed, with full documentation, rather than in the offhand manner you describe?"

"Mr. Chairman," Ben said, "I am a builder first and a senator second, although that may surprise you. I have brought to this job, and to my job with the campaign committee the same techniques—speed, directness, efficiency—that I use in paving a runway or building a bridge. I wanted money quickly available for my associates."

"And did you intend to account for this?" Senator Urban asked.

"Most certainly. After all, it has been less than five months since that contribution of $250,000 was made. I intended to write a full report covering all the transactions."

"To whom?" asked the Chairman.

"Why, to myself."

There was a pause. In those three words Ben seemed to have summed up precisely what he was, who he was. He was everything; he was anything.

"Now, Senator Hannaford, George Paxton claims you gave him *back* the $50,000 which you had originally set aside for yourself and told him to open a bank account with it. Is that correct?"

"Yes, I did."

What in heaven's name was he up to now?

"You did give him that $50,000?"

"Most certainly."

"Mr. Paxton further testified that you told him to tell this committee that this money was his payoff from Mr. Deever for consummating the deal with Mr. Krallis and his associates."

"That is not so."

"You did not so advise Mr. Paxton?"

"I did not. I am not in the habit of advising people to perjure themselves."

Shanahan stroked his chin and waited a few moments before asking the next question. "Then why was such a huge sum given to Mr. Paxton?"

"It was to be used," Ben said, "for local elections in my home state. I did not want to be in the position of directly donating campaign money to people back in Ramada. A complex relationship is involved there, and I preferred that these contributions come through a third party. Mr. Blake, who has handled these matters before, suggested we do it through Mr. Paxton."

Ah, so that was the way out. Ben owned the state. He ran Ramada. He possessed every local politician, judge, state representative. The governor waited for his orders. They had concocted a big one this time—a fund for local elections back home. And I could only guess that Paxton would be taken care of; he would be recalled and he would back this new version.

"How can you explain Mr. Paxton's story that the money came from Mr. Deever as a payoff?" asked Shanahan.

"I can't explain it. You'll have to ask him."

Webb Urban scowled. "We intend to, Senator."

Shanahan conferred a moment with Urban. Then he asked: "Senator Hannaford, were any actual campaign disbursements made from that special fund, that $250,000?"

"There were."

"How many?"

"Three."

By God, he would go through with it, right to the bitter end! He would admit everything, and then get off simply because he was Big Ben Hannaford, a King Senator among Senators!

"These were in the nature of campaign contributions to other individuals?"

"Exactly," said Ben.

Webb Urban touched Shanahan's arm lightly. "Counsel will keep in mind, as will all witnesses, that the names of other members of the Senate in any way connected with this so-called fund will not be mentioned. We are in a grave and sensitive area here, and much of what will be said will be subject to various interpretations. So for the time being, Mr. Shanahan, and Senator Hannaford, and Mr. Aubusson, and all concerned, we will not mention any other member of the Senate."

Translation: *the club must be protected at all costs.* But what was so terrible about taking a campaign contribution? I knew the answer, and I think Webb Urban suspected it. These were campaign "contributions" with a purpose: they were aimed at influencing votes.

"May I ask if these funds were requested by the three men who accepted them?"

"Of course," said Ben with some contempt. "I don't go around showering dollar bills on people. They ask, I weigh the merits, and then I act or I don't act."

What would never, never, never be asked by Shanahan—or anyone else sitting up there—was, what do you get in return for that generosity? A favorable vote on the New Wilderness Bill? A favorable vote (or two votes) on the Djarak Amendment? Such thoughts were unthinkable; they would be denied to the end. And who could prove anything?

Senator Urban shifted about in his seat. "Before resuming the direct examination of Senator Hannaford, Mr. Shanahan, I think, that for his benefit and that of the entire committee, we should discuss the matter of the letters submitted by Edward Deever yesterday."

Ben looked puzzled.

"Yes sir, I think that would be in order," Shanahan said.

"Mr. Shanahan and myself yesterday studied three letters submitted by Edward Deever. They purport to be records of his deposits and withdrawals from the Riggs National Bank. Since they deal with the names of United States Senators, I will not permit them as evidence, but I do feel they should be mentioned. They are in what we presume to be Mr. Deever's handwriting, and all bear postmarks, and date stamps with the name of the Riggs National Bank."

With that he took the three letters from a folder and arranged them in front of himself. "The first, dated June 25th, purports to record the rental of safe deposit box D-789, and the placing therein of $200,000, of which $20,000 is recorded as being Mr. Deever's. The other two purport to record withdrawals of cash from the box, in differing amounts to different people."

At that moment I was sorry I did not have a lawyer, someone to stand up and shout that the letters were real, important, truthful.

"In view of the controversial nature of these letters, the fact that they are nothing more than Mr. Deever's own accounts, and that the names mentioned are those of fellow senators, I am refusing to introduce these letters as evidence. They will be returned to Mr. Deever."

Senator Eisenberg turned to Urban. "Then why mention them at all? Either disclose their full contents—name names and amounts—or bar them altogether."

"This was not an easy decision, Senator Eisenberg," Urban said. "But it is the Chair's belief that nothing will be served by revealing the contents of these letters submitted by Mr. Deever. Senator Hannaford admits that the funds were given to these men by him as campaign contributions. We must accept his word, and we must rely on the fact that these men were United States Senators, who are not in the habit of changing votes for money, particularly money from another senator. Now I will instruct counsel to return these letters to the manila envelope, and return them to Mr. Deever."

But Maury Eisenberg was not to be put off. "Excuse me, Mr. Chairman, but I think you and I are looking at this matter in two different ways. First, both Senator Hannaford and Mr. Deever agree that the large sum of money does exist, and that sums were given to certain senators. Mr. Deever says three. So does Senator Hannaford. Now without any prejudging on our part, let's find out who the three men were, and see if there could be any cause for suspicion on our part."

"That is exactly what I seek to avoid," declared Webb Urban. "This committee, at least while I am Chairman, will not indulge in casting shadows of suspicion on other senators, or indeed on Senator Hannaford."

Eisenberg's long sallow face was not convinced. He was almost as rich as Ben, and he was, despite that rather apologetic mien that many rich Jews acquire, a man of notable courage and independence.

"Mr. Chairman, you and I and Senator Hannaford are members of the same great party, and I am reluctant to say what I am going to say. But I have been involved in fund raising for our Campaign Committee several times, and while I am not as familiar with its *modus operandi* as is Senator Hannaford, I know a little about it. And I have never heard of secret, special funds in cash, neatly set aside in safe deposit boxes, available to reward needy members of the Senate. That is not the way things are done, at least in my experience with the Campaign Committee."

"Mr. Chairman, I must associate myself with Senator Eisenberg's remarks," said Royce Henshaw—and sat back, looking miserable.

The three opposition members across the horseshoe table were silent. Three cats who had eaten canaries—Mullendore, Furman, Owens. They liked nothing better than an intra-party fight. The dirtier the better.

"May I respond to Senator Eisenberg?" Ben asked Urban.

"Of course, Senator Hannaford."

That eternal politeness, that kowtowing, that assumption that the great man had to be given special treatment! Despite Eisenberg's queries, I had the feeling all was lost. Somehow, for all the discrepancies, all the mad things that had happened since I took that quarter of a million dollars from N. Krallis, I had the feeling Ben would beat the charge. I would be a *beard* once more; first a beard for his sexual adventures, now a beard, a sacrifice, for his financial and industrial exploits. And I was voiceless, helpless, stupidly sitting there by myself, without even a lawyer.

"Senator Eisenberg," Ben was saying, "it is no secret in Washington that I operate differently from other people. Perhaps it was irregular to keep that money in cash, and not record it with the Campaign Committee. But that is the way things get done in this country. My job is to help members of my party get re-elected. I have to be given a lot of freedom. And although there isn't a darn thing wrong with their accepting this help, I am glad the Chairman is not disclosing their names. Irresponsible members of the press will only use their names to further blacken the reputation of the Senate."

"Perhaps," Royce Henshaw said, "it is time that the Senate stopped accusing its critics of trying to blacken its reputation and instead started answering certain questions."

"I'll speak only for myself," Ben said. "I'll answer any question put to me. You know that, Senator Henshaw."

Eisenberg drew in his breath. "Would you answer this, then, Senator Hannaford? Is it true, as a columnist has hinted, that one of the recipients of money from this fund later returned it, because he felt it was intended to influence a vote?"

Aubusson was on his feet. "Mr. Chairman, the implication in that question is a terrible one, and I regard it as an attack on the integrity of the entire Senate! I ask the Chairman to instruct Senator Eisenberg to withdraw his question and that it be stricken from the record!"

How badly I wanted to wave my bank book at them, the one in which I had deposited the $10,000 that Airborne Alf Kemmons had sent back to me! How sorely I wanted to tell them about that lunatic afternoon in Alf's office, when Miss Craigie and I stood around drying the $5000 he had gotten from lobbyist J. J. Mulrooney, and how the electric fan created a green storm of swirling dollars around us!

"The Chair rules Senator Eisenberg's question out of order,"

Urban said. "It is based on hearsay and hearsay from a most irresponsible source. Unless Senator Eisenberg, or counsel has any direct knowledge or evidence that that incident occurred, I bar any further questions on that matter."

Ben sat back, a smug look on his dark face. Well, he had a right to feel that way. All was going as planned. My sportswriting friends would have referred to the proceedings as "a tank job," that is to say a fixed fight. I do not mean that there had been collusion between a man of Webb Urban's uprightness and Ben. That was unthinkable. It was simply that the rules of the club were in force. I saw the distaste on Webb Urban's ashen face, and I knew he did not believe Ben's story and was not pleased that so little evidence could be introduced against him. But he was protecting the organization, engaging in what were almost reflex actions. And I was equally certain, those three beneficiaries —Alf Kemmons, Henry DiFalco, and Lester Goodchapel—would play it just as cool. They, too, would abide by the rules.

But Senator Maury Eisenberg was not appeased. Ben had once told me that there is nothing as frightened as a million dollars. Perhaps that was true of some of his Conglomerate friends. It was not true of Maury Eisenberg. He was barely in the club. Wealth and good manners and good works had given him a marginal membership. But he was not really at the heart of the organization, the way Ben or Webb Urban were.

"Mr. Chairman, I must state quite honestly to both you and our able counsel, Mr. Shanahan, that I am not at all pleased with the manner in which this hearing is progressing," Eisenberg said morosely. "We are either investigating the charge that Senator Hannaford accepted a quarter of a million dollars to kill a provision tax bill, and then used the money for unethical purposes, or we are not. If this were a court of law, Mr. Chairman, and you were the judge, and Mr. Shanahan the prosecutor, we would be a laughingstock."

Senator Urban was not happy with these remarks, but he knew there was truth in them. His answer was not as strong as I expected.

"Senator Eisenberg, I am not a judge, and you are not a juror and Mr. Shanahan is not a prosecutor. We are here to find out facts."

"Then I would suggest we are going about it very badly," Eisenberg said. "I want to know the names of those three men who accepted the money, and if any conditions were attached to their accepting it."

This was blasphemy of a most elemental nature. Aubusson was on his feet again and Ben had clasped his hands rigidly on the long table.

"Senator Eisenberg is not a lawyer," Aubusson said, "and he fails to understand the gravity of his remarks! I ask again, Mr. Chairman, that they be stricken from the record!"

Urban meditated a moment or two. "I agree," the Chairman said. "We will strike Senator Eisenberg's last comments from the record. I cannot permit these hints, these speculations on the distribution of the money Senator Hannaford received from Mr. Deever."

From Mr. Deever? As if I were the briber, the fixer! Me, poor bag man, messenger, foolish arranger of meetings in front of the gibbon cage!

As I have pointed out Ben was always in control of his temper. But now I saw a red flush paint his neck and ears, inching up the neatly barbered nape, tinting the flesh amid the black-gray hairs, scarlet and carmine. He pulled Aubusson down and, drawing himself up, his mighty chest expanding, he addressed the Chair.

"Mr. Chairman, I have a request to make," Ben said.

"By all means, Senator Hannaford."

"Mr. Chairman, I apply to disqualify Senator Eisenberg from the final deliberations of the Senate Ethics Committee in this proceeding. I ask that he be excluded from the committee vote."

It almost seemed to me, that all six—seven counting Shanahan —gasped. The overwhelming effrontery of the man! The colossal shameless gall!

"I beg the senator's pardon?" asked Urban. His Mormon face was aghast. As for Eisenberg, he stroked his pendulous lips and stared, unbelieving, at Ben.

Aubusson was whispering in Ben's ear. Ben was nodding. The tactic was Ben, pure Ben. But the ancient lawyer evidently approved, and was now adding his two cents' worth of legality, noting things on a scratch pad which he shoved in front of my ex-boss.

"Yes, Mr. Chairman, I apply to disqualify Senator Eisenberg from the final deliberation, that is to say, the committee *vote* on any resolution that may result from these hearings. I do not seek to bar him from participation in the hearing, merely from the final deliberation."

"Why do you request this?" asked Urban.

"Because, Mr. Chairman," Ben said, "it is now apparent that Senator Eisenberg has already reached conclusions on my case, and should be thus disqualified by the Chairman. I am informed by my counsel that he has, in the words of the Supreme Court, 'a constitutionally disqualifying prejudgment of guilt.'"

Aubusson seized the moment of stunned silence to add: "Ungar versus Sarapte, 1964."

At long last, Urban found his voice. It was a voice tinged with horror. "I am really not clear what you are after, gentlemen," he said.

"I'll repeat it, Mr. Chairman," Ben said. He spoke with faint contempt, with condescension. "I don't want Senator Eisenberg involved in any final decisions by this committee. I don't want him voting on my case. Is that clear?"

Aubusson joined the assault. "Mr. Chairman, permit me to point out that there is ample precedent for Senator Hannaford's request—Rex versus Benn, 1795, Capel versus Child, 1832, and Regina versus Archbishop of Canterbury, 1859."

I had the feeling that old Aubusson, that wearer of longjohns and high button shoes, was talking into the wind. For what I saw on that royal platform, around that holy table, was a withdrawal, a shrinking away.

"It seems clear from his statements," Aubusson piped, "that Senator Eisenberg is not unbiased and impartial, and has prejudged this case, and that therefore the Chair should rule him excluded from final deliberations, that is to say, any decision concerning a resolution."

The opposition trio of Mullendore, Furman and Owens looked as grim as did Urban, Henshaw, and Eisenberg. I had had sufficient experience in gauging senatorial tempers, in the way the wind blew in this great legislative body, and I sniffed the prevailing winds, and I knew they were ill winds for my boss. Don't ask me how I knew; I knew.

"Mr. Chairman," Eisenberg protested, "may I respond to these charges?"

Webb Urban turned to him, and rarely have I seen such an

expression of sympathy, of goodwill. At that moment, these two, Mormon and Jew, could truly be said to be brothers in a world where everyone else was a Gentile.

"Senator Eisenberg, I don't think that will be necessary. The motion by Senator Hannaford and his counsel was addressed to the Chair, and it is the Chair's duty to respond."

Armored with that blunt self-assurance that sustained him, Ben leaned back. I am convinced he felt he had won his point, that Maury Eisenberg would be eliminated from voting, and that the committee, sufficiently cowed, would make short shrift of the investigation. I'd be hanged; Paxton hanged; Blake reprimanded; Ben let off. Was that not the way of his world?

"Now, Senator Hannaford and Mr. Aubusson," Urban went on, "I must point out certain facts to both of you. In the first place, unless you have evidence of some sort of willful misconduct on someone's part, this committee refuses to act on your motion. That is an end of it. We do not control its membership. The members are appointed by the Vice-President of the United States. In any hearing of this nature, gentlemen, senators are not expected to sit here like marble statues and not react to the testimony and evidence.

"So I therefore will not even rule on your motion. I will simply ignore it. You have shown no proof of your allegations. And so, that motion will simply rest where it was placed, and the Chair will not recognize it, nor rule on it, nor consent to hear any other motions of that nature."

Aubusson waved his hand. "Mr. Chairman, I beg of you to hear us out—"

Urban was in the grip of an icy rage. "No, no, no, Mr. Aubusson. I speak for my colleagues here, and, for the vast majority of the men in the United States Senate, when I say we have no appetite for excluding any member of this committee from all deliberations. Your request is a reflection on the integrity and impartiality of this entire select committee, and on the United States Senate itself, and hence—"

"That was not my intent, Mr. Chairman," said Ben. For the first time in all the years I knew him I sensed a tremor in that unshakable voice.

"Do not interrupt, Senator," Urban said. "The matter has no relevance here. Your request is a futile and pointless one. The committee will just let it remain on the table, and ignore it. Mr. Shanahan you may proceed with your examination of Senator Hannaford."

Aubusson saw at once how much ground had been lost, perhaps the game itself. Like a scrambling quarterback, chased way back to his own goal line, he was now trying to pick his way along the sidelines. But Urban was in hot pursuit.

"We did not intend in any way to reflect on Senator Eisenberg," Aubusson said. "But we—"

"It does not reflect on him a jot, sir," Chairman Urban said. "You are wasting time on an irrelevant matter."

"We will cite specific examples of Senator Eisenberg's bias!" Aubusson cried.

"Mr. Chairman, I should like to hear them," Eisenberg said.

"That is unthinkable," Urban said. "I will not have these hearings obstructed every time some wild allegation is made about a member of the committee, and I do not care who makes the allegation. Mr. Shanahan, proceed."

The counsel suddenly seemed a minor, unimportant member of the group. We had just witnessed the collective wrath of the world's greatest deliberative body, in the person of Webb Urban of Wyoming, descend upon my former employer. Some desultory questioning followed; but it was anticlimax. Soon after, Urban suggested an early recess. I am sure he wanted to huddle with his members and decide what to do next. I'm not sure any of them knew. About all Ben was guilty of was rudeness, of *lèse-majesté*, and a censure resolution could hardly be returned on those grounds. But the intemperate assault on Maury Eisenberg had been a grave mistake. As I look back upon it, I think it was the only real mistake he ever made in his career in Washington. He had challenged the mythical, almighty, abstract notion of the Senate, and I had the feeling he would suffer for it. And then, I could have been wrong. Unless the ground rules were changed, unless the method of interrogation was liberalized, he might get away with his grand conniving.

"Like to do an old friend a big favor?"

It was Maria's voice on the phone. It was early evening, and I had settled down to a night of newspapers, magazines, and television in my bachelor apartment. I was getting used to seeing my photo in the papers, my pale head on the television screen. It helped foster the illusion that it was not me at all who was in crisis, but a *doppelganger* of some kind, a ghost, a spook created by the media.

"Maria! You're still in town! He's been sending out search parties for you."

"I know, I know. I've been hiding out with a girlfriend, trying to decide what to do. I've decided."

"And?"

"I'm going back to Ramada City tonight. That's why I called. You gave me my introduction to Washington—how about a decent goodbye? I need a lift to the airport."

She gave me the address of an apartment building off K Street, and I drove through the late October haze, feeling a strange sadness. Maria was standing outside the lobby of the building, her packed suitcases at her feet. I loaded them into the luggage compartment, kissed her cheek in brotherly fashion and we drove off in the fading light to the airport.

"Does the senator know?" I asked.

"No. It's been hide-and-seek for a week, Eddie. I've been changing addresses like a Communist spy. Honestly."

"Yes, honestly. Well, love came late to the big man. I suppose it confused and infuriated him, that it was something he couldn't control. Why didn't you stay on? There are worse careers than being a famous senator's girlfriend."

"Not for this girl." And she turned that classic head, that perfect profile, those dark, disarming eyes, that satiny tan skin, and my blood leaped. Yes, she had the power of beauty, that lovely arrogance. How I had misjudged her! Out of that liaison with Ben, she had suffered not a bit; and he, wretched millionaire, was bereft, shattered, by the experience. Had he at least explored and owned that glorious body, that precious face for a while—a lot more than I had ever managed in my bitter role as brother, friend, beard, and guide?

"Then you don't love him."

"I . . . I don't. I could have, but . . ."

"A bit of hesitation there," I said. "Why?"

She bit her lower lip tenderly—something I might have done on a regular basis, had not Ben moved in. "Eddie, I just can't be sure any more. That's why I decided to end it—end it for good."

She paused a moment, shaking her head. "Oh, it might have been, it might have. Without Fern. Or if he were something else than an important senator who wanted to be President some day. There's something wonderful about an older man, Eddie. I don't know how to say it."

"The father image. It's in the psychology books."

"No. No. Not that at all. Something strong, and comforting, and kind, and dependable. He's known so much—done so much —you feel you're sharing it, that his strength, and his love for you, is somehow richer, and better . . . and you want to give him so much, just because he's older. You want to make him feel good, because . . . because he's so much closer to old age and death than you are."

"A very Latin sentiment, my dear."

"I don't think so. I think it's normal. There were times when I wanted us to be together forever."

"He'll never get over you," I said.

"I know. Oh, it just might have worked out for us, it just might have."

I could think of little to say, in the way of solace, or comment, or criticism, so I tried to be fanciful. "Those things, those old man-young girl marriages can work out very well, you know. There was that old cellist Casals with the young wife, and they are very happy. And there was a composer who died some years ago, Kodaly. A Hungarian, I think he was. His first wife was older than he was, died in her late eighties. And when he was in his early eighties, widowed, he married a twenty-three-year-old girl. It was said to be a wonderfully successful marriage. Who knows? You and Ben might have made it."

"You're needling me, Edward. Maybe it's what I need. But don't ever get the idea that he was like an eighty-year-old man. He was as young in many ways as any of the Marine captains and NASA engineers I ever dated in this town."

"How about administrative assistants?"

She patted my thigh. "Oh Eddie, you were someone special! The nicest brother I ever had."

"Yes damn it, and that was all."

"I'll never forget you, Eddie. I mean it. I'll write . . . and maybe we'll be good friends for a long time."

"Fine. I have a feeling I'll be needing all the good friends I can find when they get through working me over in this town."

"Poor Eddie."

Her sympathy was appreciated. Now that she was lost to me forever, now that the Maria Valdez Incident was closing, I supposed it was proper that we settle, formally, officially, finally, into that proper relationship that had evolved, that Ben had helped create.

"What are your plans now?" I asked.

"I'm taking a job with the Hispanic League. It's all set. With my Washington contacts, what I've learned here, I can be of great help to them."

The Hispanic League was a group aimed at bettering the conditions of Mexican-Americans. They had a good reputation, a shirt-sleeve outfit that pulled a lot of weight with state legislators.

"I should think you'd be a great asset. And he knows nothing about this?"

"He hasn't even been able to find me." She shook her elegant head from side to side as we pulled into the airport parking lot. It had been a brief unsentimental trip. Unlike that memorable evening when we had toured the grand monuments and I had quoted the inspirational words of our nation's heroes, there was little time for lofty notions now. She was all business—Little Miss Hispanic League. She was escaping unhurt. And Big Ben, the man who had always gotten his way, the arm-twister and will-bender, had been the wounded party.

"He'll come down there after you," I said, as we checked her baggage at the airline counter.

We started toward the waiting room. "I don't think so. It's too close to home, Eddie. Remember, it's Fern's home also. If he still wants to be Ben Hannaford, the greatest man ever to come out of Ramada, he has to stay away from me."

"Maria, you are the coolest, most self-contained, most assured witch I have ever known. You horrify me. In a thoroughly delightful way, of course."

"Being beautiful is a help," she said. "Ever since I was twelve, men have been after me. Some were subtle, some dreadful, some clumsy, some kind, some appalling. It makes you wonder. It makes you distrustful. It makes you a little cynical."

"But he loved you, Maria."

"I'm sure he did. But I wasn't going to wait around Washington for that divorce that would never happen. It's been a good experience, but it's not for me."

Her flight was announced. I escorted her to the entrance to the runway. "What is going to happen to Ben?" she asked. "The hearings, the censure resolution."

"They've taken a bad turn. But I have a feeling he'll weather it. Doesn't he always?"

"I'm sure he will."

"The same way he'll weather this blow. You should at least have written to him."

Maria looked solemn. "No. A sudden ending is best. Maybe I'll write from Ramada. Just to congratulate him when the hearings are over and he's cleared."

We were clogging the doorway. She offered her unbearably desirable lips, and I kissed them, a full long, tender kiss, kissed her as if we were loving husband and wife, and my body ached for her, and I regretted the missed opportunities, my foolish abstinence.

"May I kiss you again?" I asked.

"Of course, but we can't keep this up all day."

"I would want to, very much," I said. "One kiss for the past, and one more for the future. That last one was the best kiss I have ever had in my life, and I expect this one to be better."

She raised her head again, and as our lips approached, she drew back a fraction. "On one condition, Eddie."

"Any condition."

"You must believe me, and believe me truly, and say it to me . . . you must believe me when I tell you that he and I never, never slept together, not once, and he never kissed me, not once."

Her wide eyes glowed at me, and I believed her. This was the damned, final, lunatic, appalling truth. Ben Hannaford, the man who had always gotten his way, gotten what he wanted, had not been able to overcome middle-aged caution, Baptist vows, marital loyalty! What a grim joke! And suddenly I felt vastly superior to him. I, at least was coming out of it with the two best kisses I have ever enjoyed—long, lingering, soft, dream-like encounters.

"I believe you, Maria. I *have* to believe you." And we kissed again, and I probed her delicious mouth, and shivered at the press of her dear breasts, the push of her young thighs. With overwhelming reluctance I released her.

She smiled at me and walked through the door to the waiting jet, her back straight, her step firm, her body breathing beauty and grace and confidence.

I hurried back to the lobby, pausing at the airport bookshop, loading up with magazines, out-of-town newspapers, a few paperbacks. I had become a fanatic reader, wallowing in my own misfortune. Distantly I heard the jet engines warming up, and I walked to the main waiting room. From the great high windows I watched the four-engined jet soar off into the night sky.

"End of Maria Valdez," I said, "and good luck to the Hispanic League of the Southwest. *Adiós, muchacha. Vaya con Dios.*"

As I turned away, laden with reading material, I saw Senator Hannaford burst into the waiting room, and look about, with the searching eye of an insurance investigator. Somehow he had tracked her down. Matt Fixx or one of his other minions had found out her plans, and here he was, in a final desperate effort to save his love.

He stood there amid the crowd, his commanding eyes darting right, then left, a burly, power-heavy figure in a well-tailored dark blue suit, his fists clenched, his body poised, a great cat ready to spring. Unfortunately, there was no mouse, no squirrel, no *pajarita* on whom he could leap in a surge of fur, muscle, and bone. The bird had flown.

Accustomed now to my soggy role of bearer of ill-tidings, of traitor, turncoat, spoiler of the wine, sourer of the cream, I walked toward Ben slowly, each arm heavy with my nocturnal sustenance. The senator saw me. And of course he realized that I had come to the airport with Maria. I moved leadenly toward the glass exit doors and his menacing frame barred my way.

"Well?" he asked.

"She's gone, Senator, gone. She doesn't want ever ever to see you again."

His burly figure started for the departure gate, then stopped. I could see his jaw working, the muscles in his ruddy cheeks pulsating.

"It's too late, Senator, she's gone. I'm sorry, Senator, I'm truly sorry."

He studied me with a kind of pained disgust. He was not really angry with me, just vaguely disgusted. "Are you really, Edward?" he asked—and his voice was husky, dim, bereft of its normal snap and force.

"Yes sir, I am. Not just about Maria, about everything."

And a strange defeated look clouded his eyes. I knew in that moment that he had, in fact, and in truth, as Maria had insisted all along, never known her young body. No man could look so lost, so filled with yearning, so poignantly frustrated. It was not the look of a man who had lost a mistress; it was the look of a man who had never known the woman he loved most in the world, the look of the jilted swain, the suitor rejected. Just about everything he had ever wanted, he had gotten. But not Maria. Not my little Latin bird.

His eyes misted, he turned from me and walked toward the airline counter. For all I knew, he would try to force them to bring the plane back; failing that, he would try to buy the airline. But there were limits to his power, there were limits. Maybe he now sensed the shrinkage of his potency. Perhaps I imagined it, but his broad back seemed to sag slightly as he talked to the girl at the counter.

There was another day of aimless sessions of the Ethics Committee. George Paxton was recalled, and this time allowed as how he had lied the first time out and that Senator Hannaford's version was the correct one. Albon Blake did a return engagement and backed him up. Ben was pulling all stops: he had now unified testimony from Paxton and Blake as to the nature of that $50,000. Only I was the apparent liar. But the committee members, in some uncanny way, that strange, almost instinctive manner in which the Senate, like certain varieties of marine life, reacts to different stimuli with predictable behavioral changes, was no longer so solicitous and helpful to him. Urban's manner was crisp; the opposing party members were silent; Eisenberg and Henshaw were on the edge of being antagonistic.

Cleo Watterson and Matt Fixx were also called. They did not directly back up everything Ben said—they pleaded no direct knowledge of many of the transactions—but in vague general ways, with bits and pieces of marginal testimony they supported his account.

Then, after the recess—I had lunched with Fred Goldstein in a greasy spoon a few blocks from the Hill—the storm broke.

Goldstein had an inkling of what was about to happen, but he was not certain what it would be. "The party Policy Committee was up late last night," he said, "without your former boss."

"Really?"

"Yup. Top-secret meeting. Old Honey-Tonsils Hopewell himself, and Webb Urban, and Walter Edgerton, and all the kings and captains."

"Have you any idea what was decided?"

"I don't know. They clammed up. Couldn't even get Hopewell to admit there was a meeting."

I tried biting my cheese sandwich. The soft bread stuck in my craw and I washed it down with Coke. "I suppose it was that attack on Eisenberg that touched it off," I said.

"Christ knows it didn't do him any good. It proves Goldstein's law, I guess."

"Which states?" I asked.

"If you're smart enough, you can pick yourself up by the scruff of the neck and throw yourself out the front door."

The afternoon session began. I could see the members were getting sick of the hearings. They seemed to squirm a little, as if the revelations were getting to them. A distasteful duty, to be sure, making the Senate look bad. At this juncture they were all grateful for Urban's decision to keep the hearings closed.

"Mr. Shanahan, you may call the first witness," the Chairman said.

I saw the counsel nod at the guard at the door. The man opened the huge double doors, and in walked two men I had never expected to see inside this hearing room. They were Senator Henry DiFalco and Senator Lester Goodchapel.

My heart performed a running broad jump. I looked at Ben, but that veteran of a thousand battles was in control of himself. He sat beside Aubusson and Matt Fixx, as immobile as the statue of Lafayette, not a flicker, not a change on his face.

Both of the newcomers took seats at one of the press tables. I knew at once what that Policy Committee meeting had been about. I suspected Ben knew. And I realized that the agonizing decision had been made. I racked my brain trying to recall previous censure hearings and I was unable to recall an instance of one senator coming forth to give testimony to the detriment of another. Certainly in the last two censure hearings within memory, such an incredible act had not taken place, such a violation of the code, so violent a departure from accepted practice. Through my fevered brain kept running rule 19, which, although it applied only to floor debate, was pretty much the sort of tribal custom that governed any Senate business: *No senator in debate shall, directly or indirectly, by any form of words impute to another senator or to other senators any conduct or motive unworthy or unbecoming a senator.* It was a rule that went back to Jefferson's manual.

"Senator Goodchapel, is it our understanding you wish to testify first?" asked Urban, in a voice so heavy with tragedy that I saw him in the robes of an Old Testament prophet, or perhaps St. Peter at the pearly gates, querying newcomers.

"Yes, Mr. Chairman," said the fat man from Indiana.

"You will have to be sworn, Senator," Urban said gloomily.

"I am aware of that, and I have no objection."

Goodchapel, his shapeless suit bagging in elephantine wrinkles, plodded forward. His shoes were unshined, and his round homely head drooped. He kept pushing his mangling eyeglasses up the bridge of his bulbous nose. A thoroughly ill-favored man. But in his march toward the witness table, I divined a determination, an attitude of decision, of firmness of purpose.

He was sworn and took his seat.

"Mr. Chairman," Senator Goodchapel said, "as the Chair is aware, I have requested in the interests of clarity and saving time, that I be permitted to read a statement. If after I have read this statement the committee and counsel wish to examine me, I am perfectly willing to respond to questions." He turned his pitted face toward Senator Hannaford and his lawyers. "And I will not object to cross-examination by counsel for Senator Hannaford."

"You may proceed, Senator," Urban said.

Goodchapel took a sheaf of papers from his pocket, breathed on his spectacles a few times, polished them on a pocket handkerchief and began.

"My statement is a brief one, Mr. Chairman," Goodchapel began. "On the 9th of October of this year, there was left in my office in this building, a large yellow envelope, and I produce it now to show to you." From his suit coat he extracted the envelope I had given him. "It was left in my office by Mr. Edward Deever, the administrative assistant to Senator Benjamin Hannaford. The envelope contained a note which read: 'My dear Senator Good-chapel, The enclosed is from Senator Hannaford, a Campaign Committee contribution, though not through the normal channels. The senator has been very much gratified via his recent talks with you.' It was signed Edward Deever.

"The envelope contained, as it does now, the sum of $20,000, that is to say, two hundred one hundred dollar bills. Mr. Chairman, that is the biggest single contribution I have ever received. I called some staff people on the Campaign Committee that afternoon, and without mentioning Senator Hannaford, or Mr. Deever, or the amount of money involved, learned that no authorization of funds to me had ever been received there.

"But that is neither here nor there. What I wish to stress is that for a week prior to my receiving this money from Mr. Deever, I was cultivated, sought out, dined, and otherwise made the object of Senator Hannaford's attentions. He and I had never been very close, although I respect him greatly. But I found myself perpetually in his company, and the burden of our conversations concerned the Djarak Amendment to the Foreign Aid Bill. I have opposed that amendment all along, although not as vigorously as other members of the Foreign Relations Committee. Every opportunity that we met, there were two major subjects of conversation—my precarious financial position in terms of the forthcoming election in Indiana and Senator Hannaford's urgent desire to see the Djarak Amendment acted upon favorably by the committee.

"I submit, Mr. Chairman, that only a blind man, only a fool, only a self-deceiving man, would fail to see the connection between these two matters. I am reluctant to put any further interpretations on these matters. But since being informed of some of the testimony offered in prior hearings, I have, with great sorrow, felt impelled to make this statement. And in connection with it, I am returning this contribution for my campaign fund to Senator Hannaford, with my sincere thanks for his interest, and with apologies for having caused him any inconvenience. That is all I have to say, Mr. Chairman."

Senator Henshaw had covered his eyes. Maury Eisenberg was staring at the chandelier. Webb Urban appeared to have at long last turned to granite.

Finally Urban spoke. "Mr. Shanahan, is it your desire to ask any questions of Senator Goodchapel?"

"No sir."

"Mr. Aubusson?"

The elderly lawyer's pouchy face was the color of white bond stationery. He raised one hand, as if trying to formulate a question, started to rise, in creaking movements. And then Ben, in a magnificent gesture of courage and resignation, tugged him down to his seat.

Goodchapel was excused. He plodded out of the chamber. Henry DiFalco took his place at the witness table. Of course it had all been cooked up at that policy meeting. Goldstein had suspected correctly that something big was in the wind. Events do not just happen in the United States Senate. Virtually everything is pre-planned, formulated, agreed upon, structured. I have often thought of senatorial procedures as having a certain life cycle—conception, gestation, birth, life, and death . . . And with a wrenched heart I suspected I was now witnessing that final fearful installment.

"Mr. Chairman," little DiFalco began after being sworn, "I will follow Senator Goodchapel's procedure, and read my statement. I will then be at your disposal for answering questions from anyone connected with this hearing. Let me begin by saying that I have a deep and abiding respect for Senator Hannaford. He and I represent different constituencies, and we have often been on opposing sides of issues. But I have never questioned his sincerity, and I still do not.

"This preamble may, in view of what I am now to report, have a hypocritical ring to it. But I find nothing contradictory in my personal attitude toward Senator Hannaford, and what I believe to be certain errors of judgment on his part, which if allowed to remain unnoticed by the Senate, may be the source of hurtful problems that will plague this great body for years to come. I can speak no plainer than that. It is essential that I be as frank as possible in this statement, even if it reflects on my own judgment. But when the reputation of the Senate itself is at stake, nothing less is in order."

DiFalco blew his nose. I felt that the blast from his Roman beak was like a signal, a call to arms. Or was it a death knell? Was it a mournful saddening sound? God knows, I have never seen six more miserable faces than those of the senators who sat in varying attitudes of melancholia at the horseshoe table. Only Shanahan—not one of their ranks, and hence not moved as much as they were—seemed unaffected. He was like a distant friend invited to a wake, at which close relatives weep and wail, while he can only observe with minimal sorrow. As for Ben, he still exercised that incredible self-control for which he was famous. I was certain, as I am to this day, that he felt no genuine malice toward Lester Goodchapel or Henry DiFalco.

"As some of you may be aware," DiFalco went on, "I am currently engaged in a bitter battle for re-election this fall. My opposition has been violent, slanderous, vicious, and unprincipled. I have been denounced, with total disregard for decency or the truth, by certain extreme elements, as a Communist, a socialist, a traitor, a race-mixer, and other choice epithets. I have fought these attacks as best I can. Many are subtle, and are almost incapable of being contested. But fought them I have, and will do so to my dying day. But as a result of these continuing slanders on me, contributions to my political campaign fund have dried up. As of August 31, the total sum of money in my campaign consisted of $1768, of which one thousand dollars represented a contribution from the Anti-Defamation League of the B'nai B'rith. In these impoverished circumstances, I was delighted when Senator Hannaford began to take an interest in my difficulties.

"He and I have never been close friends particularly since I was a leader in the fight against the increase in the oil depletion allowance, which he favored. But as I have said, we respect each other. As of the first week in October, I found myself lunching, dining, meeting more and more with Senator Hannaford. And as in the case of Senator Goodchapel, we had two main subjects of conversation—my financial difficulties, and the Djarak Amendment to the Foreign Aid Bill which Senator Hannaford wanted reported favorably out of the Foreign Relations Committee. At no time did I commit myself to a yea or nay vote on this amendment. At all times I listened to Senator Hannaford with an open mind. And may I add, my mind is still not made up on this matter, and as in every vote I have ever made in this body, only my own conscience will determine the manner in which I vote.

"I now come to a most painful matter. On the morning of the 9th of October of this year, Mr. Edward Deever arrived at my office, and presented me with this envelope, which contained twenty thousand dollars." DiFalco took it out of his coat pocket and held it up. "I accepted the money. I was grateful. But I told Mr. Deever that I was of two minds on the matter. While Mr. Deever assured me this was a contribution from the Campaign Committee, I was unhappy that there was no record of it. The cash bothered me. I was bothered, too, by Mr. Deever's insistence—at Senator Hannaford's request, he said—that the transaction remain confidential. We then discussed some of my problems with my opponents in Connecticut, and I stated that I was glad someone like Senator Hannaford was on my side, that he represented a tough and honest American tradition, which could stand up to the self-appointed super-patriots. Then, just before Mr. Deever departed, I told him to tell Senator Hannaford that while I was grateful for the money, I would have to vote my conscience on the Djarak Amendment. He said he understood."

Senator DiFalco paused, wiped his face with a handkerchief and continued. "I did not intend to make any disclosure of these events," he read, "but learning from the chairman and other committee members of the nature of these hearings, the direction they had taken, I came to the conclusion, as did Senator Goodchapel, that I had no choice but to come forward and read this statement. Let me add that I am not necessarily assuming that this money was given to me to change my vote on the Djarak Amendment. And in view of what has been here revealed, the money will be returned. Henry DiFalco's vote, like that of every single member of the United States Senate, is not for sale—"

(Except one or two or three, I thought. Airborne Alf, and maybe two others. But that is still a pretty good average.)

"—and never will be. But I am disturbed, I am deeply disturbed by the coincidences involved, the pressure exerted on me by my colleague Senator Hannaford regarding the Djarak Amendment, and the windfall of funds, brought to me in cash by his administrative assistant. It is not for me to preach to this committee, or try to move it one way or the other, since I respect all of its members, several of whom I have been closely associated with in committee work and in legislative planning. But I ask only that justice be done, that the good name of the Senate be preserved, and that compassion underscore all your deliberations. I thank the Chairman."

Shanahan had no questions. The six members of the Ethics Committee had none. Ben had none. Old Aubusson had none. There is very little to be asked after a six-ton bomb has leveled your home. Very little.

Senator DiFalco picked up his envelope, and like Goodchapel, chose to avoid the humiliating gesture of dropping the loot in front of Ben. I noticed that DiFalco's eyes were rimmed with tears. A sentimental Italian he had been pained and tormented, and I felt sorry for him.

Two days later, Senator Urban announced that the Select Committee of Standards and Ethics of the United States Senate had voted unanimously to censure Senator Hannaford for having engaged in conduct "which is contrary to accepted morals, derogates from the public trust expected of a senator, and tends to bring the Senate into dishonor and disrepute."

To make the announcement Webb Urban called an open hearing of the Select Committee. Ben was not required to be there. The Committee could not censure me, but Urban announced that it would consider my case further and also Paxton's, for possible charges of contempt of Congress and perjury.

The full text of the resolution was as follows:

> *Resolved*, That it is the judgment of the Senate that Senator Benjamin Bow Hannaford, for having engaged in a course of conduct of exercising the influence and power of his office as a United States Senator, as shown by the conclusions in the Investigation by the Select Committee on Standards and Conduct,
>
> a) to solicit, receive and sequester the sum of two hundred and fifty thousand dollars for his personal use in exchange for influence on pending legislation, and
>
> b) to use a part of this sum to influence fellow senators in the exercise of their duties as members of the Senate Foreign Relations Committee, deserves the censure of the Senate; and he is so censured for his conduct, which is contrary to accepted morals, derogates from the public trust expected of a senator, and tends to bring the Senate into dishonor and disrepute.

That curious archaic wording! Who would use the verb "sequester" but a Senate Committee? It had a wonderful Sherlock Holmes-ish sound, *The Case of the Sequestered Senator* or something like that. I noted that the specific charges were two in number: first, that Ben had finagled money for his personal use—that was our $250,000 from Mr. Norton Krallis—and secondly that he had tried to influence colleagues with part of the loot.

The word "bribe" was carefully avoided; the entire business of the Conglomerate was overlooked; the fact that he had, at worst, lied, and at best, twisted the truth until it bore no resemblance to the facts of the matter, was also ignored. Bad enough that the committee had to go as far as it did. It recommended censure, it voted unanimously on the resolution, and it turned the sticky malodorous thing over to the Senate.

In the week that passed before the censure resolution came to debate on the floor of the Senate, a variety of things occurred which can only be regarded as surrealist, fantastic, other-worldly. I moved in a drugged haze, no longer a major actor in our shabby drama. I cared, and I didn't care. As I read the headlines (we were front page, day after day) and as I watched the TV news programs, and waded through the newsmagazines, the journals, I felt I was no longer part of this mess. And in a sense I wasn't. It was Ben's show. The mighty had fallen. The giant had been brought to earth. The old gray goose shot down. To be so rich and so powerful and so arrogant and so successful! And then to come a cropper on a petty quarter of a million! But in none of the accounts could I find the interpretation I had made of that June day when he siphoned off the $50,000 for himself out of N. Krallis' attaché case. *He had come to the conclusion he could do anything he wanted to and get away with it.* And he had been right, up to a point. He had murdered the bill to lower the oil depletion allowance, had appointed judges, federal commissioners, gotten jobs for relatives and friends, owned the state house in Ramada City, ordered the President to dedicate his private road, faced up to a titan like T. E. Kape and told him off, and goodness knows what else. But I suspect the beginning of the end was his reckless battle for the New Wilderness Bill. I don't know. There is something about fighting conservationists that is dangerous, and Ben tended to disregard my advice. They are every bit as

American as corporate executives. It is almost impossible to call them Communists or traitors. You look at them and you know that they are not.

No matter. He was, for the time being, in decline. The Djarak Amendment was dead. (I thought of oily Prince Malik and his erotic passes at Judy Stapp; I imagined his most memorable experience in Washington would remain that steamy night in Georgetown when Homer Murphy threw him into "Swinging Sid's" pool.)

But to get back to those nightmarish events that followed the committee's recommendation for censure.

First there was my encounter with Senator Alford Kemmons, old Airborne Alf, the Nebraska flier. I had gone to pick up my papers and possessions—books, files, desk impedimenta, a pair of rubbers, an umbrella—from the custodian's office in the basement, and as I emerged, burdened with my gear, from the side entrance of the New Senate Office Building, there was Kemmons. Some folders slid off the top of the large cardboard box I ported, and before the breeze could pick them up and spirit them away, Alf himself gallantly stepped on them, and put them back on the box.

"Thank you, Senator. Thank you very much."

"Well, Eddie. How are you?"

"Pretty good, sir, considering."

"A terrible tragedy about Senator Hannaford," he said hoarsely. His round bald head wobbled.

"Yes, I feel very badly about it also, in spite of everything that's happened between us."

"And you were so close," Alf said in a thick voice. "He regarded you as a son, told me so many times."

"I'm sure." I started down the steps, laden with my meagre possessions, and he walked alongside me. "Eddie, now that matter of three senators who accepted funds . . ."

"Yes?"

"Well, both you and Senator Hannaford mentioned it, but only two have talked about it—DiFalco and Goodchapel." He paused, his head no longer wobbling, but firm with self-righteousness. "You don't intend to testify any further? I mean, the committee isn't going to ask . . . That is, my name . . ."

"No fear, Senator Kemmons," I said, "it's a dead issue. Besides, if it gets down to cases, you weren't even *aware* of it that day I left the $10,000 with you. And you sent it back."

"*Right!* Right! You bet your life I did! I love Ben and I'll do anything for him, but I had to stand on principle on the New Wilderness Bill! I had to!"

And he walked happily up the steps of the building. What irony! Airborne Alf, one of the truly rare birds in the Senate, a genuinely corrupt fellow, a taker, a petty schemer, he would get off the hook, he would go untouched! And courageous DiFalco and innocent Goodchapel, they had been somewhat tarnished. After all, they had taken Ben's money, then had second thoughts only after evidence was developed in the hearings—the contradictory testimony, the evasions, the coverups. But Alf Kemmons would sail on forever—double-billing, scrounging free airplane rides at the taxpayers' expense, performing favors for corporations, and canceling investigations in exchange for varieties of help.

A second interlude of lunacy: Matt Fixx, who was now filling my shoes, phoned me one evening.

"The senator wants that money, Deever," he whined.

"What money?"

"You know darn well. The balance of Mr. Krallis' contribution. Krallis has served papers on Albon Blake demanding it back."

I suddenly felt reckless, a man with nothing to lose. Besides, I could not help baiting people like Matt Fixx. "Well, let's see, Matt, you've got $90,000 of it. Just give it back. You've got twenty each from the two lucky senators, and you've got that $50,000 of Paxton's. I assume you've convinced him that it isn't his."

"That's beside the point. We want it all. The whole ball of wax."

"Doesn't Senator Hannaford always want it all? Why don't you tell Blake to give Krallis the $90,000 and tell him it's an installment."

"I don't appreciate your humor," Matt sneered. "Deever, I warn you, you'd better fork over. You're not in a one-to-one relationship here."

"Someone as rich as Senator Hannaford could easily overlook that $160,000 I still have. I think I've earned it. He can get that out of petty cash, nothing more than a day's profits for building someone's pipeline."

"You'll regret this. You'll be crisped."

"I'll regret a lot of things. But that's beside the point." I thought for a moment. "You know what I think, Matthew? I think that Senator Hannaford wants that money for himself. For Big Ben's boodle. I know that man, and I think he's laughing right now, quoting Scripture and making jokes about the whole thing. He's going to get his mitts on that special fund and try to use it to beat the Senate vote on the censure resolution. That's what I think."

"You are beneath contempt."

"No, below the salt, maybe, but not beneath contempt. Matthew, I know Hannaford. Nothing fazes him. He is shameless, without fear and without caution. You wait and see. He isn't finished spreading the green around. He'll wade right in with his money and try to beat that resolution. And you know something? I almost hope he makes it."

"Will you meet me at the bank tomorrow, Deever, and turn that money over to me?" His voice was shivering.

"No. Not a chance. That box is in my name. I have the key. I have the papers. No one gets to look at it. You tell the senator to think about it a little. Tell him to go easy on me when he gets up to defend himself, and maybe I'll reconsider. That's the trouble with dishonest money, Matt, nobody can ever prove it really belongs to him. Look at the schemer Krallis—he can't even go to the senator or to me and beg for it. He's got to scream at Blake. And he can't even go to the law. Who told him to bribe public officials?"

"I'm glad all of this amuses you. We will all enjoy a good laugh, Deever, when you are carted off to jail, where you belong." He hung up, and I found myself grinning.

After much pressure from the Washington newsmen, Ben agreed to hold a press conference. It was not like him to duck public confrontations. He was no T. E. Kape or Gordon Hackensetter, hiding behind a façade of lofty conservatism, harboring a kingly disdain for the press. He liked reporters; they liked him. But what could he say after DiFalco and Goodchapel had made their appearances? Once senators declared open season on other senators, all was lost. And there seemed to have arisen, after the release of the transcript of the closed hearings—at Chairman Urban's insistence—a moratorium on charges, accusations, bad tempers, indeed any public discussion of the Hannaford case.

I watched the conference on television. Ben asked for, and got, the magnificent caucus room in the Old Senate Building. It was mobbed; packed to the marble pilasters. Reporters and writers seeming to hang from the maroon drapes. A dozen cameras whirred at the rear of the room, live television as well, lights blinding Ben, who stood, alone, absolutely alone—no Matt Fixx, no Sid Stapp, and, of course, no Eddie Deever at his side. That was like him—brazen to the last. Just as he was trying to pry that money loose from me—not to give it back to Krallis I was certain, but to help him beat the censure vote—so, he would face up to the press and answer anything.

"Senator," a man from AP asked, starting off the questioning, "your party's Policy Committee issued a statement yesterday saying that as far as they were concerned, those contributions you made to Senators DiFalco and Goodchapel were not properly campaign contributions given by the Campaign Committee."

"A subtle distinction, son," Ben said blithely. "Who is Chairman of the Campaign Committee? I am. Do I clear everything I do with the other members? I do not. I'd be bogged down in details. As far as I was concerned they were given to help re-elect two good men."

"With no strings attached, sir?" asked the Washington *Post* man.
"None."

"But both Senators DiFalco and Goodchapel claimed you importuned them for a week on the need for their votes in favor of the Djarak Amendment."

"I tried to convince them. But not with those contributions. They were given free of any conditions."

He was unbeatable, his head bloody, but never bowed. He dominated that high-ceilinged room, a prize bull in a pasture filled with steers.

"But Senators DiFalco and Goodchapel interpreted those funds as inducements to get them to vote for the amendment," a newsmagazine writer persisted. "I believe the word arm-twisting has been used by a lot of people."

"I've never twisted an arm in my life," Ben said. His eyes were crinkled with good humor. "Where'd you hear that, son? 'He that repeateth a matter separateth friends.' "

The press roared. That was the old Ben Hannaford they knew and liked! He was no lovable Gage Hopewell sounding woodwind notes, but a truly formidable fellow, a plain-speaking man.

"Sir, the transcript of the Ethics Committee hearings shows that you challenged Senator Eisenberg's impartiality and you asked that he be removed from the final deliberations, from voting. Will you request on the floor of the Senate that some senators, whom you feel may be prejudiced against you, be disqualified from voting on the censure resolution?"

"No, there were only six on the Ethics Committee, and I figured I might make it close if I could knock off one hostile Indian at the start. Not that I have anything against the senator from Illinois. I'm personally very fond of Senator Eisenberg. I won't try to keep anyone from voting on the resolution."

"Will you be represented by Mr. Aubusson there?" a man from a Baltimore paper asked. "There's a precedent for counsel getting permission to accompany a senator to the floor during debate on censure."

"No, I'll handle it myself. After all, I'll be among friends and colleagues."

On the monochrome gray screen, Lou Parenti's bulky figure materialized. "Senator, what's going to happen to all that money you got from the Mortgage-and-Loan lobby? They must be screaming for it."

"Louis, I hate an Indian giver, being part Kiowa myself."

"You mean they don't get it back?"

"It isn't theirs," Ben said airily. "It was a contribution, and it will stay that way."

"But the hearings brought out that your ex-aide Edward Deever has it all locked up—most of it anyway—in a safe deposit box. Oh, you got some of it still, but what's going to happen with all that money? It just gonna lay around? Heck, it isn't even gathering interest."

"'The partridge sitteth on eggs and hatcheth them not,'" Senator Hannaford said. "I'll hatch those eggs in time. When I'm good and ready."

I laughed, alone in my apartment, viewing his bravura performance. And I thought: Ben, old friend, father, employer, idol, I will fight you down the line for that $160,000. You may have given me $20,000 of it to "buy some shirts with pointy collars instead of those ones with the buttons on the collar," but it was more than shirts I was after now.

"Senator, care to make any prediction on how the censure vote will go?"

Ben raised his head. "It does not stand a chance," he said, with an arrogance relieved only by his grace. "The Senate is my home and my church."

"It sounds as if you're going to preach them a sermon," Fred Goldstein said.

"Yea, Brother Goldstein," Ben replied, with a broad wink, " 'Every man's work shall be made manifest.' "

And the conference ended. He was going in fighting, armed, confident, and possibly blinded by his strength.

CHAPTER FIFTEEN

The galleries were jammed for the debate on the Ethics Committee resolution to censure Senator Ben Hannaford for conduct "tending to bring the Senate into dishonor and disrepute."

Wearing smoked glasses and an air of guilt, I was sneaked into the radio-TV section of the Senate Press Gallery by Fred Goldstein. Cringing, I settled into one of those round stools and looked around the great chamber. Across from me, in the public gallery, I saw Fern—her wheat-colored hair piled high, hard with shellac, her firm figure in a tan wool dress. She was seated with Judy Stapp, who had managed to subdue her usual extravagant appearance in deference to Ben's ordeal. Across the great hall, I could almost detect a look of relief on her cynical face—"Swinging Sid" had emerged unscathed.

In one corner of the public gallery I espied the Hungarian Ambassador, Imre Bator. No doubt he was learning, learning all the time. Back home in his socialist workers' fatherland, anyone involved in anything resembling Ben's operations would have been put away months ago. I saw little Prince Malik looking on, flanked by a brace of leggy blondes. It all made for a fine, surrealist painting, a collage, a muddled mosaic of Ben's varicolored recent past.

Before I entered to take my seat, I had been stopped in the corridor by a tall, dark man, hiding behind a pair of sunglasses bigger and rounder than my own.

"Hey Chico," he called—blowing cigar smoke at me—and I recognized former Congressman Angel López Garcia.

"Why, Congressman, what a pleasure!" I cried.

Garcia pumped my hand. "Well, I see they have catch' up weeth the beeg guy, hey, Chico?"

"Not yet, Mr. Garcia. The senator can never be counted out."

"No, Chico, they got heem now. You know why? He get too smart weeth the Establishment. *Establicimiento*. He get too fresh weeth Urban and that crowd. They don' like."

"You think he'll be censured?"

"Sure. But so wha'? He steel keep all his privileges. He steel draw salary, keep seniority, keep all committee poseetions. Sure, he ees one of the boys. *Cabron!* But not Angel López Garcia. That's the way eet goes, Chico. But you, baby, you?"

"What about me?"

Garcia grimaced, chewed on his black cigar, and patted my arm. "I theenk they throw the book at you, Chico. They give you hell, because you blow the wheestle on Ben. Yeah, that gonna be rough."

"I'm not worried. They blew the whistle on you—and you don't seem to be suffering."

"Oh, but it hurts, Chico, it hurts, way in here." And he pushed at his paunch. "Anyway, I got me a job." He winked and showed me a Senate Press Gallery pass. "Washington correspondent for the Spanish-language South American News Service. Not bad for old Angel, no?"

He swaggered off in his $250 silk suit, his cockiness worthy of my esteem.

Apart from Garcia—a quasi-newsman at best—the cream of the press corps crammed the inadequate galleries. Many syndicated columnists were present; a lot of papers in the Ramada City area had sent men to Washington for the debate and vote; and I spotted a few of the prime-time television thinkers, faces so well-known that they drew *oohs* and *ahs* and pointed fingers from the public.

President Kretz had made a personal request to Vice-President Smead Beldock that he preside over the debate. This was most unusual. But I think that the President, that genial man, was only too glad to be rid of Beldock's puritanical intransigence for a few days. Moreover, he had instructed Beldock to function in his role of presiding officer with absolute fairness, and to bend over backwards to give Ben every break possible. With typical

Kretzian guile—a guile all the more formidable because it was grounded in innocence—he had come out strongly for an Ethics Committee investigation of Ben, and had then insisted on giving Ben a more than fair shake. Thus no one could complain. No one ever complained about anything the President did.

I looked down at the great maroon-carpeted chamber I loved so well. I saw Ben seated at his desk on the majority side. He did not have a single paper, document, or news clipping with him. He had no brief case, no envelopes. His arms were folded and he looked relaxed.

The scene was too casual. Pages loitered at the edge of the president's raised dais. Assistants lounged on the waiting-room furniture in the corners—I saw Matt Fixx and Cleo together, chatting, comparing notes—senators came and left through the central doors. Some chatted in groups. It was curious how much you could learn just by watching them. Gage Hopewell, our beloved Majority Leader, sashayed about—all things to all men. Royce Henshaw and John Tyler Lord seemed to be apart, not quite full-fledged members. Was it their intellect that removed them from the heart of the club? I think it was. They studied too much. They knew too much. They were not fully to be trusted. On the other hand, people like Webb Urban and Clyde Furman and Carl Mullendore, breathing small-town courtrooms, dingy law offices, drab Main Streets surrounded by wheat farms and desert, these men seemed to be part of the furnishings, to have come with the dark brown desks, the sandboxes, the inkwells. I can't put my finger on it; some men are quintessential senators, some are not.

Beldock's gavel came down. He recognized Royce Henshaw. I thought I saw the strategy. The committee, which had voted unanimously to censure Ben, would stick together, would space its speakers, would probably save Webb Urban for last. Urban was unassailable. He was one of those people in public life beyond criticism.

"Mr. President," Senator Henshaw began, "I would hope that the Senate can dispose of this unpleasant matter in a few days. None of us is happy with the assignment thrust upon us. It is our desire to see the question of Senator Hannaford's conduct debated fairly and fully, but without repetition, unfair accusation,

delays, and windy irrelevancies. The committee has made its recommendation, let us debate it, let us vote."

Fred Goldstein whispered to me: "That crack about windy
irrelevancies won't help Henshaw. These intellectuals never learn.
What is this whole place but a windy irrelevancy?"

"Not quite, Fred," I said, "not quite."

"Mr. President," Royce Henshaw went on, "the Select Committee on Standards and Conduct has unanimously called for
the censure of Senator Hannaford on specific acts, namely that
he did solicit, receive and sequester the sum of a quarter of a
million dollars for his private use, in exchange for help in removing a section of the tax bill, and that further he did use a part of
this money to influence fellow senators in the exercise of their
functions as members of the Foreign Relations Committee, and
that in so doing he tended to bring the Senate into dishonor and
disrepute.

"The facts of this case are well known. It is inconceivable to me
that the Senate can act in any other way than to vote for the
censure resolution. Let me make a few explanatory remarks in
this connection. Should the Senate vote for censure, the senator
so rebuked will have none, I repeat, *none* of his senatorial pre-
rogatives or privileges withdrawn. He will still remain the senior
senator from his great Southwestern state.

"Further, he will continue to draw his salary and he will be
entitled to all the allowances of his office. He will retain his seniority and his position on committees.

"What then, does a censure action accomplish? It merely expresses the Senate's condemnation of the course of conduct in
which the senator has engaged. Now I have heard it argued, and
I am sure it will be argued here on the floor of the Senate, that
the committee has wrongly used *ex post facto* laws in regard to the
censure resolution's charges. In effect, it is said that there are no
laws, no statutes, no code of ethics, nothing of formal writing to
justify the wording of our resolution. I reject this. The censure
action embodies no penalties, no fines, no expulsion, no punitive measure of any kind, but merely expresses the Senate's condemnation of the senator's course of conduct. Hence, the analogy
with constitutional guarantees and *ex post facto* laws is irrelevant.

"I ask my fellow senators, does the absence of any specifically
written standard covering the senator's conduct mean that the

Senate must sit idly by and do nothing? I think not. Mr. President, the Senate is not a law unto itself. As lawmakers in the great American Republic, we dare not place ourselves above any law, above morals, above criticism. I submit, sir, that such an attitude is unthinkable.

"It is true that our individual consciences and our personal ethics must be our guides. But we are also members of a collective body, a fact that we never cease to stress. And if we are to take pride in our collegiality and protect this hallowed, this tradition-based collectivity, then we need more than personal beliefs to govern our conduct. We need a collective will toward good conduct, to moral behavior. Now, whatever the personal beliefs of any senator, whether they be on the order that 'every law favors a special interest' or 'a campaign contribution is what I say it is' —these beliefs must in some basic manner conform to what the public believes to be ethical conduct.

"Although, Mr. President, we are each elected by the citizens of our respective states, the Senate is a national institution. We are, in a sense, fiduciary agents for the whole people. More than one senator, one state, one election is involved when one of our ranks behaves in an unethical manner. This was clearly recognized by the framers of the Constitution. The power to punish or expel a member was granted to the entire Senate for just that reason, that is to say, that a member's conduct could not be judged only by his constituents.

"Mr. President, it is fatuous of me to point out to this eminent body, that because of our grave responsibilities, the misconduct of any member, particularly when that misconduct is deliberate, shameless and repeated, is a reflection on the entire body . . ."

There was a stirring. This was strong stuff, much stronger than one usually hears on the floor of the Senate. I saw Fern shaking her blond head. But Vice-President Beldock made no move to rebuke Henshaw, and there was not a word from Old Gage, who was lumbering about his apportioned area, rudely whispering to Sid Stapp and a few other cronies while Henshaw spoke. Gage had little use for professors.

". . . when the reputation of this institution itself is brought into question," Henshaw was saying, "there arise serious doubts that this institution can remain effective in the affairs of government. It is perfectly understandable why a former member of this body called it 'The Sapless Branch' and we . . ."

A drunken roar punctuated Senator Henshaw's oration. Bouncing up from his desk, where he had appeared to be in a sottish sleep was Senator Gabriel T. Tutt of Alabama. "Mistah President!" he bellowed. "Mistah President! I state to you, suh, that the senior senator from Montana is outa ordah, with his remarks, that they are a desecration and an insult to this body, and I ask that he be declared outa ordah and that those remarks about shameless deliberate conduct, I say, suh . . ."

And he raged on. Henshaw protested. "I have not yielded, Mr. President, and I ask that you permit me to finish my remarks."

"You'll do nothin' of the sort!" shouted Gabe. A bourbon flush inflamed his puffy face. Who in that chamber could guess how fast that old lecher could run? I chuckled to myself, recalling the day I had brought him down with a flying tackle in the carpeted corridors of the Sutter Hills Hotel in San Francisco. Old Gabe's voice suddenly became clogged, heavy with phlegm. Vice-President Beldock waited patiently: one did not deal rudely with so precious an old commodity as Gabe Tutt. After all, he was a Southerner, a racist, a friend to the peanut and cotton and oil lobbies, and above all a staunch defender of huge defense budgets, while unalterably opposed to welfare payments for hungry Negro children. How could such a man be bad?

"Mr. President, I would like to conclude, and I will gladly yield to Senator Tutt as soon as I have concluded," Henshaw said.

Up bobbed Tutt again. "You bet you will!" he shouted. "I'm here to defend Senator Hannaford, and I'll defend him from anyone, anyone at all! He is guilty of nothing, y'all heah? And he will not, I repeat will not, be sacrificed at the altar of the pinko-liberal-leftist conspiracy that is gnawing at the roots of our free ent'prise system!"

Henshaw shook his head—embarrassed for everyone. I saw Gage Hopewell waddle over to Senator Tutt and talk to him soothingly. The Old Medicine Man, the old vendor of Indian Vegetable Oil Soap, he could quiet Tutt. Ben, for his part, turned in his seat, where he had sat, motionless (I recalled that day when he prowled, paced, maneuvered his way around the carpeting, bending elbows, patting backs, grabbing arms, haranguing colleagues, to frustrate the cut in the oil depletion allowance!), and said a few words to Tutt.

"Probably told him to mind his own goddamn business," Goldstein whispered. "Jesus, with a friend like Tutt, Hannaford won't need any enemies."

"Mr. President," Henshaw resumed, in his soft voice, as if he were lecturing graduate students, "if we accept the right of senators to accept sums of money for vague undefined reasons, for so-called educational purposes, for presumed campaign purposes, when records are not meticulously kept, we embark down a dark and winding road, leading to dread and dangerous depths. If we accept the right of any senator, no matter how powerful, influential, industrious—and I must add, well-intentioned, for I have admired much of our colleague's labors and am aware of his considerable talents—if we accept one senator's right to lavish so-called campaign contributions on others, with even the merest hint that these funds come with a condition, with a proviso, with, I am reluctant to use the word, a *price*, then we are in sore need for self-examination, and indeed, we may have reached a point of no return in terms of the American people's view of us.

"I cannot, Mr. President, condone the actions of Senator Hannaford. His acts have been at variance with the public trust expected of a senator, and have tended to bring dishonor and disrepute on the Senate . . ."

"I wan' ask the senior senator frrom Montana," Tutt croaked, stumbling to his feet, "whut makes him think he is so free of blame, whether he ever took a dollah or moah from his liberal intellectual N'Yawk friends, and why those funds raised for him are any diff'rent from what the man under vicious attack heah today is charged with!"

"My response to the senior senator from Alabama is that I have always accounted for every single penny raised in my behalf, and that my books are open to anyone. I have no caches of hundred dollar bills in secret safe deposit boxes."

A murmur went up from the chamber. The floor was virtually filled. No absentees for this one. It was a big show. An important show. Yet despite the high attendance, the grim determination with which they all seemed gripped (apart from Senator Hopewell, who ambled about like that fellow in Thornton Wilder's play *Our Town*, smiling, nudging, gossiping, being his dear self)

I had a sense of mass humiliation, of total discomfort with their task. Henshaw was right. They would do well to get it over with as swiftly as possible, a play with a limited run.

"And so I conclude, Mr. President," Senator Henshaw said, "that with all the evidence at hand, and notably the sworn testimony of two of our own colleagues, the junior senator from Connecticut and the senior senator from Indiana, testimony which we all have read with heavy hearts, this body has no choice but to approve the resolution of censure voted unanimously by the Select Committee on Standards and Conduct."

Gabe Tutt was recognized. He shook his fist at Henshaw. "Mr. President, I am sick and tired of these holy intellectuals tellin' us in the great Senate of the United States how to run our affairs. I am sick and tired of this pinko conspiracy of the press—yes, you people up there!" And he shook his old fist at the reporters, who laughed. "Where is that traitor Parenti?" he howled. "Where is that thief in the night, who steals private papers, that besmircher of good men, that boll weevil in the cotton field, that dirty scavenging mongrel, who lusts for the bones and blood of his superiors? Let him show his face heah, so that the Senate can see the kind of evil monster who has unloosed these slanderous lies on the innocent head of one of our most distinguished members!"

At that point, Lou Parenti, with sublime contempt, rose from his seat at the rear of the Press Gallery (the gallery for newspapermen is separate from the TV-radio gallery where I sat with Goldstein) and walked to the first row. For a few seconds the columnist remained standing, his burly figure presenting itself to the legislators below, and especially to ranting Gabe Tutt, as if to say, *Shoot me, shoot me, I dare you.* He stood there a few seconds until Tutt found him, and cried: "There he is! There is the snake, the reptile, the buzzard, the worm that gnaws at our vitals! Look at him fo' whut he is!"

Parenti, with magnificent disdain, rotated his huge body and broad face so that all could see, all the time smiling, exhibiting his form, then retired.

"I want mah colleagues to see whut we are involved with heah! Who we goin' to believe?" Tutt roared. "Our dear friend from Ramada City, or that lying double-dealing thief?"

Ben looked uneasy. A few senators had turned their back on

Tutt. Even the Vice-President, who probably detested Lou Parenti as much as anyone in the chamber (Parenti, when Smead Beldock was a congressman, had nick-named him "Smokey Smead" because of his persistent efforts to liberate the tobacco industry from federal regulation), looked about for someone to recognize, someone who would not charge the electric air with additional thunderbolts. Sidney Stapp was now on his feet.

"Mr. President, I speak in defense of my friend, the senator so unfairly treated by his well-meaning colleagues, our distinguished Chairman of the Interior and Insular Affairs Committee. I wish to state, Mr. President, that the argument that he is being subjected to an *ex post facto* judgment is not so easily dismissed as the senior senator from Montana would have us believe. I submit, Mr. President, that this is a violation of Senator Hannaford's constitutional rights. The condemnation of the senator is based on standards not previously generally recognized as applicable as legal or moral principles. We are all aware of this. Until a formal code of ethics is established the Select Committee simply cannot render these arbitrary judgments!"

Sid had said this before, at a press conference. It was a pretty good argument. I wondered how many it would convince. The Swinger was a first-class lawyer, and he was popular, and he had a soothing manner. There was a good chance he could sway some members on the floor.

"The senator, Mr. President," Sid went on, "was denied due process of law, and was judged on standards so new, so extraordinary, that their usages to arrive at a severe decision, are dismaying and have the aroma of vengeance about them. I appeal to this body to think carefully before it casts its vote. I ask that that vote be in the negative. If we are the world's greatest deliberative body, then let us act in deliberate fashion—and not be swayed by emotions which cause us to cast aside the hallowed concept of due process of law and to fall into the unfair tactic of the *ex post facto* judgment."

Sid went on and I must admit he was effective. His manners were impeccable, his appeal conducted in a reasonable style. I could see Judy Stapp looking at him with admiration, whispering in Fern's ear. Yes, the Swinger was quite a man. I was glad he had gotten off clean. After all, his closeness to Ben was nothing more than the friendship of two operators, two men who had the knack for getting things done.

Unfortunately, Royce Henshaw's scholarly discourse had taken the wind out of Sid's sails. Senator Stapp had said these things in press conference, and I had the feeling that he was butting his head against a brick wall. One only had to look at Webb Urban's dour face to realize that the Establishment was behind that committee vote.

Beldock recognized Tutt again—evidently the old sot had appointed himself some kind of floor advocate for Ben—and he was ranting once more. "I advise the Senate, and you, Mr. President, that in short order, I will offer a substitute for that censure resolution, and in it, I will demand that this Select Committee set up a code of ethics once and for all, and absolve our good friend from inny, I repeat, inny wrongdoing!"

With that Tutt stepped into the aisle, and grabbed Carl Mullendore by the lapel—apparently because Senator Mullendore was the ranking minority member of the Ethics Committee—and crowed at him: "And I say to the senior senator from Iowa, the day of judgment is comin', when we all will be tried, and I will count heads and name names, and I won't forget!"

John Tyler Lord got up, his blue blood boiling. "Mr. President, I beg of you to maintain a modicum of order here. The galleries are jammed, the press is observing this, the Senate is, in effect, on trial."

But Beldock made no effort to shut Gabe up, or order him back to his seat. I reflected on this: how marvelous to be an old-fashioned Southerner in this town! The assumption, the automatic assumption is that one thus *belongs*, one is perforce a patriot, a hero, a comical but kindly fellow, an anti-Communist, and a one hundred percent American. Had Lord, or Henshaw or Eisenberg or Edgerton stumbled about the chamber waving arms and abusing people, they would have been gaveled into silence.

There followed some nit-picking debate on the wording of the resolution—none of it very conclusive, none of it delivered with anything approximating passion. As I well knew, many decisions are arrived at long before the members enter the chamber for debate, and hence debate has a prearranged, almost play-like quality. In this instance I could not truly tell which way the wind was blowing. Ben was a powerful man with many friends. Many

senators who were in his debt. But despite my doubts as to how
the censure vote would go—and the uncertainties on the floor—
the atmosphere in the great hall was aimless, irksome. No one
liked what was going on. No one appreciated the public and the
press staring down at them, naked in their own misbehavior.

A few senators—Martinson of California, O'Gara of New
Jersey, Dierking of Utah—arose to support Sid Stapp's proposal
that the Senate could not censure Ben on an *ex post facto* basis.
It seemed to be their basic strategy, and I had a suspicion it might
work, provided Gabe Tutt could be prevailed upon to shut his
drunken mouth. (I point out that while it is considered permissible
for a Southerner who favors unlimited defense appropriations
to behave in an unmannerly fashion, since he is without doubt
the greatest patriot of all, it does not follow that the Senate will
vote with him; the privileges accorded him are rather on the order
of the favors which primitive tribes accord old, looney, bad-
mannered elders.)

I now had the feeling that Ben, had he not so blatantly insulted
Maury Eisenberg, and inferentially, Webb Urban, in his bold
demand that Eisenberg disqualify himself, would have won the
day. If he could somehow paper over that impertinent move (it
was the talk of the Hill) perhaps he might survive. I could not
be sure; but Ben was a man of a thousand surprises.

I don't recall all the darts and turns that the debate took. But
by now it was impossible to divine the prevailing winds. What I
found curious was the manner in which Ben sat in his seat (how
different from the days when he had roamed the floor, playing the
bull of the woods) and listened politely. He had left his floor
fight to Senator Stapp, and Sid was a good advocate—polite, persuasive, mannerly.

"Funny thing about the Swinger," Fred Goldstein whispered to
me, "you got to like him. He's got something on the ball. Oh, I
know all about the broads in the hotel rooms, and the fees from
the movie industry, but he's still got something."

Both of us peered down at the floor, where Sid, in response to
a query from Maury Eisenberg, was explaining, in well-chosen
words, why Ben had been deprived of due process of law, and
hence his constitutional rights. They listened to each other
attentively, nodding, asking questions, I had the sense again that
things were looking up for Ben. After all, Eisenberg, that mourn-

ful millionaire, had been the butt of Ben's accusation of impartiality. Perhaps Eisenberg had forgiven him; perhaps Ben would come home free.

And then, in some peculiar manner, the wind changed again. It started with a speech, a seemingly irrelevant speech, by one of the Senate's most curious men, the junior senator from Pennsylvania, John Kovatch. This Kovatch was an odd bird. He was born in Czechoslovakia, his father a coal miner. Self-educated, he had risen to high office through the simple device of keeping quiet, observing rigid personal honesty, and taking care of ethnic minorities, first in his home district when he was a congressman, and now in terms of his entire state. He spoke several Slavic languages, and he also had a Ph.D. in education. A rare bird, this Kovatch, and one of those unpeggable, unpredictable men. "Trouble with Kovatch is," Fred Goldstein once told me, "he's been surrounded by conservatives so long, he thinks he is one. But when he was a kid congressman, there was no hotter liberal in the House. You never know how he's going to jump. He gives the party leaders fits." (As an example: in the space of one week, Senator Kovatch had voted for increased federal aid to colleges, against increased social security, for moving the United Nations to Geneva, but aaginst cutting the foreign aid appropriation for Yugoslavia.)

This inconsistent, maddeningly independent man—he was short, barrel-chested and egg-bald—also had the unnerving habit of making grandly unapropos speeches, these addresses delivered after weeks of silence, weeks when he would be the only man on the Senate floor. To this end, the presiding officer usually tried to ignore him, or to keep him waiting until a recess was imminent so that his meandering off-the-mark comments could be contained. But there had been a hiatus in debate, and Vice-President Beldock (who had no idea what to make of Kovatch) recognized him.

"Oh God," muttered Fred, "here we go with something on National Slovak Day, or the Appropriation for River Improvement in Allegheny."

And one almost heard a collective groan arising from the Senate as Kovatch's stocky figure assumed a stance and the junior senator from Pennsylvania began to speak.

"Mr. President, we have Senator Hannaford's own statement that he took a quarter of a million dollars as a campaign contribution to be used by various colleagues. We have the word of distinguished colleagues that they accepted large amounts from this donation, and we have heard that perhaps others of our number benefited from it."

I glanced quickly at Alford Kemmons, but he seemed to be half-asleep.

"Now, Mr. President, I want to talk a little in general," Senator Kovatch said, "about this matter of money, how much we need, how much we should have, what we're entitled to. I make no bones about it, I'm addressing myself to the American public, because I think someone in this chamber has to. We have often heard it said that a United States Senator is restricted in his capacity to do his work properly, let alone campaign, because of a shortage of funds. It is said that we are underpaid. That we don't get enough expenses. That the economics of being a senator are unsound, and hence we have to go around taking contributions from people like the Mortgage-and-Loan interests, or labor unions, or the veterans lobby, or other groups who have special bits of legislation they want passed—or laws they want killed. All of that came out in the Ethics Committee Hearings. I want to talk about that a little."

Have you ever seen one hundred men start to squirm at once? That is the feeling I had as I looked down, from behind my tinted specs, at the floor. Senator Tutt was on his feet again, advancing arcoss the floor to the minority side of the aisle from where Kovatch was speaking.

"A point of privilege, Mr. President," gargled Gabe Tutt, "the junior senator from Pennsylvania, Mr. President, is making remarks which reflect on the integrity of this chamber, and I—"

He was picking on the wrong man in Kovatch. There is something about an eccentric (and who was to say that John Kovatch was not *more* than merely eccentric) that defies abuse, interruption, bullying.

"Mr. President," Kovatch said, in a steely voice, "please instruct the senior senator from Alabama to stay on his side of the aisle. The rules of the Senate are clear on that matter. He can say what he wants to say when I am finished and not before."

Gabe Tutt halted in mid-step; his mouth worked stupidly, but he went back to his seat.

"Now, Mr. President, this matter of how poor most of us are alleged to be is relevant to this debate. If one senator can go around handing out huge hunks of money to others, presumably to assist them in their campaigns, then there's something rotten in Denmark. We have accepted the notion that we are all of us broke, strapped, fallen on hard times. That any money that comes our way must be taken. Well, I contest that. I don't believe it. And I intend to describe for the American people, just what the financial status of an average senator is.

"First off, we are paid $30,000 a year. Well, that doesn't sound like a whole lot especially when you consider the way salesmen and advertising people earn so much money for peddling a lot of hooey. Yes, and our expenses are heavy—a place to live in Washington, not a cheap city, a place back home, an office back home, trips back and forth to our home state. All that adds up.

"But wait a minute. The government pays an awful lot of these trips. A senator can make seven round trips home a year at government expense. He can go anywhere in the world free on what we laughingly call official business, and if he goes on military aircraft he can take his wife along at reduced rates. And when he's abroad he can get spending money to spend there, and he does not have to account for it. That's a pretty good deal all around, I'd say."

I watched the public gallery. Senator Kovatch had grabbed them. People were bent forward listening, eager to get the inside. Nothing fascinates your average American more than money.

"Oh, but that isn't all," Senator Kovatch went on—while some colleagues studied the walls, others wandered off to the rear, a few began to converse with one another as if to indicate that as far as they were concerned, the Pennsylvanian was not even present. "Let's list a few more fringe benefits that all of us are entitled to. We are allowed $2400 a year for stationery. We get free telephone and telegraph service up to $16,000. That's a lot of phone calls. We get free mail privileges all over the world. And here are a few more items we get gratis—free haircuts, free soda water, free Coca-Cola, free parking, free flowers from government greenhouses, free newspapers, free help from the Congressional Library, free gymnasium and swimming pool, free rubdowns at the gym. We also pay reduced fees at Army and Navy Hospitals.

"We are allowed $160,000 a year to pay our staff, and we can, and many of us do, put our wives, children and other relatives on our payrolls with no questions asked. Our staff members are allowed four round trips home a year at government expense. If we serve long enough, we can retire on a pension of $24,000 a year. If we die in office, our salary continues for a year and our funeral expenses are paid by the government. Thus, that $30,000 salary isn't as skimpy as it sounds. All these things I mention add up to a tidy sum, and many of our numbers, including myself, manage quite nicely on it.

"So I am getting a little annoyed with these constant references to campaign needs, and how much money we are always requiring to get by. In a sense, the senator whose fate we are debating today, a good friend to many of us, is right when he says a campaign contribution is what he decides it is. The fact of the matter is, Mr. President, that we are pretty much allowed to raise and spend money for political campaigns without making any strict accounting to anyone, unless it be our own consciences. And during a campaign, which can run for many months, in fact, can run almost as long as a senator wants it to run, we can list just about anything in the world as a campaign expense and get away with it—travel, food, laundry, hotel bills. Oh, I know it's done, and we all know it's done, and maybe it's time we stopped acting like it's perfectly all right.

"Now I know from my own experience that the vast majority of us don't do this sort of thing. Some of us do. And worst of all, that big, vague catch-all phrase 'a campaign contribution' can cover a multitude of payments. We have all heard about that attaché case filled with a quarter of a million dollars, and if someone wants to call it a campaign contribution, they can, but I have my own ideas. And as far as I'm concerned, I'm voting for the resolution offered by the Ethics Committee, and I hope it passes overwhelmingly."

So spoke Senator John Kovatch, that oddball coal miner's son from Pennsylvania. And again, as I had gauged when Ben launched his impulsive attack on Senator Eisenberg, I knew that a bridge had been crossed, a sea change taken place.

"Mr. President," Gabe Tutt muttered—he was in the middle aisle separating the two sides of the chamber, "those remarks by the junior senator from Pennsylvania are an insult to every member of this group. He should be rebuked, and if no one else will do it, I will. I ask the senator how many relatives has he got on his payroll?"

Kovatch didn't even flinch. "Not a one, Senator, nor have I ever spent two months drying out in the Bethesda Naval Hospital at government expense."

A muffled embarrassed laugh arose from the floor, from the gallery. Gabe Tutt's long drunken convalescences were too well known. The old buzzard had met his match in Kovatch.

I studied Ben. His eyes were half-shut. He seemed resigned. Kovatch's speech was a crusher—irrelevant perhaps to the immediate issues, but damning in a broad, general way. But Senator Hannaford did not seem to care. His arms were folded on his chest and he sat erect, rock-like in his chair. What could have swirled through his mind? Was he shaken at last? Was that lust for power, for manipulation, that complusion to get his own way, at long last to be frustrated?

Sid Stapp then launched an attack on Marsha Treadway, on Parenti, and on me. But it was not terribly effective, and I think I knew why. I understood that Ben did not approve this line of defense. He was a big man. He was a rich man. And in spite of all I have revealed about him, he was a decent man. He did not want to shift the blame for his fall on lesser people. Moreover, as Sid Stapp and the rest of the Senate knew, the issue of the Conglomerate papers, damning as they were, had been conveniently overlooked by the Ethics Committee. It had been as if this high-level scheming, this plot to rape the national forests had never taken place.

Senator Alford Kemmons then took the floor: a strange ally. But I had to give Airborne Alf credit. He took off on Krallis and Paxton as the real villains; but he wasn't convincing. Somehow he had his facts wrong, and his charge that Krallis was the corrupter, the snake, the villain, did not ring true. Most of the members of the Senate had read the testimony, had gotten a good look at Krallis, and they knew him for what he was—a small-timer, out of his class. Such worms did not corrupt giants like Ben Hannaford.

There was a recess. The senators seemed eager to get out of the chamber as fast as possible, to get the mess over with. There seemed little else to be debated—except for Webb Urban's speech, and the opportunity to amend the resolution or offer substitutes. The whole process was moving with unusual speed and understandably so.

"Mr. President," John Tyler Lord sniffed, just before the motion to adjourn, "let's get this over with. The longer we debate the matter, the longer we display our meaner, more irritable natures, the less the people will think of us, and they think little enough as it is."

"You speak for yo'sef!" Gabe Tutt thundered. "It's people lak you give us a bad name!"

At lunch with Fred Goldstein in a nearby sandwich shop we ran into Parenti.

"Hey, Eddie baby," he called. "What's with the big guy? He sits there like he doesn't care."

"Maybe he doesn't."

"Nah, nah, not the Master Builder. He must be saving something. He won't talk, he won't move, he don't holler. Is he sick? And Christ, what a friend he's got in that old bastard Tutt. Can't he control him?"

Uninvited, Parenti sat down with us. "What do you guess the vote will be?" Goldstein asked him.

"Oh, he'll get it, but it'll be close," Parenti said. "He might have beaten it, he just might have. But when he blasted Eisenberg, that was a blast at Urban and the committee. It just doesn't work in that place. It's like making cracks about the Pope in St. Peter's. And that's what Webb Urban is sort of, the Senate Pope." Parenti looked at me sorrowfully. "Eddie baby, I think I'll give you a break. I mean it."

"Thanks for nothing," I said, sipping my Coke.

"No, you deserve one. The way I figure this mess is you just got caught in the middle. Know what you are? You are a country boy, a babe in the woods. Your trouble is you never learned to figure out what's rotten and what's right. Anything Big Ben told you was okay. You worshiped that guy so much, you never really saw what he was up to."

"I don't care to discuss this." Inwardly I cringed.

"Yeah, Lou," Goldstein said. "Lay off Eddie."

"I like the guy!" Parenti protested. "But boy, I wouldn't want to be in your shoes when the Internal Revenue Service and the FBI and everyone else gets through examining the testimony. Someone's gonna get hit, and they'll probably decide you're the lucky one."

"I'm man enough to face up to it," I said. "Maybe I've gotten to be a little bit like my ex-boss."

Parenti looked at me, and I think he was admiring my courage. "I don't think so, kid. You shouldn't have lied about never meeting Krallis. That was a bad move. Well, you recouped a little." He cocked his swarthy head. "Hey, whatever happened to that Mexican tamale you had in the office?"

"Miss Valdez?"

"Yeah, that long legged chick. Man, that was the real thing! Hannaford's private stock. Oh, shit, Deever stop looking shocked. All I can say is you made a lousy beard. Where is she?"

"She's gone back to Ramada City."

Parenti pursed his lips. "Tough. Tough on the Big Guy. It just ain't his year."

"Thanks to you," I said.

The columnist almost looked apologetic. "Ah, what the hell, Eddie, the big guy had to foul up somewhere. His trouble is he tried to own the whole country, to run the whole government— and I don't think he was louse enough to get away with it. I mean, he's got a heart."

And it seemed to me that this, from Senator Hannaford's mortal enemy, was a rare tribute.

Debate resumed in the afternoon. The Majority Leader, Gage Hopewell, had tuned up his tonsils for the press just before the session and announced that he had gotten agreement from the leadership of both parties to conclude arguments that afternoon.

"This unseemly, divisive, yaaaaas, abrasive display of bad temper is not in the grand tradition of our beloved body," he tolled. "I think I have agreement, that is to say, an accord on an early end to these unfortunate colloquies!" And he winked at the reporters —who adored him, who publicized him, who had made of him a public figure, a funny old uncle. "Besides, I have to go to New York and make a record album—inspirational stories for little patriots. I certainly can't let anything stand in the way of my new career. Yaaaaas."

Everyone roared. But I had the feeling a lot of the laughter at old Honey-Tonsils was forced, a ritual. The truth of the matter was Senator Hopewell was becoming a dreadful bore.

But he was right about having secured agreement on a speedy

termination of debate. This became evident, when, after some more backing and filling on the wording of the resolution, Senator Urban took the floor. It was clear now, that barring amendments, substitutions, and obstructionist tactics (I did not believe Ben wanted any on his behalf) a vote was imminent.

From my spy's seat next to Goldstein, I surveyed the chamber. Across from me I saw Fern and Judy Stapp, and other close friends of Ben. For a fleeting, poignant moment I regretted that I could not be seated with them, that I could not publicly display my support of the senator. For as wild, illogical—and perhaps hypocritical—as it will sound, I was miserable about the way I had helped bring him to this unseemly pass, and I hoped that he would not be censured. I wanted him absolved. The reader will recall that early in this narrative I went to some lengths to describe the awesome mystical power surrounding a United States Senator, and the manner in which this aura affects those who work for them. I, surely, had been among the most worshipful of young men on the Hill. Old habits and attitudes were hard to break; and as I sat there awaiting the verdict, I understood that these old habits had not departed from me, and perhaps never would.

I recalled the day when Ben had unexpectedly brought the New Wilderness Bill up before the Interior and Insular Affairs Committee, and Senator Urban had sat there, impassive, his sombre face not convinced that the measure was a conservationist's dream, knowing in his bleak honest heart that it was nothing more than a grab, some of Ben's Controlled Greed. Urban was the Establishment. And I knew that if Ben were to fall, if his powers were to be diminished, the deed would be done not by the stones of the Right or Left, but by the granite of the Center.

"Mr. President," Urban said in mild voice, "I will deal first with the various defenses offered by Senator Hannaford."

He was starting right off calling him by name—which, though not unheard of in Senate debate, is unusual. One usually uses the expression "the junior senator from etc." But Urban was advertising his conviction that Ben was already *outside* the select circle.

"Let us talk about this matter of depriving him of due process of law, of *ex post facto* judgments. I reject that out of hand. The senior senator from Montana who served on the Ethics Committee with me has dealt with this in scholarly manner. I subscribe to everything he said. Either we start somewhere on this matter of ethics, or we never start. Secondly, the matter of the documents stolen from Senator Hannaford's office. Now the fact of the matter is, the resolution on censure as voted by the Ethics Committee made absolutely no use of these documents. These papers had to do with the formation of an industrial complex. The committee voted unanimously not to make use of these papers, not to cite Senator Hannaford for any actions in connection with the formation of this industrial group, as revealed in the documents.

"Finally, Senator Hannaford has contended that the money he received via Edward Deever from Norton Krallis was a campaign contribution. I can only regard this statement on his part as effrontery of the sheerest sort. I know something about Campaign Committees and campaign expenses. How many of us sitting here today have had the opportunity of getting handed to us a quarter of a million dollars for educational purposes?

"Mr. President, one would be moved to laughter were it not for the tears in our eyes—the notion of the mortgage and loan people donating $250,000 to beat a measure already dead in committee! And then wanting it back! And one of our most respected members claiming it was a donation for educational purposes, a campaign gift! Mr. President, we verge on a kind of freewheeling power-hungry anarchy if we permit these practices to continue. I am of the feeling that those of us who accepted these generous contributions from Senator Hannaford have a little soul searching to do themselves."

I glanced at Senator DiFalco—head resting in hand—and Senator Goodchapel—his eyes mangled by his eyeglasses—and I knew that they were not happy, not at all.

"Senator Hannaford has been an energetic and constructive legislator," Urban went on, "but I have doubts as to whether his tactics and his desires are always in the best interests of the Senate. It was pointed out during the debate last year on the oil depletion allowance revision, that he functioned as lobbyist, legislator and beneficiary, all in one. At that time, Mr. President, many of us, including myself, scoffed at this charge. Well, I no longer scoff at it. I no longer doubt that the senator has functioned in just that manner.

"All of us, from time to time, act in behalf of special interests. Those of us who represent wheat growers naturally act in their

behalf. Those of us who represent automotive workers will act
for them. Nothing could be more natural. But Senator Hannaford's persistent statement that *everything* that is done here is
for some special interest is wide of the mark. His interests, on too
many occasions, have been special in the very narrowest sense—
they have been designed especially to benefit *himself* and his
associates. And I, for one, am sick and tired of this sort of thing.
Senator Hannaford is not alone in this, but I am obliged to tell
the American public, that he stands in a distinct and very small
minority in the Senate.

"I am unhappy to have to make this speech. It is the most unpleasant speech I have ever made in this chamber. But if I shirked
my duty and said anything less than what I earnestly believe, I
would be less of a man, less of a United States Senator. We cannot
go on holding ourselves up to the nation as paragons of virtue,
as beyond criticism and scrutiny if we do not clean our own house.
In my view, Mr. President, this debate has dragged on too long,
and I urge swift and overwhelming approval of the Ethics Committee Resolution on Senator Hannaford. Let me state it as bluntly
as I can. Senator Hannaford deserves censure, and we have no
choice but to vote it."

Ben sat motionless—a stone figure. Sid Stapp was at his side,
whispering to him. Gage Hopewell waddled about the majority
side of the aisle. Sly fox, he was acting cool, indifferent, unaffected
by Webb Urban's speech. No matter what happened, old Honey-
Tonsils would survive. So what if his law firm drew hefty fees for
protecting railroads and tool-and-die manufacturers and dairy-
men from bothersome legislation? No one could get mad at Gage.

"Mr. President," Senator Stapp said, "I am advised by Senator
Hannaford that he will not make any statement but reserves the
right to speak after the Senate has voted, and he will ask to be
excused from voting."

"Very well," the Vice-President said, "if there are no more
statements, the Chair will entertain a motion to vote on the resolution for censure."

Silence; some shuffling; and suddenly, Gabe Tutt, blundering
drunkenly in the aisle and shouting: "Mr. President! I rise in
defense of our friend and colleague, Senator Hannaford! He is
bein' blackguarded, smeared, and tarred by sinister forces, by se-

cret conspirers against the Republic, by traitors! We must rise as
one man, united in battlin' these traitors tearin' at our guts!"

Urban was on his feet. "Point of privilege, Mr. President," he
said icily. "I will not tolerate any further insinuations of treason
or conspiracy or any other fantasy that comes into the mind of
the senior senator from Alabama."

I saw Ben shaking his head. Then he got up and put an arm
around a spuming Gabe Tutt and led him back to his seat. It was
clear that he was pleading with Gabe to stop defending him so
vigorously. To this day, I—as well as many observers of the
Washington scene—remain confounded by Gabe Tutt's behavior.
I suppose he regarded the Senate as his truest home, his sanctuary, his church, his rock, his foundation. In his cramped, fear-
ridden (Commonist and Nigras are after me) mind he saw in
the Senate a refuge from the world outside, and the censure of
Ben, one of its most forceful members, was to him an attack on
the fortress of the institution itself. If Ben could fall, could not
he be attacked, rendered vulnerable, wounded?

Tutt collapsed into his seat; he pumped Ben's hand. I could see
Ben smiling. Then all were at their desks. The motion to vote
was passed. Vice-President Beldock instructed the clerk to call
the roll.

There arrived now that moment of unbearable tension, of anticipation, of crisis. I felt the hairs prickle on the nape of my neck.
My palms sweated, but my limbs were cold. Within my chest I
tried to contain the savage erratic thumping of my heart.

"Here it goes," Fred said to me. "This is Big Casino. For all the
marbles."

"Mr. Abbott," called the clerk.

"No," said Senator Willard Abbott of Delaware. He was in
Ben's party, a regular, a down-the-liner.

"Mr. Allerdice."

"No." James Allerdice of Oregon—another regular.

I turned to Fred. "God almighty," I said. "He may beat it yet."
It appeared to me that the two calmest, most confident people
in the vast amphitheatre at that moment were Ben Hannaford
and his faithful wife Fern. They seemed above it all; people
blessed and gifted with wealth and happiness and security, who
could not be touched.

"Mr. Arnold."

"Yes."

That was normal. An opposition man, a club member from New Mexico.

"Mr. Bettenhaus."

"Yes." Another minority party regular. It would be close. But if the ranks held, if party loyalties dominated, Ben would be home safely—even if the three Ethics Committee men of his own party —Urban, Eisenberg, and Henshaw—voted for censure.

"Mr. Brady."

"No." Fine, fine, I thought. Emmett Brady of Massachusetts was safe—he was another centrist.

"Mr. DiFalco."

A pause; all waited. Then little DiFalco said weakly: "No."

But the opposition party would not break lines. As the clerk continued tolling, as each man voiced his decision on the censure of one of the great members of their august body, the minority party, President Hayward Kretz's party, held the line. About a third of the way through, as I followed the vote on Fred's tally sheet, I saw that Ben was ahead, 16–13. But, as I quickly scanned the paper, it seemed that the 38 votes contained proportionately more "Nays" from our own party. Only one or maybe two opposition senators had voted "Nay."

"Mr. Edgerton."

"Yes." That was expected: Walter Edgerton was close to Henshaw.

"Mr. Eisenberg."

"Yes."

No surprise there. Yet even as Senator Eisenberg uttered the one word, I saw his face cloud, his melting features grow more lugubrious. I knew that he liked Ben, and that his vote for censure was a difficult decision. But, like all the members of the Ethics Committee, he was above all a United States Senator, deeply concerned with the effectiveness of the grand collegium.

"Mr. Furman."

"Yes."

"Mr. Garrison."

"No."

"Mr. Gleason."

"No."

So far, the precarious balance was holding. Ben was ahead,

22–20. God, what if he made it? What if he confounded all of them? I looked across to the Press Gallery and saw Parenti looming large in the front row, a troubled young man.

"Mr. Goodchapel."

There was a pause. Henry DiFalco had already voted against censure. It was true, he had accepted the "campaign" fund, and had then gone before the committee to reveal the manner in which it was given. But Senator DiFalco could not bring himself to hurt Ben.

"Yes," Lester Goodchapel said. And as the press hummed, the gallery buzzed, I saw in my mind's eye old Lester listening to that tape recording of his night of passion in the Monroe-Plaza, the way in which Albon Blake had humiliated him and attempted to force his vote on the New Wilderness Bill. He had never forgotten. He had not forgiven. He had taken the "campaign contribution"—and then, without plotting, or malice, or I suspect any conspirator's intent (for Goodchapel was among the most innocent of men) had come full circle with Ben. Or was I doing him an injustice? Was it not possible that he disapproved on ethical grounds the manner in which Ben had tried to make the Senate his private pond? I don't know. I only know that when Lester Goodchapel cast his "yes" I felt a shuddering of the earth, that hot, uneasy calm before the storm breaks.

"Boy, that was an upset," Fred Goldstein said. "I figured DiFalco and Goodchapel had to go with the big man. It just goes to show you. You can't ever be sure."

"Mr. Henshaw."

"Yes."

"No, you can't," I said. "When you do a favor for a man, he never really forgives you."

Fred nodded solemnly. He showed me the tally sheet. The vote was tied. Ben's name was not called. He had advised the Chair he did not intend to vote.

"Mr. Hopewell."

Honey-Tonsils rose as this desk, his comic—though faintly menacing figure in command of the scene.

"Yes," said Senator Hopewell.

Now an audible gasp of shock went up from the public. Some of the senators must have known in advance that Gage was going to break party discipline, to desert his ancient friend, colleague, co-worker, fellow manipulator and controller. But there had been no inkling of it in anything Gage had said since the start of the Ethics Committee hearings. All along he had professed his faith in Ben. And now the old weathervane had changed—as he had a score of times in his illustrious career. He had sniffed the wind, he had scented a public change, he had, no doubt been in private conference with President Hayward Kretz and Kretz' millionaire backer, T. E. Kape.

It was a shock, a stunning, unforeseen blow. For the first time since the debate had begun I noticed in Ben a betrayal of uncertainty. He was staring at Gage Hopewell, seated just a few desks away, like a schoolboy who has just been tattled on by the class monitor. Almost as if trying to control himself, he had laced his fingers and had rested his massive hands on the desk. Across the floor in the opposite gallery I saw Judy Stapp whispering to Fern.

"Mr. Hopkins."

"Yes."

"Mr. Ingraham."

"Yes."

"Mr. Innis."

"Yes."

"Mr. Kemmons."

A pause; Alf looked this way and that. Then his spongy voice croaked: "Yes." Yes indeed. Gage had shown him the way.

"Mr. Kovatch."

"Yes."

"Mr. Lonsdale."

"No."

"Mr. Lord."

"Yes."

"Mr. Mullendore."

"Yes."

Goldstein arched his eyebrows. "Eddie, I think the game is over," he whispered. "Old Honey-Tonsils pointed to the road. The stampede is on."

Well, not quite. Ben had friends, he commanded loyalties. The Southerners in our party held the line. But many liberals now felt no compunction about deserting him. And the opposition appeared fixed, cemented, a band of brothers joined to do the bidding of their party leadership, to bring down the man who had been "lobbyist, legislator, and beneficiary" all in one.

"It's 30 to 32 for censure," Fred advised me. I nodded my head: and all I could think of was Gage Hopewell's act of desertion. But again, I paused. There was a very good argument to be made for censuring Ben. I was thinking with my heart, not my head. The most respected voices of the Senate—Urban, Henshaw, Edgerton —had argued for censure. Would it not be that Gage, weathervane incarnate, was acting out of principle, out of conviction? I chose to think so.

"Mr. Tutt."

"No!" Gabe yelled.

"Mr. Urban."

"Yes."

"Mr. Ussery."

"Yes."

"Mr. Valentine."

"No."

"Mr. Wagenknecht."

"Yes."

"Mr. Ziegler."

"Yes."

Fred made some notations on the tally sheet. "He's dead, Eddie," he whispered. "The big guy got it."

I looked at the sheet. The ciphers were irrevocable, as final as death. Ben had been censured, by a vote of 52 to 45. Three senators did not vote—Ben himself, and two who were absent. (Conveniently, it was later said.)

A hush descended over the chamber. I could see Fern dabbing at her eyes with a handkerchief. Royce Henshaw and Maury Eisenberg walked over to Ben and chatted with him—in a light and casual manner, as if nothing at all had happened. That was the miracle of the Senate, the way in which it moved on, surviving its convulsions.

Ben was smiling, actually *smiling* at them. He then rose, for recognition as the member present who had not voted. Had he wished, he might have cast a vote at that time. But I knew Ben. His vote, to begin with, would have been meaningless. He had been beaten. I have often wondered what Ben would have done had the vote been tied, or had he been able to effect a tie by voting. I have been unable to answer that question in my own mind. In the latter instance, I suspect he would have refrained from voting, since Vice-President Beldock, assuredly, would have voted for censure. As to the former possibility, I simply don't know. He remains to this day, an enigmatic man, capable of unexpected darts and turns. As I shall soon disclose, this capacity for the daring, the unexpected, the stunning reversal of direction, the change of tactic, was by no means diminished in him.

"Mr. President, before the final tally is announced, I formally request to be excused from voting," Ben said.

Vice-President Beldock nodded. He asked for no reasons. The presiding officer does not have the power to request such reasons.

"My reasons for not voting should be obvious to my colleagues," said Ben. "They need no elaboration. I do not intend to sit in judgment on myself."

A voice vote was taken. Ben was formally excused from voting. The Vice-President then ordered the clerk to read the final tally.

"On the Resolution of the Select Committee on Standards and Conduct to Censure Senator Hannaford," said the clerk, "Yeas, 52, Nays, 45. Not voting, 3. The Yeas have it."

Senator Hannaford was standing—an imposing, unbending figure, a hard, tough man in his middle-fifties, a rich, powerful man in a blue suit, his ruddy face tranquil. He had command presence, no question about it, and I had the peculiar feeling that had he spoken in his own defense, had he raised his own voice, he might have won the day.

"The Resolution for censure is adopted," the Vice-President said. "Chair recognizes Senator Hannaford."

Ben's eyes swept the room. He was never an impassioned orator, but a rather casual speaker, a man not given to florid phrases and rolling sentences. That was Gage Hopewell's game. (I noticed that that worthy had half-turned in his seat, to avoid Ben's gaze.)

"Mr. President, let me begin by thanking all the members of the Select Committee, notably Chairman Urban, for affording me the opportunity to make my case. That I have failed is no reflection on their impartiality. I should like particularly to apologize to the junior senator from Illinois for any misinterpretation of my comments about him in the meetings of the Select Committee." He was looking at Eisenberg. "Not for a moment did I imply that the senator was unfairly prejudiced against me, that he was, as the saying goes, out to get me. I merely felt he had already arrived at a conclusion. I regret that this motion on my part was misconstrued by many."

Fred nudged me. "Like hell. He's only sorry he didn't hang Eisenberg on that one. That's where he made his big mistake. Urban was after him from then on."

Fred was partially right. Ben had been after Eisenberg, had tried to split and confuse the committee. But that did not lessen his respect for Eisenberg.

"That is ancient history, Mr. President. The Book says to us, 'Let all things be done decently and in order,' and I am pleased that the Senate, the Senate which we all love, has acted decently and in order. But it is possible that it has acted incorrectly. Not dishonorably, not with malicious intent, but incorrectly. I am guilty of nothing more than zeal and efficiency. I have committed no crimes. No court will ever find against me. My conscience is clear."

"Jesus," whispered Goldstein, "he's said everything except, 'I give to organized charity.'"

"Mr. President, we are told by St. Paul, 'The fashion of this world passeth away' and I am sure that the fashion of this mistaken vote will pass away too, and I will be judged again by history, and I will be found innocent. I will not bother repeating again my view of the transactions I engaged in with the people mentioned in the committee hearing. Mr. President, I am a builder, a trader, an organizer, a doer, a man who gets things done. I cut corners. I work swiftly. Perhaps too swiftly for some. Perhaps that is all I am really guilty of—swift and decisive actions. I have never been a patient man, nor have I been one for devious and indirect action. Maybe that is what offended the sensibilities of some of my colleagues. But I won't linger on that, I won't speculate.

"We have gone over this ground so often—who gave what to whom and so forth—that I'm reluctant to waste the Senate's time with any more discussion of it. But I feel, that having censured me, we, all of us, one hundred good men, must start looking at ourselves and deciding who we are and what we are. Now, I know that we have among us members like the distinguished senior senator from Wyoming who was the Chairman of the

Select Committee, who buy their own postage stamps, and are uneasy at accepting free haircuts. But most of them are not that virtuous."

Webb Urban's face was expressionless. I suspect he had had enough of Ben.

"In fact, many of us are not that virtuous when it comes to the sordid matter of money, of favors, of so-called special interests. It happens that I have been hit with the first stone. But I wonder which of you is the man without sin who was permitted to cast it? I look about me, and I find it hard to answer that question, to find the white blameless garments of innocence on any of you.

"Was it you, dear friend and colleague from Wisconsin?" And Ben turned and glared at Gage Hopewell. "Was it you, my able partner in so many battles in this chamber? For if I am guilty of soliciting, receiving, and sequestering funds, what about the campaign funds I have so generously given to *you* in past years? And what of the testimonial dinners held in *your* honor —financed by the railroads of the Middle West, the tool-and-die manufacturers and the big dairies?"

"Below the belt," said Fred Goldstein. "But he's burned his bridges now."

I saw Gage Hopewell jerk upright in his seat. He had asked for it. The syrup-voiced preacher himself, the old carnie, dearly beloved by television producers and newsprint humorists, a creature of the media. But was he *really* that lovable? Beneath that façade of jolly-uncle fustian, was he not a rather shifty man, an undependable rascal, whose only loyalty was to the fat cats of industry and business? He was unassailable, dear Gage, but Ben had at last found the need and the urge to set him right before the public. (Not that it would help; tomorrow the old windbag would be back on TV, pumping out his "funny" sonorities.)

"Surely my good friend, the senior senator from Wisconsin," Ben went on, "recalls those splendid testimonial dinners, financed so readily by all those fine institutions whom he has represented so ably and faithfully both in his prestigious law firm—and in the Senate! Why, as I recall, I was the honored speaker at one such elegant affair, last January! And if I am guilty of 'soliciting, receiving, and sequestering funds' what are we to make of all those banquets to which the railroads and milk producers contributed so lavishly?"

Hopewell flopped back in his seat and tried to appear above all of this—the serene elder statesman. But his act failed. When he could not sound his vocal gong, ring that laryngeal bell, he was merely an old bore, and I suspect he was a bore even *then*, although the press had gotten so deeply rutted in its conviction that he was a cuddly comedian, that *anything* he said—no matter how dull or malignant—was interpreted as humor.

"And my good friend, the junior senator from Connecticut," Ben said, pointing at Henry DiFalco. "You, sir, went before the Ethics Committee and revealed that I had soiled your campaign kitty by enriching it by $20,000. But how strange that you did not protest when the money was given! You testified that on reflection you felt the money was intended to influence your vote—but why did it take ten days before you so decided? And you, too, my old friend from Indiana . . ."

His accusing finger pointed at Lester Goodchapel. "You, Senator, who also availed himself of $20,000, and then waited before making your speech to the Ethics Committee. Where is the evidence, in writing or in any other form, to show that I donated those funds to gain votes for an amendment to the Foreign Aid Bill? Why is it a crime to help a fellow senator in need? I am blinded suddenly by the dazzling holy light in this great hall! I am astonished by the white glittering halos, deafened by the fluttering of angels' wings!"

Goldstein shook his head. "He's dead now," he said. "Censure was bad enough—that's about as rough as it can get. But after this . . ."

"Now, we heard this afternoon from the junior senator from Pennsylvania," Hannaford went on, "who ably described the financial situation of the average senator, and pointed out all the benefits we enjoy. The implication was that most of us don't need a lot of money to run our offices, our campaigns or anything else. Where is my friend from Pennsylvania?"

Ben's angry face turned, and halted when he saw John Kovatch's gleaming bald head. "There he is! May I ask the gentleman if he will consent to a roll call of the steel producers of his great state so that they may answer the question—how much did you contribute to the gentleman's campaign, and for what purpose? Or may I ask the distinguished senior senator from Iowa, on the other side of the aisle—" He was referring to Ernest Wagenknecht, and he pointed him out. "—what was the nature of the financial assistance lavished upon him by the dairy farmers' co-operative?"

"Christ, this could last all day," Fred said to me. "He starts on every lousy dollar one of these guys got in their lives, he'll never end."

"What a performance!" I said. "They've censured him, but he'll censure all of them before he's through."

"Now let me ask the senior senator from Tennessee whom he consulted when he wanted his brother-in-law appointed to a federal judgeship in that great state," Ben stated. He was talking about Carl Mullendore, who had been the ranking minority of the Ethics Committee. I thought Mullendore would faint in his seat. "Yes, Senator, do you not recall with what plaintive voice you appealed to me to say a good word with the Justice Department for the Honorable Augustus Schmidt?

"And let me not forget my good friend the junior senator from North Carolina," he continued. This would be Stanton Betten-haus—one of the so-called "new breed" of Southerners, an Ivy League, crewcut young man, one of those who gave an aura of being "modern and progressive" but was as black a reactionary as any old-line tobacco dribbling redneck. "Yes, there you are, young man. When you wanted a dam and power plant for the Lumbee River, you had no hesitation in fawning before me, in begging favors of me, and of introducing me to all those mill owners who, as you freely confessed, helped elect you with their lint-covered dollars!

"A word, too, about the senior senator from Montana, a man whose intellect and honesty I revere above any in this great body!" And he looked at Royce Henshaw. "You, my friend, voted against me in committee, and again today. But you were not so contemptuous of me when you sought my support for the Scattered Sites provision of the Federal Housing Bill. Oh, you have all been good friends and honored colleagues! I look for the face of the senior senator from Arizona, who asked me for $10,000 to help beat the cattlemen's attack on him—and got it. Or the junior senator from Florida, who got $15,000 from me to help overcome the hatred of the White Citizens Council. Or the senior senator from Kansas, who haunted the Interior Committee until I assured him he would be able to promise his home state friends a new power plant, financed and built by the Interior Department!

"Yes, we have all played at the grand game, and I have no regrets. For isn't that what it is all about—this happy marriage of government with business, industry, labor, the people themselves? And since we have all played at it, why have I been chosen as the guilty one? Why are we not all censured, criticized, forced to reveal where our funds have come from, who gave them, why they were given, what was given in return?"

Fred pushed my knee. "I notice he left out Sid Stapp. There's one of the biggest takers in the business, but not a word about him."

I winked at Goldstein. "You don't understand Ben. He's loyal —loyal to the end."

"It has been said to me, Mr. President, that after one serves in the Senate, everything else is anticlimax. Perhaps that is so. Perhaps that is true only of lesser men. Those of us who have had active and creative lives before entering these sanctified halls, probably can survive the fall from grace somewhat easier. I suspect I shall survive."

"What the hell does he mean by that?" Fred asked me. I had no idea.

"'Let every soul be subject unto the higher powers' we are told," Ben said. "And elsewhere, the Book explains that the potter has the power to make of the same clay both honorable and dishonorable vessels. I am not a man noted for his modesty, Mr. President, and I will not play the hypocrite today. So I say to all of you, and I maintain with all my heart and power, that I have not been a dishonorable vessel, that I have served my country and this body with vigor and honor and truthfulness, and I regret nothing I have done.

"Again, I extend my gratitude to the six members of the Ethics Committee and to all my colleagues for their open-mindedness and for the tolerant manner in which they have heard me out. I thank, too, my old associate the senior senator from Alabama, for offering to defend me, for acting as my advocate—in his own peculiar way."

Gabe Tutt waved dumbly at Ben, then started down the aisle, trying to tell John Tyler Lord something.

"And so I compare what has happened to me here with the

fate of old Jonah. 'Come and let us cast lots, that we may know for whose cause this evil is upon us. So they cast lots and the lot fell upon Jonah.' But as we all know Jonah made quite a comeback, and went on to do all sorts of interesting works for the Lord, including some important preaching in Nineveh. Mr. President, it is on that Biblical note that I conclude my remarks. I thank you for your patience and your courtesy."

No one stirred for a few moments. There was a burst of applause from the public gallery. The Vice-President let it continue for several seconds.

I followed Fred into the cramped radio-TV room at the back of the gallery. There was a mad crush of bodies, a frenzy in the air. Ben was coming through to make a statement for the live television cameras. Reporters clung to him like sugar ants; a dozen microphones bobbed in front of him. He was flanked by Fern— no longer weeping, sedate, and somewhat abstracted, and Matt Fixx, whose eyes were red-rimmed and moist. I tried to shrink against the teletype machines and lower my head. I had no right to be there witnessing my idol's fall, his final disgrace. But was it disgrace? Was not Ben above everything that had happened? And what of that mocking, angry, accusing speech? One still had the feeling that he was running the show. One had the feeling that, like Lucifer, he still exercised a good deal of authority.

The mob churned and twisted, and I hid alongside a cabinet, ducking my guilty face. Ben was practically shoved into the television room—a tiny area with a bright blue curtain as background. He was seated at the desk. Matt and Fern took chairs on either side of him.

The live camera was set. A cameraman was ready, talking through his head-set to the control room. Inside the room, and clustered at the opened door, several score reporters were jammed. Parenti was there, but I could see he would not take part in the interrogation. He stood at the edge of the mob in the doorway.

A floor manager, also wearing a head-set, brandishing a clipboard, consulted his watch and waved to Senator Hannaford.

"We're on, Senator."

"Thank you. Well, I've made my speech, gentlemen. I'm sorry the Senate saw fit to censure me. It was a close thing.

Maybe if I'd spread some more of that money around I might have licked it."

They roared. Ben was at the peak of his form. He smiled at them, he patted Fern's hand. "I've already sounded my grace notes regarding the committee and my colleagues. Now let me thank my beloved wife, the finest woman in the world, who has stood by me. And let me thank young Matthew Fixx here, who is like a son to me. He's a good boy, Matt."

"What about Senator Hopewell, sir?" someone asked.

"I have nothing but affection for Senator Hopewell. He is a beloved and valiant public servant."

"But aren't you bitter, that he voted against you? I mean, after the way you and he have worked together so closely in the past?"

Ben waved his broad hand. "Oh, goodness no. I'm not given to bitterness. Senator Hopewell voted his conscience, as he always does."

There was a titter from the reporters. Ben had won them over, and I knew why. He would not apologize, would not cringe, would not weep, would not ask for sympathy, would not play the martyr.

"Senator, are you still going to push for the Djarak Amendment to the Foreign Aid bill?" asked a man from a newsmagazine. "The action seems to be hotting up there—two more Marines were killed today—and I wonder if you're still anxious to move in there with a massive aid program?"

"Yes I am, son. And I intend to push for that Amendment as hard as I can, and get it one way or the other. I'll make an ice-cream eating, movie-going, car-driving consumer out of every one of those Arabs before I'm through. We'll teach 'em a little Controlled Greed."

"But do you really think you can get that Amendment through the committee?" asked a girl reporter. "After all that's happened?"

"I may have to go *around* the committee," my ex-boss said.

"How sir?" Fred Goldstein asked. "The White House has already said it opposes the Amendment."

I saw them all lean forward. Parenti, on the fringe of the mob, looked puzzled. Ben was getting ready to stun them with something.

"I know there's opposition to my plan to upgrade and uplift

the Middle East—and incidentally make a lot of money for me and my friends, as you fellows never fail to point out. But that doesn't discourage me. I intend to work for my program, largely *outside* of government channels."

"How sir?"

"By resigning, as of this moment, from the United States Senate."

There was turmoil, a few whistles, a gasp, a shout. Several radio and TV men—those from stations not carrying the news live—flew out the door for telephones. The wire servicemen likewise fled the small room, elbowing their way out. Those who remained stared at Ben with total disbelief. Once more he had surprised everyone; and I felt that old surge of wonder.

"Resigning? Why?"

"I like the Senate. I like almost all of my colleagues. I think I've served this government and this country well and long. But I think I've reached the point where my effectiveness has been impaired. And if there is one thing I dislike, it is being ineffective. Gentlemen, I am as of this moment ex-Senator Hannaford."

They milled and clotted around him, but he had said all he wanted to say. "There'll be a formal statement issued tomorrow," he said, in a clear voice. "Matt Fixx will have it available by noon. Now if you'll excuse us, Mrs. Hannaford and I have to get back to Potomac Oaks and start packing."

And he guided Fern through the anxious, shouting, microphone-thrusting mob, into the small press room, and then into the corridors of the Capitol.

I could hear a man from a local radio station, broadcasting into a tape recorder slung over his shoulder. "An incredible end to a day of drama here in the Capitol . . . Senator Benjamin Bow Hannaford, one of the giants of the Senate, has resigned, just moments after being censured by a vote of 52 to 45 . . . an unbelievable climax to this case . . . Senator Hannaford could you tell us sir, could you tell us . . ." And his voice trailed off as he vainly chased Ben out the doors into the hallways of the Capitol.

He had shown them. He had shown them that he was bigger than any of them. If they did not like the way he did business, he would, quite simply, take his business elsewhere. And that grand contemptuous note! *He was going home to pack!*

I found myself facing Lou Parenti.

"He's got balls, that big guy," Parenti said. "I got to give him credit. Those small-timers in his party are gonna suffer now, without Big Ben to lead them through the wilderness. I mean, Hopewell is good for a few laughs, but he's no Hannaford. And what about the President? Jesus, without the Master Builder he may not even get an appropriation to cut the grass on the White House lawn from these clowns."

"It's too bad you didn't admire him so much when you were bent on destroying him," I said as we moved out of the press room into the marble hall.

"Admire him? Deever, I admire the hell out of him. I always did. I just don't like the idea of his trying to buy the United States."

Parenti walked away to the other side of the Senate Press Gallery. Camouflaged behind my dark glasses I walked—slunk might be a better word—close to the walls, down a side stairway to the ground level and toward a side exit. In a few moments I became aware of shuffling footsteps behind me. Then I thought I hear my name being called.

"Mr. Deever . . . Mr. Deever, sir . . ."

I turned and saw a tall black-clad scarecrow, scuffling along in an old man's unsteady walk, raising a trembling arm toward me. It was ancient Senator Atherton, that frail ghost out of the distant past.

"It's terrible, terrible, I say," Atherton said as he drew alongside me. "I'll be fired from the Campaign Committee now that he's gone, yes, I know they'll fire me . . ."

I steadied him with my right arm. "I wouldn't worry, Senator Atherton. Senator Hannaford will make certain that you retain that job, and if not that one, he will find you another."

He licked his cracked lips. "You think so, Mr. Deever? You really think so?"

"I am certain."

The unkempt gray head trembled. "Well, I hope so. But it's never the same again. No sir, it is never the same once you have left the Senate. The world gets smaller, and so do you. You are less of a man, and your life is less of a life. There is really nothing after the Senate, and I think Senator Hannaford will learn that."

"Senator Atherton," I said patiently, "I would say that would be true in the case of every senator that ever lived. Except Mr.

Hannaford. You see, he is larger than life, and he makes his own world."

"Yes. Yes. Maybe so."

I pumped his hand and walked briskly toward the side doors, nodding at a page I knew, at a Capitol policeman. "Say, you'll remember about my job, won't you, young man?" Atherton called after me. Poor, muddled old fellow—he did not even know I no longer worked for Ben.

CHAPTER SIXTEEN

That evening, alone again in my depressing apartment—how long had my bachelor's bed been cold, deprived of a woman's warm, soft flesh!—my viewing of the evening news was interrupted by a telephone call from Norton Krallis, that sly recorder of park bench conversations.

"Deever," he snarled, "I want that dough back, all of it."

"I don't have all of it. The senator has a good chunk."

"We'll get around to that bastard also," Krallis said. "Now you be a good guy and get what you kept—the dough in the box, and the ten grand you got in the savings bank, and bring it to me. I'm at the Fillmore Arms, Room 256."

"Mr. Krallis, it is not my money to give back. It is Senator Hannaford's. You gave it to him. You talk to him about it. I don't work for him any more but I have to respect his property."

"Lissen you little ass-kissing pimp," Krallis snarled, "I'll see to it you get worse troubles than unemployment if you don't hand that dough back. You may not look the same when I get through with you, you lousy errand boy."

"Mr. Krallis, I am a man without fear. Nothing else can happen to me. And by the way, how did you tape record that conversation in the zoo? Was the mike in your tie-tac? Your lapel? That was sneaky, Mr. Krallis. And are you recording this?"

"Screw you, Deever."

"Because *I* am," I lied. "Every word of it. And it will be given to my friend Judge Moscowitz, Director of the Federal Bureau of Investigation tomorrow. Now don't call again."

Well, a drubbing might do me good. I hadn't been getting much exercise lately. I ate cold barbecue beans from a can—a satisfying dinner when one is morbid and isolated—and listened to the newscast.

Ben's censure and resignation was the big story. I knew the whole affair, more than the newscaster did, but I did not know one bit of information which came from the network's White House man.

"It can be reliably reported," the man said, "that President Kretz himself got on the phone with Senator Hannaford immediately after he had announced his resignation and pleaded with Senator Hannaford to change his mind. The word *pleaded* is not too strong to describe the President's conversation. He explained how sorely he needs Senator Hannaford to keep the Senate in line, to get vital legislation passed. But the former Chairman of the Interior and Insular Affairs Committee was not interested. Politely but firmly, he thanked the President and said that his mind was made up, that he was through with government service, and would be going back to Ramada City within the week. . . ."

Old Ben, old defender against the tiger. Like Kretz himself, he seemed peculiarly suited to shield us from the darkest, most violent strains in our national character. They understood one another. Kretz and Ben existed, I was convinced, to keep people like T. E. Kape (I'll do anything I want to do) and Gabe Tutt and the "Kill a Commie for Christ" crowd from running the country. We walked on thin ice; and I sometimes believed that there was a gentlemen's conspiracy among the national leaders to subdue and confine the most murderous instincts in our midst.

". . . General Vasilov, commander of Soviet Army forces in Outer Mongolia said that the war against the Free Mongolia guerrillas and Inner Mongolian regulars may be reaching a turning point. 'The enemy is standing up and fighting us now, and when he does, we bloody his nose.' The general said that Red Army casualties for the week were 167, Outer Mongolian People's Army, 218, and enemy casualties, 3416. But he added, 'despite this favorable kill ratio, we need another 75,000 troops to secure lasting peace in Outer Mongolia.' He denied that his forces were using napalm against civilians, or burning peasant huts or yurts deliberately. 'We may inadvertently burn a few yurts now and then, but our bombs are directed against military installations and enemy soldiers,' the marshal said . . ."

And so on—some more sniping at the Marines in Djarak, some Negro disturbances in Toledo and New Haven.

I watched a Western, then another, then a late movie, then took the phone off the hook, wondering what it would feel like if Mr. Krallis did indeed hire goons to bloody my head and bruise my limbs. Perhaps I would have deserved it.

Deep in the cotton batting of a sleeping pill I awakened, switched on the radio and put the phone back on the hook. No sooner had I done so, than it rang.

"Edward?" a familiar voice asked—a voice rich with the easy drawl of the Southwest.

"Yes, Senator, Edward speaking."

"What's wrong with you, son? It's past ten o'clock. You still asleep? I been trying to reach you over an hour."

My tongue was furred, my lips swollen. In my discomfort, I could not fathom the lunacy of this call. Me—betrayer, Judas, traitor, informer, the man who had helped hang him—and he was calling me the day after!

"I had the phone off the hook," I said meekly. "That fellow Krallis was after me. He's threatened to have me beaten up if I don't return the money."

"Yes, that little cheapjohn called me too, but I wouldn't even talk to him. Hell, it isn't his money, it's *ours.* Caused us enough heartache, we might as well keep it. That's what I am calling you about."

"The money?" I gagged, rose from my bed and pulled the phone cord into the bathroom, where I drank two glasses of water.

"Now listen to me carefully, Edward," Ben said. "That money to begin with, is still mine."

Nothing, nothing defeated that man. "Well sir, except for the $20,000 you gave me," I said.

"I have the feeling you never wanted it."

"That's true, I suppose."

"Now, Edward, you go right to the bank and get out all the money sitting in that box, getting rusty and dusty and serving no purpose, and then withdraw that ten thousand you put in a savings bank, and you get out to Potomac Oaks at noon. Mrs.

Hannaford is fixing a fine lunch, and I want to chat with you before making further plans."

"What kind of plans?" I asked weakly. He was too much for me, Ben Hannaford was, too much for my nervous system.

"Most interesting plans, Edward. Now go on, git."

"I—ah—are we working together again, Senator? I mean, is all forgiven?"

"Not all, but just about all. Now go after that money, Edward, and bring it here."

For just a moment I paused.

"Well?" Ben demanded. "What's holding you up?"

"Senator," I asked, "do you think Lincoln ever made such a request of Herndon?"

His laughter told me we were back together again—in some strange way.

And so this narrative ends as it began with that considerable bundle of hundred dollar bills, a bribe to kill a piece of legislation already laid to rest. The grim comedy never amused me more. As I dressed, I found myself whistling. I never shaved with more care. I lavished expensive cologne on my smooth face. I slicked down my hair with perfumed stay-comb. Abruptly, I felt the desire to buy an expensive new suit, snappy shoes. I wanted to be steamed, sauna'd and massaged. Newborn, I was like a man with no worries, a schoolboy with a brand new empty notebook.

This time—my last visit to the Riggs National Bank—I made no notations, sent no self-sealing letters to myself. The guard knew me by now, and of course knew who I was. But he exercised a discreet indifference as I withdrew the thick packets, signed a chit, and then turned in my key.

Outside the bank, in the bright October sunlight, I looked about warily for suspicious strangers. Who was to say that Norton Krallis might not have his goons trailing me, to treat with me brutally and relieve me of the loot? But the coast was clear. I crossed the street, walked by four or five enormous drugstores to the savings bank, where, to the puzzlement of a clerk, I withdrew my ten thousand dollars.

"You will miss this quarter's interest, sir," the girl behind the window said.

"I'm afraid I'll have to. But I've had an emergency in the family."

"And, are you sure you want it in cash? I'll have to talk to the manager and have you fill out a form."

"A bank check will do." Time was essential. Ben wanted me out at his home at noon, and there I would be. Besides, the check made out to me, and endorsed by me, would be as good as cash.

Thus, laden with my $160,000, I drove out to Potomac Oaks—for the last time.

I parked my sports car in the gravel driveway, rang the bell and was greeted by Travis. He did not have his white butler's coat on, but wore a gray work apron. He wore it with great style and dignity—Travis always made me feel a little uneasy.

"Ah, Mr. Edward. How nice to see you again."

"And good to see you, Travis." In the soaring foyer rugs had been rolled, crates and boxes abounded. Ben was losing no time. He meant it when he said he was getting out.

"The senator is in the orangerie. He is expecting you."

The orangerie, a glassed-in room thick with rare plants and wicker furniture—was on the south side of the house. I walked through the rooms. They looked lonely, unhappy—never again to echo with Ben's firm voice, Fern's lady-like tones.

Inside the ornate hothouse I could see Ben with a guest. The guest was a very black Negro gentleman in a light gray suit. Both rose as I entered, and I recognized the caller as Mr. Dalton Warfield, the "On Our Own" community organizer from Los Angeles I had met at the Cosmos Club about six weeks ago, when Royce Henshaw had tried to get Ben to back the Scattered Sites Housing Amendment.

"Edward, you remember Mr. Warfield," the senator said.

"Indeed," I said shaking his hand. "How have you been, sir?"

"Fair enough," he responded. "I think I'll feel a lot better after this meeting with Senator Hannaford."

I sat down. Travis brought me a beer. Did I imagine it, or was there a fleeting exchange of glances between the butler and the guest? Did it signify their brotherhood? I don't know; maybe I am hypersensitive on this issue.

"Edward, let us get right to the point. Did you bring the wherewithal?"

"Yes sir. Here it is." On a glass-topped wicker table, in front of the wicker-and-chintz armchair on which Ben was seated, I deposited the thick envelope, containing $150,000—and the check to me for $10,000, which I immediately endorsed to him.

"Check, hey?" Ben asked. "That's okay. I'll get rid of it fast enough. Now, we got it all plus the $90,000 I ended up with. That's down at the office in my safe."

"So. We're back to a quarter of a million," I said. "God, it's hard to get rid of money in this town."

Warfield laughed. He did not seem surprised by what Ben was doing; he did not boggle at the sight of the cold cash. Perhaps Ben had briefed him already. Or perhaps Warfield had been so shaken up during his precarious life, that money did not move him. A man who has been bombed, burned and beaten up, and threatened regularly, may have other things on his mind.

"Now, Edward, with your permission, I am turning this fund over to Mr. Warfield here. It is a fully deductible charitable contribution. And it will be used to build a new community center, said building contract to be undertaken at cost, no profit at all, by the Hannaford-Western subsidiary in Los Angeles. I shall personally be on hand to break the ground and to make the speech, and I am going to serve as construction consultant to On Our Own, and to its President, Mr. Warfield."

"Amen," said the Negro leader. "Welcome to the Glory Train, Senator." He held up his beer glass. We joined him in a toast.

"But—but—but—this money," I stammered. "Is it ours? I mean, yours? Or Mr. Warfield's? What about Krallis?"

"To hell with him," Ben said impatiently. "To hell with all of them. He gave it to us, didn't he? He admits it. Is there any contract in writing, or even verbal, that says we got to give it back? What is his beef? His people beat that tax. Edward, that is all old stuff, a dead issue, concrete that didn't set, a burned house, a sick steer, a wheat field ruined by rust. Don't you worry about Mr. Krallis."

"But the Internal Revenue Service," I said. "There will be a big stink raised, Senator. They'll want taxes paid on this money. It's no secret anymore. My goodness, it's the most publicized quarter of a million in Washington's history . . ."

"Now Edward," Ben said, as if chiding me, "you let me worry about the Internal Revenue Service. They are just mortal men, as you and I and Mr. Warfield here, and they can be talked to. I may even set up a tax-free charitable foundation to fund this important work. I have never yet met an unreasonable Treasury Agent and I don't think I will at this late stage."

"All right, you've taken care of the tax problem," I said, "and you're convinced Krallis and his people won't make any more demands. But he may still decide he wants me beaten up, just as a final gesture."

"All you can do is take it like a man, Edward," the senator said paternally. "It won't hurt long. Warfield here is an expert on getting beaten up. Tell him, Dalton."

"Well, I'd rather get drunk than beaten up," Warfield said, "but it isn't all that bad. It sort of gives your mind focus."

"Yes, I suppose I could use some of that."

"Let me explain, Edward, that this quarter of a million dollars which you and I and our friends are donating to Mr. Warfield is just a start. Son, I am going to move into Los Angeles in a big way, and into three or four other so-called depressed areas. I intend to de-depress them in short order."

"And Djarak? And the Conglomerate?"

"I'll work something out along those lines. A few of the Conglomerate people are coming into this with me. You see, Edward, I intend to do it on a paying basis. If I build, I expect a return. Not right away—but soon enough." His eyes crinkled with that cynical sincerity of his, that talent for seeing the absurd, the phony and the valuable in every transaction. "Edward, as I have told Dalton here, I will not rest until every colored person in America is standing around his own brick barbecue in his own grassy backyard, behind his own split-level house, listening to his own custom-built hi-fi. I intend to make all those potential consumers happy in their Controlled Greed, so that my own Greed can be satisfied."

I was blinded by his vision.

"The senator is right," Warfield said. "It's never been any secret to me. The best things get done in this country for the wrong reasons. Anything that pays has got to succeed sooner or later."

"You might put it that way," Ben said. He got up. We rose also, and he put a mighty arm around each of us. "Onward, Christian soldiers," he pronounced. "Our cook has prepared enchiladas, Ramada style, and a guacamole salad without equal."

In the stadium-sized high-windowed dining room I saw Fern—
nodding her wheat-colored head of lacquered hair, smiling primly,
her hands folded just below her armored bosom. I felt I had
come home.

CHAPTER SEVENTEEN

And there it rests. I sit in my apartment, and watch television and wait. The FBI has spoken to me several times—polite young men, hand-picked by Judge Moscowitz in deference to his old friend, Ben Hannaford. And the Internal Revenue men have been to see me, but I am safe there. That money never was mine; it was Ben's; and it has gone back to him; and is now helping finance On Our Own's building campaign. Somehow Ben will get to keep it and use it.

He is running HW again in Ramada City. And he has promised to find a spot for me with one of the affiliated companies, as soon as my present problems are resolved. I have, as is well known by now, been cited for perjury and for contempt of Congress, but I don't think anyone is taking these charges very seriously. At least I hope not. In fact, Senator Eisenberg, who is one of the kindest men in the world, has spoken to me privately. He will talk to Senator Urban and other members of the committee to go easy on me. After all, while I did tell some blatant outrageous lies, I withdrew them on short notice, and then told the truth.

There is, of course, still the possibility of a federal indictment of some kind, but nobody is quite sure what kind. My lawyers tell me that this is unlikely. It will simply involve too many people, too many influential people and will not be worth the government's trouble.

I have discovered that I still have many friends here on the Hill, so that this interim period, this time of watchful waiting is not very hard to bear. Sooner or later Ben will send for me, and a new career will open for me, a new association with that enigmatic, power-bent, freewheeling man, our defender against the tiger in the streets.

His rare communications with me are brief and impersonal. Of course, he has never mentioned Maria. But she herself wrote to me the other day—and as I opened the pale blue envelope, reading her name on the return address, my heart quivered, and I thought of her on that first magic night when I had shown her the city. The letter was brief: she was working in a clinic in a Mexican-American neighborhood in a city in the western corner of the state, about 150 miles from Ramada City. And she was engaged to a young doctor there, a pediatrician named O'Keefe. She sounded as if she were very much in love with him. She had not seen Senator Hannaford since leaving Washington. I decided not to answer the letter. Prolonging the correspondence would only worsen my poignant sense of loss. I tore it up and the ripping noises of pale blue note paper sounded in my ears like that sad distant guitar I had once heard.

Ben, although usually at Hannaford-Western headquarters in Ramada City, spends a good deal of time in Los Angeles, and has visited other problem cities in the company of Dalton Warfield.

His vacant seat will be filled via a special election. I had paid little attention to this aspect of the terminaton of his public career, and was pleased to note a small item in Lou Parenti's column the other day, concerning the matter of a successor to "the Master Builder."

Well, the word is out in Ramada City. Big Ben Hannaford may have resigned from the Senate, but if there is any doubt that he is still running the show down in the land of cactus and oil, let it be dispelled. The former senator has tapped his nephew, Miles J. Cudder, a Hannaford-Western executive, to succeed him. Childless, the senator has evidently looked around for the nearest relative who would fit in nicely on Capitol Hill. Young Cudder, aged thirty-five, is the son of Mrs. Hannaford's older brother, Carlyle Cudder, a founder of Longhorn-Mideast Oil. All sound familiar? Ben's departure has left an awfully big hole in Washington. And although nephew Miles will no doubt win the special election—aided by Hannaford's fortune and influence—he'll never fill the big man's shoes. But then, who could?

I could not have agreed more with Parenti. And I sensed in the column a grudging admiration for Ben, a vague sorrow over his resignation. A lot of the Washington salt had lost its savor with Ben gone. He was, as the Book he so often quoted tells us, *one among a thousand.*